Whose Body?

Whose Body?

DOROTHY L. SAYERS

A Lord Peter Wimsey Novel

HARPER & ROW, PUBLISHERS
New York, Hagerstown, San Francisco, London

*The Singular Adventure of the
Man with the Golden Pince-Nez*

To M. J.

Dear Jim:

 This book is your fault. If it had not been for your brutal insistence, Lord Peter would never have staggered through to the end of this enquiry. Pray consider that he thanks you with his accustomed suavity.

Yours ever,

D. L. S.

CHAPTER I

"OH, DAMN!" SAID LORD PETER WIMSEY AT PICCA-
dilly Circus. "Hi, driver!"

The taxi man, irritated at receiving this appeal
while negotiating the intricacies of turning into
Lower Regent Street across the route of a 19 'bus, a
38-B and a bicycle, bent an unwilling ear.

"I've left the catalogue behind," said Lord Peter
deprecatingly. "Uncommonly careless of me. D'you
mind puttin' back to where we came from?"

"To the Savile Club, sir?"

"No—110 Piccadilly—just beyond—thank you."

"Thought you was in a hurry," said the man, overcome with a sense of injury.

"I'm afraid it's an awkward place to turn in," said
Lord Peter, answering the thought rather than the
words. His long, amiable face looked as if it had gen-
erated spontaneously from his top hat, as white mag-
gots breed from Gorgonzola.

The taxi, under the severe eye of a policeman, re-
volved by slow jerks, with a noise like the grinding
of teeth.

The block of new, perfect and expensive flats in
which Lord Peter dwelt upon the second floor, stood
directly opposite the Green Park, in a spot for many
years occupied by the skeleton of a frustrate commercial enterprise. As Lord Peter let himself in he

heard his man's voice in the library, uplifted in that throttled stridency peculiar to well-trained persons using the telephone.

"I believe that's his lordship just coming in again— if your Grace would kindly hold the line a moment."

"What is it, Bunter?"

"Her Grace has just called up from Denver, my lord. I was just saying your lordship had gone to the sale when I heard your lordship's latchkey."

"Thanks," said Lord Peter; "and you might find me my catalogue, would you? I think I must have left it in my bedroom, or on the desk."

He sat down to the telephone with an air of leisurely courtesy, as though it were an acquaintance dropped in for a chat.

"Hullo, Mother—that you?"

"Oh, there you are, dear," replied the voice of the Dowager Duchess. "I was afraid I'd just missed you."

"Well, you had, as a matter of fact. I'd just started off to Brocklebury's sale to pick up a book or two, but I had to come back for the catalogue. What's up?"

"Such a quaint thing," said the Duchess. "I thought I'd tell you. You know little Mr. Thipps?"

"Thipps?" said Lord Peter. "Thipps? Oh, yes, the little architect man who's doing the church roof. Yes. What about him?"

"Mrs. Throgmorton's just been in, in quite a state of mind."

"Sorry, Mother, I can't hear. Mrs. Who?"

"Throgmorton—Throgmorton—the vicar's wife."

10

"Oh, Throgmorton, yes?"

"Mr. Thipps rang them up this morning. It was his day to come down, you know."

"Yes?"

"He rang them up to say he couldn't. He was so upset, poor little man. He'd found a dead body in his bath."

"Sorry, Mother, I can't hear; found what, where?"

"A dead body, dear, in his bath."

"What?—no, no, we haven't finished. Please don't cut us off. Hullo! Hullo! Is that you, Mother? Hullo! —Mother!—Oh, yes—sorry, the girl was trying to cut us off. What sort of body?"

"A dead man, dear, with nothing on but a pair of pince-nez. Mrs. Throgmorton positively blushed when she was telling me. I'm afraid people do get a little narrow-minded in country vicarages."

"Well, it sounds a bit unusual. Was it anybody he knew?"

"No, dear, I don't think so, but, of course, he couldn't give her many details. She said he sounded quite distracted. He's such a respectable little man— and having the police in the house and so on, really worried him."

"Poor little Thipps! Uncommonly awkward for him. Let's see, he lives in Battersea, doesn't he?"

"Yes, dear; 59, Queen Caroline Mansions; opposite the Park. That big block just round the corner from the Hospital. I thought perhaps you'd like to run round and see him and ask if there's anything we can do. I always thought him a nice little man."

"Oh, quite," said Lord Peter, grinning at the telephone. The Duchess was always of the greatest assistance to his hobby of criminal investigation, though she never alluded to it, and maintained a polite fiction of its non-existence.

"What time did it happen, Mother?"

"I think he found it early this morning, but, of course, he didn't think of telling the Throgmortons just at first. She came up to me just before lunch—so tiresome, I had to ask her to stay. Fortunately, I was alone. I don't mind being bored myself, but I hate having my guests bored."

"Poor old Mother! Well, thanks awfully for tellin' me. I think I'll send Bunter to the sale and toddle round to Battersea now an' try and console the poor little beast. So-long."

"Good-bye, dear."

"Bunter!"

"Yes, my lord."

"Her Grace tells me that a respectable Battersea architect has discovered a dead man in his bath."

"Indeed, my lord? That's very gratifying."

"Very, Bunter. Your choice of words is unerring. I wish Eton and Balliol had done as much for me. Have you found the catalogue?"

"Here it is, my lord."

"Thanks. I am going to Battersea at once. I want you to attend the sale for me. Don't lose time—I don't want to miss the Folio Dante * nor the de

* This is the first Florence edition, 1481, by Niccolo di Lorenzo. Lord Peter's collection of printed Dantes is worth inspection. It includes, besides

12

Voragine—here you are—see? 'Golden Legend'—
Wynkyn de Worde, 1493—got that?—and, I say,
make a special effort for the Caxton folio of the 'Four
Sons of Aymon'—it's the 1489 folio and unique.
Look! I've marked the lots I want, and put my outside offer against each. Do your best for me. I shall be
back to dinner."

"Very good, my lord."

"Take my cab and tell him to hurry. He may for
you; he doesn't like me very much. Can I," said Lord
Peter, looking at himself in the eighteenth-century
mirror over the mantelpiece, "can I have the heart to
fluster the flustered Thipps further—that's very difficult to say quickly—by appearing in a top-hat and
frock-coat? I think not. Ten to one he will overlook
my trousers and mistake me for the undertaker. A
grey suit, I fancy, neat but not gaudy, with a hat to
tone, suits my other self better. Exit the amateur of
first editions; new motive introduced by solo bassoon;
enter Sherlock Holmes, disguised as a walking gentleman. There goes Bunter. Invaluable fellow—never
offers to do his job when you've told him to do somethin' else. Hope he doesn't miss the 'Four Sons of
Aymon.' Still, there *is* another copy of that—in the
Vatican.* It might become available, you never know

the famous Aldine 8vo. of 1502, the Naples folio of 1477—"edizione raris-
sima," according to Colomb. This copy has no history, and Mr. Parker's private belief is that its present owner conveyed it away by stealth from somewhere or other. Lord Peter's own account is that he "picked it up in a little
place in the hills," when making a walking-tour through Italy.

* Lord Peter's wits were wool-gathering. The book is in the possession of
Earl Spencer. The Brocklebury copy is incomplete, the last five signatures being altogether missing, but is unique in possessing the colophon.

—if the Church of Rome went to pot or Switzerland invaded Italy—whereas a strange corpse doesn't turn up in a suburban bathroom more than once in a lifetime—at least, I should think not—at any rate, the number of times it's happened, *with* a pince-nez, might be counted on the fingers of one hand, I imagine. Dear me! it's a dreadful mistake to ride two hobbies at once."

He had drifted across the passage into his bedroom, and was changing with a rapidity one might not have expected from a man of his mannerisms. He selected a dark-green tie to match his socks and tied it accurately without hesitation or the slightest compression of his lips; substituted a pair of brown shoes for his black ones, slipped a monocle into a breast pocket, and took up a beautiful Malacca walking-stick with a heavy silver knob.

"That's all, I think," he murmured to himself. "Stay—I may as well have you—you may come in useful—one never knows." He added a flat silver matchbox to his equipment, glanced at his watch, and seeing that it was already a quarter to three, ran briskly downstairs, and, hailing a taxi, was carried to Battersea Park.

Mr. Alfred Thipps was a small, nervous man, whose flaxen hair was beginning to abandon the unequal struggle with destiny. One might say that his only really marked feature was a large bruise over the left eyebrow, which gave him a faintly dissipated air incongruous with the rest of his appearance. Almost in

14

the same breath with his first greeting, he made a self-conscious apology for it, murmuring something about having run against the dining-room door in the dark. He was touched almost to tears by Lord Peter's thoughtfulness and condescension in calling.

"I'm sure it's most kind of your lordship," he repeated for the dozenth time, rapidly blinking his weak little eyelids. "I appreciate it very deeply, very deeply, indeed, and so would Mother, only she's so deaf, I don't like to trouble you with making her understand. It's been very hard all day," he added, "with the policemen in the house and all this commotion. It's what Mother and me have never been used to, always living very retired, and it's most distressing to a man of regular habits, my lord, and reely, I'm almost thankful Mother doesn't understand, for I'm sure it would worry her terribly if she was to know about it. She was upset at first, but she's made up some idea of her own about it now, and I'm sure it's all for the best."

The old lady who sat knitting by the fire nodded grimly in response to a look from her son.

"I always said as you ought to complain about that bath, Alfred," she said suddenly, in the high, piping voice peculiar to the deaf, "and it's to be 'oped the landlord'll see about it now; not but what I think you might have managed without having the police in, but there! you always were one to make a fuss about a little thing, from chicken-pox up."

"There now," said Mr. Thipps apologetically, "you see how it is. Not but what it's just as well she's settled

15

on that, because she understands we've locked up the bathroom and don't try to go in there. But it's been a terrible shock to me, sir—my lord, I should say, but there! my nerves are all to pieces. Such a thing has never 'appened—happened to me in all my born days. Such a state I was in this morning—I didn't know if I was on my head or my heels—I reely didn't, and my heart not being too strong, I hardly knew how to get out of that horrid room and telephone for the police. It's affected me, sir, it's affected me, it reely has—I couldn't touch a bit of breakfast, nor lunch neither, and what with telephoning and putting off clients and interviewing people all morning, I've hardly known what to do with myself."

"I'm sure it must have been uncommonly distressin'," said Lord Peter, sympathetically, "especially comin' like that before breakfast. Hate anything tiresome happenin' before breakfast. Takes a man at such a confounded disadvantage, what?"

"That's just it, that's just it," said Mr. Thipps, eagerly. "When I saw that dreadful thing lying there in my bath, mother-naked, too, except for a pair of eyeglasses, I assure you, my lord, it regularly turned my stomach, if you'll excuse the expression. I'm not very strong, sir, and I get that sinking feeling sometimes in the morning, and what with one thing and another I 'ad—had to send the girl for a stiff brandy, or I don't know *what* mightn't have happened. I felt so queer, though I'm anything but partial to spirits as a rule. Still, I make it a rule never to be without brandy in the house, in case of emergency, you know?"

16

"Very wise of you," said Lord Peter, cheerfully. "You're a very far-seein' man, Mr. Thipps. Wonderful what a little nip'll do in case of need, and the less you're used to it the more good it does you. Hope your girl is a sensible young woman, what? Nuisance to have women faintin' and shriekin' all over the place."

"Oh, Gladys is a good girl," said Mr. Thipps, "very reasonable indeed. She was shocked, of course; that's very understandable. I was shocked myself, and it wouldn't be proper in a young woman not to be shocked under the circumstances, but she is reely a helpful, energetic girl in a crisis, if you understand me. I consider myself very fortunate these days to have got a good, decent girl to do for me and Mother, even though she is a bit careless and forgetful about little things, but that's only natural. She was very sorry indeed about having left the bathroom window open, she reely was, and though I was angry at first, seeing what's come of it, it wasn't anything to speak of, not in the ordinary way, as you might say. Girls will forget things, you know, my lord, and reely she was so distressed I didn't like to say too much to her. All I said was: 'It might have been burglars,' I said, 'remember that, next time you leave a window open all night; this time it was a dead man,' I said, 'and that's unpleasant enough, but next time it might be burglars,' I said, 'and all of us murdered in our beds.' But the police-inspector—Inspector Sugg, they called him, from the Yard—he was very sharp with her, poor girl. Quite frightened her, and made her think he suspected her of something, though what good a body could be to her, poor girl, I can't imagine, and so I told the Inspector. He was quite rude to me, my lord—I may say I didn't like his manner at all. 'If you've got anything definite to accuse Gladys or me of, Inspector,' I said to him, 'bring it forward, that's what you have to do,' I said, 'but I've yet to learn that you're paid to be rude to a gentleman in his own 'ouse—house.' Reely," said Mr. Thipps, growing quite pink on the top of his head, "he regularly roused me, regularly roused me, my lord, and I'm a mild man as a rule."

"Sugg all over," said Lord Peter. "I know him. When he don't know what else to say, he's rude. Stands to reason you and the girl wouldn't go collectin' bodies. Who'd want to saddle himself with a body? Difficulty's usually to get rid of 'em. Have you got rid of this one yet, by the way?"

"It's still in the bathroom," said Mr. Thipps. "Inspector Sugg said nothing was to be touched till his men came in to move it. I'm expecting them at any time. If it would interest your lordship to have a look at it—"

"Thanks awfully," said Lord Peter. "I'd like to very much, if I'm not puttin' you out."

"Not at all," said Mr. Thipps. His manner as he led the way along the passage convinced Lord Peter of two things—first, that, gruesome as his exhibit was, he rejoiced in the importance it reflected upon himself and his flat, and secondly, that Inspector Sugg had forbidden him to exhibit it to anyone. The latter

18

supposition was confirmed by the action of Mr. Thipps, who stopped to fetch the door-key from his bedroom, saying that the police had the other, but that he made it a rule to have two keys to every door, in case of accident.

The bathroom was in no way remarkable. It was long and narrow, the window being exactly over the head of the bath. The panes were of frosted glass; the frame wide enough to admit a man's body. Lord Peter stepped rapidly across to it, opened it and looked out.

The flat was the top one of the building and situated about the middle of the block. The bathroom window looked out upon the back-yards of the flats, which were occupied by various small outbuildings, coal-holes, garages, and the like. Beyond these were the back gardens of a parallel line of houses. On the right rose the extensive edifice of St. Luke's Hospital, Battersea, with its grounds, and, connected with it by a covered way, the residence of the famous surgeon, Sir Julian Freke, who directed the surgical side of the great new hospital, and was, in addition, known in Harley Street as a distinguished neurologist with a highly individual point of view.

This information was poured into Lord Peter's ear at considerable length by Mr. Thipps, who seemed to feel that the neighbourhood of anybody so distinguished shed a kind of halo of glory over Queen Caroline Mansions.

"We had him round here himself this morning," he said, "about this horrid business. Inspector Sugg

19

thought one of the young medical gentlemen at the hospital might have brought the corpse round for a joke, as you might say, they always having bodies in the dissecting-room. So Inspector Sugg went round to see Sir Julian this morning to ask if there was a body missing. He was very kind, was Sir Julian, very kind indeed, though he was at work when they got there, in the dissecting-room. He looked up the books to see that all the bodies were accounted for, and then very obligingly came round here to look at this"—he indicated the bath—"and said he was afraid he couldn't help us—there was no corpse missing from the hospital, and this one didn't answer to the description of any they'd had."

"Nor to the description of any of the patients, I hope," suggested Lord Peter casually.

At this grisly hint Mr. Thipps turned pale.

"I didn't hear Inspector Sugg inquire," he said, with some agitation. "What a very horrid thing that would be—God bless my soul, my lord, I never thought of it."

"Well, if they had missed a patient they'd probably have discovered it by now," said Lord Peter. "Let's have a look at this one."

He screwed his monocle into his eye, adding: "I see you're troubled here with the soot blowing in. Beastly nuisance, ain't it? I get it, too—spoils all my books, you know. Here, don't you trouble, if you don't care about lookin' at it."

He took from Mr. Thipps's hesitating hand the

sheet which had been flung over the bath, and turned it back.

The body which lay in the bath was that of a tall, stout man of about fifty. The hair, which was thick and black and naturally curly, had been cut and parted by a master hand, and exuded a faint violet perfume, perfectly recognisable in the close air of the bathroom. The features were thick, fleshy and strongly marked, with prominent dark eyes, and a long nose curving down to a heavy chin. The clean-shaven lips were full and sensual, and the dropped jaw showed teeth stained with tobacco. On the dead face the handsome pair of gold pince-nez mocked death with grotesque elegance; the fine gold chain curved over the naked breast. The legs lay stiffly stretched out side by side; the arms reposed close to the body; the fingers were flexed naturally. Lord Peter lifted one arm, and looked at the hand with a little frown.

"Bit of a dandy, your visitor, what?" he murmured. "Parma violet and manicure." He bent again, slipping his hand beneath the head. The absurd eye-glasses slipped off, clattering into the bath, and the noise put the last touch to Mr. Thipps's growing nervousness.

"If you'll excuse me," he murmured, "it makes me feel quite faint, it reely does."

He slipped outside, and he had no sooner done so than Lord Peter, lifting the body quickly and cautiously, turned it over and inspected it with his head on one side, bringing his monocle into play with the

21

air of the late Joseph Chamberlain approving a rare orchid. He then laid the head over his arm, and bringing out the silver matchbox from his pocket, slipped it into the open mouth. Then making the noise usually written "Tut-tut," he laid the body down, picked up the mysterious pince-nez, looked at it, put it on his nose and looked through it, made the same noise again, readjusted the pince-nez upon the nose of the corpse, so as to leave no traces of interference for the irritation of Inspector Sugg; rearranged the body; returned to the window and, leaning out, reached upwards and sideways with his walking-stick, which he had somewhat incongruously brought along with him. Nothing appearing to come of these investigations, he withdrew his head, closed the window, and rejoined Mr. Thipps in the passage.

Mr. Thipps, touched by this sympathetic interest in the younger son of a duke, took the liberty, on their return to the sitting-room, of offering him a cup of tea. Lord Peter, who had strolled over to the window and was admiring the outlook on Battersea Park, was about to accept, when an ambulance came into view at the end of Prince of Wales Road. Its appearance reminded Lord Peter of an important engagement, and with a hurried "By Jove!" he took his leave of Mr. Thipps.

"My mother sent kind regards and all that," he said, shaking hands fervently; "hopes you'll soon be down at Denver again. Good-bye, Mrs. Thipps," he bawled kindly into the ear of the old lady. "Oh, no, my dear sir, please don't trouble to come down."

He was none too soon. As he stepped out of the door and turned towards the station, the ambulance drew up from the other direction, and Inspector Sugg emerged from it with two constables. The Inspector spoke to the officer on duty at the Mansions, and turned a suspicious gaze on Lord Peter's retreating back.

"Dear old Sugg," said that nobleman, fondly, "dear, dear old bird! How he does hate me, to be sure."

"EXCELLENT, BUNTER," SAID LORD PETER, SINKING with a sigh into a luxurious armchair. "I couldn't have done better myself. The thought of the Dante makes my mouth water—and the 'Four Sons of Aymon.' And you've saved me £60—that's glorious. What shall we spend it on, Bunter? Think of it—all ours, to do as we like with, for as Harold Skimpole so rightly observes, £60 saved is £60 gained, and I'd reckoned on spending it all. It's your saving, Bunter, and properly speaking, your £60. What do we want? Anything in your department? Would you like anything altered in the flat?"

"Well, my lord, as your lordship is so good"—the man-servant paused, about to pour an old brandy into a liqueur glass.

"Well, out with it, my Bunter, you imperturbable old hypocrite. It's no good talking as if you were announcing dinner—you're spilling the brandy. The voice is Jacob's voice, but the hands are the hands of Esau. What does that blessed darkroom of yours want now?"

"There's a Double Anastigmat with a set of supplementary lenses, my lord," said Bunter, with a note almost of religious fervour. "If it was a case of forgery now—or footprints—I could enlarge them right up on the plate. Or the wide-angled lens would

24

be useful. It's as though the camera had eyes at the back of its head, my lord. Look—I've got it here."

He pulled a catalogue from his pocket, and submitted it, quivering, to his employer's gaze.

Lord Peter perused the description slowly, the corners of his long mouth lifted into a faint smile.

"It's Greek to me," he said, "and £50 seems a ridiculous price for a few bits of glass. I suppose, Bunter, you'd say £750 was a bit out of the way for a dirty old book in a dead language, wouldn't you?"

"It wouldn't be my place to say so, my lord."

"No, Bunter, I pay you £200 a year to keep your thoughts to yourself. Tell me, Bunter, in these democratic days, don't you think that's unfair?"

"No, my lord."

"You don't. D'you mind telling me frankly why you don't think it unfair?"

"Frankly, my lord, your lordship is paid a nobleman's income to take Lady Worthington in to dinner and refrain from exercising your lordship's undoubted powers of repartee."

Lord Peter considered this.

"That's your idea, is it, Bunter? Noblesse oblige—for a consideration. I daresay you're right. Then you're better off than I am, because I'd have to behave myself to Lady Worthington if I hadn't a penny. Bunter, if I sacked you here and now, would you tell me what you think of me?"

"No, my lord."

"You'd have a perfect right to, my Bunter, and if I sacked you on top of drinking the kind of coffee you make, I'd deserve everything you could say of me. You're a demon for coffee, Bunter—I don't want to know how you do it, because I believe it to be witchcraft, and I don't want to burn eternally. You can buy your cross-eyed lens."

"Thank you, my lord."

"Have you finished in the dining-room?"

"Not quite, my lord."

"Well, come back when you have. I have many things to tell you. Hullo! who's that?"

The doorbell had rung sharply.

"Unless it's anybody interestin' I'm not at home."

"Very good, my lord."

Lord Peter's library was one of the most delightful bachelor rooms in London. Its scheme was black and primrose; its walls were lined with rare editions, and its chairs and Chesterfield sofa suggested the embraces of the houris. In one corner stood a black baby grand, a wood fire leaped on a wide old-fashioned hearth, and the Sèvres vases on the chimneypiece were filled with ruddy and gold chrysanthemums. To the eyes of the young man who was ushered in from the raw November fog it seemed not only rare and unattainable, but friendly and familiar, like a colourful and gilded paradise in a mediaeval painting.

"Mr. Parker, my lord."

Lord Peter jumped up with genuine eagerness.

"My dear man, I'm delighted to see you. What a beastly foggy night, ain't it? Bunter, some more of that admirable coffee and another glass and the cigars. Parker, I hope you're full of crime—nothing less than arson or murder will do for us tonight. 'On such a night as this—' Bunter and I were just sitting down to carouse. I've got a Dante, and a Caxton folio that is practically unique, at Sir Ralph Brocklebury's sale. Bunter, who did the bargaining, is going to have a lens which does all kinds of wonderful things with its eyes shut, and

> We both have got a body in a bath,
> We both have got a body in a bath—
>   For in spite of all temptations
>   To go in for cheap sensations
> We insist upon a body in a bath—

Nothing less will do for us, Parker. It's mine at present, but we're going shares in it. Property of the firm. Won't you join us? You really must put *something* in the jack-pot. Perhaps you have a body. Oh, do have a body. Every body welcome.

> Gin a body meet a body
>   Hauled before the beak,
> Gin a body jolly well knows who murdered a
>   body and that old Sugg is on the wrong tack,
>   Need a body speak?

Not a bit of it. He tips a glassy wink to yours truly and yours truly reads the truth."

"Ah," said Parker, "I knew you'd been round to Queen Caroline Mansions. So've I, and met Sugg, and he told me he'd seen you. He was cross, too. Unwarrantable interference, he calls it."

"I knew he would," said Lord Peter. "I love taking a rise out of dear old Sugg, he's always so rude. I see

27

by the *Star* that he has excelled himself by taking the girl, Gladys What's-her-name, into custody. Sugg of the evening, beautiful Sugg! But what were *you* doing there?"

"To tell you the truth," said Parker, "I went round to see if the Semitic-looking stranger in Mr. Thipps's bath was by any extraordinary chance Sir Reuben Levy. But he isn't."

"Sir Reuben Levy? Wait a minute, I saw something about that. I know! A headline: 'Mysterious disappearance of famous financier.' What's it all about? I didn't read it carefully."

"Well, it's a bit odd, though I daresay it's nothing really—old chap may have cleared for some reason best known to himself. It only happened this morning, and nobody would have thought anything about it, only it happened to be the day on which he had arranged to attend a most important financial meeting and do some deal involving millions—I haven't got all the details. But I know he's got enemies who'd just as soon the deal didn't come off, so when I got wind of this fellow in the bath, I buzzed round to have a look at him. It didn't seem likely, of course, but unlikelier things do happen in our profession. The funny thing is, old Sugg had got bitten with the idea it *is* him, and is wildly telegraphing to Lady Levy to come and identify him. But as a matter of fact, the man in the bath is no more Sir Reuben Levy than Adolf Beck, poor devil, was John Smith. Oddly enough, though, he would be really extraordinarily like Sir Reuben if he had a beard, and as Lady Levy

28

is abroad with the family, somebody may say it's him, and Sugg will build up a lovely theory, like the Tower of Babel, and destined so to perish."

"Sugg's a beautiful, braying ass," said Lord Peter. "He's like a detective in a novel. Well, I don't know anything about Levy, but I've seen the body, and I should say the idea was preposterous upon the face of it. What do you think of the brandy?"

"Unbelievable, Wimsey—sort of thing makes one believe in heaven. But I want your yarn."

"D'you mind if Bunter hears it, too? Invaluable man, Bunter—amazin' fellow with a camera. And the odd thing is, he's always on the spot when I want my bath or my boots. I don't know when he develops things—I believe he does 'em in his sleep. Bunter!"

"Yes, my lord."

"Stop fiddling about in there, and get yourself the proper things to drink and join the merry throng."

"Certainly, my lord."

"Mr. Parker has a new trick: The Vanishing Financier. Absolutely no deception. Hey, presto, pass! and where is he? Will some gentleman from the audience kindly step upon the platform and inspect the cabinet? Thank you, sir. The quickness of the 'and deceives the heye."

"I'm afraid mine isn't much of a story," said Parker. "It's just one of those simple things that offer no handle. Sir Reuben Levy dined last night with three friends at the Ritz. After dinner the friends went to the theatre. He refused to go with them on account of an appointment. I haven't yet been able to trace the appointment, but anyhow, he returned home to his house—9a, Park Lane—at twelve o'clock."

"Who saw him?"

"The cook, who had just gone up to bed, saw him on the doorstep, and heard him let himself in. He walked upstairs, leaving his greatcoat on the hall peg and his umbrella in the stand—you remember how it rained last night. He undressed and went to bed. Next morning he wasn't there. That's all," said Parker abruptly, with a wave of the hand.

"It isn't all, it isn't all. Daddy, go on, that's not *half* a story," pleaded Lord Peter.

"But it *is* all. When his man came to call him he wasn't there. The bed had been slept in. His pyjamas and all his clothes were there, the only odd thing being that they were thrown rather untidily on the ottoman at the foot of the bed, instead of being neatly folded on a chair, as is Sir Reuben's custom—looking as though he had been rather agitated or unwell. No clean clothes were missing, no suit, no boots—nothing. The boots he had worn were in his dressing-room as usual. He had washed and cleaned his teeth and done all the usual things. The housemaid was down cleaning the hall at half-past six, and can swear that nobody came in or out after that. So one is forced to suppose that a respectable middle-aged Hebrew financier either went mad between twelve and six a.m. and walked quietly out of the house in his birthday suit on a November night, or else was spirited away like the lady in the 'Ingoldsby Legends,'

30

body and bones, leaving only a heap of crumpled clothes behind him."

"Was the front door bolted?"

"That's the sort of question you *would* ask, straight off; it took me an hour to think of it. No; contrary to custom, there was only the Yale lock on the door. On the other hand, some of the maids had been given leave to go to the theatre, and Sir Reuben may quite conceivably have left the door open under the impression they had not come in. Such a thing has happened before."

"'And that's really all?"

"Really all. Except for one very trifling circumstance."

"I love trifling circumstances," said Lord Peter, with childish delight; "so many men have been hanged by trifling circumstances. What was it?"

"Sir Reuben and Lady Levy, who are a most devoted couple, always share the same room. Lady Levy, as I said before, is in Mentonne at the moment for her health. In her absence, Sir Reuben sleeps in the double bed as usual, and invariably on his own side—the outside—of the bed. Last night he put the two pillows together and slept in the middle, or, if anything, rather closer to the wall than otherwise. The housemaid, who is a most intelligent girl, noticed this when she went up to make the bed, and, with really admirable detective instinct, refused to touch the bed or let anybody else touch it, though it wasn't till later that they actually sent for the police."

"Was nobody in the house but Sir Reuben and the servants?"

"No; Lady Levy was away with her daughter and her maid. The valet, cook, parlourmaid, housemaid and kitchenmaid were the only people in the house, and naturally wasted an hour or two squawking and gossiping. I got there about ten."

"What have you been doing since?"

"Trying to get on the track of Sir Reuben's appointment last night, since, with the exception of the cook, his 'appointer' was the last person who saw him before his disappearance. There may be some quite simple explanation, though I'm dashed if I can think of one for the moment. Hang it all, a man doesn't come in and go to bed and walk away again 'mid nodings on' in the middle of the night."

"He may have been disguised."

"I thought of that—in fact, it seems the only possible explanation. But it's deuced odd, Wimsey. An important city man, on the eve of an important transaction, without a word of warning to anybody, slips off in the middle of the night, disguised down to his skin, leaving behind his watch, purse, cheque-book, and—most mysterious and important of all—his spectacles, without which he can't see a step, as he is extremely short-sighted. He—"

"That *is* important," interrupted Wimsey. "You are sure he didn't take a second pair?"

"His man vouches for it that he had only two pairs, one of which was found on his dressing-table, and the other in the drawer where it is always kept."

Lord Peter whistled.

"You've got me there, Parker. Even if he'd gone out to commit suicide he'd have taken those."

"So you'd think—or the suicide would have happened the first time he started to cross the road. However, I didn't overlook the possibility. I've got particulars of all today's street accidents, and I can lay my hand on my heart and say that none of them is Sir Reuben. Besides, he took his latchkey with him, which looks as though he'd meant to come back."

"Have you seen the men he dined with?"

"I found two of them at the club. They said that he seemed in the best of health and spirits, spoke of looking forward to joining Lady Levy later on—perhaps at Christmas—and referred with great satisfaction to this morning's business transaction, in which one of them—a man called Anderson of Wyndham's —was himself concerned."

"Then up till about nine o'clock, anyhow, he had no apparent intention or expectation of disappearing."

"None—unless he was a most consummate actor. Whatever happened to change his mind must have happened either at the mysterious appointment which he kept after dinner, or while he was in bed between midnight and 5.30 a.m."

"Well, Bunter," said Lord Peter, "what do you make of it?"

"Not in my department, my lord. Except that it is odd that a gentleman who was too flurried or unwell to fold his clothes as usual should remember to clean his teeth and put his boots out. Those are two things that quite frequently get overlooked, my lord."

"If you mean anything personal, Bunter," said Lord Peter, "I can only say that I think the speech an unworthy one. It's a sweet little problem, Parker mine. Look here, I don't want to butt in, but I should dearly love to see that bedroom tomorrow. 'Tis not that I mistrust thee, dear, but I should uncommonly like to see it. Say me not nay—take another drop of brandy and a Villar Villar, but say not, say not nay!"

"Of course you can come and see it—you'll probably find lots of things I've overlooked," said the other, equally, accepting the proffered hospitality.

"Parker, acushla, you're an honour to Scotland Yard. I look at you, and Sugg appears a myth, a fable, an idiot-boy, spawned in a moonlight hour by some fantastic poet's brain. Sugg is too perfect to be possible. What does he make of the body, by the way?"

"Sugg says," replied Parker, with precision, "that the body died from a blow on the back of the neck. The doctor told him that. He says it's been dead a day or two. The doctor told him that, too. He says it's the body of a well-to-do Hebrew of about fifty. Anybody could have told him that. He says it's ridiculous to suppose it came in through the window without anybody knowing anything about it. He says it probably walked in through the front door and was murdered by the household. He's arrested the girl because she's short and frail-looking and quite unequal to downing a tall and sturdy Semite with a

34

poker. He'd arrest Thipps, only Thipps was away in Manchester all yesterday and the day before and didn't come back till late last night—in fact, he wanted to arrest him till I reminded him that if the body had been a day or two dead, little Thipps couldn't have done him in at 10.30 last night. But he'll arrest him tomorrow as an accessory—and the old lady with the knitting, too, I shouldn't wonder."

"Well, I'm glad the little man has so much of an alibi," said Lord Peter, "though if you're only glueing your faith to cadaveric lividity, rigidity, and all the other quiddities, you must be prepared to have some sceptical beast of a prosecuting counsel walk slap-bang through the medical evidence. Remember Impey Biggs defending in that Chelsea tea-shop affair? Six bloomin' medicos contradictin' each other in the box, an' old Impey elocutin' abnormal cases from Glaister and Dixon Mann till the eyes of the jury reeled in their heads! 'Are you prepared to swear, Dr. Thingumtight, that the onset of rigor mortis indicates the hour of death without the possibility of error?' 'So far as my experience goes, in the majority of cases,' says the doctor, all stiff. 'Ah!' says Biggs, 'but this is a Court of Justice, Doctor, not a Parliamentary election. We can't get on without a minority report. The law, Dr. Thingumtight, respects the rights of the minority, alive or dead.' Some ass laughs, and old Biggs sticks his chest out and gets impressive. 'Gentlemen, this is no laughing matter. My client—an upright and honourable gentleman—is being tried for his life—for his life, gentlemen—and it is the business of the prosecution to show his guilt—if they can—without a shadow of doubt. Now, Dr. Thing-umtight, I ask you again, can you solemnly swear, without the least shadow of doubt,—probable, possible shadow of doubt—that this unhappy woman met her death neither sooner nor later than Thursday evening? A probable opinion? Gentlemen, we are not Jesuits, we are straightforward Englishmen. You cannot ask a British-born jury to convict any man on the authority of a probable opinion.' Hum of applause."

"Biggs's man was guilty all the same," said Parker.

"Of course he was. But he was acquitted all the same, an' what you've just said is libel." Wimsey walked over to the bookshelf and took down a volume of Medical Jurisprudence. " 'Rigor mortis—can only be stated in a very general way—many factors determine the result.' Cautious brute. 'On the average, however, stiffening will have begun—neck and jaw—5 to 6 hours after death'—m'm—'in all likelihood have passed off in the bulk of cases by the end of 36 hours. Under certain circumstances, however, it may appear unusually early, or be retarded unusually long!' Helpful, ain't it, Parker? 'Brown-Séquard states . . . 3½ minutes after death. . . . In certain cases not until lapse of 16 hours after death . . . present as long as 21 days thereafter.' Lord! 'Modifying factors—age—muscular state—or febrile diseases —or where temperature of environment is high'— and so on and so on—any bloomin' thing. Never mind. You can run the argument for what it's worth

to Sugg. *He* won't know any better." He tossed the
book away. "Come back to facts. What did *you* make
of the body?"

"Well," said the detective, "not very much—I was
puzzled—frankly. I should say he had been a rich
man, but self-made, and that his good fortune had
come to him fairly recently."

"Ah, you noticed the calluses on the hands—I
thought you wouldn't miss that."

"Both his feet were badly blistered—he had been
wearing tight shoes."

"Walking a long way in them, too," said Lord
Peter, "to get such blisters as that. Didn't that strike
you as odd, in a person evidently well off?"

"Well, I don't know. The blisters were two or
three days old. He might have got stuck in the sub-
urbs one night, perhaps—last train gone and no
taxi—and had to walk home."

"Possibly."

"There were some little red marks all over his back
and one leg I couldn't quite account for."

"I saw them."

"What did you make of them?"

"I'll tell you afterwards. Go on."

"He was very long-sighted—oddly long-sighted
for a man in the prime of life; the glasses were like a
very old man's. By the way, they had a very beautiful
and remarkable chain of flat links chased with a pattern. It struck me he might be traced through it."

"I've just put an advertisement in the *Times* about
it," said Lord Peter. "Go on."

"He had had the glasses some time—they had been mended twice."

"Beautiful, Parker, beautiful. Did you realize the importance of that?"

"Not specially, I'm afraid—why?"

"Never mind—go on."

"He was probably a sullen, ill-tempered man—his nails were filed down to the quick as though he habitually bit them, and his fingers were bitten as well. He smoked quantities of cigarettes without a holder. He was particular about his personal appearance."

"Did you examine the room at all? I didn't get a chance."

"I couldn't find much in the way of footprints. Sugg & Co. had tramped all over the place, to say nothing of little Thipps and the maid, but I noticed a very indefinite patch just behind the head of the bath, as though something damp might have stood there. You could hardly call it a print."

"It rained hard all last night, of course."

"Yes; did you notice that the soot on the window-sill was vaguely marked?"

"I did," said Wimsey, "and I examined it hard with this little fellow, but I could make nothing of it except that something or other had rested on the sill." He drew out his monocle and handed it to Parker.

"My word, that's a powerful lens."

"It is," said Wimsey, "and jolly useful when you want to take a good squint at somethin' and look like a bally fool all the time. Only it don't do to wear it permanently—if people see you full-face they say: 'Dear me! how weak the sight of that eye must be!' Still, it's useful."

"Sugg and I explored the ground at the back of the building," went on Parker, "but there wasn't a trace."

"That's interestin'. Did you try the roof?"

"No."

"We'll go over it tomorrow. The gutter's only a couple of feet off the top of the window. I measured it with my stick—the gentleman-scout's vade-mecum, I call it—it's marked off in inches. Uncommonly handy companion at times. There's a sword inside and a compass in the head. Got it made specially. Anything more?"

"Afraid not. Let's hear your version, Wimsey."

"Well, I think you've got most of the points. There are just one or two little contradictions. For instance, here's a man wears expensive gold-rimmed pince-nez and has had them long enough to be mended twice. Yet his teeth are not merely discoloured, but badly decayed and look as if he'd never cleaned them in his life. There are four molars missing on one side and three on the other and one front tooth broken right across. He's a man careful of his personal appearance, as witness his hair and his hands. What do you say to that?"

"Oh, these self-made men of low origin don't think much about teeth, and are terrified of dentists."

"True; but one of the molars has a broken edge so rough that it had made a sore place on the tongue. Nothing's more painful. D'you mean to tell me a man would put up with that if he could afford to get the tooth filed?"

"Well, people are queer. I've known servants endure agonies rather than step over a dentist's doormat. How did you see that, Wimsey?"

"Had a look inside; electric torch," said Lord Peter. "Handy little gadget. Looks like a matchbox. Well— I daresay it's all right, but I just draw your attention to it. Second point: Gentleman with hair smellin' of Parma violet and manicured hands and all the rest of it, never washes the inside of his ears. Full of wax. Nasty."

"You've got me there, Wimsey; I never noticed it. Still—old bad habits die hard."

"Right oh! Put it down at that. Third point: Gentleman with the manicure and the brilliantine and all the rest of it suffers from fleas."

"By Jove, you're right! Flea-bites. It never occurred to me."

"No doubt about it, old son. The marks were faint and old, but unmistakable."

"Of course, now you mention it. Still, that might happen to anybody. I loosed a whopper in the best hotel in Lincoln the week before last. I hope it bit the next occupier!"

"Oh, all these things *might* happen to anybody— separately. Fourth point: Gentleman who uses Parma

violet for his hair, etc., etc., washes his body in strong
carbolic soap—so strong that the smell hangs about
twenty-four hours later."

"Carbolic to get rid of the fleas."

"I will say for you, Parker, you've an answer for
everything. Fifth point: Carefully got-up gentleman,
with manicured, though masticated, finger-nails, has
filthy black toe-nails which look as if they hadn't
been cut for years."

"All of a piece with habits as indicated."

"Yes, I know, but such habits! Now, sixth and last
point: This gentleman with the intermittently gentlemanly habits arrives in the middle of a pouring
wet night, and apparently through the window,
when he has already been twenty-four hours dead,
and lies down quietly in Mr. Thipps's bath, unseason-
ably dressed in a pair of pince-nez. Not a hair on his
head is ruffled—the hair has been cut so recently that
there are quite a number of little short hairs stuck on
his neck and the sides of the bath—and he has shaved
so recently that there is a line of dried soap on his
cheek—"

"Wimsey!"

"Wait a minute—and *dried soap in his mouth.*"

Bunter got up and appeared suddenly at the detective's elbow, the respectful man-servant all over.

"A little more brandy, sir?" he murmured.

"Wimsey," said Parker, "you are making me feel
cold all over." He emptied his glass—stared at it as
though he were surprised to find it empty, set it

down, got up, walked across to the bookcase, turned round, stood with his back against it and said:

"Look here, Wimsey—you've been reading detective stories; you're talking nonsense."

"No, I ain't," said Lord Peter, sleepily, "uncommon good incident for a detective story, though, what? Bunter, we'll write one, and you shall illustrate it with photographs."

"Soap in his— Rubbish!" said Parker. "It was something else—some discoloration—"

"No," said Lord Peter, "there were hairs as well. Bristly ones. He had a beard."

He took his watch from his pocket, and drew out a couple of longish, stiff hairs, which he had imprisoned between the inner and the outer case.

Parker turned them over once or twice in his fingers, looked at them close to the light, examined them with a lens, handed them to the impassible Bunter, and said:

"Do you mean to tell me, Wimsey, that any man alive would"—he laughed harshly—"shave off his beard with his mouth open, and then go and get killed with his mouth full of hairs? You're mad."

"I don't tell you so," said Wimsey. "You policemen are all alike—only one idea in your skulls. Blest if I can make out why you're ever appointed. He was shaved after he was dead. Pretty, ain't it? Uncommonly jolly little job for the barber, what? Here, sit down, man, and don't be an ass, stumpin' about the room like that. Worse things happen in war. This is

42

only a blinkin' old shillin' shocker. But I'll tell you what, Parker, we're up against a criminal—*the* criminal—the real artist and blighter with imagination—real, artistic, finished stuff. I'm enjoyin' this, Parker."

CHAPTER III

LORD PETER FINISHED A SCARLATTI SONATA, AND SAT
looking thoughtfully at his own hands. The fingers
were long and muscular, with wide, flat joints and
square tips. When he was playing, his rather hard
grey eyes softened, and his long, indeterminate mouth
hardened in compensation. At no other time had he
any pretensions to good looks, and at all times he was
spoilt by a long, narrow chin, and a long, receding
forehead, accentuated by the brushed-back sleekness
of his tow-coloured hair. Labour papers, softening
down the chin, caricatured him as a typical aristocrat.

"That's a wonderful instrument," said Parker.

"It ain't so bad," said Lord Peter, "but Scarlatti
wants a harpsichord. Piano's too modern—all thrills
and overtones. No good for our job, Parker. Have
you come to any conclusion?"

"The man in the bath," said Parker, methodically,
"was *not* a well-off man careful of his personal appearance. He was a labouring man, unemployed, but
who had only recently lost his employment. He had
been tramping about looking for a job when he met
with his end. Somebody killed him and washed him
and scented him and shaved him in order to disguise
him, and put him into Thipps's bath without leaving
a trace. Conclusion: the murderer was a powerful

44

man, since he killed him with a single blow on the neck, a man of cool head and masterly intellect, since he did all that ghastly business without leaving a mark, a man of wealth and refinement, since he had all the apparatus of an elegant toilet handy, and a man of bizarre, and almost perverted imagination, as is shown in the two horrible touches of putting the body in the bath and of adorning it with a pair of pince-nez."

"He is a poet of crime," said Wimsey. "By the way, your difficulty about the pince-nez is cleared up. Obviously, the pince-nez never belonged to the body."

"That only makes a fresh puzzle. One can't suppose the murderer left them in that obliging manner as a clue to his own identity."

"We can hardly suppose that; I'm afraid this man possessed what most criminals lack—a sense. of humour."

"Rather macabre humour."

"True. But a man who can afford to be humorous at all in such circumstances is a terrible fellow. I wonder what he did with the body between the murder and depositing it chez Thipps. Then there are more questions. How did he get it there? And why? Was it brought in at the door, as Sugg of our heart suggests? or through the window, as we think, on the not very adequate testimony of a smudge on the window-sill? Had the murderer accomplices? Is little Thipps really in it, or the girl? It don't do to put the notion out of court merely because Sugg inclines to

it. Even idiots occasionally speak the truth accidentally. If not, why was Thipps selected for such an
abominable practical joke? Has anybody got a grudge
against Thipps? Who are the people in the other flats?
We must find out that. Does Thipps play the piano
at midnight over their heads or damage the reputation of the staircase by bringing home dubiously respectable ladies? Are there unsuccessful architects
thirsting for his blood? Damn it all, Parker, there
must be a motive somewhere. Can't have a crime
without a motive, you know."

"A madman—" suggested Parker, doubtfully.

"With a deuced lot of method in his madness. He
hasn't made a mistake—not one, unless leaving hairs
in the corpse's mouth can be called a mistake. Well,
anyhow, it's not Levy—you're right there. I say, old
thing, neither your man nor mine has left much clue
to go upon, has he? And there don't seem to be any
motives knockin' about, either. And we seem to be
two suits of clothes short in last night's work. Sir
Reuben makes tracks without so much as a fig-leaf,
and a mysterious individual turns up with a pince-
nez, which is quite useless for purposes of decency.
Dash it all! If only I had some good excuse for takin'
up this body case officially—"

The telephone bell rang. The silent Bunter, whom
the other two had almost forgotten, padded across
to it.

"It's an elderly lady, my lord," he said. "I think
she's deaf—I can't make her hear anything, but she's
asking for your lordship."

Lord Peter seized the receiver, and yelled into it a "Hullo!" that might have cracked the vulcanite. He listened for some minutes with an incredulous smile, which gradually broadened into a grin of delight. At length he screamed: "All right! all right!" several times, and rang off.

"By Jove!" he announced, beaming, "sportin' old bird! It's old Mrs. Thipps. Deaf as a post. Never used the 'phone before. But determined. Perfect Napoleon. The incomparable Sugg has made a discovery and arrested little Thipps. Old lady abandoned in the flat. Thipps's last shriek to her: 'Tell Lord Peter Wimsey.' Old girl undaunted. Wrestles with telephone book. Wakes up the people at the exchange. Won't take no for an answer (not bein' able to hear it), gets through, says: 'Will I do what I can?' Says she would feel safe in the hands of a real gentleman. Oh, Parker, Parker! I could kiss her, I reely could, as Thipps says. I'll write to her instead—no, hang it, Parker, we'll go round. Bunter, get your infernal machine and the magnesium. I say, we'll all go into partnership—pool the two cases and work 'em out together. You shall see my body tonight, Parker, and I'll look for your wandering Jew tomorrow. I feel so happy, I shall explode. O Sugg, Sugg, how art thou suggified! Bunter, my shoes. I say, Parker, I suppose yours are rubbersoled. Not? Tut, tut, you mustn't go out like that. We'll lend you a pair. Gloves? Here. My stick, my torch, the lampblack, the forceps, knife, pill-boxes—all complete?"

"Certainly, my lord."

"Oh, Bunter, don't look so offended. I mean no harm. I believe in you, I trust you—what money have I got? That'll do. I knew a man once, Parker, who let a world-famous poisoner slip through his fingers because the machine on the Underground took nothing but pennies. There was a queue at the booking office and the man at the barrier stopped him, and while they were arguing about accepting a five-pound-note (which was all he had) for a two-penny ride to Baker Street, the criminal had sprung into a Circle train, and was next heard of in Constantinople, disguised as an elderly Church of England clergyman touring with his niece. Are we all ready? Go!"

They stepped out, Bunter carefully switching off the lights behind them.

As they emerged into the gloom and gleam of Piccadilly, Wimsey stopped short with a little exclamation.

"Wait a second," he said. "I've thought of something. If Sugg's there he'll make trouble. I must short-circuit him."

He ran back, and the other two men employed the few minutes of his absence in capturing a taxi.

Inspector Sugg and a subordinate Cerberus were on guard at 59, Queen Caroline Mansions, and showed no disposition to admit unofficial inquirers. Parker, indeed, they could not easily turn away, but Lord Peter found himself confronted with a surly manner and what Lord Beaconsfield described as a masterly inactivity. It was in vain that Lord Peter pleaded that he had been retained by Mrs. Thipps on behalf of her son.

"Retained!" said Inspector Sugg, with a snort. "*She'll* be retained if she doesn't look out. Shouldn't wonder if she wasn't in it herself, only she's so deaf, she's no good for anything at all."

"Look here, Inspector," said Lord Peter, "what's the use of bein' so bally obstructive? You'd much better let me in—you know I'll get there in the end. Dash it all, it's not as if I was takin' the bread out of your children's mouths. Nobody paid me for finding Lord Attenbury's emeralds for you."

"It's my duty to keep out the public," said Inspector Sugg, morosely, "and it's going to stay out."

"I never said anything about your keeping out of the public," said Lord Peter, easily, sitting down on the staircase to thrash the matter out comfortably, "though I've no doubt pussyfoot's a good thing, on principle, if not exaggerated. The golden mean, Sugg, as Aristotle says, keeps you from bein' a golden ass. Ever been a golden ass, Sugg? I have. It would take a whole rose-garden to cure me, Sugg—

"'You are my garden of beautiful roses,
My own rose, my one rose, that's you!'"

"I'm not going to stay any longer talking to you," said the harassed Sugg; "it's bad enough— Hullo, drat that telephone. Here, Cawthorn, go and see what it is, if that old catamaran will let you into the room. Shutting herself up there and screaming," said the

49

Inspector, "it's enough to make a man give up crime
and take to hedging and ditching."

The constable came back:

"It's from the Yard, sir," he said, coughing apologetically; "the Chief says every facility is to be given
to Lord Peter Wimsey, sir. Um!" He stood apart non-
committally, glazing his eyes.

"Five aces," said Lord Peter, cheerfully. "The
Chief's a dear friend of my mother's. No go, Sugg,
it's no good buckin'; you've got a full house. I'm goin'
to make it a bit fuller."

He walked in with his followers.

The body had been removed a few hours previously, and when the bathroom and the whole flat had
been explored by the naked eye and the camera of
the competent Bunter, it became evident that the
real problem of the household was old Mrs. Thipps.
Her son and servant had both been removed, and it
appeared that they had no friends in town, beyond a
few business acquaintances of Thipps's, whose very
addresses the old lady did not know. The other flats
in the building were occupied respectively by a family of seven, at present departed to winter abroad, an
elderly Indian colonel of ferocious manners, who lived
alone with an Indian man-servant, and a highly respectable family on the third floor, whom the disturbance over their heads had outraged to the last
degree. The husband, indeed, when appealed to by
Lord Peter, showed a little human weakness, but Mrs.
Appledore, appearing suddenly in a warm dressing-

gown, extricated him from the difficulties into which he was carelessly wandering.

"I am sorry," she said, "I'm afraid we can't interfere in any way. This is a very unpleasant business, Mr.— I'm afraid I didn't catch your name, and we have always found it better not to be mixed up with the police. Of course, *if* the Thippses are innocent, and I am sure I hope they are, it is very unfortunate for them, but I must say that the circumstances seem to me most suspicious, and to Theophilus too, and I should not like to have it said that we had assisted murderers. We might even be supposed to be accessories. Of course you are young, Mr.—"

"This is Lord Peter Wimsey, my dear," said Theophilus mildly.

She was unimpressed.

"Ah, yes," she said, "I believe you are distantly related to my late cousin, the Bishop of Carisbrooke. Poor man! He was always being taken in by impostors; he died without ever learning any better. I imagine you take after him, Lord Peter."

"I doubt it," said Lord Peter. "So far as I know he is only a connection, though it's a wise child that knows its own father. I congratulate you, dear lady, on takin' after the other side of the family. You'll forgive my buttin' in upon you like this in the middle of the night, though, as you say, it's all in the family, and I'm sure I'm very much obliged to you, and for permittin' me to admire that awfully fetchin' thing you've got on. Now, don't you worry, Mr.

51

Appledore. I'm thinkin' the best thing I can do is to trundle the old lady down to my mother and take her out of your way, otherwise you might be findin' your Christian feelin's gettin' the better of you some fine day, and there's nothin' like Christian feelin's for upsettin' a man's domestic comfort. Good-night, sir—good-night, dear lady—it's simply rippin' of you to let me drop in like this."

"Well!" said Mrs. Appledore, as the door closed behind him.

And—

> "I thank the goodness and the grace
> That on my birth have smiled,"

said Lord Peter, "and taught me to be bestially impertinent when I choose. Cat!"

Two a.m. saw Lord Peter Wimsey arrive in a friend's car at the Dower House, Denver Castle, in company with a deaf and aged lady and an antique portmanteau.

"It's very nice to see you, dear," said the Dowager Duchess, placidly. She was a small, plump woman, with perfectly white hair and exquisite hands. In feature she was as unlike her second son as she was like him in character; her black eyes twinkled cheerfully, and her manners and movements were marked with a neat and rapid decision. She wore a charming wrap from Liberty's, and sat watching Lord Peter eat cold beef and cheese as though his arrival in such incongruous circumstances and company were the most ordinary event possible, which with him, indeed, it was.

"Have you got the old lady to bed?" asked Lord Peter.

"Oh, yes, dear. Such a striking old person, isn't she? And very courageous. She tells me she has never been in a motor-car before. But she thinks you a very nice lad, dear—that careful of her, you remind her of her own son. Poor little Mr. Thipps—whatever made your friend the inspector think he could have murdered anybody?"

"My friend the inspector—no, no more, thank you, Mother—is determined to prove that the intrusive person in Thipps's bath is Sir Reuben Levy, who disappeared mysteriously from his house last night. His line of reasoning is: We've lost a middle-aged gentleman without any clothes on in Park Lane; we've found a middle-aged gentleman without any clothes on in Battersea. Therefore they're one and the same person, Q.E.D., and put little Thipps in quod."

"You're very elliptical, dear," said the Duchess, mildly. "Why should Mr. Thipps be arrested even if they are the same?"

"Sugg must arrest somebody," said Lord Peter, "but there is one odd little bit of evidence come out which goes a long way to support Sugg's theory, only that I know it to be no go by the evidence of my own eyes. Last night at about 9.15 a young woman was strollin' up the Battersea Park Road for purposes best known to herself, when she saw a gentleman in a fur coat and top-hat saunterin' along under an umbrella, lookin' at the names of all the streets. He looked a bit out of place, so, not bein' a shy girl, you see, she walked up to him, and said: 'Good-evening.' 'Can you tell me, please,' says the mysterious stranger, 'whether this street leads into Prince of Wales Road?' She said it did, and further asked him in a jocular manner what he was doing with himself and all the rest of it, only she wasn't altogether so explicit about that part of the conversation, because she was unburdenin' her heart to Sugg, d'you see, and he's paid by a grateful country to have very pure, highminded ideals, what? Anyway, the old boy said he couldn't attend to her just then as he had an appointment. 'I've got to go and see a man, my dear,' was how she said he put it, and he walked on up Alexandra Avenue towards Prince of Wales Road. She was starin' after him, still rather surprised, when she was joined by a friend of hers, who said: 'It's no good wasting your time with him—that's Levy—I knew him when I lived in the West End, and the girls used to call him Peagreen Incorruptible'—friend's name suppressed, owing to implications of story, but girl vouches for what was said. She thought no more about it till the milkman brought news this morning of the excitement at Queen Caroline Mansions; then she went round, though not likin' the police as a rule, and asked the man there whether the dead gentleman had a beard and glasses. Told he had glasses but no beard, she incautiously said: 'Oh, then, it isn't him,' and the man said: 'Isn't who?' and collared her.

That's her story. Sugg's delighted, of course, and quodded Thipps on the strength of it."

"Dear me," said the Duchess, "I hope the poor girl won't get into trouble."

"Shouldn't think so," said Lord Peter. "Thipps is the one that's going to get it in the neck. Besides, he's done a silly thing. I got that out of Sugg, too, though he was sittin' tight on the information. Seems Thipps got into a confusion about the train he took back from Manchester. Said first he got home at 10.30. Then they pumped Gladys Horrocks, who let out he wasn't back till after 11.45. Then Thipps, bein' asked to explain the discrepancy, stammers and bungles and says, first, that he missed the train. Then Sugg makes inquiries at St. Pancras and discovers that he left a bag in the cloakroom there at ten. Thipps, again asked to explain, stammers worse an' says he walked about for a few hours—met a friend—can't say who —didn't meet a friend—can't say what he did with his time—can't explain why he didn't go back for his bag—can't say what time he *did* get in—can't explain how he got a bruise on his forehead. In fact, can't explain himself at all. Gladys Horrocks interrogated again. Says, this time, Thipps came in at 10.30. Then admits she didn't hear him come in. Can't say why she didn't hear him come in. Can't say why she said first of all that she *did* hear him. Bursts into tears. Contradicts herself. Everybody's suspicion roused. Quod 'em both."

"As you put it, dear," said the Duchess, "it all sounds very confusing, and not quite respectable.

Poor little Mr. Thipps would be terribly upset by anything that wasn't respectable."

"I wonder what he did with himself," said Lord Peter thoughtfully. "I really don't think he was committing a murder. Besides, I believe the fellow has been dead a day or two, though it don't do to build too much on doctors' evidence. It's an entertainin' little problem."

"Very curious, dear. But so sad about poor Sir Reuben. I must write a few lines to Lady Levy; I used to know her quite well, you know, dear, down in Hampshire, when she was a girl. Christine Ford, she was then, and I remember so well the dreadful trouble there was about her marrying a Jew. That was before he made his money, of course, in that oil business out in America. The family wanted her to marry Julian Freke, who did so well afterwards and was connected with the family, but she fell in love with this Mr. Levy and eloped with him. He was very handsome, then, you know, dear, in a foreign-looking way, but he hadn't any means, and the Fords didn't like his religion. Of course we're all Jews nowadays, and they wouldn't have minded so much if he'd pretended to be something else, like that Mr. Simons we met at Mrs. Porchester's, who always tells everybody that he got his nose in Italy at the Renaissance, and claims to be descended somehow or other from La Bella Simonetta—so foolish, you know, dear—as if anybody believed it; and I'm sure some Jews are very good people, and personally I'd much rather they believed something, though of course it must be very

56

inconvenient, what with not working on Saturdays and circumcising the poor little babies and everything depending on the new moon and that funny kind of meat they have with such a slang-sounding name, and never being able to have bacon for breakfast. Still, there it was, and it was much better for the girl to marry him if she was really fond of him, though I believe young Freke was really devoted to her, and they're still great friends. Not that there was ever a real engagement, only a sort of understanding with her father, but he's never married, you know, and lives all by himself in that big house next to the hospital, though he's very rich and distinguished now, and I know ever so many people have tried to get hold of him—there was Lady Mainwaring wanted him for that eldest girl of hers, though I remember saying at the time it was no use expecting a surgeon to be taken in by a figure that was all padding—they have so many opportunities of judging, you know, dear."

"Lady Levy seems to have had the knack of makin' people devoted to her," said Peter. "Look at the pea-green incorruptible Levy."

"That's quite true, dear; she was a most delightful girl, and they say her daughter is just like her. I rather lost sight of them when she married, and you know your father didn't care much about business people, but I know everybody always said they were a model couple. In fact it was a proverb that Sir Reuben was as well loved at home as he was hated abroad. I don't mean in foreign countries, you know, dear—just the

57

proverbial way of putting things—like 'a saint abroad and a devil at home'—only the other way on, reminding one of the *Pilgrim's Progress*."

"Yes," said Peter, "I daresay the old man made one or two enemies."

"Dozens, dear—such a dreadful place, the City, isn't it? Everybody Ishmaels together—though I don't suppose Sir Reuben would like to be called that, would he? Doesn't it mean illegitimate, or not a proper Jew, anyway? I always did get confused with those Old Testament characters."

Lord Peter laughed and yawned.

"I think I'll turn in for an hour or two," he said. "I must be back in town at eight—Parker's coming to breakfast."

The Duchess looked at the clock, which marked five minutes to three.

"I'll send up your breakfast at half-past six, dear," she said. "I hope you'll find everything all right. I told them just to slip a hot-water bottle in; those linen sheets are so chilly; you can put it out if it's in your way."

CHAPTER IV

"—SO THERE IT IS, PARKER," SAID LORD PETER, PUSH-
ing his coffee-cup aside and lighting his after-breakfast pipe; "you may find it leads you to something,
though it don't seem to get me any further with my
bathroom problem. Did you do anything more at that
after I left?"

"No; but I've been on the roof this morning."

"The deuce you have—what an energetic devil you
are! I say, Parker, I think this co-operative scheme is
an uncommonly good one. It's much easier to work
on someone else's job than one's own—gives one that
delightful feelin' of interferin' and bossin' about,
combined with the glorious sensation that another
fellow is takin' all one's own work off one's hands.
You scratch my back and I'll scratch yours, what?
Did you find anything?"

"Not very much. I looked for any footmarks of
course, but naturally, with all this rain, there wasn't
a sign. Of course, if this were a detective story,
there'd have been a convenient shower exactly an
hour before the crime and a beautiful set of marks
which could only have come there between two and
three in the morning, but this being real life in a
London November, you might as well expect footprints in Niagara. I searched the roofs right along—
and came to the jolly conclusion that any person in

any blessed flat in the blessed row might have done it. All the staircases open on to the roof and the leads are quite flat; you can walk along as easy as along Shaftesbury Avenue. Still, I've got some evidence that the body did walk along there.

"What's that?"

Parker brought out his pocketbook and extracted a few shreds of material, which he laid before his friend.

"One was caught in the gutter just above Thipps's bathroom window, another in a crack of the stone parapet just over it, and the rest came from the chimney-stack behind, where they had caught in an iron stanchion. What do you make of them?"

Lord Peter scrutinized them very carefully through his lens.

"Interesting," he said, "damned interesting. Have you developed those plates, Bunter?" he added, as that discreet assistant came in with the post.

"Yes, my lord."

"Caught anything?"

"I don't know whether to call it anything or not, my lord," said Bunter, dubiously. "I'll bring the prints in."

"Do," said Wimsey. "Hallo! here's our advertisement about the gold chain in the *Times*—very nice it looks: 'Write, 'phone or call 110, Piccadilly.' Perhaps it would have been safer to put a box number, though I always think that the franker you are with people, the more you're likely to deceive 'em; so unused is the modern world to the open hand and the guileless heart, what?"

"But you don't think the fellow who left that chain on the body is going to give himself away by coming here and inquiring about it?"

"I don't, fathead," said Lord Peter, with the easy politeness of the real aristocracy; "that's why I've tried to get hold of the jeweller who originally sold the chain. See?" He pointed to the paragraph. "It's not an old chain—hardly worn at all. Oh, thanks, Bunter. Now, see here, Parker, these are the finger-marks you noticed yesterday on the window-sash and on the far edge of the bath. I'd overlooked them; I give you full credit for the discovery, I crawl, I grovel, my name is Watson, and you need not say what you were just going to say, because I admit it all. Now we shall— Hullo, hullo, hullo!"

The three men stared at the photographs.

"The criminal," said Lord Peter, bitterly, "climbed over the roofs in the wet and not unnaturally got soot on his fingers. He arranged the body in the bath, and wiped away all traces of himself except two, which he obligingly left to show us how to do our job. We learn from a smudge on the floor that he wore india rubber boots, and from this admirable set of finger-prints on the edge of the bath that he had the usual number of fingers and wore rubber gloves. That's the kind of man he is. Take the fool away, gentlemen."

He put the prints aside, and returned to an examination of the shreds of material in his hand. Suddenly he whistled softly.

"Do you make anything of these, Parker?"

"They seemed to me to be ravellings of some coarse cotton stuff—a sheet, perhaps, or an improvised rope."

"Yes," said Lord Peter—"yes. It may be a mistake—it may be *our* mistake. I wonder. Tell me, d'you think these tiny threads are long enough and strong enough to hang a man?"

He was silent, his long eyes narrowing into slits behind the smoke of his pipe.

"What do you suggest doing this morning?" asked Parker.

"Well," said Lord Peter, "it seems to me it's about time I took a hand in your job. Let's go round to Park Lane and see what larks Sir Reuben Levy was up to in bed last night."

"And now, Mrs. Pemming, if you would be so kind as to give me a blanket," said Mr. Bunter, coming down into the kitchen, "and permit of me hanging a sheet across the lower part of this window, and drawing the screen across here, so—so as to shut off any reflections, if you understand me, we'll get to work."

Sir Reuben Levy's cook, with her eye upon Mr. Bunter's gentlemanly and well-tailored appearance, hastened to produce what was necessary. Her visitor placed on the table a basket, containing a water-bottle, a silver-backed hair-brush, a pair of boots, a small roll of linoleum, and the "Letters of a Self-made Merchant to His Son," bound in polished morocco. He drew an umbrella from beneath his arm and added it to the collection. He then advanced a ponderous photographic machine and set it up in the neighbourhood of the kitchen range; then, spreading a newspaper over the fair, scrubbed surface of the table, he began to roll up his sleeves and insinuate himself into a pair of surgical gloves. Sir Reuben Levy's valet, entering at the moment and finding him thus engaged, put aside the kitchen-maid, who was staring from a front-row position, and inspected the apparatus critically. Mr. Bunter nodded brightly to him, and uncorked a small bottle of grey powder.

"Odd sort of fish, your employer, isn't he?" said the valet, carelessly.

"Very singular, indeed," said Mr. Bunter. "Now, my dear," he added, ingratiatingly, to the kitchen-maid, "I wonder if you'd just pour a little of this grey powder over the edge of the bottle while I'm holding it—and the same with this boot—here, at the top—thank you, Miss—what is your name? Price? Oh, but you've got another name besides Price, haven't you? Mabel, eh? That's a name I'm uncommonly partial to—that's very nicely done, you've a steady hand, Miss Mabel—see that? That's the finger marks—three there, and two here, and smudged over in both places. No, don't you touch 'em, my dear, or you'll rub the bloom off. We'll stand 'em up here till they're ready to have their portraits taken. Now then, let's take the hair-brush next. Perhaps, Mrs.

Pemming, you'd like to lift him up very carefully by the bristles."

"By the bristles, Mr. Bunter?"

"If you please, Mrs. Pemming—and lay him here. Now, Miss Mabel, another little exhibition of your skill, *if* you please. No—we'll try lamp-black this time. Perfect. Couldn't have done it better myself. Ah! there's a beautiful set. No smudges this time. That'll interest his lordship. Now the little book—no, I'll pick that up myself—with these gloves, you see, and by the edges—I'm a careful criminal, Mrs. Pemming, I don't want to leave any traces. Dust the cover all over, Miss Mabel; now this side—that's the way to do it. Lots of prints and no smudges. All according to plan. Oh, please, Mr. Graves, you mustn't touch it—it's as much as my place is worth to have it touched."

"D'you have to do much of this sort of thing?" inquired Mr. Graves, from a superior standpoint.

"Any amount," replied Mr. Bunter, with a groan calculated to appeal to Mr. Graves's heart and unlock his confidence. "If you'd kindly hold one end of this bit of linoleum, Mrs. Pemming, I'll hold up this end while Miss Mabel operates. Yes, Mr. Graves, it's a hard life, valeting by day and developing by night —morning tea at any time from 6.30 to 11, and criminal investigation at all hours. It's wonderful, the ideas these rich men with nothing to do get into their heads."

"I wonder you stand it," said Mr. Graves. "Now there's none of that here. A quiet, orderly, domestic life, Mr. Bunter, has much to be said for it. Meals at

64

regular hours; decent, respectable families to dinner
—none of your painted women—and no valeting at
night, there's *much* to be said for it. I don't hold
with Hebrews as a rule, Mr. Bunter, and of course
I understand that you may find it to your advantage
to be in a titled family, but there's less thought of
that these days, and I will say, for a self-made man,
no one could call Sir Reuben vulgar, and my lady at
any rate is county—Miss Ford, she was, one of the
Hampshire Fords, and both of them always most
considerate."

"I agree with you, Mr. Graves—his lordship and
me have never held with being narrow-minded—
why, yes, my dear, of course it's a footmark, this is
the washstand linoleum. A good Jew can be a good
man, that's what I've always said. And regular hours
and considerate habits have a great deal to recommend them. Very simple in his tastes, now, Sir
Reuben, isn't he? for such a rich man, I mean."

"Very simple indeed," said the cook; "the meals he
and her ladyship have when they're by themselves
with Miss Rachel—well, there now—if it wasn't for
the dinners, which is always good when there's company, I'd be wastin' my talents and education here,
if you understand me, Mr. Bunter."

Mr. Bunter added the handle of the umbrella to his
collection, and began to pin a sheet across the window, aided by the housemaid.

"Admirable," said he. "Now, if I might have this
blanket on the table and another on a towel-horse
or something of that kind by way of a background—

65

you're very kind, Mrs. Pemming. . . . Ah! I wish
his lordship never wanted valeting at night. Many's
the time I've sat up till three and four, and up again
to call him early to go off Sherlocking at the other
end of the country. And the mud he gets on his
clothes and his boots!"

"I'm sure it's a shame, Mr. Bunter," said Mrs. Pemming, warmly. "Low, I calls it. In my opinion, police-
work ain't no fit occupation for a gentleman, let alone
a lordship."

"Everything made so difficult, too," said Mr.
Bunter nobly sacrificing his employer's character and
his own feelings in a good cause; "boots chucked into
a corner, clothes hung up on the floor, as they say—"

"That's often the case with these men as are born
with a silver spoon in their mouths," said Mr. Graves.
"Now, Sir Reuben, he's never lost his good old-fashioned habits. Clothes folded up neat, boots put out in
his dressing-room, so as a man could get them in the
morning, everything made easy."

"He forgot them the night before last, though."

"The clothes, not the boots. Always thoughtful for
others, is Sir Reuben. Ah! I hope nothing's happened
to him."

"Indeed, no, poor gentleman," chimed in the cook,
"and as for what they're sayin', that he'd 'ave gone
out surrepshous-like to do something he didn't ought,
well, I'd never believe it of him, Mr. Bunter, not if
I was to take my dying oath upon it."

"Ah!" said Mr. Bunter, adjusting his arc-lamps and
connecting them with the nearest electric light, "and

that's more than most of us could say of them as
pays us."

"Five foot ten," said Lord Peter, "and not an inch
more." He peered dubiously at the depression in the
bed clothes, and measured it a second time with the
gentleman-scout's vade-mecum. Parker entered this
particular in a neat pocketbook.

"I suppose," he said, "a six-foot-two man *might*
leave a five-foot-ten depression if he curled himself
up."

"Have you any Scotch blood in you, Parker?" inquired his colleague, bitterly.

"Not that I know of," replied Parker. "Why?"

"Because of all the cautious, ungenerous, deliberate
and cold-blooded devils I know," said Lord Peter,
"you are the most cautious, ungenerous, deliberate
and cold-blooded. Here am I, sweating my brains out
to introduce a really sensational incident into your
dull and disreputable little police investigation, and
you refuse to show a single spark of enthusiasm."

"Well, it's no good jumping at conclusions."

"Jump? You don't even crawl distantly within
sight of a conclusion. I believe if you caught the cat
with her head in the cream-jug you'd say it was conceivable that the jug was empty when she got there."

"Well, it would be conceivable, wouldn't it?"

"Curse you," said Lord Peter. He screwed his monocle into his eye, and bent over the pillow, breathing
hard and tightly through his nose. "Here, give me
the tweezers," he said presently. "Good heavens, man,

don't blow like that, you might be a whale." He nipped up an almost invisible object from the linen.

"What is it?" asked Parker.

"It's a hair," said Wimsey grimly, his hard eyes growing harder. "Let's go and look at Levy's hats, shall we? And you might just ring for that fellow with the churchyard name, do you mind?"

Mr. Graves, when summoned, found Lord Peter Wimsey squatting on the floor of the dressing-room before a row of hats arranged upside down before him.

"Here you are," said that nobleman cheerfully. "Now, Graves, this is a guessin' competition—a sort of three-hat trick, to mix metaphors. Here are nine hats, including three top-hats. Do you identify all these hats as belonging to Sir Reuben Levy? You do? Very good. Now I have three guesses as to which hat he wore the night he disappeared, and if I guess right, I win; if I don't, you win. See? Ready? Go. I suppose you know the answer yourself, by the way?"

"Do I understand your lordship to be asking which hat Sir Reuben wore when he went out on Monday night, your lordship?"

"No, you don't understand a bit," said Lord Peter. "I'm asking if *you* know—don't tell me, I'm going to guess."

"I do know, your lordship," said Mr. Graves, reprovingly.

"Well," said Lord Peter, "as he was dinin' at the Ritz he wore a topper. Here are three toppers. In three guesses I'd be bound to hit the right one, wouldn't I? That don't seem very sportin'. I'll take one guess. It was this one."

He indicated the hat next the window.

"Am I right, Graves—have I got the prize?"

"That *is* the hat in question, my lord," said Mr. Graves, without excitement.

"Thanks," said Lord Peter, "that's all I wanted to know. Ask Bunter to step up, would you?"

Mr. Bunter stepped up with an aggrieved air, and his usually smooth hair ruffled by the focussing cloth.

"Oh, there you are, Bunter," said Lord Peter; "look here—"

"Here I am, my lord," said Mr. Bunter, with respectful reproach, "but if you'll excuse me saying so, downstairs is where I ought to be, with all those young women about—they'll be fingering the evidence, my lord."

"I cry your mercy," said Lord Peter, "but I've quarrelled hopelessly with Mr. Parker and distracted the estimable Graves, and I want you to tell me what finger-prints you have found. I shan't be happy till I get it, so don't be harsh with me, Bunter."

"Well, my lord, your lordship understands I haven't photographed them yet, but I won't deny that their appearance is interesting, my lord. The little book off the night table, my lord, has only the marks of one set of fingers—there's a little scar on the right thumb which makes them easy recognised. The hairbrush, too, my lord, has only the same set of marks. The umbrella, the toothglass and the boots all have two sets: the hand with the scarred thumb, which I

69

Whose Body?

take to be Sir Reuben's, my lord, and a set of smudges
superimposed upon them, if I may put it that way,
my lord, which may or may not be the same hand in
rubber gloves. I could tell you better when I've got
the photographs made, to measure them, my lord.
The linoleum in front of the washstand is very gratifying indeed, my lord, if you will excuse my mentioning it. Besides the marks of Sir Reuben's boots which
your lordship pointed out, there's the print of a man's
naked foot—a much smaller one, my lord, not much
more than a tin-inch sock, I should say if you asked
me."

Lord Peter's face became irradiated with almost a
dim, religious light.

"A mistake," he breathed, "a mistake, a little one,
but he can't afford it. When was the linoleum washed
last, Bunter?"

"Monday morning, my lord. The housemaid did
it and remembered to mention it. Only remark she's
made yet, and it's to the point. The other domestics—"

His features expressed disdain.

"What did I say, Parker? Five-foot-ten and not an
inch longer. And he didn't dare to use the hair-brush.
Beautiful. But he *had* to risk the top-hat. Gentleman
can't walk home in the rain late at night without a
hat, you know, Parker. Look! what do you make of
it? Two sets of finger-prints on everything but the
book and the brush, two sets of feet on the linoleum,
and two kinds of hair in the hat!"

He lifted the top-hat to the light, and extracted the evidence with tweezers.

"Think of it, Parker—to remember the hair-brush and forget the hat—to remember his fingers all the time, and to make that one careless step on the tell-tale linoleum. Here they are, you see, black hair and tan hair—black hair in the bowler and the panama, and black and tan in last night's topper. And then, just to make certain that we're on the right track, just one little auburn hair on the pillow, on this pillow, Parker, which isn't quite in the right place. It almost brings tears to my eyes."

"Do you mean to say—" said the detective, slowly.

"I mean to say," said Lord Peter, "that it was not Sir Reuben Levy whom the cook saw last night on the doorstep. I say that it was another man, perhaps a couple of inches shorter, who came here in Levy's clothes and let himself in with Levy's latchkey. Oh, he was a bold, cunning devil, Parker. He had on Levy's boots, and every stitch of Levy's clothing down to the skin. He had rubber gloves on his hands which he never took off, and he did everything he could to make us think that Levy slept here last night. He took his chances, and won. He walked upstairs, he undressed, he even washed and cleaned his teeth, though he didn't use the hair-brush for fear of leaving red hairs in it. He had to guess what Levy did with boots and clothes; one guess was wrong and the other right, as it happened. The bed must look as if it had been slept in, so he gets in, and lies there in his victim's very pyjamas. Then, in the morning sometime, probably in the deadest hour between two and three, he gets up, dresses himself in his own clothes that he has brought with him in a bag, and creeps downstairs. If anybody wakes, he is lost, but he is a bold man, and he takes his chance. He knows that people do not wake as a rule—and they don't wake. He opens the street door which he left on the latch when he came in—he listens for the stray passer-by or the policeman on his beat. He slips out. He pulls the door quietly to with the latchkey. He walks briskly away in rubber-soled shoes—he's the kind of criminal who isn't complete without rubber-soled shoes. In a few minutes he is at Hyde Park Corner. After that—"

He paused, and added:

"He did all that, and unless he had nothing at stake, he had everything at stake. Either Sir Reuben Levy has been spirited away for some silly practical joke, or the man with the auburn hair has the guilt of murder upon his soul."

"Dear me!" ejaculated the detective, "you're very dramatic about it."

Lord Peter passed his hand rather wearily over his hair.

"My true friend," he murmured in a voice surcharged with emotion, "you recall me to the nursery rhymes of my youth—the sacred duty of flippancy:

> "There was an old man of Whitehaven
> Who danced a quadrille with a raven,
> But they said: It's absurd
> To encourage that bird—
> So they smashed that old man of Whitehaven.

That's the correct attitude, Parker. Here's a poor old buffer spirited away—such a joke—and I don't believe he'd hurt a fly himself—that makes it funnier. D'you know, Parker, I don't care frightfully about this case after all."

"Which, this or yours?"

"Both. I say, Parker, shall we go quietly home and have lunch and go to the Coliseum?"

"You can if you like," replied the detective; "but you forget I do this for my bread and butter."

"And I haven't even that excuse," said Lord Peter; "well, what's the next move? What would you do in my case?"

"I'd so some good, hard grind," said Parker. "I'd distrust every bit of work Sugg ever did, and I'd get the family history of every tenant of every flat in Queen Caroline Mansions. I'd examine all their box-rooms and rooftraps, and I would inveigle them into conversations and suddenly bring in the words 'body' and 'pince-nez,' and see if they wriggled, like those modern psyo-what's-his-names."

"You would, would you?" said Lord Peter with a grin. "Well, we've exchanged cases, you know, so just you toddle off and do it. I'm going to have a jolly time at Wyndham's."

Parker made a grimace.

"Well," he said, "I don't suppose you'd ever do it, so I'd better. You'll never become a professional till you learn to do a little work, Wimsey. How about lunch?"

"I'm invited out," said Lord Peter, magnificently.

"I'll run around and change at the club. Can't feed with Freddy Arbuthnot in these bags; Bunter!"

"Yes, my lord."

"Pack up if you're ready, and come round and wash my face and hands for me at the club."

"Work here for another two hours, my lord. Can't do with less than thirty minutes' exposure. The current's none too strong."

"You see how I'm bullied by my own man, Parker? Well, I must bear it, I suppose. Ta-ta!"

He whistled his way downstairs.

The conscientious Mr. Parker, with a groan, settled down to a systematic search through Sir Reuben Levy's papers, with the assistance of a plate of ham sandwiches and a bottle of Bass.

Lord Peter and the Honourable Freddy Arbuthnot, looking together like an advertisement for gents' trouserings, strolled into the dining-room at Wyndham's.

"Haven't seen you for an age," said the Honourable Freddy. "What have you been doin' with yourself?"

"Oh, foolin' about," said Lord Peter, languidly.

"Thick or clear, sir?" inquired the waiter of the Honourable Freddy.

"Which'll you have, Wimsey?" said that gentleman, transferring the burden of selection to his guest. "They're both equally poisonous."

"Well, clear's less trouble to lick out of the spoon," said Lord Peter.

"Clear," said the Honourable Freddy.

"Consommé Polonais," agreed the waiter. "Very nice, sir."

Conversation languished until the Honourable Freddy found a bone in the filleted sole, and sent for the head waiter to explain its presence. When this matter had been adjusted Lord Peter found energy to say:

"Sorry to hear about your gov'nor, old man."

"Yes, poor old buffer," said the Honourable Freddy; "they say he can't last long now. What? Oh! the Montrachet '08. There's nothing fit to drink in this place," he added gloomily.

After this deliberate insult to a noble vintage there was a further pause, till Lord Peter said: "How's 'Change?"

"Rotten," said the Honourable Freddy.

He helped himself gloomily to salmis of game.

"Can I do anything?" asked Lord Peter.

"Oh, no, thanks—very decent of you, but it'll pan out all right in time."

"This isn't a bad salmis," said Lord Peter.

"I've eaten worse," admitted his friend.

"What about those Argentines?" inquired Lord Peter. "Here, waiter, there's a bit of cork in my glass."

"Cork?" cried the Honourable Freddy, with something approaching animation; "you'll hear about this, waiter. It's an amazing thing a fellow who's paid to do the job can't manage to take a cork out of a bottle. What you say? Argentines? Gone all to hell.

Old Levy bunkin' off like that's knocked the bottom out of the market."

"You don't say so," said Lord Peter. "What d'you suppose has happened to the old man?"

"Cursed if I know." said the Honourable Freddy; "knocked on the head by the bears, I should think."

"P'r'aps he's gone off on his own," suggested Lord Peter. "Double life, you know. Giddy old blighters, some of these City men."

"Oh, no," said the Honourable Freddy, faintly roused; "no, hang it all, Wimsey, I wouldn't care to say that. He's a decent old domestic bird, and his daughter's a charmin' girl. Besides, he's straight enough—he'd *do* you down fast enough, but he wouldn't *let* you down. Old Anderson is badly cut up about it."

"Who's Anderson?"

"Chap with property out there. He belongs here. He was goin' to meet Levy on Tuesday. He's afraid those railway people will get in now, and then it'll be all U. P."

"Who's runnin' the railway people over here?" inquired Lord Peter.

"Yankee blighter, John P. Milligan. He's got an option, or says he has. You can't trust these brutes."

"Can't Anderson hold on?"

"Anderson isn't Levy. Hasn't got the shekels. Besides, he's only one. Levy covers the ground—he could boycott Milligan's beastly railway if he liked. That's where he's got the pull, you see."

"B'lieve I met the Milligan man somewhere," said

76

Lord Peter, thoughtfully. "Ain't he a hulking brute with black hair and a beard?"

"You're thinkin' of somebody else," said the Honourable Freddy. "Milligan don't stand any higher than I do, unless you call five-feet-ten hulking—and he's bald, anyway."

Lord Peter considered this over the Gorgonzola. Then he said: "Didn't know Levy had a charmin' daughter."

"Oh, yes," said the Honourable Freddy, with an elaborate detachment. "Met her and Mamma last year abroad. That's how I got to know the old man. He's been very decent. Let me into this Argentine business on the ground floor, don't you know?"

"Well," said Lord Peter, "you might do worse. Money's money, ain't it? And Lady Levy is quite a redeemin' point. At least, my mother knew her people."

"Oh, *she's* all right," said the Honourable Freddy, "and the old man's nothing to be ashamed of nowadays. He's self-made, of course, but he don't pretend to be anything else. No side. Toddles off to business on a 96 'bus every morning. 'Can't make up my mind to taxis, my boy,' he says. 'I had to look at every halfpenny when I was a young man, and I can't get out of the way of it now.' Though, if he's takin' his family out, nothing's too good. Rachel—that's the girl—always laughs at the old man's little economies."

"I suppose they've sent for Lady Levy," said Lord Peter.

"I suppose so," agreed the other. "I'd better pop

round and express sympathy or somethin', what? Wouldn't look well not to, d'you think? But it's deuced awkward. What am I to say?"

"I don't think it matters much what you say," said Lord Peter, helpfully. "I should ask if you can do anything."

"Thanks," said the lover, "I will. Energetic young man. Count on me. Always at your service. Ring me up any time of the day or night. That's the line to take, don't you think?"

"That's the idea," said Lord Peter.

Mr. John P. Milligan, the London representative of the great Milligan railroad and shipping company, was dictating code cables to his secretary in an office in Lombard Street, when a card was brought up to him, bearing the simple legend:

LORD PETER WIMSEY
Marlborough Club

Mr. Milligan was annoyed at the interruption, but, like many of his nation, if he had a weak point, it was the British aristocracy. He postponed for a few minutes the elimination from the map of a modest but promising farm, and directed that the visitor should be shown up.

"Good-afternoon," said that nobleman, ambling genially in, "it's most uncommonly good of you to let me come round wastin' your time like this. I'll try not to be too long about it, though I'm not awfully good at comin' to the point. My brother never would

78

let me stand for the county, y'know—said I wandered on so nobody'd know what I was talkin' about."

"Pleased to meet you, Lord Wimsey," said Mr. Milligan. "Won't you take a seat?"

"Thanks," said Lord Peter, "but I'm not a peer, you know—that's my brother Denver. My name's Peter. It's a silly name, I always think, so old-world and full of homely virtue and that sort of thing, but my god-fathers and godmothers in my baptism are responsible for that, I suppose, officially—which is rather hard on them, you know, as they didn't actually choose it. But we always have a Peter, after the third duke, who betrayed five kings somewhere about the Wars of the Roses, though come to think of it, it ain't anything to be proud of. Still, one has to make the best of it."

Mr. Milligan, thus ingeniously placed at that disadvantage which attends ignorance, manoeuvred for position, and offered his interrupter a Corona Corona.

"Thanks, awfully," said Lord Peter, "though you really mustn't tempt me to stay here burblin' all afternoon. By Jove, Mr. Milligan, if you offer people such comfortable chairs and cigars like these, I wonder they don't come an' live in your office." He added mentally: "I wish to goodness I could get those long-toed boots off you. How's a man to know the size of your feet? And a head like a potato. It's enough to make one swear."

"Say now, Lord Peter," said Mr. Milligan, "can I do anything for you?"

"Well, d'you know," said Lord Peter, "I'm wonderin' if you would. It's damned cheek to ask you, but fact is, it's my mother, you know. Wonderful woman, but don't realize what it means, demands on the time of a busy man like you. We don't understand hustle over here, you know, Mr. Milligan."

"Now don't you mention that," said Mr. Milligan; "I'd be surely charmed to do anything to oblige the Duchess."

He felt a momentary qualm as to whether a duke's mother were also a duchess, but breathed more freely as Lord Peter went on:

"Thanks—that's uncommonly good of you. Well, now, it's like this. My mother—most energetic, self-sacrificin' woman, don't you see, is thinkin' of gettin' up a sort of a charity bazaar down at Denver this winter, in aid of the church roof, y'know. Very sad case, Mr. Milligan—fine old antique—early English windows and decorated angel roof, and all that— all tumblin' to pieces, rain pourin' in and so on— vicar catchin' rheumatism at early service, owin' to the draught blowin' in over the altar—you know the sort of thing. They've got a man down startin' on it— little beggar called Thipps—lives with an aged mother in Battersea—vulgar little beast, but quite good on angel roofs and things, I'm told."

At this point, Lord Peter watched his interlocutor narrowly, but finding that this rigmarole produced in him no reaction more startling than polite interest tinged with faint bewilderment, he abandoned this line of investigation, and proceeded:

"I say, I beg your pardon, frightfully—I'm afraid I'm bein' beastly long-winded. Fact is, my mother is gettin' up this bazaar, and she thought it'd be an awfully interestin' side-show to have some lectures—sort of little talks, y'know—by eminent business men of all nations. 'How I Did It' kind of touch, y'know—'A Drop of Oil with a Kerosene King'—'Cash Conscience and Cocoa' and so on. It would interest people down there no end. You see, all my mother's friends will be there, and we've none of us any money—not what you'd call money, I mean—I expect our incomes wouldn't pay your telephone calls, would they?—but we like awfully to hear about the people who can make money. Gives us a sort of uplifted feelin', don't you know. Well, anyway, I mean, my mother'd be frightfully pleased and grateful to you, Mr. Milligan, if you'd come down and give us a few words as a representative American. It needn't take more than ten minutes or so, y'know, because the local people can't understand much beyond shootin' and huntin', and my mother's crowd can't keep their minds on anythin' more than ten minutes together, but we'd really appreciate it very much if you'd come and stay a day or two and just give us a little breezy word on the almighty dollar."

"Why, yes," said Mr. Milligan, "I'd like to, Lord Peter. It's kind of the Duchess to suggest it. It's a very sad thing when these fine old antiques begin to wear out. I'll come with great pleasure. And perhaps you'd be kind enough to accept a little donation to the Restoration Fund."

This unexpected development nearly brought Lord Peter up all standing. To pump, by means of an ingenious lie, a hospitable gentleman whom you are inclined to suspect of a peculiarly malicious murder, and to accept from him in the course of the proceedings a large cheque for a charitable object, has something about it unpalatable to any but the hardened Secret Service agent. Lord Peter temporized.

"That's awfully decent of you," he said. "I'm sure they'd be no end grateful. But you'd better not give it to me, you know. I might spend it, or lose it. I'm not very reliable, I'm afraid. The vicar's the right person—the Rev. Constantine Throgmorton, St. John-before-the-Latin-Gate Vicarage, Duke's Denver, if you like to send it there."

"I will," said Mr. Milligan. "Will you write it out now for a thousand pounds, Scoot, in case it slips my mind later?"

The secretary, a sandy-haired young man with a long chin and no eyebrows, silently did as he was requested. Lord Peter looked from the bald head of Mr. Milligan to the red head of the secretary, hardened his heart and tried again.

"Well, I'm no end grateful to you, Mr. Milligan, and so'll my mother be when I tell her. I'll let you know the date of the bazaar—it's not quite settled yet, and I've got to see some other business men, don't you know. I thought of askin' someone from one of the big newspaper combines to represent British advertisin' talent, what?—and a friend of mine promises me a leadin' German financier—very interestin' if there ain't too much feelin' against it down in the country, and I'll have to find somebody or other to do the Hebrew point of view. I thought of askin' Levy, y'know, only he's floated off in this inconvenient way."

"Yes," said Mr. Milligan, "that's a very curious thing, though I don't mind saying, Lord Peter, that it's a convenience to me. He had a cinch on my railroad combine, but I'd nothing against him personally, and if he turns up after I've brought off a little deal I've got on, I'll be happy to give him the right hand of welcome."

A vision passed through Lord Peter's mind of Sir Reuben kept somewhere in custody till a financial crisis was over. This was exceedingly possible, and far more agreeable than his earlier conjecture; it also agreed better with the impression he was forming of Mr. Milligan.

"Well, it's a rum go," said Lord Peter, "but I daresay he had his reasons. Much better not inquire into people's reasons, y'know, what? Specially as a police friend of mine who's connected with the case says the old johnnie dyed his hair before he went."

Out of the tail of his eye, Lord Peter saw the redheaded secretary add up five columns of figures simultaneously and jot down the answer.

"Dyed his hair, did he?" said Mr. Milligan.

"Dyed it red," said Lord Peter. The secretary looked up. "Odd thing is," continued Wimsey, "they can't lay hands on the bottle. Somethin' fishy there, don't you think, what?"

The secretary's interest seemed to have evaporated. He inserted a fresh sheet into his looseleaf ledger, and carried forward a row of digits from the preceding page.

"I daresay there's nothin' in it," said Lord Peter, rising to go. "Well, it's uncommonly good of you to be bothered with me like this, Mr. Milligan—my mother'll be no end pleased. She'll write you about the date."

"I'm charmed," said Mr. Milligan. "Very pleased to have met you."

Mr. Scoot rose silently to open the door, uncoiling as he did so a portentous length of thin leg, hitherto hidden by the desk. With a mental sigh Lord Peter estimated him at six-foot-four.

"It's a pity I can't put Scoot's head on Milligan's shoulders," said Lord Peter, emerging into the swirl of the city. "And what *will* my mother say?"

CHAPTER V

MR. PARKER WAS A BACHELOR, AND OCCUPIED A
Georgian but inconvenient flat at No. 12A Great
Ormond Street, for which he paid a pound a week.
His exertions in the cause of civilization were rewarded, not by the gift of diamond rings from em-
presses or munificent cheques from grateful Prime
Ministers, but by a modest, though sufficient, salary,
drawn from the pockets of the British taxpayer. He
awoke, after a long day of arduous and inconclusive
labour, to the smell of burnt porridge. Through his
bedroom window, hygienically open top and bottom,
a raw fog was rolling slowly in, and the sight of a
pair of winter pants, flung hastily over a chair the
previous night, fretted him with a sense of the sordid
absurdity of the human form. The telephone bell
rang, and he crawled wretchedly out of bed and into
the sitting-room, where Mrs. Munns, who did for him
by the day, was laying the table, sneezing as she went.

Mr. Bunter was speaking.

"His lordship says he'd be very glad, sir, if you
could make it convenient to step round to breakfast."

If the odour of kidneys and bacon had been wafted
along the wire, Mr. Parker could not have experienced
a more vivid sense of consolation.

"Tell his lordship I'll be with him in half an hour,"

he said, thankfully, and plunging into the bathroom, which was also the kitchen, he informed Mrs. Munns, who was just making tea from a kettle which had gone off the boil, that he should be out to breakfast.

"You can take the porridge home for the family," he added, viciously, and flung off his dressing-gown with such determination that Mrs. Munns could only scuttle away with a snort.

A 19 'bus deposited him in Piccadilly only fifteen minutes later than his rather sanguine impulse had prompted him to suggest, and Mr. Bunter served him with glorious food, incomparable coffee, and the *Daily Mail* before a blazing fire of wood and coal. A distant voice singing the "et iterum venturus est" from Bach's Mass in B minor proclaimed that for the owner of the flat cleanliness and godliness met at least once a day, and presently Lord Peter roamed in, moist and verbena-scented, in a bath-robe cheerfully patterned with unnaturally variegated peacocks.

"Mornin', old dear," said that gentleman. "Beast of a day, ain't it? Very good of you to trundle out in it, but I had a letter I wanted you to see, and I hadn't the energy to come round to your place. Bunter and I've been makin' a night of it."

"What's the letter?" asked Parker.

"Never talk business with your mouth full," said Lord Peter, reprovingly; "have some Oxford marmalade—and then I'll show you my Dante; they brought it round last night. What ought I to read this morning, Bunter?"

"Lord Erith's collection is going to be sold, my lord. There is a column about it in the *Morning Post*. I think your lordship should look at this review of Sir Julian Freke's new book on 'The Physiological Bases of the Conscience' in the *Times Literary Supplement*. Then there is a very singular little burglary in the *Chronicle*, my lord, and an attack on titled families in the *Herald*—rather ill-written, if I may say so, but not without unconscious humour which your lordship will appreciate."

"All right, give me that and the burglary," said his lordship.

"I have looked over the other papers," pursued Mr. Bunter, indicating a formidable pile, "and marked your lordship's after-breakfast reading."

"Oh, pray don't allude to it," said Lord Peter; "you take my appetite away."

There was silence, but for the crunching of toast and the crackling of paper.

"I see they adjourned the inquest," said Parker presently.

"Nothing else to do," said Lord Peter; "but Lady Levy arrived last night, and will have to go and fail to identify the body this morning for Sugg's benefit."

"Time, too," said Mr. Parker shortly.

Silence fell again.

"I don't think much of your burglary, Bunter," said Lord Peter. "Competent, of course, but no imagination. I want imagination in a criminal. Where's the *Morning Post?*"

After a further silence, Lord Peter said: "You might send for the catalogue, Bunter, that Apollonios Rhodios * might be worth looking at. No, I'm damned if I'm going to stodge through that review, but you can stick the book on the library list if you like. His book on crime was entertainin' enough as far as it went, but the fellow's got a bee in his bonnet. Thinks God's a secretion of the liver—all right once in a way, but there's no need to keep on about it. There's nothing you can't prove if your outlook is only sufficiently limited. Look at Sugg."

"I beg your pardon," said Parker; "I wasn't attending. Argentines are steadying a little, I see."

"Milligan," said Lord Peter.

"Oil's in a bad way. Levy's made a difference there. Tha: funny little boom in Peruvians that came on just before he disappeared has died away again. I wonder if he was concerned in it. D'you know at all?"

"I'll find out," said Lord Peter. "What was it?"

"Oh, an absolutely dud enterprise that hadn't been heard of for years. It suddenly took a little lease of life last week. I happened to notice it because my mother got let in for a couple of hundred shares a long time ago. It never paid a dividend. Now it's petered out again."

Wimsey pushed his plate aside and lit a pipe.

"Having finished, I don't mind doing some work," he said. "How did you get on yesterday?"

---

* Apollonios Rhodios. Lorenzobodi Alopa. Firenze. 1496. (4to.) The excitement attendant on the solution of the Battersea Mystery did not prevent Lord Peter from securing this rare work before his departure for Corsica.

"I didn't," replied Parker. "I sleuthed up and down those flats in my own bodily shape and two different disguises. I was a gas-meter man and a collector for a Home for Lost Doggies, and I didn't get a thing to go on, except a servant in the top flat at the Battersea Bridge Road end of the row who said she thought she heard a bump on the roof one night. Asked which night, she couldn't rightly say. Asked if it was Monday night, she thought it very likely. Asked if it mightn't have been in that high wind on Saturday night that blew my chimney-pot off, she couldn't say but what it might have been. Asked if she was sure it was on the roof and not inside the flat, said to be sure they did find a picture tumbled down next morning. Very suggestible girl. I saw your friends, Mr. and Mrs. Appledore, who received me coldly, but could make no definite complaint about Thipps except that his mother dropped her h's, and that he once called on them uninvited, armed with a pamphlet about anti-vivisection. The Indian Colonel on the first floor was loud, but unexpectedly friendly. He gave me Indian curry for supper and some very good whisky, but he's a sort of hermit, and all *he* could tell me was that he couldn't stand Mrs. Appledore."

"Did you get nothing at the house?"

"Only Levy's private diary. I brought it away with me. Here it is. It doesn't tell one much, though. It's full of entries like: 'Tom and Annie to dinner'; and 'My dear wife's birthday; gave her an old opal ring';

'Mr. Arbuthnot dropped in to tea; he wants to marry Rachel, but I should like someone steadier for my treasure.' Still, I thought it would show who came to the house and so on. He evidently wrote it up at night. There's no entry for Monday."

"I expect it'll be useful," said Lord Peter, turning over the pages. "Poor old buffer. I say, I'm not so certain now he was done away with."

He detailed to Mr. Parker his day's work.

"Arbuthnot?" said Parker. "Is that the Arbuthnot of the diary?"

"I suppose so. I hunted him up because I knew he was fond of fooling round the Stock Exchange. As for Milligan, he *looks* all right, but I believe he's pretty ruthless in business and you never can tell. Then there's the red-haired secretary—lightnin' calculator man with a face like a fish, keeps on sayin' nuthin'—got the Tarbaby in his family tree, I should think. Milligan's got a jolly good motive for, at any rate, suspendin' Levy for a few days. Then there's the new man."

"What new man?"

"Ah, that's the letter I mentioned to you. Where did I put it? Here we are. Good parchment paper, printed address of solicitor's office in Salisbury, and postmark to correspond. Very precisely written with a fine nib by an elderly business man of old-fashioned habits."

Parker took the letter and read:

Whose Body?

CRIMPLESHAM AND WICKS,
Solicitors,
MILFORD HILL, SALISBURY,
17 November, 192—.

Sir,

With reference to your advertisement today in the personal column of *The Times,* I am disposed to believe that the eyeglasses and chain in question may be those I lost on the L. B. & S. C. Electric Railway while visiting London last Monday. I left Victoria by the 5.45 train, and did not notice my loss till I arrived at Balham. This indication and the optician's specification of the glasses, which I enclose, should suffice at once as an identification and a guarantee of my bona fides. If the glasses should prove to be mine, I should be greatly obliged to you if you would kindly forward them to me by registered post, as the chain was a present from my daughter, and is one of my dearest possessions.

Thanking you in advance for this kindness, and regretting the trouble to which I shall be putting you, I am,

Yours very truly,
THOS. CRIMPLESHAM

Lord Peter Wimsey,
110, Piccadilly, W.
(Encl.)

"Dear me," said Parker, "this is what you might call unexpected."

"Either it is some extraordinary misunderstanding," said Lord Peter, "or Mr. Crimplesham is a very bold and cunning villain. Or possibly, of course, they are the wrong glasses. We may as well get a ruling on that point at once. I suppose the glasses are at the Yard. I wish you'd just ring 'em up and ask 'em to

91

send round an optician's description of them at once —and you might ask at the same time whether it's a very common prescription."

"Right you are," said Parker, and took the receiver off its hook.

"And now," said his friend, when the message was delivered, "just come into the library for a minute."

On the library table, Lord Peter had spread out a series of bromide prints, some dry, some damp, and some but half-washed.

"These little ones are the originals of the photos we've been taking," said Lord Peter, "and these big ones are enlargements all made to precisely the same scale. This one here is the footmark on the linoleum; we'll put that by itself at present. Now these finger-prints can be divided into five lots. I've numbered 'em on the prints—see?—and made a list:

"A. The finger-prints of Levy himself, off his little bedside book and his hair-brush—this and this—you can't mistake the little scar on the thumb.

"B. The smudges made by the gloved fingers of the man who slept in Levy's room on Monday night. They show clearly on the water-bottle and on the boots—superimposed on Levy's. They are very distinct on the boots—surprisingly so for gloved hands, and I deduce that the gloves were rubber ones and had recently been in water.

"Here's another interestin' point. Levy walked in the rain on Monday night, as we know, and these dark marks are mud-splashes. You see they lie *over* Levy's finger-prints in every case. Now see: on this

92

left boot we find the stranger's thumb-mark *over* the mud on the leather above the heel. That's a funny place to find a thumb-mark on a boot, isn't it? That is, if Levy took off his own boots. But it's the place where you'd expect to see it if somebody forcibly removed his boots for him. Again, most of the stranger's finger-marks come *over* the mud-marks, but here is one splash of mud which comes on top of them again. Which makes me infer that the stranger came back to Park Lane, wearing Levy's boots, in a cab, carriage or car, but that at some point or other he walked a little way—just enough to tread in a puddle and get a splash on the boots. What do you say?"

"Very pretty," said Parker. "A bit intricate, though, and the marks are not all that I could wish a finger-print to be."

"Well, I won't lay too much stress on it. But it fits in with our previous ideas. Now let's turn to:

"C. The prints obligingly left by my own particular villain on the further edge of Thipps's bath, where you spotted them, and I ought to be scourged for not having spotted them. The left hand, you notice, the base of the palm and the fingers, but not the tips, looking as though he had steadied himself on the edge of the bath while leaning down to adjust something at the bottom, the pince-nez perhaps. Gloved, you see, but showing no ridge or seam of any kind—I say rubber, you say rubber. That's that. Now see here:

"D and E come off a visiting-card of mine. There's this thing at the corner, marked F, but that you can disregard; in the original document it's a sticky mark left by the thumb of the youth who took it from me, after first removing a piece of chewing-gum from his teeth with his finger to tell me that Mr. Milligan might or might not be disengaged. D and E are the thumb-marks of Mr. Milligan and his red-haired secretary. I'm not clear which is which, but I saw the youth with the chewing-gum hand the card to the secretary, and when I got into the inner shrine I saw John P. Milligan standing with it in his hand, so it's one or the other, and for the moment it's immaterial to our purpose which is which. I boned the card from the table when I left.

"Well, now, Parker, here's what's been keeping Bunter and me up till the small hours. I've measured and measured every way backwards and forwards till my head's spinnin', and I've stared till I'm nearly blind, but I'm hanged if I can make my mind up. Question 1. Is C identical with B? Question 2. Is D or E identical with B? There's nothing to go on but the size and shape, of course, and the marks are so faint—what do you think?"

Parker shook his head doubtfully.

"I think E might almost be put out of the question," he said; "it seems such an excessively long and narrow thumb. But I think there is a decided resemblance between the span of B on the water-bottle and C on the bath. And I don't see any reason why D shouldn't be the same as B, only there's so little to judge from."

"Your untutored judgment and my measurements have brought us both to the same conclusion—if you can call it a conclusion," said Lord Peter, bitterly.

"Another thing," said Parker. "Why on earth should we try to connect B with C? The fact that you and I happen to be friends doesn't make it necessary to conclude that the two cases we happen to be interested in have any organic connection with one another. Why should they? The only person who thinks they have is Sugg, and he's nothing to go by. It would be different if there were any truth in the suggestion that the man in the bath was Levy, but we know for a certainty he wasn't. It's ridiculous to suppose that the same man was employed in committing two totally distinct crimes on the same night, one in Battersea and the other in Park Lane."

"I know," said Wimsey, "though of course we mustn't forget that Levy *was* in Battersea at the time, and now we know he didn't return home at twelve as was supposed, we've no reason to think he ever left Battersea at all."

"True. But there are other places in Battersea besides Thipps's bathroom. And he *wasn't* in Thipps's bathroom. In fact, come to think of it, that's the one place in the universe where we know definitely that he wasn't. So what's Thipps's bath got to do with it?"

"I don't know," said Lord Peter. "Well, perhaps we shall get something better to go on today."

He leaned back in his chair and smoked thoughtfully for some time over the papers which Bunter had marked for him.

"They've got you out in the limelight," he said.

"Thank Heaven, Sugg hates me too much to give me any publicity. What a dull Agony Column! 'Darling Pipsey—Come back soon to your distracted Popsey' —and the usual young man in need of financial assistance, and the usual injunction to 'Remember thy Creator in the days of thy youth.' Hullo! there's the bell. Oh, it's our answer from Scotland Yard."

The note from Scotland Yard enclosed an optician's specification identical with that sent by Mr. Crimplesham, and added that it was an unusual one, owing to the peculiar strength of the lenses and the marked difference between the sight of the two eyes.

"That's good enough," said Parker.

"Yes," said Wimsey. "Then Possibility No. 3 is knocked on the head. There remain Possibility No. 1: Accident or Misunderstanding, and No. 2: Deliberate Villainy, of a remarkably bold and calculating kind—of a kind, in fact, characteristic of the author or authors of our two problems. Following the methods inculcated at that University of which I have the honour to be a member, we will now examine severally the various suggestions afforded by Possibility No. 2. This Possibility may be again subdivided into two or more Hypotheses. On Hypothesis 1 (strongly advocated by my distinguished colleague Professor Snupshed), the criminal, whom we may designate as X, is not identical with Crimplesham, but is using the name of Crimplesham as his shield, or aegis. This hypothesis may be further subdivided into two alternatives. Alternative A: Crimplesham is an innocent and unconscious accomplice, and X is in his employment. X writes in Crimplesham's name on Crimplesham's office-paper and obtains that the object in question, i.e., the eyeglasses, be despatched to Crimplesham's address. He is in a position to intercept the parcel before it reaches Crimplesham. The presumption is that X is Crimplesham's charwoman, office-boy, clerk, secretary or porter. This offers a wide field of investigation. The method of inquiry will be to interview Crimplesham and discover whether he sent the letter, and if not, who has access to his correspondence. Alternative B: Crimplesham is under X's influence or in his power, and has been induced to write the letter by (*a*) bribery, (*b*) misrepresentation or (*c*) threats. X may in that case be a persuasive relation or friend, or else a creditor, blackmailer or assassin; Crimplesham, on the other hand, is obviously venal or a fool. The method of inquiry in this case, I would tentatively suggest, is again to interview Crimplesham, put the facts of the case strongly before him, and assure him in the most intimidating terms that he is liable to a prolonged term of penal servitude as an accessory after the fact in the crime of murder— Ah-hem! Trusting, gentlemen, that you have followed me thus far, we will pass to the consideration of Hypothesis No. 2, to which I personally incline, and according to which X is identical with Crimplesham.

"In this case, Crimplesham, who is, in the words of an English classic, a man-of-infinite-resource-and-sagacity, correctly deduces that, of all people, the last whom we shall expect to find answering our advertisement is the criminal himself. Accordingly, he plays a bold game of bluff. He invents an occasion on which the glasses may very easily have been lost or stolen, and applies for them. If confronted, nobody will be more astonished than he to learn where they were found. He will produce witnesses to prove that he left Victoria at 5.45 and emerged from the train at Balham at the scheduled time, and sat up all Monday night playing chess with a respectable gentleman well known in Balham. In this case, the method of inquiry will be to pump the respectable gentleman in Balham, and if he should happen to be a single gentleman with a deaf housekeeper, it may be no easy matter to impugn the alibi, since, outside detective romances, few ticket-collectors and 'bus-conductors keep an exact remembrance of all the passengers passing between Balham and London on any and every evening of the week.

"Finally, gentlemen, I will frankly point out the weak point of all these hypotheses, namely: that none of them offers any explanation as to why the incriminating article was left so conspicuously on the body in the first instance."

Mr. Parker had listened with commendable patience to this academic exposition.

"Might not X," he suggested, "be an enemy of Crimplesham's, who designed to throw suspicion upon him?"

"He might. In that case he should be easy to discover, since he obviously lives in close proximity to Crimplesham and his glasses, and Crimplesham in fear of his life will then be a valuable ally for the prosecution."

"How about the first possibility of all, misunderstanding or accident?"

"Well! Well, for purposes of discussion, nothing, because it really doesn't afford any data for discussion."

"In any case," said Parker, "the obvious course appears to be to go to Salisbury."

"That seems indicated," said Lord Peter.

"Very well," said the detective, "is it to be you or me or both of us?"

"It is to be me," said Lord Peter, "and that for two reasons. First, because, if (by Possibility No. 2, Hypothesis 1, Alternative A) Crimplesham is an innocent catspaw, the person who put in the advertisement is the proper person to hand over the property. Secondly, because, if we are to adopt Hypothesis 2, we must not overlook the sinister possibility that Crimplesham-X is laying a careful trap to rid himself of the person who so unwarily advertised in the daily press his interest in the solution of the Battersea Park mystery."

"That appears to me to be an argument for our both going," objected the detective.

"Far from it," said Lord Peter. "Why play into the hands of Crimplesham-X by delivering over to him the only two men in London with the evidence, such as it is, and shall I say the wits, to connect him with the Battersea body?"

"But if we told the Yard where we were going, and

we both got nobbled," said Mr. Parker, "it would afford strong presumptive evidence of Crimplesham's guilt, and anyhow, if he didn't get hanged for murdering the man in the bath he'd at least get hanged for murdering us."

"Well," said Lord Peter, "if he only murdered me you could still hang him—what's the good of wasting a sound, marriageable young male like yourself? Besides, how about old Levy? If you're incapacitated, do you think anybody else is going to find him?"

"But we could frighten Crimplesham by threatening him with the Yard."

"Well, dash it all, if it comes to that, *I* can frighten him by threatening him with *you*, which, seeing you hold what evidence there is, is much more to the point. And, then, suppose it's a wild-goose chase after all, you'll have wasted time when you might have been getting on with the case. There are several things that need doing."

"Well," said Parker, silenced but reluctant, "why can't I go, in that case?"

"Bosh!" said Lord Peter. "I am retained (by old Mrs. Thipps, for whom I entertain the greatest respect) to deal with this case, and it's only by courtesy I allow you to have anything to do with it."

Mr. Parker groaned.

"Will you at least take Bunter?" he said.

"In deference to your feelings," replied Lord Peter, "I will take Bunter, though he could be far more useully employed taking photographs or overhauling my wardrobe. When is there a good train to Salisbury, Bunter?"

"There is an excellent train at 10.50, my lord."

"Kindly make arrangements to catch it," said Lord Peter, throwing off his bath-robe and trailing away with it into his bedroom. "And, Parker—if you have nothing else to do you might get hold of Levy's secretary and look into that little matter of the Peruvian oil."

Lord Peter took with him, for light reading in the train, Sir Reuben Levy's diary. It was a simple, and in the light of recent facts, rather a pathetic document. The terrible fighter of the Stock Exchange, who could with one nod set the surly bear dancing, or bring the savage bull to feed out of his hand, whose breath devastated whole districts with famine or swept financial potentates from their seats, was revealed in private life as kindly, domestic, innocently proud of himself and his belongings, confiding, generous and a little dull. His own small economies were duly chronicled side by side with extravagant presents to his wife and daughter. Small incidents of household routine appeared, such as: "Man came to mend the conservatory roof," or "The new butler (Simpson) has arrived, recommended by the Goldbergs. I think he will be satisfactory." All visitors and entertainments were duly entered, from a very magnificent lunch to Lord Dewsbury, the Minister for Foreign Affairs, and Dr. Jabez K. Wort, the American plenipotentiary, through a series of diplomatic

101

dinners to eminent financiers, down to intimate family gatherings of persons designated by Christian names or nicknames. About May there came a mention of Lady Levy's nerves, and further reference was made to the subject in subsequent months. In September it was stated that "Freke came to see my dear wife and advised complete rest and change of scene. She thinks of going abroad with Rachel." The name of the famous nerve-specialist occurred as a diner or luncher about once a month, and it came into Lord Peter's mind that Freke would be a good person to consult about Levy himself. "People sometimes tell things to the doctor," he murmured to himself. "And, by Jove! if Levy was simply going round to see Freke on Monday night, that rather disposes of the Battersea incident, doesn't it?" He made a note to look up Sir Julian and turned on further. On September 18th, Lady Levy and her daughter had left for the south of France. Then suddenly, under the date October 5th, Lord Peter found what he was looking for: "Goldberg, Skriner and Milligan to dinner."

There was the evidence that Milligan had been in that house. There had been a formal entertainment—a meeting as of two duellists shaking hands before the fight. Skriner was a well-known picture-dealer; Lord Peter imagined an after-dinner excursion upstairs to see the two Corots in the drawing-room, and the portrait of the oldest Levy girl, who had died at the age of sixteen. It was by Augustus John, and hung in the bedroom. The name of the red-haired secretary was nowhere mentioned, unless the initial S., occurring in another entry, referred to him. Throughout September and October, Anderson (of Wyndham's) had been a frequent visitor.

Lord Peter shook his head over the diary, and turned to the consideration of the Battersea Park mystery. Whereas in the Levy affair it was easy enough to supply a motive for the crime, if crime it were, and the difficulty was to discover the method of its carrying out and the whereabouts of the victim, in the other case the chief obstacle to inquiry was the entire absence of any imaginable motive. It was odd that, although the papers had carried news of the affair from one end of the country to the other and a description of the body had been sent to every police station in the country, nobody had as yet come forward to identify the mysterious occupant of Mr. Thipps's bath. It was true that the description, which mentioned the clean-shaven chin, elegantly cut hair and the pince-nez, was rather misleading, but on the other hand, the police had managed to discover the number of molars missing, and the height, complexion and other data were correctly enough stated, as also the date at which death had presumably occurred. It seemed, however, as though the man had melted out of society without leaving a gap or so much as a ripple. Assigning a motive for the murder of a person without relations or antecedents or even clothes is like trying to visualize the fourth dimension—admirable exercise for the imagination, but arduous and inconclusive. Even if the day's interview should disclose black spots in the past or present of Mr. Crimple-

103

sham, how were they to be brought into connection with a person apparently without a past, and whose present was confined to the narrow limits of a bath and a police mortuary?

"Bunter," said Lord Peter, "I beg that in the future you will restrain me from starting two hares at once. These cases are gettin' to be a strain on my constitution. One hare has nowhere to run from, and the other has nowhere to run to. It's a kind of mental D.T., Bunter. When this is over I shall turn pussyfoot, forswear the police news, and take to an emollient diet of the works of the late Charles Garvice."

It was its comparative proximity to Milford Hill that induced Lord Peter to lunch at the Minster Hotel rather than at the White Hart or some other more picturesquely situated hostel. It was not a lunch calculated to cheer his mind; as in all Cathedral cities, the atmosphere of the Close pervades every nook and corner of Salisbury, and no food in that city but seems faintly flavoured with prayer-books. As he sat sadly consuming that impassive pale substance known to the English as "cheese" unqualified (for there are cheeses which go openly by their names, as Stilton, Camembert, Gruyère, Wensleydale or Gorgonzola, but "cheese" is cheese and everywhere the same), he inquired of the waiter the whereabouts of Mr. Crimplesham's office.

The waiter directed him to a house rather further up the street on the opposite side, adding: "But anybody'll tell you, sir; Mr. Crimplesham's very well known hereabouts."

"He's a good solicitor, I suppose?" said Lord Peter.

"Oh, yes, sir," said the waiter, "you couldn't do better than trust to Mr. Crimplesham, sir. There's folk say he's old-fashioned, but I'd rather have my little bits of business done by Mr. Crimplesham than by one of these fly-away young men. Not but what Mr. Crimplesham'll be retiring soon, sir, I don't doubt, for he must be close on eighty, sir, if he's a day, but then there's young Mr. Wicks to carry on the business, and he's a very nice, steady-like young gentleman."

"Is Mr. Crimplesham really as old as that?" said Lord Peter. "Dear me! He must be very active for his years. A friend of mine was doing business with him in town last week."

"Wonderful active, sir," agreed the waiter, "and with his game leg, too, you'd be surprised. But there, sir, I often think when a man's once past a certain age, the older he grows the tougher he gets, and women the same or more so."

"Very likely," said Lord Peter, calling up and dismissing the mental picture of a gentleman of eighty with a game leg carrying a dead body over the roof of a Battersea flat at midnight. " 'He's tough, sir, tough, is old Joey Bagstock, tough and devilish sly,' " he added, thoughtlessly.

"Indeed, sir?" said the waiter. "I couldn't say, I'm sure."

"I beg your pardon," said Lord Peter; "I was quoting poetry. Very silly of me. I got the habit at my mother's knee and I can't break myself of it."

"No, sir," said the waiter, pocketing a liberal tip. "Thank you very much, sir. You'll find the house easy. Just afore you come to Penny-farthing Street, sir, about two turnings off, on the right-hand side opposite."

"Afraid that disposes of Crimplesham-X," said Lord Peter. "I'm rather sorry; he was a fine sinister figure as I had pictured him. Still, his may yet be the brain behind the hands—the aged spider sitting invisible in the centre of the vibrating web, you know, Bunter."

"Yes, my lord," said Bunter. They were walking up the street together.

"There is the office over the way," pursued Lord Peter. "I think, Bunter, you might step into this little shop and purchase a sporting paper, and if I do not emerge from the villain's lair—say within three-quarters of an hour, you may take such steps as your perspicuity may suggest."

Mr. Bunter turned into the shop as desired, and Lord Peter walked across and rang the lawyer's bell with decision.

"The truth, the whole truth and nothing but the truth is my long suit here, I fancy," he murmured, and when the door was opened by a clerk he delivered over his card with an unflinching air.

He was ushered immediately into a confidential-

looking office, obviously furnished in the early years
of Queen Victoria's reign, and never altered since. A
lean, frail-looking old gentleman rose briskly from his
chair as he entered and limped forward to meet him.

"My dear sir," exclaimed the lawyer, "how extremely good of you to come in person! Indeed, I
am ashamed to have given you so much trouble. I
trust you were passing this way, and that my glasses
have not put you to any great inconvenience. Pray
take a seat, Lord Peter." He peered gratefully at the
young man over a pince-nez obviously the fellow of
that now adorning a dossier in Scotland Yard.

Lord Peter sat down. The lawyer sat down. Lord
Peter picked up a glass paper-weight from the desk
and weighed it thoughtfully in his hand. Subcon-
sciously he noted what an admirable set of finger-
prints he was leaving upon it. He replaced it with
precision on the exact centre of a pile of letters.

"It's quite all right," said Lord Peter. "I was here
on business. Very happy to be of service to you.
Very awkward to lose one's glasses, Mr. Crimplesham."

"Yes," said the lawyer, "I assure you I feel quite
lost without them. I have this pair, but they do not
fit my nose so well—besides, that chain has a great
sentimental value for me. I was terribly distressed on
arriving at Balham to find that I had lost them. I
made inquiries of the railway, but to no purpose. I
feared they had been stolen. There were such crowds
at Victoria, and the carriage was packed with people

all the way to Balham. Did you come across them in the train?"

"Well, no," said Lord Peter, "I found them in rather an unexpected place. Do you mind telling me if you recognized any of your fellow-travellers on that occasion?"

The lawyer stared at him.

"Not a soul," he answered. "Why do you ask?"

"Well," said Lord Peter, "I thought perhaps the—the person with whom I found them might have taken them for a joke."

The lawyer looked puzzled.

"Did the person claim to be an acquaintance of mine?" he inquired. "I know practically nobody in London, except the friend with whom I was staying in Balham, Dr. Philpots, and I should be very greatly surprised at his practising a jest upon me. He knew very well how distressed I was at the loss of the glasses. My business was to attend a meeting of shareholders in Medlicott's Bank, but the other gentlemen present were all personally unknown to me, and I cannot think that any of them would take so great a liberty. In any case," he added, "as the glasses are here, I will not inquire too closely into the manner of their restoration. I am deeply obliged to you for your trouble."

Lord Peter hesitated.

"Pray forgive my seeming inquisitiveness," he said, "but I must ask you another question. It sounds rather melodramatic, I'm afraid, but it's this. Are you aware that you have any enemy—anyone, I mean, who would profit by your—er—decease or disgrace?"

Mr. Crimplesham sat frozen into stony surprise and disapproval.

"May I ask the meaning of this extraordinary question?" he inquired stiffly.

"Well," said Lord Peter, "the circumstances are a little unusual. You may recollect that my advertisement was addressed to the jeweller who sold the chain."

"That surprised me at the time," said Mr. Crimplesham, "but I begin to think your advertisement and your behaviour are all of a piece."

"They are," said Lord Peter. "As a matter of fact I did not expect the owner of the glasses to answer my advertisement. Mr. Crimplesham, you have no doubt read what the papers have to say about the Battersea Park mystery. Your glasses are the pair that was found on the body, and they are now in the possession of the police at Scotland Yard, as you may see by this." He placed the specification of the glasses and the official note before Crimplesham.

"Good God!" exclaimed the lawyer. He glanced at the paper, and then looked narrowly at Lord Peter.

"Are you yourself connected with the police?" he inquired.

"Not officially," said Lord Peter. "I am investigating the matter privately, in the interests of one of the parties."

Mr. Crimplesham rose to his feet.

"My good man," he said, "this is a very impudent attempt, but blackmail is an indictable offence, and I advise you to leave my office before you commit yourself." He rang the bell.

"I was afraid you'd take it like that," said Lord Peter. "It looks as though this ought to have been my friend Detective Parker's job, after all." He laid Parker's card on the table beside the specification, and added: "If you should wish to see me again, Mr. Crimplesham, before tomorrow morning, you will find me at the Minster Hotel."

Mr. Crimplesham disdained to reply further than to direct the clerk who entered to "show this person out."

In the entrance Lord Peter brushed against a tall young man who was just coming in, and who stared at him with surprised recognition. His face, however, aroused no memories in Lord Peter's mind, and that baffled nobleman, calling out Bunter from the newspaper shop, departed to his hotel to get a trunk-call through to Parker.

Meanwhile, in the office, the meditations of the indignant Mr. Crimplesham were interrupted by the entrance of his junior partner.

"I say," said the latter gentleman, "has somebody done something really wicked at last? Whatever brings such a distinguished amateur of crime on our sober doorstep?"

"I have been the victim of a vulgar attempt at

blackmail," said the lawyer; "an individual passing himself off as Lord Peter Wimsey—"

"But that *is* Lord Peter Wimsey," said Mr. Wicks, "there's no mistaking him. I saw him give evidence in the Attenbury emerald case. He's a big little pot in his way, you know, and goes fishing with the head of Scotland Yard."

"Oh, dear," said Mr. Crimplesham.

Fate arranged that the nerves of Mr. Crimplesham should be tried that afternoon. When, escorted by Mr. Wicks, he arrived at the Minster Hotel, he was informed by the porter that Lord Peter Wimsey had strolled out, mentioning that he thought of attending Evensong. "But his man is here, sir," he added, "if you'd like to leave a message."

Mr. Wicks thought that on the whole it would be well to leave a message. Mr. Bunter, on inquiry, was found to be sitting by the telephone, waiting for a trunk-call. As Mr. Wicks addressed him the bell rang, and Mr. Bunter, politely excusing himself, took down the receiver.

"Hullo!" he said. "Is that Mr. Parker? Oh, thanks! Exchange! Exchange! Sorry, can you put me through to Scotland Yard? Excuse me, gentlemen, keeping you waiting.—Exchange! all right—Scotland Yard— Hullo! Is that Scotland Yard?—Is Detective Parker round there?—Can I speak to him?—I shall have done in a moment, gentlemen.—Hullo! is that you, Mr. Parker? Lord Peter would be much obliged if you could find it convenient to step down to Salisbury, sir.

Whose Body?

Oh, no, sir, he's in excellent health, sir—just stepped round to hear Evensong, sir—oh, no, I think tomorrow morning would do excellently, sir, thank you, sir."

CHAPTER VI

IT WAS, IN FACT, INCONVENIENT FOR MR. PARKER TO leave London. He had had to go and see Lady Levy towards the end of the morning, and subsequently his plans for the day had been thrown out of gear and his movements delayed by the discovery that the adjourned inquest of Mr. Thipps's unknown visitor was to be held that afternoon, since nothing very definite seemed forthcoming from Inspector Sugg's inquiries. Jury and witnesses had been convened accordingly for three o'clock. Mr. Parker might altogether have missed the event, had he not run against Sugg that morning at the Yard and extracted the information from him as one would a reluctant tooth. Inspector Sugg, indeed, considered Mr. Parker rather interfering; moreover, he was hand-in-glove with Lord Peter Wimsey, and Inspector Sugg had no words for the interferingness of Lord Peter. He could not, however, when directly questioned, deny that there was to be an inquest that afternoon, nor could he prevent Mr. Parker from enjoying the inalienable right of any interested British citizen to be present. At a little before three, therefore, Mr. Parker was in his place, and amusing himself with watching the efforts of those persons who arrived after the room was packed to insinuate, bribe or bully themselves into a position of vantage. The Coroner, a medical man of

113

precise habits and unimaginative aspect, arrived punctually, and looking peevishly round at the crowded assembly, directed all the windows to be opened, thus letting in a stream of drizzling fog upon the heads of the unfortunates on that side of the room. This caused a commotion and some expressions of disapproval, checked sternly by the Coroner, who said that with the influenza about again an un-ventilated room was a death-trap; that anybody who chose to object to open windows had the obvious remedy of leaving the court, and further, that if any disturbance was made he would clear the court. He then took a Formamint lozenge, and proceeded, after the usual preliminaries, to call up fourteen good and lawful persons and swear them diligently to inquire and a true presentment make of all matters touching the death of the gentleman with the pince-nez and to give a true verdict according to the evidence, so help them God. When an expostulation by a woman juror—an elderly lady in spectacles who kept a sweet-shop, and appeared to wish she was back there—had been summarily quashed by the Coroner, the jury departed to view the body. Mr. Parker gazed round again and identified the unhappy Mr. Thipps and the girl Gladys led into an adjoining room under the grim guard of the police. They were soon followed by a gaunt old lady in a bonnet and mantle. With her, in a wonderful fur coat and a motor bonnet of fasci-nating construction, came the Dowager Duchess of Denver, her quick, dark eyes darting hither and thither about the crowd. The next moment they had

114

lighted on Mr. Parker, who had several times visited
the Dower House, and she nodded to him, and spoke
to a policeman. Before long, a way opened magically
through the press, and Mr. Parker found himself ac-
commodated with a front seat just behind the Duchess, who greeted him charmingly, and said: "What's
happened to poor Peter?" Parker began to explain,
and the Coroner glanced irritably in their direction.
Somebody went up and whispered in his ear, at which
he coughed, and took another Formamint.

"We came up by car," said the Duchess—"so tiresome—such bad roads between Denver and Gunbury
St. Walters—and there were people coming to lunch
—I had to put them off—I couldn't let the old lady
go alone, could I? By the way, such an odd thing's
happened about the Church Restoration Fund—the
Vicar—oh, dear, here are these people coming back
again; well, I'll tell you afterwards—do look at that
woman looking shocked, and the girl in tweeds
trying to look as if she sat on undraped gentlemen
every day of her life—I don't mean that—corpses of
course—but one finds oneself being so Elizabethan
nowadays—what an awful little man the coroner
is, isn't he? He's looking daggers at me—do you think
he'll dare to clear me out of the court or commit me
for what-you-may-call-it?"

The first part of the evidence was not of great
interest to Mr. Parker. The wretched Mr. Thipps, who
had caught cold in gaol, deposed in an unhappy croak
to having discovered the body when he went in to
take his bath at eight o'clock. He had had such a

shock, he had to sit down and send the girl for brandy. He had never seen the deceased before. He had no idea how he came there.

Yes, he had been in Manchester the day before. He had arrived at St. Pancras at ten o'clock. He had cloak-roomed his bag. At this point Mr. Thipps became very red, unhappy and confused, and glanced nervously about the court.

"Now, Mr. Thipps," said the Coroner, briskly, "we must have your movements quite clear. You must appreciate the importance of the matter. You have chosen to give evidence, which you need not have done, but having done so, you will find it best to be perfectly explicit."

"Yes," said Mr. Thipps faintly.

"Have you cautioned this witness, officer?" inquired the Coroner, turning sharply to Inspector Sugg.

The Inspector replied that he had told Mr. Thipps that anything he said might be used agin' him at his trial. Mr. Thipps became ashy, and said in a bleating voice that he 'adn't—hadn't meant to do anything that wasn't right.

This remark produced a mild sensation, and the Coroner became even more acidulated in manner than before.

"Is anybody representing Mr. Thipps?" he asked, irritably. "No? Did you not explain to him that he could—that he *ought* to be represented? You did not? Really, Inspector! Did you not know, Mr. Thipps, that you had a right to be legally represented?"

Mr. Thipps clung to a chair-back for support, and said, "No," in a voice barely audible.

"It is incredible," said the Coroner, "that so-called educated people should be so ignorant of the legal procedure of their own country. This places us in a very awkward position. I doubt, Inspector, whether I should permit the prisoner—Mr. Thipps—to give evidence at all. It is a delicate position."

The perspiration stood on Mrs. Thipps's forehead.

"Save us from our friends," whispered the Duchess to Parker. "If that cough-drop-devouring creature had openly instructed those fourteen people—and what unfinished-looking faces they have—so characteristic, I always think, of the lower middle-class, rather like sheep, or calves' head (boiled, I mean), to bring in wilful murder against the poor little man, he couldn't have made himself plainer."

"He can't let him incriminate himself, you know," said Parker.

"Stuff!" said the Duchess. "How could the man incriminate himself when he never did anything in his life? You men never think of anything but your red tape."

Meanwhile Mr. Thipps, wiping his brow with a handkerchief, had summoned up courage. He stood up with a kind of weak dignity, like a small white rabbit brought to bay.

"I would rather tell you," he said, "though it's reelly very unpleasant for a man in my position. But I reelly couldn't have it thought for a moment that I'd committed this dreadful crime. I assure you, gentlemen, I *couldn't bear* that. No. I'd rather tell you the truth, though I'm afraid it places me in rather a—well, I'll tell you."

"You fully understand the gravity of making such a statement, Mr. Thipps," said the Coroner.

"Quite," said Mr. Thipps. "It's all right—I—might I have a drink of water?"

"Take your time," said the Coroner, at the same time robbing his remark of all conviction by an impatient glance at his watch.

"Thank you, sir," said Mr. Thipps. "Well, then, it's true I got to St. Pancras at ten. But there was a man in the carriage with me. He'd got in at Leicester. I didn't recognise him at first, but he turned out to be an old school-fellow of mine."

"What was this gentleman's name?" inquired the Coroner, his pencil poised.

Mr. Thipps shrank together visibly.

"I'm afraid I can't tell you that," he said. "You see —that is, you *will* see—it would get him into trouble, and I couldn't do that—no, I reelly couldn't do that, not if my life depended on it. No!" he added, as the ominous pertinence of the last phrase smote upon him, "I'm sure I couldn't do that."

"Well, well," said the Coroner.

The Duchess leaned over to Parker again. "I'm beginning quite to admire the little man," she said.

Mr. Thipps resumed.

"When we got to St. Pancras I was going home, but my friend said no. We hadn't met for a long time and we ought to—to make a night of it, was his

118

expression. I fear I was weak, and let him overpersuade me to accompany him to one of his haunts. I use the word advisedly," said Mr. Thipps, "and I assure you, sir, that if I had known beforehand where we were going I never would have set foot in the place.

"I cloak-roomed my bag, for he did not like the notion of our being encumbered with it, and we got into a taxicab and drove to the corner of Tottenham Court Road and Oxford Street. We then walked a little way, and turned into a side street (I do not recollect which) where there was an open door, with the light shining out. There was a man at a counter, and my friend bought some tickets, and I heard the man at the counter say something to him about 'Your friend,' meaning me, and my friend said, 'Oh, yes, he's been here before, haven't you, Alf?' (which was what they called me at school), though I assure you, sir"—here Mr. Thipps grew very earnest—"I never had, and nothing in the world should induce me to go to such a place again.

"Well, we went down into a room underneath, where there were drinks, and my friend had several, and made me take one or two—though I am an abstemious man as a rule—and he talked to some other men and girls who were there—a very vulgar set of people, I thought them, though I wouldn't say but what some of the young ladies were nice-looking enough. One of them sat on my friend's knee and called him a slow old thing, and told him to come on —so we went into another room, where there were a lot of people dancing all these up-to-date dances. My friend went and danced, and I sat on a sofa. One of the young ladies came up to me and said, didn't I dance, and I said 'No,' so she said wouldn't I stand her a drink then. 'You'll stand us a drink then, darling,' that was what she said, and I said, 'Wasn't it after hours?' and she said that didn't matter. So I ordered the drink—a gin and bitters it was—for I didn't like not to, the young lady seemed to expect it of me and I felt it wouldn't be gentlemanly to refuse when she asked. But it went against my conscience— such a young girl as she was—and she put her arm round my neck afterwards and kissed me just like as if she was paying for the drink—and it reelly went to my 'eart," said Mr. Thipps, a little ambiguously, but with uncommon emphasis.

Here somebody at the back said, "Cheer-oh!" and a sound was heard as of the noisy smacking of lips.

"Remove the person who made that improper noise," said the Coroner, with great indignation. "Go on, please, Mr. Thipps."

"Well," said Mr. Thipps, "about half-past twelve, as I should reckon, things began to get a bit lively, and I was looking for my friend to say good-night, not wishing to stay longer, as you will understand, when I saw him with one of the young ladies, and they seemed to be getting on altogether too well, if you follow me, my friend pulling the ribbons off her shoulder and the young lady laughing—and so on," said Mr. Thipps, hurriedly, "so I thought I'd just slip quietly out, when I heard a scuffle and a shout—and

120

before I knew what was happening there were half-a-dozen policemen in, and the lights went out, and everybody stampeding and shouting—quite horrid, it was. I was knocked down in the rush, and hit my head a nasty knock on a chair—that was where I got that bruise they asked me about—and I was dreadfully afraid I'd never get away and it would all come out, and perhaps my photograph in the papers, when someone caught hold of me—I think it was the young lady I'd given the gin and bitters to—and she said, 'This way,' and pushed me along a passage and out at the back somewhere. So I ran through some streets, and found myself in Goodge Street, and there I got a taxi and came home. I saw the account of the raid afterwards in the papers, and saw my friend had escaped, and so, as it wasn't the sort of thing I wanted made public, and I didn't want to get him into difficulties, I just said nothing. But that's the truth."

"Well, Mr. Thipps," said the Coroner, "we shall be able to substantiate a certain amount of this story. Your friend's name—"

"No," said Mr. Thipps, stoutly, "not on any account."

"Very good," said the Coroner. "Now, can you tell us what time you did get in?"

"About half-past one, I should think. Though reelly, I was so upset—"

"Quite so. Did you go straight to bed?"

"Yes, I took my sandwich and glass of milk first. I thought it might settle my inside, so to speak," added the witness, apologetically, "not being accus-

121

tomed to alcohol so late at night and on an empty stomach, as you may say."

"Quite so. Nobody sat up for you?"

"Nobody."

"How long did you take getting to bed first and last?"

Mr. Thipps thought it might have been half-an hour.

"Did you visit the bathroom before turning in?"

"No."

"And you heard nothing in the night?"

"No. I fell fast asleep. I was rather agitated, so I took a little dose to make me sleep, and what with being so tired and the milk and the dose, I just tumbled right off and didn't wake till Gladys called me."

Further questioning elicited little from Mr. Thipps. Yes, the bathroom window had been open when he went in in the morning, he was sure of that, and he had spoken very sharply to the girl about it. He was ready to answer any questions; he would be only too 'appy—happy to have this dreadful affair sifted to the bottom.

Gladys Horrocks stated that she had been in Mr. Thipps's employment about three months. Her previous employers would speak to her character. It was her duty to make the round of the flat at night, when she had seen Mrs. Thipps to bed at ten. Yes, she remembered doing so on Monday evening. She had looked into all the rooms. Did she recollect shutting the bathroom window that night? Well, no, she couldn't swear to it, not in particular, but when Mr.

Thipps called her into the bathroom in the morning it certainly *was* open. She had not been into the bathroom before Mr. Thipps went in. Well, yes, it had happened that she had left that window open before, when anyone had been 'aving a bath in the evening and 'ad left the blind down. Mrs. Thipps 'ad 'ad a bath on Monday evening, Mondays was one of her regular bath nights. She was very much afraid she 'adn't shut the window on Monday night, though she wished her 'ead 'ad been cut off afore she'd been so forgetful.

Here the witness burst into tears and was given some water, while the Coroner refreshed himself with a third lozenge.

Recovering, witness stated that she had certainly looked into all the rooms before going to bed. No, it was quite impossible for a body to be 'idden in the flat without her seeing of it. She 'ad been in the kitchen all evening, and there wasn't 'ardly room to keep the best dinner service there, let alone a body. Old Mrs. Thipps sat in the drawing-room. Yes, she was sure she'd been into the dining-room. How? Because she put Mr. Thipps's milk and sandwiches there ready for him. There had been nothing in there —that she could swear to. Nor yet in her own bedroom, nor in the 'all. Had she searched the bedroom cupboard and the box-room? Well, no, not to say searched; she wasn't use to searchin' people's 'ouses for skelintons every night. So that a man might have concealed himself in the box-room or a wardrobe? She supposed he might.

In reply to a woman juror—well, yes, she was walking out with a young man. Williams was his name, Bill Williams,—well, yes, William Williams, if they insisted. He was a glazier by profession. Well, yes, he 'ad been in the flat sometimes. Well, she supposed you might say he was acquainted with the flat. Had she ever—no, she 'adn't, and if she'd thought such a question was going to be put to a respectable girl she wouldn't 'ave offered to give evidence. The vicar of St. Mary's would speak to her character and to Mr. Williams's. Last time Mr. Williams was at the flat was a fortnight ago.

Well, no, it wasn't exactly the last time she 'ad seen Mr. Williams. Well, yes, the last time was Monday— well, yes, Monday night. Well, if she must tell the truth, she must. Yes, the officer had cautioned her, but there wasn't any 'arm in it, and it was better to lose her place than to be 'ung, though it was a cruel shame a girl couldn't 'ave a bit of fun without a nasty corpse comin' in through the window to get 'er into difficulties. After she 'ad put Mrs. Thipps to bed, she 'ad slipped out to go to the Plumbers' and Glaziers' Ball at the "Black Faced Ram." Mr. Williams 'ad met 'er and brought 'er back. 'E could testify to where she'd been and that there wasn't no 'arm in it. She'd left before the end of the ball. It might 'ave been two o'clock when she got back. She'd got the keys of the flat from Mrs. Thipps's drawer when Mrs. Thipps wasn't looking. She 'ad asked leave to go, but couldn't get it, along of Mr. Thipps bein' away that night. She was bitterly sorry she 'ad be'aved so, and she was

sure she'd been punished for it. She had 'eard nothing
suspicious when she came in. She had gone straight to
bed without looking round the flat. She wished she
were dead.

No, Mr. and Mrs. Thipps didn't 'ardly ever 'ave
any visitors; they kep' themselves very retired. She
had found the outside door bolted that morning as
usual. She wouldn't never believe any 'arm of Mr.
Thipps. Thank you, Miss Horrocks. Call Georgiana
Thipps, and the Coroner thought we had better light
the gas.

The examination of Mrs. Thipps provided more
entertainment than enlightenment, affording as it
did an excellent example of the game called "cross
questions and crooked answers." After fifteen minutes' suffering, both in voice and temper, the Coroner
abandoned the struggle, leaving the lady with the
last word.

"You needn't try to bully me, young man," said
that octogenarian with spirit, "settin' there spoilin'
your stomach with them nasty jujubes."

At this point a young man arose in court and demanded to give evidence. Having explained that he
was William Williams, glazier, he was sworn, and
corroborated the evidence of Gladys Horrocks in the
matter of her presence at the "Black Faced Ram" on
the Monday night. They had returned to the flat
rather before two, he thought, but certainly later
than 1.30. He was sorry that he had persuaded Miss
Horrocks to come out with him when she didn't

ought. He had observed nothing of a suspicious nature in Prince of Wales Road at either visit.

Inspector Sugg gave evidence of having been called in at about half-past eight on Monday morning. He had considered the girl's manner to be suspicious and had arrested her. On later information, leading him to suspect that the deceased might have been murdered that night, he had arrested Mr. Thipps. He had found no trace of breaking into the flat. There were marks on the bathroom window-sill which pointed to somebody having got in that way. There were no ladder marks or footmarks in the yard; the yard was paved with asphalt. He had examined the roof, but found nothing on the roof. In his opinion the body had been brought into the flat previously and concealed till the evening by someone who had then gone out during the night by the bathroom window, with the connivance of the girl. In that case, why should not the girl have let the person out by the door? Well, it might have been so. Had he found traces of a body or a man or both having been hidden in the flat? He found nothing to show that they might *not* have been so concealed. What was the evidence that led him to suppose that the death had occurred that night?

At this point Inspector Sugg appeared uneasy, and endeavoured to retire upon his professional dignity. On being pressed, however, he admitted that the evidence in question had come to nothing.

One of the jurors: Was it the case that any fingermarks had been left by the criminal?

126

Some marks had been found on the bath, but the criminal had worn gloves.

The Coroner: Do you draw any conclusion from this fact as to the experience of the criminal?

Inspector Sugg: Looks as if he was an old hand, sir.

The Juror: Is that very consistent with the charge against Alfred Thipps, Inspector?

The Inspector was silent.

The Coroner: In the light of the evidence which you have just heard, do you still press the charge against Alfred Thipps and Gladys Horrocks?

Inspector Sugg: I consider the whole set-out highly suspicious. Thipps's story isn't corroborated, and as for the girl Horrocks, how do we know this Williams ain't in it as well?

William Williams: Now, you drop that. I can bring a 'undred witnesses—

The Coroner: Silence, if you please. I am surprised, Inspector, that you should make this suggestion in that manner. It is highly improper. By the way, can you tell us whether a police raid was actually carried out on the Monday night on any Night Club in the neighbourhood of St. Giles's Circus?

Inspector Sugg (sulkily): I believe there was something of the sort.

The Coroner: You will, no doubt, inquire into the matter. I seem to recollect having seen some mention of it in the newspapers. Thank you, Inspector, that will do.

Several witnesses having appeared and testified to the characters of Mr. Thipps and Gladys Horrocks, the Coroner stated his intention of proceeding to the medical evidence.

"Sir Julian Freke."

There was considerable stir in the court as the great specialist walked up to give evidence. He was not only a distinguished man, but a striking figure, with his wide shoulders, upright carriage and leonine head. His manner as he kissed the Book presented to him with the usual deprecatory mumble by the Coroner's officer, was that of a St. Paul condescending to humour the timid mumbo-jumbo of superstitious Corinthians.

"So handsome, I always think," whispered the Duchess to Mr. Parker; "just exactly like William Morris, with that bush of hair and beard and those exciting eyes looking out of it—so splendid, these dear men always devoted to something or other—not but what I think socialism is a mistake—of course it works with all those nice people, so good and happy in art linen and the weather always perfect—Morris, I mean, you know—but so difficult in real life. Science is different—I'm sure if I had nerves I should go to Sir Julian just to look at him—eyes like that give one something to think about, and that's what most of these people want, only I never had any— nerves, I mean. Don't you think so?"

"You are Sir Julian Freke," said the Coroner, "and live at St. Luke's House, Prince of Wales Road, Battersea, where you exercise a general direction over the surgical side of St. Luke's Hospital?"

Sir Julian assented briefly to this definition of his personality.

"You were the first medical man to see the deceased?"

"I was."

"And you have since conducted an examination in collaboration with Dr. Grimbold of Scotland Yard?"

"I have."

"You are in agreement as to the cause of death?"

"Generally speaking, yes."

"Will you communicate your impressions to the Jury?"

"I was engaged in research work in the dissecting room at St. Luke's Hospital at about nine o'clock on Monday morning, when I was informed that Inspector Sugg wished to see me. He told me that the dead body of a man had been discovered under mysterious circumstances at 59 Queen Caroline Mansions. He asked me whether it could be supposed to be a joke perpetrated by any of the medical students at the hospital. I was able to assure him, by an examination of the hospital's books, that there was no subject missing from the dissecting room."

"Who would be in charge of such bodies?"

"William Watts, the dissecting-room attendant."

"Is William Watts present?" inquired the Coroner of the officer.

William Watts was present, and could be called if the Coroner thought it necessary.

"I suppose no dead body would be delivered to the hospital without your knowledge, Sir Julian?"

"Certainly not."

"Thank you. Will you proceed with your statement?"

"Inspector Sugg then asked me whether I would send a medical man round to view the body. I said that I would go myself."

"Why did you do that?"

"I confess to my share of ordinary human curiosity, Mr. Coroner."

Laughter from a medical student at the back of the room.

"On arriving at the flat I found the deceased lying on his back in the bath. I examined him, and came to the conclusion that death had been caused by a blow on the back of the neck, dislocating the fourth and fifth cervical vertebrae, bruising the spinal cord and producing internal haemorrhage and partial paralysis of the brain. I judged the deceased to have been dead at least twelve hours, possibly more. I observed no other sign of violence of any kind upon the body. Deceased was a strong, well-nourished man of about fifty to fifty-five years of age."

"In your opinion, could the blow have been self-inflicted?"

"Certainly not. It had been made with a heavy, blunt instrument from behind, with great force and considerable judgment. It is quite impossible that it was self-inflicted."

"Could it have been the result of an accident?"

"That is possible, of course."

"If, for example, the deceased had been looking out

of the window, and the sash had shut violently down upon him?"

"No; in that case there would have been signs of strangulation and a bruise upon the throat as well."

"But deceased might have been killed through a heavy weight accidentally falling upon him?"

"He might."

"Was death instantaneous, in your opinion?"

"It is difficult to say. Such a blow might very well cause death instantaneously, or the patient might linger in a partially paralyzed condition for some time. In the present case I should be disposed to think that deceased might have lingered for some hours. I base my decision upon the condition of the brain revealed at the autopsy. I may say, however, that Dr. Grimbold and I are not in complete agreement on the point."

"I understand that a suggestion has been made as to the identification of the deceased. *You* are not in a position to identify him?"

"Certainly not. I never saw him before. The suggestion to which you refer is a preposterous one, and ought never to have been made. I was not aware until this morning that it had been made; had it been made to me earlier, I should have known how to deal with it, and I should like to express my strong disapproval of the unnecessary shock and distress inflicted upon a lady with whom I have the honour to be acquainted."

The Coroner: It was not my fault, Sir Julian; I had nothing to do with it; I agree with you that it was unfortunate you were not consulted.

131

The reporters scribbled busily, and the court asked each other what was meant, while the jury tried to look as if they knew already.

"In the matter of the eyeglasses found upon the body, Sir Julian. Do these give any indication to a medical man?"

"They are somewhat unusual lenses; an oculist would be able to speak more definitely, but I will say for myself that I should have expected them to belong to an older man than the deceased."

"Speaking as a physician, who has had many opportunities of observing the human body, did you gather anything from the appearance of the deceased as to his personal habits?"

"I should say that he was a man in easy circumstances, but who had only recently come into money. His teeth are in a bad state, and his hands shows signs of recent manual labour."

"An Australian colonist, for instance, who had made money?"

"Something of that sort; of course, I could not say positively."

"Of course not. Thank you, Sir Julian."

Dr. Grimbold, called, corroborated his distinguished colleague in every particular, except that, in his opinion, death had not occurred for several days after the blow. It was with the greatest hesitancy that he ventured to differ from Sir Julian Freke, and he might be wrong. It was difficult to tell in any case, and when he saw the body, deceased had been dead at least twenty-four hours, in his opinion.

Inspector Sugg, recalled. Would he tell the jury what steps had been taken to identify the deceased?

A description had been sent to every police station and had been inserted in all the newspapers. In view of the suggestion made by Sir Julian Freke, had inquiries been made at all the seaports? They had. And with no results? With no results at all. No one had come forward to identify the body? Plenty of people had come forward; but nobody had succeeded in identifying it. Had any effort been made to follow up the clue afforded by the eyeglasses? Inspector Sugg submitted that, having regard to the interests of justice, he would beg to be excused from answering that question. Might the jury see the eyeglasses? The eyeglasses were handed to the jury.

William Watts, called, confirmed the evidence of Sir Julian Freke with regard to dissecting-room subjects. He explained the system by which they were entered. They usually were supplied by the workhouses and free hospitals. They were under his sole charge. The young gentlemen could not possibly get the keys. Had Sir Julian Freke, or any of the house surgeons, the keys? No, not even Sir Julian Freke. The keys had remained in his possession on Monday night? They had. And, in any case, the inquiry was irrelevant, as there was no body missing, nor ever had been? That was the case.

The Coroner then addressed the jury, reminding them with some asperity that they were not there to gossip about who the deceased could or could not have been, but to give their opinion as to the cause

133

of death. He reminded them that they should consider whether, according to the medical evidence, death could have been accidental or self-inflicted, or whether it was deliberate murder, or homicide. If they considered the evidence on this point insufficient, they could return an open verdict. In any case, their verdict could not prejudice any person; if they brought it in "murder," all the whole evidence would have to be gone through again before the magistrate. He then dismissed them, with the unspoken adjuration to be quick about it.

Sir Julian Freke, after giving his evidence, had caught the eye of the Duchess, and now came over and greeted her.

"I haven't seen you for an age," said that lady. "How are you?"

"Hard at work," said the specialist. "Just got my new book out. This kind of thing wastes time. Have you seen Lady Levy yet?"

"No, poor dear," said the Duchess. "I only came up this morning, for this. Mrs. Thipps is staying with me—one of Peter's eccentricities, you know. Poor Christine! I must run round and see her. This is Mr. Parker," she added, "who is investigating that case."

"Oh," said Sir Julian, and paused. "Do you know," he said in a low voice to Parker, "I am very glad to meet you. Have you seen Lady Levy yet?"

"I saw her this morning."

"Did she ask you to go on with the inquiry?"

"Yes," said Parker; "she thinks," he added, "that Sir Reuben may be detained in the hands of some financial rival or that perhaps some scoundrels are holding him to ransom."

"And is that *your* opinion?" asked Sir Julian.

"I think it very likely," said Parker, frankly.

Sir Julian hesitated again.

"I wish you would walk back with me when this is over," he said.

"I should be delighted," said Parker.

At this moment the jury returned and took their places, and there was a little rustle and hush. The Coroner addressed the foreman and inquired if they were agreed upon their verdict.

"We are agreed, Mr. Coroner, that deceased died of the effects of a blow upon the spine, but how that injury was inflicted we consider that there is not sufficient evidence to show."

Mr. Parker and Sir Julian Freke walked up the road together.

"I had absolutely no idea until I saw Lady Levy this morning," said the doctor, "that there was any idea of connecting this matter with the disappearance of Sir Reuben. The suggestion was perfectly monstrous, and could only have grown up in the mind of that ridiculous police officer. If I had had any idea what was in his mind I could have disabused him and avoided all this."

"I did my best to do so," said Parker, "as soon as I was called in to the Levy case—"

"Who called you in, if I may ask?" inquired Sir Julian.

"Well, the household first of all, and then Sir Reuben's uncle, Mr. Levy of Portman Square, wrote to me to go on with the investigation."

"And now Lady Levy has confirmed those instructions?"

"Certainly," said Parker in some surprise.

Sir Julian was silent for a little time.

"I'm afraid I was the first person to put the idea into Sugg's head," said Parker, rather penitently. "When Sir Reuben disappeared, my first step, almost, was to hunt up all the street accidents and suicides and so on that had turned up during the day, and I went down to see this Battersea Park body as a matter of routine. Of course, I saw that the thing was ridiculous as soon as I got there, but Sugg froze on to the idea—and it's true there was a good deal of resemblance between the dead man and the portraits I've seen of Sir Reuben."

"A strong superficial likeness," said Sir Julian. "The upper part of the face is a not uncommon type, and as Sir Reuben wore a heavy beard and there was no opportunity of comparing the mouths and chins, I can understand the idea occurring to anybody. But only to be dismissed at once. I am sorry," he added, "as the whole matter has been painful to Lady Levy. You may know, Mr. Parker, that I am an old, though I should not call myself an intimate, friend of the Levys."

"I understood something of the sort."

"Yes. When I was a young man I—in short, Mr. Parker, I hoped once to marry Lady Levy." (Mr.

136

Parker gave the usual sympathetic groan.) "I have never married, as you know," pursued Sir Julian. "We have remained good friends. I have always done what I could to spare her pain."

"Believe me, Sir Julian," said Parker, "that I sympathize very much with you and with Lady Levy, and that I did all I could to disabuse Inspector Sugg of this notion. Unhappily, the coincidence of Sir Reuben's being seen that evening in the Battersea Park Road—"

"Ah, yes," said Sir Julian. "Dear me, here we are at home. Perhaps you would come in for a moment, Mr. Parker, and have tea or a whisky-and-soda or something."

Parker promptly accepted this invitation, feeling that there were other things to be said.

The two men stepped into a square, finely furnished hall with a fireplace on the same side as the door, and a staircase opposite. The dining-room door stood open on their right, and as Sir Julian rang the bell a man-servant appeared at the far end of the hall.

"What will you take?" asked the doctor.

"After that dreadfully cold place," said Parker, "what I really want is gallons of hot tea, if you, as a nerve specialist, can bear the thought of it."

"Provided you allow of a judicious blend of China in it," replied Sir Julian in the same tone, "I have no objection to make. Tea in the library at once," he added to the servant, and led the way upstairs.

"I don't use the downstairs rooms much, except

137

the dining-room," he explained as he ushered his guest into a small but cheerful library on the first floor. "This room leads out of my bedroom and is more convenient. I only live part of my time here, but it's very handy for my research work at the hospital. That's what I do there, mostly. It's a fatal thing for a theorist, Mr. Parker, to let the practical work get behindhand. Dissection is the basis of all good theory and all correct diagnosis. One must keep one's hand and eye in training. This place is far more important to me than Harley Street, and some day I shall abandon my consulting practice altogether and settle down here to cut up my subjects and write my books in peace. So many things in this life are a waste of time, Mr. Parker."

Mr. Parker assented to this.

"Very often," said Sir Julian, "the only time I get for any research work—necessitating as it does the keenest observation and the faculties at their acutest —has to be at night, after a long day's work and by artificial light, which, magnificent as the lighting of the dissecting room here is, is always more trying to the eyes than daylight. Doubtless your own work has to be carried on under even more trying conditions."

"Yes, sometimes," said Parker; "but then you see," he added, "the conditions are, so to speak, part of the work."

"Quite so, quite so," said Sir Julian; "you mean that the burglar, for example, does not demonstrate his methods in the light of day, or plant the perfect footmark in the middle of a damp patch of sand for you to analyze."

"Not as a rule," said the detective, "but I have no doubt many of your diseases work quite as insidiously as any burglar."

"They do, they do," said Sir Julian, laughing, "and it is my pride, as it is yours, to track them down for the good of society. The neuroses, you know, are particularly clever criminals—they break out into as many disguises as—"

"As Leon Kestrel, the Master-Mummer," suggested Parker, who read railway-stall detective stories on the principle of the 'busman's holiday.

"No doubt," said Sir Julian, who did not, "and they cover up their tracks wonderfully. But when you can really investigate, Mr. Parker, and break up the dead, or for preference the living body with the scalpel, you always find the footmarks—the little trail of ruin or disorder left by madness or disease or drink or any other similar pest. But the difficulty is to trace them back, merely by observing the surface symptoms—the hysteria, crime, religion, fear, shyness, conscience, or whatever it may be; just as you observe a theft or a murder and look for the footsteps of the criminal, so I observe a fit of hysterics or an outburst of piety and hunt for the little mechanical irritation which has produced it."

"You regard all these things as physical?"

"Undoubtedly. I am not ignorant of the rise of another school of thought, Mr. Parker, but its exponents are mostly charlatans or self-deceivers. '*Sie haben sich so weit darin eingeheimnisst'* that, like Sludge the Medium, they are beginning to believe their own nonsense. I should like to have the exploring of some of their brains, Mr. Parker; I would show you the little faults and landslips in the cells—the misfiring and short-circuiting of the nerves, which produce these notions and these books. At least," he added, gazing sombrely at his guest, "at least, if I could not quite show you today, I shall be able to do so tomorrow—or in a year's time—or before I die."

He sat for some minutes gazing into the fire, while the red light played upon his tawny beard and struck out answering gleams from his compelling eyes.

Parker drank tea in silence, watching him. On the whole, however, he remained but little interested in the causes of nervous phenomena and his mind strayed to Lord Peter, coping with the redoubtable Crimplesham down in Salisbury. Lord Peter had wanted him to come: that meant, either that Crimplesham was proving recalcitrant or that a clue wanted following. But Bunter had said that tomorrow would do, and it was just as well. After all, the Battersea affair was not Parker's case; he had already wasted valuable time attending an inconclusive inquest, and he really ought to get on with his legitimate work. There was still Levy's secretary to see and the little matter of the Peruvian Oil to be looked into. He looked at his watch.

"I am very much afraid—if you will excuse me—" he murmured.

Sir Julian came back with a start to the consideration of actuality.

"Your work calls you?" he said, smiling. "Well, I
can understand that. I won't keep you. But I wanted
to say something to you in connection with your
present inquiry—only I hardly know—I hardly
like—"

Parker sat down again, and banished every indication of hurry from his face and attitude.

"I shall be very grateful for any help you can give
me," he said.

"I'm afraid it's more in the nature of hindrance,"
said Sir Julian, with a short laugh. "It's a case of destroying a clue for you, and a breach of professional
confidence on my side. But since—accidentally—a
certain amount has come out, perhaps the whole had
better do so."

Mr. Parker made the encouraging noise which,
among laymen, supplies the place of the priest's insinuating, "Yes, my son?"

"Sir Reuben Levy's visit on Monday night was to
me," said Sir Julian.

"Yes?" said Mr. Parker, without expression.

"He found cause for certain grave suspicions concerning his health," said Sir Julian, slowly, as though
weighing how much he could in honour disclose to a
stranger. "He came to me, in preference to his own
medical man, as he was particularly anxious that the
matter should be kept from his wife. As I told you,
he knew me fairly well, and Lady Levy had consulted
me about a nervous disorder in the summer."

141

"Did he make an appointment with you?" asked Parker.

"I beg your pardon," said the other, absently.

"Did he make an appointment?"

"An appointment? Oh, no! He turned up suddenly in the evening after dinner when I wasn't expecting him. I took him up here and examined him, and he left me somewhere about ten o'clock, I should think."

"May I ask what was the result of your examination?"

"Why do you want to know?"

"It might illuminate—well, conjecture as to his subsequent conduct," said Parker, cautiously. This story seemed to have little coherence with the rest of the business, and he wondered whether coincidence was alone responsible for Sir Reuben's disappearance on the same night that he visited the doctor.

"I see," said Sir Julian. "Yes. Well, I will tell you in confidence that I saw grave grounds of suspicion, but as yet, no absolute certainty of mischief."

"Thank you. Sir Reuben left you at ten o'clock?"

"Then or thereabouts. I did not at first mention the matter as it was so very much Sir Reuben's wish to keep his visit to me secret, and there was no question of accident in the street or anything of that kind, since he reached home safely at midnight."

"Quite so," said Parker.

"It would have been, and is, a breach of confidence," said Sir Julian, "and I only tell you now because Sir Reuben was accidentally seen, and because I would rather tell you in private than have you ferretting round here and questioning my servants, Mr. Parker. You will excuse my frankness."

"Certainly," said Parker. "I hold no brief for the pleasantness of my profession, Sir Julian. I am very much obliged to you for telling me this. I might otherwise have wasted valuable time following up a false trail."

"I am sure I need not ask you, in your turn, to respect this confidence," said the doctor. "To publish the matter abroad could only harm Sir Reuben and pain his wife, besides placing me in no favourable light with my patients."

"I promise to keep the thing to myself," said Parker, "except of course," he added hastily, "that I must inform my colleague."

"You have a colleague in the case?"

"I have."

"What sort of person is he?"

"He will be perfectly discreet, Sir Julian."

"Is he a police officer?"

"You need not be afraid of your confidence getting into the records at Scotland Yard."

"I see that you know how to be discreet, Mr. Parker."

"We also have our professional etiquette, Sir Julian."

On returning to Great Ormond Street, Mr. Parker found a wire awaiting him, which said: "Do not trouble to come. All well. Returning tomorrow. Wimsey."

143

CHAPTER VII

ON RETURNING TO THE FLAT JUST BEFORE LUNCH-time on the following morning, after a few confirmatory researches in Balham and the neighbourhood of Victoria Station, Lord Peter was greeted at the door by Mr. Bunter (who had gone straight home from Waterloo) with a telephone message and a severe and nursemaid-like eye.

"Lady Swaffham rang up, my lord, and said she hoped your lordship had not forgotten you were lunching with her."

"I have forgotten, Bunter, and I mean to forget. I trust you told her I had succumbed to lethargic encephalitis suddenly, no flowers by request."

"Lady Swaffham said, my lord, she was counting on you. She met the Duchess of Denver yesterday—"

"If my sister-in-law's there I won't go, that's flat," said Lord Peter.

"I beg your pardon, my lord, the Dowager Duchess."

"What's she doing in town?"

"I imagine she came up for the inquest, my lord."

"Oh, yes—we missed that, Bunter."

"Yes, my lord. Her Grace is lunching with Lady Swaffham."

"Bunter, I can't. I can't, really. Say I'm in bed with

144

whooping cough, and ask my mother to come round after lunch."

"Very well, my lord. Mrs. Tommy Frayle will be at Lady Swaffham's, my lord, and Mr. Milligan——"

"Mr. who?"

"Mr. John P. Milligan, my lord, and——"

"Good God, Bunter, why didn't you say so before? Have I time to get there before he does? All right. I'm off. With a taxi I can just——"

"Not in those trousers, my lord," said Mr. Bunter, blocking the way to the door with deferential firmness.

"Oh, Bunter," pleaded his lordship, "do let me— just this once. You don't know how important it is."

"Not on any account, my lord. It would be as much as my place is worth."

"The trousers are all right, Bunter."

"Not for Lady Swaffham's, my lord. Besides, your lordship forgets the man that ran against you with a milk-can at Salisbury."

And Mr. Bunter laid an accusing finger on a slight stain of grease showing across the light cloth.

"I wish to God I'd never let you grow into a privileged family retainer, Bunter," said Lord Peter, bitterly, dashing his walking-stick into the umbrella-stand. "You've no conception of the mistakes my mother may be making."

Mr. Bunter smiled grimly and led his victim away.

When an immaculate Lord Peter was ushered, rather late for lunch, into Lady Swaffham's drawing-room, the Dowager Duchess of Denver was seated on a sofa, plunged in intimate conversation with Mr. John P. Milligan of Chicago.

"I'm vurry pleased to meet you, Duchess," had been that financier's opening remark, "to thank you for your exceedingly kind invitation. I assure you it's a compliment I deeply appreciate."

The Duchess beamed at him, while conducting a rapid rally of all her intellectual forces.

"Do come and sit down and talk to me, Mr. Milligan," she said. "I do so love talking to you great business men—let me see, is it a railway king you are or something about puss-in-the-corner—at least, I don't mean that exactly, but that game one used to play with cards, all about wheat and oats, and there was a bull and a bear, too—or was it a horse?—no, a bear, because I remember one always had to try and get rid of it and it used to get so dreadfully crumpled and torn, poor thing, always being handed about, one got to recognise it, and then one had to buy a new pack—so foolish it must seem to you, knowing the real thing, and dreadfully noisy, but really excellent for breaking the ice with rather stiff people who didn't know each other—I'm quite sorry it's gone out."

Mr. Milligan sat down.

"Wal, now," he said, "I guess it's as interesting for us business men to meet British aristocrats as it is for Britishers to meet American railway kings, Duchess. And I guess I'll make as many mistakes talking your kind of talk as you would make if you were tryin' to

146

run a corner in wheat in Chicago. Fancy now, I called that fine lad of yours Lord Wimsey the other day, and he though I'd mistaken him for his brother. That made me feel rather green."

This was an unhoped-for lead. The Duchess walked warily.

"Dear boy," she said, "I am so glad you met him, Mr. Milligan. *Both* my sons are a *great* comfort to me, you know, though, of course, Gerald is more conventional—just the right kind of person for the House of Lords, you know, and a splendid farmer. I can't see Peter down at Denver half so well, though he is always going to all the right things in town, and very amusing sometimes, poor boy."

"I was vurry much gratified by Lord Peter's suggestion," pursued Mr. Milligan, "for which I understand you are responsible, and I'll surely be very pleased to come any day you like, though I think you're flattering me too much."

"Ah, well," said the Duchess, "I don't know if you're the best judge of that, Mr. Milligan. Not that I know anything about business myself," she added. "I'm rather old-fashioned for these days, you know, and I can't pretend to do more than know a nice *man* when I see him; for the other things I rely on my son."

The accent of this speech was so flattering that Mr. Milligan purred almost audibly, and said:

"Wal, Duchess, I guess that's where a lady with a real, beautiful, old-fashioned soul has the advantage of these modern young blatherskites—there aren't many men who wouldn't be nice—to her, and even then, if they aren't rock-bottom she can see through them."

"But that leaves me where I was," thought the Duchess. "I believe," she said aloud, "that I ought to be thanking you in the name of the vicar of Duke's Denver for a very munificent cheque which reached him yesterday for the Church Restoration Fund. He was so delighted and astonished, poor dear man."

"Oh, that's nothing," said Mr. Milligan, "we haven't any fine old crusted buildings like yours over on our side, so it's a privilege to be allowed to drop a little kerosene into the worm-holes when we hear of one in the old country suffering from senile decay. So when your lad told me about Duke's Denver I took the liberty to subscribe without waiting for the Bazaar."

"I'm sure it was very kind of you," said the Duchess. "You are coming to the Bazaar, then?" she continued, gazing into his face appealingly.

"Sure thing," said Mr. Milligan, with great promptness. "Lord Peter said you'd let me know for sure about the date, but we can always make time for a little bit of good work anyway. Of course I'm hoping to be able to avail myself of your kind invitation to stop, but if I'm rushed, I'll manage anyhow to pop over and speak my piece and pop back again."

"I hope so very much," said the Duchess. "I must see what can be done about the date—of course, I can't promise—"

"No, no," said Mr. Milligan heartily. "I know what

148

these things are to fix up. And then there's not only me—there's all the real big men of European eminence your son mentioned, to be consulted."

The Duchess turned pale at the thought that any one of these illustrious persons might some time turn up in somebody's drawing-room, but by this time she had dug herself in comfortably, and was even beginning to find her range.

"I can't say how grateful we are to you," she said; "it will be such a treat. Do tell me what you think of saying."

"Wal—" began Mr. Milligan.

Suddenly everybody was standing up and a penitent voice was heard to say:

"Really, most awfully sorry, y'know—hope you'll forgive me, Lady Swaffham, what? Dear lady, could I possibly forget an invitation from you? Fact is, I had to go an' see a man down in Salisbury—absolutely true, 'pon my word, and the fellow wouldn't let me get away. I'm simply grovellin' before you, Lady Swaffham. Shall I go an' eat my lunch in the corner?"

Lady Swaffham gracefully forgave the culprit.

"Your dear mother is here," she said.

"How do, Mother?" said Lord Peter, uneasily.

"How are you, dear?" replied the Duchess. "You really oughtn't to have turned up just yet. Mr. Milligan was just going to tell me what a thrilling speech he's preparing for the Bazaar, when you came and interrupted us."

Conversation at lunch turned, not unnaturally, on the Battersea inquest, the Duchess giving a vivid impersonation of Mrs. Thipps being interrogated by the Coroner.

" 'Did you hear anything unusual in the night?' says the little man, leaning forward and screaming at her, and so crimson in the face and his ears sticking out so—just like a cherubim in that poem of Tennyson's—or is a cherub blue?—perhaps it's a seraphim I mean—anyway, you know what I mean, all eyes, with little wings on its head. And dear old Mrs. Thipps saying, 'Of course I have, any time these eighty years,' and *such* a sensation in court till they found out she thought he'd said, 'Do you sleep without a light?' and everybody laughing, and then the Coroner said quite loudly, 'Damn the woman,' and she heard that, I can't think why, and said: 'Don't you get swearing, young man, sitting there in the presence of Providence, as you may say. I don't know what young people are coming to nowadays'—and he's sixty if he's a day, you know," said the Duchess.

By a natural transition, Mrs. Tommy Frayle referred to the man who was hanged for murdering three brides in a bath.

"I always thought that was so ingenious," she said, gazing soulfully at Lord Peter, "and do you know, as it happened, Tommy had just made me insure my life, and I got so frightened, I gave up my morning bath and took to having it in the afternoon when he was in the House—I mean, when he was *not* in the house—not at home, I mean."

"Dear lady," said Lord Peter, reproachfully, "I

have a distinct recollection that all those brides were thoroughly unattractive. But it was an uncommonly ingenious plan—the first time of askin'—only he shouldn't have repeated himself."

"One demands a little originality in these days, even from murderers," said Lady Swaffham. "Like dramatists, you know—so much easier in Shakespeare's time, wasn't it? Always the same girl dressed up as a man, and even that borrowed from Boccaccio or Dante or somebody. I'm sure if I'd been a Shakespeare hero, the very minute I saw a slim-legged young page-boy I'd have said: 'Odsbodikins! There's that girl again!' "

"That's just what happened, as a matter of fact," said Lord Peter. "You see, Lady Swaffham, if ever you want to commit a murder, the thing you've got to do is to prevent people from associatin' their ideas. Most people don't associate anythin'—their ideas just roll about like so many dry peas on a tray, makin' a lot of noise and goin' nowhere, but once you begin lettin' 'em string their peas into a necklace, it's goin' to be strong enough to hang you, what?"

"Dear me!" said Mrs. Tommy Frayle, with a little scream, "what a blessing it is none of my friends have any ideas at all!"

"Y'see," said Lord Peter, balancing a piece of duck on his fork and frowning, "it's only in Sherlock Holmes and stories like that, that people think things out logically. Or'nar'ly, if somebody tells you somethin' out of the way, you just say, 'By Jove!' or 'How sad!' an' leave it at that, an' half the time you forget about it, 'nless somethin' turns up afterwards to drive it home. F'r instance, Lady Swaffham, I told you when I came in that I'd been down to Salisbury, 'n' that's true, only I don't suppose it impressed you much; 'n' I don't suppose it'd impress you much if you read in the paper tomorrow of a tragic discovery of a dead lawyer down in Salisbury, but if I went to Salisbury again next week 'n' there was a Salisbury doctor found dead the day after, you might begin to think I was a bird of ill omen for Salisbury residents; and if I went there again the week after, 'n' you heard next day that the see of Salisbury had fallen vacant suddenly, you might begin to wonder what took me to Salisbury, an' why I'd never mentioned before that I had friends down there, don't you see, an' you might think of goin' down to Salisbury your-self, an' askin' all kinds of people if they'd happened to see a young man in plum-coloured socks hangin' round the Bishop's Palace."

"I daresay I should," said Lady Swaffham.

"Quite. An' if you found that the lawyer and the doctor had once upon a time been in business at Poggleton-on-the-Marsh when the Bishop had been vicar there, you'd begin to remember you'd once heard of me payin' a visit to Poggleton-on-the-Marsh a long time ago, an' you'd begin to look up the parish registers there an' discover I'd been married under an assumed name by the vicar to the widow of a wealthy farmer, who'd died suddenly of peritonitis, as certified by the doctor, after the lawyer'd made a will leavin' me all her money, and *then* you'd begin to think I might have very good reasons for gettin' rid of such promisin' blackmailers as the lawyer, the doctor an' the bishop. Only, if I hadn't started an association in your mind by gettin' rid of 'em all in the same place, you'd never have thought of goin' to Poggleton-on-the-Marsh, 'n' you wouldn't even have remembered I'd ever been there."

"*Were* you ever there, Lord Peter?" inquired Mrs. Tommy, anxiously.

"I don't think so," said Lord Peter; "the name threads no beads in my mind. But it might, any day, you know."

"But if you were investigating a crime," said Lady Swaffham, "you'd have to begin by the usual things, I suppose—finding out what the person had been doing, and who'd been to call, and looking for a motive, wouldn't you?"

"Oh, yes," said Lord Peter, "but most of us have such dozens of motives for murderin' all sorts of inoffensive people. There's lots of people I'd like to murder, wouldn't you?"

"Heaps," said Lady Swaffham. "There's that dreadful—perhaps I'd better not say it, though, for fear you should remember it later on."

"Well, I wouldn't if I were you," said Peter, amiably. "You never know. It'd be beastly awkward if the person died suddenly tomorrow."

"The difficulty with this Battersea case, I guess," said Mr. Milligan, "is that nobody seems to have any associations with the gentleman in the bath."

"So hard on poor Inspector Sugg," said the Duchess. "I quite felt for the man, having to stand up there and answer a lot of questions when he had nothing at all to say."

Lord Peter applied himself to the duck, having got a little behindhand. Presently he heard somebody ask the Duchess if she had seen Lady Levy.

"She is in great distress," said the woman who had spoken, a Mrs. Freemantle, "though she clings to the hope that he will turn up. I suppose you knew him, Mr. Milligan—know him, I should say, for I hope he's still alive somewhere."

Mrs. Freemantle was the wife of an eminent railway director, and celebrated for her ignorance of the world of finance. Her *faux pas* in this connection enlivened the tea parties of City men's wives.

"Wal, I've dined with him," said Mr. Milligan, good-naturedly. "I think he and I've done our best to ruin each other, Mrs. Freemantle. If this were the States," he added, "I'd be much inclined to suspect myself of having put Sir Reuben in a safe place. But we can't do business that way in your old country; no, ma'am."

"It must be exciting work doing business in America," said Lord Peter.

"It is," said Mr. Milligan. "I guess my brothers are having a good time there now. I'll be joining them again before long, as soon as I've fixed up a little bit of work for them on this side."

"Well, you mustn't go till after my bazaar," said the Duchess.

Lord Peter spent the afternoon in a vain hunt for Mr. Parker. He ran him down eventually after dinner in Great Ormond Street.

Parker was sitting in an elderly but affectionate armchair, with his feet on the mantelpiece, relaxing his mind with a modern commentary on the Epistle to the Galatians. He received Lord Peter with quiet pleasure, though without rapturous enthusiasm, and mixed him a whisky-and-soda. Peter took up the book his friend had laid down and glanced over the pages.

"All these men work with a bias in their minds, one way or other," he said; "they find what they are looking for."

"Oh, they do," agreed the detective; "but one learns to discount that almost automatically, you know. When I was at college, I was all on the other side—Conybeare and Robertson and Drews and those people, you know, till I found they were all so busy looking for a burglar whom nobody had ever seen, that they couldn't recognise the footprints of the household, so to speak. Then I spent two years learning to be cautious."

"Hum," said Lord Peter, "theology must be good exercise for the brain then, for you're easily the most cautious devil I know. But I say, do go on reading—it's a shame for me to come and root you up in your off-time like this."

"It's all right, old man," said Parker.

The two men sat silent for a little, and then Lord Peter said:

"D'you like your job?"

The detective considered the question, and replied:

"Yes—yes, I do. I know it to be useful, and I am fitted to it. I do it quite well—not with inspiration, perhaps, but sufficiently well to take a pride in it. It is full of variety and it forces one to keep up to the mark and not get slack. And there's a future to it. Yes, I like it. Why?"

"Oh, nothing," said Peter. "It's a hobby to me, you see. I took it up when the bottom of things was rather knocked out for me, because it was so damned exciting, and the worst of it is, I enjoy it—up to a point. If it was all on paper I'd enjoy every bit of it. I love the beginning of a job—when one doesn't know any of the people and it's just exciting and amusing. But if it comes to really running down a live person and getting him hanged, or even quodded, poor devil, there don't seem as if there was any excuse for me buttin' in, since I don't have to make my livin' by it. And I feel as if I oughtn't ever to find it amusin'. But I do."

Parker gave this speech his careful attention.

"I see what you mean," he said.

"There's old Milligan, f'r instance," said Lord Peter. "On paper, nothin' would be funnier than to catch old Milligan out. But he's rather a decent old bird to talk to. Mother likes him. He's taken a fancy to me. It's awfully entertainin' goin' and pumpin' him with stuff about a bazaar for church expenses, but when he's so jolly pleased about it and that, I feel a worm. S'pose old Milligan has cut Levy's throat

156

and plugged him into the Thames. It ain't my business."

"It's as much yours as anybody's," said Parker; "it's no better to do it for money than to do it for nothing."

"Yes, it is," said Peter stubbornly. "Havin' to live is the only excuse there is for doin' that kind of thing."

"Well, but look here!" said Parker. "If Milligan has cut poor old Levy's throat for no reason except to make himself richer, I don't see why he should buy himself off by giving £1,000 to Duke's Denver church roof, or why he should be forgiven just because he's childishly vain, or childishly snobbish."

"That's a nasty one," said Lord Peter.

"Well, if you like, even because he has taken a fancy to you."

"No, but—"

"Look here, Wimsey—do you think he *has* murdered Levy?"

"Well, he may have."

"But do you think he has?"

"I don't want to think so."

"Because he has taken a fancy to you?"

"Well, that biases me, of course—"

"I daresay it's quite a legitimate bias. You don't think a callous murderer would be likely to take a fancy to you?"

"Well—besides, I've taken rather a fancy to him."

"I daresay that's quite legitimate, too. You've observed him and made a subconscious deduction from your observations, and the result is, you don't think he did it. Well, why not? You're entitled to take that into account."

"But perhaps I'm wrong and he did do it."

"Then why let your vainglorious conceit in your own power of estimating character stand in the way of unmasking the singularly cold-blooded murder of an innocent and lovable man?"

"I know—but I don't feel I'm playing the game somehow."

"Look here, Peter," said the other with some earnestness, "suppose you get this playing-fields-of-Eton complex out of your system once and for all. There doesn't seem to be much doubt that something unpleasant has happened to Sir Reuben Levy. Call it murder, to strengthen the argument. If Sir Reuben has been murdered, is it a game? and is it fair to treat it as a game?"

"That's what I'm ashamed of, really," said Lord Peter. "It *is* a game to me, to begin with, and I go on cheerfully, and then I suddenly see that somebody is going to be hurt, and I want to get out of it."

"Yes, yes, I know," said the detective, "but that's because you're thinking about your attitude. You want to be consistent, you want to look pretty, you want to swagger debonairly through a comedy of puppets or else to stalk magnificently through a tragedy of human sorrows and things. But that's childish. If you've any duty to society in the way of finding out the truth about murders, you must do it in any attitude that comes handy. You want to be

158

elegant and detached? That's all right, if you find
the truth out that way, but it hasn't any value in itself, you know. You want to look dignified and consistent—what's that got to do with it? You want to
hunt down a murderer for the sport of the thing and
then shake hands with him and say, 'Well played—
hard luck—you shall have your revenge tomorrow!'
Well, you can't do it like that. Life's not a football
match. You want to be a sportsman. You can't be a
sportsman. You're a responsible person."

"I don't think you ought to read so much theology," said Lord Peter. "It has a brutalizing influence."

He got up and paced about the room, looking idly
over the bookshelves. Then he sat down again, filled
and lit his pipe, and said:

"Well, I'd better tell you about the ferocious and
hardened Crimplesham."

He detailed his visit to Salisbury. Once assured of
his bona fides, Mr. Crimplesham had given him the
fullest details of his visit to town.

"And I've substantiated it all," groaned Lord
Peter, "and unless he's corrupted half Balham, there's
no doubt he spent the night there. And the afternoon was really spent with the bank people. And half
the residents of Salisbury seem to have seen him off
on Monday before lunch. And nobody but his own
family or young Wicks seems to have anything to
gain by his death. And even if young Wicks wanted
to make away with him, it's rather far-fetched to go
and murder an unknown man in Thipps's place in

159

order to stick Crimplesham's eyeglasses on his nose."

"Where was young Wicks on Monday?" asked Parker.

"At a dance given by the Precentor," said Lord Peter, wildly. "David—his name is David—dancing before the ark of the Lord in the face of the whole Cathedral Close."

There was a pause.

"Tell me about the inquest," said Wimsey.

Parker obliged with a summary of the evidence.

"Do you believe the body could have been concealed in the flat after all?" he asked. "I know we looked, but I suppose we might have missed something."

"We might. But Sugg looked as well."

"Sugg!"

"You do Sugg an injustice," said Lord Peter; "if there had been any signs of Thipps's complicity in the crime, Sugg would have found them."

"Why?"

"Why? Because he was looking for them. He's like your commentators on Galatians. He thinks that either Thipps, or Gladys Horrocks, or Gladys Horrocks's young man did it. Therefore he found marks on the window sill where Gladys Horrocks's young man might have come in or handed something in to Gladys Horrocks. He didn't find any signs on the roof, because he wasn't looking for them."

"But he went over the roof before me."

"Yes, but only in order to prove that there were no marks there. He reasons like this: Gladys Horrocks's young man is a glazier. Glaziers come on ladders. Glaziers have ready access to ladders. Therefore Gladys Horrocks's young man had ready access to a ladder. Therefore Gladys Horrocks's young man came on a ladder. Therefore there will be marks on the window sill and none on the roof. Therefore he finds marks on the window sill but none on the roof. He finds no marks on the ground, but he thinks he would have found them if the yard didn't happen to be paved with asphalt. Similarly, he thinks Mr. Thipps may have concealed the body in the box-room or elsewhere. Therefore you may be sure he searched the box-room and all the other places for signs of occupation. If they had been there he would have found them, because he was looking for them. Therefore, if he didn't find them it's because they weren't there."

"All right," said Parker, "stop talking. I believe you."

He went on to detail the medical evidence.

"By the way," said Lord Peter, "to skip across for a moment to the other case, has it occurred to you that perhaps Levy was going out to see Freke on Monday night?"

"He was; he did," said Parker, rather unexpectedly, and proceeded to recount his interview with the nerve-specialist.

"Humph!" said Lord Peter. "I say, Parker, these are funny cases, ain't they? Every line of inquiry seems to peter out. It's awfully exciting up to a point,

161

you know, and then nothing comes of it. It's like rivers getting lost in the sand."

"Yes," said Parker. "And there's another one I lost this morning."

"What's that?"

"Oh, I was pumping Levy's secretary about his business. I couldn't get much that seemed important except further details about the Argentine and so on. Then I thought I'd just ask round in the City about those Peruvian Oil shares, but Levy hadn't even heard of them so far as I could make out. I routed out the brokers, and found a lot of mystery and concealment, as one always does, you know, when somebody's been rigging the market, and at last I found one name at the back of it. But it wasn't Levy's."

"No? Whose was it?"

"Oddly enough, Freke's. It seems mysterious. He bought a lot of shares last week, in a secret kind of way, a few of them in his own name, and then quietly sold 'em out on Tuesday at a small profit—a few hundreds, not worth going to all that trouble about, you wouldn't think."

"Shouldn't have thought he ever went in for that kind of gamble."

"He doesn't as a rule. That's the funny part of it."

"Well, you never know," said Lord Peter; "people do these things just to prove to themselves or somebody else that they could make a fortune that way if they liked. I've done it myself in a small way."

He knocked out his pipe and rose to go.

"I say, old man," he said suddenly, as Parker was

letting him out, "does it occur to you that Freke's story doesn't fit in awfully well with what Anderson said about the old boy having been so jolly at dinner on Monday night? Would you be, if you thought you'd got anything of that sort?"

"No, I shouldn't," said Parker; "but," he added with his habitual caution, "some men will jest in the dentist's waiting-room. You, for one."

"Well, that's true," said Lord Peter, and went downstairs.

LORD PETER REACHED HOME ABOUT MIDNIGHT, feeling extraordinarily wakeful and alert. Something was jigging and worrying in his brain; it felt like a hive of bees, stirred up by a stick. He felt as though he were looking at a complicated riddle, of which he had once been told the answer but had forgotten it and was always on the point of remembering.

"Somewhere," said Lord Peter to himself, "somewhere I've got the key to these two things. I know I've got it, only I can't remember what it is. Somebody said it. Perhaps I said it. I can't remember where, but I know I've got it. Go to bed, Bunter, I shall sit up a little. I'll just slip on a dressing-gown."

Before the fire he sat down with his pipe in his mouth and his jazz-coloured peacocks gathered about him. He traced out this line and that line of investigation—rivers running into the sand. They ran out from the thought of Levy, last seen at ten o'clock in Prince of Wales Road. They ran back from the picture of the grotesque dead man in Mr. Thipps's bathroom—they ran over the roof, and were lost—lost in the sand. Rivers running into the sand—rivers running underground, very far down—

> Where Alph, the sacred river, ran
> Through caverns measureless to man
> Down to a sunless sea.

By leaning his head down, it seemed to Lord Peter that he could hear them, very faintly, lipping and gurgling somewhere in the darkness. But where? He felt quite sure that somebody had told him once, only he had forgotten.

He roused himself, threw a log on the fire, and picked up a book which the indefatigable Bunter, carrying on his daily fatigues amid the excitements of special duty, had brought from the Times Book Club. It happened to be Sir Julian Freke's "Physiological Bases of the Conscience," which he had seen reviewed two days before.

"This ought to send one to sleep," said Lord Peter; "if I can't leave these problems to my subconscious I'll be as limp as a rag tomorrow."

He opened the book slowly, and glanced carelessly through the preface.

"I wonder if that's true about Levy being ill," he thought, putting the book down; "it doesn't seem likely. And yet— Dash it all, I'll take my mind off it."

He read on resolutely for a little.

"I don't suppose Mother's kept up with the Levys much," was the next importunate train of thought. "Dad always hated self-made people and wouldn't have 'em at Denver. And old Gerald keeps up the tradition. I wonder if she knew Freke well in those days. She seems to get on with Milligan. I trust Mother's judgment a good deal. She was a brick about that bazaar business. I ought to have warned her. She said something once—"

He pursued an elusive memory for some minutes, till it vanished altogether with a mocking flicker of the tail. He returned to his reading.

Presently another thought crossed his mind aroused by a photograph of some experiment in surgery.

"If the evidence of Freke and that man Watts hadn't been so positive," he said to himself, "I should be inclined to look into the matter of those shreds of lint on the chimney."

He considered this, shook his head and read with determination.

Mind and matter were one thing, that was the theme of the physiologist. Matter could erupt, as it were, into ideas. You could carve passions in the brain with a knife. You could get rid of imagination with drugs and cure an outworn convention like a disease. "The knowledge of good and evil is an observed phenomenon, attendant upon a certain condition of the brain-cells, which is removable." That was one phrase; and again:

"Conscience in man may, in fact, be compared to the sting of a hive-bee, which, so far from conducing to the welfare of its possessor, cannot function, even in a single instance, without occasioning its death. The survival-value in each case is thus purely social; and if humanity ever passes from its present phase of social development into that of a higher individualism, as some of our philosophers have ventured to speculate, we may suppose that this interesting mental phenomenon may gradually cease to appear; just as the nerves and muscles which once controlled the

movements of our ears and scalps have, in all save a
few backward individuals, become atrophied and of
interest only to the physiologist."

"By Jove!" thought Lord Peter, idly, "that's an
ideal doctrine for the criminal. A man who believed
that would never—"

And then it happened—the thing he had been half-
unconsciously expecting. It happened suddenly,
surely, as unmistakably, as sunrise. He remembered—
not one thing, nor another thing, nor a logical succession of things, but everything—the whole thing,
perfect, complete, in all its dimensions as it were and
instantaneously; as if he stood outside the world and
saw it suspended in infinitely dimensional space. He
no longer needed to reason about it, or even to think
about it. He knew it.

There is a game in which one is presented with a
jumble of letters and is required to make a word out
of them, as thus:

COSSSSRI

The slow way of solving the problem is to try out
all the permutations and combinations in turn,
throwing away impossible conjunctions of letters, as:

SSSIRC

or

SCSRSO

Another way is to stare at the inco-ordinate elements
until, by no logical process that the conscious mind
167

can detect, or under some adventitious external stimulus, the combination:

SCISSORS

presents itself with calm certainty. After that, one does not even need to arrange the letters in order. The thing is done.

Even so, the scattered elements of two grotesque conundrums, flung higgledy-piggledy into Lord Peter's mind, resolved themselves, unquestioned henceforward. A bump on the roof of the end house —Levy in a welter of cold rain talking to a prostitute in the Battersea Park Road—a single ruddy hair— lint bandages—Inspector Sugg calling the great surgeon from the dissecting-room of the hospital—Lady Levy with a nervous attack—the smell of carbolic soap—the Duchess's voice—"not really an engagement, only a sort of understanding with her father" —shares in Peruvian Oil—the dark skin and curved, fleshy profile of the man in the bath—Dr. Grimbold giving evidence, "In my opinion, death did not occur for several days after the blow"—india-rubber gloves —even, faintly, the voice of Mr. Appledore, "He called on me, sir, with an anti-vivisectionist pamphlet"—all these things and many others rang together and made one sound, they swung together like bells in a steeple, with the deep tenor booming through the clamour:

"The knowledge of good and evil is a phenomenon of the brain, and is removable, removable, removable. The knowledge of good and evil is removable."

Lord Peter Wimsey was not a young man who
habitually took himself very seriously, but this time
he was frankly appalled. "It's impossible," said his
reason, feebly; *"credo quia impossibile,"* said his interior certainty with impervious self-satisfaction. "All
right," said conscience, instantly allying itself with
blind faith, "what are you going to do about it?"

Lord Peter got up and paced the room: "Good
Lord!" he said. "Good Lord!" He took down "Who's
Who" from the little shelf over the telephone and
sought comfort in its pages:

FREKE, Sir Julian, Kt. *cr.* 1916; G.C.V.O. *cr.* 1919;
K.C.V.O. 1917; K.C.B. 1918; M.D., F.R.C.P., F.R.C.S.,
Dr. en Méd. Paris; D. Sci. Cantab.; Knight of Grace of
the Order of S. John of Jerusalem; Consulting Surgeon of
St. Luke's Hospital, Battersea. *b.* Gryllingham, 16 March,
1872, *only son* of Edward Curzon Freke, Esq., of Gryll
Court, Gryllingham. *Educ.* Harrow and Trinity Coll.,
Cambridge; Col. A.M.S.; late Member of the Advisory
Board of the Army Medical Service. *Publications:* Some
Notes on the Pathological Aspects of Genius, 1892; Sta-
tistical Contributions to the Study of Infantile Paralysis
in England and Wales, 1894; Functional Disturbances of
the Nervous System, 1899; Cerebro-Spinal Diseases, 1904;
The Borderland of Insanity, 1906; An Examination into
the Treatment of Pauper Lunacy in the United Kingdom,
1906; Modern Developments in Psycho-Therapy: A Criti-
cism, 1910; Criminal Lunacy, 1914; The Application of
Psycho-Therapy to the Treatment of Shell-Shock, 1917;
An Answer to Professor Freud, with a Description of Some
Experiments Carried Out at the Base Hospital at Amiens,
1919; Structural Modifications Accompanying the More
Important Neuroses, 1920. *Clubs:* White's; Oxford and

Cambridge; Alpine, etc. *Recreations:* Chess, Mountaineering, Fishing. *Address:* 282, Harley Street and St. Luke's House, Prince of Wales Road, Battersea Park, S.W.11."

He flung the book away. "Confirmation!" he groaned. "As if I needed it!"

He sat down again and buried his face in his hands. He remembered quite suddenly how, years ago, he had stood before the breakfast table at Denver Castle —a small, peaky boy in blue knickers, with a thunderously beating heart. The family had not come down; there was a great silver urn with a spirit lamp under it, and an elaborate coffee-pot boiling in a glass dome. He had twitched the corner of the tablecloth— twitched it harder, and the urn moved ponderously forward and all the teaspoons rattled. He seized the tablecloth in a firm grip and pulled his hardest—he could feel now the delicate and awful thrill as the urn and the coffee machine and the whole of a Sèvres breakfast service had crashed down in one stupendous ruin—he remembered the horrified face of the butler, and the screams of a lady guest.

A log broke across and sank into a fluff of white ash. A belated motor-lorry rumbled past the window.

Mr. Bunter, sleeping the sleep of the true and faithful servant, was aroused in the small hours by a hoarse whisper, "Bunter!"

"Yes, my lord," said Bunter, sitting up and switching on the light.

"Put that light out, damn you!" said the voice. "Listen—over there—listen—can't you hear it?"

"It's nothing, my lord," said Mr. Bunter, hastily getting out of bed and catching hold of his master; "it's all right, you get to bed quick and I'll fetch you a drop of bromide. Why, you're all shivering—you've been sitting up too late."

"Hush! no, no—it's the water," said Lord Peter with chattering teeth; "it's up to their waists down there, poor devils. But listen! can't you hear it? Tap, tap, tap—they're mining us—but I don't know where —I can't hear—I can't. Listen, you! There it is again —we must find it—we must stop it. . . . Listen! Oh, my God! I can't hear—I can't hear anything for the noise of the guns. Can't they stop the guns?"

"Oh, dear!" said Mr. Bunter to himself. "No, no— it's all right, Major—don't you worry."

"But I hear it," protested Peter.

"So do I," said Mr. Bunter stoutly; "very good hearing, too, my lord. That's our own sappers at work in the communication trench. Don't you fret about that, sir."

Lord Peter grasped his wrist with a feverish hand.

"Our own sappers," he said; "sure of that?"

"Certain of it," said Mr. Bunter, cheerfully.

"They'll bring down the tower," said Lord Peter.

"To be sure they will," said Mr. Bunter, "and very nice, too. You just come and lay down a bit, sir— they've come to take over this section."

"You're sure it's safe to leave it?" said Lord Peter.

"Safe as houses, sir," said Mr. Bunter, tucking his master's arm under his and walking him off to his bedroom.

Lord Peter allowed himself to be dosed and put to bed without further resistance. Mr. Bunter, looking singularly un-Bunterlike in striped pyjamas, with his stiff black hair ruffled about his head, sat grimly watching the younger man's sharp cheekbones and the purple stains under his eyes.

"Thought we'd had the last of these attacks," he said. "Been overdoin' of himself. Asleep?" He peered at him anxiously. An affectionate note crept into his voice. "Bloody little fool!" said Sergeant Bunter.

CHAPTER IX

MR. PARKER, SUMMONED THE NEXT MORNING TO
110 Piccadilly, arrived to find the Dowager Duchess
in possession. She greeted him charmingly.

"I am going to take this silly boy down to Denver
for the week-end," she said, indicating Peter, who
who was writing and only acknowledged his friend's
entrance with a brief nod. "He's been doing too much
—running about to Salisbury and places and up till
all hours of the night—you really shouldn't encourage
him, Mr. Parker, it's very naughty of you—waking
poor Bunter up in the middle of the night with scares
about Germans, as if that wasn't all over years ago,
and he hasn't had an attack for ages, but there!
Nerves are such funny things, and Peter always did
have nightmares when he was quite a little boy—
though very often of course it was only a little pill
he wanted; but he was so dreadfully bad in 1918,
you know, and I suppose we can't expect to forget all
about a great war in a year or two, and, really, I
ought to be very thankful with both my boys safe.
Still, I think a little peace and quiet at Denver won't
do him any harm."

"Sorry you've been having a bad turn, old man,"
said Parker, vaguely sympathetic; "you're looking a
bit seedy."

"Charles," said Lord Peter, in a voice entirely void

of expression, "I am going away for a couple of days because I can be no use to you in London. What has got to be done for the moment can be much better done by you than by me. I want you to take this"— he folded up his writing and placed it in an envelope —"to Scotland Yard immediately and get it sent out to all the workhouses, infirmaries, police stations, Y.M.C.A.'s and so on in London. It is a description of Thipps's corpse as he was before he was shaved and cleaned up. I want to know whether any man answering to that description has been taken in anywhere, alive or dead, during the last fortnight. You will see Sir Andrew Mackenzie personally, and get the paper sent out at once, by his authority; you will tell him that you have solved the problems of the Levy murder and the Battersea mystery"—Mr. Parker made an astonished noise to which his friend paid no attention —"and you will ask him to have men in readiness with a warrant to arrest a very dangerous and important criminal at any moment on your information. When the replies to this paper come in, you will search for any mention of St. Luke's Hospital, or of any person connected with St. Luke's Hospital, and you will send for me at once.

"Meanwhile you will scrape acquaintance—I don't care how—with one of the students at St. Luke's. Don't march in there blowing about murders and police warrants, or you may find yourself in Queer Street. I shall come up to town as soon as I hear from you, and I shall expect to find a nice ingenuous Saw-bones here to meet me." He grinned faintly.

174

"D'you mean you've got to the bottom of this thing?" asked Parker.

"Yes. I may be wrong. I hope I am, but I know I'm not."

"You won't tell me?"

"D'you know," said Peter, "honestly I'd rather not. I say I *may* be wrong—and I'd feel as if I'd libelled the Archbishop of Canterbury."

"Well, tell me—is it one mystery or two?"

"One."

"You talked of the Levy murder. Is Levy dead?"

"God—yes!" said Peter, with a strong shudder.

The Duchess looked up from where she was reading the *Tatler*.

"Peter," she said, "is that your ague coming on again? Whatever you two are chattering about, you'd better stop it at once if it excites you. Besides, it's about time to be off."

"All right, Mother," said Peter. He turned to Bunter, standing respectfully in the door with an overcoat and suitcase. "You understand what you have to do, don't you?" he said.

"Perfectly, thank you, my lord. The car is just arriving, your Grace."

"With Mrs. Thipps inside it," said the Duchess. "She'll be delighted to see you again, Peter. You remind her so of Mr. Thipps. Good-morning, Bunter."

"Good-morning, your Grace."

Parker accompanied them downstairs.

When they had gone he looked blankly at the paper

in his hand—then, remembering that it was Saturday and there was need for haste, he hailed a taxi.

"Scotland Yard!" he cried.

Tuesday morning saw Lord Peter and a man in a velveteen jacket swishing merrily through seven acres of turnip-tops, streaked yellow with early frosts. A little way ahead, a sinuous undercurrent of excitement among the leaves proclaimed the unseen yet ever-near presence of one of the Duke of Denver's setter pups. Presently a partridge flew up with a noise like a police rattle, and Lord Peter accounted for it very creditably for a man who, a few nights before, had been listening to imaginary German sappers. The setter bounded foolishly through the turnips, and fetched back the dead bird.

"Good dog," said Lord Peter.

Encouraged by this, the dog gave a sudden ridiculous gambol and barked, its ear tossed inside out over its head.

"Heel," said the man in velveteen, violently. The animal sidled up, ashamed.

"Fool of a dog, that," said the man in velveteen; "can't keep quiet. Too nervous, my lord. One of old Black Lass's pups."

"Dear me," said Peter, "is the old dog still going?"

"No, my lord; we had to put her away in the spring."

Peter nodded. He always proclaimed that he hated the country and was thankful to have nothing to do with the family estates, but this morning he enjoyed

the crisp air and the wet leaves washing darkly over
his polished boots. At Denver things moved in an
orderly way; no one died sudden and violent deaths
except aged setters—and partridges, to be sure. He
sniffed up the autumn smell with appreciation. There
was a letter in his pocket which had come by the
morning post, but he did not intend to read it just
yet. Parker had not wired; there was no hurry.

He read it in the smoking-room after lunch. His
brother was there, dozing over the *Times*—a good,
clean Englishman, sturdy and conventional, rather
like Henry VIII in his youth; Gerald, sixteenth Duke
of Denver. The Duke considered his cadet rather de-
generate, and not quite good form; he disliked his
taste for police-court news.

The letter was from Mr. Bunter.

110, Piccadilly,
W.1.

My Lord:
I write (Mr. Bunter had been carefully educated
and knew that nothing is more vulgar than a careful
avoidance of beginning a letter with the first person
singular) as your lordship directed, to inform you
of the result of my investigations.

I experienced no difficulty in becoming acquainted
with Sir Julian Freke's man-servant. He belongs to
the same club as the Hon. Frederick Arbuthnot's
man, who is a friend of mine, and was very willing
to introduce me. He took me to the club yesterday

177

(Sunday) evening, and we dined with the man, whose name is John Cummings, and afterwards I invited Cummings to drinks and a cigar in the flat. Your lordship will excuse me doing this, knowing that it is not my habit, but it has always been my experience that the best way to gain a man's confidence is to let him suppose that one takes advantage of one's employer.

("I always suspected Bunter of being a student of human nature," commented Lord Peter.)

I gave him the best old port ("The deuce you did," said Lord Peter), having heard you and Mr. Arbuthnot talk over it. ("Hum!" said Lord Peter.)

Its effects were quite equal to my expectations as regards the principal matter in hand, but I very much regret to state that the man had so little understanding of what was offered to him that he smoked a cigar with it (one of your lordship's Villar Villars). You will understand that I made no comment on this at the time, but your lordship will sympathize with my feelings. May I take this opportunity of expressing my grateful appreciation of your lordship's excellent taste in food, drink and dress? It is, if I may say so, more than a pleasure—it is an education, to valet and buttle your lordship.

Lord Peter bowed his head gravely.

"What on earth are you doing, Peter, sittin' there noddin' an' grinnin' like a what-you-may-call-it?" demanded the Duke, coming suddenly out of a snooze. "Someone writin' pretty things to you, what?"

"Charming things," said Lord Peter.

The Duke eyed him doubtfully.

"Hope to goodness you don't go and marry a chorus beauty," he muttered inwardly, and returned to the *Times*.

Over dinner I had set myself to discover Cummings's tastes, and found them to run in the direction of the music-hall stage. During his first glass I drew him out in this direction, your lordship having kindly given me opportunities of seeing every performance in London, and I spoke more freely than I should consider becoming in the ordinary way in order to make myself pleasant to him. I may say that his views on women and the stage were such as I should have expected from a man who would smoke with your lordship's port.

With the second glass I introduced the subject of your lordship's inquiries. In order to save time I will write our conversation in the form of a dialogue, as nearly as possible as it actually took place.

Cummings: You seem to get many opportunities of seeing a bit of life, Mr. Bunter.

Bunter: One can always make opportunities if one knows how.

Cummings: Ah, it's very easy for you to talk, Mr. Bunter. You're not married, for one thing.

Bunter: I know better than that, Mr. Cummings.

Cummings: So do I—*now*, when it's too late. (He sighed heavily, and I filled up his glass.)

Bunter: Does Mrs. Cummings live with you at Battersea?

Cummings: Yes, her and me we do for my governor. Such a life! Not but what there's a char comes in by the day. But what's a char? I can tell you it's dull all by ourselves in that d—d Battersea suburb.

Bunter: Not very convenient for the Halls, of course.

Cummings: I believe you. It's all right for you, here in Piccadilly, right on the spot as you might say. And I daresay your governor's often out all night, eh?

Bunter: Oh, frequently, Mr. Cummings.

Cummings: And I daresay you take the opportunity to slip off yourself every so often, eh?

Bunter: Well, what do *you* think, Mr. Cummings?

Cummings: That's it; there you are! But what's a man to do with a nagging fool of a wife and a blasted scientific doctor for a governor, as sits up all night cutting up dead bodies and experimenting with frogs?

Bunter: Surely he goes out sometimes.

Cummings: Not often. And always back before twelve. And the way he goes on if he rings the bell and you ain't there. I give you *my* word, Mr. Bunter.

Bunter: Temper?

Cummings: No-o-o—but looking through you, nasty-like, as if you was on that operating table of his and he was going to cut you up. Nothing a man could rightly complain of, you understand, Mr. Bunter, just nasty looks. Not but what I will say he's very correct. Apologizes if he's been inconsiderate.

180

But what's the good of that when he's been and gone and lost you your night's rest?

Bunter: How does he do that? Keeps you up late, you mean?

Cummings: Not him; far from it. House locked up and household to bed at half-past ten. That's his little rule. Not but what I'm glad enough to go as a rule, it's that dreary. Still, when I *do* go to bed I like to go to sleep.

Bunter: What does he do? Walk about the house?

Cummings: Doesn't he? All night. And in and out of the private door to the hospital.

Bunter: You don't mean to say, Mr. Cummings, a great specialist like Sir Julian Freke does night work at the hospital?

Cummings: No, no; he does his own work—research work, as you may say. Cuts people up. They say he's very clever. Could take you or me to pieces like a clock, Mr. Bunter, and put us together again.

Bunter: Do you sleep in the basement, then, to hear him so plain?

Cummings: No; our bedroom's at the top. But, Lord! what's that? He'll bang the door so you can hear him all over the house.

Bunter: Ah, many's the time I've had to speak to Lord Peter about that. And talking all night. And baths.

Cummings: Baths? You may well say that, Mr. Bunter. Baths? Me and my wife sleep next to the cistern-room. Noise fit to wake the dead. All hours.

When d'you think he chose to have a bath, no later than last Monday night, Mr. Bunter?

Bunter: I've known them to do it at two in the morning, Mr. Cummings.

Cummings: Have you, now? Well, this was at three. Three o'clock in the morning we was waked up. I give you *my* word.

Bunter: You don't say so, Mr. Cummings.

Cummings: He cuts up diseases, you see, Mr. Bunter, and then he don't like to go to bed till he's washed the bacilluses off, if you understand me. Very natural, too, I daresay. But what I say is, the middle of the night's no time for a gentleman to be occupying his mind with diseases.

Bunter: These great men have their own way of doing things.

Cummings: Well, all I can say is, it isn't my way.

(I could believe that, your lordship. Cummings has no signs of greatness about him, and his trousers are not what I would wish to see in a man of his profession.)

Bunter: Is he habitually as late as that, Mr. Cummings?

Cummings: Well, no, Mr. Bunter, I will say, not as a general rule. He apologized, too, in the morning, and said he would have the cistern seen to—and very necessary, in my opinion, for the air gets into the pipes, and the groaning and screeching as goes on is something awful. Just like Niagara, if you follow me, Mr. Bunter, I give you *my* word.

Bunter: Well, that's as it should be, Mr. Cummings.

One can put up with a great deal from a gentleman that has the manners to apologize. And, of course, sometimes they can't help themselves. A visitor will come in unexpectedly and keep them late, perhaps.

Cummings: That's true enough, Mr. Bunter. Now I come to think of it, there *was* a gentleman come in on Monday evening. Not that he came late, but he stayed about an hour, and may have put Sir Julian behindhand.

Bunter: Very likely. Let me give you some more port, Mr. Cummings. Or a little of Lord Peter's old brandy.

Cummings: A little of the brandy, thank you, Mr. Bunter. I suppose you have the run of the cellar here. (He winked at me.)

"Trust me for that," I said, and I fetched him the Napoleon. I assure your lordship it went to my heart to pour it out for a man like that. However, seeing we had got on the right tack, I felt it wouldn't be wasted.

"I'm sure I wish it was always gentlemen that come here at night," I said. (Your lordship will excuse me, I am sure, making such a suggestion.)

("Good God," said Lord Peter, "I wish Bunter was less thorough in his methods.")

Cummings: Oh, he's that sort, his lordship, is he? (He chuckled and poked me. I suppress a portion of his conversation here, which could not fail to be as offensive to your lordship as it was to myself. He went on:) No, it's none of that with Sir Julian. Very few

183

visitors at night, and always gentlemen. And going early as a rule, like the one I mentioned.

Bunter: Just as well. There's nothing I find more wearisome, Mr. Cummings, than sitting up to see visitors out.

Cummings: Oh, I didn't see this one out. Sir Julian let him out himself at ten o'clock or thereabouts. I heard the gentleman shout "Good-night" and off he goes.

Bunter: Does Sir Julian always do that?

Cummings: Well, that depends. If he sees visitors downstairs, he lets them out himself: if he sees them upstairs in the library, he rings for me.

Bunter: This was a downstairs visitor, then?

Cummings: Oh, yes. Sir Julian opened the door to him, I remember. He happened to be working in the hall. Though now I come to think of it, they went up to the library afterwards. That's funny. I know they did, because I happened to go up to the hall with coals, and I heard them upstairs. Besides, Sir Julian rang for me in the library a few minutes later. Still, anyway, we heard him go at ten, or it may have been a bit before. He hadn't only stayed about three-quarters of an hour. However, as I was saying, there was Sir Julian banging in and out of the private door all night, and a bath at three in the morning, and up again for breakfast at eight—it beats me. If I had all his money, curse me if I'd go poking about with dead men in the middle of the night. I'd find something better to do with my time, eh, Mr. Bunter—

184

I need not repeat any more of his conversation, as it became unpleasant and incoherent, and I could not bring him back to the events of Monday night. I was unable to get rid of him till three. He cried on my neck, and said I was the bird, and you were the governor for him. He said that Sir Julian would be greatly annoyed with him for coming home so late, but Sunday night was his night out and if anything was said about it he would give notice. I think he will be ill-advised to do so, as I feel he is not a man I could conscientiously recommend if I were in Sir Julian Freke's place. I noticed that his boot-heels were slightly worn down.

I should wish to add, as a tribute to the great merits of your lordship's cellar, that, although I was obliged to drink a somewhat large quantity both of the Cockburn '68 and the 1800 Napoleon I feel no headache or other ill effects this morning.

Trusting that your lordship is deriving real benefit from the country air, and that the little information I have been able to obtain will prove satisfactory, I remain.

With respectful duty to all the family,

Obediently yours,
MERVYN BUNTER.

"Y'know," said Lord Peter thoughtfully to himself, "I sometimes think Mervyn Bunter's pullin' my leg. What is it, Soames?"

"A telegram, my lord."

"Parker," said Lord Peter, opening it. It said:

"Description recognised Chelsea Workhouse. Unknown vagrant injured street accident Wednesday week. Died workhouse Monday. Delivered St. Luke's same evening by order Freke. Much puzzled. Parker."

"Hurray!" said Lord Peter, suddenly sparkling. "I'm glad I've puzzled Parker. Gives me confidence in myself. Makes me feel like Sherlock Holmes. 'Perfectly simple, Watson.' Dash it all, though! this is a beastly business. Still, it's puzzled Parker."

"What's the matter?" asked the Duke, getting up and yawning.

"Marching orders," said Peter, "back to town. "Many thanks for your hospitality, old bird—I'm feelin' no end better. Ready to tackle Professor Moriarty or Leon Kestrel or any of 'em."

"I do wish you'd keep out of the police courts," grumbled the Duke. "It makes it so dashed awkward for me, havin' a brother makin' himself conspicuous."

"Sorry, Gerald," said the other; "I know I'm a beastly blot on the 'scutcheon."

"Why can't you marry and settle down and live quietly, doin' something useful?" said the Duke, unappeased.

"Because that was a wash-out as you perfectly well know," said Peter; "besides," he added cheerfully, "I'm bein' no end useful. You may come to want me yourself, you never know. When anybody comes blackmailin' you, Gerald, or your first deserted wife turns up unexpectedly from the West Indies, you'll realize the pull of havin' a private detective in the

186

family. 'Delicate private business arranged with tact and discretion. Investigations undertaken. Divorce evidence a specialty. Every guarantee!' Come, now."

"Ass!" said Lord Denver, throwing the newspaper violently into his armchair. "When do you want the car?"

"Almost at once. I say, Jerry, I'm taking Mother up with me."

"Why should she be mixed up in it?"

"Well, I want her help."

"I call it most unsuitable," said the Duke.

The Dowager Duchess, however, made no objection.

"I used to know her quite well," she said, "when she was Christine Ford. Why, dear?"

"Because," said Lord Peter, "there's a terrible piece of news to be broken to her about her husband."

"Is he dead, dear?"

"Yes; and she will have to come and identify him."

"Poor Christine."

"Under very revolting circumstances, Mother."

"I'll come with you, dear."

"Thank you, Mother, you're a brick. D'you mind gettin' your things on straight away and comin' up with me? I'll tell you about it in the car."

MR. PARKER, A FAITHFUL THOUGH DOUBTING Thomas, had duly secured his medical student: a large young man like an overgrown puppy, with innocent eyes and a freckled face. He sat on the Chesterfield before Lord Peter's library fire, bewildered in equal measure by his errand, his surroundings and the drink which he was absorbing. His palate, though untutored, was naturally a good one, and he realized that even to call this liquid a drink—the term ordinarily used by him to designate cheap whisky, post-war beer or a dubious glass of claret in a Soho restaurant—was a sacrilege; this was something outside normal experience: a genie in a bottle.

The man called Parker, whom he had happened to run across the evening before in the public-house at the corner of Prince of Wales Road, seemed to be a good sort. He had insisted on bringing him round to see this friend of his, who lived splendidly in Piccadilly. Parker was quite understandable; he put him down as a government servant, or perhaps something in the City. The friend was embarrassing; he was a lord, to begin with, and his clothes were a kind of rebuke to the world at large. He talked the most fatuous nonsense, certainly, but in a disconcerting way. He didn't dig into a joke and get all the fun out of it; he made it in passing, so to speak, and skipped away to something else before your retort was ready. He had a truly terrible man-servant—the sort you read about in books—who froze the marrow in your bones with silent criticism. Parker appeared to bear up under the strain, and this made you think more highly of Parker; he must be more habituated to the surroundings of the great than you would think to look at him. You wondered what the carpet had cost on which Parker was carelessly spilling cigar ash; your father was an upholsterer—Mr. Piggott, of Piggott & Piggott, Liverpool—and you knew enough about carpets to know that you couldn't even guess at the price of this one. When you moved your head on the bulging silk cushion in the corner of the sofa, it made you wish you shaved more often and more carefully. The sofa was a monster—but even so, it hardly seemed big enough to contain you. This Lord Peter was not very tall—in fact, he was rather a small man, but he didn't look undersized. He looked right; he made you feel that to be six-foot-three was rather vulgarly assertive; you felt like Mother's new drawing-room curtains—all over great big blobs. But everybody was very decent to you, and nobody said anything you couldn't understand, or sneered at you. There were some frightfully deep-looking books on the shelves all round, and you had looked into a great folio Dante which was lying on the table, but your hosts were talking quite ordinarily and rationally about the sort of books you read yourself—clinking good love stories and detective stories. You had read a lot of those, and could give an opinion, and they

189

listened to what you had to say, though Lord Peter h. a funny way of talking about books, too, as if the author had confided in him beforehand, and told him how the story was put together, and which bit was written first. It reminded you of the way old Freke took a body to pieces.

"Thing I object to in detective stories," said Mr. Piggott, "is the way fellows remember every bloomin' thing that's happened to 'em within the last six months. They're always ready with their time of day and was it rainin' or not, and what were they doin' on such an' such a day. Reel it all off like a page of poetry. But one ain't like that in real life, d'you think so, Lord Peter?" Lord Peter smiled, and young Piggott, instantly embarrassed, appealed to his earlier acquaintance. "You know what I mean, Parker. Come now. One day's so like another, I'm sure I couldn't remember—well, I might remember yesterday, p'r'aps, but I couldn't be certain about what I was doin' last week if I was to be shot for it."

"No," said Parker, "and evidence given in police statements sounds just as impossible. But they don't really get it like that, you know. I mean, a man doesn't just say, 'Last Friday I went out at 10 a.m. to buy a mutton chop. As I was turning into Mortimer Street I noticed a girl of about twenty-two with black hair and brown eyes, wearing a green jumper, check skirt, Panama hat and black shoes, riding a Royal Sunbeam Cycle at about ten miles an hour turning the corner by the Church of St. Simon and St. Jude on the wrong side of the road riding

190

towards the market place!' It amounts to that, of course, but it's really wormed out of him by a series of questions."

"And in short stories," said Lord Peter, "it has to be put in statement form, because the real conversation would be so long and twaddly and tedious, and nobody would have the patience to read it. Writers have to consider their readers, if any, y'see."

"Yes," said Mr. Piggott, "but I bet you most people would find it jolly difficult to remember, even if you asked 'em things. I should—of course, I know I'm a bit of a fool, but then, most people are, ain't they? You know what I mean. Witnesses ain't detectives, they're just average idiots like you and me."

"Quite so," said Lord Peter, smiling as the force of the last phrase sank into its unhappy perpetrator; "you mean, if I were to ask you in a general way what you were doin'—say, a week ago today, you wouldn't be able to tell me a thing about it offhand?"

"No—I'm sure I shouldn't." He considered. "No. I was in at the Hospital as usual, I suppose, and, being Tuesday, there'd be a lecture on something or the other—dashed if I know what—and in the evening I went out with Tommy Pringle—no, that must have been Monday—or was it Wednesday? I tell you, I couldn't swear to anything."

"You do yourself an injustice," said Lord Peter gravely. "I'm sure, for instance, you recollect what work you were doing in the dissecting-room on that day, for example."

"Lord, no! not for certain. I mean, I daresay it

191

might come back to me if I thought for a long time, but I wouldn't swear to it in a court of law."

"I'll bet you half-a-crown to sixpence," said Lord Peter, "that you'll remember within five minutes."

"I'm sure I can't."

"We'll see. Do you keep a notebook of the work you do when you dissect? Drawings or anything?"

"Oh, yes."

"Think of that. What's the last thing you did in it?"

"That's easy, because I only did it this morning. It was leg muscles."

"Yes. Who was the subject?"

"An old woman of sorts; died of pneumonia."

"Yes. Turn back the pages of your drawing book in your mind. What came before that?"

"Oh, some animals—still legs; I'm doing motor muscles at present. Yes. That was old Cunningham's demonstration on comparative anatomy. I did rather a good thing of a hare's legs and a frog's, and rudimentary legs on a snake."

"Yes. Which day does Mr. Cunningham lecture?"

"Friday."

"Friday; yes. Turn back again. What comes before that?"

Mr. Piggott shook his head.

"Do your drawings of legs begin on the right-hand page or the left-hand page? Can you see the first drawing?"

"Yes—yes—I can see the date written at the top.

It's a section of a frog's hind leg, on the right-hand page."

"Yes. Think of the open book in your mind's eye. What is opposite to it?"

This demanded some mental concentration.

"Something round—coloured—oh, yes—it's a hand."

"Yes. You went on from the muscles of the hand and arm to leg- and foot-muscles?"

"Yes; that's right. I've got a set of drawings of arms."

"Yes. Did you make those on the Thursday?"

"No; I'm never in the dissecting-room on Thursday."

"On Wednesday, perhaps?"

"Yes; I must have made them on Wednesday. Yes; I did. I went in there after we'd seen those tetanus patients in the morning. I did them on Wednesday afternoon. I know I went back because I wanted to finish 'em. I worked rather hard—for me. That's why I remember."

"Yes; you went back to finish them. When had you begun them, then?"

"Why, the day before."

"The day before. That was Tuesday, wasn't it?"

"I've lost count—yes, the day before Wednesday —yes, Tuesday."

"Yes. Were they a man's arms or a woman's arms?"

"Oh, a man's arms."

"Yes; last Tuesday, a week ago today, you were

dissecting a man's arms in the dissecting-room. Six-pence, please."

"By Jove!"

"Wait a moment. You know a lot more about it than that. You've no idea how much you know. You know what kind of man he was."

"Oh, I never saw him complete, you know. I got there a bit late that day, I remember. I'd asked for an arm specially, because I was rather weak in arms, and Watts—that's the attendant—had promised to save me one."

"Yes. You have arrived late and found your arm waiting for you. You are dissecting it—taking your scissors and slitting up the skin and pinning it back. Was it very young, fair skin?"

"Oh, no—no. Ordinary skin, I think—with dark hairs on it—yes, that was it."

"Yes. A lean, stringy arm, perhaps, with no extra fat anywhere?"

"Oh, no—I was rather annoyed about that. I wanted a good, muscular arm, but it was rather poorly developed and the fat got in my way."

"Yes; a sedentary man who didn't do much manual work."

"That's right."

"Yes. You dissected the hand, for instance, and made a drawing of it. You would have noticed any hard calluses."

"Oh, there was nothing of that sort."

"No. But should you say it was a young man's arm? Firm young flesh and limber joints?"

"No—no."

"No. Old and stringy, perhaps."

"No. Middle-aged—with rheumatism. I mean, there was a chalky deposit in the joints, and the fingers were a bit swollen."

"Yes. A man about fifty."

"About that."

"Yes. There were other students at work on the same body."

"Oh, yes."

"Yes. And they made all the usual sort of jokes about it."

"I expect so—oh, yes!"

"You can remember some of them. Who is your local funny man, so to speak?"

"Tommy Pringle."

"What was Tommy Pringle's doing?"

"Can't remember."

"Whereabouts was Tommy Pringle working?"

"Over by the instrument cupboard—by sink C."

"Yes. Get a picture of Tommy Pringle in your mind's eye."

Piggott began to laugh.

"I remember now. Tommy Pringle said the old Sheeny—"

"Why did he call him a Sheeny?"

"I don't know. But I know he did."

"Perhaps he looked like it. Did you see his head?"

"No."

"Who had the head?"

"I don't know—oh, yes, I do, though. Old Freke

bagged the head himself, and little Bouncible Binns was very cross about it, because he'd been promised a head to do with old Scrooger."

"I see. What was Sir Julian doing with the head?"

"He called us up and gave us a jaw on spinal haemorrhage and nervous lesions."

"Yes. Well, go back to Tommy Pringle."

Tommy Pringle's joke was repeated, not without some embarrassment.

"Quite so. Was that all?"

"No. The chap who was working with Tommy said that sort of thing came from over-feeding."

"I deduce that Tommy Pringle's partner was interested in the alimentary canal."

"Yes; and Tommy said, if he'd thought they'd feed you like that he'd go to the workhouse himself."

"Then the man was a pauper from the workhouse?"

"Well, he must have been, I suppose."

"Are workhouse paupers usually fat and well-fed?"

"Well, no—come to think of it, not as a rule."

"In fact, it struck Tommy Pringle and his friend that this was something a little out of the way in a workhouse subject?"

"Yes."

"And if the alimentary canal was so entertaining to these gentlemen, I imagine the subject had come by his death shortly after a full meal."

"Yes—oh, yes—he'd have had to, wouldn't he?"

"Well, I don't know," said Lord Peter. "That's in

your department, you know. That would be your inference, from what they said."

"Oh, yes. Undoubtedly."

"Yes; you wouldn't, for example, expect them to make that observation if the patient had been ill for a long time and fed on slops."

"Of course not."

"Well, you see, you really know a lot about it. On Tuesday week you were dissecting the arm muscles of a rheumatic middle-aged Jew, of sedentary habits, who had died shortly after eating a heavy meal, of some injury producing spinal haemorrhage and nervous lesions, and so forth, and who was presumed to come from the workhouse?"

"Yes."

"And you could swear to those facts, if need were?"

"Well, if you put it in that way, I suppose I could."

"Of course you could."

Mr. Piggott sat for some moments in contemplation.

"I say," he said at last, "I did know all that, didn't I?"

"Oh, yes—you knew it all right—like Socrates's slave."

"Who's he?"

"A person in a book I used to read as a boy."

"Oh—does he come in 'The Last Days of Pompeii'?"

"No—another book—I daresay you escaped it. It's rather dull."

197

"I never read much except Henty and Fenimore Cooper at school. . . . But—have I got rather an extra good memory, then?"

"You have a better memory than you credit yourself with."

"Then why can't I remember all the medical stuff? It all goes out of my head like a sieve."

"Well, why can't you?" said Lord Peter, standing on the hearthrug and smiling down at his guest.

"Well," said the young man, "the chaps who examine one don't ask the same sort of questions you do."

"No?"

"No—they leave you to remember all by yourself. And it's beastly hard. Nothing to catch hold of, don't you know? But, I say—how did you know about Tommy Pringle being the funny man and—"

"I didn't, till you told me."

"No; I know. But how did you know he'd be there if you did ask? I mean to say—I say," said Mr. Piggott, who was becoming mellowed by influences themselves not unconnected with the alimentary canal—"I say, are you rather clever, or am I rather stupid?"

"No, no," said Lord Peter, "it's me. I'm always askin' such stupid questions, everybody thinks I must mean somethin' by 'em."

This was too involved for Mr. Piggott.

"Never mind," said Parker, soothingly, "he's always like that. You mustn't take any notice. He can't help it. It's premature senile decay, often observed in the families of hereditary legislators. Go away, Wimsey, and play us the 'Beggar's Opera,' or something."

"That's good enough, isn't it?" said Lord Peter, when the happy Mr. Piggott had been despatched home after a really delightful evening.

"I'm afraid so," said Parker. "But it seems almost incredible."

"There's nothing incredible in human nature," said Lord Peter; "at least, in educated human nature. Have you got that exhumation order?"

"I shall have it tomorrow. I thought of fixing up with the workhouse people for tomorrow afternoon. I shall have to go and see them first."

"Right you are; I'll let my mother know."

"I begin to feel like you, Wimsey, I don't like this job."

"I like it a deal better than I did."

"You are really certain we're not making a mistake?"

Lord Peter had strolled across to the window. The curtain was not perfectly drawn, and he stood gazing out through the gap into lighted Piccadilly. At this he turned round:

"If we are," he said, "we shall know tomorrow, and no harm will have been done. But I rather think you will receive a certain amount of confirmation on your way home. Look here, Parker, d'you know, if I were you I'd spend the night here. There's a spare bedroom; I can easily put you up."

Parker stared at him.

"Do you mean—I'm likely to be attacked?"

"I think it very likely indeed."

"Is there anybody in the street?"

"Not now; there was half-an-hour ago."

"When Piggott left?"

"Yes."

"I say—I hope the boy is in no danger."

"That's what I went down to see. I don't think so. Fact is, I don't suppose anybody would imagine we'd exactly made a confidant of Piggott. But I think you and I are in danger. You'll stay?"

"I'm damned if I will, Wimsey. Why should I run away?"

"Bosh!" said Peter. "You'd run away all right if you believed me, and why not? You don't believe me. In fact, you're still not certain I'm on the right tack. Go in peace, but don't say I didn't warn you."

"I won't; I'll dictate a message with my dying breath to say I was convinced."

"Well, don't walk—take a taxi."

"Very well, I'll do that."

"And don't let anybody else get into it."

"No."

It was a raw, unpleasant night. A taxi deposited a load of people returning from the theatre at the block of flats next door, and Parker secured it for himself. He was just giving the address to the driver, when a man came hastily running up from a side street. He was in evening dress and an overcoat. He rushed up, signalling frantically.

"Sir—sir!—dear me! why, it's Mr. Parker! How

fortunate! If you would be so kind—summoned from the club—a sick friend—can't find a taxi—everybody going home from the theatre—if I might share your cab—you are returning to Bloomsbury? I want Russell Square—if I might presume—a matter of life and death."

He spoke in hurried gasps, as though he had been running violently and far. Parker promptly stepped out of the taxi.

"Delighted to be of service to you, Sir Julian," he said; "take my taxi. I am going down to Craven Street myself, but I'm in no hurry. Pray make use of the cab."

"It's extremely kind of you," said the surgeon. "I am ashamed—"

"That's all right," said Parker, cheerily. "I can wait." He assisted Freke into the taxi. "What number? 24 Russell Square, driver, and look sharp."

The taxi drove off. Parker remounted the stairs and rang Lord Peter's bell.

"Thanks, old man," he said. "I'll stop the night, after all."

"Come in," said Wimsey.

"Did you see that?" asked Parker.

"I saw something. What happened exactly?"

Parker told his story. "Frankly," he said, "I've been thinking you a bit mad, but now I'm not quite so sure of it."

Peter laughed.

"Blessed are they that have not seen and yet have believed. Bunter, Mr. Parker will stay the night."

"Look here, Wimsey, let's have another look at this business. Where's that letter?"

Lord Peter produced Bunter's essay in dialogue. Parker studied it for a short time in silence.

"You know, Wimsey, I'm as full of objections to this idea as an egg is of meat."

"So'm I, old son. That's why I want to dig up our Chelsea pauper. But trot out your objections."

"Well—"

"Well, look here, I don't pretend to be able to fill in all the blanks myself. But here we have two mysterious occurrences in one night, and a complete chain connecting the one with another through one particular person. It's beastly, but it's not unthinkable."

"Yes, I know all that. But there are one or two quite definite stumbling-blocks."

"Yes, I know. But, see here. On the one hand, Levy disappeared after being last seen looking for Prince of Wales Road at nine o'clock. At eight next morning a dead man, not unlike him in general outline, is discovered in a bath in Queen Caroline Mansions. Levy, by Freke's own admission, was going to see Freke. By information received from Chelsea workhouse a dead man, answering to the description of the Battersea corpse in its natural state, was delivered that same day to Freke. We have Levy with a past, and no future, as it were; an unknown vagrant with a future (in the cemetery) and no past, and Freke stands between their future and their past."

"That looks all right—"

202

"Yes. Now, further: Freke has a motive for getting rid of Levy—an old jealousy."

"Very old—and not much of a motive."

"People have been known to do that sort of thing.* You're thinking that people don't keep up old jealousies for twenty years or so. Perhaps not. Not just primitive, brute jealousy. That means a word and a blow. But the thing that rankles is hurt vanity. That sticks. Humiliation. And we've all got a sore spot we don't like to have touched. I've got it. You've got it. Some blighter said hell knew no fury like a woman scorned. Stickin' it on to women, poor devils. Sex is every man's loco spot—you needn't fidget, you know it's true—he'll take a disappointment, but not a humiliation. I knew a man once who'd been turned down—not too charitably—by a girl he was engaged to. He spoke quite decently about her. I asked what had become of her. 'Oh,' he said, 'she married the other fellow.' And then burst out—couldn't help himself. 'Lord, yes!' he cried. 'To think of it—jilted for a Scotchman!' I don't know why he didn't like Scots, but that was what got him on the raw. Look at Freke. I've read his books. His attacks on his antag-

---

* Lord Peter was not without authority for his opinion: "With respect to the alleged motive, it is of great importance to see whether there was a motive for committing such a crime, or whether there was not, or whether there is an improbability of its having been committed so strong as not to be overpowered by positive evidence. But *if there be any motive which can be assigned, I am bound to tell you that the inadequacy of that motive is of little importance.* We know, from the experience of criminal courts, that atrocious crimes of this sort have been committed from very slight motives; *not merely from malice and revenge,* but to gain a small pecuniary advantage, and to drive off for a time pressing difficulties."—L. C. J. Campbell, summing up in Reg. v. Palmer, Shorthand Report, p. 308 C. C. C., May, 1856, Sess. Pa. 5. (Italics mine. D. L. S.)

onists are savage. And he's a scientist. Yet he can't bear opposition, even in his work, which is where any first-class man is most sane and open-minded. Do you think he's a man to take a beating from any man on a side-issue? On a man's most sensitive side-issue? People are opinionated about side-issues, you know. I see red if anybody questions my judgment about a book. And Levy—who was nobody twenty years ago—romps in and carries off Freke's girl from under his nose. It isn't the girl Freke would bother about—it's having his aristocratic nose put out of joint by a little Jewish nobody.

"There's another thing. Freke's got another side-issue. He likes crime. In that criminology book of his he gloats over a hardened murderer. I've read it, and I've seen the admiration simply glaring out between the lines whenever he writes about a callous and successful criminal. He reserves his contempt for the victims or the penitents or the men who lose their heads and get found out. His heroes are Edmond de la Pommerais, who persuaded his mistress into becoming an accessory to her own murder, and George Joseph Smith of Brides-in-a-bath fame, who could make passionate love to his wife in the night and carry out his plot to murder her in the morning. After all, he thinks conscience is a sort of vermiform appendix. Chop it out and you'll feel all the better. Freke isn't troubled by the usual conscientious deterrent. Witness his own hand in his books. Now again. The man who went to Levy's house in his place knew the house: Freke knew the house; he was a red-haired man, smaller than Levy, but not much smaller, since he could wear his clothes without appearing ludicrous: you have seen Freke—you know his height—about five-foot-eleven, I suppose, and his auburn mane; he probably wore surgical gloves: Freke is a surgeon; he was a methodical and daring man: surgeons are obliged to be both daring and methodical. Now take the other side. The man who got hold of the Battersea corpse had to have access to dead bodies. Freke obviously had access to dead bodies. He had to be cool and quick and callous about handling a dead body. Surgeons are all that. He had to be a strong man to carry the body across the roofs and dump it in at Thipps's window. Freke is a powerful man and a member of the Alpine Club. He probably wore surgical gloves and he let the body down from the roof with a surgical bandage. This points to a surgeon again. He undoubtedly lived in the neighbourhood. Freke lives next door. The girl you interviewed heard a bump on the roof of the end house. That is the house next to Freke's. Every time we look at Freke, he leads somewhere, whereas Milligan and Thipps and Crimplesham and all the other people we've honoured with our suspicion simply led nowhere."

"Yes; but it's not quite so simple as you make out. What was Levy doing in that surreptitious way at Freke's on Monday night?"

"Well, you have Freke's explanation."

"Rot, Wimsey. You said yourself it wouldn't do."

"Excellent. It won't do. Therefore Freke was lying.

Why should he lie about it, unless he had some object in hiding the truth?"

"Well, but why mention it at all?"

"Because Levy, contrary to all expectation, had been seen at the corner of the road. That was a nasty accident for Freke. He thought it best to be beforehand with an explanation—of sorts. He reckoned, of course, on nobody's ever connecting Levy with Battersea Park."

"Well, then, we come back to the first question: Why did Levy go there?"

"I don't know, but he was got there somehow. Why did Freke buy all those Peruvian Oil shares?"

"I don't know," said Parker in his turn.

"Anyway," went on Wimsey, "Freke expected him, and made arrangements to let him in himself, so that Cummings shouldn't see who the caller was."

"But the caller left again at ten."

"Oh, Charles! I did not expect this of you. This is the purest Suggery! Who saw him go? Somebody said 'Good-night' and walked away down the street. And you believe it was Levy because Freke didn't go out of his way to explain that it wasn't."

"D'you mean that Freke walked cheerfully out of the house to Park Lane, and left Levy behind—dead or alive—for Cummings to find?"

"We have Cummings's word that he did nothing of the sort. A few minutes after the steps walked away from the house, Freke rang the library bell and told Cummings to shut up for the night."

"Then—"

"Well—there's a side door to the house, I suppose—in fact, you know there is—Cummings said so—through the hospital."

"Yes—well, where was Levy?"

"Levy went up into the library and never came down. You've been in Freke's library. Where would you have put him?"

"In my bedroom next door."

"Then that's where he did put him."

"But suppose the man went in to turn down the bed?"

"Beds are turned down by the housekeeper, earlier than ten o'clock."

"Yes. . . . But Cummings heard Freke about the house all night."

"He heard him go in and out two or three times. He'd expect him to do that, anyway."

"Do you mean to say Freke got all that job finished before three in the morning?"

"Why not?"

"Quick work."

"Well, call it quick work. Besides, why three? Cummings never saw him again till he called him for eight o'clock breakfast."

"But he was having a bath at three."

"I don't say he didn't get back from Park Lane before three. But I don't suppose Cummings went and looked through the bathroom keyhole to see if he was in the bath."

Parker considered again.

"How about Crimplesham's pince-nez?" he asked.

"That is a bit mysterious," said Lord Peter.

"And why Thipps's bathroom?"

"Why, indeed? Pure accident, perhaps—or pure devilry."

"Do you think all this elaborate scheme could have been put together in a night, Wimsey?"

"Far from it. It was conceived as soon as that man who bore a superficial resemblance to Levy came into the workhouse. He had several days."

"I see."

"Freke gave himself away at the inquest. He and Grimbold disagreed about the length of the man's illness. If a small man (comparatively speaking) like Grimbold presumes to disagree with a man like Freke, it's because he is sure of his ground."

"Then—if your theory is sound—Freke made a mistake."

"Yes. A very slight one. He was guarding, with unnecessary caution, against starting a train of thought in the mind of anybody—say, the work-house doctor. Up till then he'd been reckoning on the fact that people don't think a second time about anything (a body, say) that's once been accounted for."

"What made him lose his head?"

"A chain of unforeseen accidents. Levy's having been recognised—my mother's son having foolishly advertised in the *Times* his connection with the Battersea end of the mystery—Detective Parker (whose photograph has been a little prominent in the illustrated press lately) seen sitting next door to the

Duchess of Denver at the inquest. His aim in life was to prevent the two ends of the problem from linking up. And there were two of the links, literally side by side. Many criminals are wrecked by over-caution."

Parker was silent.

CHAPTER XI

"A REGULAR PEA-SOUPER, BY JOVE," SAID LORD PETER.

Parker grunted, and struggled irritably into an overcoat.

"It affords me, if I may say so, the greatest satisfaction," continued the noble lord, "that in a collaboration like ours all the uninteresting and disagreeable routine work is done by you."

Parker grunted again.

"Do you anticipate any difficulty about the warrant?" inquired Lord Peter.

Parker grunted a third time.

"I suppose you've seen to it that all this business is kept quiet?"

"Of course."

"You've muzzled the workhouse people?"

"Of course."

"And the police?"

"Yes."

"Because, if you haven't there'll probably be nobody to arrest."

"My dear Wimsey, do you think I'm a fool?"

"I had no such hope."

Parker grunted finally and departed.

Lord Peter settled down to a perusal of his Dante. It afforded him no solace. Lord Peter was hampered in his career as a private detective by a public-school education. Despite Parker's admonitions, he was not always able to discount it. His mind had been warped in its young growth by "Raffles" and "Sherlock Holmes," or the sentiments for which they stand. He belonged to a family which had never shot a fox.

"I am an amateur," said Lord Peter.

Nevertheless, while communing with Dante, he made up his mind.

In the afternoon he found himself in Harley Street. Sir Julian Freke might be consulted about one's nerves from two till four on Tuesdays and Fridays. Lord Peter rang the bell.

"Have you an appointment, sir?" inquired the man who opened the door.

"No," said Lord Peter, "but will you give Sir Julian my card? I think it possible he may see me without one."

He sat down in the beautiful room in which Sir Julian's patients awaited his healing counsel. It was full of people. Two or three fashionably dressed women were discussing shops and servants together, and teasing a toy griffon. A big, worried-looking man by himself in a corner looked at his watch twenty times a minute. Lord Peter knew him by sight. It was Wintrington, a millionaire, who had tried to kill himself a few months ago. He controlled the finances of five countries, but he could not control his nerves. The finances of five countries were in Sir Julian Freke's capable hands. By the fireplace sat a soldierly-looking young man, of about Lord Peter's own age.

211

His face was prematurely lined and worn; he sat bolt upright, his restless eyes darting in the direction of every slightest sound. On the sofa was an elderly woman of modest appearance, with a young girl. The girl seemed listless and wretched; the woman's look showed deep affection, and anxiety tempered with a timid hope. Close beside Lord Peter was another younger woman, with a little girl, and Lord Peter noticed in both of them the broad cheekbones and beautiful grey, slanting eyes of the Slav. The child, moving restlessly about, trod on Lord Peter's patent-leather toe, and the mother admonished her in French before turning to apologize to Lord Peter.

"Mais je vous en prie, madame," said the young man, "it is nothing."

"She is nervous, pauvre petite," said the young woman.

"You are seeking advice for her?"

"Yes. He is wonderful, the doctor. Figure to yourself, monsieur, she cannot forget, poor child, the things she has seen." She leaned nearer, so that the child might not hear. "We have escaped—from starving Russia—six months ago. I dare not tell you —she has such quick ears, and then, the cries, the tremblings, the convulsions—they all begin again. We were skeletons when we arrived—mon Dieu!— but that is better now. See, she is thin, but she is not starved. She would be fatter but for the nerves that keep her from eating. We who are older, we forget— enfin, on apprend à ne pas y penser—but these children! When one is young, monsieur, tout ça impressionne trop."

Lord Peter, escaping from the thraldom of British good form, expressed himself in that language in which sympathy is not condemned to mutism.

"But she is much better, much better," said the mother, proudly; "the great doctor, he does marvels."

"C'est un homme précieux," said Lord Peter.

"Ah, monsieur, c'est un saint qui opère des miracles! Nous prions pour lui, Natasha et moi, tous les jours. N'est-ce pas, chérie? And consider, monsieur, that he does it all, ce grand homme, cet homme illustre, for nothing at all. When we come here, we have not even the clothes upon our backs—we are ruined, famished. Et avec ça que nous sommes de bonne famille—mais hélas! monsieur, en Russie, comme vous savez, ça ne vous vaut que des insultes—des atrocités. Enfin! the great Sir Julian sees us, he says—'Madame, your little girl is very interesting to me. Say no more. I cure her for nothing—pour ses beaux yeux,' a-t-il ajouté en raint. Ah, monsieur, c'est un saint, un véritable saint! and Natasha is much, much better."

"Madame, je vous en félicite."

"And you, monsieur? You are young, well, strong—you also suffer? It is still the war, perhaps?"

"A little remains of shell-shock," said Lord Peter.

"Ah, yes. So many good, brave, young men—"

"Sir Julian can spare you a few minutes, my lord, if you will come in now," said the servant.

Lord Peter bowed to his neighbour, and walked

213

across the waiting-room. As the door of the consulting-room closed behind him, he remembered having once gone, disguised, into the staff-room of a German officer. He experienced the same feeling—the feeling of being caught in a trap, and a mingling of bravado and shame.

He had seen Sir Julian Freke several times from a distance, but never close. Now, while carefully and quite truthfully detailing the circumstances of his recent nervous attack, he considered the man before him. A man taller than himself, with immense breadth of shoulder, and wonderful hands. A face beautiful, impassioned and inhuman; fanatical, compelling eyes, bright blue amid the ruddy bush of hair and beard. They were not the cool and kindly eyes of the family doctor, they were the brooding eyes of the inspired scientist, and they searched one through.

"Well," thought Lord Peter, "I shan't have to be explicit, anyhow."

"Yes," said Sir Julian, "yes. You had been working too hard. Puzzling your mind. Yes. More than that, perhaps—troubling your mind, shall we say?"

"I found myself faced with a very alarming contingency."

"Yes. Unexpectedly, perhaps "

"Very unexpected indeed."

"Yes. Following on a period of mental and physical strain."

"Well—perhaps. Nothing out of the way."

214

"Yes. The unexpected contingency was—personal to yourself?"

"It demanded an immediate decision as to my own actions—yes, in that sense it was certainly personal."

"Quite so. You would have to assume some responsibility, no doubt."

"A very grave responsibility."

"Affecting others besides yourself?"

"Affecting one other person vitally, and a very great number indirectly."

"Yes. The time was night. You were sitting in the dark?"

"Not at first. I think I put the light out afterwards."

"Quite so—that action would naturally suggest itself to you. Were you warm?"

"I think the fire had died down. My man tells me that my teeth were chattering when I went in to him."

"Yes. You live in Piccadilly?"

"Yes."

"Heavy traffic sometimes goes past during the night, I expect."

"Oh, frequently."

"Just so. Now this decision you refer to—you had taken that decision."

"Yes."

"Your mind was made up?"

"Oh, yes."

"You had decided to take the action, whatever it was."

215

"Yes."

"Yes. It involved perhaps a period of inaction."

"Of comparative inaction—yes."

"Of suspense, shall we say?"

"Yes—of suspense, certainly."

"Possibly of some danger?"

"I don't know that that was in my mind at the time."

"No—it was a case in which you could not possibly consider yourself."

"If you like to put it that way."

"Quite so. Yes. You had these attacks frequently in 1918?"

"Yes—I was very ill for some months."

"Quite. Since then they have recurred less frequently?"

"Much less frequently."

"Yes—when did the last occur?"

"About nine months ago."

"Under what circumstances?"

"I was being worried by certain family matters. It was a question of deciding about some investments, and I was largely responsible."

"Yes. You were interested last year, I think, in some police case?"

"Yes—in the recovery of Lord Attenbury's emerald necklace."

"That involved some severe mental exercise?"

"I suppose so. But I enjoyed it very much."

"Yes. Was the exertion of solving the problem attended by any bad results physically?"

"None."

"No. You were interested, but not distressed."

"Exactly."

"Yes. You have been engaged in other investigations of the kind?"

"Yes. Little ones."

"With bad results for your health?"

"Not a bit of it. On the contrary. I took up these cases as a sort of distraction. I had a bad knock just after the war, which didn't make matters any better for me, don't you know."

"Ah! you are not married?"

"No."

"No. Will you allow me to make an examination? Just come a little nearer to the light. I want to see your eyes. Whose advice have you had till now?"

"Sir James Hodges'."

"Ah! yes—he was a sad loss to the medical profession. A really great man—a true scientist. Yes. Thank you. Now I should like to try you with this little invention."

"What's it do?"

"Well—it tells me about your nervous reactions. Will you sit here?"

The examination that followed was purely medical. When it was concluded, Sir Julian said:

"Now, Lord Peter, I'll tell you about yourself in quite untechnical language—"

"Thanks," said Peter, "that's kind of you. I'm an awful fool about long words."

"Yes. Are you fond of private theatricals, Lord Peter?"

"Not particularly," said Peter, genuinely surprised. "Awful bore as a rule. Why?"

"I thought you might be," said the specialist, drily. "Well, now. You know quite well that the strain you put on your nerves during the war has left its mark on you. It has left what I may call old wounds in your brain. Sensations received by your nerve-endings sent messages to your brain, and produced minute physical changes there—changes we are only beginning to be able to detect, even with our most delicate instruments. These changes in their turn set up sensations; or I should say, more accurately, that sensations are the names we give to these changes of tissue when we perceive them: we call them horror, fear, sense of responsibility and so on."

"Yes, I follow you."

"Very well. Now, if you stimulate those damaged places in your brain again, you run the risk of opening up the old wounds. I mean, that if you get nerve-sensations of any kind producing the reactions which we call horror, fear, and sense of responsibility, they may go on to make disturbance right along the old channel, and produce in their turn physical changes which you will call by the names you were accustomed to associate with them—dread of German mines, responsibility for the lives of your men, strained attention and the inability to distinguish small sounds through the overpowering noise of guns."

218

"I see."

"This effect would be increased by extraneous circumstances producing other familiar physical sensations—night, cold or the rattling of heavy traffic, for instance."

"Yes."

"Yes. The old wounds are nearly healed, but not quite. The ordinary exercise of your mental faculties has no bad effect. It is only when you excite the injured part of your brain."

"Yes, I see."

"Yes. You must avoid these occasions. You must learn to be irresponsible, Lord Peter."

"My friends say I'm only too irresponsible already."

"Very likely. A sensitive nervous temperament often appears so, owing to its mental nimbleness."

"Oh!"

"Yes. This particular responsibility you were speaking of still rests upon you?"

"Yes, it does."

"You have not yet completed the course of action on which you have decided?"

"Not yet."

"You feel bound to carry it through?"

"Oh, yes—I can't back out of it now."

"No. You are expecting further strain?"

"A certain amount."

"Do you expect it to last much longer?"

"Very little longer now."

"Ah! Your nerves are not all they should be."

"No?"

"No. Nothing to be alarmed about, but you must exercise care while undergoing this strain, and afterwards you should take a complete rest. How about a voyage in the Mediterranean or the South Seas or somewhere?"

"Thanks. I'll think about it."

"Meanwhile, to carry you over the immediate trouble I will give you something to strengthen your nerves. It will do you no permanent good, you understand, but it will tide you over the bad time. And I will give you a prescription."

"Thank you."

Sir Julian got up and went into a small surgery leading out of the consulting-room. Lord Peter watched him moving about—boiling something and writing. Presently he returned with a paper and a hypodermic syringe.

"Here is the prescription. And now, if you will just roll up your sleeve, I will deal with the necessity of the immediate moment."

Lord Peter obediently rolled up his sleeve. Sir Julian Freke selected a portion of his forearm and anointed it with iodine.

"What's that you're goin' to stick into me. Bugs?"

The surgeon laughed.

"Not exactly," he said. He pinched up a portion of flesh between his finger and thumb. "You've had this kind of thing before, I expect."

"Oh, yes," said Lord Peter. He watched the cool fingers, fascinated, and the steady approach of the needle. "Yes—I've had it before—and, d'you know—I don't care frightfully about it."

He had brought up his right hand, and it closed over the surgeon's wrist like a vice.

The silence was like a shock. The blue eyes did not waver; they burned down steadily upon the heavy white lids below them. Then these slowly lifted; the grey eyes met the blue—coldly, steadily—and held them.

When lovers embrace, there seems no sound in the world but their own breathing. So the two men breathed face to face.

"As you like, of course, Lord Peter," said Sir Julian, courteously.

"Afraid I'm rather a silly ass," said Lord Peter, "but I never could abide these little gadgets. I had one once that went wrong and gave me a rotten bad time. They make me a bit nervous."

"In that case," replied Sir Julian, "it would certainly be better not to have the injection. It might rouse up just those sensations which we are desirous of avoiding. You will take the prescription, then, and do what you can to lessen the immediate strain as far as possible."

"Oh, yes—I'll take it easy, thanks," said Lord Peter. He rolled his sleeve down neatly. "I'm much obliged to you. If I have any further trouble I'll look in again."

"Do—do—" said Sir Julian, cheerfully. "Only

Whose Body?

make an appointment another time. I'm rather rushed these days. I hope your mother is quite well. I saw her the other day at that Battersea inquest. You should have been there. It would have interested you."

CHAPTER XII

THE VILE, RAW FOG TORE YOUR THROAT AND RAV-
aged your eyes. You could not see your feet. You
stumbled in your walk over poor men's graves.

The feel of Parker's old trench-coat beneath your
fingers was comforting. You had felt it in worse
places. You clung on now for fear you should get
separated. The dim people moving in front of you
were like Brocken spectres.

"Take care, gentlemen," said a toneless voice out
of the yellow darkness, "there's an open grave just
hereabouts."

You bore away to the right, and floundered in a
mass of freshly turned clay.

"Hold up, old man," said Parker.

"Where is Lady Levy?"

"In the mortuary; the Duchess of Denver is with
her. Your mother is wonderful, Peter."

"Isn't she?" said Lord Peter.

A dim blue light carried by somebody ahead wavered and stood still.

"Here you are," said a voice.

Two Dantesque shapes with pitchforks loomed
up.

"Have you finished?" asked somebody.

"Nearly done, sir." The demons fell to work again
with the pitchforks—no, spades.

Somebody sneezed. Parker located the sneezer and introduced him.

"Mr. Levett represents the Home Secretary. Lord Peter Wimsey. We are sorry to drag you out on such a day, Mr. Levett."

"It's all in the day's work," said Mr. Levett, hoarsely. He was muffled to the eyes.

The sound of the spades for many minutes. An iron noise of tools thrown down. Demons stooping and straining.

A black-bearded spectre at your elbow. Introduced. The Master of the Workhouse.

"A very painful matter, Lord Peter. You will forgive me for hoping you and Mr. Parker may be mistaken."

"I should like to be able to hope so too."

Something heaving, straining, coming up out of the ground.

"Steady, men. This way. Can you see? Be careful of the graves—they lie pretty thick hereabouts. Are you ready?"

"Right you are, sir. You go on with the lantern. We can follow you."

Lumbering footsteps. Catch hold of Parker's trench-coat again. "That you, old man? Oh, I beg your pardon, Mr. Levett—thought you were Parker."

"Hullo, Wimsey—here you are."

More graves. A headstone shouldered crookedly aslant. A trip and jerk over the edge of the rough grass. The squeal of gravel under your feet.

"This way, gentlemen, mind the step."

The mortuary. Raw red brick and sizzling gas-jets. Two women in black, and Dr. Grimbold. The coffin laid on the table with a heavy thump.

" 'Ave you got that there screw-driver, Bill? Thank 'ee. Be keerful wi' the chisel now. Not much substance to these 'ere boards, sir."

Several long creaks. A sob. The Duchess's voice, kind but peremptory.

"Hush, Christine. You mustn't cry."

A mutter of voices. The lurching departure of the Dante demons—good, decent demons in corduroy.

Dr. Grimbold's voice—cool and detached as if in the consulting room.

"Now—have you got that lamp, Mr. Wingate? Thank you. Yes, here on the table, please. Be careful not to catch your elbow in the flex, Mr. Levett. It would be better, I think, if you came on this side. Yes—yes—thank you. That's excellent."

The sudden brilliant circle of an electric lamp over the table. Dr. Grimbold's beard and spectacles. Mr. Levett blowing his nose. Parker bending close. The Master of the Workhouse peering over him. The rest of the room in the enhanced dimness of the gas-jets and the fog.

A low murmur of voices. All heads bent over the work.

Dr. Grimbold again—beyond the circle of the lamplight.

"We don't want to distress you unnecessarily, Lady Levy. If you will just tell us what to look for—the—?

225

Whose Body?

Yes, yes, certainly—and—yes—stopped with gold?
Yes—the lower jaw, the last but one on the right?
Yes—no teeth missing—no—yes? What kind of a
mole? Yes—just over the left breast? Oh, I beg your
pardon, just under—yes—appendicitis? Yes—a long
one—yes—in the middle? Yes, I quite understand—
a scar on the arm? Yes, I don't know if we shall be
able to find that—yes—any little constitutional
weakness that might—? Oh, yes—arthritis—yes—
thank you, Lady Levy—that's very clear. Don't
come unless I ask you to. Now, Wingate."

A pause. A murmur. "Pulled out? After death,
you think—well, so do I. Where is Dr. Colegrove?
You attended this man in the workhouse? Yes. Do
you recollect—? No? You're quite certain about
that? Yes—we mustn't make a mistake, you know.
Yes, but there are reasons why Sir Julian can't be
present; I'm asking *you*, Dr. Colegrove. Well, you're
certain—that's all I want to know. Just bring the
light closer, Mr. Wingate, if you please. These miserable shells let the damp in so quickly. Ah! what
do you make of this? Yes—yes—well, that's rather
unmistakable, isn't it? Who did the head? Oh, Freke
—of course. I was going to say they did good work
at St. Luke's. Beautiful, isn't it, Dr. Colegrove? A
wonderful surgeon—I saw him when he was at Guy's.
Oh, no, gave it up years ago. Nothing like keeping
your hand in. Ah—yes, undoubtedly that's it. Have
you a towel handy, sir? Thank you. Over the head,
if you please—I think we might have another here.
Now, Lady Levy—I am going to ask you to look at

226

a scar, and see if you recognise it. I'm sure you are going to help us by being very firm. Take your time —you won't see anything more than you absolutely must."

"Lucy, don't leave me."

"No, dear."

A space cleared at the table. The lamplight on the Duchess's white hair.

"Oh, yes—oh, yes! No, no—I couldn't be mistaken. There's that funny little kink in it. I've seen it hundreds of times. Oh, Lucy—Reuben!"

"Only a moment more, Lady Levy. The mole—"

"I—I think so—oh, yes, that is the very place."

"Yes. And the scar—was it three-cornered, just above the elbow?"

"Yes, oh, yes."

"Is this it?"

"Yes—yes—"

"I must ask you definitely, Lady Levy. Do you, from these three marks identify the body as that of your husband?"

"Oh! I must, mustn't I? Nobody else could have them just the same in just those places? It is my husband. It is Reuben. Oh—"

"Thank you, Lady Levy. You have been very brave and very helpful."

"But—I don't understand yet. How did he come here? Who did this dreadful thing?"

"Hush, dear," said the Duchess; "the man is going to be punished."

227

"Oh, but—how cruel! Poor Reuben! Who could have wanted to hurt him? Can I see his face?"

"No, dear," said the Duchess. "That isn't possible. Come away—you mustn't distress the doctors and people."

"No—no—they've all been so kind. Oh, Lucy!"

"We'll go home, dear. You don't want us any more, Dr. Grimbold?"

"No, Duchess, thank you. We are very grateful to you and to Lady Levy for coming."

There was a pause, while the two women went out, Parker, collected and helpful, escorting them to their waiting car. Then Dr. Grimbold again:

"I think Lord Peter Wimsey ought to see—the correctness of his deductions—Lord Peter—very painful—you may wish to see—yes, I was uneasy at the inquest—yes—Lady Levy—remarkably clear evidence—yes—most shocking case—ah, here's Mr. Parker—you and Lord Peter Wimsey entirely justified—do I really understand—? Really? I can hardly believe it—so distinguished a man—as you say, when a great brain turns to crime—yes—look here! Marvellous work—marvellous—somewhat obscured by this time, of course—but the most beautiful sections —here, you see, the left hemisphere—and here— through the corpus striatum—here again—the very track of the damage done by the blow—wonderful —guessed it—saw the effect of the blow as he struck it, you know—ah, I should like to see *his* brain, Mr. Parker—and to think that—heavens, Lord Peter, you don't know what a blow you have struck at the whole profession—the whole civilized world! Oh, my dear sir! Can you ask me? My lips are sealed of course— all our lips are sealed."

The way back through the burial ground. Fog again, and the squeal of wet gravel.

"Are your men ready, Charles?"

"They have gone. I sent them off when I saw Lady Levy to the car."

"Who is with them?"

"Sugg."

"Sugg?"

"Yes—poor devil. They've had him up on the mat at headquarters for bungling the case. All that evidence of Thipps's about the night club was corroborated, you know. That girl he gave the gin-and-bitters to was caught, and came and identified him, and they decided their case wasn't good enough, and let Thipps and the Horrocks girl go. Then they told Sugg he had overstepped his duty and ought to have been more careful. So he ought, but he can't help being a fool. I was sorry for him. It may do him some good to be in at the death. After all, Peter, you and I had special advantages."

"Yes. Well, it doesn't matter. Whoever goes won't get there in time. Sugg's as good as another."

But Sugg—an experience rare in his career—was in time.

Parker and Lord Peter were at 110 Piccadilly. Lord Peter was playing Bach and Parker was reading Origen when Sugg was announced.

229

"We've got our man, sir," said he.

"Good God!" said Peter. "Alive?"

"We were just in time, my lord. We rang the bell and marched straight up past his man to the library. He was sitting there doing some writing. When we came in, he made a grab for his hypodermic, but we were too quick for him, my lord. We didn't mean to let him slip through our hands, having got so far. We searched him thoroughly and marched him off."

"He is actually in gaol, then?"

"Oh, yes—safe enough—with two warders to see he doesn't make away with himself."

"You surprise me, Inspector. Have a drink."

"Thank you, my lord. I may say that I'm very grateful to you—this case was turning out a pretty bad egg for me. If I was rude to your lordship—"

"Oh, it's all right, Inspector," said Lord Peter, hastily. "I don't see how you could possibly have worked it out. I had the good luck to know something about it from other sources."

"That's what Freke says." Already the great surgeon was a common criminal in the inspector's eyes —a mere surname. "He was writing a full confession when we got hold of him, addressed to your lordship. The police will have to have it, of course, but seeing it's written for you, I brought it along for you to see first. Here it is."

He handed Lord Peter a bulky document.

"Thanks," said Peter. "Like to hear it, Charles?"

"Rather."

Accordingly Lord Peter read it aloud.

230

DEAR LORD PETER—WHEN I WAS A YOUNG MAN I used to play chess with an old friend of my father's. He was a very bad, and a very slow, player, and he could never see when a checkmate was inevitable, but insisted on playing every move out. I never had any patience with that kind of attitude, and I will freely admit now that the game is yours. I must either stay at home and be hanged or escape abroad and live in an idle and insecure obscurity. I prefer to acknowledge defeat.

If you have read my book on "Criminal Lunacy," you will remember that I wrote: "In the majority of cases, the criminal betrays himself by some abnormality attendant upon this pathological condition of the nervous tissues. His mental instability shows itself in various forms: an overweening vanity, leading him to brag of his achievement; a disproportionate sense of the importance of the offence, resulting from the hallucination of religion, and driving him to confession; egomania, producing the sense of horror or conviction of sin, and driving him to headlong flight without covering his tracks; a reckless confidence, resulting in the neglect of the most ordinary precautions, as in the case of Henry Wainwright, who left a boy in charge of the murdered woman's remains while he went to call a cab, or on the other hand, a nervous distrust of apperceptions in the past, causing him to revisit the scene of the crime to assure himself that all traces have been as safely removed as *his own judgment knows them to be*. I will not hesitate to assert that a perfectly sane man, not intimidated by religious or other delusions, could always render himself perfectly secure from detection, provided, that is, that the crime were sufficiently premeditated and that he were not pressed for time or thrown out in his calculations by purely fortuitous coincidence.

You know as well as I do, how far I have made this assertion good in practice. The two accidents which betrayed me, I could not by any possibility have foreseen. The first was the chance recognition of Levy by the girl in the Battersea Park Road, which suggested a connection between the two problems. The second was that Thipps should have arranged to go down to Denver on the Tuesday morning, thus enabling your mother to get word of the matter through to you before the body was removed by the police and to suggest a motive for the murder out of what she knew of my previous personal history. If I had been able to destroy these two accidentally forged links of circumstance, I will venture to say that you would never have so much as suspected me, still less obtained sufficient evidence to convict.

Of all human emotions, except perhaps those of hunger and fear, the sexual appetite produces the most violent, and, under some circumstances, the most persistent reactions; I think, however, I am

232

right in saying that at the time when I wrote my book, my original sensual impulse to kill Sir Reuben Levy had already become profoundly modified by my habits of thought. To the animal lust to slay and the primitive human desire for revenge, there was added the rational intention of substantiating my own theories for the satisfaction of myself and the world. If all had turned out as I had planned, I should have deposited a sealed account of my experiment with the Bank of England, instructing my executors to publish it after my death. Now that accident has spoiled the completeness of my demonstration, I entrust the account to you, whom it cannot fail to interest, with the request that you will make it known among scientific men, in justice to my professional reputation.

The really essential factors of success in any undertaking are money and opportunity, and as a rule, the man who can make the first can make the second. During my early career, though I was fairly well-off, I had not absolute command of circumstance. Accordingly I devoted myself to my profession, and contented myself with keeping up a friendly connection with Reuben Levy and his family. This enabled me to remain in touch with his fortunes and interests, so that, when the moment for action should arrive, I might know what weapons to use.

Meanwhile, I carefully studied criminology in fiction and fact—my work on "Criminal Lunacy" was a side-product of this activity—and saw how, in every murder, the real crux of the problem was the

233

disposal of the body. As a doctor, the means of death were always ready to my hand, and I was not likely to make any error in that connection. Nor was I likely to betray myself on account of any illusory sense of wrong-doing. The sole difficulty would be that of destroying all connection between my personality and that of the corpse. You will remember that Michael Finsbury, in Stevenson's entertaining romance, observes: "What hangs people is the unfortunate circumstance of guilt." It became clear to me that the mere leaving about of a superfluous corpse could convict nobody, provided that nobody was guilty in connection *with that particular corpse*. Thus the idea of substituting the one body for the other was early arrived at, though it was not till I obtained the practical direction of St. Luke's Hospital that I found myself perfectly unfettered in the choice and handling of dead bodies. From this period on, I kept a careful watch on all the material brought in for dissection.

My opportunity did not present itself until the week before Sir Reuben's disappearance, when the medical officer at the Chelsea workhouse sent word to me that an unknown vagrant had been injured that morning by the fall of a piece of scaffolding, and was exhibiting some very interesting nervous and cerebral reactions. I went round and saw the case, and was immediately struck by the man's strong superficial resemblance to Sir Reuben. He had been heavily struck on the back of the neck, dislocating the fourth and fifth cervical vertebrae and heavily bruising the spinal cord. It seemed highly unlikely that he could ever recover, either mentally or physically, and in any case there appeared to me to be no object in indefinitely prolonging so unprofitable an existence. He had obviously been able to support life until recently, as he was fairly well nourished, but the state of his feet and clothing showed that he was unemployed, and under present conditions he was likely to remain so. I decided that he would suit my purpose very well, and immediately put in train certain transactions in the City which I had already sketched out in my own mind. In the meantime, the reactions mentioned by the workhouse doctor were interesting, and I made careful studies of them, and arranged for the delivery of the body to the hospital when I should have completed my preparations.

On the Thursday and Friday of that week I made private arrangements with various brokers to buy the stock of certain Peruvian Oil-fields, which had gone down almost to waste-paper. This part of my experiment did not cost me very much, but I contrived to arouse considerable curiosity, and even a mild excitement. At this point I was of course careful not to let my name appear. The incidence of Saturday and Sunday gave me some anxiety lest my man should after all die before I was ready for him, but by the use of saline injections I contrived to keep him alive and, late on Sunday night, he even manifested disquieting symptoms of at any rate a partial recovery.

On Monday morning the market in Peruvians opened briskly. Rumours had evidently got about

that somebody knew something, and this day I wa'
not the only buyer in the market. I bought a couple
of hundred more shares in my own name, and left
the matter to take care of itself. At lunch time I
made my arrangements to run into Levy accidentally
at the corner of the Mansion House. He expressed
(as I expected) his surprise at seeing me in that part
of London. I simulated some embarrassment and suggested that we should lunch together. I dragged him
to a place a bit off the usual beat, and there ordered
a good wine and drank of it as much as he might suppose sufficient to induce a confidential mood. I asked
him how things were going on 'Change. He said, "Oh,
all right," but appeared a little doubtful, and asked
me whether I did anything in that way. I said I had
a little flutter occasionally, and that, as a matter of
fact, I'd been put on to rather a good thing. I glanced
round apprehensively at this point, and shifted my
chair nearer to his.

"I suppose you don't know anything about Peruvian Oil, do you?" he said.

I started and looked round again, and leaning
across to him, said, dropping my voice:

"Well, I do, as a matter of fact, but I don't want
it to get about. I stand to make a good bit on it."

"But I thought the thing was hollow," he said;
"it hasn't paid a dividend for umpteen years."

"No," I said, "it hasn't, but it's going to. I've got
inside information." He looked a bit unconvinced,
and I emptied off my glass, and edged right up to his
ear.

"Look here," I said, "I'm not giving this away to everyone, but I don't mind doing you and Christine a good turn. You know, I've always kept a soft place in my heart for her, ever since the old days. You got in ahead of me that time, and now it's up to me to heap coals of fire on you both."

I was a little excited by this time, and he thought I was drunk.

"It's very kind of you, old man," he said, "but I'm a cautious bird, you know, always was. I'd like a bit of proof."

And he shrugged up his shoulders and looked like a pawnbroker.

"I'll give it to you," I said, "but it isn't safe here. Come round to my place tonight after dinner, and I'll show you the report."

"How d'you get hold of it?" said he.

"I'll tell you tonight," said I. "Come round after dinner—any time after nine, say."

"To Harley Street?" he asked, and I saw that he meant coming.

"No," I said, "to Battersea—Prince of Wales Road; I've got some work to do at the hospital. And look here," I said, "don't you let on to a soul that you're coming. I bought a couple of hundred shares today, in my own name, and people are sure to get wind of it. If we're known to be about together, someone'll twig something. In fact, it's anything but safe talking about it in this place."

"All right," he said, "I won't say a word to any-

237

body. I'll turn up about nine o'clock. You're sure it's a sound thing?"

"It can't go wrong," I assured him. And I meant it.

We parted after that, and I went round to the workhouse. My man had died at about eleven o'clock. I had seen him just after breakfast, and was not surprised. I completed the usual formalities with the workhouse authorities, and arranged for his delivery at the hospital at about seven o'clock.

In the afternoon, as it was not one of my days to be in Harley Street, I looked up an old friend who lives close to Hyde Park, and found that he was just off to Brighton on some business or other. I had tea with him, and saw him off by the 5.35 from Victoria. On issuing from the barrier it occurred to me to purchase an evening paper, and I thoughtlessly turned my steps to the bookstall. The usual crowds were rushing to catch suburban trains home, and on moving away I found myself involved in a contrary stream of travellers coming up out of the Underground, or bolting from all sides for the 5.45 to Battersea Park and Wandsworth Common. I disengaged myself after some buffeting and went home in a taxi; and it was not till I was safely seated there that I discovered somebody's gold-rimmed pince-nez involved in the astrakhan collar of my overcoat. The time from 6.15 to seven I spent concocting something to look like a bogus report for Sir Reuben.

At seven I went through to the hospital, and found the workhouse van just delivering my subject at the

side door. I had him taken straight up to the theatre,
and told the attendant, William Watts, that I intended to work there that night. I told him I would
prepare the body myself—the injection of a pre-
servative would have been a most regrettable com-
plication. I sent him about his business, and then
went home and had dinner. I told my man that I
should be working in the hospital that evening, and
that he could go to bed at 10.30 as usual, as I could
not tell whether I should be late or not. He is used
to my erratic ways. I only keep two servants in the
Battersea house—the man-servant and his wife, who
cooks for me. The rougher domestic work is done by
a charwoman, who sleeps out. The servants' bedroom
is at the top of the house, overlooking Prince of Wales
Road.

As soon as I had dined I established myself in the
hall with some papers. My man had cleared dinner
by a quarter past eight, and I told him to give me
the syphon and tantalus; and sent him downstairs.
Levy rang the bell at twenty minutes past nine, and
I opened the door to him myself. My man appeared
at the other end of the hall, but I called to him that
it was all right, and he went away. Levy wore an
overcoat with evening dress and carried an umbrella.
"Why, how wet you are!" I said. "How did you
come?" "By 'bus," he said, "and the fool of a conductor forgot to put me down at the end of the
road. It's pouring cats and dogs and pitch-dark—I
couldn't see where I was." I was glad he hadn't taken
a taxi, but I had rather reckoned on his not doing so.

239

"Your little economies will be the death of you one of these days," I said. I was right there, but I hadn't reckoned on their being the death of me as well. I say again, I could not have foreseen it.

I sat him down by the fire, and gave him a whisky. He was in high spirits about some deal in Argentines he was bringing off the next day. We talked money for about a quarter of an hour and then he said:

"Well, how about this Peruvian mare's-nest of yours?"

"It's no mare's-nest," I said; "come and have a look at it."

I took him upstairs into the library, and switched on the centre light and the reading lamp on the writing table. I gave him a chair at the table with his back to the fire, and fetched the papers I had been faking, out of the safe. He took them, and began to read them, poking over them in his short-sighted way, while I mended the fire. As soon as I saw his head in a favourable position I struck him heavily with the poker, just over the fourth cervical. It was delicate work calculating the exact force necessary to kill him without breaking the skin, but my professional experience was useful to me. He gave one loud gasp, and tumbled forward on to the table quite noise-lessly. I put the poker back, and examined him. His neck was broken, and he was quite dead. I carried him into my bedroom and undressed him. It was about ten minutes to ten when I had finished. I put him away under my bed, which had been turned down for the night, and cleared up the papers in the

library. Then I went downstairs, took Levy's umbrella, and let myself out at the hall door, shouting
"Good-night" loudly enough to be heard in the basement if the servants should be listening. I walked
briskly away down the street, went in by the hospital
side door, and returned to the house noiselessly by
way of the private passage. It would have been awkward if anybody had seen me then, but I leaned over
the back stairs and heard the cook and her husband
still talking in the kitchen. I slipped back into the
hall, replaced the umbrella in the stand, cleared up
my papers there, went up into the library and rang
the bell. When the man appeared I told him to lock
up everything except the private door to the hospital.
I waited in the library until he had done so, and about
10.30 I heard both servants go up to bed. I waited
a quarter of an hour longer and then went through
to the dissecting-room. I wheeled one of the stretcher
tables through the passage to the house door, and
then went to fetch Levy. It was a nuisance having
to get him downstairs, but I had not liked to make
away with him in any of the ground-floor rooms, in
case my servant should take a fancy to poke his head
in during the few minutes that I was out of the
house, or while locking up. Besides, that was a flea-
bite to what I should have to do later. I put Levy on
the table, wheeled him across to the hospital and substituted him for my interesting pauper. I was sorry
to have to abandon the idea of getting a look at the
latter's brain, but I could not afford to incur suspicion. It was still rather early, so I knocked down a

241

few minutes getting Levy ready for dissection. Then
I put my pauper on the table and trundled him over
to the house. It was now five past eleven, and I
thought I might conclude that the servants were in
bed. I carried the body into my bedroom. He was
rather heavy, but less so than Levy, and my Alpine
experience had taught me how to handle bodies. It is
as much a matter of knack as of strength, and I am,
in any case, a powerful man for my height. I put the
body into the bed—not that I expected anyone to
look in during my absence, but if they should they
might just as well see me apparently asleep in bed.
I drew the clothes a little over his head, stripped, and
put on Levy's clothes, which were fortunately a little
big for me everywhere, not forgetting to take his
spectacles, watch and other oddments. At a little before half-past eleven I was in the road looking for a
cab. People were just beginning to come home from
the theatre, and I easily secured one at the corner of
Prince of Wales Road. I told the man to drive me to
Hyde Park Corner. There I got out, tipped him well,
and asked him to pick me up again at the same place
in an hour's time. He assented with an understanding
grin, and I walked on up Park Lane. I had my own
clothes with me in a suitcase, and carried my own
overcoat and Levy's umbrella. When I got to No. 9A
there were lights in some of the top windows. I was
very nearly too early, owing to the old man's having
sent the servants to the theatre. I waited about for a
few minutes, and heard it strike the quarter past mid-

night. The lights were extinguished shortly after, and I let myself in with Levy's key.

It had been my original intention, when I thought over this plan of murder, to let Levy disappear from the study or the dining-room, leaving only a heap of clothes on the hearth-rug. The accident of my having been able to secure Lady Levy's absence from London, however, made possible a solution more misleading, though less pleasantly fantastic. I turned on the hall light, hung up Levy's wet overcoat and placed his umbrella in the stand. I walked up noisily and heavily to the bedroom and turned off the light by the duplicate switch on the landing. I knew the house well enough, of course. There was no chance of my running into the man-servant. Old Levy was a simple old man, who liked doing things for himself. He gave his valet little work, and never required any attendance at night. In the bedroom I took off Levy's gloves and put on a surgical pair, so as to leave no tell-tale finger-prints. As I wished to convey the impression that Levy had gone to bed in the usual way, I simply went to bed. The surest and simplest method of making a thing appear to have been done is to do it. A bed that has been rumpled about with one's hands, for instance, never looks like a bed that has been slept in. I dared not use Levy's brush, of course, as my hair is not of his colour, but I did everything else. I supposed that a thoughtful old man like Levy would put his boots handy for his valet, and I ought to have deduced that he would fold up his clothes. That was a mistake, but not an important one. Remembering that well-thought-out little work of Mr. Bentley's, I had examined Levy's mouth for false teeth, but he had none. I did not forget, however, to wet his tooth-brush.

At one o'clock I got up and dressed in my own clothes by the light of my own pocket torch. I dared not turn on the bedroom lights, as there were light blinds to the windows. I put on my own boots and an old pair of goloshes outside the door. There was a thick Turkey carpet on the stairs and hall-floor, and I was not afraid of leaving marks. I hesitated whether to chance the banging of the front door, but decided it would be safer to take the latchkey. (It is now in the Thames. I dropped it over Battersea Bridge the next day.) I slipped quietly down, and listened for a few minutes with my ear to the letter-box. I heard a constable tramp past. As soon as his steps had died away in the distance I stepped out and pulled the door gingerly to. It closed almost soundlessly, and I walked away to pick up my cab. I had an overcoat of much the same pattern as Levy's, and had taken the precaution to pack an opera hat in my suitcase. I hoped the man would not notice that I had no umbrella this time. Fortunately the rain had diminished for the moment to a sort of drizzle, and if he noticed anything he made no observation. I told him to stop at 50 Overstrand Mansions, and I paid him off there, and stood under the porch till he had driven away. Then I hurried round to my own side door and let myself in. It was about a quarter to two, and the harder part of my task still lay before me.

My first step was so to alter the appearance of my subject as to eliminate any immediate suggestion either of Levy or of the workhouse vagrant. A fairly superficial alteration was all I considered necessary, since there was not likely to be any hue-and-cry after the pauper. He was fairly accounted for, and his deputy was at hand to represent him. Nor, if Levy was after all traced to my house, would it be difficult to show that the body in evidence was, as a matter of fact, not his. A clean shave and a little hair-oiling and manicuring seemed sufficient to suggest a distinct personality for my silent accomplice. His hands had been well washed in hospital, and though calloused, were not grimy. I was not able to do the work as thoroughly as I should have liked, because time was getting on. I was not sure how long it would take me to dispose of him, and moreover, I feared the onset of *rigor mortis*, which would make my task more difficult. When I had him barbered to my satisfaction, I fetched a strong sheet and a couple of wide roller bandages, and fastened him up carefully, padding him with cotton wool wherever the bandages might chafe or leave a bruise.

Now came the really ticklish part of the business. I had already decided in my own mind that the only way of conveying him from the house was by the roof. To go through the garden at the back in this soft wet weather was to leave a ruinous trail behind us. To carry a dead man down a suburban street in

245

the middle of the night seemed outside the range of practical politics. On the roof, on the other hand, the rain, which would have betrayed me on the ground, would stand my friend.

To reach the roof, it was necessary to carry my burden to the top of the house, past my servants' room, and hoist him out through the trap-door in the box-room roof. Had it merely been a question of going quietly up there myself, I should have had no fear of waking the servants, but to do so burdened by a heavy body was more difficult. It would be possible, provided that the man and his wife were soundly asleep, but if not, the lumbering tread on the narrow stair and the noise of opening the trap-door would be only too plainly audible. I tiptoed delicately up the stair and listened at their door. To my disgust I heard the man give a grunt and mutter something as he moved in his bed.

I looked at my watch. My preparations had taken nearly an hour, first and last, and I dared not be too late on the roof. I determined to take a bold step and, as it were, bluff out an alibi. I went without precaution against noise into the bathroom, turned on the hot and cold water taps to the full and pulled out the plug.

My household has often had occasion to complain of my habit of using the bath at irregular night hours. Not only does the rush of water into the cistern disturb any sleepers on the Prince of Wales Road side of the house, but my cistern is afflicted with peculiarly loud gurglings and thumpings, while frequently the pipes emit a loud groaning sound. To my delight, on this particular occasion, the cistern was in excellent form, honking, whistling and booming like a railway terminus. I gave the noise five minutes' start, and when I calculated that the sleepers would have finished cursing me and put their heads under the clothes to shut out the din, I reduced the flow of water to a small stream and left the bathroom, taking good care to leave the light burning and lock the door after me. Then I picked up my pauper and carried him upstairs as lightly as possible.

The box-room is a small attic on the side of the landing opposite to the servants' bedroom and the cistern-room. It has a trap-door, reached by a short, wooden ladder. I set this up, hoisted up my pauper and climbed up after him. The water was still racing into the cistern, which was making a noise as though it were trying to digest an iron chain, and with the reduced flow in the bathroom the groaning of the pipes had risen almost to a hoot. I was not afraid of anybody hearing other noises. I pulled the ladder through on to the roof after me.

Between my house and the last house in Queen Caroline Mansions there is a space of only a few feet. Indeed, when the Mansions were put up, I believe there was some trouble about ancient lights, but I suppose the parties compromised somehow. Anyhow, my seven-foot ladder reached well across. I tied the body firmly to the ladder, and pushed it over till the far end was resting on the parapet of the opposite house. Then I took a short run across the cistern-room and the box-room roof, and landed easily on the other side, the parapet being happily both low and narrow.

The rest was simple. I carried my pauper along the flat roofs, intending to leave him, like the hunchback in the story, on someone's staircase or down a chimney. I had got about half-way along when I suddenly thought, "Why, this must be about little Thipps's place," and I remembered his silly face, and his silly chatter about vivisection. It occurred to me pleasantly how delightful it would be to deposit my parcel with him and see what he made of it. I lay down and peered over the parapet at the back. It was pitch-dark and pouring with rain again by this time, and I risked using my torch. That was the only incautious thing I did, and the odds against being seen from the houses opposite were long enough. One second's flash showed me what I had hardly dared to hope—an open window just below me.

I knew those flats well enough to be sure it was either the bathroom or the kitchen. I made a noose in a third bandage that I had brought with me, and made it fast under the arms of the corpse. I twisted it into a double rope, and secured the end to the iron stanchion of a chimney-stack. Then I dangled our friend over. I went down after him myself with the aid of a drain-pipe and was soon hauling him in by Thipps's bathroom window.

By that time I had got a little conceited with myself, and spared a few minutes to lay him out prettily and make him shipshape. A sudden inspiration suggested that I should give him the pair of pince-nez which I had happened to pick up at Victoria. I came across them in my pocket while I was looking for a penknife to loosen a knot, and I saw what distinction they would lend his appearance, besides making it more misleading. I fixed them on him, effaced all traces of my presence as far as possible, and departed as I had come, going easily up between the drain-pipe and the rope.

I walked quietly back, re-crossed my crevasse and carried in my ladder and sheet. My discreet accomplice greeted me with a reassuring gurgle and thump. I didn't make a sound on the stairs. Seeing that I had now been having a bath for about three-quarters of an hour, I turned the water off, and enabled my deserving domestics to get a little sleep. I also felt it was time I had a little myself.

First, however, I had to go over to the hospital and make all safe there. I took off Levy's head, and started to open up the face. In twenty minutes his own wife could not have recognised him. I returned, leaving my wet goloshes and mackintosh by the garden door. My trousers I dried by the gas stove in my bedroom, and brushed away all traces of mud and brickdust. My pauper's beard I burned in the library.

I got a good two hours' sleep from five to seven, when my man called me as usual. I apologized for having kept the water running so long and so late, and added that I thought I would have the cistern seen to.

I was interested to note that I was rather extra

hungry at breakfast, showing that my night's work had caused a certain wear-and-tear of tissue. I went over afterwards to continue my dissection. During the morning a peculiarly thick-headed police inspector came to inquire whether a body had escaped from the hospital. I had him brought to me where I was, and had the pleasure of showing him the work I was doing on Sir Reuben Levy's head. Afterwards I went round with him to Thipps's and was able to satisfy myself that my pauper looked very convincing.

As soon as the Stock Exchange opened I telephoned my various brokers, and by exercising a little care, was able to sell out the greater part of my Peruvian stock on a rising market. Towards the end of the day, however, buyers became rather unsettled as a result of Levy's death, and in the end I did not make more than a few hundreds by the transaction.

Trusting I have now made clear to you any point which you may have found obscure, and with congratulations on the good fortune and perspicacity which have enabled you to defeat me, I remain, with kind remembrances to your mother,

Yours very truly,
JULIAN FREKE

Post-Scriptum: My will is made, leaving my money to St. Luke's Hospital, and bequeathing my body to the same institution for dissection. I feel sure that my brain will be of interest to the scientific world. As I shall die by my own hand, I imagine that there may be a little difficulty about this. Will you do me the favour, if you can, of seeing the persons concerned in the inquest, and obtaining that the brain is not damaged by an unskilful practitioner at the post-mortem, and that the body is disposed of according to my wish?

By the way, it may be of interest to you to know that I appreciated your motive in calling this afternoon. It conveyed a warning, and I am acting upon it in spite of the disastrous consequences to myself. I was pleased to realize that you had not underestimated my nerve and intelligence, and refused the injection. Had you submitted to it, you would, of course, never have reached home alive. No trace would have been left in your body of the injection, which consisted of a harmless preparation of strychnine, mixed with an almost unknown poison, for which there is at present no recognised test, a concentrated solution of sn—

At this point the manuscript broke off.

"Well, that's all clear enough," said Parker.

"Isn't it queer?" said Lord Peter. "All that coolness, all those brains—and then he couldn't resist writing a confession to show how clever he was, even to keep his head out of the noose."

"And a very good thing for us," said Inspector Sugg, "but Lord bless you, sir, these criminals are all alike."

"Freke's epitaph," said Parker, when the Inspector had departed. "What next, Peter?"

"I shall now give a dinner party," said Lord Peter, "to Mr. John P. Milligan and his secretary and to Messrs. Crimplesham and Wicks. I feel they deserve it for not having murdered Levy."

"Well, don't forget the Thippses," said Mr. Parker.

"On no account," said Lord Peter, "would I deprive myself of the pleasure of Mrs. Thipps's company. Bunter!"

"My lord?"

"The Napoleon brandy."

MURDER MUST ADVERTISE

MURDER
Must Advertise

by
DOROTHY L. SAYERS

HARPER & ROW, PUBLISHERS
New York, Hagerstown, San Francisco, London

CONTENTS

MURDER MUST ADVERTISE

CHAPTER I

DEATH COMES TO PYM'S PUBLICITY

AND by the way," said Mr. Hankin, arresting Miss Rossiter as she rose to go, "there is a new copy-writer coming in today."

"Oh, yes, Mr. Hankin?"

"His name is Bredon. I can't tell you much about him; Mr. Pym engaged him himself; but you will see that he is looked after."

"Yes, Mr. Hankin."

"He will have Mr. Dean's room."

"Yes, Mr. Hankin."

"I should think Mr. Ingleby could take him in hand and show him what to do. You might send Mr. Ingleby along if he can spare me a moment."

"Yes, Mr. Hankin."

"That's all. And, oh, yes! Ask Mr. Smayle to let me have the Dairyfields guard-book."

"Yes, Mr. Hankin."

Miss Rossiter tucked her note-book under her arm, closed the glass-panelled door noiselessly after her and tripped smartly down the corridor. Peeping through another glass-panelled door, she observed Mr. Ingleby seated on a revolving chair with his feet on the cold radiator, and talking with great animation to a young woman in green, perched on the corner of the writing-table.

"Excuse me," said Miss Rossiter, with perfunctory civility, "but Mr. Hankin says can you spare him a moment, Mr. Ingleby?"

"If it's Tom-Boy Toffee," replied Mr. Ingleby defensively,

"it's being typed. Here! you'd better take these two bits along and make it so. That will lend an air of verisimilitude to an otherwise—"

"It isn't Tom-Boy. It's a new copy-writer."

"What, already?" exclaimed the young woman. "Before those shoes were old! Why, they only buried little Dean on Friday."

"Part of the modern system of push and go," said Mr. Ingleby. "All very distressing in an old-fashioned, gentlemanly firm. Suppose I've got to put this blighter through his paces. Why am I always left with the baby?"

"Oh, rot!" said the young woman, "you've only got to warn him not to use the directors' lav., and not to tumble down the iron staircase."

"You are the most callous woman, Miss Meteyard. Well, as long as they don't put the fellow in with me—"

"It's all right, Mr. Ingleby. He's having Mr. Dean's room."

"Oh! What's he like?"

"Mr. Hankin said he didn't know, Mr. Pym took him on."

"Oh, gosh! friend of the management." Mr. Ingleby groaned.

"Then I think I've seen him," said Miss Meteyard. "Tow-coloured, supercilious-looking blighter. I ran into him coming out of Pymmie's room yesterday. Horn-rims. Cross between Ralph Lynn and Bertie Wooster."

"Death, where is thy sting? Well, I suppose I'd better push off and see about it."

Mr. Ingleby lowered his feet from the radiator, prised up his slow length from the revolving chair, and prowled unhappily away.

"Oh, well, it makes a little excitement," said Miss Meteyard.

"Oh, don't you think we've had rather too much of that lately? By the way, could I have your subscription for the wreath? You told me to remind you."

"Yes, rather. What is it? A bob? Here's half-a-crown, and you'd better take the sweep-money out of it as well."

"Thanks awfully, Miss Meteyard. I do hope you get a horse this time."

"High time I did. I've been five years in this beastly office and never even been placed. I believe you wangle the draw."

"Indeed we don't, Miss Meteyard, or we shouldn't let all the horses go to those people in the Printing. Wouldn't you like to come and draw for us this time? Miss Parton's just typing out the names."

"All right." Miss Meteyard scrambled down leggily and followed Miss Rossiter to the typists' room.

This was a small, inconvenient cubicle, crowded at the moment to bursting-point. A plump girl in glasses, with head tilted back and brows twisted to keep the smoke of a cigarette out of her eyes, was rattling off the names of Derby runners on her type-writer, assisted by a bosom-friend who dictated the list from the columns of the *Morning Star*. A languid youth in shirt-sleeves was cutting the names of sweep-subscribers from a typed sheet, and twisting the papers into secretive little screws. A thin, eager young man, squatting on an upturned waste-paper basket, was turning over the flimsies in Miss Rossiter's tray and making sarcastic comments upon the copy to a bulky, dark youth in spectacles, immersed in a novel by P. G. Wodehouse and filching biscuits from a large tin. Draped against the door-posts and blocking the entrance to all comers, a girl and another young man, who seemed to be visitors from another department, were smoking gaspers and discussing lawn-tennis.

"Hullo, angels!" said Miss Rossiter, brightly. "Miss Meteyard's going to draw for us. And there's a new copy-writer coming."

The bulky young man glanced up to say "Poor devil!" and retreated again into his book.

"Bob for the wreath and sixpence for the sweep," went on Miss Rossiter, scrabbling in a tin cash-box. "Has anybody got two shillings for a florin? Where's your list, Parton? Scratch Miss Meteyard off, will you? Have I had your money, Mr. Garrett?"

"No money till Saturday," said the Wodehouse-reader.

"Hark at him!" cried Miss Parton, indignantly. "You'd think we were millionaires, the way we have to finance this department."

"Pick me a winner," replied Mr. Garrett, "and you can knock it off the prize-money. Hasn't that coffee come yet?"

"Have a look, Mr. Jones," suggested Miss Parton, addressing the gentleman on the door-post, "and see if you can see the boy. Just check these runners over with me, duckie. Meteor Bright, Tooralooral, Pheidippides II, Roundabout—"

"Roundabout's scratched," said Mr. Jones. "Here's the boy just coming."

"Scratched? No, when? What a shame! I put him down in the *Morning Star* competition. Who says so?"

"*Evening Banner* lunch special. Slip in the stable."

"Damn!" said Miss Rossiter, briefly. "There goes my thousand quid! Oh, well, that's life. Thank you, sonnie. Put it on the table. Did you remember the cucumber? Good boy. How much? One-and-five? Lend me a penny, Parton. There you are. Mind out a minute, Mr. Willis, do you mind? I want a pencil and rubber for the new bloke."

"What's his name?"

"Bredon."

"Where's he come from?"

"Hankie doesn't know. But Miss Meteyard's seen him. She says he's like Bertie Wooster in horn-rims."

"Older, though," said Miss Meteyard. "A well-preserved forty."

"Oh, gosh! When's he coming?"

" 'Smorning. If I'd been him I'd have put it off till to-morrow and gone to the Derby. Oh, here's Mr. Ingleby. He'll know. Coffee, Mr. Ingleby? Have you heard anything?"

"Star of Asia, Twinkletoes, Sainte-Nitouche, Duke Humphrey . . ."

"Forty-two," said Mr. Ingleby. "No sugar, thanks. Never been in advertising before. *Balliol.*"

"Golly!" said Miss Meteyard.

"As you say. If there is one thing more repulsive than another it is Balliolity," agreed Mr. Ingleby, who was a Trinity man.

> "Bredon went to Balliol
> And sat at the feet of Gamaliel,"

chanted Mr. Garrett, closing his book.

> "And just as he ought
> He cared for nought,"

added Miss Meteyard. "I defy you to find another rhyme for Balliol."

"Flittermouse, Tom Pinch, Fly-by-Night . . ."

> "And his language was sesquipedalial."

"It isn't sesquipedalial, it's sesquipedalian."

"Bother!"

"Twist those papers up tight, duckie. Put them in the lid of the biscuit-tin. Damn! that's Mr. Armstrong's buzzer. Stick a saucer over my coffee. Where's my note-book?"

". . . two double-faults running, so I said . . ."

". . . I can't find the carbon of that Magnolia wholetreble . . ."

". . . started at fifty to one . . ."

"Who's bagged my scissors?"

"Excuse me, Mr. Armstrong wants his Nutrax carbons . . ."

". . . and shake 'em up well . . ."

". . . hail you all, impale you all, jail you all . . ."

"Mr. Ingleby, can you spare me a moment?"

At Mr. Hankin's mildly sarcastic accents, the scene dislimned as by magic. The door-post drapers and Miss Parton's bosom-friend melted out into the passage, Mr. Willis, rising hurriedly with the tray of carbons in his hand, picked a paper out at random and frowned furiously at it, Miss Parton's cigarette dropped unostentatiously to the floor, Mr. Garrett, unable to get rid of his coffee-cup, smiled vaguely and tried to look as though he had picked it up by accident and didn't know it was there, Miss Meteyard, with great presence of mind, put the sweep counterfoils on a chair and sat on them, Miss Rossiter, clutching Mr. Armstrong's carbons in her hand, was able to look businesslike, and did so. Mr. Ingleby alone, disdaining pretence, set down his cup with a slightly impudent smile and advanced to obey his chief's command.

"This," said Mr. Hankin, tactfully blind to all evidences of disturbance, "is Mr. Bredon. You will—er—show him what he has to do. I have had the Dairyfields guard-books sent along to his room. You might start him on margarine. Er—I don't think Mr. Ingleby was up in your time, Mr. Bredon—he was at Trinity. Your Trinity, I mean, not ours." (Mr. Hankin was a Cambridge man.)

Mr. Bredon extended a well-kept hand.

"How do you do?"

"How do you do?" echoed Mr. Ingleby. They gazed at one another with the faint resentment of two cats at their first meeting. Mr. Hankin smiled kindly at them both.

"And when you've produced some ideas on margarine, Mr. Bredon, bring them along to my room and we'll go over them."

"Right-ho!" said Mr. Bredon, simply.

Mr. Hankin smiled again and padded gently away.

"Well, you'd better know everybody," said Mr. Ingleby, rapidly. "Miss Rossiter and Miss Parton are our guardian angels—type our copy, correct our grammar, provide us with pencils and paper and feed us on coffee and cake. Miss Parton is the blonde and Miss Rossiter the brunette. Gentlemen prefer blondes but personally I find them both equally seraphic."

Mr. Bredon bowed.

"Miss Meteyard—of Somerville. One of the brighter or-

naments of our department. She makes the vulgarest limericks ever recited within these chaste walls."

"Then we shall be friends," said Mr. Bredon cordially.

"Mr. Willis on your right, Mr. Garrett on your left—both
comrades in affliction. That is the whole department, except
Mr. Hankin and Mr. Armstrong who are directors, and Mr.
Copley, who is a man of weight and experience and does
not come and frivol in the typists' room. He goes out for
his elevenses, and assumes seniority though he hath it not."

Mr. Bredon grasped the hands extended to him and murmured politely.

"Would you like to be in on the Derby sweep?" inquired
Miss Rossiter, with an eye to the cash-box. "You're just in
time for the draw."

"Oh, rather," said Mr. Bredon. "How much?"

"Sixpence."

"Oh, yes, rather. I mean, it's jolly good of you. Of course,
absolutely—must be in on the jolly old sweep, what?"

"That brings the first prize up to a pound precisely," said
Miss Rossiter, with a grateful sigh. "I was afraid I should
have to take two tickets myself. Type Mr. Bredon's for him,
Parton. B,R,E,D,O,N—like summer-time on Bredon?"

"That's right."

Miss Parton obligingly typed the name and added another
blank ticket to the collection in the biscuit-box.

"Well, I suppose I'd better take you along to your dog-
kennel," said Mr. Ingleby, with gloom.

"Right-ho!" said Mr. Bredon. "Oh, rather. Yes."

"We're all along this corridor," added Mr. Ingleby, leading the way. "You'll find your way about in time. That's
Garrett's room and that's Willis's, and this is yours, between Miss Meteyard and me. That iron staircase opposite
me goes down to the floor below; mostly group managers
and conference rooms. Don't fall down it, by the way. The
man whose room you've got tumbled down it last week and
killed himself."

"No, did he?" said Mr. Bredon, startled.

"Bust his neck and cracked his skull," said Mr. Ingleby. "On one of those knobs."

"Why do they put knobs on staircases?" expostulated Mr. Bredon. "Cracking fellows' skulls for them? It's not right."

"No, it isn't," said Miss Rossiter, arriving with her hands full of scribbling-blocks and blotting-paper. "They're supposed to prevent the boys from sliding down the hand-rail, but it's the stairs themselves that are so—oh, I say, push on. There's Mr. Armstrong coming up. They don't like too much being said about the iron staircase."

"Well, here you are," said Mr. Ingleby, adopting this advice. "Much the same as the rest, except that the radiator doesn't work very well. Still, that won't worry you just at present. This was Dean's room."

"Chap who fell downstairs?"

"Yes."

Mr. Bredon gazed round the small apartment, which contained a table, two chairs, a rickety desk and a bookshelf, and said:

"Oh!"

"It *was* awful," said Miss Rossiter.

"It must have been," agreed Mr. Bredon, fervently.

"Mr. Armstrong was just giving me dictation when we heard the most *frightful* crash. He said, 'Good God, what's that?' I thought it must be one of the boys, because one of them fell down last year carrying an Elliot-Fisher typewriter and it sounded exactly like it, only worse. And I said, 'I think one of the boys must have fallen downstairs, Mr. Armstrong,' and he said, 'Careless little devil,' and went on dictating and my hand was so shaky I could hardly make my outlines and then Mr. Ingleby ran past and Mr. Daniels' door opened and then we heard the most terrific shriek, and Mr. Armstrong said, 'Better go and see what's happened,' so I went out and looked down and I couldn't see anything because there was such a bunch of people standing round and then Mr. Ingleby came tearing up, with *such* a look on his face—you were as white as a sheet, Mr. Ingleby, you really were."

"Possibly," said Mr. Ingleby, a little put out. "Three years in this soul-searing profession have not yet robbed me of all human feeling. But that will come in time."

"Mr. Ingleby said, 'He's killed himself!' And I said, 'Who?' and he said, 'Mr. Dean,' and I said, 'You don't mean that,' and he said, 'I'm afraid so,' and I went back to Mr. Armstrong and said, 'Mr. Dean's killed himself,' and he said, 'What do you mean, killed himself?' and then Mr. Ingleby came in and Mr. Armstrong gave one look at him and went out and I went down by the other staircase and saw them carrying Mr. Dean along to the board-room and his head was all hanging sideways."

"Does this kind of thing happen often?" inquired Mr. Bredon.

"Not with such catastrophic results," replied Mr. Ingleby, "but that staircase is definitely a death-trap."

"I fell down it myself one day," said Miss Rossiter, "and tore the heels off both my shoes. It was awfully awkward, because I hadn't another pair in the place and—"

"I've drawn a horse, darlings!" announced Miss Meteyard, arriving without ceremony. "No luck for you, Mr. Bredon, I'm afraid."

"I always was unlucky."

"You'll feel unluckier still after a day with Dairyfields Margarine," said Mr. Ingleby, gloomily. "Nothing for me, I suppose?"

"Nothing, I'm afraid. Of course Miss Rawlings has drawn the favourite—she always does."

"I hope it breaks its beastly leg," said Mr. Ingleby. "Come in, Tallboy, come in. Do you want me? Don't mind butting in on Mr. Bredon. He will soon become used to the idea that his room is a public place within the meaning of the act. This is Mr. Tallboy, group-manager for Nutrax and a few other wearisome commodities. Mr. Bredon, our new copy-writer."

"How do you do?" said Mr. Tallboy, briefly. "Look here, about this Nutrax 11-inch double. Can you possibly cut out about thirty words?"

"No, I can't," said Mr. Ingleby. "I've cut it to the bone already."

"Well, I'm afraid you'll have to. There isn't room for all this guff with a two-line sub-head."

"There's plenty of room for it."

"No, there isn't. We've got to get in the panel about the Fifty-six Free Chiming Clocks."

"Damn the clocks and the panel! How do they expect to display all that in a half-double?"

"Dunno, but they do. Look here, can't we take out this bit about 'When your nerves begin to play tricks on you,' and start off with 'Nerves need Nutrax'?"

"Armstrong liked that bit about playing tricks. Human appeal and all that. No, take out that rot about the patent spring-cap bottle."

"They won't stand for dropping that," said Miss Mete-yard. "That's their pet invention."

"Do they think people buy nerve-food for the sake of the bottle? Oh, well! I can't do it straight away. Hand it over."

"The printer wants it by two o'clock," said Mr. Tallboy, dubiously.

Mr. Ingleby damned the printer, seized the proof and began cutting the copy, uttering offensive ejaculations between his teeth.

"Of all beastly days of the week," he observed, "Tuesday is the foulest. There's no peace till we get this damned 11-inch double off our chests. There! I've cut out twenty-two words, and you'll have to make it do. You can take that 'with' up into the line above and save a whole line, and that gives you the other eight words."

"All right, I'll try," agreed Mr. Tallboy. "Anything for a quiet life. It'll look a bit tight, though."

"Wish *I* was tight," said Mr. Ingleby. "Take it away, for God's sake, before I murder anybody."

"I'm going, I'm going," said Mr. Tallboy, and vanished hastily. Miss Rossiter had departed during the controversy, and Miss Meteyard now took herself out of the way, remarking, "If Pheidippides wins, you shall have a cake for tea."

"Now we'd better start *you* off," observed Mr. Ingleby. "Here's the guard-book. You'd better have a look through it to see the kind of thing, and then think up some head-lines. Your story is, of course, that Dairyfields' 'Green Pastures' Margarine is everything that the best butter ought to be and only costs ninepence a pound. And they like a cow in the picture."

"Why? Is it made of cow-fat?"

"Well, I daresay it is, but you mustn't say so. People wouldn't like the idea. The picture of the cow suggests the taste of butter, that's all. And the name—Green Pastures—suggests cows, you see."

"It suggests Negroes to me," said Mr. Bredon. "The play, you know."

"You mustn't put Negroes in the copy," retorted Mr. Ingleby. "Nor, of course, religion. Keep Psalm 23 out of it. Blasphemous."

"I see. Just something about 'Better than Butter and half the price.' Simple appeal to the pocket."

"Yes, but you mustn't knock butter. They sell butter as well."

"Oh!"

"You can say it's as good as butter."

"But in that case," objected Mr. Bredon, "what does one find to say in favour of butter? I mean, if the other stuff's as good and doesn't cost so much, what's the argument for buying butter?"

"You don't need an argument for buying butter. It's a natural, human instinct."

"Oh, I see."

"Anyway, don't bother about butter. Just concentrate on Green Pastures Margarine. When you've got a bit done, you take it along and get it typed, and then you buzz off to Mr. Hankin with the result. See? Are you all right now?"

"Yes, thanks," said Mr. Bredon, looking thoroughly be-wildered.

"And I'll push along about 1 o'clock and show you the decentest place for lunch."

"Thanks frightfully."

"Well, cheerio!" Mr. Ingleby returned to his own room. "*He* won't stay the course," he said to himself. "Goes to a damned good tailor, though. I wonder—"

He shrugged his shoulders and sat down to concoct a small, high-class folder about Slider's Steel Office Tables.

Mr. Bredon, left alone, did not immediately attack the subject of margarine. Like a cat, which, in his soft-footed inquisitiveness, he rather resembled, he proceeded to make himself acquainted with his new home. There was not very much to see in it. He opened the drawer in his writing-table and found a notched and inky ruler, some bitten-looking pieces of india-rubber, a number of bright thoughts on tea and margarine scribbled on scraps of paper, and a broken fountain-pen. The book-case contained a dictionary, a repellent volume entitled *Directory of Directors,* a novel by Edgar Wallace, a pleasingly got-up booklet called *All about Cocoa, Alice in Wonderland,* Bartlett's *Familiar Quotations,* the *Globe* edition of the *Works of Wm. Shakespeare,* and five odd numbers of the *Children's Encyclopædia.* The interior of the sloping desk offered more scope for inquiry; it was filled with ancient and dusty papers, including a Government Report on the Preservatives in Food (Restrictions) Act of 1926, a quantity of rather (in every sense) rude sketches by an amateur hand, a bundle of pulls of advertisements for Dairyfields commodities, some private correspondence and some old bills. Mr. Bredon, dusting fastidious fingers, turned from this receptacle, inventoried a hook and a coat-hanger on the wall and a battered paper-file in a corner, and sat down in the revolving-chair before the table. Here, after a brief glance at a paste-pot, a pair of scissors, a new pencil and a blotting-pad, two scribbling-blocks and a grubby cardboard box-lid full of oddments, he propped up the Dairyfields guard-book before him, and fell to studying his predecessor's masterpieces on the subject of Green Pastures Margarine.

An hour later, Mr. Hankin pushed open the door and looked in upon him.

"How are you getting on?" he inquired kindly.

Mr. Bredon sprang to his feet.

"Not frightfully well, I'm afraid. I don't seem to get the atmosphere altogether, if you follow me."

"It will come," said Mr. Hankin. He was a helpfully-minded man, who believed that new copy-writers throve on encouragement. "Let me see what you are doing. You are starting with the headlines? Quite right. The headline is more than half the battle. IF YOU WERE A COW—no, no, I'm afraid we mustn't call the customer a cow. Besides, we had practically the same headline in—let me see—about 1923, I think. Mr. Wardle put it up, you'll find it in the last guard-book but three. It went 'IF YOU KEPT A COW IN THE KITCHEN you could get no better bread-spread than G. P. Margarine'—and so on. That was a good one. Caught the eye, made a good picture, and told the whole story in a sentence."

Mr. Bredon bowed his head, as one who hears the Law and the Prophets. The copy-chief ran a thoughtful pencil over the scribbled list of headlines, and ticked one of them.

"I like that.

BIGGER AND BUTTER
VALUE FOR MONEY

That has the right feel about it. You might write copy for that, and perhaps for this one,

YOU'D BE READY TO BET
IT WAS BUTTER—

though I'm not quite sure about it. These Dairyfields people are rather strait-laced about betting."

"Oh, are they? What a pity! I'd done several about that. 'HAVE A BIT ON—' Don't you like that one?"

Mr. Hankin shook his head regretfully.

"I'm afraid that's too direct. Encouraging the working classes to waste their money."

"But they all do it—why, all these women like a little flutter."

"I know, I know. But I'm sure the client wouldn't stand for it. You'll soon find that the biggest obstacle to good advertising is the client. They all have their fads. That headline would do for Darling's, but it won't do for Dairy-fields. We did very well with a sporting headline in '26—'PUT YOUR SHIRT ON Darling's Non-collapsible Towel-Horse' —sold 80,000 in Ascot week. Though that was partly accident, because we mentioned a real horse in the copy and it came in at 50 to 1, and all the women who'd won money on it rushed out and bought Non-collapsible Towel-Horses out of sheer gratitude. The public's very odd."

"Yes," said Mr. Bredon. "They must be. There seems to be more in advertising than, so to speak, meets the eye."

"There is," said Mr. Hankin, a little grimly. "Well, get some copy written and bring it along to me. You know where to find my room?"

"Oh, yes—at the end of the corridor, near the iron staircase."

"No, no, that's Mr. Armstrong. At the other end of the corridor, near the other staircase—not the iron staircase. By the way—"

"Yes?"

"Oh, nothing," said Mr. Hankin, vaguely. "That is to say —no, nothing."

Mr. Bredon gazed after his retreating figure, and shook his fair head in a meditative manner. Then, applying himself to his task, he wrote out, rather quickly, a couple of paragraphs in praise of margarine and wandered out with them. Turning to the right, he paused opposite the door of Ingleby's room and stared irresolutely at the iron staircase. As he stood there, the glass door of a room on the opposite side of the corridor opened and a middle-aged man shot out. Seeing Bredon, he paused in his rush for the stairhead and inquired:

"Do you want to know how to get anywhere or anything?"

"Oh! thanks awfully. No—I mean, yes. I'm the new copywriter. I'm looking for the typists' room."

"Other end of the passage."

"Oh, I see, thanks frightfully. This place is rather confusing. Where does this staircase go to?"

"Down to a whole lot of departments—mostly groupmanagers' rooms and board-rooms and Mr. Pym's room and several of the Directors' rooms and the Printing."

"Oh, I see. Thanks ever so. Where does one wash?"

"That's downstairs too. I'll show you if you like."

"Oh, thanks—thanks most awfully."

The other man plunged down the steep and rattling spiral as though released by a spring. Bredon followed more gingerly.

"A bit precipitous, isn't it?"

"Yes, it is. You'd better be careful. One fellow out of your department smashed himself up here the other day."

"No, really?"

"Broke his neck. Dead when we picked him up."

"No, did he? was he? How on earth did he come to do that? Couldn't he see where he was going?"

"Slipped, I expect. Must have been going too fast. There's nothing really wrong with the staircase. I've never had an accident. It's very well-lit."

"Well-lit?" Mr. Bredon gaped vaguely at the skylight and up and down the passage, surrounded, like the one on the floor above, with glass partitions. "Oh, yes, to be sure. It's very well-lit. Of course he must have slipped. Dashed easy thing to slip on a staircase. Did he have nails in his shoes?"

"I don't know. I wasn't noticing his shoes. I was thinking about picking up the pieces."

"Did you pick him up?"

"Well, I heard the racket when he went down, and rushed out and got there one of the first. My name's Daniels, by the way."

"Oh, is it? Daniels, oh, yes. But didn't it come out at the inquest about his shoes?"

"I don't remember anything about it."

"Oh! then I suppose he didn't have nails. I mean, if he had, somebody would have mentioned it. I mean, it would be a sort of excuse, wouldn't it?"

"Excuse for whom?" demanded Daniels.

"For the firm; I mean, when people put up staircases and other people come tumbling down them, the insurance people generally want to know why. At least, I'm told so. I've never fallen down any staircases myself—touch wood."

"You'd better not try," retorted Daniels, evading the question of insurance. "You'll find the wash-place through that door and down the passage on the left."

"Oh, thanks frightfully."

"Not at all."

Mr. Daniels darted away into a room full of desks, leaving Mr. Bredon to entangle himself in a heavy swing door.

In the lavatory, Bredon encountered Ingleby.

"Oh!" said the latter. "You've found your way. I was told off to show you, but I forgot."

"Mr. Daniels showed me. Who's he?"

"Daniels? He's a group-manager. Looks after a bunch of clients—Sliders and Harrogate Bros. and a few more. Sees to the lay-outs and sends the stereos down to the papers and all that. Not a bad chap."

"He seems a bit touchy about the iron staircase. I mean, he was quite matey till I suggested that the insurance people would want to look into that fellow's accident—and then he kind of froze on me."

"He's been a long time in the firm and doesn't like any nasturtiums cast at it. Certainly not by a new bloke. As a matter of fact, it's better not to throw one's weight about here till one's been ten years or so in the place. It's not encouraged."

"Oh? Oh, thanks awfully for telling me."

"This place is run like a Government office," went on

Ingleby. "Hustle's not wanted and initiative and curiosity are politely shown the door."

"That's right," put in a pugnacious-looking red-headed man, who was scrubbing his fingers with pumice-stone as though he meant to take the skin off. "I asked them for £50 for a new lens—and what was the answer? Economy, please, in all departments—the Whitehall touch, eh?—and yet they pay you fellows to write more-you-spend-more-you-save copy! However, I shan't be here long, that's one comfort."

"This is Mr. Prout, our photographer," said Ingleby. "He has been on the point of leaving us for the last five years, but when it comes to the point he realizes that we couldn't do without him and yields to our tears and entreaties."

"Tcha!" said Mr. Prout.

"The management think Mr. Prout so precious," went on Ingleby, "that they have set his feet in a large room—"

"That you couldn't swing a kitten in," said Mr. Prout, "and no ventilation. Murder, that's what they do here. Black holes of Calcutta and staircases that break people's heads open. What we want in this country is a Mussolini to organize trade conditions. But what's the good of talking? All the same, one of these days, you'll see."

"Mr. Prout is our tame firebrand," observed Ingleby, indulgently. "You coming up, Bredon?"

"Yes. I've got to take this stuff to be typed."

"Right-ho! Here you are. Round this way and up this staircase by the lift, through the Dispatching and here you are—right opposite the home of British Beauty. Children, here's Mr. Bredon with a nice bit of copy for you."

"Hand it here," said Miss Rossiter, "and oh! Mr. Bredon, do you mind putting down your full name and address on this card—they want it downstairs for the file."

Bredon took the card obediently.

"Block letters please," added Miss Rossiter, glancing with some dismay at the sheets of copy she had just received.

"Oh, do you think my handwriting's awful? I always

think it's rather neat, myself. Neat, but not gaudy. However, if you say so—"

"Block letters," repeated Miss Rossiter, firmly. "Hullo! here's Mr. Tallboy. I expect he wants you, Mr. Ingleby."

"What, again?"

"Nutrax have cancelled that half-double," announced Mr. Tallboy with gloomy triumph. "They've just sent up from the conference to say that they want something special to put up against the new Slumbermalt campaign, and Mr. Hankin says will you get something out and let him have it in half an hour."

Ingleby uttered a loud yell, and Bredon, laying down the index-card, gazed at him open-mouthed.

"Damn and blast Nutrax," said Ingleby. "May all its directors get elephantiasis, locomotor ataxy and ingrowing toe-nails!"

"Oh, quite," said Tallboy. "You'll let us have something, won't you? If I can get it passed before 3 o'clock the printer— Hullo!"

Mr. Tallboy's eye, roving negligently round, had fallen on Bredon's index-card. Miss Rossiter's glance followed his. Neatly printed on the card stood the one word

DEATH

"Look at that!" said Miss Rossiter.

"Oh!" said Ingleby, looking over her shoulder. "That's who you are, is it, Bredon? Well, all I can say is, your stuff ought to come home to everybody. Universal appeal, and so forth."

Mr. Bredon smiled apologetically.

"You startled me so," he said. "Pooping off that howl in my ear." He took up the card and finished his inscription:

DEATH BREDON,
12A, Great Ormond Street,
W.C.1

CHAPTER II

EMBARRASSING INDISCRETION
OF TWO TYPISTS

FOR the twentieth time, Mr. Death Bredon was studying the report of the coroner's inquest on Victor Dean.

There was the evidence of Mr. Prout, the photographer: "It would be about tea-time. Tea is served at 3.30, more or less. I was coming out of my room on the top floor, carrying my camera and tripod. Mr. Dean passed me. He was coming quickly along the passage in the direction of the iron staircase. He was not running—he was walking at a good pace. He was carrying a large, heavy book under one arm. I know now that it was *The Times Atlas*. I turned to walk in the same direction that he was going. I saw him start down the iron staircase; it is rather a steep spiral. He had taken about half a dozen steps when he seemed to crumple together and disappear. There was a tremendous crash. You might call it a clatter—a prolonged crashing noise. I started to run, when Mr. Daniels' door opened and he came out and collided with the legs of my tripod. While we were mixed up together, Mr. Ingleby ran past us down the corridor. I heard a shrill scream from below. I put the camera down and Mr. Daniels and I went to the head of the staircase together. Some other people joined us—Miss Rossiter, I think, and some of the copy-writers and clerks. We could see Mr. Dean lying huddled together at the foot of the staircase. I could not say whether he had fallen down the stairs or through the banisters. He was lying all in a heap. The staircase is a right-handed spiral, and makes one complete turn. The treads are composed of pierced iron-work. The hand-rail has a number of iron knobs on it, about the size of small walnuts. The stairs are apt to be slippery. The stair is well lit. There is a sky-light above, and it receives light through the glass panels of Mr. Daniels' room and also from the glass-panelled corridor on the floor below. I have here a photograph taken by myself at 3.30 p.m. yesterday—that is the day after the accident. It shows the head of the spiral staircase. It was taken by ordinary daylight. I used an Actinax Special Rapid plate with the H & D number 450. The exposure was ⅕ second with the lens stopped down to f.16. The light was then similar to what it was at the time of Mr. Dean's death. The sun was shining on both occasions. The corridor runs, roughly, north and south. As deceased went down the staircase, the light would be coming from above and behind him; it is not possible that he could have the sun in his eyes."

Then came Mr. Daniels' account:

"I was standing at my desk consulting with Mr. Freeman about an advertising lay-out. I heard the crash. I thought one of the boys must have fallen down again. A boy did fall down that staircase on a previous occasion. I do not consider it a dangerous structure. I consider that the boy was going too fast. I do not recollect hearing Mr. Dean go along the passage. I did not see him. My back was to the door. People pass along that passage continuously; I should not be paying attention. I went quickly out when I heard the noise of the fall. I encountered Mr. Prout and tripped over his tripod. I did not exactly fall down, but I stumbled and had to catch hold of him to steady myself. There was nobody in the corridor when I came out except Mr. Prout. I will swear to that. Mr. Ingleby came past us while we were recovering from the collision. He did not come from his own room, but from the south end of the passage. He went down the iron staircase and Mr. Prout and I followed as quickly as we could. I heard somebody shriek downstairs. I think it was just before, or just after I ran into Mr. Prout. I was rather confused at the time and cannot say for certain. We saw Mr. Dean lying at the bottom of the staircase. There were a number of people standing round. Then Mr. Ingleby came up the stairs very hastily and called out: 'He's dead!' or 'He's killed himself.' I cannot speak to the exact words. I did not believe him at first; I thought he was exaggerating. I went on down the staircase. Mr. Dean was lying bundled together, head downwards. His legs were partly up the staircase. I think somebody had already tried to lift him before I got there. I have had some experience of death and accidents. I was a stretcher-bearer in the War. I examined him and gave it as my opinion that he was dead. I believe Mr. Atkins had already expressed a similar opinion. I helped to lift the body and carry it into the Board-room. We laid him on the table and endeavoured to administer first-aid, but I never had any doubt that he was dead. It did not occur to us to leave him where he was till the police were summoned, because, of course, he might not have been dead, and we could not leave him head downwards on the staircase."

Then came Mr. Atkins, who explained that he was a group-secretary, working in one of the downstairs rooms.

"I was just coming out of my room, the door of which commands a view of the iron staircase. It is not directly opposite the foot of the staircase, but it commands a view of the lower half of the staircase. Any one coming down the staircase would have his back turned to me as he stepped off. I heard a loud crash, and saw the deceased falling all of a heap down the stairs. He did not appear to make any attempt to save himself. He was clutching a large book in his arms. He did not loose his grip of the book as he fell. He seemed to cannon from one side of the staircase to the other and fall like a sack of potatoes, so to speak. He pitched on his head at the bottom. I was carrying a large tray full of glass jars. I set this down and ran towards him. I endeavoured to lift him up, but the moment I touched him I felt sure that he was dead. I formed the opinion that he had broken his neck. Mrs. Crump was in the passage at the time. Mrs. Crump is the head charwoman. I said to her: 'Good God! he's broken his neck,' and she screamed loudly. A number of other people arrived almost immediately upon the scene. Somebody said, 'Perhaps it's only dislocated.' Mr. Daniels said to me: 'We can't leave him here.' I think it was Mr. Armstrong who suggested that he should be taken into the Board-room. I assisted to carry him there. The book was held by the deceased in such a tight grip that we had difficulty in getting it away from him. He made no movement of any kind after he fell, and no attempt at speech. I never had the least doubt that he was dead from the moment that he fell."

Mrs. Crump confirmed this account to the best of her ability. She said: "I am head charwoman to the firm of Pym's Publicity, Ltd. It is my duty to take the tea-waggon round the office building at about 3.30 each afternoon. That is, I start my round at about 3.15 and finish at about 3.45. I had nearly finished doing the first floor, and was returning on my way to the lift to take tea up to the top floor. That would make the time about 3.30. I was coming along the corridor and was facing the foot of the iron staircase. I saw Mr. Dean fall. He fell all in a bunch-like. It was dreadful. He did not shout out or make any exclamation in falling. He fell like a dead thing. My heart seemed to stop. I was struck so I couldn't move for a minute or two. Then Mr. Atkins came running along to pick him up. He said: 'He's broke his neck,' and I let out a scream. I couldn't help myself, I was that upset. I think that staircase is a wicked dangerous place. I am always warning the other women against it. If you was to slip you couldn't hardly save yourself, not if you was carrying anything. People run up and downstairs on it all day, and the edges of the steps gets that polished you wouldn't believe, and some of them is wore down at the edges."

The medical evidence was given by Dr. Emerson. "I reside in Queen's Square, Bloomsbury. It is about five minutes from my house to the offices of Pym's Publicity in Southampton Row. I received a telephone message at 3.40 p.m. and went round immediately. Deceased was dead when I arrived. I concluded that he had then been dead about 15 minutes. His neck was broken at the fourth cervical ver-

tebra. He also had a contused wound on the right temple
which had cracked the skull. Either of these injuries was
sufficient to cause death. I should say he had died instantly
upon falling. He had also the tibia of the left leg broken,
probably through catching in the banister of the staircase.
There were also, of course, a quantity of minor scratches
and contusions. The wound on the head is such as might
be caused through pitching upon one of the knobs on the
handrail in falling. I could not say whether this or the
broken vertebra was the actual cause of death, but in either
case, death would be instantaneous. I agree that it is not a
matter of great importance. I found no trace of any heart
disease or any other disease which might suggest that deceased was subject to vertigo or fainting-fits. I observed no
traces of alcoholic tendency or of addiction to drugs. I have
seen the staircase, and consider that it would be very easy
to slip upon it. So far as I can tell, deceased's eyesight would
appear to have been normal."

Miss Pamela Dean, sister of deceased, gave evidence that
her brother had been in good health at the time of the accident, and that he had never been subject to fits or fainting.
He was not short-sighted. He occasionally suffered from liv-
erish attacks. He was a good dancer and usually very neat
and nimble on his feet. He had once sprained his ankle as
a boy, but so far as she knew, no permanent weakness of
the joint had resulted.

Evidence was also called which showed that accidents had
occurred on several previous occasions to persons descend-
ing the staircase; other witnesses expressed the opinion that
the staircase was not dangerous to anybody exercising reasonable care. The jury returned a verdict of accidental
death, with a rider to the effect that they thought the iron
spiral should be replaced by a more solid structure.

Mr. Bredon shook his head. Then he drew a sheet of
paper from the rack before him and wrote down:

1. He seemed to crumple together.
2. He did not make any attempt to save himself.

3. He did not loose his grip of the book.
4. He pitched on his head at the bottom.
5. Neck broken, skull cracked; either injury fatal.
6. Good health; good sight; good dancer.

He filled himself a pipe and sat for some time staring at this list. Then he searched in a drawer and produced a piece of notepaper, which seemed to be an unfinished letter, or the abandoned draft of one.

"DEAR MR. PYM,—I think it only right that you should know that there is something going on in the office which is very undesirable, and might lead to serious—"

After a little more thought, he laid this document aside and began to scribble on another sheet, erasing and re-writing busily. Presently a slow smile twitched his lips.

"I'll swear there's something in it," he muttered, "something pretty big. But the job is, to handle it. One's got to go for the money—but where's it coming from? Not from Pym, I fancy. It doesn't seem to be his personal show, and you can't blackmail a whole office. I wonder, though. After all, he'd probably pay a good bit to prevent—"

He relapsed into silence and meditation.

"And what," demanded Miss Parton, spearing another chocolate éclair, "do you think of our Mr. Bredon?"

"The Pimlico Pet?" said Miss Rossiter. "You'll put on pounds and pounds if you eat all that sweet stuff, duckie. Well, I think he's rather a lamb, and his shirts are simply too marvellous. He won't be able to keep that up on Pym's salary, bonus or no bonus. Or the silk socks either."

"He's been brought up silk-lined all right," agreed Miss Parton. "One of the new poor, I expect. Lost all his money in the slump or something."

"Either that, or his family have got tired of supporting him and pushed him out to scratch for himself," suggested

Miss Rossiter. She slimmed more strenuously than her colleague, and was less inclined to sentiment. "I sort of asked him the other day what he did before he came here, and he said, all sorts of things, and mentioned that he'd had a good bit to do with motors. I expect he's been one of these gilded johnnies who used to sell cars on commission, and the bottom's dropped out of that and he's got to do a job of work— if you call copy-writing work."

"I think he's very clever," said Miss Parton. "Did you see that idiotic headline he put up for Margarine yesterday: 'IT'S A FAR, FAR BUTTER THING'? Hankie nearly sniggered himself sick. I think the Pet was pulling his leg. But what I mean is, he wouldn't think of a silly thing like that if he hadn't got brains."

"He'll make a copy-writer," declared Miss Rossiter, firmly. She had seen so many new copy-writers come and pass like ships in the night, that she was as well able to size them up as the copy-chiefs themselves. "He's got the flair if you know what I mean. He'll stay all right."

"I hope he does," said Miss Parton. "He's got beautiful manners. Doesn't chuck the stuff at you as if you were dirt like young Willis. And he pays his tea-bill like a little gentleman."

"Early days," said Miss Rossiter. "He's paid *one* tea-bill. Gives me the pip, the way some of them make a fuss about it. There's Garrett. He was quite rude when I went to him on Saturday. Hinted that I made money out of the teas. I suppose he thinks it's funny. I don't."

"He means it for a joke."

"No, he doesn't. Not altogether. And he's always grumbling. Whether it's Chelsea buns or jam roll, there's always something wrong with it. I said to him, 'Mr. Garrett,' I said, 'if *you* like to give up *your* lunch-time every day to trying to find something that *everybody* will enjoy, you're welcome to do it.' 'Oh, no,' he said, 'I'm not the office-boy.' 'And who do you think I am,' I said, 'the errand-girl?' So he told me not to lose my temper. It's all very well, but you get very tired of it, especially this hot weather, fagging round."

Miss Parton nodded. The teas were a perennial grievance. "Anyhow," she said, "friend Bredon is no trouble. A plain biscuit and a cup of tea every day. That's his order. And he said he was quite ready to pay the same subscription as everybody else, though really he ought to be let off with sixpence. I do like a man to be generous and speak to you nicely."

"Oh, the Pet's tongue runs on ball-bearings," said Miss Rossiter. "And talk of being a nosey-parker!"

"They all are," replied Miss Parton. "But I say, do you know what I did yesterday? It was dreadful. Bredon came in and asked for Mr. Hankin's carbons. I was in an awful rush with some of old Copley's muck—he always wants everything done in five minutes—and I said, 'Help yourself.' Well, what do you think? Ten minutes afterwards I went to look for something on the shelf and I found he'd gone off with Mr. Hankin's private letter-file. He must have been blind, because it's marked PRIVATE in red letters an inch high. Of course Hankie'd be in an awful bait if he knew. So I hared off to Bredon and there he was, calmly reading Hankie's private letters, if you please! 'You've got the wrong file, Mr. Bredon,' I said. And he wasn't a bit ashamed. He just handed it back with a grin and said, 'I was beginning to think I might have. It's very interesting to see what salary everybody gets.' And, my dear, he was reading Hankie's departmental list. And I said, 'Oh, Mr. Bredon, you *oughtn't* to be reading that. It's frightfully confidential.' And he said, 'Is it?' He seemed quite surprised."

"Silly ass!" said Miss Rossiter. "I hope you told him to keep it to himself. They *are* all so sensitive about their salaries. I'm sure I don't know why. But they're all dying to find out what the others get and terrified to death anybody should find out what they get themselves. If Bredon goes round shooting his mouth off, he'll stir up some awful trouble."

"I warned him," said Miss Parton, "and he seemed to think it was awfully funny and asked how long it would take him to reach Dean's salary."

"Let's see, how much was Dean getting?"

"Six," replied Miss Parton, "and not worth much more in my opinion. The department will be better-tempered without him, I must say. He did rile 'em sometimes."

"If you ask me," said Miss Rossiter, "I don't think this business of mixing the University people with the other sort works very well. With the Oxford and Cambridge lot it's all give-and-take and bad language, but the others don't seem to fit in with it. They always think they're being sneered at."

"It's Ingleby upsets them. He never takes anything seriously."

"None of them do," said Miss Rossiter, putting an unerring and experienced finger on the point of friction. "It's all a game to them, and with Copley and Willis it's all deadly serious. When Willis starts on metaphysics, Ingleby recites limericks. Personally, I'm broadminded. I rather like it. And I will say the 'varsity crowd don't quarrel like the rest of them. If Dean hadn't fallen downstairs, there'd have been a good old bust-up between him and Willis."

"I never could understand what that was all about," observed Miss Parton, thoughtfully stirring her coffee.

"*I* believe there was a girl in it," said Miss Rossiter. "Willis used to go about with Dean quite a lot at the week-end, and then it all stopped suddenly. They had an awful row one day last March. Miss Meteyard heard them going at it hammer and tongs in Dean's room."

"Did she hear what the fuss was?"

"No. Being Miss Meteyard, she first pounded on the partition and then went in and told them to shut up. She's no use for people's private feelings. Funny woman. Well, I suppose we'd better push off home, or we shan't be fit for anything in the morning. It was quite a good show, wasn't it? Where's the check? You had two cakes more than me. Yours is one-and-a-penny and mine's ninepence. If I give you a bob and you give me twopence and the waitress twopence and settle up at the desk, we shall be all square."

The two girls left the Corner House by the Coventry

Street entrance, and turned to the right and crossed the Piccadilly merry-go-round to the Tube entrance. As they regained the pavement, Miss Rossiter clutched Miss Parton by the arm:

"Look! the Pet! got up regardless!"

"Go on!" retorted Miss Parton. "It isn't the Pet. Yes, it is! Look at the evening cloak and the gardenia, *and*, my dear, the monocle!"

Unaware of this commentary, the gentleman in question was strolling negligently towards them, smoking a cigarette. As he came abreast of them, Miss Rossiter broke into a cheerful grin and said, "Hullo!"

The man raised his hat mechanically and shook his head. His face was a well-bred blank. Miss Rossiter's cheeks became flooded with a fiery crimson.

"It isn't him. How *awful!*"

"He took you for a tart," said Miss Parton, with some confusion and perhaps a little satisfaction.

"It's an extraordinary thing," muttered Miss Rossiter, vexed. "I could have sworn—"

"He's not a bit like him, really, when you see him close to," said Miss Parton, wise after the event. "I told you it wasn't him."

"You said it was him." Miss Rossiter glanced back over her shoulder, and was in time to see a curious little incident.

A limousine car came rolling gently along from the direction of Leicester Square and drew up close to the kerb, opposite the entrance to the Criterion Bar. The man in dress-clothes stepped up to it and addressed a few words to the occupant, flinging his cigarette away as he did so, and laying one hand on the handle of the door, as though about to enter the car. Before he could do so, two men emerged suddenly and silently from a shop-entrance. One of them spoke to the chauffeur; the other put his hand on the gentleman's elegant arm. A brief sentence or two were exchanged; then the one man got up beside the chauffeur while the second man opened the door of the car. The man in dress-clothes got in, the other man followed, and the whole party drove off. The whole thing was so quickly done that almost before Miss Parton could turn round in answer to Miss Rossiter's exclamation, it was all over.

"An arrest!" breathed Miss Rossiter, her eyes shining. "Those two were detectives. I wonder what our friend in the monocle's been doing."

Miss Parton was thrilled.

"And we actually spoke to him and thought it was Bredon."

"*I* spoke to him," corrected Miss Rossiter. It was all very well for Miss Parton to claim the credit, but only a few minutes back she had rather pointedly dissociated herself from the indiscretion and she could not be allowed to have it both ways.

"You did, then," agreed Miss Parton. "I'm surprised at you, Rossie, trying to get off with a smart crook. Anyhow, if Bredon doesn't turn up tomorrow, we'll know it was him after all."

But it could hardly have been Mr. Bredon, for he was in his place the next morning just as usual. Miss Rossiter asked him if he had a double.

"Not that I know of," said Mr. Bredon. "One of my cousins is a bit like me."

Miss Rossiter related the incident, with slight modifica-tions. On consideration, she thought it better not to men-tion that she had been mistaken for a lady of easy virtue.

"Oh, I don't think that would be my cousin," replied Mr. Bredon. "He's a frightfully proper person. Well known at Buckingham Palace, and all that."

"Go on," said Miss Rossiter.

"I'm the black sheep of the family," said Mr. Bredon. "He never even sees me in the street. It must have been some one quite different."

"Is your cousin called Bredon, too?"

"Oh, yes," said Mr. Bredon.

CHAPTER III

INQUISITIVE INTERVIEWS OF A NEW COPY-WRITER

MR. BREDON had been a week with Pym's Publicity, and had learnt a number of things. He learned the average number of words that can be crammed into four inches of copy; that Mr. Armstrong's fancy could be caught by an elaborately-drawn lay-out, whereas Mr. Hankin looked on art-work as waste of a copy-writer's time; that the word "pure" was dangerous, because, if lightly used, it laid the client open to prosecution by the Government inspectors, whereas the words "highest quality," "finest ingredients," "packed under the best conditions" had no legal meaning, and were therefore safe; that the expression "giving work to umpteen thousand British employees in our model works at so-and-so" was not by any means the same thing as "British made throughout"; that the north of England liked its butter and margarine salted, whereas the south preferred it fresh; that the *Morning Star* would not accept any advertisements containing the word "cure," though there was no objection to such expressions as "relieve" or "ameliorate," and that, further, any commodity that professed to "cure" anything might find itself compelled to register as a patent medicine and use an expensive stamp; that the most convincing copy was always written with the tongue in the cheek, a genuine conviction of the commodity's worth producing—for some reason—poverty and flatness of style; that if, by the most far-fetched stretch of ingenuity, an indecent meaning could be read into a headline, that was the meaning that the great British Public would infallibly read into it; that the great aim and object of the studio artist was to crowd the copy out of the advertisement and that, conversely, the copy-writer was a designing villain whose ambition was to cram the space with verbiage and leave no room for the sketch; that the lay-out man, a meek ass between two burdens, spent a miserable life trying to reconcile these opposing parties; and further, that all departments alike united in hatred of the client, who persisted in spoiling good lay-outs by cluttering them up with coupons, free-gift offers, lists of local agents and realistic portraits of hideous and uninteresting cartons, to the detriment of his own interests and the annoyance of everybody concerned.

He also learned to find his way without assistance over the two floors occupied by the agency, and even up on to the roof, where the messenger boys did their daily physical jerks under the eye of the Sergeant, and whence a fine view of London might be obtained on a clear day. He became acquainted with a number of the group-managers, and was sometimes even able to remember off-hand which clients' accounts were in the control of which manager, while with most of the members of his own department he found himself established on a footing of friendly intimacy. There were the two copy-chiefs, Mr. Armstrong and Mr. Hankin, each brilliant in his own way and each with his own personal fads. Mr. Hankin, for example, would never accept a headline containing the word "magnificent"; Mr. Armstrong disliked any lay-out which involved the picture of a judge or a Jew, and was rendered so acutely wretched when the proprietors of "Whifflets" put out a new brand of smoke called "Good Judge" Mixture that he was obliged to hand the whole account over, lock, stock and barrel to Mr. Hankin. Mr. Copley, an elderly, serious-minded man, who had entered the advertising profession before the modern craze set in for public-school-and-University-trained copy-writers, was remarkable for a tendency to dyspepsia and a perfectly miraculous knack of writing appetizing copy for tinned and packeted foodstuffs. Anything that came out of a tin or a packet was poison to him, and his diet consisted of undercooked beef-steak, fruit and whole-meal bread. The only copy he really enjoyed writing was that for Bunbury's Whole-Meal Flour, and he was perennially depressed when his careful eulogiums, packed with useful medical detail, were scrapped in favour of some light-headed foolishness of Ingleby's, on the story that Bunbury's Whole-Meal Flour took the Ache out of Baking. But on Sardines and Tinned Salmon he was unapproachable.

Ingleby specialized in snobbish copy about Twentyman's Teas ("preferred by Fashion's Favourites"), Whifflets ("in the Royal Enclosure at Ascot, in the Royal Yacht Club at Cowes, you find the discriminating men who smoke Whifflets") and Farley's Footwear ("Whether it's a big shoot or a Hunt Ball, Farley puts you on a sound footing"). He lived in Bloomsbury, was communistic in a literary way, and dressed almost exclusively in pull-overs and grey flannels. He was completely and precociously disillusioned and one of the most promising copy-writers Pym's had ever fathered. When released from Whifflets and fashionable footwear, he could be amusing on almost any subject, and had a turn for "clever" copy, wherever cleverness was not out of place.

Miss Meteyard, with a somewhat similar mental make-up, could write about practically anything except women's goods, which were more competently dealt with by Mr. Willis or Mr. Garrett, the former of whom in particular, could handle corsets and face-cream with a peculiar plaintive charm which made him more than worth his salary. The copy department on the whole worked happily together, writing each other's headlines in a helpful spirit and invading each other's rooms at all hours of the day. The only two men with whom Bredon was unable to establish genial relations were Mr. Copley, who held aloof from everybody, and Mr. Willis, who treated him with a reserve for which he was unable to account. Otherwise he found the department a curiously friendly place.

And it talked. Bredon had never in his life encountered a set of people with such active tongues and so much apparent leisure for gossip. It was a miracle that any work ever got done, though somehow it did. He was reminded of his Oxford days, when essays mysteriously wrote themselves in the intervals of club-meetings and outdoor sports, and when most of the people who took firsts boasted of never having worked more than three hours of any day. The atmosphere suited him well enough. He was a bonhomous soul, with the insatiable curiosity of a baby elephant, and nothing pleased him better than to be interrupted in his encomiums of Sopo ("makes Monday, Fun-day") or the Whoosh Vacuum-cleaner ("one Whoosh and it's clean") by a fellow-member of the department, fed-up with advertising and spoiling for a chat.

"Hullo!" said Miss Meteyard one morning. She had dropped in to consult Bredon about googlies—the proprietors of Tomboy Toffee having embarked upon a series of cricket advertisements which, starting respectively from "Lumme, what a Lob!" or "Yah! that's a Yorker!" led up by devious routes to the merits of Toffee—and had now reached the point when "Gosh! it's a Googly" had to be tackled. Bredon had demonstrated googlies with pencil and paper, and also in the corridor with a small round tin of Good Judge tobacco (whereby he had nearly caught Mr. Armstrong on the side of the head), and had further discussed the relative merits of "Gosh" and "Golly" in the headline; but Miss Meteyard showed no symptoms of departing. She had sat down at Bredon's table and was drawing caricatures, in which she displayed some skill, and was rummaging in the pencil-tray for an india-rubber when she remarked, as above mentioned, "Hullo!"

"What?"

"That's little Dean's scarab. It ought to have been sent back to his sister."

"Oh, that! Yes, I knew that was there, but I didn't know whom it belonged to. It's not a bad thing. It's real onyx, though of course it's not Egyptian and it's not even very old."

"Probably not, but Dean adored it. He thought it was a sure-fire mascot. He always had it in his waistcoat pocket

or sitting in front of him while he worked. If he'd had it
on him that day, he wouldn't have tumbled downstairs—at
least, that's what he'd have said himself."

Bredon poised the beetle on the palm of his hand. It
was as big as a man's thumb-nail, heavy and shallowly
carved, smooth except for a slight chip at one side.

"What sort of chap was Dean?"

"Well. *De mortuis,* and all that, but I wasn't exactly keen
on him. I thought he was rather an unwholesome little
beast."

"What way?"

"For one thing, I didn't like the people he went about
with."

Bredon twitched an interrogative eyebrow.

"No," said Miss Meteyard, "I don't mean what you mean.
At least, I mean, I can't tell you about that. But he used to
tag round with that de Momerie crowd. Thought it was
smart, I suppose. Luckily, he missed the famous night when
that Punter-Smith girl did away wih herself. Pym's would
never have held its head up again if one of its staff had been
involved in a notorious case. Pym's is particular."

"How old did you say this blighter was?"

"Oh, twenty-six or -seven, I should think."

"How did he come to be here?"

"Usual thing. Needed cash, I suppose. Had to have some
sort of job. You can't lead a gay life on nothing, and he
wasn't anybody, you know. His father was a bank-manager,
or something, deceased, so I suppose young Victor had to
push out and earn his keep. He knew how to look after
himself all right."

"Then how did he get in with that lot?"

Miss Meteyard grinned at him.

"Somebody picked him up, I should think. He had a certain kind of good looks. There is a *nostalgie de la banlieue*
as well as *de la boue.* And you're pulling my leg, Mr. Death
Bredon, because you know that as well as I do."

"Is that a compliment to my sagacity or a reflection on
my virtue?"

"How *you* came here is a good deal more interesting than how Victor Dean came here. They start new copy-writers without experience at four quid a week—about enough to pay for a pair of your shoes."

"Ah!" said Bredon, "how deceptive appearances can be! But it is evident, dear lady, that you do not do your shopping in the true West End. You belong to the section of society that pays for what it buys. I revere, but do not imitate you. Unhappily, there are certain commodities which cannot be obtained without cash. Railway fares, for example, or petrol. But I am glad you approve of my shoes. They are supplied by Rudge in the Arcade and, unlike Farley's Fashion Footwear, are actually of the kind that is to be seen in the Royal Enclosure at Ascot and wherever discriminating men congregate. They have a ladies' department, and if you will mention my name—"

"I begin to see why you chose advertising as a source of supply." The look of doubt left Miss Meteyard's angular face, and was replaced by a faintly derisive expression. "Well, I suppose I'd better get back to Tomboy Toffee. Thanks for your dope about googlies."

Bredon shook his head mournfully as the door closed after her. "Careless," he muttered. "Nearly gave the game away. Oh, well, I suppose I'd better do some work and look as genuine as possible."

He pulled towards him a guard-book pasted up with pulls of Nutrax advertising and studied its pages thoughtfully. He was not left long in peace, however, for after a couple of minutes Ingleby slouched in, a foul pipe at full blast and his hands thrust deep into his trousers-pockets.

"I say, is Brewer here?"

"Don't know him. But," added Bredon, waving his hand negligently, "you have my permission to search. The priest's hole and the concealed staircase are at your service."

Ingleby rooted in the bookcase in vain.

"Somebody's bagged him. Anyway, how do you spell Chrononhotonthologos?"

"Oh! I can do that. And Aldiborontophoscophornio, too. Crossword? Torquemada?"

"No, headline for Good Judges. Isn't it hot? And now I suppose we're going to have a week's dust and hammering."

"Why?"

"The fiat has gone forth. The iron staircase is condemned."

"Who by?"

"The Board."

"Oh, rot! they mustn't do that."

"What d'you mean?"

"Admission of liability, isn't it?"

"Time, too."

"Well, I suppose it is."

"You looked quite startled. I was beginning to think you had some sort of personal feeling in the matter."

"Good lord, no, why should I? Just a matter of principle. Except that the staircase does seem to have had its uses in eliminating the unfit. I gather that the late Victor Dean was not universally beloved."

"Oh, I don't know. I never saw much harm in him, except that he wasn't exactly pukka and hadn't quite imbibed the Pym spirit, as you may say. Of course the Meteyard woman loathed him."

"Why?"

"Oh! she's a decent sort of female, but makes no allowances. My motto is, live and let live, but protect your own interests. How are you getting on with Nutrax?"

"Haven't touched it yet. I've been trying to get out a name for Twentyman's shilling tea. As far as I can make Hankin out, it has no qualities except cheapness to recommend it, and is chiefly made of odds and ends of other teas. The name must suggest solid worth and respectability."

"Why not call it 'Domestic Blend'? Nothing could sound more reliable and obviously nothing could suggest so much dreary economy."

"Good idea. I'll put it up to him." Bredon yawned. "I've

had too much lunch. I don't think anybody ought to have to work at half-past two in the afternoon. It's unnatural."

"Everything's unnatural in this job. Oh, my God! Here's somebody with something on a tray! Go away! go a-*way!*"

"I'm sorry," said Miss Parton, brightly, entering with six saucers filled with a grey and steaming mess. "But Mr. Hankin says, will you please taste these samples of porridge and report upon them?"

"My dear girl, look at the time!"

"Yes, I know, it's awful, isn't it? They're numbered A, B and C, and here's the questionnaire paper, and if you'll let me have the spoons back I'll get them washed for Mr. Copley."

"I shall be sick," moaned Ingleby. "Who's this? Pea-body's?"

"Yes—they're putting out a tinned porridge, 'Piper Par-ritch.' No boiling, no stirring—only heat the tin. Look for the Piper on the label."

"Look here," said Ingleby, "run away and try it on Mr. McAllister."

"I did, but his report isn't printable. There's sugar and salt and a jug of milk."

"What we suffer in the service of the public!" Ingleby attacked the mess with a disgusted sniff and a languid spoon. Bredon solemnly rolled the portions upon his tongue, and detained Miss Parton.

"Here, taken this down while it's fresh in my mind. Vintage A: Fine, full-bodied, sweet nutty flavour, fully ma-tured; a grand masculine porridge. Vintage B: extra-sec, refined, delicate character, requiring only—"

Miss Parton emitted a delighted giggle, and Ingleby, who hated gigglers, fled.

"Tell me, timeless houri," demanded Mr. Bredon, "what was wrong with my lamented predecessor? Why did Miss Meteyard hate him and why does Ingleby praise him with faint damns?"

This was no problem to Miss Parton.

"Why, because he didn't play fair. He was always snooping round other people's rooms, picking up their ideas and showing them up as his own. And if anybody gave him a headline and Mr. Armstrong or Mr. Hankin liked it, he never said whose it was."

This explanation seemed to interest Bredon. He trotted down the passage and thrust his head round Garrett's door. Garrett was stolidly making out his porridge report, and looked up with a grunt.

"I hope I'm not interrupting you at one of those moments of ecstasy," bleated Bredon, "but I just wanted to ask you something. I mean to say, it's just a question of etiquette, don't you know, and what's done, so to speak. I mean, look here! You see, Hankie-pankie told me to get out a list of names for a shilling tea and I got out some awful rotten ones, and then Ingleby came in and I said, 'What would you call this tea?' just like that, and he said, 'Call it Domestic Blend,' and I said, 'What-ho! that absolutely whangs the nail over the crumpet.' Because it struck me, really, as being the caterpillar's boots."

"Well, what about it?"

"Well, just now I was chatting to Miss Parton about that fellow Dean, the one who fell downstairs you know, and why one or two people here didn't seem to be fearfully keen on him, and she said, it was because he got ideas out of other people and showed them up with his own stuff. And what I wanted to know was, isn't it done to ask people? Ingleby didn't say anything, but of course, if I've made a floater—"

"Well, it's like this," said Garrett. "There's a sort of unwritten law—at our end of the corridor, anyway. You take any help you can get and show it up with your initials on it, but if Armstrong or whoever it is simply goes all out on it and starts throwing bouquets about, you're rather expected to murmur that it was the other bird's suggestion really, and you thought rather well of it yourself."

"Oh, I see. Oh, thanks frightfully. And if, on the other hand, he goes right up in the air and says it's the damnsilliest thing he's seen since 1919, you stand the racket, I suppose."

"Naturally. If it's as silly as that you ought to have known better than to put it up to him anyway."

"Oh, yes."

"The trouble with Dean was that he first of all snitched people's ideas without telling them, and then didn't give them the credit for it with Hankin. But, I say, I wouldn't go asking Copley or Willis for too much assistance if I were you. They weren't brought up to the idea of lending round their lecture notes. They've a sort of board-school idea that everybody ought to paddle his own canoe."

Bredon thanked Garrett again.

"And if I were you," continued Garrett, "I wouldn't mention Dean to Willis at all. There's some kind of feeling—I don't know quite what. Anyway, I just thought I'd warn you."

Bredon thanked him with almost passionate gratitude.

"It's so easy to put your foot in it in a new place, isn't it? I'm really most frightfully obliged to you."

Clearly Mr. Bredon was a man of no sensibility, for half an hour later he was in Willis's room, and had introduced the subject of the late Victor Dean. The result was an unequivocal request that Mr. Bredon would mind his own business. Mr. Willis did not wish to discuss Mr. Dean at all. In addition to this, Bredon became aware that Willis was suffering from an acute and painful embarrassment, almost as though the conversation had taken some indecent turn. He was puzzled, but persisted. Willis, after sitting for some moments in gloomy silence, fidgeting with a pencil, at last looked up.

"If you're on Dean's game," he said, "you'd better clear out. I'm not interested."

He might not be, but Bredon was. His long nose twitched with curiosity.

"What game? I didn't know Dean. Never heard of him till I came here. What's the row?"

"If you didn't know Dean, why bring him up? He went about with a gang of people I didn't care about, that's all, and from the look of you, I should have said you belonged to the same bright crowd."

"The de Momerie crowd?"

"It's not much use your pretending you don't know all about it, is it?" said Willis, with a sneer.

"Ingleby told me Dean was a hanger-on of that particular bunch of Bright Young People," replied Bredon, mildly. "But I've never met any of them. They'd think me terribly ancient. They would, really. Besides, I don't think they're nice to know. Some of them are really naughty. Did Mr. Pym know that Dean was a Bright Young Thing?"

"I shouldn't think so, or he'd have buzzed him out double quick. What business is Dean of yours, anyway?"

"Absolutely none. I just wondered about him, that's all. He seems to have been a sort of misfit here. Not quite imbued with the Pym spirit, if you see what I mean."

"No, he wasn't. And if you take my advice, you'll leave Dean and his precious friends alone, or you won't make yourself too popular. The best thing Dean ever did in his life was to fall down that staircase."

"Nothing in life became him like the leaving it? But it seems a bit harsh, all the same. Somebody must have loved him. 'For he must be somebody's son,' as the dear old song says. Hadn't he any family? There is a sister, at least, isn't there?"

"Why the devil do you want to know about his sister?"

"I don't. I just asked, that's all. Well, I'd better tootle off, I suppose. I've enjoyed this little talk."

Willis scowled at his retreating form, and Mr. Bredon went away to get his information elsewhere. As usual, the typists' room was well informed.

"Only the sister," said Miss Parton. "She's something to do with Silkanette Hosiery. She and Victor ran a little flat together. Smart as paint, but rather silly, I thought, the only time I saw her. I've an idea our Mr. Willis was a bit smitten in that direction at one time, but it didn't seem to come to anything."

"Oh, I see," said Mr. Bredon, much enlightened.

He went back to his own room and the guard-books. But his attention wandered. He paced about, sat down, got up, stared out of the window, came back to the desk. Then, from a drawer, he pulled out a sheet of paper. It bore a list of dates in the previous year, and to each date was appended a letter of the alphabet, thus:

Jan. 7 G
" 14 O ?
" 21 A
" 28 P
Feb. 5 G

There were other papers in the desk in the same hand-writing—presumably Victor Dean's—but this list seemed to interest Mr. Bredon unaccountably. He examined it with an attention that one would have thought it scarcely deserved, and finally folded it carefully away in his pocket-book.

"Who dragged whom, how many times, at the wheels of what, round the walls of where?" demanded Mr. Bredon of the world at large. Then he laughed. "Probably some sublime scheme for selling Sopo to sapheads," he remarked, and this time set himself soberly to work upon his guard-books.

Mr. Pym, the presiding genius of Pym's Publicity, Ltd., usually allowed a week or so to elapse before interviewing new members of his staff. His theory was that it was useless to lecture people about their work till they had acquired some idea of what the work actually was. He was a conscientious man, and was particularly careful to keep before his mind the necessity for establishing a friendly personal relation with every man, woman and child in his employment, from the heads of departments down to the messenger-boys and, not being gifted with any spontaneous ease and charm of social intercourse, had worked out a rigid formula for dealing with this necessity. At the end of a week or so, he sent for any newly-joined recruits, interrogated them about their work and interests, and delivered his famous sermon on Service in Advertising. If they survived this frightful ordeal, under which nervous young typists had been known to collapse and give notice, they were put on the list for the monthly tea-party. This took place in the Little Conference Room. Twenty persons, selected from all ranks and departments, congregated under Mr. Pym's official eye to consume the usual office tea, supplemented by ham sandwiches from the canteen, and cake supplied at cost by Dairyfields, Ltd., and entertained one another for an exact hour. This function was supposed to promote inter-departmental cordiality, and by its means the entire staff, including the Outside Publicity, passed under scrutiny once in every six months. In addition to these delights there were, for department and group managers, informal dinners at Mr. Pym's private residence, where six victims were turned off at a time, the proceedings being hilariously concluded by the formation of two bridge-tables, presided over by Mr. and Mrs. Pym respectively. For the group-secretaries, junior copywriters and junior artists, invitations were issued to an At Home twice a year, with a band and dancing till 10 o'clock; the seniors were expected to attend these and exercise the functions of stewards. For the clerks and typists, there was the Typists' Garden-Party, with tennis and badminton; and for the office-boys, there was the Office-Boys' Christmas Treat. In May of every year there was the Grand Annual Dinner and Dance for the whole staff, at which the amount of the staff bonus was announced for the year, and the health of Mr. Pym was drunk amid expressions of enthusiastic loyalty.

In accordance with the first item on this onerous programme, Mr. Bredon was summoned to the Presence within ten days of his first appearance at Pym's.

"Well, Mr. Bredon," said Mr. Pym, switching on an automatic smile and switching it off again with nervous abruptness, "and how are you getting on?"

"Oh, pretty well, thank you, sir."

"Find the work hard?"

"It is a little difficult," admitted Bredon, "till you get the hang of it, so to speak. A bit bewildering, if you know what I mean."

"Quite so, quite so," said Mr. Pym. "Do you get on all right with Mr. Armstrong and Mr. Hankin?"

Mr. Bredon said he found them very kind and helpful.

"They give me very good accounts of you," said Mr. Pym. "They seem to think you will make a good copy-writer." He smiled again and Bredon grinned back impudently.

"That's just as well, under the circumstances, isn't it?"

Mr. Pym rose suddenly to his feet and threw open the door which separated his room from his secretary's cubicle.

"Miss Hartley, do you mind going along to Mr. Vickers and asking him to look up the detailed appropriation for Darling's and let me have it? You might wait and bring it back with you."

Miss Hartley, realizing that she was to be deprived of hearing Mr. Pym's discourse on Service in Advertising, which—owing to the thinness of the wooden partition and the resonant quality of Mr. Pym's voice—was exceedingly familiar to her, rose and departed obediently. This meant that she would be able to have a nice chat with Miss Rossiter and Miss Parton while Mr. Vickers was getting his papers together. And she would not hurry herself, either. Miss Rossiter had hinted that Mr. Willis had hinted all kinds of frightful possibilities about Mr. Bredon, and she wanted to know what was up.

"Now," said Mr. Pym, passing his tongue rapidly across his lips and seeming to pull himself together to face a disagreeable interview. "What have you got to tell me?"

Mr. Bredon, very much at his ease, leaned across with his elbows on the Managing Director's desk, and spoke for some considerable time in a low tone, while Mr. Pym's cheek grew paler and paler.

CHAPTER IV

REMARKABLE ACROBATICS
OF A HARLEQUIN

IT HAS already been hinted that Tuesday was a day of
general mortification in Pym's copy-department. The trouble was caused by Messrs. Toule & Jollop, proprietors of
Nutrax, Maltogene, and Jollop's Concentrated Lactobeef
Tablets for Travellers. Unlike the majority of clients who,
though all tiresome in their degree, exercised their tiresomeness by post from a reasonable distance and at reasonable intervals, Messrs. Toule & Jollop descended upon Pym's
every Tuesday for a weekly conference. While there, they
reviewed the advertising for the coming week, rescinding the
decisions taken at the previous week's conference, springing
new schemes unexpectedly upon Mr. Pym and Mr. Armstrong, keeping those two important men shut up in the
Conference Room for hours on end, to the interruption of
office-business, and generally making nuisances of themselves. One of the items discussed at this weekly séance was
the Nutrax 11-inch double for Friday's *Morning Star*, which
occupied an important position in that leading news-organ
on the top right-hand corner of the Home page, next to the
special Friday feature. It subsequently occupied other posi-
tions in other journals, of course, but Friday's *Morning Star*
was the real matter of importance.

The usual procedure in respect of this exasperating advertisement was as follows. Every three months or so, Mr.
Hankin sent out an S O S to the copy-department to the effect that more Nutrax copy was urgently required. By the
united ingenuity of the department, about twenty pieces of

copy were forthwith produced and submitted to Mr. Hankin. Under his severely critical blue-pencil, these were reduced to twelve or so, which went to the Studio to be laid
out and furnished with illustrative sketches. They were then
sent or handed to Messrs. Toule & Jollop, who fretfully rejected all but half-a-dozen, and weakened and ruined the
remainder by foolish alterations and additions. The copy-
department was then scourged into producing another
twenty efforts, of which, after a similar process of elimination and amendment, a further half-dozen contrived to survive criticism, thus furnishing the necessary twelve half-
doubles for the ensuing three months. The department
breathed again, momentarily, and the dozen lay-outs were
stamped in purple ink "Passed by Client," and a note was
made of the proposed order of their appearance.

On Monday of each week, Mr. Tallboy, group-manager
for Nutrax, squared his shoulders and settled down to the
task of getting Friday's half-double safely into the *Morning
Star*. He looked out the copy for the week and sent round
to collect the finished sketch from the Studio. If the finished
sketch was really finished (which seldom happened), he sent
it down to the block-makers, together with the copy and a
carefully drawn lay-out. The block-makers, grumbling that
they never were allowed proper time for the job, made a
line-block of the sketch. The thing then passed to the
printers, who set up the headlines and copy in type, added
a name-block of the wrong size, locked the result up in a
forme, pulled a proof and returned the result to Mr. Tallboy, pointing out in a querulous note that it came out
half an inch too long. Mr. Tallboy corrected the misprints,
damned their eyes for using the wrong name-block, made
it clear to them that they had set the headlines in the wrong
fount, cut the proof to pieces, pasted it up again into the
correct size and returned it. By this time it was usually
11 o'clock on Tuesday morning, and Mr. Toule or Mr.
Jollop, or both of them, were closeted in the Conference
Room with Mr. Pym and Mr. Armtsrong, calling loudly and
repeatedly for their 11-inch double. As soon as the new

proof arrived from the printer's, Mr. Tallboy sent it down
to the Conference Room by a boy, and escaped, if he could,
for his elevenses. Mr. Toule or Mr. Jollop then pointed out
to Mr. Pym and Mr. Armstrong a great number of weaknesses in both sketch and copy. Mr. Pym and Mr. Armstrong, sycophantically concurring in everything the client
said, confessed themselves at a loss and invited suggestions
from Mr. Toule (or Mr. Jollop). The latter, being, as most
clients are, better at destructive than constructive criticism,
cudgelled his brains into stupor, and thus reduced himself
to a condition of utter blankness, upon which the per-
suasiveness of Mr. Pym and Mr. Armstrong could work
with hypnotic effect. After half an hour of skilled treatment,
Mr. Jollop (or Mr. Toule) found himself returning with a
sense of relief and refreshment to the rejected lay-out. He
then discovered that it was really almost exactly what he
required. It only needed the alteration of a sentence and
the introduction of a panel about gift-coupons. Mr. Armstrong then sent the lay-out up again to Mr. Tallboy, with a
request that he would effect these necessary alterations. Mr.
Tallboy, realizing with delight that these involved nothing
more drastic than the making of a new lay-out and the
complete re-writing of the copy, sought out the copy-writer
whose initials appeared on the original type-script, instructing him to cut out three lines and incorporate the client's
improvements, while he himself laid the advertisement out
afresh.

When all this had been done, the copy was returned to
the printer to be re-set, the forme was sent to the block-
makers, a complete block was made of the whole advertisement, and a fresh proof was returned. If, by any lucky
chance, there turned out to be no defects in the block, the
stereotypers got to work and made a sufficient number of
stereos to be sent out to the other papers carrying the
Nutrax advertising, with a proof to accompany each. On
Thursday afternoon, the stereos were distributed by the
despatching department to the London papers by hand, and
to the provincial papers by post and train, and if nothing

went wrong with these arrangements, the advertisement duly appeared in Friday's *Morning Star* and in other papers on the dates provided for. So long and arduous a history it is, that lies behind those exhortations to "Nourish your Nerves with Nutrax," which smite the reader in the eye as he opens his *Morning Star* in the train between Gidea Park and Liverpool Street.

On this particular Tuesday, exasperation was intensified. To begin with, the weather was exceptionally close, with a thunderstorm impending, and the top floor of Pym's Publicity was like a slow oven beneath the broad lead roof and the great glass skylights. Secondly, a visit was expected from two directors of Brotherhoods, Ltd., that extremely old-fashioned and religiously-minded firm who manufacture boiled sweets and non-alcoholic liquors. A warning had been sent round that all female members of the staff must refrain from smoking, and that any proofs of beer or whisky advertising must be carefully concealed from sight. The former restriction bore hardly upon Miss Meteyard and the copy-department typists, whose cigarettes were, if not encouraged, at least winked at in the ordinary way by the management. Miss Parton had been further upset by a mild suggestion from Mr. Hankin that she was showing rather more arm and neck than the directors of Brotherhoods, Ltd., would think seemly; out of sheer perversity, she had covered the offending flesh with a heavy sweater, and was ostentatiously stewing and grumbling and snapping the head off every one who approached her. Mr. Jollop, who was, if anything, slightly more captious than Mr. Toule, had arrived particularly early for the weekly Nutrax conference, and had distinguished himself by firmly killing no less than three advertisements which Mr. Toule had previously passed. This meant that Mr. Hankin had been obliged to send out his S O S nearly a month earlier than usual. Mr. Armstrong had toothache, and had been exceptionally short with Miss Rossiter, and something had gone wrong with Miss Rossiter's type-writer, so that its spacing was completely unreliable.

To Mr. Ingleby, perspiring over his guard-books, entered the detested form of Mr. Tallboy, a sheet of paper in his hand.

"Is this your copy?"

Mr. Ingleby stretched out a languid hand, took the paper, glanced at it and returned it.

"How often have I got to tell you blasted incompetents," he demanded amiably, "that those initials are on the copy for the purpose of identifying the writer? If you think my initials are DB you're either blind or potty."

"Who is DB anyway?"

"New fellow, Bredon."

"Where is he?"

Mr. Ingleby jerked his thumb in the direction of the next room.

"Empty," announced Mr. Tallboy, after a brief excursion.

"Well, have a look for him," suggested Ingleby.

"Yes, but look here," said Mr. Tallboy, persuasively, "I only want a suggestion. What the devil are the Studio to do with this? Do you mean to say Hankin passed that headline?"

"Presumably," said Ingleby.

"Well, how does he or Bredon or anybody suppose we're going to get it illustrated? Has the client seen it? They'll never stand for it. What's the point in laying it out? I can't think how Hankin came to pass it."

Ingleby stretched his hand out again.

"Brief, bright and brotherly," he observed. "What's the matter with it?"

The headline was:

————!

IF LIFE'S A BLANK
TAKE NUTRAX

"And in any case," grumbled Tallboy, "the *Morning Star* won't take it. They won't put in anything that looks like bad language."

"Your look-out," said Ingleby. "Why not ask 'em?"

Tallboy muttered something impolite.

"Anyway, if Hankin's passed it, it'll have to be laid out, I suppose," said Ingleby. "Surely the Studio—oh! hullo! here's your man. You'd better worry him. Bredon!"

"That's me!" said Mr. Bredon. "All present and correct!"

"Where've you been hiding from Tallboy? You knew he was on your tail."

"I've been on the roof," admitted Bredon, apologetically. "Cooler and all that. What's the matter. What have I done?"

"Well, this headline of yours, Mr. Bredon. How do you expect them to illustrate it?"

"I don't know. I left it to their ingenuity. I always believe in leaving scope to other people's imagination."

"How on earth are they to draw a blank?"

"Let 'em take a ticket in the Irish Sweep. That'll larn 'em," said Ingleby.

"I should think it would be rather like a muchness," suggested Bredon. "Lewis Carroll, you know. Did you ever see a drawing of a muchness?"

"Oh, don't fool," growled Tallboy. "We've got to do something with it. Do you really think it's a good head-line, Mr. Bredon?"

"It's the best I've written yet," said Bredon enthusiastically, "except that beauty Hankie wouldn't pass. Can't they draw a man looking blank? Or just a man with a blank face, like those 'Are these missing features yours?' advertisements?"

"Oh, I suppose they could," admitted Tallboy, discontentedly. "I'll put it up to them anyhow. Thanks," he added, belatedly, and bounced out.

"Cross, isn't he?" said Ingleby. "It's this frightful heat. Whatever made you go up on the roof? It must be like a gridiron."

"So it is, but I thought I'd just try it. As a matter of fact, I was chucking pennies over the parapet to that brass band. I got the bombardon twice. The penny goes down with a tremendous whack, you know, and they look up all over the place to see where it comes from and you dodge down behind the parapet. It's a tremendous high parapet, isn't it? I suppose they wanted to make the building look even higher than it is. It's the highest in the street in any case. You do get a good view from up there. 'Earth hath not anything to show more fair.' It's going to rain like billy-ho in about two ticks. See how black it's come over."

"You seem to have come over pretty black, if it comes to that," remarked Ingleby. "Look at the seat of your trousers."

"You do want a lot," complained Bredon, twisting his spine alarmingly. "It is a bit sooty up there. I was sitting on the skylight."

"You look as if you'd been shinning up a pipe."

"Well, I did shin down a pipe. Only one pipe—rather a nice pipe. It took my fancy."

"You're loopy," said Ingleby, "doing acrobatics on dirty pipes in this heat. Whatever made you?"

"I dropped something," said Mr. Bredon, plaintively. "It went down on to the glass roof of the wash-place. I nearly put my foot through. Wouldn't old Smayle have been surprised if I'd tumbled into the wash-basin on top of him? And then I found I needn't have gone down the pipe after all; I came back by the staircase—the roof-door was open on both floors."

"They generally keep them open in hot weather," said Ingleby.

"I wish I'd known. I say, I could do with a drink."

"All right, have a glass of Sparkling Pompayne."

"What's that?"

"One of Brotherhood's non-alcoholic refreshers," grinned Ingleby. "Made from finest Devon apples, with the crisp, cool sparkle of champagne. Definitely anti-rheumatic and non-intoxicant. Doctors recommend it."

Bredon shuddered.

"I think this is an awfully immoral job of ours. I do, really. Think how we spoil the digestions of the public."

"Ah, yes—but think how earnestly we strive to put them

right again. We undermine 'em with one hand and build
'em up with the other. The vitamins we destroy in the
canning, we restore in Revito, the roughage we remove
from Peabody's Piper Parritch we make up into a package
and market as Bunbury's Breakfast Bran; the stomachs we
ruin with Pompayne, we re-line with Peplets to aid digestion. And by forcing the damn-fool public to pay twice
over—once to have its food emasculated and once to have
the vitality put back again, we keep the wheels of com-
merce turning and give employment to thousands—including you and me."

"This wonderful world!" Bredon sighed ecstatically.
"How many pores should you say there were in the human
skin, Ingleby?"

"Damned if I know. Why?"

"Headline for Sanfect. Could I say, at a guess, ninety
million? It sounds a good round number. 'Ninety Million
Open Doors by which Germs can Enter—Lock Those
Doors with Sanfect.' Sounds convincing, don't you think?
Here's another: 'Would you Leave your Child in a Den of
Lions?' That ought to get the mothers."

"It'd make a good sketch— Hullo! here comes the storm
and no mistake."

A flash of lightning and a tremendous crack of thunder
broke without warning directly over their heads.

"I expected it," said Bredon. "That's why I did my roof-
walk."

"How do you mean, that's why?"

"I was on the look-out for it," explained Bredon. "Well,
it's here. Phew! that was a good one. I do adore thunder-
storms. By the way, what has Willis got up against me?"

Ingleby frowned and hesitated.

"He seems to think I'm not nice to know," explained
Bredon.

"Well—I warned you not to talk to him about Victor
Dean. He seems to have got it into his head you were a
friend of his, or something."

"But what *was* wrong with Victor Dean?"

"He kept bad company. Why are you so keen to know about Dean, anyway?"

"Well, I suppose I'm naturally inquisitive. I always like to know about people. About the office-boys, for instance. They do physical jerks on the roof, don't they? Is that the only time they're allowed on the roof?"

"They'd better not let the Sergeant catch 'em up there in office-hours. Why?"

"I just wondered. They're a mischievous lot, I expect; boys always are. I like 'em. What's the name of the red-headed one? He looks a snappy lad."

"That's Joe—they call him Ginger, of course. What's he been doing?"

"Oh, nothing. I suppose you get a lot of cats prowling about this place."

"Cats? I've never seen any cats. Except that I believe there's a cat that lives in the canteen, but she doesn't seem to come up here. What do you want a cat for?"

"I don't—anyway, there must be dozens of sparrows, mustn't there?"

Ingleby began to think that the heat had affected Bredon's brain. His reply was drowned in a tremendous crash of thunder. A silence followed, in which the street noises came thinly up from without; then heavy drops began to spit upon the panes. Ingleby got up and shut the window.

The rain came down like rods and roared upon the roof. In the lead gutters it danced and romped, rushing in small swift rivers into the hoppers. Mr. Prout, emerging from his room in a hurry, received a deluge of water down his neck from the roof and yelled for a boy to run along and shut the skylights. The oppression of heat and misery lifted from the office like a cast-off eiderdown. Standing at the window of his own room, Bredon watched the hurrying foot-passengers six stories below, open their umbrellas to the deluge, or, caught defenceless, scurry into shop doorways. Down below, in the Conference Room, Mr. Jollop suddenly smiled and

passed six lay-outs and a three-colour folder, and consented
to the omission of the Fifty-six Free Chiming Clocks from
the current week's half-double. Harry, the lift-man, usher-
ing a dripping young woman into the shelter of the cage,
expressed sympathy with her plight, and offered her a wipe-
down with a duster. The young woman smiled at him, assured him that she was quite all right and asked if she
could see Mr. Bredon. Harry handed her on to Tompkin,
the reception clerk, who said he would send up, and what
was her name, please?

"Miss Dean—Miss Pamela Dean—on private business."

The clerk became full of sympathetic interest.

"Our Mr. Dean's sister, miss?"

"Yes."

"Oh, yes, miss. A dreadful sad thing about Mr. Dean,
miss. We were all very sorry to lose him like that. If you'll
just take a seat, miss, I'll tell Mr. Bredon you're here."

Pamela Dean sat down and looked about her. The recep-
tion-hall was on the lower floor of the agency and contained
nothing but the clerk's semi-circular desk, two hard chairs,
a hard settle and a clock. It occupied the space which, on
the upper floor, was taken up by the Dispatching, and just
outside the door was the lift and the main staircase, which
wound round the lift-shaft and went the whole way to the
roof, though the lift itself went no further than the top
floor. The clock pointed to 12.45, and already a stream of
employees was passing through the hall, or clattering down
from the floor above for a wash and brush-up before going
out to lunch. A message from Mr. Bredon arrived to say
that he would be down in a moment, and Pamela Dean entertained herself by watching the various members of the
staff as they passed. A brisk, neat young man, with an immaculate head of wavy brown hair, a minute dark moustache and very white teeth (Mr. Smayle, had she known it,
group-manager for Dairyfields, Ltd.); a large, bald man
with a reddish, clean-shaven face and a masonic emblem
(Mr. Harris of the Outdoor Publicity); a man of thirty-five,
with rather sulky good looks and restless light eyes (Mr.

Tallboy, brooding on the iniquities of Messrs. Toule & Jollop); a thin, prim, elderly man (Mr. Daniels); a plump little man with a good-natured grin and fair hair, chatting to a square-jawed, snub-nosed red-head (Mr. Cole, group-manager for Harrogate Bros. of soap fame, and Mr. Prout, the photographer); a handsome, worried, grey-haired man in the forties, accompanying a prosperous baldpate in an overcoat (Mr. Armstrong escorting Mr. Jollop away to a mollifying and expensive lunch); an untidy, saturnine person with both hands in his trousers-pockets (Mr. Ingleby); a thin, predatory man with a stoop and jaundiced eyeballs (Mr. Copley, wondering whether his lunch was going to agree with him); then a lean, fair-haired, anxious-looking youth, who, at sight of her, stopped dead in his tracks, flushed, and then passed on. This was Mr. Willis; Miss Dean gave him a glance and a cool nod, which was as coolly returned. Tompkin, the reception clerk, who missed nothing, saw the start, the flush, the glance and the nods and mentally added another item to his fund of useful knowledge. Then came a slim man of forty or so, with a long nose and straw-coloured hair, wearing horn-rimmed glasses and a pair of well-cut grey trousers which seemed to have received recent ill-treatment; he came up to Pamela and said, more as a statement than as a question:

"Miss Dean."

"Mr. Bredon?"

"Yes."

"You ought not to have come here," said Mr. Bredon, shaking his head reproachfully, "it's a little indiscreet, you know. However—hullo, Willis, want me?"

It was evidently not Mr. Willis' lucky day. He had con-quered his nervous agitation and turned back with the ob-vious intention of addressing Pamela, just in time to find Bredon in possession. He replied, "Oh, no, not at all"—with such patent sincerity that Tompkin made another ecstatic mental note, and was, indeed, forced to dive hur-riedly behind his counter to conceal his radiant face.

Bredon grinned amiably and Willis, after a moment's hesitation, fled through the doorway.

"I'm sorry," said Miss Dean. "I didn't know—"

"Never mind," said Bredon, and then, in a louder tone: "You've come for those things of your brother's, haven't you? I've got them here; I'm working in his room, don't you know. I say, er, how about, er, coming out and honouring me by taking in a spot of lunch with me, what?"

Miss Dean agreed; Bredon fetched his hat and they passed out.

"Ho!" said Tompkin in confidence to himself. "Ho! what's the game, I wonder? She's a smart jane all right, all right. Given the youngster a chuck and now she's out after the new bloke, I shouldn't be surprised. *And* I don't know as I blame her."

Mr. Bredon and Miss Dean went sedately down together in silence, affording no pasture for the intelligent ears of Harry the liftman, but as they emerged into Southampton Row, the girl turned to her companion:

"I was rather surprised when I got your letter . . ."

Mr. Willis, lurking in the doorway of a neighbouring tobacconist's shop, heard the words and scowled. Then, pulling his hat over his eyebrows and buttoning his mackintosh closely about him, he set out in pursuit. They walked through the lessening rain to the nearest cab-rank and engaged a taxi. Mr. Willis, cunningly waiting till they were well started, engaged the next.

"Follow that taxi," he said, exactly like somebody out of a book. And the driver, nonchalant as though he had stepped from the pages of Edgar Wallace, replied, "Right you are, sir," and slipped in his clutch.

The chase offered no excitement, ending up in the tamest possible manner at Simpson's in the Strand. Mr. Willis paid off his taxi, and climbed, in the wake of the couple, to that upper room where ladies are graciously permitted to be entertained. The quarry found a table near the window; Mr. Willis, ignoring the efforts of a waiter to pilot him to a quiet corner, squeezed in at the table next to them, where a man and woman, who obviously wanted to lunch alone, made way for him indignantly. Even so, he was not very well placed, for, though he could see Bredon and the girl, they had their backs to him, and their conversation was perfectly inaudible.

"Plenty of room at the next table, sir," suggested the waiter.

"I'm all right here," replied Willis, irritably. His neighbour glared, and the waiter, with a glance as much as to say, 'Loopy—but what can a man do?' presented the bill of fare. Willis vaguely ordered saddle of mutton and red-currant jelly with potatoes and gazed at Bredon's slim back.

". . . very nice today, sir."

"What?"

"The cauliflower, sir—very nice today."

"Anything you like."

The little black hat and the sleek yellow poll seemed very close together. Bredon had taken some small object out of his pocket and was showing it to the girl. A ring? Willis strained his eyes—

"What will you drink, sir?"

"Lager," said Willis, at random.

"Pilsener, sir, or Barclay's London Lager?"

"Oh, Pilsener."

"Light or dark, sir?"

"Light—dark—no, I mean light."

"Large light Pilsener, sir?"

"Yes, yes."

"Tankard, sir?"

"Yes, no—damn it! Bring it in anything that's got a hole in the top." There seemed no end to the questions that could be asked about beer. The girl had taken the object, and was doing something with it. What? For heaven's sake, what?

"Roast or new potatoes, sir?"

"New." The man had gone, thank goodness. Bredon was holding Pamela Dean's hand—no, he was turning over the object that lay on her palm. The woman opposite Willis

was stretching across for the sugar-basin—her head ob-
structed his view—deliberately, as it seemed to him. She
moved back. Bredon was still examining the object—

A large dinner-wagon, laden with steaming joints under
great silver covers was beside him. A lid was lifted—the
odour of roast mutton smote him in the face.

"A little more fat, sir? You like it underdone?"

Great God! What monster helpings they gave one at this
place! What sickening stuff mutton was! How vile were
these round yellow balls of potato that the man kept heap-
ing on his plate! What disgusting stuff cauliflower could be
—a curdle of cabbage! Willis, picking with nauseated reluctance at the finest roast saddle in London, felt his stomach
cold and heavy, his feet a-twitch.

The hateful meal dragged on. The indignant couple finished their gooseberry pie and went their affronted way
without waiting for coffee. Now Willis could see better. The
other two were laughing now and talking eagerly. In a sudden lull a few words of Pamela's floated clearly back to
him: "It's to be fancy dress, so you'll slip in all right." Then
she dropped her voice again.

"Will you take any more mutton, sir?"

Try as he would, Willis could catch nothing more. He
sat on in Simpson's until Bredon, glancing at his watch,
appeared to remind himself and his companion that advertising copy-writers must work sometimes. Willis was ready
for them. His bill was paid. He had only to shelter behind
the newspaper he had brought in with him until they had
passed him and then—what? Follow them out? Pursue them
again in a taxi, wondering all the time how closely they
were clasped together, what they were saying to one another, what appointments they were making, what new
devilment there was still in store for Pamela, now that
Victor Dean was out of the way, and what he would or
could do next to make the world safe for her to live in?

He was spared the decision. As the two came abreast of
them, Bredon, suddenly popping his head over the Lunch
Edition of the *Evening Banner,* observed cheerfully:

"Hullo, Willis! enjoyed your lunch? Excellent saddle, what? But you should have tried the peas. Can I give you a lift back to the tread-mill?"

"No, thanks," growled Willis; and then realized that if he had said, "Yes, please," he would at least have made an ardent tête-à-tête in the taxi impossible. But ride in the same taxi with Pamela Dean and Bredon he could not.

"Miss Dean, unhappily, has to leave us," went on Bredon. "You might come and console me by holding my hand."

Pamela was already half-way out of the room. Willis could not decide whether she knew to whom her escort was speaking and had studied to avoid him, or whether she supposed him to be some friend of Bredon's unknown to her. Quite suddenly he made up his mind.

"Well," he said, "it is getting a bit late. If you're having a taxi, I'll share it with you."

"That's the stuff," said Bredon. Willis rose and joined him and they moved on to where Pamela was waiting.

"I think you know our Mr. Willis?"

"Oh, yes," Pamela smiled a small, frozen smile. "Victor and he were great friends at one time."

The door. The stairs. The entrance. They were outside at last.

"I must be getting along now. Thank you so much for my lunch, Mr. Bredon. And you won't forget?"

"I certainly will not. 'Tisn't likely, is it?"

"Good afternoon, Mr. Willis."

"Good afternoon."

She was gone, walking briskly in her little, high-heeled shoes. The roaring Strand engulfed her. A taxi purred up to them.

Bredon gave the address and waved Willis in before him.

"Pretty kid, young Dean's sister," he remarked, cheerfully.

"See here, Bredon; I don't know quite what your game is, but you'd better be careful. I told Dean and I tell you— if you get Miss Dean mixed up with that dirty business of yours—"

"What dirty business?"

"You know well enough what I mean."

"Perhaps I do. And what then? Do I get my neck broken, like Victor Dean?"

Bredon slewed round as he spoke and looked Willis hard in the eye.

"You'll get—" Willis checked himself. "Never mind," he said darkly, "you'll get what's coming to you. I'll see to that."

"I've no doubt you'll do it very competently, what?" replied Bredon. "But do you mind telling me exactly where you come into it? From what I can see, Miss Dean does not seem to welcome your championship with any great enthusiasm."

Willis flushed a dusky red.

"It's no business of mine, of course," went on Bredon, airily, while their taxi chugged impatiently in a traffic jam at Holborn Tube Station, "but then, on the other hand, it doesn't really seem to be any business of yours, does it?"

"It is my business," retorted Willis. "It's every decent man's business. I heard Miss Dean making an appointment with you," he went on, angrily.

"What a detective you would make," said Bredon, admiringly. "But you really ought to take care, when you are shadowing anybody, that they are not sitting opposite a mirror, or anything that will serve as a mirror. There is a picture in front of the table where we were sitting, that reflects half the room. Elementary, my dear Watson. No doubt you will do better with practice. However, there is no secret about the appointment. We are going to a fancy dress affair on Friday. I am meeting Miss Dean for dinner at Boulestin's at 8 o'clock and we are going on from there. Perhaps you would care to accompany us?"

The policeman dropped his arm, and the taxi lurched forward into Southampton Row.

"You'd better be careful," growled Willis, "I might take you at your word."

"I should be charmed, personally," replied Bredon. "You

will decide for yourself whether Miss Dean would or would not be put in an embarrassing position if you joined the party. Well, well, here we are at our little home from home. We must put aside this light badinage and devote ourselves to Sopo and Pompayne and Peabody's Piper Parritch. A delightful occupation, though somewhat lacking in incident. But let us not complain. We can't expect battle, murder and sudden death more than once a week or so. By the way, where were you when Victor Dean fell downstairs?"

"In the lavatory," said Willis, shortly.

"Were you, indeed?" Bredon looked at him once more attentively. "In the lavatory? You interest me strangely."

The atmosphere of the copy-department was much less strained by tea-time. Messrs. Brotherhood had been and gone, having seen nothing to shock their sense of propriety; Mr. Jollop, mellowed by his lunch, had passed three large poster designs with almost reckless readiness and was now with Mr. Pym, being almost persuaded to increase his appropriation for the autumn campaign. The suffering Mr. Armstrong, released from attendance on Mr. Jollop, had taken himself away to visit his dentist. Mr. Tallboy, coming in to purchase a stamp from Miss Rossiter for his private correspondence, announced with delight that the Nutrax half-double had gone to the printer's.

"Is that 'KITTLE CATTLE'?" asked Ingleby. "You surprise me. I thought we should have trouble with it."

"I believe we did," said Tallboy. "Was it Scotch, and would people know what it meant? Would it suggest that we were calling women cows? And wasn't the sketch a little modernistic? But Armstrong got it shoved through somehow. May I drop this in your 'Out' basket, Miss Rossiter?"

"Serpently," replied the lady, with gracious humour, presenting the basket to receive the latter. "All billy-doos receive our prompt attention and are immediately forwarded to their destination by the quickest and surest route."

"Let's see," said Garrett. "I bet it's to a lady, and him

a married man, too! No, you don't, Tallboy, you old devil
—stand still, will you? Tell us who it is, Miss Rossiter."

"K. Smith, Esq.," said Miss Rossiter. "You lose your bet."

"What a swizz! But I expect it's all camouflage. I suspect
Tallboy of keeping a harem somewhere. You can't trust
these handsome blue-eyed men."

"Shut up, Garrett. I never," said Mr. Tallboy, extricating
himself from Garrett's grasp and giving him a playful punch
in the wind, "in my life, met with such a bunch of buttin-
skis as you are in this department. Nothing is sacred to
you, not even a man's business correspondence."

"How should anything be sacred to an advertiser?" demanded Ingleby, helping himself to four lumps of sugar.
"We spend our whole time asking intimate questions of
perfect strangers and it naturally blunts our finer feelings.
'Mother! has your Child Learnt Regular Habits?' 'Are you
Troubled with Fullness after Eating?' 'Are you satisfied
about your Drains?' 'Are you *Sure* that your Toilet-Paper is
Germ-free?' 'Your most Intimate Friends dare not Ask you
this question.' 'Do you Suffer from Superfluous Hair?' 'Do
you Like them to Look at your Hands?' 'Do you ever ask
yourself about Body-Odour?' 'If anything Happened to
You, would your Loved Ones be Safe?' 'Why Spend so much
Time in the Kitchen?' 'You think that Carpet is Clean—
but is it?' 'Are you a Martyr to Dandruff?' Upon my soul, I
sometimes wonder why the long-suffering public doesn't rise
up and slay us."

"They don't know of our existence," said Garrett. "They
all think advertisements write themselves. When I tell people I'm in advertising, they always ask whether I design
posters—they never think about the copy."

"They think the manufacturer does it himself," said Ingleby.

"They ought to see some of the suggestions the manufacturer does put up when he tries his hand at it."

"I wish they could." Ingleby grinned. "That reminds me.
You know that idiotic thing Darling's put out the other

day—the air-cushion for travellers with a doll that fits into the middle and sits up holding an 'ENGAGED' label?"

"What for?" asked Bredon.

"Well, the idea is, that you plank the cushion down in the railway carriage and the doll proclaims that the place is taken."

"But the cushion would do that without the doll."

"Of course it would, but you know how silly people are. They like superfluities. Well, anyway, they—Darling's, I mean—got out an ad. for the rubbish all by their little selves, and were fearfully pleased with it. Wanted us to put it through for them, till Armstrong burst into one of his juicy laughs and made them blush."

"What was it?"

"Picture of a nice girl bending down to put the cushion in the corner of a carriage. And the headline? 'DON'T LET THEM PINCH YOUR SEAT.' "

"Attaboy!" said Mr. Bredon.

The new copy-writer was surprisingly industrious that day. He was still in his room, toiling over Sanfect ("Wherever there's Dirt there's Danger!" "The Skeleton in the Water-closet," "Assassins Lurk in your Scullery!" "Deadlier than Shell-Fire—GERMS!!!") when Mrs. Crump led in her female army to attack the day's accumulated dirt—armed, one regrets to say, not with Sanfect, but with plain yellow soap and water.

"Come in, come in!" cried Mr. Bredon, genially, as the good lady paused reverently at his door. "Come and sweep me and my works away with the rest of the rubbish."

"Well, I'm sure, sir," said Mrs. Crump, "I've no need to be disturbing you."

"I've finished, really," said Bredon. "I suppose there's an awful lot of stuff to clear out here every day."

"That there is, sir—you'd hardly believe. Paper—well, I'm sure paper must be cheap, the amount they waste. Sackfuls and sackfuls every evening goes out. Of course, it's disposed

of to the mills, but all the same it must be a dreadful expense. And there's boxes and boards and odds and ends—
you'd be surprised, the things we picks up. I sometimes
think the ladies and gentlemen brings up all their cast-offs
on purpose to throw 'em away here."

"I shouldn't wonder."

"And mostly chucked on the floor," resumed Mrs. Crump,
warming to her theme, "hardly ever in the paper-baskets,
though goodness knows they makes 'em big enough."

"It must give you a lot of trouble."

"Lor', sir, we don't think nothing of it. We just sweeps
the lot up and sends the sacks down by the lift. Though
sometimes we has a good laugh over the queer things we
finds. I usually just give the stuff a look through to make
sure there's nothing valuable got dropped by mistake. Once
I found two pound-notes on Mr. Ingleby's floor. He's a careless one and no mistake. And not so long ago—the very
day poor Mr. Dean had his sad accident, I found a kind
of carved stone lying round in the passage—looked as though
it might be a charm or a trinket or something of that. But
I think it must have tumbled out of the poor gentleman's
pocket as he fell, because Mrs. Doolittle said she'd seen it
in his room, so I brought it in here, sir, and put it in that
there little box."

"Is this it?" Bredon fished in his waistcoat pocket and
produced the onyx scarab, which he had unaccountably
neglected to return to Pamela Dean.

"That's it, sir. A comical-looking thing, ain't it? Like it
might be a beedle or such. It was lying in a dark corner
under the iron staircase and at first I thought it was just a
pebble like the other one."

"What other one?"

"Well, sir, I found a little round pebble in the very same
place only a few days before. I said at the time, 'Well, I
said, 'that's a funny thing to find there.' But I reckon that
one must have come from Mr. Atkins's room, him having
taken his seaside holiday early this year on account of hav-

ing been ill, and you know how people do fill up their pockets with sea-shells and pebbles and such."

Bredon hunted in his pocket again.

"Something like that, was it?" He held out a smooth, water-rounded pebble, about the size of his thumbnail.

"Very like it, sir. Did that come out of the passage, sir, might I ask?"

"No—I found that up on the roof."

"Ah!" said Mrs. Crump. "It'll be them boys up to their games. When the Sergeant's eye is off them you never know what they're after."

"They do their drill up there, don't they? Great stuff. Hardens the muscles and develops the figure. When do they perform? In the lunch-hour?"

"Oh, no, sir. Mr. Pym won't have them running about after their dinners. He says it spoils their digestions and gives them the colic. Very particular, is Mr. Pym. Half-past eight regular they has to be on duty, sir, in their pants and singlets. Twenty minutes they has of it and then changed and ready for their dooties. After dinner they sets a bit in the boys' room and has a read or plays somethink quiet, as it might be, shove ha'penny or tiddley-winks or such. But in their room they must stay, sir; Mr. Pym won't have nobody about the office in the dinner-hour, sir, not without, of course, it's the boy that goes round with the disinfectant, sir."

"Ah, of course! Spray with Sanfect and you're safe."

"That's right, sir, except that they uses Jeyes' Fluid."

"Oh, indeed," said Mr. Bredon, struck afresh by the curious reluctance of advertising firms to use the commodities they extol for a living. "Well, we're very well looked after here, Mrs. Crump, what?"

"Oh, yes, sir. Mr. Pym pays great attention to 'ealth. A very kind gentleman, is Mr. Pym. Next week, sir, we has the Charwomen's Tea, down in the canteen, with an egg-and-spoon race and a bran-tub, and bring the kiddies. My daughter's little girls always look forward to the tea, sir."

"I'm sure they must," said Mr. Bredon, "and I expect

they'd like some new hair-ribbons or something of that sort—"

"It's very kind of you, sir," said Mrs. Crump, much gratified.

"Not at all." A couple of coins clinked. "Well, I'll push off now and leave you to it."

A very nice gentleman, in Mrs. Crump's opinion, and not at all proud.

It turned out precisely as Mr. Willis had expected. He had tracked his prey from Boulestin's, and this time he felt quite certain he had not been spotted. His costume—that of a member of the Vehmgericht, with its black cossack and black, eyeleted hood covering the whole head and shoulders—was easily slipped on over his every-day suit. Muffled in an old burberry, he had kept watch behind a convenient van in Covent Garden until Bredon and Pamela Dean came out; his taxi had been in waiting just round the corner. His task was made the easier by the fact that the others were driving, not in a taxi, but in an enormous limousine, and that Bredon had taken the wheel himself. The theatre rush was well over before the chase started, so that there was no need to keep suspiciously close to the saloon. The trail had led westward through Richmond and still west, until it had ended at a large house, standing in its own grounds on the bank of the river. Towards the end of the journey they were joined by other cars and taxis making in the same direction; and on arrival they found the drive a parking-place for innumerable vehicles. Bredon and Miss Dean had gone straight in, without a glance behind them.

Willis, who had put on his costume in the taxi, anticipated some difficulty about getting in, but there was none. A servant had met him at the door and asked if he was a member. Willis had replied boldly that he was and given the name of William Brown, which seemed to him an ingenious and plausible invention. Apparently the club was full of William Browns, for the servant raised no difficulty, and he was ushered straight in to a handsomely furnished hall. Immediately in front of him, on the skirts of a crowd of people drinking cocktails, was Bredon, in the harlequin black and white which had been conspicuous as he stepped into his car after dinner. Pamela Dean, in an exiguous swan's-down costume representing a powder-puff, stood beside him. From a room beyond resounded the strains of a saxophone.

"The place," said Mr. Willis to himself, "is a den of iniquity." And for once, Mr. Willis was not far wrong.

He was amazed by the slackness of the organization. Without question or hesitation, every door was opened to him. There was gambling. There was drink in oceans. There was dancing. There were what Mr. Willis had heard described as orgies. And at the back of it all, he sensed something else, something that he did not quite understand; something that he was not precisely kept out of, but to which he simply had not the key.

He was, of course, partnerless, but he soon found himself absorbed into a party of exceedingly bright young people, and watching the evolutions of a *danseuse* whose essential nakedness was enhanced and emphasized by the wearing of a top hat, a monocle and a pair of patent-leather boots. He was supplied with drinks—some of which he paid for, but the majority of which were thrust upon him, and he suddenly became aware that he would have made a better detective had he been more hardened to mixed liquors. His head began to throb, and he had lost sight of Bredon and Pamela. He became obsessed with the idea that they had departed into one of the sinister little cubicles he had seen—each heavily curtained and furnished with a couch and a mirror. He broke away from the group surrounding him and began a hurried search through the house. His costume was hot and heavy, and the sweat poured down his face beneath the stifling black folds of his hood. He found a conservatory full of amorous drunken couples, but the pair he was looking for was not among them. He pushed open a door and found himself in the garden. Cries and

splashes attracted him. He plunged down a rose-scented
alley beneath a pergola and came out upon an open space
with a round fountain-pool in the centre.

A man with a girl in his arms came reeling past him,
flushed and hiccuping with laughter, his leopard-skin tunic
half torn from his shoulders and the vine-leaves scattering
from his hair as he ran. The girl was shrieking like a steam-
engine. He was a broad-shouldered man, and the muscles of
his back gleamed in the moonlight as he swung his protesting burden from him and tossed her, costume and all, into
the pool. Yells of laughter greeted this performance, renewed as the girl, draggled and dripping, crawled back over
the edge of the basin and burst into a stream of abuse. Then
Willis saw the black-and-white harlequin.

He was climbing the statue-group in the centre of the
pool—an elaborate affair of twined mermaids and dolphins,
supporting a basin in which crouched an amorino, blowing
from a conch-shell a high spout of dancing water. Up and
up went the slim chequered figure, dripping and glittering
like a fantastic water-creature. He caught the edge of the
upper basin with his hands, swung for a moment and lifted.
Even in that moment, Willis felt a pang of reluctant admiration. It was the easy, unfretted motion of the athlete,
a display of muscular strength without jerk or effort. Then
his knee was on the basin. He was up and climbing upon
the bronze cupid. Yet another moment and he was kneeling upon the figure's stooped shoulders—standing upright
upon them, the spray of the fountain blowing about him.

"Good God!" thought Willis, "the fellow's a tight-rope
walker—or he's too drunk to fall." There were yells of applause, and a girl began to shriek hysterically. Then a very
tall woman, in a moonlight frock of oyster satin, who had
made herself the centre of the most boisterous of all the
parties, pushed past Willis and stood out on the edge of
the basin, her fair hair standing out like a pale aureole
round her vivid face.

"Dive!" she called out, "dive in! I dare you to! Dive in!"

"Shut up, Dian!" One of the soberer of the men caught

her round the shoulders and put his hand over her mouth.
"It's too shallow—he'll break his neck."

She pushed him away.

"You be quiet. He shall dive. I want him to. Go to hell,
Dickie. You wouldn't dare do it, but he will."

"I certainly wouldn't. Stow it."

"Come on, Harlequin, dive!"

The black and white figure raised its arms above its fantastic head and stood poised.

"Don't be a fool, man," bawled Dickie.

But the other women were fired with the idea and their
screams drowned his voice.

"Dive, Harlequin, dive."

The slim body shot down through the spray, struck the
surface with scarcely a splash and slid through the water
like a fish. Willis caught his breath. It was perfectly done.
It was magnificent. He forgot his furious hatred of the man
and applauded with the rest. The girl Dian ran forward
and caught hold of the swimmer as he emerged.

"Oh, you're marvellous, you're marvellous!" She clung to
him, the water soaking into her draggled satin.

"Take me home, Harlequin—I adore you!"

The Harlequin bent his masked face and kissed her. The
man called Dickie tried to pull him away, but was neatly
tripped and fell with a jerk into the pool, amid a roar of
laughter. The Harlequin tossed the tall girl across his
shoulder.

"A prize!" he shouted. "A prize!"

Then he swung her lightly to her feet and took her hand.
"Run," he called, "run! Let's run away, and let them catch
us if they can."

There was a sudden stampede. Willis saw the angry face
of Dickie as he lurched past him and heard him swearing.
Somebody caught his hand. He ran up the rose-alley, panting. Something caught his foot, and he tripped and fell.
His companion abandoned him, and ran on, hooting. He
sat up, found his head enveloped in his hood and struggled
to release himself.

A hand touched his shoulder.

"Come on, Mr. Willis," said a mocking voice in his ear, "Mr. Bredon says I am to escort you home."

He succeeded in dragging the black cloth from his head and scrambled to his feet.

Beside him stood Pamela Dean. She had taken off her mask, and her eyes were alight with mischief.

CHAPTER V

SURPRISING METAMORPHOSIS
OF MR. BREDON

LORD PETER WIMSEY had paid a call upon Chief-Inspector Parker of Scotland Yard, who was his brother-in-law.

He occupied a large and comfortable arm-chair in the Chief-Inspector's Bloomsbury flat. Opposite him, curled upon the chesterfield, was his sister, Lady Mary Parker, in dustriously knitting an infant's vest. On the window-seat, hugging his knees and smoking a pipe, was Mr. Parker himself. On a convenient table stood a couple of decanters and a soda siphon. On the hearthrug was a large tabby cat. The scene was almost ostentatiously peaceful and domestic.

"So you have become one of the world's workers, Peter," said Lady Mary.

"Yes; I'm pulling down four solid quid a week. Amazin' sensation. First time I've ever earned a cent. Every week when I get my pay-envelope, I glow with honest pride."

Lady Mary smiled, and glanced at her husband, who grinned cheerfully back. The difficulties which are apt to arise when a poor man marries a rich wife had, in their case, been amicably settled by an ingenious arrangement, under which all Lady Mary's money had been handed over to her brothers in trust for little Parkers to come, the trustee having the further duty of doling out each quarter to the wife a sum precisely equal to the earnings of the husband during that period. Thus a seemly balance was maintained between the two principals; and the trifling anomaly that Chief-Inspector Parker was actually a mere pauper in com-

72

parison with small Charles Peter and still smaller Mary Lucasta, now peacefully asleep in their cots on the floor above, disturbed nobody one whit. It pleased Mary to have the management of their moderate combined income, and incidentally did her a great deal of good. She now patronized her wealthy brother with all the superiority which the worker feels over the man who merely possesses money.

"But what *is* the case all about, exactly?" demanded Parker.

"Blest if I know," admitted Wimsey, frankly. "I got hauled into it through Freddy Arbuthnot's wife—Rachel Levly that was, you know. She knows old Pym, and he met her at dinner somewhere and told her about this letter that was worrying him, and she said, Why not get somebody in to investigate it, and he said, Who? So she said she knew somebody—not mentioning my name, you see—and he said would she ask me to buzz along, so I buzzed and there I am."

"Your narrative style," said Parker, "though racy, is a little elliptical. Could you not begin at the beginning and go on until you come to the end, and then, if you are able to, stop?"

"I'll try," said his lordship, "but I always find the stopping part of the business so difficult. Well, look! On a Monday afternoon—the 25th of May, to be particular, a young man, Victor Dean by name, employed as a copy-writer in the firm of Pym's Publicity, Ltd., Advertising Agents, fell down an iron spiral staircase on their premises, situated in the upper part of Southampton Row, and died immediately of injuries received, to wit: one broken neck, one cracked skull, one broken leg and minor cuts and contusions, various. The time of this disaster was, as nearly as can be ascertained, 3.30 in the afternoon."

"Hum!" said Parker. "Pretty extensive injuries for a fall of that kind."

"So I thought, before I saw the staircase. To proceed. On the day after this occurrence, the sister of deceased sends to Mr. Pym a fragment of a half-finished letter which she

has found on her brother's desk. It warns him that there is
something of a fishy nature going on in the office. The letter
is dated about ten days previous to the death, and appears
to have been laid aside as though the writer wanted to think
over the wording a bit more carefully. Very good. Now,
Mr. Pym is a man of rigid morality—except, of course, as
regards his profession, whose essence is to tell plausible lies
for money—"

"How about truth in advertising?"

"Of course, there is *some* truth in advertising. There's
yeast in bread, but you can't make bread with yeast alone.
Truth in advertising," announced Lord Peter sententiously,
"is like leaven, which a woman hid in three measures of
meal. It provides a suitable quantity of gas, with which to
blow out a mass of crude misrepresentation into a form that
the public can swallow. Which incidentally brings me to
the delicate and important distinction between the words
'with' and 'from.' Suppose you are advertising lemonade,
or, not to be invidious, we will say perry. If you say 'Our
perry is made from fresh-plucked pears only,' then it's got
to be made from pears only, or the statement is actionable;
if you just say it is made 'from pears,' without the 'only,'
the betting is that it is probably made chiefly of pears; but
if you say, 'made *with* pears,' you generally mean that you
use a peck of pears to a ton of turnips, and the law cannot
touch you—such are the niceties of our English tongue."

"Make a note, Mary, next time you go shopping, and buy
nothing that is not 'from, only.' Proceed, Peter—and let us
have a little less of your English tongue."

"Yes. Well, here is a young man who starts to write a
warning letter. Before he can complete it, he falls downstairs and is killed. Is that, or is it not, a darned suspicious
circumstance?"

"So suspicious that it is probably the purest coincidence.
But since you have a fancy for melodrama, we will allow
it to be suspicious. Who saw him die?"

"I, said the fly. Meaning one Mr. Atkins and one Mrs.
Crump, who saw the fall from below, and one Mr. Prout

who saw it from above. All their evidence is interesting. Mr. Prout says that the staircase was well-lit, and that deceased was not going extra fast, while the others say that he fell all of a heap, forwards, clutching *The Times Atlas* in so fierce a grip that it could afterwards hardly be prised from his fingers. What does that suggest to you?"

"Only that the death was instantaneous, which it would be if one broke one's neck."

"I know. But look here! You are going downstairs and your foot slips. What happens? Do you crumple forwards and dive down head first? Or do you sit down suddenly on your tail and do the rest of the journey that way?"

"It depends. If it was actually a slip, I should probably come down on my tail. But if I tripped, I should very likely dive forwards. You can't tell, without knowing just how it happened."

"All right. You always have an answer. Well now—do you clutch what you're carrying with a deathly grip—or do you chuck it, and try to save yourself by grabbing hold of the banisters?"

Mr. Parker paused. "I should probably grab," he said, slowly, "unless I was carrying a tray full of crockery, or anything. And even then . . . I don't know. Perhaps it's an instinct to hold on to what one's got. But equally it's an instinct to try and save one's self. I don't know. All this arguing about what you and I would do and what the reasonable man would do is very unsatisfactory."

Wimsey groaned. "Put it this way, doubting Thomas. If the death-grip was due to instantaneous rigor, he must have been dead so quickly that he couldn't think of saving himself. Now, there are two possible causes of death—the broken neck, which he must have got when he pitched on his head at the bottom, and the crack on the temple, which is attributed to his hitting his skull on one of the knobs on the banisters. Now, falling down a staircase isn't like falling off a roof—you do it in instalments, and have time to think about it. If he killed himself by hitting the banisters, he must have fallen first and hit himself afterwards. The same thing applies, with still more force, to his breaking his neck. Why, when he felt himself going, didn't he drop everything and break his fall?"

"I know what you want me to say," said Parker. "That he was sandbagged first and dead before he fell. But I don't see it. I say he would have caught his toe in something and tripped forwards and struck his head straight away and died of that. There's nothing impossible about it."

"Then I'll try again. How's this? That same evening, Mrs. Crump, the head charwoman, picked up this onyx scarab in the passage, just beneath the iron staircase. It is, as you see, rounded and smooth and heavy for its size, which is much about that of the iron knobs on the staircase. It has, as you also see, a slight chip on one side. It belonged to the dead man, who was accustomed to carry it in his waistcoat pocket or keep it sitting on the desk beside him while he worked. What about it?"

"I should say it fell from his pocket when he fell."

"And the chip?"

"If it wasn't there before—"

"It wasn't; his sister says she's sure it wasn't."

"Then it got chipped in falling."

"You think that?"

"I do."

"I think you were meant to think that. To continue: some few days earlier, Mrs. Crump found a smooth pebble of much the same size as the scarab lying in the same passage at the foot of the same iron staircase."

"Did she?" said Parker. He uncurled himself from the window-seat and made for the decanters. "What does she say about it?"

"Says that you'd scarcely believe the queer odds and ends she finds when she's cleaning out the office. Attributes the stone to Mr. Atkins, he having taken his seaside holiday early on account of ill-health."

"Well," said Parker, releasing the lever of the soda-siphon, "and why not?"

"Why not, indeed? This other pebble, which I here pro-

duce, was found by me on the roof of the lavatory. I had
to shin down a pipe to get it, and ruined a pair of flannel
bags."

"Oh, yeah?"

"Okay, captain. That's where I found it. I also found a
place where the paint had been chipped off the skylight."

"What skylight?"

"The skylight that is directly over the iron staircase. It's
one of those pointed things, like a young greenhouse, and it
has windows that open all round—you know the kind I
mean—which are kept open in hot weather. It was hot
weather when young Dean departed this life."

"The idea being that somebody heaved a stone at him
through the skylight?"

"You said it, chief. Or, to be exact, not *a* stone, but *the*
stone. Meaning the scarab."

"And how about the other stones?"

"Practice shots. I've ascertained that the office is always
practically empty during the lunch-hour. Nobody much ever
goes on the roof, except the office-boys for their P.J.'s at
8.30 ack emma."

"People who live in glass skylights shouldn't throw stones.
Do you mean to suggest that by chucking a small stone like
this at a fellow, you're going to crack his skull open and
break his neck for him?"

"Not if you just throw it, of course. But how about a
sling or a catapult?"

"Oh, in that case, you've only got to ask the people in
the neighbouring offices if they've seen anybody enjoying a
spot of David and Goliath exercise on Pym's roof, and
you've got him."

"It's not as simple as that. The roof's quite a good bit
higher than the roofs of the surrounding buildings, and it
has a solid stone parapet all round about three feet high—
to give an air of still greater magnificence, I suppose. To
sling a stone through on to the iron staircase you'd have to
kneel down in a special position between that skylight and
the next, and you can't be seen from anywhere—unless

somebody happened to be *on* the staircase looking up—which nobody obviously was, except Victor Dean, poor lad. It's safe as houses."

"Very well, then. Find out if any member of the staff has frequently stayed in at lunch-time."

Wimsey shook his head.

"No bon. The staff clock in every morning, but there are no special tabs kept on them at 1 o'clock. The reception clerk goes out to his lunch, and one of the elder boys takes his place at the desk, just in case any message or parcel comes in, but he's not there necessarily every moment of the time. Then there's the lad who hops round with Jeyes' Fluid in a squirt, but he doesn't go on to the roof. There's nothing to prevent anybody from going up, say at half-past twelve, and staying there till he's done his bit of work and then simply walking out down the staircase. The lift-man, or his locum tenens, would be on duty, but you've only to keep on the blind side of the lift as you pass and he couldn't possibly see you. Besides, the lift might quite well have gone down to the basement. All the bloke would have to do would just be to bide his time and walk out. There's nothing in it. Similarly, on the day of the death. He goes through towards the lavatory, which is reached from the stairs. When the coast is clear, he ascends to the roof. He lurks there, till he sees his victim start down the iron stair-case, which everybody does, fifty times a day. He whangs off his bolt and departs. Everybody is picking up the body and exclaiming over it, when in walks our friend, innocently, from the lav. It's as simple as pie."

"Wouldn't it be noticed, if he was out of his own room all that time?"

"My dear old man, if you knew Pym's! Everybody is always out of his room. If he isn't chatting with the copy-department, or fooling round the typists, he's in the studio, clamouring for a lay-out, or in the printing, complaining about a folder, or in the press-department, inquiring about an appropriation, or in the vouchers, demanding back numbers of something, or if he isn't in any of those places, he's somewhere else—slipping out for surreptitious coffee or haircuts. The word alibi has no meaning in a place like Pym's."

"You're going to have a lovely time with it all, I can see that," said Parker. "But what sort of irregularity could possibly be going on in a place like that, which would lead to murder?"

"Now we're coming to it. Young Dean used to tag round with the de Momerie crowd—"

Parker whistled.

"Sinning above his station in life?"

"Very much so. But you know Dian de Momerie. She gets more kick out of corrupting the bourgeois—she enjoys the wrestle with their little consciences. She's a bad lot, that girl. I took her home last night, so I ought to know."

"Peter!" said Lady Mary. "Quite apart from your morals, which alarm me, how did you get into that gang? I should have thought they'd as soon have taken up with Charles, here, or the Chief Commissioner."

"Oh, I went incog. A comedy of masks. And you needn't worry about my morals. The young woman became incapably drunk on the way home, so I pushed her inside her dinky little maisonette in Garlic Mews and tucked her up on a divan in the sitting-room to astonish her maid in the morning. Though she's probably past being astonished. But the point is that I found out a good bit about Victor Dean."

"Just a moment," interrupted Parker, "did he dope?"

"Apparently not, though I'll swear it wasn't Dian's fault if he didn't. According to his sister, he was too strong-minded. Possibly he tried it once and felt so rotten that he didn't try it again. . . . Yes—I know what you're thinking. If he was dopey, he might have fallen downstairs on his own account. But I don't think that'll work. These things have a way of coming out at post-mortems. The question was raised . . . no; it wasn't that."

"Did Dian have any opinion on the subject?"

"She said he wasn't a sport. All the same, she seems to have kept him in tow from about the end of November to the end of April—nearly six months, and that's a long time for Dian. I wonder what the attraction was. I suppose the whelp must have had something engaging about him."

"Is that the sister's story?"

"Yes; but she says that Victor 'had great ambitions.' I don't quite know what she thinks he meant by that."

"I suppose she realized that Dian was his mistress. Or wasn't she?"

"Must have been. But I rather gather his sister thought he was contemplating matrimony."

Parker laughed.

"After all," said Lady Mary, "he probably didn't tell his sister everything."

"Damned little, I should imagine. She was quite honestly upset by last night's show. Apparently the party Dean took her to wasn't quite so hot. Why did he take her? That's another problem. He said he wanted her to meet Dian, and no doubt the kid imagined she was being introduced to a future-in-law. But Dean—you'd think he'd want to keep his sister out of it. He couldn't, surely, really have wanted to corrupt her, as Willis said."

"Who is Willis?"

"Willis is a young man who foams at the mouth if you mention Victor Dean, who was once Victor Dean's dearest friend, who is in love with Victor Dean's sister, is furiously jealous of me, thinks I'm tarred with the same brush as Victor Dean, and dogs my footsteps with the incompetent zeal of fifty Watsons. He writes copy about face-cream and corsets, is the son of a provincial draper, was educated at a grammar school and wears, I deeply regret to say, a double-breasted waistcoat. That is the most sinister thing about him—except that he admits to having been in the lavatory when Victor Dean fell downstairs, and the lavatory, as I said before, is the next step to the roof."

"Who else was in the lavatory?"

"I haven't asked him yet. How can I? It's horribly hampering to one's detective work when one isn't supposed to be detecting, because one daren't ask any questions, much. But if whoever it was knew I was detecting, then whatsoever questions I asked, I shouldn't get any answers. It wouldn't matter if only I had the foggiest notion whom or what I was detecting, but looking among about a hundred people for the perpetrator of an unidentified crime is rather difficult."

"I thought you were looking for a murderer."

"So I am—but I don't think I shall ever get the murderer till I know why the murder was done. Besides, what Pym engaged me to do was to look for the irregularity in the office. Of course, murder is an irregularity, but it's not the one I'm commissioned to hunt for. And the only person I can fix a motive for the murder on to is Willis—and it's not the sort of motive I'm looking for."

"What was Willis's row with Dean?"

"Damn silliest thing in the world. Willis used to go home with Dean at week-ends. Dean lived in a flat with his sister, by the way—no parents or anything. Willis fell in love with sister. Sister wasn't sure about him. Dean took sister to one of Dian's hot parties. Willis found out. Willis, being a boob, talked to sister like a Dutch uncle. Sister called Willis a disgusting, stuck-up, idiotic, officious prig. Willis rebuked Dean. Dean told Willis to go to hell. Loud row. Sister joined in. Dean family united in telling Willis to go and bury himself. Willis told Dean that if he (Dean) persisted in cor-rupting his (Dean's) sister he (Willis) would shoot him like a dog. His very words, or so I am told."

"Willis," said Mary, "appears to think in clichés."

"Of course he does—that's why he writes such good corset-copy. Anyhow, there it was. Dean and Willis at daggers drawn for three months. Then Dean fell downstairs. Now Willis has started on me. I told off Pamela Dean to take him home last night, but I don't know what came of it. I've explained to her that those hot-stuff parties are genu-inely dangerous, and that Willis has some method in his madness, though a prize juggins as regards tact and knowl-edge of the sex. It was frightfully comic to see old Willis sneaking in after us in a sort of Ku Klux Klan outfit—in-credibly stealthy, and wearing the same shoes he wears in the office and a seal-ring on his little finger that one could identify from here to the Monument."

"Poor lad! I suppose it wasn't Willis who tipped friend Dean down the staircase?"

"I don't think so, Polly—but you never know. He's such a melodramatic ass. He might consider it a splendid sin. But I don't think he'd have had the brains to work out the details. And if he had done it, I fancy he'd have gone straight round to the police-station, smitten the double-breasted waistcoat a resounding blow and proclaimed 'I did it, in the cause of purity.' But against that, there's the un-doubted fact that Dean's connection with Dian and Co. defi-nitely came to an end in April—so why should he wait till the end of May to strike the blow? The row with Dean took place in March."

"Possibly, Peter, the sister has been leading you up the garden. The connection may not have stopped when she said it did. She may have kept it up on her own. She may even be a drug-taker or something herself. You never know."

"No; but generally one can make a shrewd guess. No; I don't think there's anything like that wrong with Pamela Dean. I'll swear her disgust last night was genuine. It was pretty foul, I must say. By the way, Charles, where the devil do these people get their stuff from? There was enough dope floating about that house to poison a city."

"If I knew that," said Mr. Parker, sourly, "I should be on velvet. All I can tell you is, that it's coming in by the boat-load from somewhere or other, and is being distributed broadcast from somewhere or other. The question is, where? Of course, we could lay hands tomorrow on half a hundred of the small distributors, but where would be the good of that? They don't know themselves where it comes from, or who handles it. They all tell the same tale. It's handed to them in the street by men they've never seen before and couldn't identify again. Or it's put in their pockets in omni-buses. It isn't always that they won't tell; they honestly don't know. And if you did catch the man immediately above them in the scale, he would know nothing either. It's heart-breaking. Somebody must be making millions out of it."

"Yes. Well, to go back to Victor Dean. Here's another problem. He was pulling down six pounds a week at Pym's. How does one manage to run with the de Momerie crowd on £300 a year? Even if he wasn't much of a sport, it couldn't possibly be done for nothing."

"Probably he lived on Dian."

"Possibly he did, the little tick. On the other hand, I've got an idea. Suppose he really did think he had a chance of marrying into the aristocracy—or what he imagines to be the aristocracy. After all, Dian is a de Momerie, though her people have shown her the door, and you can't blame them. Put it that he was spending far more than he could afford in trying to keep up the running. Put it that it took longer than he thought and that he had got heavily dipped. And then see what that half-finished letter to Pym looks like in the light of that theory."

"Well," began Parker.

"Oh, do step on the gas!" broke in Mary. "How you two darlings do love going round and round a subject, don't you? Blackmail, of course. It's perfectly obvious. I've seen it coming for the last hour. This Dean creature is looking round for a spot of extra income and he discovers somebody at Pym's doing something he shouldn't—the head-cashier cooking the accounts, or the office-boy pilfering from the petty cash, or something. So he says, 'If you don't square me, I'll tell Pym,' and starts to write a letter. Probably, you know, he never meant that letter to get to Mr. Pym, at all; it was just a threat. The other man stops him for the moment by paying up something on account. Then he thinks: 'This is hopeless, I'd better slug the little beast.' So he slugs him. And there you are."

"Just as simple as that," said Wimsey.

"Of course it's simple, only men love to make mysteries."

"And women love to jump to conclusions."

"Never mind the generalizations," said Parker, "they always lead to bad reasoning. Where do I come into all this?"

"You give me your advice, and stand by ready to rally round with your myrmidons in case there's any rough-housing. By the way, I can give you the address of that house we went to last night. Dope and gambling to be had for the asking, to say nothing of nameless orgies."

He mentioned the address and the Chief-Inspector made a note of it. "Though we can't do much," he admitted. "It's a private house, belonging to a Major Milligan. We've had our eye on it for some time. And even if we could get in on it, it probably wouldn't help us to what we want. I don't suppose there's a soul in that gang who knows where the dope comes from. Still, it's something to have definite evidence that that's where it goes. By the way, we got the goods on that couple you helped us to arrest the other night. They'll probably get seven years."

"Good. I was pretty nearly had that time, though. Two of Pym's typists were fooling round and recognized me. I gave them a fishy stare and explained next morning that I had a cousin who closely resembled me. That notorious fellow Wimsey, of course. It's a mistake to be too well known."

"If the de Momerie crowd get wise to you, you'll find yourself in Queer Street," said Parker. "How did you get so pally with Dian?"

"Dived off a fountain into a fish-pond. It pays to advertise. She thinks I'm the world's eighth wonder. Absolutely the lobster's dress-shirt."

"Well, don't kill yourself," said Mary, gently. "We rather like you, and small Peter couldn't spare his best uncle."

"It will do you no end of good," remarked his brother-in-law, callously, "to have a really difficult case for once. When you've struggled for a bit with a death that might have been caused by anybody for any imaginable motive, you may be less sniffy and superior about the stray murders all over the country that the police so notoriously fail to avenge. I hope it will be a lesson to you. Have another spot?"

"Thanks; I'll try to profit by it. In the meantime, I'll go on gulling the public and being Mr. Bredon, to be heard of at your address. And let me know of any developments with the Momerie-Milligan lot."

"I will. Should you care to make one in our next dope-raid?"

"Sure thing. When do you expect it?"

"We've had information about cocaine-smuggling on the Essex coast. Worst thing the Government ever did was to abolish the coast-guard service. It doubles our trouble, especially with all these privately-owned motor-boats about. If you're out for an evening's fun any time, you could come along—and you might bring that car of yours. It's faster than anything we've got."

"I see. Two for yourselves and one for me. Right you are. I'm on. Send me a line any time. I cease work at 5.30."

In the meantime, three hearts were being wrung on Mr. Death Bredon's account.

Miss Pamela Dean was washing a pair of silk stockings in her solitary flat.

"Last night was rather marvellous. . . . I suppose I oughtn't to have enjoyed it, with poor old Victor only just buried, the darling . . . but, of course, I really went for Victor's sake . . . I wonder if that detective man will find out anything about it . . . he didn't say much, but I believe he thinks there was something funny about Victor being killed like that . . . anyhow, Victor suspected there was something wrong, and he'd *want* me to do everything I could to ferret it out. . . . I didn't know private detectives were like that. . . . I thought they were nasty, furtive little men . . . vulgar . . . I like his voice . . . and his hands . . . oh, dear! there's a hole . . . I'll have to catch it together before it runs up the instep . . . and beautiful manners, only I'm afraid he was cross with me for coming to Pym's . . . he must be fearfully athletic to climb up that fountain . . . he swims like a fish . . . my new bathing-dress . . . sun-bathing . . . thank goodness I've got decent legs . . . I'll really have to get some more stockings, these won't go on much longer . . . I wish I didn't look so washed-out in black. . . . Poor Victor! . . . I wonder what I can possibly do with Alec Willis . . . if only he wasn't such a prig. . . . I don't mind Mr. Bredon . . . he's quite right about that crowd being no good, but then he really knows what he's talking about, and it isn't just prejudice. . . . Why will Alec be so jealous and tiresome? . . . And looking so silly in that black thing . . . following people about. . . . Incompetent—I do like people to be competent. . . . Mr. Bredon looks terribly competent . . . no, he doesn't exactly look it, but he is . . . he looks as though he never did anything but go to dinner-parties. . . . I suppose high-class detectives have to look like that. . . . Alec would make a rotten detective. . . . I don't like ill-tempered men . . . I wonder what happened when Mr. Bredon went off with Dian de Momerie . . . she is beautiful . . . damn her, she's lovely . . . she does drink an awful lot . . . they say it makes you look old before your time . . . you get coarse . . . my complexion's all right, but I'm not the fashionable type . . . Dian de Momerie is perfectly crazy about people who do mad things . . . I don't like aluminium blondes . . . I wonder if I could get an aluminium bleach. . . ."

Alec Willis, hammering a rather hard pillow into a more comfortable shape in his boarding-house bedroom, sought slumber in vain:

"Gosh! what a head I had this morning . . . that damned, sleek brute! . . . there's something up between Pamela and him . . . helping her with some business of Victor's my foot! . . . He's out to make trouble . . . and going off with that white-headed bitch . . . it's a damned insult . . . of course Pamela would lick his boots . . . women . . . put up with anything . . . wish I hadn't had all those drinks . . . damn this bed! damn this foul place . . . I'll have to chuck Pym's . . . it isn't safe. . . . Murder? . . . anybody interfering with Pamela . . . Pamela. . . . She wouldn't let me kiss her . . . that swine Bredon . . . down the iron staircase . . . get my hands on

his throat. . . . What a hope! damned posturing acrobat
. . . Pamela . . . I'd like to show her . . . money, money,
money . . . if I wasn't so damned hard up . . . Dean was
a little squirt anyway . . . I only told her the truth . . .
blast all women! . . . They like rotters . . . I haven't paid
for that last suit . . . oh, hell! I wish I hadn't had those
drinks . . . I forgot to get any bicarbonate . . . I haven't
paid for those boots . . . all those naked women in the
swimming-pool . . . black and silver . . . he spotted me,
damn his eyes! . . . 'Hullo, Willis!' this morning, as cool as
a fish . . . dives like a fish . . . fish don't dive . . . fish
don't sleep . . . or do they? . . . I can't sleep . . . 'Mac-
beth hath murdered sleep.' . . . Murder . . . down the
iron staircase . . . get my hands on his throat . . . oh,
damn! damn! damn! . . ."

Dian de Momerie was dancing:
"My God! I'm bored. . . . Get off my feet, you clumsy
cow. . . . Money, tons of money . . . but I'm bored. . . .
Can't we do something else? . . . I'm sick of that tune . . .
I'm sick of everything . . . he's working up to get all mushy
. . . suppose I'd better go through with it . . . I was soz-
zled last night . . . wonder where the Harlequin man went
to . . . wonder who he was . . . that little idiot Pamela
Dean . . . these women . . . I'll have to make up to her,
I suppose, if I'm ever to get his address . . . I got him
away from her, any old how . . . wish I hadn't been so
squiffy . . . I can't remember . . . climbing up the fountain . . . black and silver . . . he's got a lovely body . . .
I think he could give me a thrill . . . my God! how bored
I am . . . he's exciting . . . rather mysterious . . . I'll
have to write to Pamela Dean . . . silly little fool . . .
expect she hates me . . . rather a pity I chucked little Victor . . . fell downstairs and broke his silly neck . . . damn
good riddance . . . ring her up . . . she's not on the
'phone . . . so suburban not to be on the 'phone . . . if
this tune goes on, I shall scream . . . Milligan's drinks are
rotten . . . why does one go there? . . . Must do some-

thing . . . Harlequin . . . don't even know his name. . . . Weedon . . . Leader . . . something or other . . . oh, hell! perhaps Milligan knows . . . I can't stand this any longer . . . black and silver . . . thank God! that's over!"

All over London the lights flickered in and out, calling on the public to save its body and purse: SOPO SAVES SCRUB-BING—NUTRAX FOR NERVES—CRUNCHLETS ARE CRISPER—EAT PIPER PARRITCH—DRINK POMPAYNE—ONE WHOOSH AND IT'S CLEAN—OH, BOY! IT'S TOMBOY TOFFEE—NOURISH NERVES WITH NUTRAX—FARLEY'S FOOTWEAR TAKES YOU FURTHER—IT ISN'T DEAR, IT'S DARLING—DARLING'S FOR HOUSEHOLD APPLIANCES—MAKE ALL SAFE WITH SANFECT—WHIFFLETS FASCINATE. The presses, thundering and growling, ground out the same appeals by the million: ASK YOUR GROCER—ASK YOUR DOCTOR—ASK THE MAN WHO'S TRIED IT—MOTHER'S! GIVE IT TO YOUR CHILDREN—HOUSEWIVES! SAVE MONEY—HUSBANDS! INSURE YOUR LIVES—WOMEN! DO YOU REALIZE?—DON'T SAY SOAP, SAY SOPO! Whatever you're doing, stop it and do something else! Whatever you're buying, pause and buy something different! Be hectored into health and prosperity! Never let up! Never go to sleep! Never be satisfied. If once you are satisfied, all our wheels will run down. Keep going—and if you can't, Try Nutrax for Nerves!

Lord Peter Wimsey went home and slept.

CHAPTER VI

SINGULAR SPOTLESSNESS OF A LETHAL WEAPON

Y OU know," said Miss Rossiter to Mr. Smayle, "our newest copy-writer is perfectly potty."

"Potty?" Mr. Smayle, showing all his teeth in an engaging smile, "you don't say so, Miss Rossiter? How, potty?"

"Well, loopy," explained Miss Rossiter. "Goofy. Blah. He's always up on the roof, playing with a catapult. I don't know *what* Mr. Hankin would say if he knew."

"With a catapult?" Mr. Smayle looked pained. "That doesn't seem quite the thing. But we in other spheres, Miss Rossiter, always envy, if I may say so, the happy youthful spirit of the copy-department. Due, no doubt," added Mr. Smayle, "to the charming influence of the ladies. Allow me to get you another cup of tea."

"Thanks awfully, I wish you would." The monthly tea was in full swing, and the Little Conference Room was exceedingly crowded and stuffy. Mr. Smayle edged away gallantly in pursuit of tea, and against the long table, presided over by Mrs. Johnson (the indefatigable lady who ruled the Dispatching, the office-boys and the first-aid cupboard) found himself jostled by Mr. Harris of the Outdoor Publicity.

"Pardon, old fellow," said Mr. Smayle.

"Granted," said Mr. Harris, "fascinating young fellows like you are privileged to carry all before them. Ha, ha, *ha!* I saw you doing the polite to Miss Rossiter—getting on like a house afire, eh?"

Mr. Smayle smirked deprecatingly.

"Wouldn't you like three guesses at our conversation?" he suggested. "One milk and no sugar and one milk and sugar, Mrs. J., please."

"Three's two too many," replied Mr. Harris. "I can tell you. You were talking about Miss Rossiter and Mr. Smayle, hey? Finest subjects of conversation in the world—to Mr. Smayle and Miss Rossiter, hey?"

"Well, you're wrong," said Mr. Smayle, triumphantly. "We were discussing another member of this community. The new copy-writer, in fact. Miss Rossiter was saying he was potty."

"They're all potty in that department, if you ask me," said Mr. Harris, waggling his chins. "Children. Arrested development."

"It looks like it," agreed Mr. Smayle. "Cross-words I am not surprised at, for everybody does them, nor drawing nursery pictures, but playing with catapults on the roof is really childish. Though what with Miss Meteyard bringing her Yo-Yo to the office with her—"

"I'll tell you what it is, Smayle," pronounced Mr. Harris, taking his colleague by the lapel and prodding him with his forefinger, "it's all this University education. What does it do? It takes a boy, or a young woman for that matter, and keeps him in leading-strings in the playground when he ought to be ploughing his own furrow in the face of reality—Hullo, Mr. Bredon! Was that your toe? Beg pardon, I'm sure. This room's too small for these social gatherings. I hear you are accustomed to seek the wide, open spaces on the roof."

"Oh, yes. Fresh air and all that, you know. Exercise. Do you know, I've been taking pot-shots at the sparrows with a catapult. Frightfully good training for the eye and that sort of thing. Come up one day and we'll have a competition."

"Not for me, thanks," replied Mr. Harris. "Getting too old for that kind of thing. Though when I was a boy I remember putting a pebble through my old aunt's cucumber-frame. Lord! how she did scold, to be sure!"

Mr. Harris suddenly looked rather wistful.

"I haven't had a catapult in my hand for thirty years, I don't suppose," he added.

"Then it's time you took it up again." Mr. Bredon half pulled a tangle of stick and rubber from his side-pocket and pushed it back again, with a wink and a grimace at the back of Mr. Pym, who now came into view, talking condescendingly to a lately-joined junior. "Between you and me, Harris, don't you find this place a bit wearisome at times?"

"Wearisome?" put in Mr. Tallboy, extricating himself from the crowd at the table, and nearly upsetting Mr. Smayle's two cups of tea, now at length achieved, "wearisome? You people don't know the meaning of the word. Nobody but a lay-out man knows what a lay-out man's feelings is."

"You should frivol with us," said Mr. Bredon. "If the lay-out lays you out, rejuvenate your soul in Roof Revels with Copy-writers. I bagged a starling this morning."

"What do you mean, bagged a starling?"

"Father, I cannot tell a lie. I did it with my little catapult. But if it's found," added Mr. Bredon earnestly, "I expect they will lay the blame on the canteen cat."

"—apult," said Mr. Harris. He looked at Mr. Tallboy to see if this play upon words had been appreciated, and seeing that that gentleman looked more than ordinarily blank and unreceptive, he proceeded to rub it in.

"Like the old joke, eh? 'O take a pill! O take a pill! O take a pilgrim home!' "

"What do you say?" asked Mr. Tallboy, frowning in the effort to concentrate.

"O blame the cat, don't you see," persisted Mr. Harris, "O blame the cat! O blame the catapult! Got me?"

"Ha, ha! very good!" said Mr. Tallboy.

"There was another," Mr. Harris went on, "O for a man! O for a—"

"Are you a good hand with a catapult, Tallboy?" inquired

Mr. Bredon, rather hastily, as though he feared something might explode unless he caused a diversion.

"I haven't the eye for it." Mr. Tallboy shook his head, regretfully.

"Eye for what?" demanded Miss Rossiter.

"For a catapult."

"Oh, go on, Mr. Tallboy! And you such a tennis champion!"

"It's not quite the same thing," explained Mr. Tallboy.

"A games' eye is a games' eye, surely!"

"An eye's an eye for a' that," said Mr. Harris, rather vaguely. "Ever done anything at darts, Mr. Bredon?"

"I won the pewter pot three years running at the Cow and Pump," replied that gentleman, proudly. "With right of free warren—I mean free beer every Friday night for a twelvemonth. It came rather expensive, though, because every time I had my free pot of beer I had to stand about fifteen to the pals who came to see me drink it. So I withdrew myself from the competition and confined myself to giving exhibition displays."

"What's that about darts?"

Mr. Daniels had roamed into view. "Have you ever seen young Binns throw darts? Really quite remarkable."

"I haven't yet the pleasure of Mr. Binns' acquaintance," acknowledged Mr. Bredon. "I am ashamed to say that there are still members of this great staff unknown to me except by sight. Which, of all the merry faces I see flitting about the passages, is the youthful Mr. Binns?"

"You wouldn't have seen him, I don't expect," said Miss Rossiter. "He helps Mr. Spender in the Vouchers. Go along there one day and ask for a back number of some obscure periodical, and Mr. Binns will be sent to fetch it. He's a terrific dab at any sort of game."

"Except bridge," said Mr. Daniels, with a groan. "I drew him one night at a tournament—you remember, Miss Rossiter, the last Christmas party but two, and he went three no trumps on the ace of spades singleton, five hearts to the king, queen and—"

"What a memory you have, Mr. Daniels! You'll never forget or forgive those three no trumps. Poor Mr. Binns! He must miss Mr. Dean—they often lunched together."

Mr. Bredon seemed to pay more attention to this remark than it deserved, for he looked at Miss Rossiter as though he were about to ask her a question, but the conclave was broken up by the arrival of Mrs. Johnson, who, having served out the tea and handed the teapot over to the canteen cook felt that the time had come for her to join in the social side of the event. She was a large, personable widow, with a surprising quantity of auburn hair and a high complexion, and being built on those majestic lines was, inevitably and unrelentingly, arch.

"Well, well," she said, brightly. "And how is Mr. Daniels today?"

Mr. Daniels, having suffered this method of address for nearly twelve years, bore up tolerably well under it, and merely replied that he was quite well.

"This is the first time you have been at one of our monthly gatherings, Mr. Bredon," pursued the widow. "You're *supposed* to make the acquaintance of the rest of the staff, you know, but I see you haven't strayed far from your own department. Ah, well, when we're fat and forty"—here Mrs. Johnson giggled—"we can't expect the same attention from the gentlemen that these young things get."

"I assure you," said Mr. Bredon, "that nothing but an extreme awe of your authority has hitherto prevented me from forcing my impertinent attentions upon you. To tell you the truth, I've been misbehaving myself, and I expect you would give me a rap over the knuckles if you knew what I'd been doing."

"Not unless you've been upsetting my boys," returned Mrs. Johnson, "the young scamps! Take your eye off them a minute and they're up to their games. Would you believe it, that little wretch they call Ginger brought a Yo-Yo to the office with him and broke the window in the boys' room practising 'Round the World' in his lunch-hour. That'll come out of young Ginger's wages."

"I'll pay up when I break a window," promised Mr. Bredon, handsomely. "I shall say: I did it with my little catapult—"

"Catapult!" cried Mrs. Johnson, "I've had quite enough of catapults. There was that Ginger, not a month ago— Let me catch you at it once again, I said."

Mr. Bredon, with raised and twisted eyebrows, exhibited his toy.

"You've been at my desk, Mr. Bredon!"

"Indeed I have not; I shouldn't dare," protested the accused. "I'm far too pure-minded to burgle a lady's desk."

"I should hope so," said Mr. Daniels. "Mrs. Johnson keeps all her letters from her admirers in that desk."

"That's quite enough of that, Mr. Daniels. But I really did think for a moment that was Ginger's catapult, but I see now it's a bit different."

"Have you still got that poor child's catapult? You are a hard-hearted woman."

"I have to be."

"That's bad luck on all of us," said Mr. Bredon. "Look here, let the kid have it back. I like that boy. He says 'Morning, sir,' in a tone that fills me with a pleasant conceit of myself. And I like red hair. To oblige *me*, Mrs. Johnson, let the child have his lethal weapon."

"Well," said Mrs. Johnson, yielding, "I'll hand it over to *you*, Mr. Bredon, and if any more windows are broken it's you will be responsible. Come along to me when the tea-party's over. Now I must go and talk to that other new member."

She bustled away, no doubt to tell Mr. Newbolt, Mr. Hamperley, Mr. Sidebotham, Miss Griggs and Mr. Woodhurst about the childish proclivities of copy-writers. The tea-party dwindled to its hour's end, when Mr. Pym, glancing at the Greenwich-controlled electric clock-face on the wall, bustled to the door, casting vague smiles at all and sundry as he went. The chosen twenty, released from durance, surged after him into the corridor. Mrs. Johnson found Mr. Bredon's slim form drooping deprecatingly beside her.

"Shall I come for the catapult before we both forget about it?"

"Certainly, if you like; you *are* in a hurry," said Mrs. Johnson.

"It promises me a few more minutes in your company," said Mr. Bredon.

"You *are* a flatterer," said Mrs. Johnson, not altogether ill-pleased. After all, she was not very much older than Mr. Bredon, and a plump widowhood has its appeal. She led the way upstairs to the Dispatching department, took a bunch of keys from her handbag and opened a drawer.

"You're careful with your keys, I see. Secrets in the drawer and all that, I suppose?"

"Stamp-money, that's all," said Mrs. Johnson, "and any odds and ends I have to confiscate. Not but what anybody *might* get at my keys if they wanted to, because I often leave my bag on the desk for a few moments. But we've got a very honest set of boys here."

She lifted out a sheet of blotting-paper and a cash-box, and began to rummage at the back of the drawer. Mr. Bredon detained her by laying his left hand on hers.

"What a pretty ring you're wearing."

"Do you like it? It belonged to my mother. Garnets, you know. Old-fashioned, but quaint, don't you think?"

"A pretty ring, and it suits the hand," said Mr. Bredon, gallantly. He held the hand pensively in his. "Allow me." He slipped his right hand into the drawer and brought out the catapult. "This appears to be the engine of destruction —a good, strong one, from the look of it."

"Have you cut your finger, Mr. Bredon?"

"It's nothing; my penknife slipped and it's opened up again. But I think it has stopped bleeding."

Mr. Bredon unwound his handkerchief from his right hand, wrapped it carelessly round the catapult, and dropped both together into his pocket. Mrs. Johnson inspected the finger he held out to her.

"You'd better have a bit of sticking-plaster for that," she pronounced. "Wait a moment, and I'll get you some from the first-aid cupboard." She took up her keys and departed.

Mr. Bredon, whistling thoughtfully to himself, looked round. On a bench at the end of the room sat four messenger-boys, waiting to be sent upon any errand that might present itself. Conspicuous among them was Ginger Joe, his red head bent over the pages of the latest *Sexton Blake*.

"Ginger!"

"Yessir."

The boy ran up and stood expectantly by the desk.

"When do you get off duty tonight?"

"'Bout a quarter to six, sir, when I've taken the letters down and cleared up here."

"Come along then and find me in my room. I've got a small job for you. You need not say anything about it. Just a private matter."

"Yessir." Ginger grinned confidentially. A message to a young lady, his experience told him. Mr. Bredon waved him back to his bench as Mrs. Johnson's footsteps approached.

The sticking-plaster was fixed in its place.

"And now," said Mrs. Johnson, playfully, "you must run away, Mr. Bredon. I see Mr. Tallboy's got a little spot of trouble for me, and I've got fifty stereos to pack and dispatch."

"I want this got down to the printer urgently," said Mr. Tallboy, approaching with a large envelope.

"Cedric!" cried Mrs. Johnson.

A boy ran up. Another lad, arriving from the staircase, dumped a large tray full of stereo-blocks on the desk. The interlude was over. Mrs. Johnson addressed herself briskly to the important task of seeing that the right block went to the right newspaper, and that all were safely packed in corrugated cardboard and correctly stamped.

Punctually at a quarter to six, Ginger Joe presented himself at Mr. Bredon's door. The office was almost empty; the cleaners had begun their rounds, and the chink of pails, the slosh of soap and water and the whirr of the vacuum-cleaner resounded through the deserted corridors.

"Come in, Ginger; is this your catapult?"

"Yessir."

"It's a good one. Made it yourself?"

"Yessir."

"Good shot with it?"

"Pretty fair, sir."

"Like to have it back?"

"Yes, please, sir."

"Well, don't touch it for the moment. I want to see whether you're the sort of fellow to be trusted with a catapult."

Ginger grinned a little sheepishly.

"Why did Mrs. Johnson take it away from you?"

"We ain't supposed to carry them sort of things in our uniform pockets, sir. Mrs. Johnson caught me a-showin' it to the other fellows, sir, and constickated it."

"Confiscated."

"Confiscated it, sir."

"I see. Had you been shooting with it in the office, Ginger?"

"No, sir."

"H'm. You're the bright lad who's broken a window, aren't you?"

"Yessir. But that wasn't with a catapult. It was a Yo-Yo, sir."

"Quite so. You're sure you've never used a catapult in the office?"

"Oh, no, sir, never, sir."

"What made you bring this thing to the office at all?"

"Well, sir—" Ginger stood on one leg. "I'd been telling the other chaps about me shooting me Aunt Emily's tom-cat, sir, and they wanted to see it, sir."

"You're a dangerous man, Ginger. Nothing is safe from you. Tom-cats and windows and maiden aunts—they're all your victims, aren't they?"

"Yessir." Understanding this to be in the nature of a jest, Joe sniggered happily.

"How long ago did this bereavement take place, Ginger?"

"Bereavement, sir? Did you mean Auntie's cat?"

"No, 1 meant, how long ago was your catapult confiscated?"

"Bit over a month ago, it would be, sir."

"About the middle of May?"

"That's right, sir."

"And you've never laid hands on it since?"

"No, sir."

"Have you any other catapult?"

"No, sir."

"Has any of the other boys got a catapult?"

"No, sir."

"Or a sling, or any other infernal machine for projecting stones?"

"No, sir; leastways, not here, sir. Tom Faggott has a pea-shooter at home, sir."

"I said stones, not peas. Did you ever shoot with this, or any other catapult, on the roof?"

"On the roof of the office, sir?"

"Yes."

"No, sir."

"Or anybody else that you know of?"

"No, sir."

"Are you absolutely sure?"

"Nobody that I know of, sir."

"Now, look here, son; I've got an idea that you're a straight sort of fellow, that mightn't like to split on a pal. You're quite sure there isn't anything at all about this catapult that you know and don't like to tell me? Because, if there is, I shall quite understand, and I'll explain to you exactly why it would be better that you should tell me."

Ginger's eyes opened very wide in bewilderment.

"Honest injun, sir," he said, with earnest sincerity, "I don't know nothing at all about no catapult, bar Mrs. Johnson taking that one and putting it away in her desk. Cross me heart and wish I may die, sir."

"All right. What was that book I saw you reading just now?"

Ginger, accustomed to the curious habit grown-up people

have of interrogating their youngers and betters on any un-related subjects that happen to strike a roving fancy, replied without hesitation or surprise:

"*The Clue of the Crimson Star*, sir. About Sexton Blake; he's a detective, you know, sir. It's a top-hole yarn."

"Like detective-stories, Ginger?"

"Oh, yes, sir. I reads a lot of them. I'm going to be a detective one day, sir. My eldest brother's in the police, sir."

"Is he? Splendid fellow. Well, the first thing a detective has to learn to do is to keep his mouth shut. You know that?"

"Yessir."

"If I show you something now, can you keep quiet about it?"

"Yessir."

"Very well. Here's a ten-bob note. Hop out to the nearest chemist and get me some grey powder and an insufflator."

"What sort of powder, sir?"

"Grey powder—mercury powder—the man will know. And an insufflator; it's a little rubber bulb with a nozzle to it."

"Yessir."

Ginger Joe hopped with speed.

"An ally," said Mr. Bredon to himself, "an ally—indispensable, I fear, and I fancy I've picked the right one."

Ginger came panting back in record time. He scented adventure. Mr. Bredon, in the meantime, had attached a discreet curtain of brown paper to the glass panel of his door. Mrs. Crump was not surprised. That proceeding was familiar to her. It usually meant that a gentleman was going out, and wished to change his trousers in a decent privacy.

"Now," said Mr. Bredon, shutting the door, "we will see whether your catapult can tell us anything about its adventures since it left your hands." He filled the insufflator with the grey powder and directed an experimental puff upon the edge of the desk. On blowing away the surplus powder, he thus disclosed a surprising collection of greasy finger-prints. Ginger was enthralled.

"Cool!" he said, reverently. "Are you going to test the catapult for prints, sir?"

"I am. It will be interesting if we find any, and still more interesting if we find none."

Ginger, goggle-eyed, watched the proceedings. The catapult appeared to have been well polished by use and presented an admirable surface for finger-prints, had there been any, but though they covered every half-inch of the thick Y-fork with powder, the result was a blank. Ginger looked disappointed.

"Ah!" said Bredon. "Now is it that it will not, or that it cannot speak? We will make that point clear. Catch hold of the thing, Ginger, as though you were whanging a shot off."

Ginger obeyed, clutching grimly with his greasy little paw.

"That ought to give 'em," said his new friend, "the whole of the palms of the fingers round the handle and the ball of the thumb in the fork. Now we'll try again."

The insufflator came once more into play, and this time a noble set of markings sprang into view.

"Ginger," said Mr. Bredon, "what do you, as a detective, deduce from this?"

"Mrs. Johnson must a-wiped it, sir."

"Do you think that's very likely, Ginger?"

"No, sir."

"Then go on deducing."

"Somebody else must a-wiped it, sir."

"And why should somebody else do that?"

Ginger knew where he was now.

"So that the police couldn't fix nothing on him, sir."

"The police, eh?"

"Well, sir, the police—or a detective—or somebody like as it might be yourself, sir."

"I can find no fault with that deduction, Ginger. Can you go further and say why this unknown catapult artist should have gone to all that trouble?"

"No, sir."

"Come, come."

"Well, sir, it ain't as though he stole it—and besides, it ain't worth nothing."

"No; but it looks as though somebody had borrowed it, if he didn't steal it. Who could do that?"

"I dunno, sir. Mrs. Johnson keeps that drawer locked."

"So she does. Do you think Mrs. Johnson has been having a little catapult practice on her own?"

"Oh, no, sir. Women ain't no good with catapults."

"How right you are. Well, now, suppose somebody had sneaked Mrs. Johnson's keys and taken the catapult and broken a window or something with it, and was afraid of being found out?"

"There ain't been nothing broke in this office, not between Mrs. Johnson pinching my catapult and me breaking the window with the Yo-Yo. And if one of the boys had took the catapult, I don't think they'd think about fingerprints, sir."

"You never know. He might have been playing burglars or something and just wiped his fingerprints away out of dramatic instinct, if you know what that is."

"Yessir," agreed Ginger, in a dissatisfied tone.

"Particularly if he'd done some really bad damage with it. Or of course, it might be more than dramatic instinct. Do you realize, Ginger, that a thing like this might easily kill anybody, if it happened to catch him in just the right spot?"

"Kill anybody? Would it, sir?"

"I wouldn't like to try the experiment. Was your aunt's tom-cat killed?"

"Yessir."

"That's nine lives at a blow, Ginger, and a man has only one. You're quite sure, sonnie, that nobody you know of was larking about with this catapult the day Mr. Dean fell downstairs?"

Ginger flushed and turned pale; but apparently only with excitement. His small voice was hoarse as he answered:

"No, sir. Wish I may die, sir, I never see nothing of that. You don't think somebody catapulted Mr. Dean, sir?"

"Detectives never 'think' anything," replied Mr. Bredon, reprovingly. "They collect facts and make deductions—God forgive me!" The last three words were a whispered lip-service to truth. "Can you remember who might have happened to be standing round or passing by when Mrs. Johnson took that catapult from you and put it in her desk?"

Ginger considered.

"I couldn't say right off, sir. I was just coming upstairs to the Dispatching when she spotted it. She was behind me, you see, sir, and it made me pocket stick out, like. A-jawing me, she was, all up the stairs, and took it off of me at the top and sent me down again with the basket to Mr. 'Ornby. I never see her put it away. But some of the other boys may have. 'Course, I knowed it was there, because all the things as is confisticated—"

"Confiscated."

"Yessir—confiscated, gets put in there. But I'll ask round, sir."

"Don't let them know why you're asking."

"No, sir. Would it do if I said I believed somebody had been borrowing of it and spiled the elastic for me?"

"That would do all right, provided—"

"Yessir. Provided I recollecks to spile the elastic."

Mr. Bredon, who had already jabbed a penknife into his own finger that afternoon in the sacred cause of verisimilitude, smiled lovingly upon Ginger Joe.

"You are the kind of man I am proud to do business with," he said. "Here's another thing. You remember when Mr. Dean was killed. Where were you at the time?"

"Sittin' on the bench in the Dispatching, sir. I got an alibi." He grinned.

"Find out for me, if you can, how many other people had alibis."

"Yessir."

"It's rather a job, I'm afraid."

"I'll do me best, sir. I'll make up somefin', don't you

worry. It's easier for me to do it than it is for you, I see that, sir. I say, sir!"

"Yes?"

"Are you a Scotland Yard 'tec?"

"No, I'm not from Scotland Yard."

"Oh! Begging your pardon for asking, sir. But I thought, if you was, you might be able, excuse me, sir, to put in a word for my brother."

"I might be able to do that, all the same, Ginger."

"Thank you, sir."

"Thank *you*," replied Mr. Bredon, with the courtesy which always distinguished him. "And mum's the word, remember."

"Wild 'orses," declared Ginger, finally and completely losing his grasp of the aitches with which a careful nation had endowed him at the expense of the tax-payer, "wild 'orses wouldn't get a word out o' me when I've give me word to 'old me tongue."

He ran off. Mrs. Crump, coming along the passage with a broom, was surprised to find him still hanging about the place. She challenged him, received an impudent answer, and went her way, shaking her head. A quarter of an hour later, Mr. Bredon emerged from his seclusion. As she had expected, he was in evening dress and looking, she thought, very much the gentleman. She obliged by working the lift for him. Mr. Bredon, the ever-polite, expanded and assumed his gibus during the descent, apparently for the express purpose of taking it off to her when he emerged.

In a taxi rolling south-west, Mr. Bredon removed his spectacles, combed out his side-parting, stuck a monocle in his eye, and by the time he reached Piccadilly Circus was again Lord Peter Wimsey. With a vacant wonder he gazed upon the twinkling sky-signs, as though, ignorant astronomer, he knew nothing of the creative hands that had set these lesser lights to rule the night.

CHAPTER VII

ALARMING EXPERIENCE OF A CHIEF-INSPECTOR

ON THAT same night, or rather in the early hours of the following morning, a very disagreeable adventure befell Chief-Inspector Parker. He was the more annoyed by it, in that he had done absolutely nothing to deserve it.

He had had a long day at the Yard—no thrills, no interesting disclosures, no exciting visitors, not so much as a dis-diamonded rajah or a sinister Chinaman—only the reading and summarizing of twenty-one reports of interviews with police narks, five hundred and thirteen letters from the public in response to a broadcast S O S about a wanted man, and a score or so of anonymous letters, all probably written by lunatics. In addition, he had had to wait for a telephone call from an inspector who had gone down to Essex to investigate some curious movements of motor-boats in and about the estuary of the Blackwater. The message, if favourable, might call for immediate action, on which account Mr. Parker thought it better to wait for it in his office than go home to bed, with the prospect of being hawked out again at 1 o'clock in the morning. There, then, he sat, as good as gold, collating information and drawing up a schedule of procedure for the following day's activities, when the telephone duly rang. He glanced at the clock, and saw that it pointed to 1.10. The message was brief and unsatisfactory. There was nothing to report; the suspected boat had not arrived with that tide; no action was therefore called for; Chief-Inspector Parker could go home and get what sleep he could out of the small hours.

Mr. Parker accepted disappointment as philosophically as the gentleman in Browning's poem, who went to the trouble and expense of taking music lessons just in case his lady-love might demand a song with lute *obbligato*. Waste of time, as it turned out, but—suppose it hadn't been. It was all in the day's work. Putting his papers tidily away and locking his desk, the Chief-Inspector left the building, walked down to the Embankment, took a belated tram through the subway to Theobald's Road and thence walked soberly to Great Ormond Street.

He opened the front door with his latch-key and stepped inside. It was the same house in which he had long occupied a modest bachelor flat, but on his marriage he had taken, in addition, the flat above his own, and thus possessed what was, in effect, a seven-roomed maisonette, although, on account of a fiddling L.C.C. regulation about access to the roof for the first-floor tenants in case of fire, he was not permitted to shut his two floors completely off by means of a door across the staircase.

The front hall, common to all the tenants, was in darkness when he got in. He switched on the light and hunted in the little glass-fronted box labelled "Flat 3—Parker" for letters. He found a bill and a circular and deduced, quite correctly, that his wife had been at home all evening and too tired or too slack to go down to fetch the 9.30 post. He was turning to go upstairs, when he remembered that there might be a letter for Wimsey, under the name of Bredon, in the box belonging to Flat 4. As a rule, of course, this box was not used, but when Wimsey had begun his impersonation at Pym's, his brother-in-law had provided him with a key to fit it and had embellished the box itself with a written label "Bredon," for the better information of the postman.

There was one letter in the "Bredon" box—the kind that novelists used to call a "dainty missive"; that is to say, the envelope was tinted mauve, had a gilt deckle-edge and was addressed in a flourishing feminine handwriting. Parker took it out, intending to enclose it with a note which he

was sending to Wimsey in the morning, pushed it into his
pocket and went on up to the first floor. Here he switched
out the hall-light which, like the staircase lights, was fitted
with two-way wiring, and proceeded to the second floor,
containing Flat 3, which comprised his living-room, dining-
room and kitchen. Here he hesitated, but, rather unfortunately for himself, decided that he did not really want soup
or sandwiches. He switched off the lower light behind him
and pressed down the switch that should have supplied light
to the top flight. Nothing nappened. Parker growled but was
not surprised. The staircase lights were the affair of the
landlord, who had a penurious habit of putting in cheap
bulbs and leaving them there till the filament broke. By
this means he alienated his tenants' affections, besides wasting more in electricity than he saved in bulbs, but then he
was that kind of man. Parker knew the stairs as well as he
knew the landlord's habits; he went on up in the dark, not
troubling to light a match.

Whether the little incident had, however, put his professional subconsciousness on the alert, or whether some faint
stir of breath or movement gave him last-minute warning,
he never afterwards knew. He had his key in his hand, and
was about to insert it in the lock when he dodged suddenly
and instinctively to the right, and in that very instant the
blow fell, with murderous violence, on his left shoulder. He
heard his collar-bone crack as he flung himself round to
grapple with the villainous darkness, and even as he did so
he found himself thinking: "If I hadn't dodged, my bowler
would have broken the blow and saved my collar-bone."
His right hand found a throat, but it was protected by a
thick muffler and a turned-up collar. He struggled to get
his fingers inside this obstacle, at the same time that, with
his semi-disabled left arm, he warded off the second blow
which he felt was about to descend upon him. He heard the
other man panting and cursing. Then the resistance suddenly gave way, and, before he could loose his grip he
was lurching forward, while a jerked knee smote him with
brutal violence in the stomach, knocking the wind out of

him. He staggered, and his opponent's fist crashed upon his jaw. In his last seconds of consciousness before his head struck the ground, he thought of the weapon in the other's hand and gave up hope.

Probably his being knocked out saved his life. The crash of his fall woke Lady Mary. For a stunned moment she lay, wondering. Then her mind rushed to the children, asleep in the next room. She turned on the light, calling out as she did so to ask whether they were all right. Receiving no answer, she sprang up, threw on a dressing-gown and ran into the nursery. All was peace. She stood puzzled, and asking herself whether she had dreamed the crash. Then she heard feet running down the staircase at headlong speed. She ran back into the bedroom, pulled out the revolver which always lay loaded in the dressing-table drawer and flung open the door which gave upon the landing. The light streaming from behind her showed her the crumpled body of her husband, and as she stared aghast at this unnerving sight, she heard the street-door slam heavily.

"What you ought to have done," said Mr. Parker, acidly, "was not to have bothered about me, but dashed to the window and tried to get a squint at the bloke as he went down the street."

Lady Mary smiled indulgently at this absurd remark, and turned to her brother.

"So that's all I can tell you about it, and he's uncommonly lucky to be alive, and ought to be jolly well thankful instead of grumbling."

"You'd grumble all right," said Parker, "with a bust collar-bone and a headache like nothing on earth and a feeling as though bulls of Bashan had been trampling on your tummy."

"It beats me," said Wimsey, "the way these policemen give way over a trifling accident. In the Sexton Blake book that my friend Ginger Joe has just lent me, the great detective, after being stunned with a piece of lead-piping and trussed up for six hours in ropes which cut his flesh nearly to the bone, is taken by boat on a stormy night to a remote house on the coast and flung down a flight of stone steps into a stone cellar. Here he contrives to release himself from his bonds after three hours' work on the edge of a broken wine-bottle, when the villain gets wise to his activities and floods the cellar with gas. He is most fortunately rescued at the fifty-ninth minute of the eleventh hour and, pausing only to swallow a few ham sandwiches and a cup of strong coffee, instantly joins in a prolonged pursuit of the murderers by aeroplane, during which he has to walk out along the wing and grapple with a fellow who has just landed on it from a rope and is proposing to chuck a hand-grenade into the cockpit. And here is my own brother-in-law—a man I have known for nearly twenty years —giving way to bad temper and bandages because some three-by-four crook has slugged him one on his own comfortable staircase."

Parker grinned ruefully.

"I'm trying to think who it could have been," he said. "It wasn't a burglar or anybody like that—it was a deliberate attempt at murder. The light-bulb had been put out of action beforehand and he had been hiding for hours behind the coal-bunker. You can see the marks of his feet. Now, who in the name of goodness have I got it in for to that extent? It can't be Gentleman Jim or Dogsbody Dan, because that's not their line of country at all. If it had happened last week, it might well have been Knockout Wally—he uses a cosh—but we jailed him good and hard for that business down in Limehouse on Saturday night. There are one or two bright lads who have it in for me one way or another, but I can't exactly fit it on to any of them. All I know is, that whoever it was, he must have got in here before 11 p.m., when the housekeeper shuts the street door and puts out the hall light. Unless, of course, he had a latch-key, but that's not so likely. He wasn't obliging enough to leave anything behind to identify him, except a Woolworth pencil."

"Oh, he left a pencil, did he?"

"Yes—one of those pocket propelling things—not a wooden one—you needn't hope for a handy mould of his front teeth on it, or anything like that."

"Show, show!" pleaded Wimsey.

"All right; you can see it if you like. I've tried it for finger-prints, but I can't get much—only vague smudges, very much superimposed. I've had our finger-print wallah round to look at 'em, but he doesn't seem to have made anything of 'em. See if you can find the pencil, Mary dear, for your little brother. Oh, and by the way, Peter, there's a letter for you. I've only just remembered. In my left coat-pocket, Mary. I'd just taken it out of the Flat 4 box when all this happened."

Mary sped away, and returned in a few minutes with the pencil and the coat.

"I can't find any letter."

Parker took the coat and, with his available hand, searched all the pockets carefully.

"That's funny," he said. "I know it was there. One of those fancy long-shaped mauve envelopes with gilt edges, and a lady's fist, rather sprawly."

"Oh!" said Wimsey, "the letter's gone, has it?" His eyes glinted with excitement. "That's very remarkable. And what's more, Charles, this isn't a Woolworth pencil—it's one of Darling's."

"I meant Darling's—same thing. Anybody might carry one of them."

"Ah!" said Wimsey, "but this is where my expert knowl-edge comes in. Darling's don't sell these pencils—they give them away. Anybody buying more than a pound's worth of goods gets a pencil as a good-conduct prize. You observe that it carries an advertising slogan: IT ISN'T DEAR, IT'S DARLING. (One of Pym's best efforts, by the way.) The idea is that, every time you make a note on your shopping list, you are reminded of the superior economy of purchasing your household goods from Darling's. And a very remark-able firm it is, too," added his lordship, warming to the subject. "They've carried the unit system to the pitch of a fine art. You can sit on a Darling chair, built up in shilling and sixpenny sections and pegged with patent pegs at sixpence a hundred. If Uncle George breaks the leg, you buy a new leg and peg it in. If you buy more clothes than will go into your Darling chest of drawers, you unpeg the top, purchase a new drawer for half a crown, peg it on and replace the top. Everything done by numbers, and kindness. And, as I say, if you buy enough, they give you a pencil. If you mount up to five pounds' worth, they give you a fountain pen."

"That's very helpful," said Parker, sarcastically. "It ought to be easy to identify a criminal who has bought a pound's worth of goods at Darling's within the last six months or so."

"Wait a bit; I said I had expert knowledge. This pencil—a natty scarlet, as you observe, with gold lettering—didn't come from any of Darling's branches. It's not on the market yet. There are only three places it could have come from: one, from the pencil manufacturer's; two, from Darling's head office; three, from our place."

"Do you mean Pym's?"

"I do. This is the new pencil design, with an improved propelling mechanism. The old ones only propelled; this repels also, with a handy twist of the what-d'ye-call. Darling's obligingly presented us with half a gross of them to try out."

Mr. Parker sat up so suddenly that he jarred his shoulder and his head, and groaned dismally.

"I think it highly improbable," went on Lord Peter, lusciously, "that you have a deadly enemy at the pencil manufacturer's or at Darling's head office. It seems to me much more likely that the gentleman with the cosh, or knuckle-duster, or sand-bag, or lead-piping, in short, the blunt instrument, came from Pym's, guided by the address which, with your usual amiability, you kindly allowed me to give as mine. Observing my name neatly inscribed on the letter-box of Flat 4, he mounted confidently, armed with his cosh, knuckle—"

"Well, I'm dashed!" exclaimed Lady Mary, "do you mean to say that it's really you, you devil, who ought to be lying there mangled and bruised in the place of my afflicted husband?"

"I think so," said Wimsey, with satisfaction, "I certainly do think so. Particularly as the assailant seems to have walked off with my private correspondence. I know who—or to be grammatical, whom—that letter was from, by the way."

"Who?" demanded Parker, disregarding the grammatical nicety.

"Why, from Pamela Dean, to be sure. I recognize your description of the envelope."

"Pamela Dean? The victim's sister?"

"As you say."

"Willis's young woman?"

"Precisely."

"But how should he know about the letter?"

"I don't suppose he did. I rather fancy this is the result of a little bit of self-advertisement I put in yesterday afternoon at the office tea-party. I made it clear to all and sundry that I had been experimenting on the roof with a catapult."

"Did you? Who, exactly, were the all and sundry?"

"The twenty people taking tea and all the other people they mentioned it to."

"Rather a wide limit."

"M'm, yes. I thought I might get some reaction. What a pity it reacted on you and not on me."

"A very great pity," agreed Mr. Parker, with feeling.

"Still, it might have been worse. We've got three lines to go upon. The people who heard about the catapult. The people who knew, or inquired for, my address. And, of course, the bloke who's lost his pencil. But, I say—" Wimsey broke off with a shout of laughter—"what a shock it must have been for whoever it was when I turned up this morning without so much as a black eye! Why in the name of creation didn't you let me have all the details first thing this morning, so that I could have kept a look-out?"

"We were otherwise employed," said Lady Mary.

"Besides, we didn't think it had anything to do with you."

"You should have guessed. Wherever trouble turns up, there am I at the bottom of it. But I'll overlook it this time. You have been sufficiently punished, and no one shall say that a Wimsey could not be magnanimous. But this blighter —you didn't manage to mark him, Charles, did you?"

"Afraid not. I got a clutch on his beastly throat, but he was all muffled up."

"You did that badly, Charles. You should have socked him one. But, as I said before, I forgive you. I wonder if our friend will have another shot at me."

"Not at this address, I hope," said Mary.

"*I* hope not. I'd like to have him under my own eye next time. He must have been pretty smart to get that letter. Why in the world—ah! now I understand."

"What?"

"Why nobody fainted at the sight of me this morning. He must have had a torch with him. He knocks you down and turns on the torch to see if you're properly dead. The first thing he spots is the letter. He grabs that—why? Because—we'll come back to that. He grabs it and then looks at your classic features. He realizes that he's slugged the wrong man, and at that very moment he hears Mary making a hullabaloo. So he clears. That's perfectly plain now. But the letter? Would he have taken any letter that happened to be there, or did he know the writing? When was that letter delivered? Yes, of course, the 9.30 post. Suppose, when he came in to look for my flat, he saw the letter in the box and recognized whom it was from. That opens up a wide field of speculation, and possibly even offers us another motive."

"Peter," said Lady Mary, "I don't think you ought to sit here exciting Charles with all this speculation. It'll send his temperature up."

"So it will, by Jove! Well, look here, old boy, I'm really fearfully sorry you copped that packet that was meant for me. It's perfectly damnable luck and I'm dashed thankful it was no worse. I'll buzz off now. I've got to, anyhow. I've got a date. So-long."

Wimsey's first action after leaving the flat was to ring up Pamela Dean, whom he fortunately found at home. He explained that her letter had been lost in transmission, and asked what was in it.

"Only a note from Dian de Momerie. She wants to know who you are. You seem to have made a remarkable hit."

"We aim to please," said Peter. "What have you done about it?"

"Nothing. I didn't know what you would like me to do."

"You didn't give her my address?"

"No. That was what she was asking for. I didn't want to make another mistake, so I passed it all on to you."

"Quite right."

"Well?"

"Tell her—does she know that I'm at Pym's?"

"No, I was very careful to say absolutely nothing about you. Except your name. I did tell her that, but she seems to have forgotten it."

"Good. Listen, now. Tell bright Dian that I'm a most mysterious person. You never know where to find me yourself. Hint that I'm probably miles away—in Paris or Vienna, or anything that sounds fruity. You can convey the right impression, I know. Phillips Oppenheim, with a touch of Ethel M. Dell and Elinor Glyn."

"Oh, yes, I can do that."

"And you might say that she will probably see me some time when she least expects it. Suggest, if you don't mind being so vulgar, that I am a sort of yellow-dog dingo, very truly run after and hard to catch. Be stimulating. Be intriguing."

"I will. Am I at all jealous, by the way?"

"Yes, if you like. Give the impression that you're sort of putting her off. It's a hard chase and you're not keen on competitors."

"All right. That won't be difficult."

"What did you say?"

"Nothing. I said I could manage that all right."

"I know you'll do it beautifully. I rely on you very much."

"Thank you. How is the enquiry getting on?"

"So-so."

"Tell me all about it some time, won't you?"

"Rather! As soon as there's anything to report."

"Will you come to tea one Saturday or Sunday?"

"I should love to."

"I'll keep you to that."

"Oh, yes, rather! Well, goodnight."

"Goodnight—Yellow-Dog Dingo."

"Bung-ho!"

Wimsey put down the receiver. "I hope," he thought, "she isn't going to make an awkwardness. You cannot trust these young women. No fixity of purpose. Except, of course, when you particularly want them to be yielding."

He grinned with a wry mouth, and went out to keep his date with the one young woman who showed no signs of yielding to him, and what he said or did on that occasion is in no way related to this story.

Ginger Joe hoisted himself cautiously up in bed and looked round the room.

His elder brother—not the policeman, but sixteen-year-old Bert, the nosey one—was reassuringly asleep, curled up dog-fashion, and dreaming, no doubt, of motor-cycles. The faint light from the street lamp outlined the passive hump he made in the bedclothes, and threw a wan gleam across Ginger's narrow bedstead.

From beneath his pillow, Ginger drew out a penny exercise book and a stubby pencil. There was very little privacy in Ginger's life, and opportunities had to be seized when they occurred. He licked the pencil, opened the book, and headed a page in a large, round hand: "Report."

There he paused. It was desirable to do this thing really creditably, and the exercises in English composition they had given him at school did not seem to help. "My Favourite Book," "What I Should Like to Do when I Grow Up," "What I Saw at the Zoo"—very good subjects but not of great assistance to a rising young detective. He had once been privileged to take a glimpse at Wally's note-book (Wally being the policeman), and remembered that the items had all begun somewhat in this fashion: "At 8.30 p.m., as I was proceeding along Wellington Street"—a good opening, but not applicable to the present case. The style of *Sexton Blake,* also, though vigorous, was more suited for the narration of stirring adventures than for the compilation of a catalogue of names and facts. And on the top of all this, there was the awkward question of spelling—always a stumbling-block. Ginger felt vaguely that an ill-spelt report would have an untrustworthy appearance.

In this emergency, he consulted his native commonsense, and found it a good guide.

"I better just begin at the beginning," he said to himself, and, pressing heavily upon the paper and frowning desperately, began to write.

"REPORT
by Joseph L. Potts
(aged 14½)"

On consideration, he thought this needed a little more corroborative detail, and added his address and the date. The report then proceeded:

"I had a talk with the boys about the *catter* (erased) cattapult. Bill Jones says he reckollects of me standing in the Dispatch and Mrs. Johnson collering of the cattapult. Sam Tabbit and George Pyke was there too. What I says to them was as Mr. Bredon give me back the cattapult and it have the bit of leather tore and I wants to know who done it. They all says they never been to Mrs. Johnson's draw and I think they was tellin the truth sir because Bill and Sam is good sorts and you can always tell if George is fibbing because of the way he looks and he was looking alright. So then I says could it have been any of the others and they says they have not seen none of them with catta-pults so I makes out to be very angry and says it's a pitty a boy can't have his cattapult *confist* confiskcated without somebody goes and tears of it. And then Clarence Metcalfe comes along which he is head boy sir and asks what's up so I tells him and he says if anybody's been at Mrs. John-sons draw its very serious. So he gets arsking them all and they all says no but Jack Bolter remembers of Mrs. Johnson leaving her bag on the desk one day and Miss Parton pick-ing it up and taking of it down to the canteen. I says when? And he says it was about two days after my cattapult was *confik* took away, and the time just after lunch sir. So you see sir it would have been laying there an hour sir when no-body was about.

Now sir about who else was there and might have seen it took. Now I comes to think I remember Mr. Prout was there at the head of the stairs because he passed a remark to Mrs. Johnson and pulled my ear and there was one of the young ladies I think it was Miss Hartley waiting to get a messenger. And after I gone down to Mr. Hornby Sam says as Mr. Wedderburn came along and him and Mrs. Johnson had a bit of a joke about it. But sir I expecks lots of people knew about it because Mrs. Johnson would tell them in the canteen. She is always telling tales on we boys sir I suppose she thinks its funny.

This is all I has to report about the cattapult sir. I has not yet made any inquiry about the other matter thinking one was enough at a time or they might think I was askin a lot of questions but I have thought of a plan for that.

Yours respeckfully

J. POTTS.

"What the devil are you doing there, Joe?"

Ginger, too absorbed in his report to have kept a proper look-out upon Bert, started violently, and thrust the exercise book under his pillow.

"Never you mind," he said, nervously. "It's private."

"Oh, is it?"

Bert flung the bedclothes aside and advanced, a threatening figure.

"Writing poitry?" he demanded, with contempt.

"It's nothing to do with you," retorted Ginger. "You leave me be."

" 'And that there book over," said Bert.

"No, I won't."

"You won't, won't you?"

"No, I won't. Get out!"

Ginger clasped the document with agitated hands.

"I'm going to 'ave a look—leggo!"

Ginger was a wiry child for his years and spirited, but his hands were hampered by the book, and the advantages of height, weight and position were with Bert. The struggle was noisy.

"Let me go, you beastly great bully."

"I'll teach you to call names! Cheeky little beast."

"Ow!" wailed Ginger. "I won't, I won't, I tell you! it's private!"

Whack! wallop!

"Nah then!" said a stately voice, "wot's all this?"

"Wally, tell Bert to leave me be."

"He didn't oughter cheek me. I only wanted ter know wot he was doin', sittin' up writin' poitry w'en he oughter a-bin asleep."

"It's private," persisted Ginger. "Really and truly, it's frightfully private."

"Can't yer leave the kid alone?" said P. C. Potts, magisterially, "makin' all this noise. You'll wake Dad and then you'll both get a 'iding. Now both of you 'op back to bed or I'll 'ave ter take you up for disturbing the peace. And you did oughter be asleep, Joe, and not writing poitry."

"It ain't poitry. It's something I was doing for a gentle-man at the office and he said I wasn't to tell nobody."

"Well, see here," said Wally Potts, extending a vast of-ficial fist. "You 'and over that there book to me, see? I'll put it away in my drawer and you can 'ave it again in the morning. And now go to sleep for goodness' sake, both on yer."

"You won't read it, will yer, Wally?"

"All right, I won't read it if you're so bloomin' per-ticler."

Ginger, reluctant but confident of Wally's honour, re-luctantly released the exercise-book.

"That's right," said Wally, "and if I 'ear any more larkin' about you're for it, both of yer. See wot I mean?"

He stalked away, gigantic in his striped pyjamas.

Ginger Joe, rubbing the portions of himself which had suffered in the assault, rolled the bed-clothes about him and took comfort in telling himself a fresh instalment of that nightly narrative of which he was both author and hero.

"Bruised and battered, but unshaken in his courage, the famous detective sank back on his straw pallet in the rat-ridden dungeon. In spite of the pain of his wounds, he was happy, knowing that the precious documents were safe. He laughed to think of the baffled Crime King, gnashing his teeth in his gilded oriental saloon. 'Foiled yet again, Hawk-eye!' growled the villainous doctor, 'but it will be my turn next!' Meanwhile . . ."

The life of a detective is a hard one.

CHAPTER VIII

CONVULSIVE AGITATION
OF AN ADVERTISING AGENCY

IT WAS on the Friday of the week in which all these stirring incidents occurred that Pym's Publicity, Ltd. became
convulsed by the Great Nutrax Row, which shook the
whole office from the highest to the lowest, turned the peaceful premises into an armed camp and very nearly ruined
the Staff Cricket Match against Brotherhood's, Ltd.

The hardworking and dyspeptic Mr. Copley was the
prime mover of all the trouble. Like most fomenters of
schism, he acted throughout with the best intentions—and
indeed, when one looks back upon the disturbance in the
serene perspective of distance and impartiality, it is difficult
to see what he could have done, other than what he did.
But as Mr. Ingleby observed at the time, "It isn't what
Copley *does,* it's the way he does it"; and in the heat and
fury of the battle, when the passions of strong men are
aroused, judgment easily becomes warped.

The thing started in this way:

At a quarter past six on the Thursday evening, the office
was deserted, except for the cleaners and Mr. Copley, who,
by an altogether exceptional accident, was left working
overtime upon a rush series of cut-price advertisements for
Jamboree Jellies. He was getting along nicely, and hoped to
be through by half-past six and home in good time for 7.30
supper, when the telephone in the Dispatching rang violently and insistently.

"Dash it!" said Mr. Copley, annoyed by the din, "they
119

ought to know the office is closed. You'd think they expected us to work all night."

He went on working, trusting that the nuisance would
cease of itself. Presently it did cease, and he heard the shrill
voice of Mrs. Crump informing the caller that there was
nobody in the office. He took a soda-mint tablet. His sentence was shaping itself beautifully. "The authentic flavour
of the fresh home-grown orchard fruit—of apricots ripening
in the sunny warmth of an old, walled garden . . ."

"Excuse me, sir."

Mrs. Crump, shuffling apologetically in her carpet slip-
pers, poked a nervous head round the door.

"What is it now?" said Mr. Copley.

"Oh, if you please, sir, it's the *Morning Star* on the telephone very urgent, asking for Mr. Tallboy. I told them they
was all gone 'ome, but they says it's very important, sir, so I
thought I'd better ask you."

"What's it all about?"

"Somethink about the advertisement for tomorrow morning, sir—somethink's gone wrong and they say, did it ought
to be left out altogether or can we send them somethink
else, sir?"

"Oh, well!" said Mr Copley, resigned, "I suppose I'd better come and speak to them."

"I dunno whether I done right, sir," continued Mrs.
Crump, anxiously pattering after him, "but I thought, sir,
if there *is* a gentleman in the office I ought to tell him
about it, because I didn't know but what it mightn't be important—"

"Quite right, Mrs. Crump, quite right," said Mr. Copley.
"I daresay I can settle it."

He strode competently to the telephone and grasped the
receiver.

"Hullo!" he said, petulantly, "Pym's here. What's the
matter?"

"Oh!" said a voice. "Is that Mr. Tallboy?"

"No. Mr. Tallboy's gone home. Everybody's gone home
You ought to know that by this time. What is it?"

"Well," said the voice, "it's about that Nutrax half-double for tomorrow's feature page."

"What about it? Haven't you had it?"

(Just like Tallboy, thought Mr. Copley. No organization. You never could trust these younger men.)

"Yes, we've got it," said the voice, doubtfully, "but Mr. Weekes says we can't put it in. You see—"

"Can't put it in?"

"No. You see, Mr.—"

"I'm Mr. Copley. It's not in my department. I really know nothing about it. What's the matter with it?"

"Well, if you had it there before you, you'd see what I mean. You know the headline—"

"No, I don't," snapped Mr. Copley, exasperated. "I tell you it's not my business and I've never seen the thing."

"Oh!" said the voice, with irritating cheerfulness. "Well, the headline is: ARE YOU TAKING TOO MUCH OUT OF YOUR-SELF? And, taken in conjunction with the sketch, Mr. Weekes thinks it might lay itself open to an unfortunate interpretation. If you had it there before you, I think you'd see what he means."

"I see," said Mr. Copley, thoughtfully. Fifteen years' experience told him that this was disaster. There was no arguing with it. If the *Morning Star* got it into their heads that an advertisement contained some lurking indelicacy, that advertisement would not be printed, though the skies fell. Indeed, it was better that it should not. Errors of this kind lowered the prestige of the product and of the agency responsible. Mr. Copley had no fancy for seeing copies of *Morning Star* sold at half-a-crown a time in the Stock Exchange to provide a pornographer's holiday.

In the midst of his annoyance, he felt the inward exultation of the Jeremiah whose prophecies have come true. He had always said that the younger generation of advertising writers were No Good. Too much of the new-fangled University element. Feather-headedness. No solid business sense. No thought. But he was well-trained. He carried the war instantly into the enemy's camp.

"You ought to let us know earlier," he said, severely. "It's ridiculous to ring up at a quarter past six, when the office is closed. What do you expect us to do about it?"

"Not our fault," said the voice, brightly. "It only came in ten minutes ago. We're always asking Mr. Tallboy to let us have the blocks in better time, just to prevent this kind of situation."

More and more confirmation of Mr. Copley's prophecies. General slackness—that was what it was. Mr. Tallboy had left promptly at 5.30. Mr. Copley had seen him go. Clock-watchers, the whole lot of them. Tallboy had no business to leave before he had got an assurance from the paper that the block was received and that all was in order. Moreover, if the messenger had not delivered the parcel to the *Morning Star* till 6.5, he had either started too late, or had dawdled on the way. More bad management. That Johnson woman —no control, no discipline. Before the War there would have been no women in advertising offices, and none of these silly mistakes.

Still, something must be done.

"Very unfortunate," said Mr. Copley. "Well, I'll see if I can get hold of somebody. What's your last moment for making an alteration?"

"Must have it down here by 7 o'clock," said the voice, ineluctably. "As a matter of fact, the foundry is waiting for that sheet now. We only want your block to lock the forme. But I've spoken to Wilkes, and he says he can give you till seven."

"I'll ring you," said Mr. Copley, and rang off.

Rapidly his mind raced over the list of people who were fitted to cope with the situation. Mr. Tallboy, the Group-manager; Mr. Wedderburn, his Group-secretary; Mr. Armstrong, the copy-chief responsible; the writer of the copy, whoever he was; in the last resort, Mr. Pym. It was a most unfortunate moment. Mr. Tallboy lived at Croydon, and was probably still swaying and sweltering in the train; Mr. Wedderburn—he really had no idea where he lived, except that it was probably in some still more remote suburb. Mr.

Armstrong lived in Hampstead; he was not in the tele-
phone-book, but his private number would doubtless be
on the telephone-clerk's desk; there was some hope of catching him. Mr. Copley hurried downstairs, found the list and
the number and rang up. After two wrong numbers, he got
the house. Mr. Armstrong's housekeeper replied. Mr. Armstrong was out. She could not say where he had gone or
when he would return. Could she take a message? Mr. Copley replied that it didn't matter and rang off again. Half-
past six.

He consulted the telephonist's list again. Mr. Wedderburn did not appear upon it and presumably was not on
the 'phone. Mr. Tallboy's name was there. Without much
hope, Mr. Copley got on to the Croydon number, only to
hear, as he expected, that Mr. Tallboy had not yet returned.
His heart sinking, Mr. Copley rang up Mr. Pym's house.
Mr. Pym had just that minute left. Where for? It was
urgent. Mr. and Mrs. Pym were dining at Frascati's with
Mr. Armstrong. This sounded a little more hopeful. Mr.
Copley rang up Frascati's. Oh, yes. Mr. Pym had engaged a
table for 7.30. He had not yet arrived. Could they give a
message when he did arrive? Mr. Copley left a message to
ask Mr. Pym or Mr. Armstrong to ring him up at the office
before 7 o'clock if possible, but he felt convinced that nothing could possibly come of it. No doubt these gadding directors had gone to a cocktail party somewhere. He looked
at the clock. It was 6.45. As he looked, the telephone rang
again.

It was, as he had expected, the *Morning Star,* impatient
for instructions.

"I can't get hold of anybody," explained Mr. Copley.

"What are we to do? Leave it out altogether?"

Now, when you see in a newspaper a blank white space,
bearing the legend: "THIS SPACE RESERVED FOR SO-AND-SO
LTD.," it may mean nothing very much to you, but to those
who know anything of the working of advertising agencies,
those words carry the ultimate, ignominious brand of in-
competency and failure. So-and-so's agents have fallen down

on their job; nothing can be alleged in mitigation. It is the Thing That Must Not Happen.

Mr. Copley, therefore, while savagely reflecting that it would serve the whole bunch of slackers and half-wits right if the space *was* left blank, ejaculated hastily: "No, no! on no account. Hold the line one moment. I'll see what I can do." In so doing he acted very properly, for it is the first and almost the only rule of business morality that the Firm must come first.

Dashing hastily along the passage, he entered Mr. Tallboy's room, which was on the same floor as the Dispatching and Copy departments, on the far side of the iron staircase. One minute brought him there; another minute, spent rummaging in Mr. Tallboy's drawers, gave him what he wanted —an advance proof of the wretched Nutrax half-double. A glance showed him that Mr. Weekes's doubts were perfectly justified. Each harmless enough in itself, sketch and headline together were deadly. Without waiting to wonder how so obvious a gaffe had escaped the eagle eyes of the department chiefs, Mr. Copley sat down and pulled out his pocket pencil. Nothing now could be done about the sketch; it must stand; his job was to find a new headline which would suit the sketch and the opening line of the copy, and contain approximately the same number of letters as the original.

Hurriedly he jotted down ideas and crossed them out. "WORK AND WORRY SAP NERVE-STRENGTH"—that was on the right lines, but was a few letters short. It was rather flat, too; and besides, it wasn't quite true. Not work—over-work was what the copy was talking about. "WORRY AND OVERWORK"—no good, it lacked rhythm. "OVERWORK AND OVERWORRY"—far better, but too long. As it stood, the headline filled three lines (too much, thought Mr. Copley, for a half-double), being spaced thus:

Are you Taking
TOO MUCH OUT
OF YOURSELF?

He scribbled desperately, trying to save a letter here and there. "NERVOUS FORCE"? "NERVE-FORCE"? "NERVE-POWER"? The minutes were flying. Ah? how about this?

OVER-WORK &

OVER-WORRY—

waste Nerve-Power!

Not brilliant, but dead on the right note, unexceptionable and offering no difficulties about spacing. On the point of rushing back to the 'phone it occurred to him that the instrument on Mr. Tallboy's desk might have been left connected to the switchboard. He removed the receiver; a reassuring buzz assured him that it was so. He spoke urgently:

"Are you there?"

"Yes."

"Look here. Can you cut away the headline and re-set in Goudy Bold?"

"Ye-es—Yes, we can just do that if we get it at once."

"I'll dictate it."

"Right-ho! Fire away."

"Start exactly where you start now with 'ARE YOU TAKING.' First line in caps, same size as the caps you've got there for 'TOO MUCH OUT.' Right. This is the line: 'OVER-WORK &'— with hyphen in Over-work and an ampersand. Got that?"

"Yes."

"Next line. Same size. Start two ems further in. 'OVER-WORRY.' Hyphen. Dash. Got that?"

"Yes."

"Now, third line, Goudy 24-point upper and lower. Start under the W. 'Waste Nerve-Power!' Capital N, capital P, and screamer. Got that?"

"Yes; I'll repeat. First line Goudy caps., starting level with cap A of present headline. O,V,E,R, hyphen, W,O,R,K, ampersand; second line, same fount, 2 ems to the right, O,V,E,R, hyphen, W,O,R,R,Y, dash. Third line. Start under W, Goudy 24 point upper and lower: lower-case w,a,s,t,e, capital N,e,r,v,e, hyphen, capital P,o,w,e,r, screamer. That O.K.?"

"That's right. Much obliged."

"Not at all. Much obliged to you. Sorry to bother you. Good-bye."

"Good-bye."

Mr. Copley sank back, mopping his brow. It was done. The firm was saved. Men had been decorated for less. When it came to an emergency, when all the jumped-up jacks-in-office had deserted their posts, it was on him, Mr. Copley, the old-fashioned man of experience, that Pym's Publicity had to depend. A man who could grapple with a situation. A man not afraid of responsibility. A man whose heart and soul were wrapped up in his job. Suppose he had rushed off home on the stroke of half-past five, like Tallboy, caring nothing whether his work was done or not—what would have happened? Pym's would have been in the cart. He would have something to say about it in the morning. He hoped it would be a jolly good lesson to them.

He pulled the roll-top of Mr. Tallboy's desk down again over the disgracefully untidy set of pigeon-holes and the cluttered mass of paper that it nightly concealed, and as he did so, received fresh proof of the disorderliness of Mr. Tallboy's habits. From some mysterious nook where it had become caught up, a registered envelope dislodged itself, and fell with a plump little flop to the floor.

Mr. Copley stooped at once and picked it up. It was addressed in block letters to J. Tallboy, Esq., at the Croydon address, and had already been opened. Peeping in at the slit end, Mr. Copley observed what could be nothing but a thickish wad of green currency notes. Yielding to a not unnatural impulse, Mr. Copley pulled them out, and counted, to his astonishment and indignation, no less than fifty of them.

If there was one action more than another which Mr. Copley condemned as Thoughtless and Unfair (long advertising practice had given him a trick of thinking in capital letters), it was Putting Temptation in People's Way.

Here was the colossal sum of Fifty Pounds, so carelessly secured that the mere opening of the desk sent it skittering to the floor, for Mrs. Crump and her corps of charladies to find. No doubt they were all very honest women, but in these Hard Times, a working woman could hardly be blamed if she succumbed. Worse still, suppose the precious envelope had got swept up and destroyed. Suppose it had fallen into the wastepaper basket and thence made its way to the sack and the paper-makers, or, still worse, to the furnace. Some innocent person might have been Falsely Accused, and laboured for the rest of her life under a Stigma. It was intolerable of Mr. Tallboy. It was Really Wicked.

Of course, Mr. Copley realized exactly what had happened. Mr. Tallboy had received this Large Sum (from whom? there was no covering letter; but that was hardly Mr. Copley's business. Possibly these were winnings on dog-races, or something equally undesirable) and had brought it to the office, intending to bank it at the Metropolitan & Counties Bank at the corner of Southampton Row, where the majority of the staff kept their accounts. By some accident, he had been prevented from doing this before the Bank closed. Instead of bestowing the envelope safely in his pocket, he had thrust it into his desk, and at 5.30 had rushed off home in his usual helter-skelter way, and forgotten all about it. And if he had since given another thought to it, reflected Mr. Copley indignantly, it was probably only to assume that it would be "perfectly all right." The man really ought to be given a lesson.

Very well, he *should* be given a lesson. The notes should be placed in safe custody and he, Mr. Copley, would give Mr. Tallboy a good talking-to in the morning. He hesitated for a moment as to the best plan. If he took the notes away with him, there was the possibility that he might have his pocket picked on the way home, which would be very unfortunate and expensive. It would be better to take them to his own room and lock them securely in the bottom drawer of his own desk. Mr. Copley congratulated himself upon the conscientious foresight that had prompted him to ask for a drawer with a proper lock.

He accordingly carried the packet to his room, put it safely away underneath a quantity of confidential papers dealing with future campaigns for tinned food and jellies, tidied up his own desk and locked it, pocketed the keys, brushed his hat and coat and took his virtuous departure, not forgetting to replace the telephone receiver upon its hook as he passed through the Dispatching.

He emerged from the doorway into the street, and crossed the road before turning south to the Theobalds Road tram-terminus. On gaining the opposite pavement, he happened to glance back, and saw the figure of Mr. Tallboy coming up on the other side from the direction of Kingsway. Mr. Copley stood still and watched him. Mr. Tallboy turned into Pym's entrance and disappeared.

"Aha!" said Mr. Copley to himself, "he's remembered about the money after all."

It is at this point that Mr. Copley's conduct is perhaps open to censure. A charitable fellow-feeling would, one imagines, have prompted him to dodge back through the traffic, to return to Pym's, to take the lift to the top floor, to seek out the anxious Mr. Tallboy and to say to him: "Look here, old man, I found a registered packet of yours sculling about and put it away in safety and, by the bye, about that half-double for Nutrax—" But he did not.

Let us remember, in mitigation, that it was now half-past seven, that there was no chance of his getting back to his evening meal much before half-past eight, that he was of dyspeptic habit and dependent upon regular hours, and that he had had a long day, concluding with an entirely unnecessary piece of worry and hustle occasioned by Mr. Tallboy's tiresomeness.

"Let him suffer for it," said Mr. Copley, grimly. "It serves him right."

He caught his tram and departed on his tedious way to a remote northern suburb. As he jolted and ground along, he planned to himself how, next day, he would score over Mr.

Tallboy and earn commendations from the powers that
were.

There was one factor with which Mr. Copley, in his an-
ticipatory triumph, had failed to reckon; namely, that to
obtain the full effect and splendour of his *coup de théâtre*
it was necessary for him to get to the office before Mr. Tallboy. In his day-dream, he had taken this for granted—
naturally so, since he was a punctual man at all times, and
Mr. Tallboy was apt to be more punctual in departing than
in arriving. Mr. Copley's idea was that, after making a
stately report to Mr. Armstrong at 9 o'clock, in the course
of which Mr. Tallboy would be called in and admonished,
he should then take the repentant Group-manager privately to one side, read him a little lecture on orderliness
and thought for others, and hand him over his fifty pounds
with a paternal caution. Meanwhile, Mr. Armstrong would
mention the Nutrax incident to the other directors, who
would congratulate themselves on having so reliable, experienced, and devoted a servant. The words sang themselves into a little slogan in Mr. Copley's head: "You can
Count on Copley in a Crisis."

But things did not turn out that way. To begin with, Mr.
Copley's late arrival on the Thursday night plunged him
into a domestic storm which lasted into the night and still
muttered with thunderous reverberations on the following
morning.

"I suppose," said Mrs. Copley, acidly, "that while you
were telephoning to all these people, it was too much trouble to think of your *wife*. I don't count at all, naturally.
It's nothing to *you* that I should be left imagining all kinds
of things. Well, don't blame *me* if the chicken is roasted to
a chip and the potatoes are sodden, and you get indigestion."

The chicken *was* roasted to a chip; the potatoes *were*
sodden; and, in consequence, Mr. Copley did get a violent
indigestion, to which his wife was obliged to minister with
soda-mint and bismuth and hot-water bottles, voicing her
opinion of him at every application. Not until six o'clock in

the morning did he fall into a heavy and unrefreshing slumber, from which he was aroused at a quarter to eight by hearing Mrs. Copley say:

"If you are going to the office today, Frederick, you had better get up. If you are *not* going, you may as well say so, and I will send a message. I have called you three times, and your breakfast is getting cold."

Mr. Copley, with a bilious headache over his right eye and a nasty taste in his mouth, would gladly have authorized her to send the message—gladly have turned over upon his pillow and buried his woes in sleep, but the recollection of the Nutrax half-double and the fifty pounds rushed over him in a flood and swept him groaning from between the sheets. Seen in the morning light, to the accompaniment of black spots dancing before his eyes, the prospect of his triumph had lost much of its glamour. Still, he could not let it go with a mere explanation by telephone. He must be on the spot. He shaved hastily, with a shaking hand and cut himself. The flow of blood would not be staunched. It invaded his shirt. He snatched the garment off, and called to his wife for a clean one. Mrs. Copley supplied it—not without reprimand. It seemed that the putting on of a clean shirt on a Friday morning upset the entire economy of the household. At ten minutes past eight, he came down to a breakfast he could not eat, his cheek ludicrously embellished with a tuft of cotton-wool and his ears ringing with migraine and conjugal rebuke.

It was impossible, now, to catch the 8.15. Sourly, he caught the 8.25.

At a quarter to nine, the 8.25 was hung up for twenty minutes outside King's Cross on account of an accident to a goods train.

At 9.30, Mr. Copley crawled drearily into Pym's, wishing he had never been born.

As he entered the office from the lift, the reception-clerk greeted him with a message that Mr. Armstrong would like to see him at once. Mr. Copley, savagely signing his name far away below the red line which divided the punctual from the dilatory, nodded, and then wished he had not, as a pang of agony shot through his aching head. He mounted the stair and encountered Miss Parton, who said brightly:

"Oh, *here* you are, Mr. Copley! We thought you were lost. Mr. Armstrong would like to see you."

"I'm just going," said Mr. Copley, savagely. He went to his room and took off his coat, wondering whether a phenacetin would cure his headache or merely make him sick. Ginger Joe knocked at the door.

"If you please, sir, Mr. Armstrong says, could you spare him a moment."

"All right, all right," said Mr. Copley. He tottered out into the passage, and nearly fell into the arms of Mr. Ingleby.

"Hullo!" said the latter, "you're wanted, Copley! We were just sending out the town-crier. You'd better nip along to Armstrong pronto. Tallboy's out for your blood."

"Ar'rh!" said Mr. Copley.

He shouldered Mr. Ingleby aside and went on his way, only to encounter Mr. Bredon, lurking at the door of his own room, armed with an imbecile grin and a jew's harp.

"See the conquering hero comes," cried Mr. Bredon, following up this remark with a blast upon his instrument.

"Jackanapes!" said Mr. Copley. Whereupon, to his horror, Mr. Bredon executed three handsome cart-wheels before him down the passage, finishing up accurately before Mr. Armstrong's door, and just out of Mr. Armstrong's line of sight.

Mr. Copley knocked upon the glass panel, through which he could see Mr. Armstrong, seated at his desk, Mr. Tallboy, upright and indignant, and Mr. Hankin standing, with his usual air of mild hesitation, on the far side of the room. Mr. Armstrong looked up and beckoned Mr. Copley in.

"Ah!" said Mr. Armstrong, "here's the man we want. Rather late this morning, aren't you, Mr. Copley?"

Mr. Copley explained that there had been an accident on the line.

"Something must be done about these accidents on **the**

line," said Mr. Armstrong. "Whenever Pym's staff travels, the trains break down. I shall have to write to the Superintendent of the line. Ha, ha!"

Mr. Copley realized that Mr. Armstrong was in one of his frivolous and tiresome moods. He said nothing.

"Now, Mr. Copley," said Mr. Armstrong, "what's all this about the Nutrax half-double? We've just had an agitated telegram from Mr. Jollop. I can't get hold of the *Morning Star* man—what's his name?"

"Weekes," said Mr. Tallboy.

"Weekes—golly, what a name! But I understand—or Mr. Tallboy understands—from somebody or other, that you altered the Nutrax headline last night. I've no doubt you've got an excellent explanation, but I should like to know just what we've got to say to Mr. Jollop."

Mr. Copley pulled himself together and embarked on an account of the previous night's crisis. He felt that he was not doing himself justice. Out of the tail of his eye, he could see the dab of cotton-wool on his cheek waggling absurdly as he spoke. He pointed out with emphasis and acerbity the extremely unfortunate suggestion conveyed by the sketch and the original headline.

Mr. Armstrong burst into a hoot of laughter.

"My God!" he shouted. "They've got us there, Tallboy! Ho, ho, ho! Who wrote the headline? I must tell Mr. Pym about this. Why the devil didn't you catch it, Tallboy?"

"It never occurred to me," said Mr. Tallboy, unaccountably crimson in the face. Mr. Armstrong hooted again.

"I think Ingleby wrote it," added Mr. Tallboy.

"Ingleby, of all people!" Mr. Armstrong's mirth was not to be restrained. He pushed the buzzer on his desk. "Miss Parton, ask Mr. Ingleby to step in here."

Mr. Ingleby arrived, cool and insolent as ever. Mr. Armstrong, half speechless with joy, thrust the original pull of the advertisement at him, with a comment so barbarically outspoken that Mr. Copley blushed.

Mr. Ingleby, unabashed, capped the comment with a remark still more immodest, and Miss Parton, lingering, note-book in hand, gave a refined snigger.

"Well, sir," said Ingleby, "it's not my fault. My original rough was illustrated with a very handsome sketch of a gentleman overwhelmed with business cares. If the inno-cents in the Studio choose to turn down my refined sugges-tion in favour of a (male epithet) and a (female epithet) who look as though they'd been making a night of it, I re-fuse to be responsible."

"Ha, ha!" said Mr. Armstrong. "That's Barrow all over. I don't suppose Barrow—"

The end of the sentence was more complimentary to the Studio-chief's virtue than to his virility. Mr. Hankin sud-denly exploded into a loud snicker of laughter.

"Mr. Barrow is rather fond of cashiering any suggestion put forward by the Copy Department," said Mr. Copley. "I hardly like to suggest that there is any inter-depart-mental jealousy behind it, but the fact remains—"

But Mr. Armstrong was feeling hilarious, and paid no attention. He recited a limerick, amid applause.

"Well, it's all right, Mr. Copley," he said, when he had partially recovered himself. "You did quite right. I'll send an explanation to Mr. Jollop. He'll have a fit."

"He'll be surprised that *you* passed it," said Mr. Hankin.

"Well he may be," agreed Mr. Armstrong, pleasantly. "It isn't often I overlook anything indecent. I must have been off-colour that day. So must you, Tallboy. Oh, dear! Mr. Pym will have something to say about it. I shall enjoy seeing his face. I only wish it had gone through. He'd have sacked the whole department."

"It would have been very serious," said Mr. Copley.

"Of course it would. I'm very glad the *Morning Star* spotted it. All right. Now that's settled. Mr. Hankin, about that whole page for Sopo—"

"I hope," said Mr. Copley, "you are satisfied with what I did. There wasn't much time—"

"Quite all right, quite all right," said Mr. Armstrong. "Very much obliged to you. But, by the way, you might have let somebody know. I was left rather up in the air this morning."

Mr. Copley explained that he had endeavoured to get into touch with Mr. Pym, Mr. Armstrong, Mr. Tallboy and Mr. Wedderburn, but without success.

"Yes, yes, I see," said Mr. Armstrong. "But why didn't you ring up Mr. Hankin?"

"I am always at home by six," added Mr. Hankin, "and it is very seldom that I go out. When I do, I always leave directions where I am to be found." (This was a dig at Mr. Armstrong.)

Dismay seized upon Mr. Copley. He had clean forgotten Mr. Hankin, and he knew well enough that Mr. Hankin, mild as were his manners, was quick to resent anything in the nature of a slight.

"Of course," he stammered. "Of course, yes, I might have done that. But Nutrax being your client, Mr. Armstrong— I thought—it never occurred to me that Mr. Hankin—"

This was a bad tactical error. It was, to begin with, contrary to the great Pym Principle that any member of the Copy Department was supposed to be ready to carry on with any part of the work at any time, if called upon. And it also suggested that Mr. Hankin was, in that respect, less versatile than Mr. Copley himself.

"Nutrax," said Mr. Hankin, in a thin manner, "is certainly not a favourite account of mine. But I have coped with it in my time." (This was another side-blow at Mr. Armstrong, who had temperamental periods when he was apt to hand all his clients over to Mr. Hankin, pleading nervous exhaustion.) "It is really no further outside my scope than that of the junior copy-writers."

"Well, well," said Mr. Armstrong, perceiving that Mr. Hankin was on the point of doing the undesirable thing, and ticking off a member of the department before a member of another department, "it's not of any great consequence, and you did your best in an awkward crisis. Nobody can think of everything. Now, Mr. Hankin"—he dismissed the small fry with a nod—"let's get this Sopo question settled once and for all. Don't go, Miss Parton, I want you to take a note. I'll see to Nutrax, Mr. Tallboy. Don't worry."

The door closed behind Mr. Copley, Mr. Ingleby and Mr. Tallboy.

"My God!" said Ingleby, "what a howl! Went with a bang from start to finish. It only wanted Barrow to make it complete. That reminds me, I'll have to go and pull his leg. This'll teach him to turn down my intelligent suggestions. Hullo! there's the Meteyard. I must tell her what Armstrong said about old Barrow."

He dived into Miss Meteyard's room, from which unlady-like shouts of mirth were soon heard to proceed. Mr. Copley, feeling as though his head were filled with hard knobs of spinning granite that crashed with sickening thuds against his brain-pan, walked stiffly away to his own quarters. As he passed the Dispatching, he had a vision of Mrs. Crump, in tears, standing before Mrs. Johnson's desk, but he paid no attention. His one agonized yearning was to shake off Mr. Tallboy, who padded grimly at his heels.

"Oh, Mr. Tallboy!"

Mrs. Johnson's rather shrill voice came to Mr. Copley like an order of release. He shot home like a bolting rabbit. He must try phenacetin and chance the consequences. Hastily he swallowed three tablets without even troubling to fetch a glass of water, sat down in his revolving chair and closed his eyes.

Crash, crash, crash, went the lumps of granite in his brain. If only he could remain where he was, quite quietly, for half an hour—

The door was flung violently open.

"Look here, Copley," said Mr. Tallboy, in a voice like a pneumatic drill, "when you were hugger-muggering round with my desk last night did you have the unprintable bloody impertinence to interfere with my private belongings?"

"For heaven's sake," moaned Mr. Copley, "don't make such a row. I've got a splitting headache."

"I don't care a highly-coloured damn if you've got a headache or not," retorted Mr. Tallboy, flinging the door to behind him with a slam like the report of an 11-inch gun. "There was an envelope in my desk last night with fifty pounds in it, and it's gone, and that old (epithet) Mrs. Crump says she saw you (vulgar word)-ing about among my papers."

"I have your fifty pounds here," replied Mr. Copley, with as much dignity as he could muster. "I put it away safely for you, and I must say, Tallboy, that I consider it extremely thoughtless of you to leave your property about for the charwomen to find. It's not fair. You should have more consideration. And I did not rummage about in your desk as you suggest. I merely looked for the pull of the Nutrax half-double, and when I was closing the desk, this envelope fell out upon the floor."

He stooped to unlock the drawer, experiencing a ghastly qualm as he did so.

"You mean to tell me," said Mr. Tallboy, "that you had the all-fired cheek to take my money away to your own damned room—"

"In your own interests," said Mr. Copley.

"Interests be damned! Why the devil couldn't you leave it in a pigeon-hole and not be so blasted interfering?"

"You do not realize—"

"I realize this," said Mr. Tallboy, "that you're an expurgated superannuated interfering idiot. What you wanted to come poking your blasted nose in for—"

"Really, Mr. Tallboy—"

"What business was it of yours, anyway?"

"It was anybody's business," said Mr. Copley—so angry that he almost forgot his headache—"who had the welfare of the firm at heart. I am considerably older than you, Tallboy, and in my day, a Group-manager would have been ashamed to leave the building before ascertaining that all was well with his advertisement for the next day's paper. How you came to let such an advertisement pass in the first place is beyond my understanding. You were then late with the block. Perhaps you do not know that it was not received by the *Morning Star* till five minutes past six—*five minutes past six.* And instead of being at your post to consider any necessary corrections—"

"I don't want you to teach me my job," said Mr. Tallboy.

"Pardon me, I think you do."

"Anyhow, what's that got to do with it? The point is, you stick your nose into my private affairs—"

"I did not. The envelope fell out—"

"That's a bloody lie."

"Pardon me, it is the truth."

"Don't keep saying 'pardon me' like a bloody kitchenmaid."

"Leave my room!" shrieked Mr. Copley.

"I'm not going to leave your damned room till I get an apology."

"I think I ought to receive the apology."

"*You?*" Mr. Tallboy became almost inarticulate. "You—! Why the hell couldn't you have had the decency to ring me up and tell me, anyway?"

"You weren't at home."

"How do you know? Did you try?"

"No. I knew you were out, because I saw you in Southampton Row."

"You saw me in Southampton Row, and you hadn't the ordinary common decency to get hold of me and tell me what you'd been after? Upon my word, Copley, I believe you jolly well *meant* to get me into a row. And collar the cash for yourself, too, I shouldn't wonder."

"How dare you suggest any such thing?"

"And all your rot about consideration for the charwomen! It's sheer damned hypocrisy. Of course I thought one of them had had it. I told Mrs. Crump—"

"You accused Mrs. Crump?"

"I didn't accuse her. I told her I had missed fifty pounds."

"That just shows you," began Mr. Copley.

"And fortunately she'd seen you at my desk. Otherwise, I suppose I should never have heard anything more about my money."

"You've no right to say that."

"I've a damn sight more right to say it than you had to steal the money."

"Are you calling me a thief?"

"Yes, I am."

"And I call you a scoundrel," gasped Mr. Copley, beside himself, "an insolent scoundrel. And I say that if you came by the money honestly, which I doubt, sir, which I very much doubt—"

Mr. Bredon poked his long nose round the door.

"I say," he bleated anxiously, "sorry to butt in, and all that, but Hankie's compliments and he says, would you mind talking a little more quietly? He's got Mr. Simon Brotherhood next door."

A pause followed, in which both parties realized the thinness of the beaverboard partition between Mr. Hankin's room and Mr. Copley's. Then Mr. Tallboy thrust the recovered envelope into his pocket.

"All right, Copley," he said. "I shan't forget your kind interference." He bounced out.

"Oh, dear, oh, dear," moaned Mr. Copley, clasping his head in his hands.

"Is anything up?" queried Mr. Bredon.

"Please go away," pleaded Mr. Copley, "I'm feeling horribly ill."

Mr. Bredon withdrew on catlike feet. His inquisitive face beamed with mischief. He pursued Mr. Tallboy into the Dispatching, and found him earnestly talking to Mrs. Johnson.

"I say, Tallboy," said Mr. Bredon, "what's wrong with Copley? He looks jolly fed-up. Have you been twisting his tail?"

"It's no affair of yours, anyway," retorted Mr. Tallboy, sullenly. "All right, Mrs. J., I'll see Mrs. Crump and put it right with her."

"I hope you will, Mr. Tallboy. And another time, if you have any valuables, I should be obliged if you would bring them to me and let me put them in the safe downstairs.

These upsets are not pleasant, and Mr. Pym would be greatly annoyed if he knew about it."

Mr. Tallboy fled for the lift without vouchsafing any reply.

"Atmosphere seems a bit hectic this morning, Mrs. Johnson," observed Mr. Bredon, seating himself on the edge of the good lady's desk. "Even the presiding genius of the Dispatching looks a trifle ruffled. But a righteous indignation becomes you. Gives sparkle to the eyes and a clear rosiness to the complexion."

"Now that'll do, Mr. Bredon. What will my boys think if they hear you making fun of me? Really, though, some of these people are *too* trying. But I must stand up for my women, Mr. Bredon, and for my boys. There isn't one of them that I wouldn't trust, and it isn't right to bring accusations with nothing to support them."

"It's simply foul," agreed Mr. Bredon. "Who's been bringing accusations?"

"Well, I don't know if I ought to tell tales out of school," said Mrs. Johnson, "but it's really only justice to poor Mrs. Crump to say—"

Naturally, in five minutes' time, the insinuating Mr. Bredon was in possession of the whole story.

"But you needn't go and spread it all round the office," said Mrs. Johnson.

"Of course I needn't," said Mr. Bredon. "Hullo! is that the lad with our coffee?"

He sprang alertly from his perch and hastened into the typists' room, where Miss Parton was detailing to a prick-eared audience the more juicy details of the morning's scene with Mr. Armstrong.

"That's nothing," announced Mr. Bredon. "You haven't heard the latest development."

"Oh, *what* is it?" cried Miss Rossiter.

"I've promised not to tell," said Mr. Bredon.

"Shame, shame!"

"At least, I didn't exactly promise. I was asked not to."

"Is it about Mr. Tallboy's money?"

"You do know, then? What a disappointment!"

"I know that poor little Mrs. Crump was crying this morning because Mr. Tallboy had accused her of taking some money out of his desk."

"Well, if you know that," said Mr. Bredon artlessly, "in justice to Mrs. Crump—"

His tongue wagged busily.

"Well, I think it's too bad of Mr. Tallboy," said Miss Rossiter. "He's always being rude to poor old Copley. It's a shame. And it's rotten to accuse the charwomen."

"Yes, it is," agreed Miss Parton, "but I've no patience with that Copley creature. He's a tiresome old sneak. He went and told Hankie once that he'd seen me at the dog-races with a gentleman friend. As if it was any business of his what a girl does out of business hours. He's too nosey by half. Just because anybody's a mere typist it doesn't mean one's a heathen slave. Oh! here's Mr. Ingleby. Coffee, Mr. Ingleby? I say, *have* you heard about old Copley pinching Mr. Tallboy's fifty quid?"

"You don't say so," exclaimed Mr. Ingleby, shooting a miscellaneous collection of oddments out of the waste-paper basket as a preliminary to up-turning it and sitting upon it. "Tell me quickly. Golly! what a day we're having!"

"Well," said Miss Rossiter, lusciously taking up the tale, "somebody sent Mr. Tallboy fifty pounds in a registered envelope—"

"What's all this?" interrupted Miss Meteyard, arriving with some sheets of copy in one hand and a bag of bulls' eyes in the other. "Here are some lollipops for my little ones. Now let's hear it all from the beginning. I only wish people would send *me* fifty poundses in registered envelopes. Who was the benefactor?"

"I don't know. Do you know, Mr. Bredon?"

"Haven't the foggiest. But it was all in currency notes, which is suspicious, for a start."

"And he brought them to the office, meaning to take them to the Bank."

"But he was busy," chimed in Miss Parton, "and forgot all about them."

"Catch me forgetting about fifty pounds," said Miss Parton's bosom-friend from the Printing.

"Oh, we're only poor hardworking typists. Fifty pounds or so is nothing to Mr. Tallboy, obviously. He put them in his desk—"

"Why not in his pocket?"

"Because he was working in his shirt-sleeves, and didn't like to leave all that wealth hanging on a coat-peg—"

"Nasty suspicious nature the man's got—"

"Yes; well, he forgot them at the lunch-hour. And in the afternoon, he found that the blockmaker had done something silly with the Nutrax block—"

"Was that what delayed it?" inquired Mr. Bredon.

"Yes, that was it. And, I say, I've found out something else. Mr. Drew—"

"Who's Mr. Drew?"

"That stout man from the Cormorant Press. He said to Mr. Tallboy he thought the headline was a bit hot. And Mr. Tallboy said he had a nasty mind and anyhow, everybody had passed it and it was too late to alter it then—"

"Jiminy!" said Mr. Garrett, suddenly bursting into speech, "it's a good thing Copley didn't get hold of that. He'd have rubbed it in, all right. I must say, I think Tallboy ought to have done something about it."

"Who told you that?"

"Mr. Wedderburn. Drew asked him about it this morning. Said he noticed they'd thought better of it after all."

"Well, get on with the story."

"By the time Mr. Tallboy had had the block put right, the Bank was shut. So he forgot about it again, and went off, leaving the fifty quid in his desk."

"Does he often do that sort of thing?"

"Goodness knows. And old Copley was working late on his jellies—"

Clack, clack, clack. The story lost nothing in the telling.

"—poor old Mrs. Crump was weeping like a sponge—"

"—Mrs. Johnson was in *such* a bait—"

"—making a most *awful* row. Mr. Bredon heard them. What did he call him, Mr. Bredon?"

"—accused him of stealing the money—"

"—thief and scoundrel—"

"—what Mr. Brotherhood must have thought—"

"—give them the sack, I shouldn't wonder—"

"—my dear, the *thrills* we get in this place!"

"And, by the way," observed Mr. Ingleby, maliciously, "I pulled Barrow's leg all right about that sketch."

"You *didn't* tell him what Mr. Armstrong said?"

"No. At least, I didn't tell him Mr. Armstrong said it. But I gave him a hint to that effect off my own bat."

"You are awful!"

"He's out for the blood of this department—especially Copley's."

"Because Copley went to Hankie last week about a Jamboree display and complained that Barrow didn't follow his directions, and so now he thinks this business is a plot of Copley's to—"

"Shut up!"

Miss Rossiter leapt at her typewriter and began to pound the keys deafeningly.

Amid a pointed silence of tongues, Mr. Copley made his entrance.

"Is that Jelly copy of mine ready, Miss Rossiter? There doesn't seem to be much work being done here this morning."

"You've got to take your turn, Mr. Copley. I have a report of Mr. Armstrong's to finish."

"I shall speak to Mr. Armstrong about the way the work is done," said Mr. Copley. "This room is a bear-garden. It's disgraceful."

"Why not give Mr. Hankin a turn?" snapped Miss Parton, unpleasantly.

"No, but really, Copley, old sport," pleaded Mr. Bredon, earnestly. "You mustn't let these little things get your goat. It's not done, old thing. Positively not done. You watch me squeeze copy out of Miss Parton. She eats out of my hand. A little kindness and putting her hair in papers will work wonders with her. Ask her nicely and she'll do anything for you."

"A man of your age, Bredon, should know better," said Mr. Copley, "than to hang round here all day. Am I the only person in this office with work to do?"

"If you only knew it," replied Mr. Bredon, "I'm working away like anything. Look here," he added, as the unhappy Mr. Copley withdrew, "do the poor old blighter's muck for him. It's a damned shame to tease him. He's looking horribly green about the gills."

"Right-ho!" said Miss Parton, amiably, "I don't mind if I do. May as well get it over."

The typewriters clacked again.

CHAPTER IX

UNSENTIMENTAL MASQUERADE
OF A HARLEQUIN

DIAN DE MOMERIE was holding her own. True, the big Chrysler and the Bentley ahead of her had more horsepower, but young Spenlow was too drunk to last out, and Harry Thorne was a notoriously rotten driver. She had only to tail them at a safe distance till they came to grief. She only wished "Spot" Lancaster would leave her alone. His clumsy grabs at her waist and shoulders interfered with her handling of the car. She eased the pressure of her slim sandal on the accelerator, and jabbed an angry elbow into his hot face.

"Shut up, you fool! you'll have us into the ditch, and then they'd beat us."

"I say! protested Spot, "don't do that. It hurts."

She ignored him, keeping her eye on the road. Everything was perfect tonight. There had been a most stimulating and amusing row at Tod Milligan's, and Tod had been very definitely told where he got off. All the better. She was getting tired of Tod's hectoring. She was keyed up just enough and not too much. The hedges flashed and roared past them; the road, lit by the raking headlights, showed like a war-worn surface of holes and hillocks, which miraculously smoothed themselves out beneath the spinning wheels. The car rode the earth-waves like a ship. She wished it were an open car and not this vulgar, stuffy saloon of Spot's.

The Chrysler ahead was lurching perilously, thrashing her great tail like a fighting salmon. Harry Thorne had no business with a car like that; he couldn't hold it on the road. And there was a sharp S-bend coming. Dian knew that. Her senses seemed unnaturally sharpened—she could see the road unrolled before her like a map. Thorne was taking the first bend—far too wide—and young Spenlow was cutting in on the left. The race was hers now—nothing could prevent it. Spot was drinking again from a pocket-flask. Let him. It left her free. The Chrysler, wrenched brutally across the road, caught the Bentley on the inner edge of the bend, smashing it against the bank and slewing it round till it stood across the road. Was there room to pass? She pulled out, her off wheels bumping over the grass verge. The Chrysler staggered on, swaying from the impact—it charged the bank and broke through the hedge. She heard Thorne yell—saw the big car leap miraculously to earth without overturning, and gave an answering cry of triumph. And then the road was suddenly lit up as though by a search-light, whose powerful beam swallowed her own headlights like a candle in sunlight.

She leant over to Spot.

"Who's that behind us?"

"Dunno," grunted Spot, twisting ineffectually to stare through the small pane at the rear of the car. "Some blighter or other."

Dian set her teeth. Who the hell, who the *hell* had a car like that? The driving mirror showed only the glare of the enormous twin lights. She drove the accelerator down to its limit, and the car leaped forward. But the pursuer followed easily. She swung out on the crown of the road. Let him crash if he wanted to. He held on remorselessly. A narrow, hump-backed bridge sprang out of the darkness. She topped it and seemed to leap the edge of the world. A village, with a wide open square. This would be the man's chance. He took it. A great dark shape loomed up beside her, long, low and open. Out of the tail of her eye she sought the driver. For five seconds he held beside her, neck and neck, and she saw the black mask and skull-cap and the flash of black and silver. Then, in the narrowing of the street, he swept ahead. She remembered what Pamela Dean had told her:

"You will see him when you least expect him."

Whatever happened, she must hold on to him. He was running ahead now, lightly as a panther, his red tail-lamp tantalizingly only a few yards away. She could have cried with exasperation. He was playing with her.

"Is this all your beastly Dutch-oven will do?"

Spot had fallen asleep. His head rolled against her arm and she shook it off violently. Two miles, and the road plunged beneath over-arching trees, with a stretch of woodland on either side. The leading car turned suddenly down a side-road and thence through an open gate beneath the trees; it wound its way into the heart of the wood, and then abruptly stopped; all its lights were shut off.

She jammed on her brakes and was out upon the grass. Overhead the treetops swung together in the wind. She ran to the other car; it was empty.

She stared round. Except for the shaft of light thrown by her own headlamps, the darkness was Egyptian. She stumbled over her long skirts among briars and tufts of bracken. She called:

"Where are you? Where are you hiding? Don't be so *silly!*"

There was no answer. But presently, far off and mockingly, there came the sound of a very high, thin fluting. No jazz tune, but one which she remembered from nursery days:

> *Tom, Tom the piper's son*
> *Learned to play when he was young,*
> *And the only tune that he could play*
> *Was: "Over the hills and far away—"*

"It's too *stupid*," said Dian.

> *Over the hills and a great way off*
> *The wind is blowing my top-knot off.*

The sound was so bodiless that it seemed to have no abiding-place. She ran forward, and it grew fainter; a thick bramble caught her, tearing her ankles and her sheer silk stockings. She wrenched herself pettishly away and started off in a new direction. The piping ceased. She suddenly became afraid of the trees and the darkness. The good, comforting drinks were taking back the support they gave and offering her instead a horrible apprehensiveness. She remembered Spot's pocket-flask and began scrambling back towards the car. Then the beaconing lights went out, leaving her alone with the trees and the wind.

The high spirits induced by gin and cheerful company do not easily survive siege by darkness and solitude. She was running now, desperately, and screaming as she ran. A root, like a hand about her ankles, tripped her, and she dropped, cowering.

The thin tune began again.

Tom, Tom the piper's son—

She sat up.

"The terror induced by forests and darkness," said a mocking voice from somewhere over her head, "was called by the Ancients, Panic fear, or the fear of the great god Pan. It is interesting to observe that modern progress has not altogether succeeded in banishing it from ill-disciplined minds."

Dian gazed upwards. Her eyes were growing accustomed to the night, and in the branches of the tree above her she caught the pale gleam of silver.

"What do you want to behave like an idiot for?"

"Advertisement, chiefly. One must be different. I am always different. That is why, my dear young lady, I am the pursued and not the pursuer. You may say it is a cheap way of producing an effect, and so it is; but it is good enough for gin-soaked minds. On such as you, if you will pardon my saying so, subtlety would be wasted."

"I wish you would come down."

"Possibly. But I prefer to be looked up to."

"You can't stay there all night. Think how silly you would look in the morning."

"Ah! but by comparison with yourself I shall retain an almost bandbox perfection of appearance. My costume is better suited than yours to acrobatic exercise in a wood at midnight."

"Well, what are you doing it for, anyway?"

"To please myself—which is the only reason you would admit for doing anything."

"Then you can sit up there and do it all alone. I'm going home."

"Your shoes aren't very suitable for a long walk—but if it amuses you, go home by all means."

"Why should I have to walk?"

"Because I have the ignition keys of both cars in my pocket. A simple precaution, my dear Watson. Nor do I think it will be very much good to try to send a message by your companion. He is plunged in the arms of Morpheus— an ancient and powerful god, though not so ancient as Pan."

"I hate you," said Dian.

"Then you are on the high road to loving me—which is only natural. We needs must love the highest when we see it. Can you see me?"

"Not very well. I could see you better if you came down."

"And love me better, perhaps?"

"Perhaps."

"Then I am safer where I am. Your lovers have a knack of coming to bad ends. There was young Carmichael—"

"I couldn't help that. He drank too much. He was an idiot."

"And Arthur Barrington—"

"I told him it wasn't any good."

"Not a bit of good. But he tried, all the same, and blew his brains out. Not that they were very good brains, but they were all the brains he had. And Victor Dean—"

"The little rotter! That wasn't anything to do with me."

"Wasn't it?"

"Why, he fell down a staircase, didn't he?"

"So he did. But why?"

"I haven't the faintest idea."

"Haven't you? I thought you might have. Why did you send Victor Dean about his business?"

"Because he was a silly little bore and just like all the rest."

"You like them to be different?"

"I like everything to be different."

"And when you find them different, you try to make them all alike. Do you know anybody who is different?"

"Yes; you're different."

"Only so long as I stay on my branch, Circe. If I come down to your level, I should be just like all the rest."

"Come down and try."

"I know when I am well off. You had better come up to me."

"You know I can't."

"Of course you can't. You can only go down and down."

"Are you trying to insult me?"

"Yes, but it's very difficult."

"Come down, Harlequin—I want you here."

"That's a new experience for you, isn't it? To want what you can't get. You ought to be grateful to me."

"I always want what I can't get."

"What do you want?"

"Life—thrills—"

"Well, you're getting them now. Tell me all about Victor Dean."

"Why do you want to know about him?"

"That's a secret."

"If I tell you, will you come down?"

"Perhaps."

"What a funny thing to want to know about."

"I'm famous for being funny. How did you pick him up?"

"We all went out one night to some frightful sort of suburban dancing place. We thought it would be such a scream."

"And was it?"

"No, it was rather dull really. But he was there, and he fell for me and I thought he was rather a pet. That's all."

"A simple story in words of one syllable. How long was he your pet?"

"Oh, about six months. But he was terribly, terribly boring. And such a prig. Imagine it, Harlequin darling. He got all cross and wanted bread and cheese and kisses. Are you laughing?"

"Hilariously."

"He wasn't any fun. He was all wet."

"My child, you are telling this story very badly. You made him drink and it upset his little tummy. You made him play high, and he said he couldn't afford it. And you tried to make him take drugs and he didn't like it. Anything else?"

"He was a little beast, Harlequin, really he was. He was out for what he could get."

"Aren't you?"

"Me?" Dian was really surprised. "I'm terribly generous. I gave him everything he wanted. I'm like that when I'm fond of anybody."

"He took what he could get but didn't spend it like a gentleman?"

"That's it. Do you know, he actually called himself a gentleman. Wouldn't that make you laugh? Like the middle ages, isn't it? Ladies and Gentlemen. He said we needn't think he wasn't a gentleman because he worked in an office. Too mirth-making, Harlequin, darling, wasn't it?"

She rocked herself backwards and forwards in amusement.

"Harlequin! Listen! I'll tell you something funny. One night Tod Milligan came in and I told him: 'This is Victor Dean, and he's a gentleman, and he works for Pym's Publicity.' Tod said: 'Oh, you're the chap, are you?' and looked too utterly murderous. And afterwards he asked me, just like you, how I got hold of Victor. That's queer. Did Tod send you out here to ask me?"

"No. No one ever sends me. I go where I like."

"Well, then, why do you all want to know about Victor Dean?"

"Too mystery-making, isn't it? What did Milligan say to Dean?"

"Nothing much, but he told me to string him along. And afterwards, quite suddenly, he told me to give him the push."

"And you did as you were told, like a good girl?"

"I was fed up with Victor, anyhow. And it doesn't do to get wrong with Tod."

"No—he might cut off supplies, mightn't he? Where does he get it from?"

"Coke, do you mean? I don't know."

"No, I suppose you don't. And you can't get him to tell you, either. Not with all your charms, Circe."

"Oh, Tod! he doesn't give anything away. He's a dirty swine. I loathe him. I'd do anything to get away from Tod. But he knows too much. And besides, he's got the stuff. Lots of people have tried to chuck Tod, but they always go back again—on Fridays and Saturdays."

"That's when he hands it out, is it?"

"Mostly. But—" she began to laugh again—"you weren't there tonight, were you? It was too amusing. He'd run short, or something. There was a hellish row. And that septic woman Babs Woodley was screaming all over the place. She scratched him. I do hope he gets blood-poisoning. He promised it would be there tomorrow, but he looked the most perfect idiot, with blood running down his chin. She said she'd shoot him. It was too marvellous."

"Rabelaisian, no doubt."

"Fortunately I'd got enough, so I gave her enough to keep her quiet, and then we thought we'd have a race. I won—at least, I should have, if it hadn't been for you. How did you happen along?"

"Oh, I just happened along. I always happen."

"You don't. You only seem to happen occasionally. You aren't one of Tod's regular lot, are you?"

"Not at present."

"Do you want to be? Because, don't. I'll get the stuff for you if you want it. But Tod's a beast. You'd better keep clear of him."

"Are you warning me for my good?"

"Yes, I am."

"What devotion!"

"No, I mean it. Life's hell, anyway, but it's worse if you get mixed up with Tod."

"Then why don't you cut loose from Tod?"

"I can't."

"Afraid of him?"

"Not so much of him. It's the people behind him. Tod's afraid too. He'd never let me go. He'd kill me first."

"How fascinating! I think I must know Tod better."

"You'd end by being afraid, too."

"Should I? Well, there's a kick in being afraid."

"Come down here, Harlequin, and I'll show you how to get a kick out of life."

"Could you?"

"Try and see."

There was a rustle among the leaves, and he slid down to stand beside her.

"Well?"

"Lift me up. I'm all cramped."

He lifted her, and she felt his hands hard as iron under her breast. She was tall, and as she turned to look at him she could see the glint of his eyeballs, level with her own.

"Well, will I do?"

"For what?"

"For you?"

"For me? What are you good for, to me?"

"I'm beautiful."

"Not so beautiful as you were. In five years' time you will be ugly."

"Five years? I wouldn't want you for five years."

"I wouldn't want you for five minutes."

The cold daybreak was beginning to filter through the leaves; it showed her only a long, implacable chin and the thin curl of a smiling mouth. She made a snatch at his mask, but he was too quick for her. Very deliberately he turned her towards him, putting both her arms behind her back and holding them there.

"What next?" she demanded, mockingly.

"Nothing. I shall take you home."

"You will? Ah, you will, then?"

"Yes, as I did once before."

"Exactly as you did before?"

"Not exactly, because you were drunk then. You are sober now. With that trifling difference, the programme will be carried out according to precedent."

"You might kiss me, Harlequin."

"Do you deserve kissing? Once, for your information. Twice, for your disinterested effort to save me from the egregious Mr. Milligan. And the third time, because the fancy takes me that way."

He bestowed the kisses like deliberate insults. Then he picked her up bodily, still holding her arms imprisoned, and dumped her into the back of the open car.

"Here's a rug for you. You'll need it."

She said nothing. He started up the engine, turned the car and drove it slowly along the path. As they came abreast of the saloon, he leaned out and tossed the ignition key on to the knees of Spot Lancaster, happily snoring in his seat. In a few minutes, they had turned out from the wood into the main road. The sky was faintly streaked with the ghostly glimmer of the false dawn.

Dian de Momerie slid from under the rug and leaned forward. He was driving easily, slumped down in his seat, his black poll leaning carelessly back, his hand slack on the wheel. With a twist, she could send him and herself into the ditch, and he would deserve it.

"Don't do it," he said, without turning his head.

"You devil!"

He stopped the car.

"If you don't behave, I shall leave you by the roadside, sitting on a milestone, like the bailiff's daughter of Islington. Or, if you prefer it, I can tie you up. Which is it to be?"

"Be kind to me."

"I am being kind. I have preserved you from boredom for two solid hours. I beg you not to plunge us both into the horrors of an anti-climax. What are you crying for?"

"I'm tired—and you won't love me."

"My poor child, pull yourself together. Who would believe that Dian de Momerie could fall for a fancy-dress and a penny whistle?"

"It isn't that. It's you. There's something queer about you. I'm afraid of you. You aren't thinking about me at all. You're thinking of something horrible. What is it? What is it? Wait!"

She put out a cold hand and clutched his arm.

"I'm seeing something that I can't make out. I've got it now. Straps. They are strapping his elbows and dropping a white bag over his head. The hanged man. There's a hanged man in your thoughts. Why are you thinking of hanging?"

She shrank away from him and huddled into the farthest corner of the car. Wimsey re-started the engine and let in the clutch.

"Upon my word," he thought, "that's the oddest after-effect of drink and drugs I've met yet. Very interesting. But not very safe. Quite a providential interposition in one way. We may get home without breaking our necks. I didn't know I carried such a graveyard aura about with me."

Dian was fast asleep when he lifted her out of the car. She half woke, and slipped her arms round his neck.

"Darling, it's been lovely." Then she came to with a little start. "Where have we got to? What's happened?"

"We're home. Where's your latch-key?"

"Here. Kiss me. Take that mask off."

"Run along in. There's a policeman thinking we look rather disreputable." He opened the door.

"Aren't you coming in?"

She seemed to have forgotten all about the hanged man.
He shook his head.

"Well, good-bye, then."

"Good-bye."

He kissed her gently this time and pushed her into the
house. The policeman, stumping inquisitively nearer, revealed a face that Wimsey knew. He smiled to himself as
the official gaze swept over him.

"Good morning, officer."

"Morning, sir," said the policeman, stolidly.

"Moffatt, Moffatt," said his lordship, reprovingly, "you
will never get promotion. If you don't know me, you should
know the car."

"Good lord, your lordship, I beg your pardon. Didn't
somehow expect to see you here."

"Not so much of the lordship. Somebody might be listening. You on your beat?"

"Just going home, my—sir."

"Jump in and I'll drive you there. Ever see a fellow called
Milligan round this way?"

"Major Tod Milligan? Yes, now and then. He's a bad
hat, he is, if ever there was one. Runs that place down by
the river. Mixed up with that big drug-gang as Mr. Parker's
after. We could pull him in any day, but he's not the real
big noise."

"Isn't he, Moffatt?"

"No, my lord. This car's a treat, ain't she? Shouldn't think
there's much catches *you* on the road. No. What Mr. Parker
wants is to get him to lead us to the top man of all, but
there don't seem to be much chance of it. They're as cunning as weasels, they are. Don't suppose he knows himself
who the other fellow is."

"How's it worked, Moffatt?"

"Well, my lord, as far as we've been told, the stuff is
brought in from the coast once or twice a week and run up
to London. We've had a try at catching it on the way more
than once, that is to say, Mr. Parker's special squad have,

but they've always given us the slip. Then it'll be taken somewhere, but where we don't know, and distributed out again to the big distributors. From them it goes to all kinds of places. We could lay hands on it there—but lord! what's the use? It'd only be in another place next week."

"And whereabouts does Milligan come into it?"

"We think he's one of the high-up distributors, my lord. He hands it out at that house of his, and in other places."

"In the place where you found me, for instance?"

"That's one of them."

"But the point is, where does Milligan get his supplies?"

"That's it, my lord."

"Can't you follow him and find out?"

"Ah! but he don't fetch it for himself, my lord. There's others does that. And you see, if we was to open his parcels and search his tradesmen and so on, they'd just strike him off their list, and we'd be back where we was before."

"So you would. How often does he give parties in that house of his?"

"Most evenings, my lord. Seems to keep open house, like."

"Well, keep an eye open on Friday and Saturday nights, Moffatt."

"Fridays and Saturdays, my lord?"

"Those are the nights when things happen."

"Is that so, my lord? I'm much obliged to you. We didn't know that. That's a good tip, that is. If you'll drop me at the next corner, my lord, that'll do me champion. I'm afraid I've took your lordship out of your way."

"Not a bit, Moffatt, not a bit. Very glad to have seen you. And, by the way, you have not seen me. Not a question of my morals, you understand, but I've a fancy that Major Milligan might not approve of my visiting that particular house."

"That's all right, my lord. Not being on duty at the time, I ain't bound to put it in a report. Good morning, my lord, and thank you."

CHAPTER X

DISTRESSING DEVELOPMENTS
OF AN OFFICE ROW

ALL very well for you to talk, Bill Jones," said Ginger
Joe, "but bet you sixpence if you was called as a witness in
a case, you'd get into a 'owling mess. Why, they might ask
you what you was doin' a month ago and what'd you know
about that?"

"Bet you I'd know all right."

"Bet you you wouldn't."

"All right, bet you anything I would."

"Bet you if I was a 'tec—"

"Cor lumme, you'd be a good 'tec, you would."

"Bet you I would, anyhow."

" 'Oo ever 'eard of a carrotty-'eaded 'tec?"

This objection appeared to Ginger to be irrelevant. He
replied, however, automatically:

"Bet you I'd be a better 'tec 'or you."

"Bet you you wouldn't."

"Bet you if I was a 'tec and arst you w'ere you was when
Mr. Dean fell downstairs, you wouldn't 'ave no alleybi."

"That's silly, that is," said Bill Jones. "I wouldn't want
no alleybi for Mr. Dean falling downstairs, 'cause it was
accidental death."

"All right, Suet-face. I was only sayin', supposin' I *was*
a 'tec an' I was investigatin' Mr. Dean's fallin' downstairs,
and I arst you wot you was a-doin' of, you wouldn't be able
to tell me."

"Bet you I would, then. I was on the lift, that's where I

was, and 'Arry could prove it. So just you stick that in your silly face and shut up."

"Oh, you was on the lift, was you? 'Ow d'you know that was when it was?"

"When wot was?"

"When Mr. Dean fell downstairs?"

" 'Cos the first thing I 'ears when I comes off of the lift is Mr. Tompkin a-telling Sam there all about it. Didn't I, Sam?"

Sam Tabbitt glanced up from a copy of *Radio for Amateurs* and nodded briefly.

"That don't prove nothing," persisted Ginger. "Not without you know 'ow long it took Mr. Tompkin to shoot 'is mouth off."

"Not long it didn't," said Sam. "I'd just come out of the Big Conference room—takin' tea to Mr. Pym and two clients, I was—Muggleton's, if you want ter know—and I hears an awful screeching and I says to Mr. Tompkin, 'Coo, lumme!' I says, 'wot's up?' An' he says as Mr. Dean's fallen down and broke 'is neck an' they've jest rung up for a doctor."

"That's right," added Cyril, who was the boy in attendance on the Executive and the Switchboard. "Mr. Stanley comes running along full pelt into our place and says, 'Oh, Miss Fearney, Mr. Dean's fell downstairs and we're afraid he's killed himself and you're to telephone for a doctor.' So Miss Fearney tells Miss Beit to put the call through and I hops out quick through the other door so as Miss Fearney can't see me—that's the door behind Mr. Tompkin's desk—and I says, 'Mr. Dean's tumbled down and killed hisself,' and he says, 'Run and see what's happened, Cyril.' So I runs and I see Sam jest a-comin' out from the Big Conference room. Didn't I, Sam?"

Sam agreed.

"And that's when I heard the screeching," he added.

"Who was a-screeching?"

"Mrs. Crump was a-screeching in the Executive. Said she'd just seen Mr. Dean fall down and kill hisself and they was a-bringin' 'im along. So I looked into the passage and there they was, a-carryin' of him. He did look awful."

"And that was when I come up," said Bill, sticking to the point at issue. "I hears Mr. Tompkin telling Sam about it, and I runs after Sam and I calls to Mr. Tompkin as they're a-bringing him through, and he comes and looks on too. So they takes him into the Board-room, and Miss Fearney says, 'What about telling Mr. Pym?' and Mr. Tompkin says, 'He's still in the conference,' and she says, 'I know he is. We don't want the clients to hear about it.' So Mr. Tompkin says, 'Better telephone through to him.' So she does and then she gets hold of me and says, 'Bill, get a sheet of brown paper and run along to the Board-room and tell them to put it over the glass door,' and just as I was a-going, Mr. Atkins comes along and says, 'Is there any dust-sheets?' he says. 'He's gone,' he says, 'and we got to have somethink to put over him.' And Miss Fearney says, sharp-like, 'Dust-sheets is nothing to do with this department,' she says, 'what are you thinking about? Go up and ask Mrs. Johnson.' Coo! that was a set-out, that was." Bill grinned, as one who looks back to a grand gala-day, a brilliant green oasis in a desert of drudgery. Then he remembered once more what the dispute had been about.

"So where's your blinkin' alleybi?" he demanded, sternly.

"Where's yours, Ginger, if it comes to that?"

By such methods, serpentine but effective, Ginger Joe pursued his inquiries. The eyes of the office-boy are everywhere, and his memory is retentive. Five days of inquiry brought the whole inside staff of Pym's under review—all that was necessary, since the day of Dean's death had not been the day that brought the Outside Publicity men into the office.

Out of the ninety-odd inside members of the staff, only ten remained unaccounted or partially unaccounted for. These were: in the Copy Department:

Mr. Willis. He had arrived from the outside staircase about five minutes after the accident, had gone straight through the hall, up the stair to the Dispatching and so into his own room, speaking to nobody. About a quarter of an hour later, he had gone to Mr. Dean's room and, not finding him, had gone back to the typists' room. Here, on asking for Mr. Dean, he had been greeted with the news, which appeared to startle and horrify him. (Witness: the boy George Pyke, who had heard Miss Rossiter telling Mrs. Johnson all about it.)

Mr. Hankin. He had been absent from the office since half-past two, on private business, and did not return till half-past four. Harry had informed him of the catastrophe as soon as he came in, and, as soon as he stepped out of the lift, Mr. Tompkin had requested him to go and see Mr. Pym. (Witnesses: Harry and Cyril.)

Mr. Copley. Presumably in his room all the time, but this could not be substantiated, since he never took tea and was accustomed to work at his "slope," which was set against the inner wall and not visible to any one casually passing his door. He was an assiduous worker, and was not likely to emerge from his room, however much noise or running about there might be in the passages. At a quarter to five, he had walked in the most ordinary way into the typists' room to ask why his copy had not been typed. Miss Parton had told him, rather tartly, that she didn't see how he could expect anything to be ready under the circumstances. He had then asked what circumstances and, on being told about Mr. Dean's fatal accident, had expressed astonishment and regret, but added that he could see no reason why the work of the department should not be carried on. (Witnesses: four boys who, on separate occasions, had heard this shocking exhibition of callousness discussed with and by Mrs. Johnson.)

In the Vouchers:

Mr. Binns. An elegant youth who had gone out at 3 o'clock to inquire for last September's number of the *Connoisseur* for Mr. Armstrong, and had unaccountably taken an hour and a half over the transaction. (Witness: Sam, whose elder sister was a typist in the Vouchers, and had given it as her opinion that young Binns had had a date for tea with his best girl.) (Note: Mr. Binns was already known to Mr. Bredon as the darts expert who had often lunched with Victor Dean.)

In the various Group-managers' offices:

Mr. Haagedorn (Sopo and allied products). Leave of absence all day to attend aunt's funeral. But said to have been seen during the afternoon attending a matinée at the Adelphi. (Witnesses: Jack Dennis, the boy who thought he had seen him, and Mr. Tompkin's attendance-register consulted by Cyril.)

Mr. Tallboy. Exact location at the moment of the action not quite certain. At 3.30 or thereabouts, Mr. Wedderburn had come down to the Vouchers to ask for certain back numbers of the *Fishmonger's Gazette,* saying that Mr. Tallboy wanted them in a hurry. On returning ten minutes later, after having the required numbers sorted out for him, Mr. Wedderburn had run into all the excitement about Mr. Dean and had forgotten the *Fishmonger's Gazette.* He had, in fact, been talking to Miss Fearney in the Executive, when Mr. Tallboy had come in and rather abruptly asked whether he was expected to wait all night for them. Mr. Wedderburn had explained that the alarm about Mr. Dean had put the matter out of his head, and Mr. Tallboy had replied that the work had got to be done, notwithstanding. (Witnesses: Horace, the messenger-boy in the Vouchers, and Cyril.)

Mr. McAllister. Group-secretary to Dairyfields, Ltd., under Mr. Smayle. Absent all afternoon on visit to dentist. (Witness: Mr. Tompkin's register.)

In the Studio:

Mr. Barrow. At British Museum, studying Greek vases with view to advertising display for Klassika Corsets. (Witness: Mr. Barrow's time-sheet.)

Mr. Vibart. Supposed to be at Westminster, making a sketch of the Terrace of the House of Commons for Farley's Footwear. ("The feet that tread this historic pavement are more often than not, clad in Farley Fashion Footwear.")

Absent 2.30-4.30. (Witnesses: Mr. Vibart's time-sheet and the sketch itself.)

Wilfred Cotterill. At 3 o'clock complained of nose-bleeding and sent to lie down by himself in the Boys' Room, the other boys being told to leave him alone. Completely forgotten by everybody till 5 o'clock, when he was discovered, asleep, by the boys going in to change their tunics. Alleged that he had slept through the whole of the excitement. (Witnesses: All the other boys.) Wilfred Cotterill was a small, pale, excitable child of fourteen, but looking much younger. When told what he had missed he merely remarked "Oo-er!"

A very creditable piece of work on Ginger Joe's part, thought Mr. Bredon, if we may continue so to call him during office-hours, but leaving much room for further inquiry. His own investigations were not going too well. In his search for Darling Special Pencils he had been brought face to face with the practical communism of office life. The Copy Department preferred 5B or even 6B drawing-pencils for writing its roughs, and was not much interested in Darling's product, except, of course, Mr. Garrett, who had been drawing up a little panel for display in Darling's advertisements, calling attention to the generous offer of the pencil. He had two specimens, and four, in various stages of decay, were found in the typists' room. There was one on Mr. Armstrong's desk. Mr. Hankin had none. Mr. Ingleby admitted to having thrown his out of the window in a fit of temper, and Miss Meteyard said she thought she had one somewhere if Mr. Bredon really wanted it, but he had better ask Miss Parton. The other departments were even worse. The pencils had been taken home, lost, or thrown away. Mr. McAllister, mysteriously but characteristically, said he had no less than six. Mr. Wedderburn had lost his, but produced one which he had bagged from Mr. Tallboy. Mr. Prout said he couldn't be bothered; the pencil was a silly, gimcrack thing anyway; if Bredon really wanted a propelling pencil he ought to get an Eversharp. He (Mr. Prout) had never seen the thing since he'd had it to photograph; he added that for a first-class photographer to spend his life photographing tin pencils and jelly cartons was enough to drive any sensitive person to suicide. It was heart-breaking work.

In the matter of his own address, Bredon did get one piece of information. Mr. Willis had asked for it one day. Discreet questioning fixed the date to within a day or so, one way or another, of Chief-Inspector Parker's unfortunate encounter on the stairs. Nearer than this, Miss Beit (the telephonist, who also presided over the office address-book) could not go. It was all rather unnerving as well as exasperating. Mr. Bredon hoped that the assailant would have been sufficiently alarmed by the failure of his first attempt to forswear blunt instruments and violence for the future; nevertheless, he developed a habit of keeping a careful lookout for following footsteps whenever he left the office. He went home by circuitous routes, and when engaged on his daily duties, found himself avoiding the iron staircase.

Meanwhile, the great Nutrax row raged on with undiminished vigour, developing as it went an extraordinary number of offshoots and ramifications, of which the most important and alarming was a violent breach between Mr. Smayle and Mr. Tallboy.

It began, rather absurdly, at the bottom of the lift, where Mr. Tallboy and Miss Meteyard were standing, waiting for Harry to return and waft them to their sphere of toil above. To them, enter Mr. Smayle, fresh and smiling, his teeth gleaming as though cleaned with Toothshine, a pink rosebud in his buttonhole, his umbrella neatly rolled.

"Morning, Miss Meteyard, morning, morning," said Mr. Smayle, raising his bowler, and replacing it at a jaunty angle. "Fine day again."

Miss Meteyard agreed that it was a fine day. "If only," she added, "they wouldn't spoil it with income-tax demands."

"Don't talk about income-tax," replied Mr. Smayle with

a smile and a shudder. "I said to the wife this morning, 'My dear, we shall have to take our holiday in the back garden, I can see.' And I'm sure it's a fact. Where the money for our usual little trip to Eastbourne is to come from, I don't know."

"The whole thing's iniquitous," said Mr. Tallboy. "As for this last budget—"

"Ah! *you* must be paying super-tax, old man," said Mr. Smayle, giving Mr. Tallboy a prod in the ribs with his umbrella.

"Don't do that," said Mr. Tallboy.

"Tallboy needn't worry," said Mr. Smayle, with a rallying air. "He's got more money than he knows what to do with. We all know that, don't we, Miss Meteyard?"

"He's luckier than most, then," said Miss Meteyard.

"He can afford to chuck his quids over the office, fifty at a time," pursued Mr. Smayle. "Wish I knew where he gets it from. Daresay the income-tax authorities would like to know too. I'll tell you what, Miss Meteyard, this man's a dark horse. I believe he runs a dope-den or a bucket-shop on the sly, eh? You're a one, you are," said Mr. Smayle, extending a roguish forefinger and jabbing it into Mr. Tallboy's second waistcoat button. At this moment the lift descended and Miss Meteyard stepped into it. Mr. Tallboy, rudely thrusting Mr. Smayle aside, stepped in after her.

"Here!" said Mr. Smayle, "manners, manners! The trouble with you, old man," he went on, "is that you can't take a joke. No offence meant, I'm sure—and none taken, I hope."

He clapped Mr. Tallboy on the shoulder.

"Do you mind keeping your hands off me, Smayle," said Mr. Tallboy.

"Oh, all right, all right, your Highness. Got out of bed the wrong side, hasn't he?" He appealed to Miss Meteyard, being troubled by an obscure feeling that men should not quarrel before ladies, and that it was somehow up to him to preserve the decencies by turning the whole thing into a joke.

"Money's a sore point with us all, I'm afraid, Mr. Smayle," replied Miss Meteyard. "Let's talk about something jollier. That's a nice rose you've got there."

"Out of my own garden," replied Mr. Smayle, with pride. "Mrs. Smayle's a wonder with the roses. I leave it all to her, bar the digging and mulching, of course." They emerged from the lift and signed their names at the desk. Miss Meteyard and Mr. Smayle passed on through the ante-room and turned by common consent to the left up the stair by the Dispatching. Mr. Tallboy shouldered past them and took a lone and frosty course down the main corridor to ascend by the iron staircase.

"I'm reelly very sorry," said Mr. Smayle, "that Tallboy and I should have indulged in anything approaching to words in your presence, Miss Meteyard."

"Oh, that's nothing. He seems a little irritable. I don't think he likes that little upset of his with Mr. Copley to be talked about."

"No, but reelly," said Mr. Smayle, lingering at the door of Miss Meteyard's room, "if a man can't take a harmless joke, it's a great pity, isn't it?"

"It is," said Miss Meteyard. "Hullo! What are all you people doing here?"

Mr. Ingleby and Mr. Bredon, seated on Miss Meteyard's radiator with a volume of the *New Century Dictionary* between them, looked up unabashed.

"We're finishing a Torquemada cross-word," said Ingleby, "and naturally the volume we wanted was in your room. Everything always is."

"I forgive you," said Miss Meteyard.

"But I do wish you wouldn't bring Smayle in here with you," said Mr. Bredon. "The mere sight of him makes me think of Green Pastures Margarine. You haven't come to dun me for that copy, have you? Because don't, there's a good fellow. I haven't done it and I can't do it. My brain has dried up. How you can live all day with Margarine and always look so fresh and cheerful passes my understanding."

"I assure you it's an effort," said Mr. Smayle, displaying

his teeth. "But it reelly is a great refreshment to see you copy-writers all so cheerful and pleasant together. Not like some people I could name."

"Mr. Tallboy has been unkind to Mr. Smayle," said Miss Meteyard.

"I like to be agreeable with everybody," said Mr. Smayle, "but reelly, when it comes to shoving your way past a person into the lift as if one wasn't there and then telling you to keep your hands off as if a person was dirt, a man may be excused for taking offence. I suppose Tallboy thinks I'm not worth speaking to, just because he's been to a public school and I haven't."

"Public school," said Mr. Bredon, "first I've heard of it. What public school?"

"He was at Dumbleton," said Mr. Smayle, "but what I say is, I went to a Council School and I'm not ashamed of it."

"Where's Dumbleton?" demanded Ingleby. "I shouldn't worry, Smayle. Dumbleton isn't a public school, within the meaning of the act."

"Isn't it?" said Mr. Smayle, hopefully. "Well, you and Mr. Bredon have had college educations, so you know all about it. What schools do *you* call public schools?"

"Eton," said Mr. Bredon, promptly, "—and Harrow," he added, magnanimously, for he was an Eton man.

"Rugby," suggested Mr. Ingleby.

"No, no," protested Bredon, "that's a railway junction."

Ingleby delivered a brisk left-hander to Bredon's jaw, which the latter parried neatly.

"And I've heard," Bredon went on, "that there's a decentish sort of place at Winchester, if you're not too particular."

"I once met a man who'd been to Marlborough," suggested Ingleby.

"I'm sorry to hear that," said Bredon. "They get a terrible set of hearty roughs down there. You can't be too careful of your associates, Ingleby."

"Well," said Mr. Smayle, "Tallboy always says that Dumbleton is a public school."

"I daresay it is—in the sense that it has a Board of Governors," said Ingleby, "but it's nothing to be snobbish about."

"What is, if you come to that?" said Bredon. "Look here, Smayle, if only you people could get it out of your heads that these things matter a damn, you'd be a darn sight happier. You probably got a fifty times better education than I ever did."

Mr. Smayle shook his head. "Oh, no," he said, "I'm not deceiving myself about that, and I'd give anything to have had the same opportunities as you. There's a difference, and I know there's a difference, and I don't mind admitting it. But what I mean is, some people make you feel it and others don't. I don't feel it when I'm talking to either of you, or to Mr. Armstrong or Mr. Hankin, though you've been to Oxford and Cambridge and all that. Perhaps it's just because you've been to Oxford and Cambridge."

He struggled with the problem, embarrassing the other two men by his wistful eyes.

"Look here," said Miss Meteyard, "I know what you mean. But it's just that these two here never think twice about it. They don't have to. And you don't have to, either. But the minute anybody begins to worry about whether he's as good as the next man, then he starts a sort of uneasy snobbish feeling and makes himself offensive."

"I see," said Mr. Smayle. "Well, of course, Mr. Hankin doesn't have to try and prove that he's better than me, because he is and we both know it."

"Better isn't the right word, Smayle."

"Well, better educated. You know what I mean."

"Don't worry about it," said Ingleby. "If I were half as good at my job as you are at yours, I should feel superior to everybody in this tom-fool office."

Mr. Smayle shook his head, but appeared comforted.

"I do wish they wouldn't start that kind of thing," said Ingleby when he had gone, "I don't know what to say to them."

"I thought you were a Socialist, Ingleby," said Bredon, "it oughtn't to embarrass you."

"So I am a Socialist," said Ingleby, "but I can't stand this stuff about Old Dumbletonians. If everybody had the same State education, these things wouldn't happen."

"If everybody had the same face," said Bredon, "there'd be no pretty women."

Miss Meteyard made a grimace.

"If you go on like that, I shall be getting an inferiority complex too."

Bredon looked at her gravely.

"I don't think you'd care to be called pretty," he said, "but if I were a painter I should like to make a portrait of you. You have very interesting bones."

"Good God!" said Miss Meteyard. "I'm going. Let me know when you've finished with my room."

There was a mirror in the typists' room, and in this Miss Meteyard curiously studied her face.

"What's the matter, Miss Meteyard?" asked Miss Rossiter. "Got a spot coming?"

"Something of the sort," said Miss Meteyard, absently. "Interesting bones indeed!"

"Pardon?" said Miss Rossiter.

"Smayle is getting unbearable," grumbled Mr. Tallboy to Mr. Wedderburn. "Vulgar little tick. I hate a fellow who digs you in the ribs."

"He means no harm," rejoined Mr. Wedderburn. "He's quite a decent sort, really."

"Can't stand those teeth," grumbled Mr. Tallboy. "And why must he put that stinking stuff on his hair?"

"Oh, well," said Mr. Wedderburn.

"I'm not going to have him playing in the cricket match, anyhow," pursued Mr. Tallboy, viciously. "Last year he wore white suède shoes with crocodile vamps, and an incredible blazer with Old Borstalian colours."

Mr. Wedderburn looked up, rather startled.

"Oh, but you're not going to leave him out? He's quite a good bat and very nippy on the ball in the field."

"We can do without him," said Mr. Tallboy, firmly. Mr. Wedderburn said no more. There was no regular cricket eleven at Pym's, but every summer a scratch team was got together to play a couple of matches, the selection being entrusted to Mr. Tallboy, who was energetic and had once carried his bat out for 52 against Sopo. He was supposed to submit a list of cricketers for Mr. Hankin's final decision, but Mr. Hankin seldom questioned his selection, for the sufficient reason that there were seldom more than eleven candidates available to choose from. The important point was that Mr. Hankin should bat third, and field at mid-on. If these points were taken note of, he raised no further objections.

Mr. Tallboy pulled out a list.

"Ingleby," he said, "and Garrett. Barrow. Adcock. Pinchley. Hankin. Myself. Gregory can't play; he's going away for the week-end, so we'd better have McAllister. And we can't very well leave out Miller. I wish we could, but he's a Director. Yourself."

"Leave me out," said Mr. Wedderburn. "I haven't touched a bat since last year and I didn't put up much of a show then."

"We've nobody else who can bowl slow spinners," said Mr. Tallboy. "I'll put you down No. 11."

"All right," said Mr. Wedderburn, gratified by the recognition accorded to his bowling, but irrationally provoked by being put down No. 11. He had expected his companion to say, "Oh, but that was just a fluke," and send him in higher up the list. "How about a wicket-keeper? Grayson says he won't do it again, not after getting his front tooth knocked out last year. He seems to have got the wind up properly."

"We'll make Haagedorn do it. He's got hands like a pair of hams. Who else? Oh, that chap in the printing—Beesely—he's not much good with a bat, but we can rely on him for a few straight balls."

"What about that new fellow in the Copy Department? Bredon? He's a public school man. Is he any good?"

"Might be. He's a bit ancient, though. We've got two aged stiffs already in Hankin and Miller."

"Aged stiff be blowed. That chap can move, I've seen him do it. I wouldn't be surprised if he could show us a bit of style."

"Well, I'll find out. If he's any good, we'll stick him in instead of Pinchley."

"Pinchley can swipe 'em up," said Mr. Wedderburn.

"He never does anything but swipe. He's jam for the fielders. He gave them about ten chances last year and was caught both innings."

Mr. Wedderburn agreed that this was so.

"But he'll be awfully hurt if he's left out," he said.

"I'll ask about Bredon," said Mr. Tallboy.

He sought out that gentleman, who was, for once, in his own room, singing soup-slogans to himself.

> *A meal begun with Blagg's Tomato*
> *Softens every husband's heart-oh!*
>
> *Hubbies hold those wives most dear*
> *Who offer them Blagg's Turtle Clear.*
>
> *Fit for an Alderman—serve it up quick—*
> *Rum-ti-ty, tum-ti-ty, Blagg's Turtle Thick.*

"Rum-ti-ty, tum-ti-ty," said Mr. Bredon. "Hullo, Tallboy, what's the matter? Don't say Nutrax has developed any more innuendos."

"Do you play cricket?"

"Well, I used to play for—" Mr. Bredon coughed; he had been about to say, "for Oxford," but remembered in time that these statements could be checked. "I've played a good deal of country-house cricket in the old days. But I'm rapidly qualifying to be called a Veteran. Why?"

"I've got to scrape up an eleven for a match against Brotherhood's. We play one every year. They always beat us, of course, because they have their own playing-fields and play together regularly, but Pym likes it to be done. He thinks it fosters fellow-feeling between client and agent and all that sort of thing."

"Oh! when does it come off?"

"Saturday fortnight."

"I daresay I might keep my end up for a bit, if you can't get anybody better."

"You anything of a bowler?"

"Nothing."

"Better with the willow than the leather, eh?"

Mr. Bredon, wincing a little at this picturesqueness, admitted that, if he was anything, he was a batsman.

"Right. You wouldn't care to open the ball with Ingleby, I suppose?"

"I'd rather not. Put me down somewhere near the tail."

Tallboy nodded.

"Just as you like."

"Who captains this Eleven?"

"Well, I do, as a rule. At least, we always ask Hankin or Miller, just out of compliment, but they generally decline with thanks. Well, righty-ho; I'll just buzz round and see that the others are O.K."

The selected team went up on the office notice-board at lunch-time. At ten minutes past two, the trouble began with Mr. McAllister.

"I observe," said he, making a dour appearance in Mr. Tallboy's room, "that ye're no askin' Smayle to play for ye, and I'm thinkin' it'll be a wee bit awkward for me if I play and he does not. Workin' in his room all day and under his orders, it will make my poseetion not just so very comfortable."

"Position in the office has nothing to do with playing cricket," said Mr. Tallboy.

"Ay, imph'm, that's so. But I just do not care for it. So ye'll oblige me by leavin' my name oot."

"Just as you like," said Tallboy, annoyed. He struck Mr. McAllister's name off the list, and substituted that of Mr. Pinchley. The next defection was that of Mr. Adcock, a stolid youth from the Voucher Department. He inconsiderately fell off a step-ladder in his own home, while assisting his mother to hang a picture, and broke the small bone of his leg.

In this extremity, Mr. Tallboy found himself compelled to go and eat humble pie to Mr. Smayle, and request him to play after all. But Mr. Smayle had been hurt in his feelings by being omitted from the first list, and showed no eagerness to oblige.

Mr. Tallboy, who was, indeed, a little ashamed of himself, endeavoured to gloss the matter over by making it appear that his real object in leaving out Mr. Smayle had been to make room for Mr. Bredon, who had been to Oxford and was sure to play well. But Mr. Smayle was not deceived by this specious reasoning.

"If you had come to me in the first instance," he complained, "and put the matter to me in a friendly way, I should say nothing about it. I like Mr. Bredon, and I appreciate that he has had advantages that I haven't had. He's a very gentlemanly fellow, and I should be happy to make way for him. But I do not care for having things done behind my back in a hole-and-corner fashion."

If Mr. Tallboy had said at this point, "Look here, Smayle, I'm sorry; I was rather out of temper at the time over that little dust-up we had, and I apologize"—then Mr. Smayle, who was really an amiable creature enough, would have given way and done anything that was required of him. But Mr. Tallboy chose to take a lofty tone. He said:

"Come, come, Smayle. You're not Jack Hobbs, you know."

Even this might have passed over with Mr. Smayle's ready admission that he was not England's premier batsman, had not Mr. Tallboy been unhappily inspired to say:

"Of course, I don't know about you, but *I* have always been accustomed to have these things settled by whoever was appointed to select the team, and to play or not, according as I was put down."

"Oh, yes," retorted Mr. Smayle, caught on his sensitive point, "you would say that. I am quite aware, Tallboy, that

I never was at a public school, but that is no reason why I shouldn't be treated with ordinary, common courtesy. And from those who have been to real public schools, I get it, what's more. You may think a lot of Dumbleton, but it isn't what *I* call a public school."

"And what do *you* call a public school?" inquired Mr. Tallboy.

"Eton," retorted Mr. Smayle, repeating his lesson with fatal facility, "and Harrow, and—er—Rugby, and Winchester and places like those. Places where they send gentlemen's sons to."

"Oh, do they?" said Mr. Tallboy. "I suppose you are sending *your* family to Eton, then."

At this, Mr. Smayle's narrow face became as white as a sheet of paper.

"You cad!" he said, choking. "You unspeakable swine. Get out of here or I'll kill you."

"What the devil's the matter with you, Smayle?" cried Mr. Tallboy, in considerable surprise.

"Get out!" said Mr. Smayle.

"Now, I'd just like a word wi' ye, Tallboy," interposed Mr. McAllister. He laid a large, hairy hand on Mr. Tallboy's arm and propelled him gently from the room.

"What on airth possessed ye to say such a thing to him?" he asked, when they were safely in the passage. "Did ye not know that Smayle has but the one boy and him feebleminded, the poor child?"

Mr. Tallboy was really aghast. He was stricken with shame, and, like many shame-stricken people, took refuge in an outburst of rage against the nearest person handy.

"No, I didn't know. How should I be expected to know anything about Smayle's family? Good God! I'm damned sorry and all that, but why must the fellow be such an ass? He's got a mania about public schools. Eton, indeed! I don't wonder the boy's feeble-minded if he takes after his father."

Mr. McAllister was deeply shocked. His Scottish sense of decency was outraged.

"Ye ought to be damn well ashamed o' yersel'," he said, severely, and releasing Tallboy's arm, stepped back into the room he shared with Mr. Smayle and slammed the door.

Now, it is not very clear at the first glance what this disagreement between Mr. Tallboy and Mr. Smayle about a cricket match had to do with the original disagreement between the former and Mr. Copley. True, one may trace a remote connection at the beginning of things, since the Tallboy-Smayle row may be said to have started with Mr. Smayle's indiscreet jest about Mr. Tallboy's fifty pounds. But this fact has no very great importance. What is really important is that as soon as Mr. McAllister made known all the circumstances of the Tallboy-Smayle affair (which he did as soon as he could find a listener), public opinion, which, in the Tallboy-Copley dispute had been largely on Mr. Tallboy's side, veered round. It was felt that since Mr. Tallboy could behave with so much unkindness to Mr. Smayle, he was probably not guiltless towards Mr. Copley. The office staff was divided like the Red Sea and rose up in walls on either hand. Only Mr. Armstrong, Mr. Ingleby, and Mr. Bredon, sardonic Gallios, held themselves apart, caring little, but fomenting the trouble for their own amusement. Even Miss Meteyard, who abominated Mr. Copley, experienced an unwonted uprush of feminine pity for him, and pronounced Mr. Tallboy's behaviour intolerable. Old Copley, she said, might be an interfering old nuisance, but he wasn't a cad. Mr. Ingleby said he really didn't think Tallboy could have meant what he said to Smayle. Miss Meteyard said: "Tell that to the marines," and, having said so, noted that the phrase would make a good headline for something-or-other. But Mr. Ingleby said, "No, that had been done."

Miss Parton, of course, was an anti-Copleyite whom nothing could move, and therefore smiled on Mr. Tallboy when he happened into the typists' room to borrow a stamp. But Miss Rossiter, though superficially more peppery, prided

herself on possessing a well-balanced mind. After all, she
insisted, Mr. Copley had probably meant well over the matter of the fifty pounds and, when you came to think of it,
he had got Tallboy and all the rest of the Nutrax con-
tingent out of a very tiresome sort of mess. She thought
that Mr. Tallboy thought rather a lot of himself, and he
had certainly had no business to speak as he had done to
poor Mr. Smayle.

"And," said Miss Rossiter, "I don't like his lady friends."

"Lady friends?" said Miss Parton.

"Well, I'm not one to talk, as you know," replied Miss
Rossiter, "but when you see a married man coming out of
a restaurant at past midnight with somebody who is obviously not his wife—"

"No!" exclaimed Miss Parton.

"My dear! and got up regardless . . . one of those little
hats with an eye-veil . . . three-inch diamanté heels . . .
such bad taste with a semi-toilette . . . fish-net stockings
and all. . . ."

"Perhaps it was his sister."

"My *dear*! . . . And his wife's having a baby, too. . . .
He didn't see me. . . . Of course, I wouldn't say a word,
but I do think . . ."

Thus the typewriters clacked.

Mr. Hankin, though officially impartial, was a Tallboyite.
Himself a precise and efficient man, he was nevertheless
perennially irritated by the precision and efficiency of Mr.
Copley. He suspected, what was quite true, that Mr. Copley
criticized the conduct of the department and would have
liked to be given a measure of authority. Mr. Copley had a
way of coming to him with suggestions: "Would it not be
better, Mr. Hankin, if . . ." "If you will excuse my making
a suggestion, Mr. Hankin, could not a stricter control be
kept . . . ?" "Of course, I know I am in an entirely subordinate position here, Mr. Hankin, but I have had over
thirty years' experience of advertising, and in my humble
opinion . . ."—excellent suggestions, always, and having
only the one drawback that they threatened either to annoy

Mr. Armstrong, or to involve a quantity of tedious and time-wasting supervision, or to embroil the whole tempera-mental Copy Department and put it off its stroke. Mr. Hankin grew weary of saying: "Quite so, Mr. Copley, but Mr. Armstrong and I find it works better, on the whole, to have as few restrictions as possible." Mr. Copley had a way of saying that he quite understood, which always left Mr. Hankin with the impression that Mr. Copley thought him weak and ineffectual, and this impression had been confirmed by the Nutrax incident. When a point had arisen about which Mr. Hankin might, and ought to, have been consulted, Mr. Copley had passed him over—conclusive proof to Mr. Hankin that all Mr. Copley's valuable sug-gestions about departmental management were so much window-dressing, put forward to show how brilliant Mr. Copley was, and not in the least with the desire of aiding Mr. Hankin or the department. In this, Mr. Hankin's shrewdness saw much more clearly into Mr. Copley's motives than did Mr. Copley himself. He was quite right. Consequently, he was not inclined to bother himself about Mr. Copley, and was determined to give any necessary support to Mr. Tallboy. The Smayle incident was, natu-rally, not reported to him; he therefore made no comment upon the Cricket Eleven except to ask, mildly, why Mr. Smayle and Mr. McAllister were excluded. Mr. Tallboy replied briefly that they were unable to play, and that was the end of the matter.

Mr. Tallboy had a further ally in Mr. Barrow, who dis-liked the whole Copy Department on principle, because, as he complained, they were a conceited lot who were always trying to interfere with his artists and dictate to him about his displays. He admitted that, as a general proposition, the sketch was supposed to illustrate the copy, but he main-tained (and with truth) that the displays suggested by the copy-writers were often quite impracticable and that the copy-writers took unnecessary offence over the very neces-sary modifications which he had to make in their "roughs." Further, he had been deeply insulted by Mr. Armstrong's remarks about himself, too faithfully reported by Mr.

Ingleby, whom he detested. In fact, he was within an ace of refusing altogether to play in the same match as Mr. Ingleby.

"Oh, but, look here!" protested Mr. Tallboy, "you simply can't let me down like that! You're the best bat we've got."

"Can't you leave Ingleby out?"

This was more than awkward, for in fact Mr. Barrow, though a good and reliable bat, was by no means so good a bat as Mr. Ingleby. Mr. Tallboy hesitated:

"I don't quite see how I can do that. He made 63 last year. But I'll tell you what. I'll put him in fourth and leave you to open with somebody else—say Pinchley. Will you start with Pinchley?"

"You can't put Pinchley in first. He's nothing but a slogger."

"Who else is there?"

Mr. Barrow scanned the list mournfully.

"It's a weak bunch, Tallboy. Is that really the best you can do?"

"Afraid so."

"Pity you've managed to get across Smayle and McAllister."

"Yes—but that can't be helped now. You'll *have* to play, Mr. Barrow, or we'll have to scratch—one or the other!"

"I know what you'd better do. Put yourself in first with me."

"They won't like that. They'll think it's swank."

"Then put Garrett in."

"Very well. You'll play, then?"

"I suppose I must."

"That's very sporting of you, Mr. Barrow."

Mr. Tallboy ran down, sighing, to pin the revised list on the board:

MATCH AGAINST BROTHERHOOD'S

1. Mr. Barrow
2. Mr. Garrett

3. Mr. Hankin
4. Mr. Ingleby
5. Mr. Tallboy (Captain)
6. Mr. Pinchley
7. Mr. Miller
8. Mr. Beeseley
9. Mr. Bredon
10. Mr. Haagedorn
11. Mr. Wedderburn

He stood for a moment looking at it rather hopelessly. Then he went back to his room and took up a large sheet of foolscap, with the intention of marking off the figures for a client's appropriation over the next three months. But his mind was not on the figures. Presently he pushed the sheet aside, and sat staring blankly out of the window across the grey London roofs.

"What's up, Tallboy?" inquired Mr. Wedderburn.

"Life's the devil," said Mr. Tallboy. Then, in a sudden outburst:

"My God! how I hate this blasted place. It gets on my nerves."

"Time you had your holiday," said Mr. Wedderburn, placidly. "How's the wife?"

"All right," rejoined Mr. Tallboy, "but we shan't be able to get away till September."

"That's the worst of being a family man," replied Mr. Wedderburn. "And that reminds me. Have you done anything about that series for *The Nursing Times* about 'Nutrax for Nursing Mothers'?"

Mr. Tallboy thoughtlessly cursed the nursing mothers, dialled Mr. Hankin's room on the inter-office 'phone and in a mournful tone put in a requisition for six 4-inch doubles on that inspiring subject.

CHAPTER XI

INEXCUSABLE INVASION OF A DUCAL
ENTERTAINMENT

To LORD PETER WIMSEY, the few weeks of his life
spent in unravelling the Problem of the Iron Staircase
possessed an odd dreamlike quality, noticeable at the time
and still more insistent in retrospect. The very work that
engaged him—or rather, the shadowy simulacrum of himself that signed itself on every morning in the name of
Death Bredon—wafted him into a sphere of dim platonic
archetypes, bearing a scarcely recognizable relationship to
anything in the living world. Here those strange entities,
the Thrifty Housewife, the Man of Discrimination, the
Keen Buyer and the Good Judge, for ever young, for ever
handsome, for ever virtuous, economical and inquisitive,
moved to and fro upon their complicated orbits, comparing
prices and values, making tests of purity, asking indiscreet
questions about each other's ailments, household expenses,
bed-springs, shaving cream, diet, laundry work and boots,
perpetually spending to save and saving to spend, cutting
out coupons and collecting cartons, surprising husbands
with margarine and wives with patent washers and vacuum
cleaners, occupied from morning to night in washing, cooking, dusting, filing, saving their children from germs, their
complexions from wind and weather, their teeth from
decay and their stomachs from indigestion, and yet adding
so many hours to the day by labour-saving appliances that
they had always leisure for visiting the talkies, sprawling on
the beach to picnic upon Potted Meats and Tinned Fruit,
and (when adorned by So-and-so's Silks, Blank's Gloves,

Dash's Footwear, Whatnot's Weatherproof Complexion Cream and Thingummy's Beautifying Shampoos), even attending Ranelagh, Cowes, the Grand Stand at Ascot, Monte Carlo and the Queen's Drawing-Rooms. Where, Bredon asked himself, did the money come from that was to be spent so variously and so lavishly? If this hell's-dance of spending and saving were to stop for a moment, what would happen? If all the advertising in the world were to shut down tomorrow, would people still go on buying more soap, eating more apples, giving their children more vitamins, roughage, milk, olive oil, scooters and laxatives, learning more languages by gramophone, hearing more virtuosos by radio, re-decorating their houses, refreshing themselves with more non-alcoholic thirst-quenchers, cooking more new, appetizing dishes, affording themselves that little extra touch which means so much? Or would the whole desperate whirligig slow down, and the exhausted public relapse upon plain grub and elbow-grease? He did not know. Like all rich men, he had never before paid any attention to advertisements. He had never realized the enormous commercial importance of the comparatively poor. Not on the wealthy, who buy only what they want when they want it, was the vast superstructure of industry founded and built up, but on those who, aching for a luxury beyond their reach and for a leisure for ever denied them, could be bullied or wheedled into spending their few hardly won shillings on whatever might give them, if only for a moment, a leisured and luxurious illusion. Phantasmagoria—a city of dreadful day, of crude shapes and colours piled Babel-like in a heaven of harsh cobalt and rocking over a void of bankruptcy—a Cloud Cuckooland, peopled by pitiful ghosts, from the Thrifty Housewife providing a Grand Family Meal for Fourpence with the aid of Dairyfields Butter Beans in Margarine, to the Typist capturing the affections of Prince Charming by a liberal use of Muggins's Magnolia Face Cream.

Among these phantasms, Death Bredon, driving his pen

across reams of office foolscap, was a phantasm too, emerging from this nightmare toil to a still more fantastical existence amid people whose aspirations, rivalries and modes of thought were alien, and earnest beyond anything in his waking experience. Nor, when the Greenwich-driven clocks had jerked on to half-past five, had he any world of reality to which to return; for then the illusionary Mr. Bredon dislimned and became the still more illusionary Harlequin of a dope-addict's dream; an advertising figure more crude and fanciful than any that postured in the columns of the *Morning Star;* a thing bodiless and absurd, a mouthpiece of stale clichés shouting in dull ears without a brain. From this abominable impersonation he could not now free himself, since at the sound of his name or the sight of his unmasked face, all the doors in that other dream-city—the city of dreadful night—would be closed to him.

From one haunting disquietude, Dian de Momerie's moment of inexplicable insight had freed him. She no longer desired him. He thought she rather dreaded him; yet, at the note of the penny whistle she would come out and drive with him, hour after hour, in the great black Daimler, till night turned to daybreak. He sometimes wondered whether she believed in his existence at all; she treated him as though he were some hateful but fascinating figure in a hashish-vision. His fear now was that her unbalanced fancy might topple her over the edge of suicide. She asked him once what he was and what he wanted, and he told her stark truth, so far as it went.

"I am here because Victor Dean died. When the world knows how he died, I shall go back to the place from which I came."

"To the place from which you came. I've heard that said before, but I can't remember where."

"If you ever heard a man condemned to death, then you heard it said then."

"My God, yes! That was it. I went to a murder trial once. There was a horrible old man, the Judge—I forget his

name. He was like a wicked old scarlet parrot, and he
said it as though he liked it. 'And may the Lord have
mercy upon your soul.' Do we have souls, Harlequin, or is
that all nonsense? It is nonsense, isn't it?"

"So far as you are concerned, it probably is."

"But what have I got to do with Victor's death?"

"Nothing, I hope. But you ought to know."

"Of course I had nothing to do with it."

And indeed, she might not have. This was the most
phantasmal part of the illusion—the border where day-
dream and night-dream marched together in an eternal twilight. The man had been murdered—of that he was now
certain; but what hand had struck the blow and why was
still beyond all guessing. Bredon's instinct told him to hold
fast to Dian de Momerie. She was the guardian of the
shadow-frontier; through her, Victor Dean, surely the most
prosaic denizen of the garish city of daylight, had stepped
into the place of bright flares and black abysses, whose
ministers are drink and drugs and its monarch death. But
question her as he might, he could get no help from her.
She had told him one thing only, and over and over again
he pondered it, wondering how it fitted into the plot.
Milligan, the sinister Milligan, knew something about
Pym's, or somebody who worked at Pym's. He had known
of this before he met Dean, for he had said on meeting
him: "So you're the chap, are you?" What connection was
there? What had Dean, at Pym's, had to do with Milligan,
before Milligan knew him? Was it merely that Dian had
boasted, laughing, of having a lover from that respectable
agency? Had Victor Dean died merely because of Dian's
fancy for him?

Wimsey could not believe it; the fancy had died first, and
the death of Dean was, after that, surely superfluous. Besides, when they of the city of night slay for passion's sake,
they lay no elaborate schemes, wipe off no fingerprints and
hold no discreet tongues before or after. Brawls and
revolver-shots, with loud sobs and maudlin remorse, are the

signs and tokens of fatal passion among leaders of the bright life.

One other piece of information Dian had indeed given him, but at that moment he could not interpret it, and was not even aware that he held. it. He could only wait, like a cat at a mouse-hole, till something popped out that he could run after. And so he passed his nights very wearily, driving the car and playing upon a penny whistle, and snatching his sleep in the small hours, before taking up the daily grind at Pym's.

Wimsey was quite right about Dian de Momerie's feeling for him. He excited her and frightened her, and, on the whole, she got a sensation of rather titillating horror at the sound of the penny whistle. But the real reason of her anxiety to propitiate him was founded on a coincidence that he could not have known and that she did not tell him.

On the day after their first encounter, Dian had backed an outsider called Acrobat, and it had come in at 50 to 1. Three days after the adventure in the woods, she had backed another outsider called Harlequin, each way, and it had come in second at 100 to 1. Thereafter, she had entertained no doubt whatever that he was a powerful and heaven-sent mascot. The day after a meeting with him was her lucky day, and it was a fact that on those days she usually succeeded in winning money in one way or another. Horses, after those first two brilliant coups, had been rather disappointing, but her fortune with cards had been good. How much of this good fortune had been due to sheer self-confidence and the will to win, only a psychologist could say; the winnings were there, and she had no doubt at all about the reason for them. She did not tell him that he was a mascot, from a superstitious feeling that to do so would be to break the luck, but she had been to a crystal-gazer, who, reading her mind like a book, had encouraged her in the belief that a mysterious stranger would bring her good fortune.

Major Milligan, sprawling upon the couch in Dian's flat with a whisky-and-soda, turned on her a pair of rather bilious eyes. He was a large, saturnine man, blank as to morals but comparatively sober in his habits, as people must be who make money out of other people's vices.

"Ever see anything of that Dean girl nowadays, Dian?"

"No, darling," said Dian, absently. She was getting rather tired of Milligan, and would have liked to break with him, if only he had not been so useful, and if she had not known too much to make a break-away healthy.

"Well, I wish you would."

"Oh, why? She's one of Nature's worst bores, darling."

"I want to know if she knows anything about that place where Dean used to work."

"The advertising place? But, Tod, how too yawn-making. Why do you want to know about advertising?"

"Oh, never mind why. I was on to something rather useful there, that's all."

"Oh!" Dian considered. This, she thought, was interesting. Something to be made out of this, perhaps. "I'll give her a ring if you like. But she's about as wet as a drowned eel. *What* do you want to know?"

"That's my business."

"Tod, I've often wanted to ask you. Why did you say I'd got to chuck Victor? Not that I cared about him, the poor fish, but I just wondered, especially after you'd told me to string him along."

"Because," replied Major Milligan, "the young what-not was trying to double-cross me."

"Good heavens, Tod—you ought to go on the talkies as Dog-faced Dick the Dope-King of the Underworld. Talk sense, darling."

"That's all very well, my girl, but your little Victor was getting to be a nuisance. Somebody had been talking to him —probably you."

"Me? that's good! There wasn't anything I could tell him. You never tell me anything, Tod."

"No—I've got some sense left."

"How rude you are, darling. Well, you see, I couldn't have split to Victor. Did you bump Victor off, Tod?"

"Who says he was bumped off?"

"A little bird told me."

"Is that your friend in the black and white checks?"

Dian hesitated. In an expansive and not very sober moment, she had told Tod about her adventure in the woods, and now rather wished she had not. Milligan took her silence for consent and went on:

"Who is that fellow, Dian?"

"Haven't the foggiest."

"What's he want?"

"He doesn't want me, at any rate," said Dian. "Isn't that humiliating, Tod?"

"It must be." Milligan grinned. "But what's the big idea?"

"I think he's on Victor's lay, whatever that was. He said he wouldn't be here if Victor hadn't popped off. Too thrilling, don't you think?"

"Um," said Milligan. "I think I'd like to meet this friend of yours. When's he likely to turn up?"

"Damned if I know. He just arrives. I don't think I'd have anything to do with him, Tod, if I were you. He's dangerous—queer, somehow. I've got a hunch about him."

"Your brain's going to mush, sweetest," said Milligan, "and he's trading on it, that's all."

"Oh, well," said Dian, "he amuses me, and you don't any more. You're getting to be a bit feeding, Tod." She yawned and trailed over to the looking-glass, where she inspected her face narrowly. "I think I'll give up dope, Tod. I'm getting puffy under the eyes. Do you think it would be amusing to go all good?"

"About as amusing as a Quaker meeting. Has your friend been trying to reform you? That's damn good."

"Reform me, nothing. But I'm looking horribly hag-like tonight. Oh, hell! what's the odds, anyway? Let's do something."

"All right. Come on round to Slinker's. He's throwing a party."

"I'm sick of Slinker's parties. I say, Tod, let's go and gate-crash something really virtuous. Who's the stickiest old cat in London that's got anything on?"

"Dunno."

"Tell you what. We'll scoop up Slinker's party and go round and look for striped awnings, and crash the first thing we see."

"Right-ho! I'm on."

Half an hour later, a noisy gang, squashed into five cars and a taxi, were whooping through the quieter squares of the West End. Even today, a few strongholds of the grimly aristocratic are left in Mayfair, and Dian, leaning from the open window of the leading car, presently gave tongue before a tall, old-fashioned house, whose entrance was adorned with a striped awning, a crimson carpet and an array of hothouse plants in tubs upon the steps.

"Whoopee! Hit it up, boys! Here's something! Whose is it?"

"My God!" said Slinger Braithwaite. "We've hit the bull, all right. It's Denver's place."

"You won't get in there," said Milligan. "The Duchess of Denver is heaven's prize frozen-face. Look at the chucker-out in the doorway. Better try something easier."

"Easier be damned. We said the first we came to, and this is the first. No ratting, darlings."

"Well, look here," said Milligan, "we'd better try the back entrance. There's a gate into the garden round the other side, opening on the car-park. We've more chance there."

From the other side, the assault turned out to be easy enough. The cars were parked in a back street, and on approaching the garden gate, they found it wide open, displaying a marquee, in which supper was being held. A bunch of guests came out just as they arrived, while, almost on their heels, two large cars drove up and disgorged a large party of people.

"Blow being announced," said an immaculate person, "we'll just barge right in and dodge the Ambassadors."

"Freddy, you can't."

"Can't I? You watch me." Freddy tucked his partner's arm firmly under his own and marched with determination up to the gate. "We're certain to barge into old Peter or somebody in the garden."

Dian nipped Milligan's arm, and the pair of them fell in behind the new arrivals. The gate was passed—but a footman just inside presented an unexpected obstacle.

"Mr. and Mrs. Frederick Arbuthnot," said the immaculate gentleman. "And party," he added, waving a vague hand behind him.

"Well, *we're* in, anyhow," exulted Dian.

Helen, Duchess of Denver, looked round with satisfaction upon her party. It was all going very nicely indeed. The Ambassador and his wife had expressed delight at the quality of the wine. The band was good, the refreshments more than adequate. A tone of mellow decorum pervaded the atmosphere. Her own dress, she thought, became her, although her mother-in-law, the Dowager Duchess, had said something rather acid about her spine. But then, the Dowager was always a little tiresome and incalculable. One must be fashionable, though one would not, of course, be vulgarly immodest. Helen considered that she was showing the exact number of vertebrae that the occasion demanded. One less would be incorrect; one more would be over-modern. She thanked Providence that at forty-five she still kept her figure—as indeed, she did, having been remarkably flat on both aspects the whole of her life.

She was just raising a well-earned glass of champagne to her lips when she paused, and set it down again. Something was wrong. She glanced hurriedly round for her husband. He was not there, but a few paces off an elegant black back and smooth, straw-coloured head of hair announced the presence of her brother-in-law, Wimsey. Hastily excusing herself to Lady Mendip, with whom she had been discussing the latest enormities of the Government, she edged her way through the crowd and caught Wimsey's arm.

"Peter! Look over there. Who are those people?"

Wimsey turned and stared in the direction pointed by the Duchess' fan.

"Good God, Helen! You've caught a pair of ripe ones this time! That's the de Momerie girl and her tame dope-merchant."

The Duchess shuddered.

"How horrible! Disgusting woman! How in the world did they get in? . . . Do you know them?"

"Not officially, no."

"Thank goodness! I was afraid you'd let them in. I never know what you're going to do next; you know so many impossible people."

"Not guilty this time, Helen."

"Ask Bracket how he came to let them in."

"I fly," said Wimsey, "to obey your behest."

He finished the drink he had in his hand, and set off in a leisurely manner in pursuit of the footman. Presently he returned.

"Bracket says they came with Freddy Arbuthnot."

"Find Freddy."

The Hon. Freddy Arbuthnot, when found, denied all knowledge of the intruders. "But there was a bit of a scrum at the gate, you know," he admitted, ingenuously, "and I daresay they barged in with the crowd. The de Momerie girl, eh, what? Where is she? I must have a look at her. Hot stuff and all that, what?"

"You will do nothing of the sort, Freddy. Where in the world is Gerald? Not here. He never is when he's wanted. You'll have to go and turn them out, Peter."

Wimsey, who had had time for a careful calculation, asked nothing better.

"I will turn them out," he announced, "like one John Smith. Where are they?"

The Duchess, who had kept a glassy eye upon them,

waved a stern hand in the direction of the terrace. Wimsey ambled off amiably.

"Forgive me, dear Lady Mendip," said the Duchess, returning to her guest. "I had a little commission to give to my brother-in-law."

Up the dimly-lit terrace steps went Wimsey. The shadow of a tall pillar-rose fell across his face and chequered his white shirt-front with dancing black; and as he went he whistled softly: "Tom, Tom, the piper's son."

Dian de Momerie clutched Milligan's arm as she turned. Wimsey stopped whistling.

"Er—good evening," he said, "excuse me. Miss de Momerie, I think."

"Harlequin!" cried Dian.

"I beg your pardon?"

"Harlequin. So here you are. I've got you this time. And I'm going to see your face properly if I die for it."

"I'm afraid there is some mistake," said Wimsey.

Milligan thought it time to interfere.

"Ah!" said he, "the mysterious stranger. I think it's time you and I had a word, young man. May I ask why you have been tagging round after this lady in a mountebank get-up?"

"I fear," said Wimsey, more elaborately, "that you are labouring under a misapprehension, sir, whoever you are. I have been dispatched by the Duchess on a—forgive me—somewhat distasteful errand. She regrets that she has not the honour of this lady's acquaintance, nor, sir, of yours, and wishes me to ask you by whose invitation you are here."

Dian laughed, rather noisily.

"You do it marvellously, darling," she said. "We gate-crashed on the dear old bird—same as you did, I expect."

"So the Duchess inferred," replied Wimsey. "I am sorry. I'm afraid I must ask you to leave at once."

"That's pretty good," said Milligan, insolently. "I'm afraid it won't work. It may be a fact that we weren't invited here, but we aren't going to turn out for a nameless acrobat who's afraid to show his face."

"You must be mistaking me for a friend of yours," said

Wimsey. "Allow me." He stepped across to the nearest pillar and pressed a switch, flooding that end of the terrace with light. "My name is Peter Wimsey; I am Denver's brother, and my face—such as it is, is entirely at your service."

He fixed his monocle in his eye and stared unpleasantly at Milligan.

"But aren't you my Harlequin?" protested Dian. "Don't be such an ass—I know you are. I know your voice perfectly well—and your mouth and chin. Besides, you were whistling that tune."

"This is very interesting," said Wimsey. "Is it possible—I fear it is—I think you must have encountered my unfortunate cousin Bredon."

"That was the name—" began Dian, uncertainly, and stopped.

"I am glad to hear it," replied Wimsey. "Sometimes he gives mine, which makes it very awkward."

"See here, Dian," broke in Milligan, "you seem to have dropped a brick. You'd better apologize and then we'll clear. Sorry we crashed in, and all that—"

"One moment," said Wimsey. "I should like to hear more about this. Be good enough to come into the house for a moment. This way."

He ushered them courteously round the corner of the terrace, up a side path and by way of a French window into a small ante-room, laid out with tables and a cocktail bar.

"What will you drink? Whiskies? I might have known it. The abominable practice of putting whisky on top of mixed drinks late at night is responsible for more ruined complexions and reputations than any other single cause. There is many a woman now walking the streets of London through putting whisky on top of gin cocktails. Two stiff whiskies, Tomlin, and a liqueur brandy."

"Very good, my lord."

"You perceive," said Wimsey, returning with the drinks, "the true object of this hospitable gesture. I have established my identity, by the evidence of the reliable Tomlin. Let us now seek a spot less open to interruption. I suggest

the library. This way. My brother, being an English gentleman, possesses a library in all his houses, though he never
opens a book. This is called fidelity to ancient tradition.
The chairs, however, are comfortable. Pray be seated. And
now, tell me all about your encounter with my scandalous
cousin."

"One moment," said Milligan, before Dian could speak.
"I think I know the stud-book pretty well. I was not aware
that you had a cousin Bredon."

"It is not every puppy that appears in the kennel-book,"
replied Wimsey carelessly, "and it is a wise man that knows
all his own cousins. But what matter? Family is family,
though indicated by the border compony (or gobony if you
prefer that form of the word) or by the bend or baton sinister, called by most writers of fiction the bar sinister, for
reasons which I am unable to determine. My regrettable
cousin Bredon, having no particular right to one family
name more than another, makes it his practice to employ
them all in turn, thus displaying a happy absence of favour-
itism. Please help yourselves to smokes. You will find the
cigars passable, Mr.—er—"

"Milligan."

"Ah! the notor—the well-known Major Milligan? You
have a residence on the river, I fancy. Charming, charming.
Its fame has reached me from time to time through my good
brother-in-law, Chief-Inspector Parker of Scotland Yard.
A beautiful, retired spot, I believe?"

"Just so," said Milligan. "I had the pleasure of entertaining your cousin there one night."

"Did he gate-crash on you? That is exactly what he
would do. And you have retorted upon my dear sister-in-
law. Poetic justice, of course. I appreciate it—though possibly the Duchess will take a different view of the matter."

"No; he was brought by a lady of my acquaintance."

"He is improving. Major Milligan, painful though it may
be to me, I feel that I ought to warn you against that cousin
of mine. He is definitely not nice to know. If he has been
thrusting his attentions upon Miss de Momerie, it is

probably with some ulterior object. Not," added Wimsey, "that any man would need an ulterior object for such attentions. Miss de Momerie is an object in herself—"

His eye wandered over Dian, scantily clothed and slightly intoxicated, with a cold appraisement which rendered the words almost impertinent.

"But," he resumed, "I know my cousin Bredon—too well. Few people know him better. And I must confess that he is the last man to whom I should look for a disinterested attachment. I am unhappily obliged, in self-defence, to keep an eye on Cousin Bredon's movements, and I should be deeply grateful to be informed of the details of his latest escapade."

"All right, I'll tell you," said Dian. The whisky had strung her up to recklessness, and she became suddenly voluble, disregarding Milligan's scowls. She poured out the tale of her adventures. The incident of the fountain-dive seemed to cause Lord Peter Wimsey acute distress.

"Vulgar ostentation!" he said, shaking his head. "How many times have I implored Bredon to conduct himself in a quiet and reasonable manner."

"I thought he was too marvellous," said Dian, and proceeded to relate the encounter in the wood.

"He always plays 'Tom, Tom, the piper's son,' so of course, when you came along whistling it, I thought it was him."

Wimsey's face darkened in a most convincing manner. "Disgusting," he said.

"Besides, you are so much alike—the same voice and the same face as far as one can see it, you know. But of course he never took off his mask—"

"No wonder," said Wimsey, "no wonder." He heaved a deep sigh. "The police are interested in my cousin Bredon."

"How thrilling!"

"What for?" demanded Milligan.

"For impersonating me, among other things," said Wimsey, now happily launched and well away. "I cannot tell you in the brief time at our disposal, the distress and humiliation I have been put to on Bredon's account. Bailing him out at police stations—honouring cheques drawn in my name—rescuing him from haunts of infamy—I am telling you all these distressing details in confidence, of course."

"We won't split," said Dian.

"He trades upon our unfortunate resemblance," went on Wimsey. "He copies my habits, smokes my favourite brand of cigarettes, drives a car like mine, even whistles my favourite air—one, I may say, peculiarly well adapted for performance upon the penny whistle."

"He must be pretty well off," said Dian, "to drive a car like that."

"*That*," said Wimsey, "is the most melancholy thing of all. I suspect him—but perhaps I had better not say anything about that."

"Oh, do tell," urged Dian, her eyes dancing with excitement. "It sounds too terribly breath-taking."

"I suspect him," said Wimsey, in solemn and awful tones, "of having to do with—*smug-druggling*—I mean, dash it all—drug-smuggling."

"You don't say so," said Milligan.

"Well, I can't prove it. But I have received warnings from a certain quarter. You understand me." Wimsey selected a fresh cigarette and tapped it, with the air of one who has closed the coffin-lid upon a dead secret and is nailing it down securely. "I don't want to interfere in your affairs in any way at all, Major Milligan. I trust that I shall never be called upon to do so." Here he transfixed Milligan with another hard stare. "But you will perhaps allow me to give you, and this lady, a word of warning. Do not have too much to do with my cousin Bredon."

"I think you're talking rot," said Dian. "Why, you can't even get him to—"

"Cigarette, Dian?" interrupted Milligan, rather sharply.

"I do not say," resumed Wimsey, raking Dian slowly with his eyes, and then turning again to Milligan, "that my deplorable cousin is himself an addict to cocaine or heroin or anything of that description. In some ways, it would be almost more respectable if he were. The man or woman who can batten on the weaknesses of his fellow-creatures without sharing them is, I admit, to me a singularly disgusting object. I may be old-fashioned, but there it is."

"Quite so," said Milligan.

"I do not know, and do not wish to know," went on Wimsey, "how you came to allow my cousin Bredon into your house, nor what, on his side, can have brought him there. I prefer not to suppose that he found there any other attraction than good drinks and good company. You may think, Major Milligan, that because I have interested myself in certain police cases, I am a consistent busybody. That is not the case. Unless I am forced to take an interest in another man's business, I greatly prefer to let him alone. But I think it only fair to tell you that I *am* forced to take an interest in my cousin Bredon and that he is a person whose acquaintance might prove—shall I say, embarrassing? —to any one who preferred to live a quiet life. I don't think I need say any more, need I?"

"Not at all," said Milligan. "I am much obliged to you for the warning, and so, I am sure, is Miss de Momerie."

"Of course, I'm frightfully glad to know all about it," said Dian. "Your cousin sounds a perfect lamb. I like 'em dangerous. Pompous people are too terribly moribund, aren't they?"

Wimsey bowed.

"My dear lady, your choice of friends is entirely at your own discretion."

"I'm glad to hear it. I got the impression that the Duchess wasn't too fearfully anxious to have both arms round my neck."

"Ah! the Duchess—no. There, I fear, all the discretion is on the other side, what? Which reminds me—"

"Quite right," said Milligan. "We have trespassed on your hospitality too long. We must really apologize and remove ourselves. By the way, there were some other members of our party—"

"I expect my sister-in-law will have dealt with them by

now," said Wimsey with a grin. "If not, I will make a point of seeing them and telling them that you have gone on to—where shall I say?"

Dian gave her own address.

"You'd better come round and have a drink, too," she suggested.

"Alas!" said Wimsey, "duty and all that sort of thing, what? Can't leave my sister-in-law in the lurch, greatly as I should enjoy the entertainment." He rang the bell. "You will excuse me now, I trust. I must see to our other guests. Porlock, show this lady and gentleman out."

He returned to the garden by way of the terrace, whistling a passage of Bach, as was his way when pleased.

"Nun gehn wir wo der Tudelsack, der Tudel, tudel, tudel, tudel, tudelsack . . ."

"I wonder, was the fly too big and gaudy? Will he rise to it? We shall see."

"My dear Peter," said the Duchess, fretfully, "what a terrible time you have been. Please go and fetch Mme. de Framboise-Douillet an ice. And tell your brother I want him."

CHAPTER XII

SURPRISING ACQUISITION OF A JUNIOR
REPORTER

VERY early one morning, a junior reporter on the *Morning Star,* of no importance to anybody except himself and his widowed mother, walked out of that great newspaper's palatial new offices and into the affairs of Chief-Inspector Parker. This nonentity's name was Hector Puncheon, and he was in Fleet Street at that time because a fire had broken out the previous night in a large City warehouse, destroying a great deal of valuable property and involving the spectacular escapes of three night watchmen and a cat from the roofs of the adjacent buildings. Hector Puncheon, summoned to the scene for the excellent reason that he had lodgings in the West Central district and could be transported to the scene of action in a comparatively brief time, had written a short stop-press notice of the disaster for the early country editions, a longer and more exciting account for the London edition, and then a still longer and more detailed report, complete with the night-watchmen's and eye-witnesses' stories and a personal interview with the cat, for the early editions of the *Evening Comet,* twin-organ to the *Morning Star* and housed in the same building.

After completing all this toil, he was wakeful and hungry. He sought an all-night restaurant in Fleet Street, accustomed to catering for the untimely needs of pressmen, and, having previously armed himself with a copy of the *Morning Star* as it poured out damp from the machines, sat down to a 3 a.m. breakfast of grilled sausages, coffee and rolls.

He ate with leisurely zest, pleased with himself and his good fortune, and persuaded that not even the most distinguished of the senior men could have turned in a column more full of snap, pep and human interest than his own. The interview with the cat had been particularly full of appeal. The animal was, it seemed, an illustrious rat-catcher, with many famous deeds to her credit. Not only that, but she had been the first to notice the smell of fire and had, by her anguished and intelligent mewings, attracted the attention of night-watchman number one, who had been in the act of brewing himself a cup of tea when the outbreak took place. Thirdly, the cat, an ugly black-and-white creature with a spotted face, was about to become a mother for the tenth time, and Hector Puncheon by a brilliant inspiration had secured the reversion of the expected family for the *Morning Star*, so that half a dozen or so fortunate readers might, by applying to their favourite paper and enclosing a small donation for the Animals' Hospital, become the happy owners of kittens with a pre-natal reputation and a magnificent rat-catching pedigree. Hector Puncheon felt that he had done well. He had been alert and courageous, offering the night-watchman ten shillings on his own responsibility the very moment the big idea occurred to him, and the night-editor had okayed the stunt and even remarked that it would do quite well.

Filled with sausages and contentment, Hector Puncheon lingered over his paper, reading the Special Friday Feature with approval and appreciating the political cartoon. At length, he folded the sheet, stuffed it in his pocket, tipped the waiter extravagantly with sixpence and emerged into Fleet Street.

The morning was fine, though chilly, and he felt that after his night's labours, a little walk would do him good. He strolled happily along, past the Griffin at Temple Bar and the Law Courts and the churches of St. Clement Danes and St. Mary-le-Strand, and made his way up Kingsway. It was only when he got to the turning into Great Queen Street that he became aware of something lacking in an otherwise satisfactory universe. Great Queen Street led into Long Acre; off Long Acre lay Covent Garden; already the vans and lorries laden with fruit and flowers were rumbling in from all over the country and rumbling out again. Already the porters were unloading their stout sacks, huge crates, round baskets, frail punnets and long flat boxes filled with living scent and colour, sweating and grumbling over their labours as though their exquisite burdens were so much fish or pig-iron. And for the benefit of these men the pubs would be open, for Covent Garden interprets the London licensing regulations to suit its own topsy-turvy hours of labour. Hector Puncheon had had a successful night and had celebrated his success with sausages and coffee; but there are, dash it all! more suitable methods of celebration.

Hector Puncheon, swinging blithely along in his serviceable grey flannel bags and tweed jacket, covered by an old burberry, suddenly realized that he owned the world, including all the beer in Covent Garden Market. He turned into Great Queen Street, traversed half the length of Long Acre, dodged under the nose of a van horse at the entrance to the Underground Station, and set his face towards the market, picking his way cheerfully between the boxes and baskets and carts and straw that littered the pavement. Humming a lively tune, he turned in through the swing doors of the White Swan.

Although it was only a quarter past four, the Swan was already doing a brisk trade. Hector Puncheon edged his way up to the bar between two enormous carters and waited modestly for the landlord to finish serving his habitual customers before calling attention to himself. A lively discussion was going on about the merits of a dog named Forked Lightning. Hector, always ready to pick up a hint about anything that was, or might conceivably be turned into news, pulled his early *Morning Star* from his pocket and pretended to read it, while keeping his ears open.

"And what I say is," said Carter the First, "—same again, Joe—what I say is, when a dawg that's fancied like that dawg is, stops dead 'arf way round the course like as if 'e'd a-bin shot, wot I say is, I likes to know wot's at the back of it."

"Ar," said Carter the Second.

"Mind you," went on Carter the First, "I ain't sayin' as animals is always to be relied on. They 'as their off-days, same as you an' me, but wot I says is—"

"That's a fact," put in a smaller man, from the other side of Carter the Second, "that's a fact, that is. An' wot's more, they 'as their fancies. I 'ad a dawg once as couldn't abide the sight of a goat. Or maybe it was the smell. I dunno. But show 'im a goat any time, and 'e got a fit of the trembles. Couldn't run all day. I remember one time when I was bringin' 'im up to run at the White City, there was a bloke in the street leadin' two goats on a string—"

"Wot did a bloke want with two goats?" demanded Carter the Second, suspiciously.

"'Ow should I know wot 'e wanted with goats?" retorted the little man, indignantly. "They wasn't my goats, was they? Well, that there dawg—"

"That's different," said Carter the First. "Nerves is nerves, and a thing like a goat might 'appen to anybody, but wot I says is—"

"What's yours, sir?" inquired the landlord.

"Oh, I think I'll have a Guinness," said Hector. "Guinness is good for you—particularly on a chilly morning. Perhaps," he added, feeling pleased with himself and the world, "these gentlemen will join me."

The two carters and the little man expressed their gratification, and ordered beer.

"It's a queer thing, this business of nerves," said the little man. "Talking of Guinness, now, my old aunt had a parrot. Some bird it was, too. Learnt to speak from a sailor. Fortunately the old lady couldn't 'ear 'alf of wot it said, and didn't understand the other 'alf. Now, that there bird—"

"You seem to have had a wide experience with livestock," observed Hector Puncheon.

"I 'ave that," said the little man. "That there bird, as I was going to say, got fits of nerves as would surprise you. 'Unched 'isself up on 'is perch like, and shivered fit to shake 'isself to pieces. And wot was the reason of that, do you think?"

"Beggared if I know," said Carter the Second. "Your 'ealth, sir."

"Mice," said the little man, triumphantly. "Couldn't stand the sight of a mouse. And wot do you think we 'ad to give it to pull it round, like?"

"Brandy," suggested Carter the First. "Nothing like brandy for parrots. We got one at 'ome—one o' them green sort. My wife's brother brought it 'ome with 'im—"

"They ain't such good talkers as the grey ones," said Carter the Second. "There was a parrot at the old Rose & Crown dahn Seven Dials way—"

"Brandy?" scoffed the little man, "not 'im. 'E wouldn't look at brandy."

"Wouldn't 'e now?" said Carter the First. "Now, you show our old bird brandy, an' 'e'll 'op right out of 'is cage for it same as a Christian. Not too much, mind you, but give it 'im neat in a teaspoon—"

"Well, it wasn't brandy," persisted the little man. "Aunt's was a teetotal bird, 'e was. Now, I'll give you three guesses, an' if you gets it right, I'll stand drinks all round, and I can't say fairer 'an that."

"Aspirin?" suggested the landlord, anxious that the round of drinks should be stood by somebody.

The little man shook his head.

"Ginger," said Carter the Second. "Birds is sometimes wonderful fond o' ginger. Stimulates the innards. Though, mind you, some says it's too 'eatin', an' brings their fevvers aht."

"Nutrax for Nerves," suggested Hector Puncheon, a little wildly, his eye having been caught by that morning's half-double, which carried the intriguing headline: "WHY BLAME THE WOMAN?"

"Nutrax nothing," snorted the little man, "nor none o'

yer patent slops. No. Strong coffee wiv' cayenne pepper in
it—that's wot that bird liked. Put 'im right in a jiff, it did.
Well, seein' as the drinks ain't on me this time—"

He looked wistful, and Hector obliged again with the
same all round. Carter the Second, jerking his beer off at
one gulp and offering a general salute to the company,
shouldered his way out, and the little man moved up closer
to Hector Puncheon to make way for a florid person in evening dress, who had just shot his way in through the door
and now stood swaying a little uncertainly against the bar.

"Scotch-and-soda," said this person, without preface,
"double Scotch and not too bloody much soda."

The landlord looked at him keenly.

"Thass all right," said the newcomer, "I know what
you're thinking, my boy, but I'm not drunk. Norra bittovit.
Nerves a liddleoutavorder, 'tsall." He paused, evidently conscious that his speech was getting a little ahead of itself.
"Been sittin' up with a sick friend," he explained, carefully. "Very trying to the system, sittin' up all night. Very
hard on the conshi-conshishushion—excuse me—slight acshi-
dent to my dental plate, mush gettitsheento."

He leaned one elbow on the bar, pawed vaguely with his
foot for the brass rail, pushed his silk hat well to the back
of his head and beamed pleasantly upon the company.

The landlord of the Swan looked at him again with a
practised eye, calculated that his customer could probably
carry one more Scotch-and-soda without actual disaster, and
fulfilled his order.

"Thanks verrimush, old feller," said the stranger. "Well,
goo' luck, all. What are these gentlemen taking?"

Hector Puncheon excused himself politely, explaining
that he had really had all he wanted and must now be
going home.

"No, no," said the other, hurt. "Mustn't say that. Not-
time to gome yet. Night yet young." He flung an affectionate arm round Hector's neck. "I like your face. You're the
sortafeller I like. You must come along one day 'n see my
little place. Roses roun' the porch an' all that. Give you my

card." He hunted in his pockets and produced a note-case, which he flapped open on the bar-counter. A quantity of small pieces of paper flew out right and left.

"Dashitall," said the gentleman in dress clothes, "what I mean, dashit." Hector stooped to pick up some of the scattered oddments, but the little man was before him.

"Thanks, thanks," said the gentleman. "Wheresh card? Thatsh not card, thatsh my wife's shopping-list—you gorra-wife?"

"Not yet," admitted Hector.

"Lucky devil," replied the stranger with emphasis. "No wife, no damned shopping-list." His vagrant attention was caught and held by the shopping-list, which he held up in one hand and tried, unsuccessfully, to focus with a slightly squinting gaze. "Alwaysh bringing home parcels like a blurry errand-boy. Where'd I put that parcel now?"

"You 'adn't no parcel when you come in 'ere, guv'nor," said Carter the First. The question of drinks seemed to have been shelved, and the worthy man no doubt felt it was time to remind the gentleman that there were others in the bar, besides the abstemious Mr. Puncheon. "Dry work," he added, "cartin' parcels round."

"Damn dry," said the married gentleman. "Mine's a Scotch-and-soda. Whaddid you say you'd have, ol' boy?" He again embraced Hector Puncheon, who gently disentangled himself.

"I really don't want—" he began; but, seeing that this reiterated refusal might give offence, he gave way and asked for a half-tankard of bitter.

"Talking about parrots," said a thin voice behind them. Hector started and, looking round, observed a dried-up old man seated at a small table in the corner of the bar, absorbing a gin-and-potash. He must have been there all the time, thought Hector.

The gentleman in dress clothes swung round upon him so sharply that he lost his balance and had to cling to the little man to save himself.

"I never mentioned parrots," he said, enunciating the

words very distinctly. "I shouldn't think of talking about parrots."

"I once knowed a parson wot 'ad a parrot," continued the old man. "Joey, they called 'im."

"Wot, the parson?" asked the little man.

"No, the parrot," said the old fellow, mildly, "and that there parrot hadn't ever been out of the parson's family. Joined in family prayers, he did and said 'Amen' like a Christian. Well, one day this here parson—"

A rush of customers entering from the market drew the landlord's attention away and drowned the next sentence or so of the story. The carter hailed some acquaintances and joined them in a fresh round of beer. Hector, shaking off the intoxicated gentleman, who seemed now to be inviting him to join a cozy little fishing party in Scotland, turned to go, but found himself caught and held by the old man.

"—and old parson found the bishop sitting over the cage with a lump of sugar in his fingers, saying, 'Come on, Joey, say it! B . . . b . . . b . . . !' And that, mind you," said the old man, "was a Church of England bishop. And what do you think the bishop did then?"

"I can't imagine," said Hector.

"Made the parson a canon," said the old man, triumphantly.

"Never!" said Hector.

"But that's nothing," pursued the old man. "There was a parrot I knew down in Somerset—"

Hector felt he really could not bear to hear about the parrot down in Somerset. He extricated himself politely and fled.

His next activity was to go home and have a bath, after which he coiled himself up on his bed and slept placidly till his normal breakfast-time at nine.

He breakfasted in his dressing-gown, and it was when he was transferring his various possessions from his grey flannels to his navy lounge suit that he came upon the little packet. It was neatly done up with sealing-wax in white paper, and bore the innocent label "Bicarbonate of Soda." He stared at it in surprise.

Hector Puncheon was a young man with a hearty and healthy digestion. He had heard, of course, of sodium bicarb, and its virtues, but only as a wealthy man hears of hire-purchase. For the moment he thought he must have accidentally picked the little package up in the bathroom and slipped it into his pocket unaware. Then he remembered that he had not taken his coat into the bathroom that morning, and that he had emptied out the pockets the previous night. He distinctly recollected that, when the summons to the fire had reached him, he had had to tumble hurriedly into them the few odds and ends he habitually carried about him—handkerchief, keys, loose cash, pencils and what-not, taken from his dressing-table. It was quite inconceivable that there should have been any bicarbonate on his dressing-table.

Hector Puncheon was puzzled. A glance at the clock, however, reminded him that he had no time for puzzlement just then. He had to get down to St. Margaret's, Westminster, by 10.30 to report the wedding of a fashionable beauty who was being married in the strictest secrecy at that unfashionable hour. He had then to hasten back to report a political meeting in Kingsway Hall, and thence he must gallop round the corner to attend a luncheon given to a distinguished airman in the Connaught Rooms. If the speeches were over by 3 o'clock, he could then make a dash for a train and get out to Esher, where a royalty was opening a new school and inaugurating it with a children's tea-party. After which, if he were still alive, and had contrived to get his copy written up in the train, he could turn it in at the office and find time to think.

This strenuous programme was carried out without more than the usual number of exasperating hitches, and not until he had pushed the last sheet of copy over to the subeditor, and was sitting, tired but conscious of work well done, in the Cock Tavern, tackling a beef-steak, did he give another thought to the mysterious packet of sodium bicarb. And now, the more he thought about it, the odder the incident became.

He ran over in his mind the various activities of the previous night. At the fire, he remembered now quite distinctly, he had put on his burberry and buttoned it up, by way of protecting his light grey flannels against showers of smuts and the spray of the firemen's hoses. The mysterious package could hardly have been placed in his jacket-pocket then. After that, there had been interviews with various people—including the cat—the writing of his copy in the *Morning Star* offices and his breakfast in the Fleet Street eating-house. To suppose that he had accidentally found and pocketed four ounces of bicarbonate on any of these occasions seemed to him fantastic. Unless, of course, one of his newspaper colleagues had put the thing there for a joke. But who? And why?

He went on to consider the walk home and the conversation in the White Swan. His exhilarated acquaintance in dress clothes was the kind of man, he thought, who might from time to time require the assistance of a mild digestive and carminative. Possibly in one of his more affectionate moments he might have slipped the packet into Hector's coat-pocket by mistake for his own. The two carters would not, Mr. Puncheon felt sure, be carrying drugs round with them. . . .

Drugs. As the word shaped itself in his mind—for Hector Puncheon usually thought articulately, and often, indeed, conversed quite sensibly aloud with his own soul—an enormous query shot up in his brain. Bicarbonate of soda, hell! He was ready to stake his journalistic reputation it was nothing of the sort. His fingers sought the packet, which he had thrust back into the pocket where he had found it, and he was on the point of opening it and investigating the contents when a better idea struck him. Leaving his rump-steak half finished, and muttering to the astonished waiter that he would be back in a minute, he ran out hatless to the establishment of the nearest chemist, one Mr. Tweedle, who knew him well.

Mr. Tweedle's shop was shut, but a light still burned within, and Hector hammered violently until the door was opened by an assistant. Was Mr. Tweedle in? Yes, he was in, but he was just going. On being assured that Mr. Puncheon wanted to see Mr. Tweedle personally, the assistant volunteered to see what could be done.

Mr. Tweedle, hatted and coated, appeared from the inner recesses of the shop with just enough delay to make Hector feel that he had acted with some precipitation and had probably started out upon a wild-goose chase. Once started, however, he had to go through with it.

"Look here, Tweedle," he said, "I'm sorry to bother you, and there's probably nothing in it, but I wish you'd have a look at this for me. It came into my hands in rather a curious way."

The chemist received the packet and held it balanced in his hand for a moment.

"What's wrong with it?"

"I don't know that anything's wrong with it. I want you to tell me."

"Bicarbonate of soda," said Mr. Tweedle, glancing at the label and at the sealed flaps of the package. "No chemist's name—the ordinary printed label. You don't seem to have opened it."

"No, I haven't, and I want you to bear witness to that, if necessary. It appears to be just as it came from the chemist, doesn't it?"

"It appears to be, certainly," rejoined Mr. Tweedle in some surprise. "The label seems to be the original label and the ends have apparently only been sealed once, if that is what you want to know."

"Yes, and I couldn't have sealed it up like that, could I? I mean, it looks professional."

"Quite."

"Well, now, if you're quite satisfied about that, open it."

Mr. Tweedle carefully inserted a penknife beneath one flap, broke the wax and opened up the paper. The packet was, as might have been expected, filled with a fine white powder.

"What next?" inquired Mr. Tweedle.

"Well, is it bicarbonate of soda?"

Mr. Tweedle shook some of the powder out into the palm of his hand, looked closely at it, smelt it, moistened his finger and took up a few grains, and then carried them to his tongue. Then his face changed. He took out his handkerchief, wiped his mouth, poured the powder from his palm carefully back into the paper and asked:

"**How did** you get hold of this?"

"**I'll** tell you in a moment," said Hector. "What is it?"

"Cocaine," said Mr. Tweedle.

"Are you sure?"

"Positive."

"My God!" cried Hector, jubilantly. "I'm on to something! What a day! Here, Tweedle, can you spare a moment? I want you to come round to our place and tell Hawkins about this."

"Where? What?" demanded Mr. Tweedle.

Hector Puncheon wasted no more words, but grabbed him by the arm. Thus, on Mr. Hawkins, news-editor of the *Morning Star*, there burst an agitated member of his own staff, with a breathless witness in tow, and an exhibit of cocaine.

Mr. Hawkins was a keen newspaper man and rejoiced in a stunt. He had, nevertheless, a certain conscience in such matters, so far as giving information to the police was concerned. For one thing, it does a newspaper no good to be on bad terms with the police, and, for another, there had only recently been trouble about another case in which information had been held up. Having, therefore, heard Hector Puncheon's story and scolded him soundly for having waited so long before examining the mysterious package, he telephoned to Scotland Yard.

Chief-Inspector Parker, with his arm in a sling and his nerves very much on edge, received the information in his own home, just as he thought his day's work was happily done with. He grumbled horribly; but there had been a good deal of fuss made lately at the Yard about dope-gangs, and things had been said which he resented. He irritably called a taxi and trundled down to the *Morning Star* offices, accompanied by a morose person called Sergeant Lumley, who disliked him, and whom he disliked, but who happened to be the only sergeant available.

By this time, Hector Puncheon's excitement had rather worn off. He was getting sleepy and stupid after a broken night and a hard day's work. He could not control his yawns, and the Chief-Inspector snapped at him. In answer to questions he managed, however, to give a fairly complete account of his movements during the night and early morning.

"Actually, then," said Parker, when the tale was finished, "you can't say with any certainty when you received this packet?"

"No, I can't," said Hector, resentfully. He could not help feeling that it was very clever of him to have received the packet at all, and that everybody ought, somehow, to be grateful to him. Instead of which, they almost seemed to think he was to blame for something.

"You say you found it in your right hand coat-pocket. Did you at no time previously to that put your hand in that pocket for anything?"

"I should think I must have," said Hector. He yawned. "But I can't exactly remember. He yawned again, uncontrollably.

"What do you keep in that pocket?"

"Odds and ends," said Hector. He dipped into the pocket and drew out a mixed collection—a pencil, a box of matches, a pair of nail-scissors, some string, a thing for opening beer-bottles with patent caps, a corkscrew for opening ordinary beer-bottles, a very dirty handkerchief and some crumbs.

"If you could remember using any of those things during the night—" suggested Parker.

"I must have used the handkerchief," said Hector, gaz-

ing at it in some dismay. "I meant to take a clean one out
this morning. I did, too. Where is it? Oh, in my trousers-
pocket. Here it is. But of course," he added, helpfully,
"this isn't the suit I wore last night. I had my old tweed
jacket on then. I must have put the dirty handkerchief in
this pocket with the other things instead of into the clothes-
basket. I know it's the one I had at the fire. Look at the
soot on it."

"Quite so," said Parker, "but can you remember *when*
you used this handkerchief last night? Surely, if you had
felt in your pocket at any time, you couldn't have failed
to come on the packet if it was there."

"Oh, yes, I could," said Hector, brightly. "I shouldn't
notice. I'm so accustomed to having a lot of junk in my
pocket. I can't help you there, I'm afraid."

Another frightful yawn attacked him. He stifled it manfully, and it forced itself painfully out at his nose, nearly
breaking his ear-drums on the way. Parker gazed crossly
at his grimacing countenance.

"Do try to keep your mind on what I am asking you,
Mr. Firkin," he said. "If only—"

"Puncheon," said Hector, annoyed.

"Puncheon," said Parker, "I beg your pardon. Did you
at any time, Mr. Puncheon—?"

"I don't know," interrupted Hector. "I honestly don't
know. It's no good asking. I can't tell you. I would if I
could, but I simply can't."

Mr. Hawkins, looking from one to the other, discovered
in himself a little elementary knowledge of human nature.

"I think," he said, "a small drink is indicated."

He fetched a bottle of Johnnie Walker and some glasses
from a locker and set them on the desk, together with a
siphon. Parker thanked him and, suddenly ashamed of
himself and his bad temper, apologized.

"I'm sorry," he said. "I'm afraid I was a bit curt. I got
my collar-bone broken a little time ago and it still aches
a bit and makes me abominably peevish. Let's go about
this business another way. Why do you suppose, Mr. Punch-

eon, that anybody should have picked you out to take charge of this hefty dose of dope?"

"I thought whoever it was must have mistaken me for some one else."

"So I should imagine. And you think that's more likely to have happened at the pub than anywhere else?"

"Yes; unless it was in the crowd at the fire. Because in the other places—I mean in this office and when I was interviewing people, everybody knew me, or at least they knew what I was there for."

"That seems sound," agreed Parker. "How about this restaurant where you had your sausages?"

"There's that, of course. But I can't recollect anybody coming near enough to me to shove things in my pocket. And it couldn't have been during the fire either, because I had my burberry on, buttoned up. But in the pub, I had my burberry open, and there were at least four people barging up against me—one of two carters who were there before me, and a little man who looked like a bookmaker's tout or something, and the drunken chap in dress clothes and the old boy sitting in the corner. I don't think it can have been the carter, though; he looked quite genuine."

"Had you ever been to the White Swan before?"

"Once, I think, ages ago. Certainly not often. And I think there's a new landlord since then."

"Well, then," said Parker, "what is there about you, Mr. Puncheon, that induces people to hand you out valuable cargoes of dope on sight and without payment?"

"Goodness knows," said Hector.

The desk telephone buzzed furiously, and Mr. Hawkins, snatching the receiver, plunged into a long conversation with some unknown person. The two policemen with their witness retired into a distant corner and carried on the inquiry in low tones.

"Either," said Parker, "you must be the dead spit of some habitual dope-peddler, or you must have led them in some way to imagine that you were the person they expected to see. What did you talk about?"

Hector Puncheon racked his brains.

"Greyhounds," he said at last, "and parrots. Chiefly parrots. Oh, yes—and goats."

"Greyhounds, parrots and goats?"

"We were swapping stories about parrots," said Hector Puncheon. "No, wait, we began about dogs. The little tout person said he'd had a dog that couldn't abide goats and that led on to parrots and mice (I'd forgotten the mice) — and doping parrots with coffee and cayenne."

"Doping?" said Parker, quickly. "Was that word used?"

"No, I don't know that it was. The parrot was frightened of mice, and they had to cure it of shock by giving it coffee."

"Whose parrot?"

"The little fellow's aunt's, I think. The old boy knew a parrot, too, but that belonged to a clergyman, and the bishop tried to teach it to swear and promoted the parson. I don't know whether it was blackmail, or just that he liked the parrot."

"But what did you contribute to the conversation?"

"Hardly anything. I just listened and paid for the drinks."

"And the man in dress clothes?"

"Oh, he talked about his wife's shopping-list and a parcel—yes, there was something about a parcel he ought to have brought with him."

"Was the parcel produced?"

"No, he never had a parcel."

"All right," said Parker, after a little more of this unsatisfactory conversation. "We'll go into the matter, Mr. Puncheon. We're very much obliged to you and Mr.—er—Hawkins for having called our attention to the matter. We will take charge of the packet, and if we want you again, we'll let you know."

He rose to his feet. Mr. Hawkins shot across from his desk.

"Got all you want? You don't want this story to go in, I suppose?" he added, wistfully.

"No; you mustn't say anything about it at present," said Parker, firmly. "But we're very much indebted to you, and if anything comes of it, you shall have the story first with all the details we can give you. I can't say fairer than that."

He left the office with Sergeant Lumley, mournful and silent, at his heels.

"It's a thousand pities, Lumley, that we didn't get this information earlier. We could have put a man in at that pub for the rest of the day. It's too late to do anything now."

"Yes, sir, it is," said Sergeant Lumley.

"The pub's the place, I fancy."

"Very likely, sir."

"The cargo of dope was a pretty large one. That means that it was meant for some one who distributes the stuff on a fairly extensive scale. And it didn't have to be paid for. That suggests to me that the man they expected to see was only a messenger for this distributor, who, no doubt, settles up direct with the top man by some other route."

"Very possibly, sir," said Sergeant Lumley, in an unbelieving tone.

"The thing is, what are we to do? We could raid the place, of course, but I don't think that would be advisable. We probably shouldn't find anything, and we should merely give the alarm to no purpose."

"That wouldn't be anything unusual," grunted the Sergeant, disagreeably.

"Too true. We haven't anything against the White Swan so far, have we?"

"Not that I know of, sir."

"We shall have to make certain about it first. The landlord may or may not be concerned in the business. Quite possibly he isn't, but we shall have to make sure. You had better arrange for at least two men to investigate the Swan. They mustn't make themselves conspicuous. They can drop in from time to time and talk about parrots and goats and see if anything peculiar happens to them. And they can try and get a line on those people—the little chap, and the old man, and the fellow in the boiled shirt. It ought not to be difficult. Put on two sensible, tactful men who are not teetotallers, and if they don't get anything in the course of a day or two, change them for two others. And see that they look like what they're supposed to be and don't wear regulation boots or anything foolish."

"Very well, sir."

"And for God's sake, Lumley, look a little more cheerful about it," said the Chief-Inspector. "I like to see duties undertaken in a pleasant spirit."

"I do my best," replied Sergeant Lumley, offended.

Chief-Inspector Parker went resolutely home to bed.

CHAPTER XIII

EMBARRASSING ENTANGLEMENT
OF A GROUP-MANAGER

Excuse me, miss," said Tompkin, the reception-clerk, to Miss Rossiter, "but do you happen to have seen Mr. Wedderburn anywhere? He's not in his room."

"I think I saw him in with Mr. Ingleby."

"Thank you very much, miss."

Tompkin's cheerful face looked worried; and all the more so, when he reached Mr. Ingleby's room and found nobody there but Mr. Ingleby himself and Mr. Bredon.

He repeated his inquiry.

"He's just gone down to Bream's Buildings about an insertion in some magazine or other," said Ingleby.

"Oh!" Tompkin looked so non-plussed that Ingleby added, "Why, what's up?"

"Well, sir, as a matter of fact and strictly between you and I, a rather awkward thing has happened. I don't quite know what to do about it."

"In all social difficulties," said Bredon, "ask Uncle Ugly. Do you want to know how many buttons there should be on a dress waistcoat? how to eat an orange in public? how to introduce your first-wife-that-was to your third-wife-to-be? Uncle Ugly will put you right."

"Well, sir, if you will treat the matter in confidence, you and Mr. Ingleby—"

"Say on, Tompkin. We will be silent as a pre-talkie movie. Any sum from £5 to £5,000 advanced on your note of hand alone. No embarrassing investigations. No security required—or offered. What's your trouble?"

214

"Not mine, sir. As a matter of fact, sir, there's a young woman here, asking for Mr. Tallboy, and he's in conference with Mr. Armstrong and Mr. Toule, and I don't like to send a message."

"Well," said Ingleby, "tell her to wait."

"That's just it, sir, I did, and she said I was only saying that to put her off, while Mr. Tallboy got out of the building, and she took on terribly and said she was going to speak to Mr. Pym. Well, sir, of course I don't know what the trouble is"—here Tompkin looked unnaturally blank and innocent—"but I don't think Mr. Tallboy would care for that, nor Mr. Pym neither. So I thought, seeing that Mr. Wedderburn is the gentleman who sees most of Mr. Tallboy, so to speak—"

"I see," said Ingleby. "Where is the young woman?"

"Well, I've put her in the Little Conference Room," said Tompkin, dubiously, with an accent on the "put," "but of course, if she was to come out again (and there's nothing to stop her) and was to go to Mr. Pym, or even to Miss Fearney— You see, sir, when parties like Miss Fearney are in an official position, they have to take notice of things, as you may say, whether they like to or not. It isn't the same as you or me, sir." Tompkin glanced from Ingleby to Bredon, dividing the "sir" impartially between them.

Bredon, who was drawing patterns on his blotter, looked up.

"What is she like?" he asked. "I mean"—as Tompkin hesitated—"do you think she is genuinely in distress or merely out to make trouble?"

"Well, sir," said Tompkin, "since you ask me, I should say she was a tough jane."

"I'll go and keep her quiet," said Bredon. "Be sure you tell Mr. Tallboy the moment he is free."

"Very good, sir."

"And try not to let it get round the office. It may be nothing at all."

"Quite so, sir. I'm not one to talk. But there's the boy on the desk, sir—"

"Oh! Well, tell him to hold his tongue."

"Yes, sir."

Bredon went out, looking as though he did not care for his self-imposed task. By the time he arrived at the door of the Little Conference Room, however, his face bore nothing but an expression of amiable helpfulness. He entered briskly, and in the first glance his practised eye took in every detail about the young woman who sprang up to face him, from her hard eyes and shrewish mouth to her blood-red, pointed finger-nails and over-elaborate shoes.

"Good afternoon," he said, brightly. "You want Mr. Tallboy, I think. He won't be long, but he's been called in to a conference with some clients and we can't rescue him, so they've sent me down to entertain you till he comes. Will you smoke, Miss—er—the clerk didn't mention your name?"

"It's Vavasour—Miss Ethel Vavasour. Who're you? Are you Mr. Pym?"

Bredon laughed.

"Good lord, no. I'm a very unimportant person—one of the junior copy-writers, that's all."

"Oh, I see. You a pal of Jim's?"

"Of Tallboy's? Not specially. I just happened to be there, so I came along, don't you know. They told me there was a very beautiful young lady asking for Tallboy, and I thought, What-ho! Why not buzz along and cheer her weary hours of waiting?"

"I'm sure it's frightfully good of you," said Miss Vavasour, laughing rather shrilly. "I expect what you mean is, that Jim's sent you along to see if you can talk me round. That's just like Jim. I suppose he's sneaked off the back way."

"I assure you, my dear young lady, that I haven't seen or spoken to Tallboy this afternoon. And I expect, when he hears that I've been along to have a chat with you, he'll be very fed-up with me. And no wonder. If you'd come to see me, I should loathe any other blighter who came and barged in."

"You can can that stuff," retorted Miss Vavasour. "I know your sort. You'd talk the hind leg off a donkey. But I can tell you this: if Jim Tallboy thinks he's going to get round me by sending his flash friends to shoot off a lot of hot air, he's mistaken."

"My dear Miss Vavasour, will nothing rid you of this misapprehension? In other words, you got me all wrong. I'm not here to forward Tallboy's interests in any way— except, perhaps, by offering the suggestion that this office is possibly not the most suitable spot for interviews of a personal and confidential kind. If I might presume to advise you, would not an appointment for some other place and time—?"

"Ah!" said Miss Vavasour. "I dare say. But if a fellow won't answer your letters or come and see you, and you don't even know where he lives, what is a girl to do? I'm sure I don't want to make trouble."

Here Miss Vavasour sniffed and applied a small handkerchief carefully to her made-up eye-lashes.

"Good heavens!" said Bredon. "How unkind and abominable!"

"You may well say so," said Miss Vavasour. "It's not what anybody would expect of a gentleman, is it? But there! When a fellow's telling the tale to a girl it's one thing, and when he's got her into trouble it's another. A girl doesn't hear so much about him marrying her then. Well, you tell him he's got to do it, see? Or I'll scream my way into old Pym's office and make him. A girl's got to look after herself these days. I'm sure I only wish I had somebody to do it for me, and now poor Auntie's dead, I haven't got a soul to stick up for me."

The handkerchief came into play again.

"But, my dear girl," said Bredon, "even Mr. Pym, great autocrat as he is, couldn't make Tallboy marry you. He's married already."

"Married?" Miss Vavasour took away the handkerchief revealing a pair of perfectly dry and very angry eyes, "the dirty beast! So *that's* why he never asked me to his home.

Talking a lot of eye-wash about only one room and his landlady being very particular. I don't care, though. He's got to do it. His wife can divorce him. Goodness knows she's got cause. I've got his letters."

Her eyes turned, irresistibly, to her large and ornate handbag. It was a false move and she realized it instantly and gazed appealingly at Bredon, but he knew where he was now.

"So you've got them there with you. That was very—far-sighted of you. See here, Miss Vavasour, what's the use of talking like this? You may just as well be frank with me. Your idea was to threaten to show those letters to Mr. Pym if Tallboy didn't pay up, wasn't it?"

"No, of course it wasn't."

"You're so devoted to Tallboy that you always carry his correspondence about with you?"

"Yes—no. I never said I'd got the letters with me."

"No? But you've admitted it now, you know. Now, you take the advice of a man double your age." (This was a generous estimate, for Miss Vavasour was an easy twenty-eight.) "If you make a disturbance here, nothing will happen, except that Tallboy will possibly lose his job and have no money at all for you or anybody. And if you try to sell him those letters—there's a name for that, and it's not a pretty one."

"That's all very well," said Miss Vavasour, sullenly, "but how about this trouble he's got me into? I'm a manne-quin, see? And if a girl's got to chuck her job, and her figure ruined for life—"

"Are you sure you're not mistaken about that?"

" 'Course I'm sure. What do you take me for? An inno-cent?"

"Surely not," said Bredon. "No doubt Tallboy will be ready to come to a suitable arrangement. But—if I may presume to advise you—no threats and no disturbance. And —forgive me—there are other people in the world."

"Yes, there are," said Miss Vavasour, frankly, "but they're not so keen to take over a girl with encumbrances, if you know what I mean. You wouldn't yourself now, would you?"

"Oh, me? I'm not in the running," said Bredon, with perhaps more promptness and emphasis than was quite complimentary. "But, speaking generally, I'm sure you'll find it better not to make an explosion—not here, at any rate. I mean to say, you know, that's the point. Because this is one of those old-fashioned firms that don't like anything unpleasant or—er—undesirable to happen on their premises."

"You bet they don't," said Miss Vavasour, shrewdly, "that's why I'm here."

"Yes, but take it from me, you'll do no good by making a fuss. Really not. And—ah! here is the missing gentleman. I'll be pushing along. Hullo, Tallboy—I've just been entertaining the lady in your absence."

Tallboy, his eyes burning in a very white face and his lips twitching, looked at Bredon for a moment or two in silence. Then:

"Thanks very much," he said, in a stifled tone.

"No, don't thank me," said Bredon. "The gratification is entirely on my side."

He went out and shut the door upon the pair of them.

"Now, I wonder," said Mr. Bredon, reverting to his own detective personality as he went slowly upstairs to his room, "I wonder if it's possible that I'm all wrong about our friend Victor Dean. Can it be that he was merely a common or garden blackmailer, intent on turning his colleague's human weaknesses to his own advantage? Would that be worth cracking a fellow's skull for him and hurling him down a staircase, iron, one, murderers for the use of? The chap who could probably tell me is Willis, but somehow the good Willis is deaf as an adder to my well-known charm of speech. Is it any use sounding him again? If only I could be sure that he was not the gentleman who sandbagged my poor brother-in-law Charles and that he

was not still harbouring designs upon my unworthy car-
case. Not that I mind having designs harboured on me,
but I don't want to make a confidant of the fellow I'm
after, like the fat-headed hero in one of those detective
stories where the detective turns out to be the villain. If
only I had ever seen Willis engaged in any game or sport,
I should know better where I stood, but he seems to de-
spise the open-air life—and that in itself, if you come to
think of it, is sinister."

After a little more thought, he went along to Willis'
room.

"Oh, I say, Willis," he said, "am I disturbing you?"

"No. Come in."

Willis looked up from a sheet of paper which bore the
engaging headlines: "MAGNOLIA-WHITE, MAGNOLIA-SOFT—
that's what they'll say of your hands." He looked depressed
and ill.

"See here, Willis," said Bredon, "I want your advice. I
know we don't seem to hit it off very well—"

"No—it's my fault," said Willis. He seemed to struggle
with himself for a moment, and then brought his words
out with a rush, as though they had been violently forced
from him: "I fancy I owe you some sort of apology. I appear to have been mistaken."

"What exactly did you have against me? I never could
make out what it was, to tell you the truth."

"I thought you belonged to Victor Dean's beastly doping
and drinking crowd, and thought you were trying to get
Pamela—Miss Dean—in among them again. She tells me
that's not the case. But I saw you there with her, and now
she tells me it's my fault that you—that you—oh, hell!"

"What *is* the matter?"

"I'll tell you what's the matter," said Willis, violently.
"You went and forced yourself on Miss Dean—God knows
what you told her, and she won't tell me. You made out
you were a friend of her brother's, or something—was that
true, to start with?"

"Not quite, as you put it. I made Miss Dean's acquaintance over a matter connected with her brother, but I had never met him, and she knows that."

"What had it got to do with him, then?"

"I'm afraid I can't tell you that."

"It sounds damned queer to me," said Willis, his face darkening with suspicion. Then he seemed to recollect that he was supposed to be making an apology, and went on:

"Well, anyway, you took her to that disgusting place down there by the river."

"That's not altogether true, either. I asked her to take me, because I couldn't very well have got in without an introduction."

"That's a lie; I got in all right."

"Miss Dean told them to let you in."

"Oh!" Willis was disconcerted for a moment. "Well, in any case, you had no business to ask a decent girl to do anything of the kind. That was exactly what Dean and I had trouble about. A house like that is no fit place for her, and you know it."

"I do; and I regretted the necessity which compelled me to ask her to go there. You may have noticed that I took care nothing should happen to her."

"I don't know that," grumbled Willis.

"You aren't a very good detective," said Bredon with a smile. "You must take my word for it that she was quite safe."

"I won't take your word, but I'd take hers. She says so, and I suppose I've got to believe it. But if you're not an out-and-out rotter yourself, why did you want to be taken there?"

"That's another thing I can't tell you. But I can offer you one or two reasonable explanations that might fit the case. I might be a journalist, commissioned to write an inside story about the newest kind of night-club. Or I might be a detective, engaged in tracking down dope-smugglers. Or I might be a zealot with a new brand of religion, trying to save the souls of post-war society sinners. Or I might be in love with somebody—say, if you like, the notorious Dian de

Momerie—and threatening to commit suicide unless I got an introduction to her. I present you with those four solutions on the spur of the moment, and I dare say I could think of others, if I was put to it."

"You might be a dope-merchant yourself," said Willis.

"I hadn't thought of that. But if I were, I doubt if I should need Miss Dean's introduction to that particular crowd."

Willis muttered something unintelligible.

"But I gather," said Bredon, "that Miss Dean has more or less absolved me of being anything hopelessly corrupt. So what's the trouble?"

"The trouble is," groaned Willis, "that you've—my God! you swine—you've thrown her over and she says it's my fault."

"You oughtn't to say a thing like that, old son," said Bredon, really distressed. "It's not done."

"No—I dare say I'm not quite a gentleman. I've never been—"

"If you tell me you've never been to a public school," said Bredon, "I shall scream. What with Copley and Smayle, and all the other pathetic idiots who go about fostering inferiority complexes, and weighing up the rival merits of this place and that place, when it doesn't matter a damn anyway, I'm fed up. Pull yourself together. Anybody, wherever he's been educated, ought to know better than to say a thing like that about any girl. Particularly when there isn't the slightest foundation for it."

"Ah, but there is," said Willis. "You don't realize it, but I do. I know a man's a man for a' that and all the rest of it, but people like you have a sort of glamour about them and women fall for it, every time. I know I'm as good a man as you are, but I don't look it, and that's where it is."

"I can only assure you, Willis—"

"I know, I know. You've never made love to Miss Dean —that's what you're going to say—never by word, look or deed and so forth and so on, given her the slightest ground —bah! I know it. She admits it. It makes it all the worse."

"I am afraid," said Mr. Bredon, "that you are a very foolish pair of people And I really think you must be quite mistaken in Miss Dean's feelings."

"That's damned likely."

"I think so. In any case, you oughtn't to have said anything to me about it. And in any case, there's nothing I can do."

"She asked me," said Willis, miserably, "to apologize to you and bring you—and ask you—and put the matter right."

"There's nothing to put right. Miss Dean knows quite well that my interviews with her were merely a matter of business. And all I can say is, Willis, if you accepted any such commission, she must think you as soft as a pancake. Why on earth didn't you tell her you'd see me at the devil first? That's probably what she expected you to do."

"Do you think so?"

"Sure of it," said Bredon, who was not sure at all, but thought it best to appear so. "You mustn't go about creating intolerable situations, you know. It's very awkward for me, and I'm sure Miss Dean would be horribly upset if she knew what you'd been saying about her. All she meant was, I expect, that you'd taken quite a wrong view of a perfectly ordinary business acquaintanceship and been unnecessarily antagonistic and so on, and that she wanted you to put the thing straight, so that, if I needed her help again, there wouldn't be any awkwardness about it. Isn't that, in other words, what she said to you?"

"Yes," said Willis. It was a lie, and he knew that Bredon knew that it was a lie, but he lied manfully. "Of course that was what she actually said. But I'm afraid I put another interpretation on it."

"All right," said Bredon, "that's settled. Tell Miss Dean that my business is progressing very well, and that when I need her kind help again I shall have no hesitation in calling her to my assistance. Now, is that all?"

"Yes, that's all."

"You're sure—while you are about it—that there's nothing else you want to get off your chest?"

"N-no."

"You don't sound very sure about it. You've been trying to say all this to me for some time, I dare say."

"No, not very long. A few days."

"Since the day of the monthly tea-party, shall we say?"

Willis started violently. Bredon, with a wary eye on him, followed up his advantage.

"Was that what you came round to Great Ormond Street that night to tell me?"

"How do you know about that?"

"I didn't know, I guessed. As I have said before, you would not make a good detective. You lost a pencil on that occasion, I believe?"

He drew the pencil from his pocket and held it out.

"A pencil? Not that I know of. Where did you find that?"

"In Great Ormond Street."

"I don't think it's mine. I don't know. I think I've still got mine."

"Well, never mind. You came round that night intending to apologize?"

"No—I didn't. I came round to have an explanation with you. I wanted to bash your face in, if you must know. I went round there just before ten—"

"Did you ring the bell of my flat?"

"No, I didn't. I'll tell you why. I looked in your letter-box, and I saw a letter there from Miss Dean, and I—I didn't dare go upstairs. I was afraid I might let myself go. I felt like murdering you. So I went off and wandered about till I was too done-up to think."

"I see. You didn't make any attempt to get hold of me at all?"

"No."

"Oh, well, that's that." Bredon dismissed the matter with a wave of the hand. "It's quite all right. It doesn't matter. I was only a little bit puzzled about the pencil."

"The pencil?"

"Yes. I found it on the top landing, you see, just outside my door. I couldn't quite understand how it got there, that's all."

"It wasn't me. I didn't go upstairs."

"How long did you stay in the house?"

"Only a few minutes."

"In the front hall downstairs all the time?"

"Yes."

"Oh, well then, it can't have been your pencil. It's very odd, because those pencils aren't on the market, as you know."

"Perhaps you dropped it yourself."

"Well, perhaps I did. That seems the likeliest explanation, doesn't it? It's not of any importance."

There was a short and rather uncomfortable pause. Willis broke it by asking in a constrained tone:

"What did you want to ask my advice about?"

"About the old subject," said Bredon; "perhaps, now that we've had this little explanation, you may find it easier to tell me what I want to know. Circumstances have brought me up against the Dean family, and I feel a certain amount of curiosity about the late lamented Victor. From his sister I gather that he was a good, kind brother, but unfortunately a little wild in his morals—which means, I take it, that he became infatuated with Dian de Momerie. According to her, he took his sister to various places to meet the fair Dian; you interfered; Miss Dean then realized what the situation was, and withdrew from the association, while quite naturally and illogically resenting your interference; and finally Dian de Momerie shut down on Victor and sent him off home. That's true, as far as it goes, I imagine?"

"Yes," said Willis, "except that I don't believe Dean ever was really infatuated with the de Momerie woman. I think he was flattered, and I think he thought he could make something out of her. As a matter of fact, he was a mean little beast."

"Did she give him money?"

"Yes, she did; but he didn't get much out of that, because he found that crowd so expensive to run with. He wasn't naturally one of that sort. He didn't enjoy gambling, though he had to do it, to keep in with them; and he wasn't a drinker. In some ways, I'd have liked him better if he had been. He wouldn't dope, either. I expect that's why Miss de Momerie got tired of him. The worst of that crowd, you know, is that they can't rest till they've made everybody they have to do with as bad as themselves. If they'd only drug themselves into their graves and have done with it, the sooner they did it the better it would be for every one. I'd cheerfully hand the stuff over to them by the cartload. But they get hold of quite decent people and ruin them for life. That's why I got so worried about Pamela."

"But you say that Victor managed to remain undefiled."

"Yes, but Pamela's different. She's rather impulsive and easily—no, not easily led, but easily excited about things. She's high-spirited and likes to try everything once. If she once gets a sort of enthusiasm for a person, she wants to do the same as they do. She needs somebody—well, never mind that. I don't want to discuss Pamela. I only mean that Victor was just the opposite. He was very careful of himself, and he had a very good eye for the main chance."

"Do you mean that he was the sort of man who makes what he can out of his friends?"

"He was the kind of man who never has his own cigarettes, and never happens to be there, if he can help it, when it's his turn to stand the drinks. And he'd pick your brains every time."

"He must have had a pretty good reason, then, for going round with Dian de Momerie's lot. As you say, they're expensive."

"Yes; he must have seen something remunerative in the distance. And when it came to sacrificing his sister—"

"Exactly. Well, that's all rather by the way. What I

wanted to know from you was this: supposing he found out that somebody—say somebody in this office—as it might be yourself—had a skeleton in the closet, to use the pretty old metaphor, was Victor Dean the kind of fellow to—er—to dispose of that skeleton to an anatomist?"

"Blackmail, do you mean?" asked Willis, bluntly.

"That's a strong word. But call it that."

"I don't quite know," said Willis, after a few moments' consideration. "It's a devil of a thing to suggest about anybody, isn't it? But I can only say that the question gives me no shock. If you were to tell me that he had blackmailed somebody, it wouldn't surprise me very much. Only, as it's a pretty serious offence, it would have to be a very safe kind of blackmail, with the sort of victim who couldn't possibly afford to face a court of law. Mind you, I haven't the least reason to suppose he ever did anything of the kind. And he certainly never seemed to be particularly flush of cash. Not that that's much to go by, with a careful fellow like him. *He* wouldn't have let wads of bank-notes come tumbling out his desk."

"You think the tumbling about of notes affords a presumption of innocence?"

"Not a bit. Only of carelessness, and Dean certainly wasn't careless."

"Well, thanks for speaking so frankly."

"That's all right. Only, for goodness' sake, don't let Pamela know what I've been saying about Victor. I've had trouble enough about that."

Bredon assured him that he need not fear any such fantastic indiscretion, and took his leave, polite but still puzzled.

Mr. Tallboy was lying in wait for him at the end of the passage.

"Oh, Bredon, I'm very much obliged to you, of course. I'm sure I can rely on you not to spread the thing any further than it's gone already. All quite absurd, of course. That fool Tompkin seems to have lost his head completely. I've ticked him off properly."

"Oh, yes, absolutely," replied Bredon. "Just so. Much ado about nothing. No real necessity for me to have butted in at all. But you never know. I mean to say, if you'd been detained and Miss Vavasour had got tired of waiting or—well, you know what I mean."

"Yes." Tallboy licked his dry lips. "It might have been very awkward. When girls get hysterical and so on, they sometimes say more than they mean. I've been a bit of a fool, as I dare say you've gathered. I'm cutting it all out now. I've settled everything all right. Worrying, of course, but nothing really desperate." He laughed uncomfortably.

"You're looking a bit over-done."

"I feel it. The fact is, I was up all night. My wife—well, the fact is, my wife had a baby last night. That was partly why—oh, hell, what's it matter, anyhow?"

"I quite understand," said Bredon. "Very wearing business. Why didn't you take the day off?"

"I didn't want to do that. It's my busy day. Much better to occupy one's mind. Besides, there wasn't any necessity. Everything went all right. I suppose you think I'm an awful swine."

"You're not the first, by any means," said Bredon.

"No—it's rather usual, I believe. It's not going to happen again, I can tell you."

"It must have put you in a hell of a hole—all this."

"Yes—at least—not so bad. As you say, I'm not the only man it's ever happened to. It doesn't do to let one's self be upset, does it? Well, as I said, thanks very much and—that's all, isn't it?"

"Absolutely. There's nothing whatever to thank me about. Well, sonnie, what do you want?"

"Any letters to go, sir?"

"No, thanks," said Bredon.

"Oh, stop a minute," said Tallboy. "Yes, I've got one." He searched in his breast-pocket and pulled out an envelope, all ready sealed. "Lend me a pen one moment, Bredon. Here, boy, take this penny-halfpenny and run along to Miss Rossiter and ask her for a stamp."

He took the pen Bredon held out, and bending over the

desk addressed the envelope hurriedly to "T. Smith, Esq."
Bredon, idly watching him, was caught by his eye in the
act, and apologized.

"I beg your pardon; I was snooping. Beastly habit. One
catches it in the typists' room."

"All right—it's only a note to a stockbroker."

"Lucky man to have anything to stockbroke."

Tallboy laughed, stamped the letter and tossed it to the
waiting boy.

"And so ends an exhausting day," he observed.

"Toule very tiresome?"

"Not more so than usual. He turned down 'Like Niobe,
all Tears.' Said he didn't know who Niobe was and he
didn't suppose anybody else did either. But he passed this
week's 'Tears, Idle Tears,' because when he was a boy his
father used to read Tennyson aloud to the family circle."

"That's one saved from the wreck, anyhow."

"Oh, yes. He liked the general idea of the poetical quotations. Said he thought they gave his advertisements class.
You'll have to think up some more. He likes the ones that
illustrate well."

"All right. 'Like Summer Tempest came her Tears.'
That's Tennyson, too. Picture of the nurse of ninety years
setting his babe upon her knee. Babies always go well.
(Sorry, we don't seem able to get off babies.) Start the
copy, 'Tears are often a relief to overwrought nerves, but
when they flow too often, too easily, it is a sign that you
need Nutrax.' I'll do that one. Bassanio and Antonio: 'I
know not Why I am so Sad.' Carry the quote on into the
copy. 'Causeless depression, like Antonio's, wearies both the
sufferer and his friends. Go to the root of the matter and
tone up the overstrung Nerves with Nutrax.' I can do that
sort of thing by the hour."

Mr. Tallboy smiled wanly.

"It's a pity we can't cure ourselves with our own nos-
trums, isn't it?"

Mr. Bredon surveyed him critically.

"What *you* need," he said, "is a good dinner and a bottle of fizz."

CHAPTER XIV

HOPEFUL CONSPIRACY OF TWO
BLACK SHEEP

THE gentleman in the harlequin costume removed his mask with quiet deliberation, and laid it on the table.

"Since," he said, "my virtuous cousin Wimsey has let the cat out of the bag, I may as well take this off. I am afraid"—he turned to Dian—"my appearance will disappoint you. Except that I am handsomer and less rabbity-looking, the woman who has seen Wimsey has seen me. It is a heavy handicap to carry, but I can't help it. The resemblance, I am happy to say, is only skin-deep."

"It's almost incredible," said Major Milligan. He bent forward to examine the other's face more closely, but Mr. Bredon extended a languid arm and, without apparently using any force at all, pushed him back into his seat.

"You needn't come too close," he observed, insolently. "Even a face like Wimsey's is better than yours. Yours is spotty. You eat and drink too much."

Major Milligan, who had, indeed, been distressed that morning by the discovery of a few small pimples on his forehead, but had hoped they were not noticeable, grunted angrily. Dian laughed.

"I take it," pursued Mr. Bredon, "that you want to get something out of me. People of your sort always do. What is it?"

"I've no objection to being frank with you," replied Major Milligan.

"How nice it is to hear anybody say that. It always prepares one for a lie to follow. Fore-warned is fore-armed, isn't it?"

"If you choose to think so. But I think you'll find it to your advantage to listen."

"Financial advantage?"

"What other kind is there?"

"What indeed? I begin to like your face a trifle better."

"Oh, do you? Perhaps you may like it well enough to answer a few questions?"

"Possibly."

"How do you come to know Pamela Dean?"

"Pamela? A charming girl, isn't she? I obtained an introduction to her through what the great public—seduced by the unfortunate example of that incomparable *vulgarisateur*, Charles Dickens—abominably calls a mutual friend. I admit that my object in obtaining the introduction was a purely business one; I can only say that I wish all business acquaintances were so agreeable."

"What was the business?"

"The business, my dear fellow, was concerned with another mutual friend of us all—with the late Victor Dean, who died, deeply regretted, upon a staircase. A remarkable young man, was he not?"

"In what way?" asked Milligan, quickly.

"Don't you know? I thought you did. Otherwise, why am I here?"

"You two idiots make me tired," broke in Dian. "Where's the sense of going round and round each other like this? Your pompous cousin told us all about you, Mr. Bredon—I suppose you've got a Christian name, by the way?"

"I have. It's spelt Death. Pronounce it any way you like. Most of the people who are plagued with it make it rhyme with teeth, but personally I think it sounds more picturesque when rhymed with breath. What did my amiable cousin say about me?"

"He said you were a dope-runner."

"Where my cousin Wimsey gets his information from, I am damned if I know. Sometimes he is correct."

"And you know perfectly well that one can get what one wants at Tod's place. So why not come to the point?"

"As you say, why not? Is that the particular facet of my brilliant personality that interests you, Milligan?"

"Is that the particular facet of Victor Dean's personality that interests *you?*"

"One point to me," said Mr. Bredon. "Till this moment, I was not sure that it was a facet of his personality. Now I do. Dear me! How interesting it all is, to be sure."

"If you can find out exactly how Victor Dean was involved in that show," said Mr. Milligan, "it might be worth something to you and to me."

"Say on."

Major Milligan reflected a little and seemed to make up his mind to lay his cards on the table.

"Did you learn from Pamela Dean what her brother's job was?"

"Yes, of course. He wrote advertising copy at a place called Pym's. There's no secret about that."

"That's just what there is. And if that infernal young fool hadn't gone and got killed, we might have found out what it was and done ourselves a lot of good. As it is—"

"But look here, Tod," said Dian. "I thought it was the other way round. I thought you were afraid of *his* finding out too much."

"That's true," said Milligan, scowling. "What would be the use of it if he found out first?"

"I don't follow all this," said Bredon. "Wasn't it his secret? Why not stop talking like a sensation novel and give us the dope straight?"

"Because I don't believe you know even as much as I do about the fellow."

"I don't. I never met him in my life. But I know a good deal about Pym's Publicity, Ltd."

"How?"

"I work there."

"What?"

"I work there."

"Since when?"

"Since Dean's death."

"Because of Dean's death, do you mean?"

"Yes."

"How did that happen?"

"I received information, as my dear cousin Wimsey's police pals would say, that Dean was on to something fishy about Pym's. So, since most fish have gold in their mouths like St. Peter's, I thought it wouldn't do any harm to try a cast or two over that particular pool."

"And what did you find?"

"My dear Milligan, you would make a cat laugh. I don't give away information. I dispose of it—advantageously."

"So do I."

"As you like. You invited me here tonight. I wasn't looking for you. But there's one thing I don't mind telling you, because I've already told Miss de Momerie, and that is, that Victor Dean was bumped off deliberately to prevent him from talking. So far, the only person I can discover who wanted him out of the way was yourself. The police might be interested to know that fact."

"The police?"

"Oh! I quite agree. I don't like the police. They pay very badly and ask a hell of a lot of questions. But it might be useful, for once, to get on the right side of them."

"That's all punk," said Milligan. "You're barking up the wrong tree. I didn't kill the fellow. I didn't want him killed."

"Prove that," said the other, coolly.

He watched Milligan's impassive face, and Milligan watched his.

"Give it up," suggested Bredon, after a few minutes of this mutual scrutiny. "I can play poker just as well as you. But this time I fancy I hold a straight flush."

"Well, what do you want to know?"

"I want to know what you think Dean was in a position to find out."

"I can tell you that. He was trying to find out—"

"Had found out."

"How do you know?"

"If you want instruction in detective methods, you must pay extra. I say he had found out."

"Well, then, he had found out who was running the show from Pym's end."

"The dope-show?"

"Yes. And he may have found out, too, the way it's worked."

"*Is* worked?"

"Yes."

"It's still being worked the same way, then?"

"So far as I know."

"So far as you know? You don't seem to know much."

"Well, how much do you know about the way your own gang run the show?"

"Nothing whatever. Instructions are issued—"

"By the way, how did you get into it?"

"Sorry. Can't tell you that. Not even if you pay extra."

"How do I know I can trust you, then?"

Bredon laughed.

"Perhaps you'd like me to supply you," he said. "If you're not satisfied with your distribution, you can inscribe yourself upon the roll of my customers. Deliveries Sunday and Thursday. Meanwhile—and as a sample—you may be interested in the collar of my cloak. It is handsome, is it not? A rich velvet. A little ostentatious, perhaps you think—a little over-much buckram? Possibly you are right. But very well made. The opening is almost invisible. We delicately insert the forefinger and thumb, pull the tab gently, and produce this dainty bag of oiled silk—fine as an onion-skin, but remarkably tough. Within it, you will discover sufficient inspiration for quite a number of enthusiasts. A magician's cloak. Such stuff as dreams are made on."

Milligan examined the contents of the little bag in silence. They were, in fact, a portion of the famous packet obtained by Mr. Hector Puncheon at the White Swan.

"All right, so far. Where do you get it from?"

"I got it in Covent Garden."

"Not at Pym's?"

"No."

Milligan looked disappointed.

"What day did you get it?"

"Friday morning. Like yourself, I get it on a Friday."

"Look here," said Milligan, "you and I have got to be together on this. Dian, my child, run away and play. I'm going to talk business with your friend."

"That's a nice way to treat me in my own house," grumbled Miss de Momerie, but, seeing that Milligan meant what he said, she gathered up herself and her wraps and retreated into the bedroom. Milligan leaned forwards over the table.

"I'm going to tell you what I know," he said. "If you double-cross me, it's at your own risk. I don't want any funny business with that damned cousin of yours."

Mr. Bredon expressed his opinion of Lord Peter Wimsey in a few well-chosen words.

"All right," said Milligan. "You have been warned. Now, see here. If we can find out who works this thing and how it's worked, we can get in at the top. It pays fairly well as it is, in one way, but it's a devil of a risk and a lot of trouble, and it's expensive. Look at that place I have to keep up. It's the man in the centre of the ring that makes the big profits. I know, and you know, what we pay for the stuff, and then there's the bore of handing it out to all these fools and collecting the cash. Now, here's what I know. The whole stunt is worked from that advertising place of yours—Pym's. I found that out from a man who's dead now. I won't tell you how I fell in with him—it's a long story. But I'll tell you what he told me. I was dining with him one night at the Carlton, and he was a bit lit-up. A chap came in with a party, and this man said to me:

'Know who that is?'—'Not from Adam,' I said. He said:
'Well, it's old Pym, the publicity agent.' And then he
laughed and said: 'If he only knew what his precious agency
was doing, he'd have a fit.' 'How's that?' I said. 'Why,' said
he, 'didn't you know? All this dope-traffic is worked from
there.' Naturally, I started to ask him how he knew and all
about it, but he suddenly got an attack of caution and
started to be mysterious, and I couldn't get another word
out of him."

"I know that brand of drunkenness," said Bredon. "Do
you think he really knew what he was talking about?"

"Yes, I think so. I saw him again next day, but he was
sober then, and got the shock of his life when I told him
what he'd said. But he admitted it was true, and implored
me to keep quiet about it. That was all I could get out of
him, and the same evening he was run over by a lorry."

"Was he? How remarkably well-timed."

"I thought so myself," said Milligan. "It made me rather
nervous."

"But how does Victor Dean come into it?"

"There," admitted Milligan, "I dropped a bad brick.
Dian brought him along one evening—"

"Just a minute. When did this conversation with your
indiscreet friend take place?"

"Nearly a year ago. Naturally, I'd been trying to follow
the matter up, and when Dian introduced Dean and said
he worked at Pym's, I thought he must be the man. Apparently he wasn't. But I'm afraid he got an idea about
the thing from me. After a bit, I found out he was trying
to horn in on my show, and I told Dian to shut down on
him."

"In fact," said Mr. Bredon, "you tried to pump him, just
as you are trying to pump me, and you found out that he
was pumping you instead."

"Something like that," confessed Milligan.

"And shortly after that he fell down a staircase."

"Yes; but I didn't push him down it. You needn't think
that. I didn't want him snuffed out. I only wanted him

kept out of the way. Dian's too much of a chatterer, especially when she's ginned up. The trouble is, you're never safe with these people. You'd think common sense would tell them to keep quiet in their own interests, but they've got no more sense than a cageful of monkeys."

"Well," said Bredon, "if we fill them up with stuff that notoriously saps their self-control, I suppose we can't grumble at the consequences."

"I suppose not, but it's a damned nuisance sometimes. They're as cunning as weasels in one way, and sheer idiots in another. Spiteful, too."

"Yes. Dean never became an addict, did he?"

"No. If he had, we'd have had more control over him; but unfortunately, his head was screwed on the right way. All the same, he knew pretty well that he'd have been well paid for any information."

"Very likely. The trouble is that he was taking money from the other side as well—at least, I think he was."

"Don't you try that game," said Milligan.

"I've no wish to fall down staircases. What you want, I take it, is the way the trick's worked and the name of the man who works it. I dare say I can find that out for you. How about terms?"

"My idea is, that we use the information to get into the inside ring ourselves, and each strike our own bargain."

"Just so. Alternatively, I suppose, we put the screw on the gentleman at Pym's, when we've got him, and divide the spoil. In which case, as I'm doing most of the work and taking the biggest risk, I suggest I take 75 per cent."

"Not on your life. Fifty-fifty. I shall conduct the negotiations."

"Will you? That's pretty good. Why should I bring you into it at all? You can't negotiate till I tell you whom to negotiate with. You don't think I was born yesterday."

"No. But knowing what I do, I could get you shifted from Pym's tomorrow, couldn't I? If Pym knew who you were, do you suppose he'd keep you on his virtuous premises for another day?"

"Well, look here. We conduct the negotiations together, and I take 60 per cent."

Milligan shrugged his shoulders.

"Well, leave it at that for the moment. I'm hoping it won't pan out that way. What we want to aim at is getting the reins into our own hands."

"As you say. When we've done that, it will be time enough to decide which of us is going to crack the whip."

When he had gone, Tod Milligan went into the bedroom, and found Dian kneeling on the window-seat, staring down into the street.

"Have you fixed things up with him?"

"Yes. He's a twister, but I'll be able to make him see that it'll pay him to be straight with me."

"You had much better leave him alone."

"You're talking rubbish," said Milligan, using a coarser term.

Dian turned round and faced him.

"I've warned you," she said. "Not that I care a damn what happens to you. You're getting on my nerves, Tod. It's going to be great fun to see you come to smash. But you'd better keep off that man."

"Thinking of selling me, are you?"

"I shan't need to."

"You'd better not. Lost your head over this theatrical gentleman in tights, haven't you?"

"Why do you have to be so vulgar?" she asked, contemptuously.

"What's the matter with you, then?"

"I'm frightened, that's all. Unlike me, isn't it?"

"Frightened of that advertising crook?"

"Really, Tod, you're a fool sometimes. You can't see a thing when it's under your nose. It's written too big for you to see, I suppose."

"You're drunk," said Milligan. "Just because you haven't quite managed to get off with this joker of yours—"

"Shut up," said Dian. "Get off with him? I'd as soon get off with the public hangman."

"I dare say you would. Any new sensation would do for you. What do you want? A row? Because, if so, I'm afraid I can't be bothered to oblige you."

There is a dreary convention which decrees that the final collapse of a sordid liaison shall be preceded by a series of no less sordid squabbles. But on this occasion, Miss de Momerie seemed ready to dispense with convention.

"No. I'm through with you, that's all. I'm cold. I'm going to bed. . . . Tod, *did* you kill Victor Dean?"

"I did not."

Major Milligan dreamed that night that Death Bredon, in his harlequin dress, was hanging him for the murder of Lord Peter Wimsey.

CHAPTER XV

SUDDEN DECEASE OF A MAN
IN DRESS CLOTHES

CHIEF-INSPECTOR PARKER continued to be disturbed in his mind. There had been another fiasco in Essex. A private motor-boat, suspected of being concerned in the drug-traffic, had been seized and searched without result—except, of course, the undesired result of giving the alarm to the parties concerned, if they were concerned. Further, a fast car, which had attracted attention by its frequent midnight excursions from the coast to the capital, had been laboriously tracked to its destination, and proved to belong to a distinguished member of the diplomatic corps, engaged on extremely incognito visits to a lady established in a popular seaside resort. Mr. Parker, still incapacitated from personal attendance upon midnight expeditions, was left with the gloomy satisfaction of saying that everything always went wrong when he wasn't there himself. He was also unreasonably annoyed with Wimsey, as the original cause of his incapacity.

Nor had the investigation at the White Swan so far borne very much fruit. For a week in succession, tactful and experienced policemen had draped themselves over its bar, chatting to all and sundry about greyhounds, goats, parrots and other dumb friends of man, without receiving any return in the shape of mysterious packets.

The old man with the parrot-story had been traced easily enough. He was an habitué. He sat there every morning and every afternoon, and had a fund of such stories. The patient police made a collection of them. The proprietor—

against whose character nothing could be proved—knew this customer well. He was a superannuated Covent Garden porter, who lived on an old-age pension, and every corner of his inoffensive life was open to the day. This excellent old gentleman, when questioned, recalled the conversation with Mr. Hector Puncheon, but was positive that he had never seen any of the party before, except the two carters, whom he knew well enough. These men also agreed that the gentleman in dress clothes and the little man who had talked about greyhounds were equally unknown to them. It was not, however, unusual for gentlemen in dress clothes to drop in at the Swan by way of a good finish to a lively night—or for gentlemen without dress clothes, either. Nothing threw any light on the mystery of the packet of cocaine.

Parker was, however, roused to some enthusiasm by Wimsey's report of his conversations with Milligan.

"What incredible luck you do have, Peter. People who, in the ordinary way, would avoid you like the plague, gate-crash into your parties at the psychological moment and offer you their noses to lead them by."

"Not so much luck, old man," said Wimsey. "Good guidance, that's all. I sent the fair Dian an anonymous letter, solemnly warning her against myself and informing her that if she wanted to know the worst about me, she had only to inquire at my brother's address. It's a curious thing, but people *cannot* resist anonymous letters. It's like free sample offers. They appeal to all one's lower instincts."

"You are a devil," said Parker. "One of these days you'll get into trouble. Suppose Milligan had recognized you."

"I prepared his mind to accept a striking resemblance."

"I wonder he didn't see through it. Family resemblances don't usually extend to details of teeth and so on."

"I never let him get close enough to study details."

"That ought to have made him suspicious."

"No, because I was rude to him about it. He believed me all the time, simply because I was rude. Everybody suspects an eager desire to curry favour, but rudeness, for some reason, is always accepted as a guarantee of good faith. The only man who ever managed to see through rudeness was St. Augustine, and I don't suppose Milligan reads the *Confessions.* Besides, he wanted to believe in me. He's greedy."

"Well, no doubt you know your own business. But about this Victor Dean affair. Do you really believe that the head of this particular dope-gang is on Pym's staff? It sounds quite incredible."

"That's an excellent reason for believing it. I don't mean in a *credo quia impossible* sense, but merely because the staff of a respectable advertising agency would be such an excellent hiding-place for a big crook. The particular crookedness of advertising is so very far removed from the crookedness of dope-trafficking."

"Why? As far as I can make out, all advertisers are dope-merchants."

"So they are. Yes, now I come to think of it, there is a subtle symmetry about the thing which is extremely artistic. All the same, Charles, I must admit that I find it difficult to go the whole way with Milligan. I have carefully reviewed the staff of Pym's, and I have so far failed to find any one who looks in the least like a Napoleon of crime."

"But you seem convinced that the murder of Victor Dean was an inside job. Or do you now think that some stranger was hiding on the roof and did away with Dean because he was on the point of splitting on the gang? I suppose an outsider could get access to Pym's roof?"

"Oh, easily. But that wouldn't explain the catapult in Mrs. Johnson's desk."

"Nor the attack on me."

"Not if the same person that killed Dean attacked you too."

"Meaning that it might have been Willis? I take it that Willis is not the Napoleon of crime, anyhow."

"Willis isn't a Napoleon of anything. Nor, I fancy, is the chap with the catapult. If he had been, he'd have had the common sense to use his own catapult and burn it afterwards. As I see him, he is a person of considerable ingenuity but limited foresight; a person who snatches at the first thing that is offered him and does his best with it, but lacks just that little extra bit of consideration that would make the thing a real success. He lives from hand to mouth, as you may say. I dare say I could spot him without much difficulty—but that's not what you want, is it? You'd rather have the Napoleon of the dope-traffic, wouldn't you? If he exists, that is."

"Certainly I should," said Parker, emphatically.

"That's what I thought. What, if you come to think of it, is a trifle like an odd murder or assault, compared with a method of dope-running that baffles Scotland Yard? Nothing at all."

"It isn't, really," replied Parker, seriously. "Dope-runners are murderers, fifty times over. They slay hundreds of people, soul and body, besides indirectly causing all sorts of crimes among the victims. Compared with that, slugging one inconsiderable pip-squeak over the head is almost meritorious."

"Really, Charles! for a man of your religious upbringing, your outlook is positively enlightened."

"Not so irreligious, either. Fear not him that killeth, but him that hath power to cast into hell. How about it?"

"How indeed? Hang the one and give the other a few weeks in jail—or, if of good social position, bind him over or put him on remand for six months under promise of good behaviour."

Parker made a wry mouth.

"I know, old man, I know. But where would be the good of hanging the wretched victims or the smaller fry? There would always be others. We want the top people. Take even this man, Milligan, who's a pest of the first water—with no excuse for it, because he isn't an addict himself—but suppose we punish him here and now. They'd only start again, with a new distributor and a new house for him to run his show in, and what would anybody gain by that?"

"Exactly," said Wimsey. "And how much better off will you be, even if you catch the man above Milligan? The same thing will apply."

Parker made a hopeless gesture.

"I don't know, Peter. It's no good worrying about it. My job is to catch the heads of the gangs if I can, and, after that, as many as possible of the little people. I can't overthrow cities and burn the population."

" 'Tis the Last Judgment's fire must cure this place," said Wimsey, "calcine its clods and set its prisoners free. There are times, Charles, when even the unimaginative decency of my brother and the malignant virtue of his wife appear to me admirable. I could hardly say more."

"You have a certain decency of your own, Peter," replied Parker, "which I like better, because it is not negative." Having given voice to this atrocious outburst of sentiment, he became extremely red in the face, and hastened to cover up his lapse from good taste. "But at the present moment I must say you are not being very helpful. You have been investigating a crime—if it is a crime—for some weeks now, and the only tangible result is a broken collar-bone for me. If you could confine yourself to breaking your own collar-bone—"

"It has been broken before now," said Wimsey, "and in no less good a cause. You shouldn't shove your beastly collar-bone into my affairs."

At this moment, the telephone-bell rang.

It was half-past eight in the morning, and Wimsey had been consuming an early breakfast with his brother-in-law, prior to their departure each to his own place of business. Lady Mary, who had been supplying their bodily necessities and leaving them to their argument, took up the receiver.

"It's from the Yard, darling. Something about that man Puncheon."

Parker took the instrument and plunged into an animated discussion, which ended with his saying:

"Send Lumley and Eagles along at once, and tell Puncheon to keep in touch with you. I'm coming."

"What's up?" inquired Wimsey.

"Our little friend Puncheon has seen his bloke in dress clothes again," said Parker, cursing as he tried to get his coat over his damaged shoulder. "Saw him hanging about the *Morning Star* offices this morning, buying an early paper or something. Been chasing him ever since, apparently. Landed out at Finchley, of all places. Says he couldn't get on to the 'phone before. I must push off. See you later. Cheerio, Mary dear. Bung-ho, Peter."

He bounced out in a hurry.

"Well, well," said Wimsey. He pushed back his chair and sat staring vacantly at the wall opposite, on which hung a calendar. Then, emptying the sugar-bowl on the table-cloth with a jerk, he began, frowning hideously, to built a lofty tower with its contents. Mary recognized the signs of inspiration and stole quietly away to her household duties.

Forty-five minutes afterwards she returned. Her brother had gone, and the banging of the flat-door after him had flung his column of sugar-lumps in disorder across the table, but she could see that it had been a tall one. Mary sighed.

"Being Peter's sister is rather like being related to the public hangman," she thought, echoing the words of a lady with whom she had otherwise little in common. "And being married to a policeman is almost worse. I suppose the hangman's relatives are delighted when business is looking up. Still," she thought, being not without humour, "one might be connected with an undertaker, and rejoice over the deaths of the righteous, which would be infinitely worse."

Sergeant Lumley and P.C. Eagles found no Hector Puncheon at the small eating-house in Finchley from which he had telephoned. They did, however, find a message.

"He has had breakfast and is off again," said the note, written hurriedly on a page torn from the reporter's note-book. "I will telephone to you here as soon as I can. I'm afraid he knows I am following him."

"There," said Sergeant Lumley, gloomily. "That's an amachoor all over. 'Course 'e lets the bloke know 'e's bein' followed. If one of these newspaper fellows was a blue-bottle and 'ad to follow an elephant, 'e'd get buzzin' in the elephant's ear, same as 'e'd know what 'e was up to."

P.C. Eagles was struck with admiration at this flight of fancy, and laughed heartily.

"Ten to one 'e'll lose 'im for keeps, now," pursued Sergeant Lumley. "Gettin' us pushed off 'ere without our breakfusses."

"There ain't no reason why we shouldn't have our breakfusses, seein' as we are here," said his subordinate, who was of that happy disposition that makes the best of things. "'Ow about a nice pair o' kippers?"

"I don't mind if I do," said the sergeant, "if only we're allowed to eat 'em in peace. But you mark my words, 'e'll start ringin' up again afore we 'as time to swallow a bite. Which reminds me. I better ring up the Yard and stop me lord Parker from traipsin' up 'ere. 'E mustn't be put about. Oh, no!"

P.C. Eagles ordered the kippers and a pot of tea. He used his jaws more readily for eating than for talking. The sergeant got his call, and returned, just as the eatables were placed on the table.

"Says, if 'e rings up from anywhere else, we better take a taxi," he announced. "Save time, 'e says. 'Ow's 'e think we're goin' to pick up a taxi 'ere. Nothing but blinkin' trams."

"Order the taxi now," suggested Mr. Eagles, with his mouth full, "so's to be in readiness, like."

"And 'ave it tickin' up the thruppences for nothing? Think they'll call that legitimate expenses? Not 'arf. 'You pay that out of your own pocket, my man,' that's what they'll say, the lousy skin-flints."

"Well, 'ave yer grub," suggested Mr. Eagles, pacifically.

Sergeant Lumley inspected his kipper narrowly.

" 'Ope it's a good one, that's all," he muttered. "Looks oily, it do. 'Ope it's cooked. Eat a kipper what ain't properly cooked through and you gets kipper on your breath for the rest of the day." He forked a large portion into his mouth without pausing to remove the bones, and was obliged to expend a painful minute rescuing them with his fingers. "Tcha! it beats me why Godamighty wanted to put such a lot of bones into them things."

P.C. Eagles was shocked.

"You didn't oughter question the ways of Godamighty," he said, reprovingly.

"You keep a civil tongue in your 'ed, my lad," retorted Sergeant Lumley, unfairly intruding his official superiority into this theological discussion, "and don't go forgettin' what's due to my position."

"There ain't no position in the eyes of Godamighty," said P.C. Eagles, stoutly. His father and his sister happened to be noted lights in the Salvation Army, and he felt himself to be on his own ground here. "If it pleases 'Im to make you a sergeant, that's one thing, but it won't do you no good when you comes before 'Im to answer to the charge of questionin' 'Is ways with kippers. Come to think of it, in 'Is sight you an' me is just the same as worms, with no bones at all."

"Not so much about worms," said Sergeant Lumley. "You oughter know better than to talk about worms when a man's eating his breakfuss. It's enough to take any one's appetite away. And let me tell you, Eagles, worm or no worm, if I have any more lip from you— Drat that telephone! What did I tell you?"

He pounded heavily across to the insanitary little cupboard that held the instrument, and emerged in a minute or two, dismally triumphant.

"That's 'im. Kensington, this time. You 'op out an' get that taxi, while I settle up 'ere."

"Wouldn't the Underground be quicker?"

"They said taxi, so you damn well make it taxi," said Sergeant Lumley. While Eagles fetched the taxi, the serg-

eant took the opportunity to finish his kipper, thus aveng-
ing his defeat in religious controversy. This cheered him so
much that he consented to take the Underground at the
nearest suitable point, and they journeyed in comparative
amity as far as South Kensington Station, and thence to
the point indicated by Hector Puncheon, which was, in
fact, the entrance to the Natural History Museum.

There was nobody in the entrance-hall who resembled
Hector Puncheon in the least.

"Suppose 'e's gone on already?" suggested P.C. Eagles.

"Suppose 'e 'as," retorted the sergeant. "I can't 'elp that.
I told 'im to telephone 'ere if 'e did or to let them know
at the Yard. I can't do no more, can I? I better take a
walk round, and you sit 'ere to see as they don't come out.
If they do, you be ready to take up this other bird's trail
and tell Puncheon to set 'ere till I come. An' don't let your
bird see you talking to Puncheon, neether. And if they
comes out and you see me a-follerin' of them, then you
foller on be'ind an' keep yourself outer sight, see?"

Mr. Eagles saw clearly—as indeed he well might, for he
knew quite as much about his duties as Sergeant Lumley.
But the worm still ranked in the sergeant's breast. Mr.
Eagles strolled over to a case of humming-birds and gazed
at it with absorbed interest, while Mr. Lumley went heavily
up the steps, looking as much as possible like a country
cousin bent on seeing the sights.

He had been in the entrance-hall about ten minutes,
and had almost exhausted the humming-birds, when he saw
something reflected in the glass case which made him sidle
softly round so as to command a view of the staircase.
A portly person in an overcoat and a top-hat was coming
slowly down, one hand thrust deep into his overcoat pocket,
the other swinging carelessly at his side. P.C. Eagles looked
past him up the stair; there was no sign, either of Hector
Puncheon or of Sergeant Lumley, and for a moment the
constable hesitated. Then something caught his eye. In
the gentleman's left-hand overcoat pocket was a folded copy
of the *Morning Star*.

There is nothing unusual about seeing a gentleman with a copy of the *Morning Star*. The readers of that great organ periodically write to the editor, giving statistics of the number of passengers on the 8.15 who read the *Morning Star* in preference to any other paper, and their letters are printed for all to read. Nevertheless, P.C. Eagles determined to take the risk. He scribbled a hasty note on the back of an envelope and walked across to the doorkeeper.

"If you see my friend that came in with me," he said, "you might give him that and tell him I can't wait any longer. I got to get along to my work."

Out of the corner of his eye, he saw the gentleman in the overcoat pass out through the swing-door. Unobtrusively, he followed him.

Upstairs, at the top of a dark staircase barred by a trestle bearing the words "No Entrance," Sergeant Lumley was bending anxiously over the inanimate form of Hector Puncheon. The reporter was breathing heavily in a way the sergeant did not like, and there was a nasty contused wound on his temple.

"Trust your amachoors to make a mess of it," reflected Sergeant Lumley, bitterly. "I only 'ope as that Eagles 'as got 'is 'ead screwed on the right way. But there you are. I can't be in two places at once."

The man in the overcoat walked quietly down the street towards the Underground Station. He did not look back. A few yards behind him, P. C. Eagles sauntered casually along in his wake. His eyes were on his quarry. Neither of them saw a third man, who emerged from nowhere in particular and followed a few yards behind P.C. Eagles. No passer-by gave so much as a second glance to the little procession as it crossed Cromwell Road and debouched upon the station.

The man in the overcoat glanced at the taxi-rank; then he seemed to change his mind. For the first time, he looked back. All he saw was P.C. Eagles purchasing a newspaper, and in this sight there was nothing alarming. The other follower he could not have seen, because, like the Spanish Fleet, he was not yet in sight, though P.C. Eagles might have seen him, had he been looking in his direction. The gentleman appeared to reject the notion of a taxi and turned into the station entrance. Mr. Eagles, his eyes apparently intent upon a headline about Food-Taxes, wandered in after him, and was in time to follow his example in taking a ticket for Charing Cross. Pursued and pursuer entered the lift together, the gentleman walking across to the farther gate, Eagles remaining modestly on the hither side. There were already about half a dozen people, mostly women, in the lift, and just as the gate was shutting, another man came in hurriedly. He passed Eagles and took up a central position among the group of women. At the bottom of the shaft, they all emerged in a bunch, the strange man pressing rather hastily past the man in the overcoat, and leading the way towards the platform, where an eastward-bound train was just running in.

What exactly happened then, P.C. Eagles was not quite clear about at the time, though, in the light of after events he saw plainly one or two things that were not obvious to him then. He saw the third man standing close to the edge of the platform, carrying a thin walking-stick. He saw the man in the overcoat walk past him and then suddenly stop and stagger in his walk. He saw the man with the stick fling out his hand and grasp the other by the arm, saw the two waver together on the edge and heard a shriek from a woman. Then both toppled together under the advancing train.

Through the uproar, Eagles shouldered his way.

" 'Ere," he said, "I'm an officer of the law. Stand aside, please."

They stood aside, with the exception of a porter and another man, who were hauling out something between the train and the platform. An arm came up, and then a head—then the battered body of the third man, the one who had

had the walking-stick. They laid him down on the platform bruised and bloody.

"Where's the other?"

"Gone, poor chap."

"Is that one dead?"

"Yes."

"No, he ain't."

"Oh, Betty, I'm going to faint."

"He's all right—see! He's opening his eyes."

"Yes, but how about the other?"

"Do stop shoving."

"Look out, that's a policeman."

"That's the live rail down there."

"Where's a doctor? Send for a doctor."

"Stand back, please. Stand right back."

"Why don't they shut off the electricity?"

"They have. That feller ran off to do it."

"How'll they get 'im out without moving the train?"

"Expect he's all in little bits, pore chap."

"That one tried to save 'im."

"Looked as if he was took ill, or drunk-like."

"Drunk, this time in the morning?"

"They ought to give 'im brandy."

"Clear all this lot out," said Eagles. "This one'll do all right. The other's done for, I suppose."

"Smashed all to blazes. 'Orrible."

"Then you can't do him any good. Clear the station and get an ambulance and another police officer."

"Right you are."

"This one's coming round," put in the man who had helped to haul the victim up. "How are you feeling now, sir?"

"Bloody," said the rescued man, faintly. Then, seeming to realize where he was, he added:

"What happened?"

"Why, sir, a poor gentleman fell off the platform and took you over with him."

"Yes, of course. Is he all right?"

"Afraid he's badly knocked about, sir. Ah!" as somebody ran up with a flask. "Take a pull at this, sir. Gently, you. Lift his head up. Don't jerk him. Now then."

"Ah!" said the man. "That's better. All right. Don't fuss. My spine's all right and I don't think anything's broken to speak of." He moved his arms and legs experimentally.

"Doctor'll be here in a minute, sir."

"Doctor be damned. I'm a doctor myself. Limbs all correct. Head apparently sound, though it aches like hell. Ribs —not so sure about those. Something gone there, I'm afraid. Pelvis intact, thank goodness."

"Very glad to hear that," said Eagles.

"It's the footboard of the train that got me, I fancy. I remember being rolled round and round like a pat of butter between two whatsinames," said the stranger, whose damaged ribs did not seem to impede his breathing altogether. "And I saw the wheels of the train get slower and stop, and I said to myself: 'This is it. You're for it, my lad. Time's stopped and this is Eternity.' But I see I was mistaken."

"Happily so, sir," said Eagles.

"Wish I'd been able to stop that other poor devil, though."

"I'm sure you did your best, sir." Eagles produced his note-book. "Excuse me, sir, but I'm a police-officer, and if you could manage to tell me just how it occurred—"

"Damned if I know myself," replied the other. "All I know is, I was standing just about here when the fellow passed me." He paused, catching his breath a little. "I noticed he was looking rather queer. Heart subject, I should think. He suddenly stopped and staggered and then came towards me. I caught hold of his arm and then he lurched over with all his weight and dragged me over with him. And then I can't remember anything but the noise of the train and the tremendous size of its wheels and the feeling of having the breath squeezed out of me. I must have dropped him, I suppose."

"And no wonder," said Eagles, sympathetically.

"My name's Garfield," went on the rescuer. "Dr. Herbert Garfield." He gave an address in Kensington and another in Harley Street. "I think I see one of my professional brethren arriving, and he'll probably say I'm not to talk." He grinned faintly. "Anyhow, I shall be filed for reference for the next few weeks, if you want more information."

P.C. Eagles thanked Dr. Garfield, and then turned to the body of the man in the overcoat, which had by now been disentangled from between the wheels of the train and laid upon the platform. It was an unpleasant sight. Even Eagles, accustomed as he was to casualties, felt a violent distaste for the necessary job of searching the dead man's pockets for evidence of identity. Curiously enough, he found none in the shape of visiting cards or papers. There was a note-case with a few pound-notes, a silver cigarette-case filled with a popular brand of Turks, a little loose change, an unmarked handkerchief, and an H.T. & V. latch-key. Moreover—and this pleased him very much—in the overcoat pocket was a little rubber cosh, such as is sold for use against motor-bandits. He was in the act of hunting over the suit for the tailor's tab, when he was hailed by a local inspector of police, who had arrived with the ambulance.

Eagles was relieved to have the support of a colleague. He knew that he ought to get in touch with Sergeant Lumley and with Scotland Yard. An hour's energetic action on the part of all resulted in a happy reunion at the nearest police-station, where, in fact, Lumley had already arrived, after depositing the unconscious Mr. Puncheon in hospital. Chief-Inspector Parker came hot-foot to Kensington, heard the statements of Lumley and Eagles, reviewed the scene of the disaster and the remains of the mysterious man in dress clothes, and was annoyed. When a man whom you have been elaborately chasing all over London has the impudence to be killed just as you are on the point of catching him, and turns out to have no tailor's name on his clothes and nothing to identify him by; when, moreover, he has thoughtlessly permitted his face to be smashed into pulp by an electric train, so that you cannot usefully circulate his photograph for recognition, your satisfaction in feeling that there is something wrong about him is cancelled by the thought of the weary work that his identification is going to involve.

"There's nothing for it," said Chief-Inspector Parker, "but his laundry-mark, I suppose. And, of course, his dentistry, if any."

Irritatingly enough, the deceased turned out to have an excellent set of teeth and at least three laundry-marks. Nor were his shoes helpful, being ready-made, though by an excellent and much-advertised firm. In fact, the wretched man had gone to meet his Maker in Farley's Footwear, thus upholding to the last the brave assertion that, however distinguished the occasion, Farley's Footwear will carry you through.

In this extremity, Mr. Parker—perhaps stimulated by the thought of Messrs. Farley's advertising—rang up Pym's Publicity and desired to speak with Mr. Bredon.

That gentleman was closeted with Mr. Armstrong when the call came through. Whifflets were causing trouble. The sales of Whifflets had been considerably affected by the publicity methods of a rival brand, Puffin Cigarettes. The manufacturers of Puffins had had a brain-wave. They were giving away aeroplanes. In every packet of Puffins they enclosed a coupon, bearing the name of a component part of a popular little touring 'plane, suitable for amateur use. When you had collected your complete set of parts (numbering one hundred) you sent up your coupons, together with a brief essay on the importance of air-mindedness for British boys. The writer of the best essay each day became the recipient of a private 'plane, and a course of free instruction enabling him or her to take out an air-pilot's certificate. This happy scheme was supported by heavy advertising of a modern and stimulating kind: "The Future is with the Air-

Minded"—"The Highest Flight in Modern Cigarette Manu‐
facture"—"Puff Puffins, and Reach the Height of your
Ambition"—and so forth. If you were incapacitated, by
reason of age or infirmity, from enjoying the ownership
of an aeroplane, you received instead a number of shares
in the new issue of the Aeroplane Company involved. The
scheme had the support of several notable airmen, whose
faces, adorned with flying helmets, stared and grinned
from every page of the press in conjunction with their
considered opinions that Puffins were doing a valuable work
in helping to establish British Supremacy in the Air.

Whifflets were upset. They demanded, with some annoy‐
ance, why Pym's had not had this brilliant idea first.
They clamoured for an aeroplane scheme of their own, with
a larger plane and a hangar to keep it in. Mr. Armstrong
pointed out to them that the sole result of this would be to
confuse the public mind between Whifflets and Puffins,
which were already quite sufficiently similar in quality and
appearance to confuse anybody.

"They're all alike," he said to Bredon, not meaning the
cigarettes, but the manufacturers. "They follow each other
like sheep. If Whifflets use large heads of film-stars, Puffin's
want to come out with still larger heads of still more im‐
portant stars. If Gasperettes give away timepieces, Puffins
follow on with grandfather clocks and Whifflets with
chronometers. If Whifflets announce that they don't damage
the lungs, Puffins claim that they strengthen the pulmonary
system and Gasperettes quote doctors who recommend them
in cases of tuberculosis. They will try to snatch each other's
thunder—and what happens? The public smoke them all in
turn, just as they did before."

"Isn't that a good thing for trade?" asked Mr. Bredon,
innocently. "If one of them got all the sales, the others
would go bankrupt."

"Oh, no, they wouldn't," said Mr. Armstrong. "They'd
merely amalgamate. But it would be bad for us, because
then they'd all use the same agency."

"Well, what about it, then?" queried Bredon.

"We've got to cope. We must head them off aeroplanes. For one thing, the boom won't last. The country isn't ready to be cluttered up with aeroplanes, and fathers of families are beginning to complain about it. Even today, few fathers care about having private aeroplanes delivered to their daughters in quiet suburban areas. What we want is a new scheme, on similar lines but with more family appeal. But it must boost Britain. We've got to have the patriotic note."

It was in that moment, and while Chief-Inspector Parker was arguing over the line with the office telephonist, that Mr. Death Bredon conceived that magnificent idea that everybody remembers and talks about today—the scheme that achieved renown as "Whiffling Round Britain"—the scheme that sent up the sales of Whifflets by five hundred per cent in three months and brought so much prosperity to British Hotel-keepers and Road and Rail Transport. It is not necessary to go into details. You have probably Whiffled yourself. You recollect how it was done. You collected coupons for everything—railway fares, charabancs, hotel-bills, theatre-tickets—every imaginable item in a holi-day programme. When you had collected enough to cover the period of time you wished to spend in travelling, you took your coupons with you (no sending up to Whifflets, nothing to post or fill in) and started on your tour. At the railway station you presented coupons entitling you to so many miles of first-class travel and received your ticket to the selected town. You sought your hotel (practically all the hotels in Britain fell eagerly in with the scheme) and there presented coupons entitling you to so many nights' board and lodging on special Whifflet terms. For your charabanc outings, your sea-bathing, your amusements, you paid in Whifflet coupons. It was all exceedingly simple and trouble-free. And it made for that happy gregariousness which is the joy of the travelling middle-class. When you asked for your packet of Whifflets in the bar, your next-door neighbour was almost sure to ask, "Are you Whiffling too?" Whiffling parties arranged to Whiffle together, and ex-

changed Whifflet coupons on the spot. The great Whifflers'
Club practically founded itself, and Whifflers who had
formed attachments while Whiffling in company, secured
special Whifflet coupons entitling them to a Whifflet wedding with a Whifflet cake and their photographs in the
papers. When this had happened several times, arrangements were made by which Whiffler couples could collect
for a Whifflet house, whose Whifflet furniture included a
handsome presentation smoking cabinet, free from advertising matter and crammed with unnecessary gadgets. After
this, it was only a step to a Whifflet Baby. In fact, the
Whifflet Campaign is and remains the outstanding example
of Thinking Big in Advertising. The only thing that you
cannot get by Whiffling is a coffin; it is not admitted that
any Whiffler could ever require such an article.

It is not to be supposed that the great Whiffle-Way, in all
its comprehensive perfection, sprang fully armed from Mr.
Bredon's brain when Mr. Armstrong uttered the words,
Family Appeal. All that then happened was a mental
association with the phrase Family Hotel, coupled with a
faint consciousness of inner illumination. He replied,
humbly, "Yes, I see; I'll try to work out something,"
gathered up some sheets of paper on which Mr. Armstrong
had scribbled a few illegible notes and a thing that looked
like a hedgehog, and made his way out. He had taken six
steps down the passage when the idiotic slogan: "If that's
what you want, you can Whiffle for it," took possession of
his brain; two steps further on, this repellent sentence had
recast itself as: "All you Want by Whiffling," and on the
threshold of his own room, the first practical possibility of
Whiffledom struck him like a sledge-hammer. Fired with
excitement, he hurled himself at his desk, snatched a scribbling-block, and had written the word "WHIFFLE" in
capitals an inch high, when Miss Rossiter arrived with the
message that Mr. Parker urgently requested Mr. Bredon to
ring him up on the Whitehall number. Lord Peter Wimsey
was so intimately in the skin of Mr. Death Bredon that he
said: "Damn!" loudly and heartily.

Nevertheless, he obeyed the call, presented himself with leave of absence on urgent private business, and went down to Scotland Yard, where he surveyed the clothes and effects of the man in the dress suit.

"No doubt we shall end by having to circularize the laundries," said Parker. "Perhaps a photograph in some of the London and provincial papers would be as well. I loathe newspapers, but they do advertise one's requirements, and some of these laundry-marks may come from outside London. . . ."

Wimsey looked at him.

"Advertisement, my dear Charles, may be desirable in the case of laundries, but for people like ourselves it does not exist. A gentleman whose clothes are so well cut, and who yet deprives his tailor of the credit for them is, like ourselves, not of the advertising sort. This, I see, is his top-hat, mysteriously uninjured."

"It had rolled beyond the train, on to the farther line."

"Quite. Here again the maker's golden imprint has been removed. How absurd, Charles! One does not—at least, you and I and this gentleman do not—consider the brand to be the guarantee of quality. For us, the quality guarantees the brand. There are two hatters in London who could have made this hat, and you have doubtless already observed that the crown is markedly dolichocephalic, while the curve of the brim is also characteristic. It is a thought behind the present fashion; yet the article is undoubtedly of recent manufacture. Send one of your sleuths to each of these two establishments and ask for the customer with the elongated head who has a fancy for this type of brim. Do not waste your time on laundry-marks, which are, at best, tedious and, at worst, deceptive."

"Thanks," said Parker. "I thought you might be able to put your finger either on the hatter or the tailor."

The first hatter they visited proved to be the right man. He directed their researches to the flat of a Mr. Horace

Mountjoy, who lived in Kensington. They armed them·
selves with a search-warrant and visited the flat.

Mr. Mountjoy, they ascertained from the commissionaire,
was a bachelor of quiet habits, except that he was frequently out rather late at night. He lived alone, and was
waited upon and valeted by the staff belonging to the block
of flats.

The commissionaire came on duty at 9 o'clock. There was
no night porter. Between 11 p.m. and 9 a.m. the outer door
was locked and could be opened by the tenants with their
own keys, without disturbing him in his basement flat. He
had seen Mr. Mountjoy go out the previous evening at
about 7.45, in evening dress. He had not seen him return.
Withers, the valet, would probably be able to say whether
Mr. Mountjoy had been in that night.

Withers was able to say positively that he had not. Nobody had entered Mr. Mountjoy's flat but himself, and the
chambermaid who did the rooms. The bed had not been
slept in. That was nothing unusual with Mr. Mountjoy.
He was frequently out all night, though he generally returned to breakfast at 9.30.

Parker displayed his official card, and they went upstairs
to a flat on the third floor. Withers was about to open the
door with his pass-key, which, as he explained, he was accustomed to use in the mornings, to avoid disturbing the
tenants, but Parker stopped him and produced the two
keys which had been taken from the corpse. One of them
fitted the lock and established, without much doubt, that
they had come to the right place.

Everything in the flat was in perfect order. There was a
desk in the sitting-room, containing a few bills and some
notepaper, but its drawers were all unlocked and it appeared to hold no secrets. Nor was there anything remarkable about the bedroom or the small dining-room. In the
bathroom was a little cupboard containing the usual toilet
articles and household medicines. Parker made a rapid
inventory of these, pausing for a few minutes over a packet
labelled "Bicarbonate of Soda," but touch and taste soon

assured him that this contained exactly what it purported to contain. The only thing that could be considered in the slightest degree out of the ordinary in the whole establishment was the presence (also in the bathroom cupboard) of several packets of cigarette papers.

"Did Mr. Mountjoy roll his own cigarettes?"

"I never saw him do so," replied Withers. "He smoked Turkish Abdullas as a rule."

Parker nodded and impounded the cigarette-papers. A further search disclosed no loose tobacco. A number of boxes of cigars and cigarettes were retrieved from the dining-room sideboard. They looked innocent and a few, which Parker promptly slit open, proved to contain excellent tobacco and nothing else. Parker shook his head.

"You'll have to go through everything very carefully, Lumley."

"Yes, sir."

"Any letters by the first post?"

There were none.

"Any visitors today?"

"No, sir. Not unless you count the man from the post-office."

"Oh? What did *he* want?"

"Nothing," replied Withers, "except to bring the new telephone directory." He indicated the two clean volumes which lay upon the sitting-room desk.

"Oh!" said Parker. This did not sound promising. "Did he come into the room?"

"No, sir. He knocked at the door when Mrs. Trabbs and I were both here. Mrs. Trabbs was sweeping, sir, and I was brushing Mr. Mountjoy's lounge suit. I took the books in, sir, and handed him out the old ones."

"I see. All right. And beyond sweeping and brushing and so on, you disturbed nothing?"

"No, sir."

"Anything in the waste-paper basket?"

"I could not say, sir. Mrs. Trabbs would know."

Mrs. Trabbs, produced, said there had been nothing in

the waste-paper basket except a wine-merchant's circular.
Mr. Mountjoy wrote very little and did not receive many
letters.

Satisfied that there had been no interference with the flat
since the occupant had left the night before, Parker turned
his attention to the wardrobe and chest of drawers, where
he found various garments, all properly marked with the
names of the tailor or shirt-maker responsible for them. He
noticed that all were by first-class artists in their own line.
Another silk hat, similar to the one now resting at Scotland
Yard, but with sweat-band and crown undisfigured, was
found in a hat-box; there were also several felt hats and a
bowler, all by first-class makers.

"Mr. Mountjoy was a rich man?"

"He appeared to be in very easy circumstances, sir. He
did himself well; the best of everything. Especially during
the last year or so."

"What was his profession?"

"I think he was a gentleman of independent means. I
never heard of him being engaged in any business."

"Did you know that he had a silk hat from which the
maker's name had been removed?"

"Yes, sir. He was very angry about it. Said that some
friend of his had damaged the hat for a rag. I offered several
times to get it put right, sir, but when he had cooled down
he said it didn't matter. It wasn't a hat he very often used,
sir. And besides, he said, why should he be a walking
advertisement for his hatter?"

"Did you know that his dress suit had also lost the
tailor's tab?"

"Had it indeed, sir? No, I can't say I noticed it."

"What sort of man was Mr. Mountjoy?"

"A very pleasant gentleman, sir. I'm very sorry to hear
he has met with such a sad accident."

"How long has he lived here?"

"Six or seven years, I believe, sir. I've been here four
years myself."

"When was the practical joke played on his silk hat?"

"About eighteen months ago, sir, if I remember rightly."

"As long ago as that? I fancied the hat looked newer."

"Well, sir, as I say, he didn't wear it above once or twice a week, sir. And Mr. Mountjoy didn't trouble about the fashion of his hats. There was one particular shape he fancied, and he had all his hats specially made to that pattern."

Parker nodded. He knew this already from the hatter and from Wimsey, but it was well to check matters up. He reflected that he had never yet caught Wimsey tripping in any fact pertaining to dress.

"Well," he said, "as you may have guessed, Withers, there will have to be an inquiry about Mr. Mountjoy's death. You had better say as little as possible to any outside person. You will give me all the keys of the flat, and I shall be leaving the police in charge here for a day or two."

"Very good, sir."

Parker waited to ascertain the name and address of the proprietor of the flats, and left Lumley to his investigations. From the proprietor he gained very little information. Mr. Mountjoy, of no profession, had taken the flat six years previously. He had paid his rent regularly. There had been no complaints. Nothing was known of Mr. Mountjoy's friends or relations. It was regrettable that so good a tenant should have come to so sudden and sad an end. It was much to be hoped that nothing would transpire of a scandalous nature, as those flats had always been extremely respectable.

Parker's next visit was to Mr. Mountjoy's bank. Here he encountered the usual obstructive attitude, but eventually succeeded in getting access to the books. There was a regular income of about a thousand a year derived from sound investments. No irregularities. No mysterious fluctuations. Parker came away with an uneasy impression that Mr. Hector Puncheon had discovered a mare's nest.

CHAPTER XVI

ECCENTRIC BEHAVIOUR
OF A POST-OFFICE DEPARTMENT

THE Chief-Inspector voiced this opinion to Wimsey the same evening. His lordship, whose mind was still divided between detection and the new Whifflet campaign, which had taken clear shape during the afternoon, was curt with him:

"Mare's nest? Then what knocked Puncheon out? A kick from the mare's heel?"

"Perhaps Mountjoy merely got fed up with him. You'd get fed up yourself if you were pursued all over London by a Puncheon."

"Possibly. But I shouldn't knock him out and leave him to his fate. I should give him in charge. How is Puncheon?"

"Still unconscious. Concussion. He seems to have got a violent blow on the temple and a nasty crack on the back of the head."

"Um. Knocked up against the wall, probably, when Mountjoy got him with the cosh."

"No doubt you're right."

"I am always right. I hope you are keeping an eye on the man Garfield."

"He won't move for a bit. Why?"

"Well—it's odd that Mountjoy should have been snuffed out so inconveniently for you."

"You don't suppose that Garfield had anything to do with it? Why, the man was nearly killed himself. Besides, we've looked into him. He's a well-known Harley Street man, with a large West-end practice."

"Among the dope-maniacs, perhaps?"

"He specializes in nervous complaints."

"Exactly."

Parker whistled.

"That's what you think, is it?"

"See here," said Wimsey, "your grey matter isn't function-ing as it ought. Are you tired at the end of the day? Do you suffer from torpor and lethargy after meals? Try Sparkletone, the invigorating vegetable saline that stimu-lates while it cleanses. Some accidents are too accidental to be true. When a gentleman removes his tailor's tab and takes the trouble to slice his hatter's imprint away with a razor, and goes skipping, for no reason at all, from Finchley to South Kensington Museum in his dress suit at unearthly hours in the morning, it's because he has something to hide. If he tops up his odd behaviour by falling under a train without the smallest apparent provocation, it's because somebody else is interested in getting the things hidden, too. And the more risks somebody else takes in the process, the more certain it is that the thing is worth hiding."

Parker looked at him and grinned quietly.

"You're a great guesser, Peter. Would you be surprised to hear that you're not the only one?"

"No, I shouldn't. You're holding something out on me. What is it? A witness to the assault, what? Somebody who was on the platform? Somebody you weren't inclined to pay much attention to? You old leg-puller, I can see it in your face. Out with it now—who was it? A woman. A hysterical woman. A middle-aged, hysterical spinster. Am I right?"

"Curse you, yes."

"Go on, then. Tell me all about it."

"Well, when Eagles took the depositions of the witnesses at the station, they all agreed that Mountjoy had walked several paces past Garfield and then suddenly staggered; that Garfield had caught him by the arm and that both had fallen together. But this female, Miss Eliza Tebbutt by name, 52, unmarried, housekeeper, living in Kensington, says that she was standing a little way beyond them both and that she distinctly heard what she describes as a 'dreadful voice' say, 'Punch away, you're *for* it!' That Mountjoy immediately stopped as though he had been shot, and that Garfield 'with a terrible face,' took him by the arm and tripped him up. It may increase your confidence in this good lady when you hear that she is subject to nervous disorders, has once been confined in a mental home and is persuaded that Garfield is a prominent member of a gang whose object is to murder all persons of British birth and establish the supremacy of the Jews in England."

"Jews in England be damned. Because a person has a monomania she need not be wrong about her facts. She might have imagined or invented a good deal, but she couldn't possibly imagine or invent anything so fantastic as 'Punch away,' which is obviously her mishearing of the name 'Mountjoy.' Garfield's your man—though I admit that you're going to have some difficulty in fixing anything on him. But if I were you, I'd have his premises searched—if it isn't too late by now."

"I'm afraid it probably is too late. We didn't get any sense out of Miss Tebbutt for an hour or so; by which time the heroic Dr. Garfield had, naturally, telephoned both to his home and to his consulting room to explain what had happened to him. Still, we'll keep an eye on him. The immediate matter of importance is Mountjoy. Who was he? What was he up to? Why did he have to be suppressed?"

"It's pretty clear what he was up to. He was engaged in the dope traffic and he was suppressed because he had been fool enough to let Puncheon recognize and follow him. Somebody must have been on the watch; this gang apparently keeps tabs on all its members. Or the wretched Mountjoy may have asked for help and been helped out of the world as the speediest method of disposing of the difficulty. It's a pity Puncheon can't talk—he could tell us whether Mountjoy had telephoned or spoken to anybody during his dash round town. Anyhow, he made a mistake, and people who make mistakes are not permitted to survive. The odd thing, to my mind, is that you heard nothing of any visit to the flat. You'd rather expect the gang to have made some sort of investigation there, just to make sure. I suppose those servants are to be trusted?"

"I think so. We've made inquiries. They've all got good histories. The commissionaire has an army pension and an excellent record. The valet and chambermaid are highly respectable—nothing whatever against them."

"H'm. And you've found nothing but a packet of cigarette-papers. Handy, of course, for wrapping up a grain or so of cocaine but, in themselves, no proof of anything."

"I thought you'd see the significance of the cigarette-papers."

"I am not yet blind or mentally deficient."

"But where is the dope?"

"The dope? Really, Charles! He was going to fetch the dope when friend Puncheon butted in. Haven't you yet grasped that this is part of the Milligan crowd and that Friday is their day for distributing dope? The Milligans get it on Friday and give house-parties on Friday night and Saturday, when it goes into the hands of the actual addicts. Dian de Momerie told me so."

"I wonder," said Parker, "why they stick to one day? It must add to the risk."

"It's obviously an integral part of the system. The stuff comes into the country—say on Thursdays. That's your part of the story. You don't seem to have done much about that, by the way. It is taken to—somewhere or the other— that night. Next day it is called for by the Mountjoys and sent on to the Milligans, none of whom probably knows any of the others by sight. And by Saturday the whole lot is pushed out and everybody has a happy week-end."

"That sounds plausible. It certainly explains why we found no trace of anything either in the flat or on Mount-joy's body. Except cigarette-papers. By the way, is that right? If Mountjoy has the cigarette-papers, he ought to be the one who distributes to the addicts."

"Not necessarily. He gets it himself in bulk—done up as Bicarbonate of Soda or what not. He divides it into small packets and parcels them out—so many to Milligan, so many to the next retailer and so forth; when, or how, I don't know. Nor do I know how the payments are worked."

"Glad to hear there's something you don't know."

"I said I didn't know; not that I couldn't guess. But I won't bother you with guesses. All the same, it's rather surprising that Garfield & Co. left that flat alone."

"Perhaps Garfield meant to go there afterwards, if he hadn't got knocked out."

"No; he'd not leave it so late. Tell me again about the flat."

Parker patiently repeated the account of his visit and the interviews with the servants. Before he was half-way through, Wimsey had sat up in his chair and was listening with fascinated attention.

"Charles! What imbeciles we are! Of course, that's it!"

"What's what?"

"The Telephone Directory, of course. The man who brought the new volumes and took the old away. Since when has the Post Office taken to getting *both* new volumes out at once?"

"By Jove!" exclaimed Parker.

"I should think it was, by Jove. Ring up now and find out whether two new volumes were sent round to Mountjoy's address today."

"It'll be a job to get hold of O.C. Directories at this time of night."

"So it will. Wait a moment. Ring up the flats and ask if anybody else received any Directories this morning. My experience is that even Government departments do these things in batches, and don't make a special journey to every subscriber."

Parker acted on this suggestion. After a little trouble, he succeeded in getting into touch with three other occupants in the same block as Mountjoy's flat. All three gave the same answer. They had received a new L-Z volume about a fortnight previously. The new A-K volume was not yet due to be issued. One man went further. His name was Barrington, and he had only recently moved in. He had inquired when the new A-K volume would be out with his new 'phone number, and had been told that it would probably be issued in October.

"That settles it," said Wimsey. "Our friend Mountjoy kept his secrets in the telephone directory. That great work contains advertisements, post-office regulations and names and addresses, but particularly names and addresses. May we conclude that the secret nestled among the names and addresses? I think we may."

"It seems reasonable."

"Very reasonable. Now, how do we set about discovering those names and addresses?"

"Bit of a job. We can probably get a description of the man who called for the books this morning—"

"And comb London's teeming millions for him? Had we but world enough and time. Where do good telephone directories go when they die?"

"The pulping-mills, probably."

"And the last exchange of the L-Z volume was made a fortnight ago. There's a chance that it hasn't been pulped yet. Get on to it, Charles. There's more than a chance that it, too, was marked, and that the markings were transferred at each exchange from the old book to the new one."

"Why? Mountjoy might easily have kept the old marked set by him."

"I fancy not, or we should have either found it or heard about it from the manservant. The stranger came; the two current volumes were handed to him and he went away satisfied. As I see the plan, the whole idea would be to use the current volume, so as to rouse no suspicion, have nothing to conceal and provide a convenient mechanism for getting rid of the evidence at short notice."

"You may be right. It's a chance, as you say. I'll get on to the telephone people first thing in the morning."

The tide of luck seemed to have turned. A morning's strenuous work revealed that the old directories had already been dispatched by the sackful to the pulping-mills, but had not, so far, been pulped. Six workers, toiling over the week-end among L-Z volumes collected from the Kensington District, brought to light the pleasing fact that nine people out of ten marked their directories in some way or another. Reports came pouring in. Wimsey sat with Parker in the latter's office at Scotland Yard and considered these reports.

Late on Sunday night, Wimsey raised his head from a sheaf of papers.

"I think this is it, Charles."

"What is it?" Parker was weary and his eyes blood-shot with strain, but a note of hope was in his voice.

"This one. A whole list of public-houses in Central London have been ticked off—three in the middle of the L's, two near the end of the M's, one in the N's, one in the O's, and so forth and so on, including two in the middle of the W's. The two in the W's are the White Stag in Wapping and the White Stoat off Oxford Street. The next W after that is the White Swan in Covent Garden. I would bet any money that in the new volume that was carried away, the White Swan was duly ticked off in its turn."

"I'm not quite sure what you're driving at."

"I'm making rather a long cast, but I suggest this. When the stuff comes up to London of a Thursday, I think it is taken to which ever pub. stands next on the list in the directory. One week it will be a pub. with a name in A—say the Anchor. Next week it will be a B—the Bull & Dog, or the Brickmaker's Arms. The week after that, it will be a C, and so on to W, X, Y, Z—if there are any. The people who have to call for their dope wander into the pub. indicated, where it is slipped to them by the head distributor and his agents, probably quite without the knowledge of the proprietor. And since it never comes twice to the same place, your pretty policemen can go and talk parrots and goats in the White Swan till they are blue in the face. They

ought to have been at the Yellow Peril or the York &
Lancaster."

"That's an idea, Peter. Let's look at that list again."

Wimsey handed it over.

"If you're right, then this week was W week, and next
week will be X week. That's unlikely. Say Y week. The
next Y after the last one ticked is the Yelverton Arms in
Soho. Wait a minute, though. If they have been taking them
in alphabetical order, why have they got right down to the
end of the M's in one case and only to WH in the other?"

"They must have been through the W's once, and be
starting again."

"Yes—I suppose there are quite a lot of M's. But then
there are hundreds of W's. Still, we'll try it, Peter, any way.
What is it, Lumley?"

"Report from the hospital, sir. Puncheon has come
round."

Parker glanced through the report.

"Much what we expected," he said, handing the paper
to Wimsey. "Mountjoy evidently knew he was being followed. He put through a telephone call at Piccadilly Tube
Station, and started off on a wild scamper across London."

"That was how the gang came to be ready for him."

"Yes. Finding he couldn't shake Puncheon off, he lured
him into the Museum, got him into a quiet corner and laid
him out. Puncheon thinks he was slugged with a weapon
of some kind. So he was. He did not speak to Mountjoy.
In fact, this report tells us nothing we didn't know, except
that, when Puncheon first saw him, Mountjoy was buying
an early copy of the *Morning Star* from a man outside the
office."

"Was he? That's interesting. Well, keep your eye on the
Yelverton Arms."

"And you keep your eye on Pym's. Do remember that
what we want is the man at the top."

"So does Major Milligan. The man at the top is very
much sought after. Well, cheerio! If I can't do anything

more for you, I think I'll tootle off to bed. I've got my Whifflets scheme to get out tomorrow."

"I like this scheme, Mr. Bredon," said Mr. Pym, tapping his finger on the drafts submitted to him. "It has Breadth. It has Vision. More than anything else, Advertising needs Vision and Breadth. That is what determines Appeal. In my opinion, this scheme of yours has Appeal. It is going to be expensive, of course, and needs some working out. For instance, if all these vouchers were cashed in at once, it would send up the cost per packet issued to a figure that the profits could not possibly cover. But I think that can be got over."

"They won't all be cashed in at once," said Mr. Armstrong. "Not if we mix them up sufficiently. People will want time to collect and exchange. That will give us a start. They've got to look on the cost of the thing as so much advertising expenditure. We shall want a big press splash to start it, and after that, it will run itself quite happily in small spaces."

"That's all very well, Armstrong, but we've got to think of ourselves."

"That's all right. We make all the arrangements with the hotels and railways and so forth and charge our fee or commission on the work. All we've got to do is to average the thing out so that the claims won't amount to more than their estimated appropriation for the month. If the thing goes big they'll be willing enough to increase the appropriation. The other thing we've got to do is to see that each coupon bears more or less the same actual cash value, so as not to get into trouble with the Lottery Act. The whole thing comes down to this. How much of the profit on each shilling packet are they prepared to spend in advertising? Remembering that this scheme, if properly put through, is going to sweep every other fag off the market for the time being. Then we make our coupons up to that value minus an appropriation for the opening press campaign. At pres-

ent their appropriation is sixty thousand and their sales
. . . have we got that report on sales?"

The two directors plunged into a maze of facts and
figures. Mr. Bredon's attention wandered.

"Printing costs . . . see that they have a sufficient distribution . . . bonus to the tobacconists . . . free displays
. . . tackle the hotels first . . . news-value . . . get the
Morning Star to give it a show . . . no, I know, but there's
the Boost Britain side of it . . . I can wangle Jenks . . .
reduce overheads by . . . call it £200 a day . . . Puffin's
aeroplanes must be costing them that . . . front-page splash
and five free coupons . . . well, that's a matter of detail. . . ."

"In any case, we've got to do *something*." Mr. Armstrong
emerged from the argument with a slightly flushed face.
"It's no use telling people that the cost of the advertising
has to come out of the quality of the goods. They don't
care. All they want is something for nothing. Pay? Yes,
of course they pay in the end, but somebody's got to pay.
You can't fight free gifts with solemn assertions about
Value. Besides, if Whifflets lose their market they'll soon
lose their quality too—or what are we here for?"

"You needn't tell me that, Armstrong," said Mr. Pym.
"Whether people like it or not, the fact remains that unless
you continually increase sales you must either lose money
or cut down quality. I hope we've learnt that by this time."

"What happens," asked Mr. Bredon, "when you've increased sales to saturation point?"

"You mustn't ask those questions, Bredon," said Mr.
Armstrong, amused.

"No, but really. Suppose you push up the smoking of
every man and woman in the Empire till they must either
stop or die of nicotine poisoning?"

"We're a long way off that," replied Mr. Pym, seriously.
"And that reminds me. This scheme should carry a strong
appeal to women. 'Give your children that seaside holiday
by smoking Whifflets.' That sort of thing. We want to get
women down to serious smoking. Too many of them play

about with it. Take them off scented stuff and put them on to the straightforward Virginia cigarette—"

"The gasper, in fact."

"Whifflets," said Mr. Pym. "You can smoke a lot more of them in the day without killing yourself. And they're cheaper. If we increase women's smokes by 500 per cent —there's plenty of room for it—"

Mr. Bredon's attention wandered again.

"—all right, date the coupons. Let them run for three months only. That will give us plenty of duds to play with. And they'll have to see that their stockists are kept up to date with fresh goods. By the way, that makes a selling point—"

Mr. Bredon fell into a dream.

"—but you must have a good press campaign as well. Posters are good and cheap, but if you really want to tell people something, you've got to have a press campaign. Not a big one, necessarily, after the first big bang. But a good, short, snappy reminder week by week—"

"Very well, Mr. Bredon." The creator of the Whifflet scheme came out of his doze with a start. "We'll put this up to Whifflets. Will you see if you can get out some copy? And you'd better put a few other people on to it as well, Armstrong. Ingleby—it's rather his line. And Miss Mete-yard. We want to get something out by the end of the week. Tell Mr. Barrow to put everything else aside and rough out some really striking displays." Mr. Pym gave the signal of dismissal, and then, as a thought struck him, called Bredon back.

"I want a word with you, Bredon. I'd almost forgotten what you were really here for. Has any progress been made in that matter?"

"Yes." The Whifflets campaign receded from Lord Peter Wimsey, dying along the distance of his mind. "In fact, the investigation is turning out to be of so much im-portance that I don't quite know how I can take even you into my confidence."

"That's nonsense," said Mr. Pym. "I am employing you—"

"No. There's no question of employment. I'm afraid it's a police job."

The shadows of disquiet gathered and deepened in Mr. Pym's eyes.

"Do you mean that those earlier suspicions you mentioned to me were actually justified?"

"Oh, yes. But it's a bigger thing than that."

"I don't want any scandal."

"Possibly not. But I don't quite see how it's to be avoided, if the thing comes to trial."

"Look here, Bredon," said Mr. Pym, "I don't like your behaviour. I put you in here as my private inquiry agent. I admit that you have made yourself very useful in other capacities, but you are not indispensable. If you insist on going beyond your authority—"

"You can sack me. Of course. But would that be wise?"

Mr. Pym mopped his forehead.

"Can you tell me this," he inquired anxiously, after a silence in which he seemed to be digesting the meaning of his employee's question. "Do your suspicions point to any particular person? Is it possible to remove that person promptly from our staff? You see my point. If, before this scandal breaks—whatever it is—and I really think I ought to be told—but so long as we can say that the person is no longer on the staff, it makes a difference. The firm's name might even be kept out of it—mightn't it? The good name of Pym's means a great deal to me, Mr. Bredon—"

"I can't tell you," said Wimsey; "a few days ago, I thought I knew, but just lately, other facts have come to my knowledge which suggest that the man I originally suspected may not be the right one. And until I know definitely, I can't do or say anything. At the moment it might be anybody. It might even be yourself."

"This is outrageous," cried Mr. Pym. "You can take your money and go."

Wimsey shook his head.

"If you get rid of me, the police will probably want to put somebody in my place."

"If I had the police here," retorted Mr. Pym, "I should at least know where I was. I know nothing about you, except that Mrs. Arbuthnot recommended you. I never cared for the idea of a private detective, though I certainly thought at first that you were of a somewhat superior type to the usual inquiry agent. But insolence I cannot and will not put up with. I shall communicate at once with Scotland Yard, and they will, I imagine, require you to state plainly what you imagine yourself to have discovered."

"They know it."

"Do they? You do not seem to be a model of discretion, Mr. Bredon." He pressed his buzzer. "Miss Hartley, will you please get Scotland Yard on the 'phone, and ask them to send up a reliable detective."

"Very well, Mr. Pym."

Miss Hartley danced away. This was meat and drink. She had always said there was something funny about Mr. Bredon, and now he had been caught. Pinching the cash, perhaps. She dialled the switch-board and asked for White-hall 1212.

"Just one moment," said Wimsey, when the door had closed upon her. "If you really want Scotland Yard, tell her to ask for Chief-Inspector Parker and say that Lord Peter Wimsey would like to speak to him. Then he'll know what it's about."

"You are—? Why didn't you tell me?"

"I thought it might raise difficulties about the salary and prove embarrassing. I took the job on because I thought advertising might be rather good fun. So it is," added Wimsey, pleasantly, "so it is."

Mr. Pym put his head into Miss Hartley's room.

"I'll take that call in here," he said, briefly.

They sat mute till the call came through. Mr. Pym asked for Chief-Inspector Parker.

"There is a man here on my staff, calling himself—"

The conversation was a brief one. Mr. Pym handed the receiver to Wimsey.

"They want to speak to you."

"Hullo, Charles! That you? Have you established my credit? All right. . . . No, no trouble, only Mr. Pym feels he ought to know what it's all about. . . . Shall I tell him? . . . Not wise? . . . Honestly, Charles, I don't think he's our man. . . . Well, that's a different question. . . . The Chief-Inspector wants to know whether you can hold your tongue, Mr. Pym."

"I only wish to God everybody could hold his tongue," groaned Mr. Pym.

Wimsey passed on the reply. "I think I'll risk it, Charles. If anybody is going to be slugged in the dark after this, it won't be you, and I can look after myself."

He rang off and turned to Mr. Pym.

"Here's the brutal fact," he said. "Somebody's running an enormous dope-traffic from this office. Who is there that has far more money than he ought to have, Mr. Pym? We're looking for a very rich man. Can you help us?"

But Mr. Pym was past helping anybody. He was chalk-white.

"Dope? From this office? What on earth will our clients say? How shall I face the Board? The publicity . . ."

"Pym's Publicity," said Lord Wimsey, and laughed.

CHAPTER XVII

LACHRYMOSE OUTBURST
OF A NOBLEMAN'S NEPHEW

THAT week passed quietly. On Tuesday, Mr. Jollop
passed, quite amiably, another of the new "Quotations"
series for Nutrax "—And Kissed Again with Tears" ("But
Tears, and Fallings-Out, however poetical, are nearly always a sign of Nerve-Strain"); on Wednesday, Green Pastures Margarine was Reduced in Price though Improved in
Quality ("It might seem impossible to improve on Perfection, but we have done it!"); Sopo adopted a new advertising figure ("Let Susan Sopo do the Dirty Work");
Tomboy Toffee finished up its Cricket Campaign with a
huge display containing the portraits of a complete Eleven
of Famous Cricketers all eating Tomboy; five people went
on holiday; Mr. Prout created a sensation by coming to the
office in a black shirt; Miss Rossiter lost a handbag containing her bonus money and recovered it from the Lost
Property Office, and a flea was found in the ladies' cloakroom, causing dire upheaval, some ill-founded accusations
and much heart-burning. In the typists' room, the subject
of the flea almost ousted for the moment the juicier and
more speculative topic of Mr. Tallboy's visitor. For, whether
by the indiscretion of Tompkin or of the boy at the desk,
or of some other person (though not of Mr. Ingleby or Mr.
Bredon, who surely knew better) the tale had somehow
seeped through.

"And how he does it on his salary I don't know," observed Miss Parton. "I do think it's a shame. His wife's a

nice little woman. You remember, we met her last year at
the Garden Party."

"Men are all alike," said Miss Rossiter, scornfully. "Even
your Mr. Tallboy. I told you, Parton, that I didn't think
old Copley was so much to blame as you thought in that
other business, and now, perhaps, you'll believe me. What
I say is, if a man does one ungentlemanly thing, he'll do
another. And as for doing it on his salary, how about that
fifty pounds in an envelope? It's pretty obvious where *that*
went to."

"It's always obvious where money goes to," said Miss
Meteyard, sardonically. "The point is, where does it come
from?"

"That's what Mr. Dean used to say," said Miss Rossiter.
"You remember how he used to chip Mr. Tallboy about
his stockbrokers?"

"The famous firm of Smith," said Mr. Garrett. "Smith,
Smith, Smith, Smith, Smith & Smith Unlimited."

"Money-lenders, if you ask me," said Miss Rossiter. "Are
you going to the cricket-match, Miss Meteyard? In *my*
opinion, Mr. Tallboy ought to resign and leave somebody
else to captain it. You can't wonder that people aren't keen
to play under him, with all these stories going about. Don't
you feel the same, Mr. Bredon?"

"Not a bit of it," said Mr. Bredon. "Provided the man
can captain, I don't care a bit if he has as many wives as
Solomon, and is a forger and swindler into the bargain.
What's it matter?"

"It would matter to me," said Miss Rossiter.

"How feminine she is," said Mr. Bredon, plaintively, to
the world at large. "She *will* let the personal element come
into business."

"I dare say," said Miss Rossiter, "but you bet, if Hankie
or Pymmy knew, there'd soon be an end of Mr. Tallboy."

"Directors are the last people to hear anything about the
staff. Otherwise," said Miss Meteyard, "they wouldn't be
able to stand on their hind legs at the Staff Dinner and

shoot off the speeches about co-operation, and all being one happy family."

"Family quarrels, family quarrels." Mr. Ingleby waved his hand. "Little children, love one another and don't be such little nosey-parkers. What's Hecuba's bank-balance to you, or yours to Hecuba?"

"Bank-balance? Oh, you mean Mr. Tallboy's. Well, *I* don't know anything, except what little Dean used to say."

"And how did Dean know so much about it?"

"He was in Mr. Tallboy's office for a few weeks. Learning the work of other departments, they call it. I expect you'll be pushed round the office before long, Mr. Bredon. You'll have to mind your P's and Q's in the Printing. Mr. Thrale's a perfect tartar. Won't even allow you to slip out for coffee."

"I shall have to come to you for it."

"They won't let Mr. Bredon out of this department for a bit," said Miss Meteyard. "They're all up in the air about his Whifflets stunt. Everybody always hoped Dean would do better somewhere else. He was like a favourite book—you liked him so well that you were always yearning to lend him to somebody else."

"What a savage woman you are," observed Ingleby, coolly amused. "It's that kind of remark that gets the university woman a bad name." He glanced at Willis, who said:

"It isn't the savagery. It's the fact that there's no animosity behind it. You are all like that."

"You agree with Shaw—whenever you beat your child, be sure that you do it in anger."

"Shaw's Irish," said Bredon. "Willis has put his finger on the real offensiveness of the educated Englishman—that he will not even trouble to be angry."

"That's right," said Willis. "It's that awful, bleak, blank—" he waved his hands helplessly—"the façade."

"Meaning Bredon's face?" suggested Ingleby, mischievously.

"Icily regular, splendidly null," said Bredon, squinting into Miss Rossiter's mirror. "Strange, to think that a whole

Whifflets campaign seethes and burgeons behind this solid ivory brow."

"Mixed metaphor," said Miss Meteyard. "Pots seethe, plants burgeon."

"Of course; it is a flower of rhetoric culled from the kitchen-garden."

"It's no use, Miss Meteyard," said Ingleby, "you might as well argue with an eel."

"Talking of eels," said Miss Meteyard, abandoning the position, "what's the matter with Miss Hartley?"

"The hipless wonder? Why?"

"She came up the other day to inform the world that the police were coming to arrest somebody."

"What?" said Willis.

"You mean, whom?"

"Whom, then?"

"Bredon."

"Mr. Bredon?" said Miss Parton. "What next, I wonder."

"You mean, what for? Why don't you people say what you do mean?"

Miss Rossiter turned on her chair and gazed at Mr. Bredon's gently twitching mouth.

"That's funny," she said. "Do you know, Mr. Bredon, we never told you, but Parton and I thought we saw you actually being arrested one evening, in Piccadilly Circus."

"Did you?"

"It wasn't you, of course."

"Well, as a matter of fact, it wasn't. Still, cheer up—it may happen yet. Only I suppose Pymmy doesn't keep his millions in the office safe."

"Nor yet in registered envelopes," said Miss Meteyard, casually.

"Don't say they're after our Mr. Copley!"

"I hope not. Bread-and-skilly wouldn't suit him at all."

"But what was Bredon being arrested for?"

"Loitering, perhaps," said a mild voice in the doorway. Mr. Hankin poked his head round the corner and smiled sarcastically. "I am sorry to interrupt you, but if Mr.

Bredon could favour me with his attention for a moment
on the subject of Twentyman's Teas—"

"I beg your pardon, sir," said Mr. Bredon, springing to
attention and allowing himself to be marched off.

Miss Rossiter shook her head.

"You mark my words, there's a mystery about Mr.
Bredon."

"He's a darling," objected Miss Parton, warmly.

"Oh, Bredon's all right," said Ingleby.

Miss Meteyard said nothing. She went downstairs to the
Executive and borrowed the current volume of *Who's Who*.
She ran her finger through the W's, till she came to the
entry beginning: "WIMSEY, Peter Death Bredon (Lord),
D.S.O., born 1890; second *s.* of Mortimer Gerald Bredon
Wimsey, 15th Duke of Denver, and Honoria Lucasta, *d.*
of Francis Delagardie of Bellingham Manor, Bucks. *Educ.*
Eton College and Balliol." She read it through.

"So that's it," said Miss Meteyard to herself. "I thought
so. And now what? Does one do anything? I think not. Better leave it alone. But there's no harm in putting out feel-
ers for another job. One's got to look after one's self."

Mr. Bredon, unaware that his disguise had been penetrated, gave but a superficial consideration to the interests
of Twentyman's Teas. He meekly accepted the instruction
to prepare a window-bill with two streamers on the subject
of a richer infusion with fewer spoonfuls, and a gentle
rebuke in the matter of wasting time in the typists' room.
His mind was in Old Broad Street.

"You are playing for us on Saturday, I see," said Mr.
Hankin, at the conclusion of the interview.

"Yes, sir."

"I hope the weather will hold. You have played in first-
class cricket, I believe?"

"A long time ago."

"You will be able to show them a bit of style," said Mr.
Hankin, happily. "Style—one sees so little of it nowadays.

I am afraid you will find us a scratch lot, and for some reason, several of our best players seem unable to attend this match. A pity. But you will find Mr. Tallboy very good. An excellent all-round man, and quite remarkable in the field."

Mr. Bredon said that it was all too rare to find proper attention given to fielding. Mr. Hankin agreed with him.

"Mr. Tallboy is excellent at all games; it's a pity he can't give more time to them. Personally, I should like to see more organization of the athletic side of our social functions here. But Mr. Pym thinks it would perhaps be too absorbing, and I dare say he is right. Still, I can't help feeling that the cultivation of the team-spirit would do this office good. I don't know whether you, as a newcomer, have noticed a certain tension from time to time—"

Bredon admitted that he had noticed something of the sort.

"You know, Mr. Bredon," said Mr. Hankin, a little wistfully, "it is sometimes difficult for the directors to get the atmosphere of situations in the office. You people keep us rather in cotton-wool, don't you? It can't be helped, naturally, but I sometimes fancy that there are currents beneath the surface. . . ."

Evidently, thought Bredon, Mr. Hankin had realized that something was on the point of breaking. He felt suddenly sorry for him. His eyes strayed to a strip poster, printed in violent colours and secured by drawing-pins to Mr. Hankin's notice-board:

EVERY ONE EVERYWHERE ALWAYS AGREES
ON THE FLAVOUR AND VALUE OF TWENTYMAN'S TEAS

No doubt it was because agreement on any point was so rare in a quarrelsome world, that the fantastical announcements of advertisers asserted it so strongly and so absurdly. Actually, there was no agreement, either on trivialities like tea or on greater issues. In this place, where from morning till night a staff of over a hundred people hymned the praises of thrift, virtue, harmony, eupepsia and domestic contentment, the spiritual atmosphere was clamorous with financial storm, intrigue, dissension, indigestion and marital infidelity. And with worse things—with murder wholesale and retail, of soul and body, murder by weapon and by poison. These things did not advertise, or, if they did, they called themselves by other names.

He made some vague answer to Mr. Hankin.

At one o'clock he left the office and took a taxi citywards. He was suddenly filled with a curiosity to visit Mr. Tallboy's stockbroker.

At twenty minutes past one, he was standing on the pavement in Old Broad Street, and his blood was leaping with the excitement which always accompanies discovery.

Mr. Tallboy's stockbroker inhabited a small tobacconist's shop, the name over which was not Smith but Cummings.

"An accommodation address," observed Lord Peter Wimsey. "Most unusual for a stockbroker. Let us probe this matter further."

He entered the shop, which was narrow, confined and exceedingly dark. An elderly man stepped forward to serve him. Wimsey went immediately to the point.

"Can I see Mr. Smith?"

Mr. Smith doesn't live here."

"Then perhaps you would kindly let me leave a note for him."

The elderly man slapped his hand on the counter.

"If I've said it once, I've said it five hundred times," he snapped irritably. "There's no Mr. Smith here, and never was, to my knowledge. And if you're the gentleman that addresses his letters here, I'd be glad if you'd take that for an answer. I'm sick and tired of handing his letters back to the postman."

"You surprise me. I don't know Mr. Smith myself, but I was asked by a friend to leave a message for him."

"Then tell your friend what I say. It's no good sending

letters here. None whatever. Never has been. People seem to think I've got nothing better to do than hand out letters to postmen. If I wasn't a conscientious man, I'd burn the lot of them. That's what I'd do. Burn 'em. And I will, if it goes on any longer. You can tell your friend that from me."

"I'm very sorry," said Wimsey. "There seems to be some mistake."

"Mistake?" said Mr. Cummings, angrily. "I don't believe it's a mistake at all. It's a stupid practical joke, that's what it is. And I'm fed up with it, I can tell you."

"If it is," said Wimsey, "I'm the victim of it. I've been sent right out of my way to deliver a message to somebody who doesn't exist. I shall speak to my friend about it."

"I should, if I were you," said Mr. Cummings. "A silly, tom-fool trick. You tell your friend to come here himself, that's all. I'll know what to say to him."

"That's a good idea," said Wimsey. "And you tell him off."

"You can lay your last penny I shall, sir." Mr. Cummings, having blown off his indignation, seemed a little appeased. "If your friend should turn up, what name will he give, sir?"

Wimsey, on the point of leaving the shop, pulled up short. Mr. Cummings, he noticed, had a pair of very sharp eyes behind his glasses. A thought struck him.

"Look here," he said, leaning confidentially over the counter. "My friend's name is Milligan. That mean anything to you? He told me to come to you for a spot of the doings. See what I mean?"

That got home; a red glint in Mr. Cummings' eye told Wimsey as much.

"I don't know what you are talking about," was what Mr. Cummings actually said. "I never heard of a Mr. Milligan, and I don't want to. And I don't want any of your sauce, neither."

"Sorry, old thing, sorry," said Wimsey.

"And what's more," said Mr. Cummings, "I don't want you. See?"

"I see," said Wimsey. "I see perfectly. Good-morning."

"That's torn it," he thought. "I'll have to work quickly now. St. Martin's-le-Grand comest next, I fancy."

A little pressure at head-quarters produced what was required. The postmen who carried letters to Old Broad Street were found and interrogated. It was quite true that they frequently delivered letters for a Mr. Smith to Mr. Cummings' shop, and that these letters invariably were returned, and marked "Not known." Where did they go then? To the Returned Letter Office. Wimsey rang up Pym's, explained that he was unavoidably detained, and sought the Returned Letter Office. After a little delay, he found the official who knew all about it.

The letters for Mr. Smith came regularly every week. They were never returned to the sender in the ordinary course. Why? Because they bore no sender's name. In fact, they never contained anything but a sheet of blank paper.

"Had they last Tuesday's letter there?" No; it had already been opened and destroyed. Would they keep the next one that arrived and send it on to him? Seeing that Lord Peter Wimsey had Scotland Yard behind him, they would. Wimsey thanked the official, and went his way, pondering.

On leaving the office at 5.30, he walked down Southampton Row to Theobald's Road. There was a newsvendor at the corner. Wimsey purchased an *Evening Comet* and glanced carelessly through the news. A brief paragraph in the Stop Press caught his eye.

CLUBMAN KILLED IN PICCADILLY

At 3 o'clock this afternoon a heavy lorry skidded and mounted the pavement in Piccadilly, fatally injuring Major "Tod" Milligan, the well-known clubman, who was standing on the kerb.

"They work quickly," he thought with a shudder. "Why, in God's name, am I still at large?" He cursed his own

recklessness. He had betrayed himself to Cummings; he had
gone into the shop undisguised; by now they knew who he
was. Worse, they must have followed him to the General
Post Office and to Pym's. Probably they were following him
now. From behind the newspaper he cast a swift glance
about the crowded streets. Any one of these loitering men
might be *the* man. Absurd and romantic plans flitted
through his mind. He would lure his assassins into some se-
cluded spot, such as the Blackfriars subway or the steps
beneath Cleopatra's Needle, and face them there and kill
them with his hands. He would ring up Scotland Yard and
get a guard of detectives. He would go straight home to his
own flat in a taxi ("not the first nor the second that presents itself," he thought, with a fleeting recollection of Professor Moriarty), barricade himself in and wait—for what?
For air-guns? . . . In this perplexity he suddenly caught
sight of a familiar figure—Chief-Inspector Parker himself,
apparently taking his early way home, and carrying a fishmonger's bag in one hand and an attaché case in the other.

He lowered the paper and said, "Hullo!"

Parker stopped. "Hullo!" he replied, tentatively. He was
obviously not quite certain whether he was being hailed by
Lord Peter Wimsey or by Mr. Death Bredon. Wimsey strode
forward and relieved him of the fish-bag.

"Well met. You come most carefully upon your cue, to
prevent me from being murdered. What's this, lobster?"

"No, turbot," said Parker, placidly.

"I'm coming to eat it with you. They will hardly attack
both of us. I've made a fool of myself and given the game
away, so we may as well be open and cheerful about it."

"Good. I'd like to feel cheerful."

"What's wrong? Why so early home?"

"Fed-up. The Yelverton Arms is a wash-out, I'm afraid."

"Did you raid it?"

"Not yet. Nothing happened during the morning, but
during the lunch-hour crush, Lumley saw something being
smuggled into a fellow's hands by a chap who looked like
a tout. They stopped the fellow and searched him. All they

found was some betting-slips. It's quite possible that nothing is timed to happen before this evening. If nothing turns up, I'll have the place searched. Just before closing-time will be best. I'm going down there myself. Thought I'd step home for an early supper."

"Right. I've got something to tell you."

They walked to Great Ormond Street in silence.

"Cummings?" said Parker, when Wimsey had told his tale. "Don't know anything about him. But you say he knew Milligan's name?"

"He certainly did. Besides, here's the proof of it."

He showed Parker the stop-press item.

"But this fellow, Tallboy—is he the bird you're after?"

"Frankly, Charles, I don't understand it. I can't see him as the Big Bug in all this business. If he were, he'd be too well-off to get into difficulties with a cheap mistress. And his money wouldn't be coming to him in fifty-pound instalments. But there's a connection. There must be."

"Possibly he's only a small item in the account."

"Possibly. But I can't get over Milligan. According to his information, the whole show was run from Pym's."

"Perhaps it is. Tallboy may be merely the cat's paw for one of the others. Pym himself—he's rich enough, isn't he?"

"I don't think it's Pym. Armstrong, possibly, or even quiet little Hankie. Of course, Pym's calling me in may have been a pure blind, but I don't somehow think he has quite that kind of brain. It was so unnecessary. Unless he wanted to find out, through me, how much Victor Dean really knew. In which case, he's succeeded," added Wimsey, ruefully. "But I can't believe that any man would be such a fool as to put himself in the power of one of his own staff. Look at the opportunities for blackmail! Twelve years' penal servitude is a jolly threat to hold over a man. Still—blackmail. Somebody was being blackmailed, that's almost a certainty. But Pym can't have slugged Dean; he was in conference at the time. No, I think we must acquit Pym."

"What I don't quite see," said Lady Mary, "is why Pym's is brought into it at all. Somebody *at* Pym's is one thing, but if you say that the show is 'run from Pym's,' it suggests something quite different—to me, anyhow. It sounds to me as though they were using Pym's organization for something—doesn't it to you?"

"Well, it does," agreed her husband. "But how? And why? What has advertising got to do with it? Crime doesn't want to advertise, far from it."

"I don't know," said Wimsey, suddenly and softly. "I don't know." His nose twitched, rabbit-fashion. "Pymmy was saying only this morning that to reach the largest number of people all over the country in the shortest possible time, there was nothing like a press campaign. Wait a second, Polly—I'm not sure that you haven't said something useful and important."

"Everything I say is useful and important. Think it over while I go and tell Mrs. Gunner how to cook turbot."

"And the funny thing is," said Parker, "she seems to like telling Mrs. Gunner how to cook turbot. We could perfectly well afford more servants—"

"My dear old boy," said Wimsey. "Servants are the devil. I don't count my man Bunter, because he's exceptional, but it's a treat to Polly to kick the whole boiling out of the house at night. Don't you worry. When she wants servants, she'll ask for them."

"I admit," said Parker, "I was glad myself when the kids were old enough to dispense with a resident nurse. But look here, Peter, it seems to me you'll be wanting a resident nurse yourself, if you want to avoid nasty accidents."

"That's just it. Here I am. Why? What are they keeping me for? Something unusually nasty?"

Parker moved quietly across to the window and peered out from a little gap in the short net blind.

"He's there, I think. A repellent-looking young man in a check cap, playing with a Yo-Yo on the opposite pavement. Playing darned well, too, with a circle of admiring kids round him. What a grand excuse for loitering. There he

goes. Three-leaf clover, over the falls, non-stop lift, round
the world. Quite masterly. I must tell Mary to have a look
at him, and take a lesson. You'd better sleep here tonight,
old man."

"Thanks. I think I will."

"And stop away from the office tomorrow."

"I should, in any case. I've got to play in a cricket match
at Brotherhood's. Their place is down at Romford."

"Cricket-match be damned. I don't know, though. It's
nice and public. Provided the fast bowler doesn't knock
you out with a swift ball, it may be as safe as anywhere else.
How are you going?"

"Office charabanc."

"Good. I'll see you round to the starting-point."

Wimsey nodded. Nothing further was said about dope or
danger until supper was over and Parker had departed for
the Yelverton Arms. Then Wimsey gathered up a calendar,
the telephone directory, a copy of the official report on the
volume retrieved from Mountjoy's flat, a scribbling-block
and a pencil, and curled himself up on the couch with a
pipe.

"You don't mind, do you, Polly? I want to brood."

Lady Mary dropped a kiss on the top of his head.

"Brood on, old thing. I won't disturb you. I'm going up
to the nursery. And if the telephone rings, take care it isn't
the mysterious summons to the lonely warehouse by the
river, or the bogus call to Scotland Yard."

"All right. And if the door-bell rings, beware of the
disguised gas-inspector and the plain-clothes cop without a
warrant-card. I need scarcely warn you against the golden-
haired girl in distress, the slit-eyed Chink or the distinguished grey-haired man wearing the ribbon of some foreign order."

He brooded.

He took from his pocket-book the paper he had removed,
weeks earlier, from Victor Dean's desk, and compared the
dates with the calendar. They were all Tuesdays. After a
little further cogitation, he added the date of the previous

Tuesday week, the day when Miss Vavasour had called at the office and Tallboy had borrowed his pen to address a letter to Old Broad Street. To this date he appended the initial "T." Then, his mind working slowly backwards, he remembered that he had come to Pym's on a Tuesday, and that Tallboy had come into the typists' room for a stamp. Miss Rossiter had read out the name of his addressee—what had the initial been? "K," of course. He wrote this down also. Then, with rather more hesitation, he looked up the date of the Tuesday preceding Mr. Puncheon's historic adventure at the White Swan, and wrote "W?"

So far, so good. But from "K" to "T" there were nine letters—there had not been nine weeks. Nor should "W" have come between "K" and "T." What was the rule governing the letter-sequence? He drew thoughtfully at his pipe and sank into a reverie that was almost a pipe-dream, till he was aroused by a very distinct sound of yells and conflict from the floor above. Presently the door opened and his sister appeared, rather flushed.

"I'm sorry, Peter. Did you hear the row? Your young namesake was being naughty. He heard Uncle Peter's voice and refused to stay in bed. He wants to come down and see you."

"Very flattering," said Wimsey.

"But very exhausting," said Mary. "I do hate disciplining people. Why shouldn't he see his uncle? Why should uncle be busy with dull detective business when his nephew is so much more interesting?"

"Quite so," said Wimsey. "I have often asked myself the same question. I gather that you hardened your heart."

"I compromised. I said that if he was a good boy and went back to bed, Uncle Peter might come up to say good night to him."

"And has he been a good boy?"

"Yes. In the end. That is to say, he is in bed. At least, he was when I came down."

"Very well," said Wimsey, putting down his paraphernalia. "Then I will be a good uncle."

He mounted the stairs obediently and found Peterkin, aged three, technically in bed. That is to say, he was sitting bolt upright with the blankets cast off, roaring lustily.

"Hullo!" said Wimsey, shocked.

The roaring ceased.

"What is all this?" Wimsey traced the course of a fat, down-rolling drop with a reproachful finger. "Tears, idle tears? Great Scott!"

"Uncle Peter! I got a naeroplane." Peterkin tugged violently at the sleeve of a suddenly unresponsive uncle. "Look at my naeroplane, Uncle! Naeroplane, naeroplane!"

"I beg your pardon, old chap," said Wimsey, recollecting himself. "I wasn't thinking. It's a beautiful aeroplane. Does it fly? . . . Hi! you needn't get up and show me now. I'll take your word for it."

"Mummie make it fly."

It flew very competently, effecting a neat landing on the chest of drawers. Wimsey watched it with vague eyes.

"Uncle Peter!"

"Yes, son, it's splendid. Listen, would you like a speed-boat?"

"What's peed-boat?"

"A boat that will run in the water—chuff, chuff—like that."

"Will it float in my barf?"

"Yes, of course. It'll sail right across the Round Pond."

Peterkin considered.

"Could I have it in my barf wiv' me?"

"Certainly, if Mummie says so."

"I'd like a boat in my barf."

"You shall have one, old man."

"When, now?"

"Tomorrow."

"Weally tomowwow?"

"Yes, promise."

"Say thank-you, Uncle Peter."

"Fank-you, Uncle Peter. Will it be tomowwow soon?"

"Yes, if you lie down now and go to sleep."

Peterkin, who was a practically-minded child, shut his eyes instantly, wriggled under the bed-clothes, and was promptly tucked in by a firm hand.

"Really, Peter, you shouldn't bribe him to go to sleep. How about my discipline?"

"Discipline be blowed," said Peter, at the door.

"Uncle!"

"Good night!"

"Is it tomowwow yet?"

"Not yet. Go to sleep. You can't have tomorrow till you've been to sleep."

"Why not?"

"It's one of the rules."

"Oh! I'm asleep now, Uncle Peter."

"Good. Stick to it." Wimsey pulled his sister out after him and shut the nursery door.

"Polly, I'll never say kids are a nuisance again."

"What's up? I can see you're simply bursting with something."

"I've got it! Tears, idle Tears. That kid deserves fifty speed-boats as a reward for howling."

"Oh, dear!"

"I couldn't tell him that, though, could I? Come downstairs, and I'll show you something."

He dragged Mary at full speed into the sitting-room, took up his list of dates and jabbed at it with a jubilant pencil.

"See that date? That's the Tuesday before the Friday on which coke was being served out at the White Swan. On that Tuesday, the Nutrax headline was finally passed for the following Friday. And what," asked Wimsey, rhetorically, "was that headline?"

"I haven't the faintest idea. I never read advertisements."

"You should have been smothered at birth. The headline was, 'Why Blame the Woman?' You will note that it begins with a 'W.' White Swan also begins with a 'W.' Got that?"

"I think so. It seems fairly simple."

"Just so. Now on this date, the Nutrax headline was 'Tears, idle Tears'—a quotation from the poets."

"I follow you so far."

"This is the date on which the headline was passed for press, you understand."

"Yes."

"Also a Tuesday."

"I have grasped that."

"On that same Tuesday, Mr. Tallboy, who is Group-manager for Nutrax, wrote a letter addressed to 'T. Smith, Esq.' You get that?"

"Yes."

"Very good. That advertisement appeared on a Friday."

"Are you trying to explain that these advertisements are all passed for press on a Tuesday and all appear on a Friday?"

"Exactly."

"Then why not say so, instead of continually repeating yourself?"

"All right. But now perpend. Mr. Tallboy has a habit of sending letters on a Tuesday, addressed to a Mr. Smith —who, by the way, doesn't exist."

"I know. You told us all about that. Mr. T. Smith is Mr. Cummings; only Mr. Cummings denies it."

"He denies it, said the King. Leave out that part. The point is that Mr. Smith isn't always Mr. T. Smith. Sometimes he's other kinds of Mr. Smith. But on the day that the Nutrax headline began with a 'T,' Mr. Smith was Mr. T. Smith."

"And what sort of Mr. Smith was he on the day that the Nutrax headline began with a 'W'?"

"Unfortunately I don't know. But I can guess that he was Mr. W. Smith. In any case, on this date here, which was the day I came to Pym's, the Nutrax headline was 'Kittle Cattle.' On that day, Mr. Smith—"

"Stop! I can guess this one. He was Mr. K. Smith."

"He was. Kenneth, perhaps, or Kirkpatrick, or Killarney. Killarney Smith would be a lovely name."

"And was coke distributed the next Friday from the King's Head?"

"I'm betting my boots it was. What do you think of that?"

"I think you want a little more evidence on that point. You don't seem to have any instance where you can point to the initial, the headline and the pub. all together."

"That's the weak point," confessed Wimsey. "But look here. This Tuesday which I now write down is the date on which the great Nutrax row occurred, and the headline was altered at the last moment on Thursday night. On the Friday of that week, something went wrong with the supply of dope to Major Milligan. It never turned up."

"Peter, I do believe you've got hold of something."

"Do you, Polly? Well, so do I. But I wasn't sure if it would sound plausible to anybody but me. And, look here! I remember another day." Wimsey began to laugh. "I forget which date it was, but the headline was simply a blank line and an exclamation mark, and Tallboy was horribly peeved about it. I wonder what they did that week. I should think they took the initial of the sub-head. What a joke!"

"But how is it worked, Peter?"

"Well, I don't know the details, but I imagine it's done this way. On the Tuesday, as soon as the headline is decided, Tallboy sends an envelope to Cummings' shop addressed to A. Smith, Esq., or B. Smith, Esq., according to the initial of the headline. Cummings looks at it, snorts at it and hands it back to the postman. Then he informs the head distributing agent, or agents. I don't know how. Possibly he advertises too, because the great point of this scheme, as I see it, is to have as little contact as possible between the various agents. The stuff is run across on Thursday, and the agent meets it and packets it up as Bicarbonate of Soda, or something equally harmless. Then he gets the London Telephone Directory and looks up the next pub. on the list whose name begins with the letter of which Cummings has advised him. As soon as the pub.

opens on Friday morning, he is there. The retail agents, if we may call them so, have meanwhile consulted the *Morning Star* and the Telephone Directory. They hasten to the pub. and the packets are passed to them. The late Mr. Mountjoy must have been one of these gentry."

"How does the wholesaler recognize the retailer?"

"There must be some code or other, and our battered friend Hector Puncheon must have given the code-word by accident. We must ask about that. He's a *Morning Star* man, and it may be something to do with the *Morning Star*. Mountjoy, by the way, evidently believed in being early on the job, because he seems to have made a practice of getting his copy of the paper the second it was off the machine, which accounts for his having been in full working order at 4.30 a.m. in Covent Garden, and hanging round Fleet Street again in the small hours of the following Friday. He must have given the code-signal, whatever it was; Puncheon may remember about it. After that, he would make his supply up into smaller packets (hence his supply of cigarette-papers) and proceed with the distribution according to his own taste and fancy. Of course, there are a lot of things we don't know yet. How the payments are made, for instance. Puncheon wasn't asked for money. Tallboy seems to have got his particular share in Currency Notes. But that's a detail. The ingenuity of the thing is that the stuff is never distributed twice from the same place. No wonder Charles had difficulties with it. By the way, I've sent him to the wrong place tonight, poor devil. How he must be cursing me!"

Mr. Parker cursed solidly enough on his return.

"It's entirely my fault," said Wimsey, blithely. "I sent you to the Yelverton Arms. You ought to have been at the Anchor or the Antelope. But we'll pull it off next week— if we live so long."

"If," said Parker, seriously, "we live so long."

CHAPTER XVIII

UNEXPECTED CONCLUSION
OF A CRICKET MATCH

THE party from Pym's filled a large charabanc; in addition, a number of people attended in their own Austins. It was a two-innings match, starting at 10 a.m., and Mr. Pym liked to see it well attended. A skeleton staff was left to hold the fort at the office during the Saturday morning, and it was expected that as many of them as possible would trundle down to Romford by the afternoon train. Mr. Death Bredon, escorted by Lady Mary and Chief-Inspector Parker, was one of the last to scramble into the charabanc.

The firm of Brotherhood believed in ideal conditions for their staff. It was their pet form of practical Christianity; in addition to which, it looked very well in their advertising literature and was a formidable weapon against the trade unions. Not, of course, that Brotherhood's had the slightest objection to trade unions as such. They had merely discovered that comfortable and well-fed people are constitutionally disinclined for united action of any sort—a fact which explains the asinine meekness of the income-tax payer.

In Brotherhood's régime of bread and circuses, organized games naturally played a large part. From the pavilion overlooking the spacious cricket-field floated superbly a crimson flag, embroidered with the Brotherhood trademark of two clasped hands. The same device adorned the crimson blazers and caps of Brotherhood's cricket eleven. By contrast, the eleven advertising cricketers were but a poor advertisement for themselves. Mr. Bredon was, in-

deed, a bright spot on the landscape, for his flannels were
faultless, while his Balliol blazer, though ancient, carried
with it an air of authenticity. Mr. Ingleby also was correct,
though a trifle shabby. Mr. Hankin, beautifully laundered,
had rather spoilt his general effect by a brown felt hat,
while Mr. Tallboy, irreproachable in other respects, had an
unfortunate tendency to come apart at the waist, for which
his tailor and shirt-maker were, no doubt, jointly responsible. The dress of the remainder varied in combining
white flannels with brown shoes, white shoes with the
wrong sort of shirt, tweed coats with white linen hats, down
to the disgraceful exhibition of Mr. Miller, who, disdaining
to put himself out for a mere game, affronted the sight in
grey flannel trousers, a striped shirt and braces.

The day began badly with Mr. Tallboy's having lost his
lucky half-crown and with Mr. Copley's observing, offensively, that perhaps Mr. Tallboy would prefer to toss with
a pound-note. This flustered Mr. Tallboy. Brotherhood's
won the toss and elected to go in first. Mr. Tallboy, still
flustered, arranged his field, forgetting in his agitation Mr.
Hankin's preference for mid-on and placing him at cover-
point. By the time this error was remedied, it was discovered that Mr. Haagedorn had omitted to bring his wicket-
keeper's gloves, and a pair had to be borrowed from the
pavilion. Mr. Tallboy then realized that he had put on his
two fast bowlers together. He remedied this by recalling
Mr. Wedderburn from the deep field to bowl his slow
"spinners," and dismissing Mr. Barrow in favour of Mr.
Beeseley. This offended Mr. Barrow, who retired in
dudgeon to the remotest part of the field and appeared to
go to sleep.

"What's all the delay about?" demanded Mr. Copley.

Mr. Willis said he thought Mr. Tallboy must have got a
little confused about the bowling order.

"Lack of organization," said Mr. Copley. "He should
make out a list and stick to it."

The first Brotherhood innings passed off rather unevent-
fully. Mr. Miller missed two easy catches and Mr. Barrow,

to show his resentment at the placing of the field, let a really quite ordinary ball go to the boundary instead of running after it. The eldest Mr. Brotherhood, a spry old gentleman of seventy-five, came doddering cheerfully round from the pavilion and sat down to make himself agreeable to Mr. Armstrong. He did this by indulging in reminiscences of all the big cricket matches he had ever seen in a long life, and as he had been devoted to the game since his boyhood, and had never missed a game of any importance, this took him some time and was excessively wearisome to Mr. Armstrong, who thought cricket a bore and only attended the staff match out of compliment to Mr. Pym's prejudices. Mr. Pym, whose enthusiasm was only equalled by his ignorance of the game, applauded bad strokes and good strokes indifferently.

Eventually the Brotherhoods were dismissed for 155, and the Pym Eleven gathered themselves together from the four corners of the field; Messrs. Garrett and Barrow, both rather ill-tempered, to buckle on their pads, and the remainder of the team to mingle with the spectators. Mr. Bredon, languid in movement but cheerful, laid himself down at Miss Meteyard's feet, while Mr. Tallboy was collared by the aged Mr. Brotherhood, thus releasing Mr. Armstrong, who promptly accepted the invitation of a younger Brotherhood to inspect a new piece of machinery.

The innings opened briskly. Mr. Barrow, who was rather a showy bat, though temperamental, took the bowling at the factory end of the pitch and cheered the spirits of his side by producing a couple of twos in the first over. Mr. Garrett, canny and cautious, stonewalled perseveringly through five balls of the following over and then cut the leather through the slips for a useful three. A single off the next ball brought the bowling back to Mr. Barrow, who, having started favourably, exhibited a happy superiority complex and settled down to make runs. Mr. Tallboy breathed a sigh of relief. Mr. Barrow, confident and successful, could always be relied upon for some good work; Mr. Barrow, put off his stroke by a narrowly missed catch,

or the sun in his eyes, or a figure crossing the screens, was apt to become defeatist and unreliable. The score mounted blithely to thirty. At this point, Brotherhood's captain, seeing that the batsmen had taken the measure of the bowling, took off the man at the factory end and substituted a short, pugnacious-looking person with a scowl, at sight of whom Mr. Tallboy quaked again.

"They're putting on Simmonds very early," he said. "I only hope nobody gets hurt."

"Is this their demon bowler?" inquired Bredon, seeing the wicket-keeper hurriedly retire to a respectful distance from the wicket.

Tallboy nodded. The ferocious Simmonds wetted his fingers greedily, pulled his cap fiercely over his eyes, set his teeth in a snarl of hatred, charged like a bull and released the ball with the velocity of a 9-inch shell in Mr. Barrow's direction.

Like most fast bowlers, Simmonds was a little erratic in the matter of length. His first missile pitched short, rocketed up like a pheasant, whizzed past Mr. Barrow's ear and was adroitly fielded by long-stop, a man with a phlegmatic countenance and hands of leather. The next two went wide. The fourth was pitched straight and with a good length. Mr. Barrow tackled it courageously. The impact affected him like an electric shock; he blinked and shook his fingers, as though not quite sure whether his bones were still intact. The fifth was more manageable; he smote it good and hard and ran.

"Again!" yelled Mr. Garrett, already half-way down the pitch for the second time. Mr. Barrow accordingly ran and once again stood ready for the onslaught. It came; it ran up his bat like a squirrel, caught him viciously on the knuckle and glanced off sharply, offering a chance to point, who, very fortunately, fumbled it. The field crossed over, and Mr. Barrow was able to stand aside and nurse his injuries.

Mr. Garrett, pursuing a policy of dogged-does-it, proceeded systematically to wear down the bowling by blocking the first four balls of the next over. The fifth produced two runs; the sixth, which was of much the same calibre, he contented himself with blocking again.

"I don't like this slow-motion cricket," complained the aged Mr. Brotherhood. "When I was a young man—"

Mr. Tallboy shook his head. He knew very well that Mr. Garrett suffered from a certain timidity when facing fast bowling. He knew, too, that Garrett had some justification, because he wore spectacles. But he knew equally well what Mr. Barrow would think about it.

Mr. Barrow, irritated, faced the redoubtable Simmonds with a sense of injury. The first ball was harmless and useless; the second was a stinger, but the third he could hit and did. He whacked it away lustily to the boundary for four, amid loud cheers. The next kept out of the wicket only by the grace of God, but the sixth he contrived to hook round to leg for a single. After which, he adopted Mr. Garrett's tactics, stonewalled through an entire over, and left Mr. Garrett to face the demon.

Mr. Garrett did his best. But the first ball rose perpendicularly under his chin and unnerved him. The second came to earth about half-way down the pitch and bumped perilously over his head. The third, pitched rather longer, seemed to shriek as it rushed for him. He stepped out, lost heart, flinched and was bowled as clean as a whistle.

"Dear, dear!" said Mr. Hankin. "It seems that it is up to me." He adjusted his pads and blinked a little. Mr. Garrett retired gloomily to the pavilion. Mr. Hankin, with exasperating slowness, minced his way to the crease. He had his own methods of dealing with demon bowlers and was not alarmed. He patted the turf lengthily, asked three times for middle and off, adjusted his hat, requested that a screen might be shifted, asked for middle and off again and faced Mr. Simmonds with an agreeable smile and a very straight bat, left elbow well forward and his feet correctly placed. The result was that Simmonds, made nervous, bowled an atrocious wide, which went to the boundary, and followed it up by two mild balls of poor length, which Mr. Hankin very properly punished. This behaviour cheered Mr. Barrow and steadied him. He hit out with confidence, and the score mounted to fifty. The applause had scarcely subsided when Mr. Hankin, stepping briskly across the wicket to a slow and inoffensive-looking ball pitched rather wide to the off, found it unaccountably twist from under his bat and strike him on the left thigh. The wicket-keeper flung up his hands in appeal.

"Out!" said the umpire.

Mr. Hankin withered him with a look and stalked very slowly and stiffly from the field, to be greeted by a chorus of: "Bad luck, indeed, sir!"

"It *was* bad luck," replied Mr. Hankin. "I am surprised at Mr. Grimbold." (Mr. Grimbold was the umpire, an elderly and impassive man from Pym's Outdoor Publicity Department.) "The ball was an atrocious wide. It could never have come anywhere near the wicket."

"It had a bit of a break on it," suggested Mr. Tallboy.

"It certainly had a break on it," admitted Mr. Hankin, "but it would have gone wide nevertheless. I don't think anybody can accuse me of being unsporting, and if I *had* been leg before, I should be the first to admit it. Did you see it, Mr. Brotherhood?"

"Oh, I saw it all right," said the old gentleman, with a chuckle.

"I put it to you," said Mr. Hankin, "whether I was l.b.w. or not."

"Of course not," said Mr. Brotherhood. "Nobody ever is. I have attended cricket matches now for sixty years, for sixty years, my dear sir, and that goes back to a time before you were born or thought of, and I've never yet known anybody to be really out l.b.w.—according to himself, that is." He chuckled again. "I remember in 1892 . . ."

"Well, sir," said Mr. Hankin, "I must defer to your experienced judgment. I think I will have a pipe." He wandered away and sat down by Mr. Pym.

"Poor old Brotherhood," he said, "is getting very old and doddery. Very doddery indeed. I doubt if we shall see him here another year. That was a very unfortunate decision of Grimbold's. Of course it is easy to be deceived in these matters, but you could see for yourself that I was no more l.b.w. than he was himself. Very vexing, when I had just settled down nicely."

"Shocking luck," agreed Mr. Pym, cheerfully. "There's Ingleby going in. I always like to watch him. He puts up a very good show, doesn't he, as a rule?"

"No style," said Mr. Hankin, morosely.

"Hasn't he?" said Mr. Pym, placidly. "You know best about that, Hankin. But he always hits out. I like to see a batsman hitting out, you know. There! Good shot! Good shot! Oh, dear!"

For Mr. Ingleby, hitting out a little too vigorously, was caught at cover-point and came galloping out rather faster than he had gone in.

"Quack, quack," said Mr. Bredon.

Mr. Ingleby threw his bat at Mr. Bredon, and Mr. Tallboy, hurriedly muttering, "Bad luck!" went to take his place.

"What a nuisance," said Miss Rossiter, soothingly. "I think it was very brave of you to hit it at all. It was a frightfully fast one."

"Um!" said Mr. Ingleby.

The dismissal of Mr. Ingleby had been the redoubtable Simmonds' swan-song. Having exhausted himself by his own ferocity, he lost his pace and became more erratic than usual, and was taken off, after an expensive over, in favour of a gentleman who bowled leg-breaks. To him, Mr. Barrow fell a victim, and retired covered with glory, with a score of twenty-seven. His place was taken by Mr. Pinchley, who departed, waving a jubilant hand and declaring his intention of whacking hell out of them.

Mr. Pinchley indulged in no antics of crease-patting or taking middle. He strode vigorously to his post, raised his bat shoulder-high and stood four-square to whatever it might please Heaven to send him. Four times did he loft the ball sky-high to the boundary. Then he fell into the hands of the Philistine with the leg-break and lofted the ball into the greedy hands of the wicket-keeper.

"Short and sweet," said Mr. Pinchley, returning with his ruddy face all grins.

"Four fours are very useful," said Mr. Bredon, kindly.

"Well, that's what I say," said Mr. Pinchley. "Make 'em quick and keep things going, that's my idea of cricket. I can't stand all this pottering and poking about."

This observation was directed at Mr. Miller, whose cricket was of the painstaking sort. A tedious period followed, during which the score slowly mounted to 83, when Mr. Tallboy, stepping back a little inconsiderately to a full-pitch, slipped on the dry turf and sat down on his wicket.

Within the next five minutes Mr. Miller, lumbering heavily down the pitch in gallant response to an impossible call by Mr. Beeseley, was run out, after compiling a laborious 12. Mr. Bredon, pacing serenely to the wicket, took counsel with himself. He reminded himself that he was still, in the eyes of Pym's and Brotherhood's at any rate, Mr. Death Bredon of Pym's. A quiet and unobtrusive mediocrity, he decided, must be his aim. Nothing that could recall the Peter Wimsey of twenty years back, making two centuries in successive innings for Oxford. No fancy cuts. Nothing remarkable. On the other hand, he had claimed to be a cricketer. He must not make a public exhibition of incompetence. He decided to make twenty runs, not more and, if possible, not less.

He might have made his mind easy; the opportunity was not vouchsafed him. Before he had collected more than two threes and a couple of demure singles, Mr. Beeseley had paid the penalty of rashness and been caught at mid-on. Mr. Haagedorn, with no pretensions to being a batsman, survived one over and was then spread-eagled without remorse or question. Mr. Wedderburn, essaying to cut a twisty one which he would have done well to leave alone, tipped the ball into wicket-keeper's gloves and Pym's were disposed of for 99, Mr. Bredon having the satisfaction of carrying out his bat for 14.

"Well played all," said Mr. Pym. "One or two people had bad luck, but of course, that's all in the game. We must try and do better after lunch."

"There's one thing," observed Mr. Armstrong, confidently to Mr. Miller, "they always do one very well. Best part of the day, to my thinking."

Mr. Ingleby made much the same remark to Mr. Bredon. "By the way," he added, "Tallboy's looking pretty rotten."

"Yes, and he's got a flask with him," put in Mr. Garrett, who sat beside them.

"He's all right," said Ingleby. "I will say for Tallboy, he can carry his load. He's much better off with a flask than with this foul Sparkling Pomayne. All wind. For God's sake, you fellows, leave it alone."

"Something's making Tallboy bad-tempered, though," said Garrett. "I don't understand him; he seems to have gone all to pieces lately, ever since that imbecile row with Copley."

Mr. Bredon said nothing to all this. His mind was not easy. He felt as though thunder was piling up somewhere and was not quite sure whether he was fated to feel or to ride the storm. He turned to Simmonds the demon bowler, who was seated on his left, and plunged into cricket talk.

"What's the matter with our Miss Meteyard today?" inquired Mrs. Johnson, archly, across the visitors' table. "You're very silent."

"I've got a headache. It's very hot. I think it's going to thunder."

"Surely not," said Miss Parton. "It's a beautiful clear day."

"*I* believe," asserted Mrs. Johnson, following Miss Meteyard's gloomy gaze, "*I* believe she's more interested in the *other* table. Now, Miss Meteyard, confess, who is it? Mr. Ingleby? I hope it's not my favourite Mr. Bredon. I simply *can't* have anybody coming between us, you know."

The joke about Mr. Bredon's reputed passion for Mrs. Johnson had become a little stale, and Miss Meteyard received it coldly.

"She's offended," declared Mrs. Johnson. "I believe it *is* Mr. Bredon. She's blushing! When are we to offer our congratulations, Miss Meteyard?"

"Do you," demanded Miss Meteyard, in a suddenly harsh and resonant voice, "recollect the old lady's advice to the bright young man?"

"Why, I can't say that I do. What was it?"

"Some people can be funny without being vulgar, and some can be both funny and vulgar. I should recommend you to be either the one or the other."

"Oh, really?" said Mrs. Johnson, vaguely. After a moment's reflection she gathered the sense of the ancient gibe and said, "Oh, really!" again, with a heightened colour. "Dear me, how rude we can be when we try. I do hate a person who can't take a joke."

Brotherhood's second innings brought some balm to the feelings of the Pymmites. Whether it was the Sparkling Pomayne, or whether it was the heat ("I do believe you were right about the thunder," remarked Miss Parton), more than one of their batsmen found his eye a little out and his energy less than it had been. Only one man ever looked really dangerous, and this was a tall, dour-faced person with whipcord wrists and a Yorkshire accent, whom no bowling seemed to daunt, and who had a nasty knack of driving extremely hard through gaps in the field. This infuriating man settled down grimly and knocked up a score of fifty-eight, amid the frenzied applause of his side. It was not only his actual score that was formidable, but the extreme exhaustion induced in the field.

"I've had—too much—gas," panted Ingleby, returning past Garrett after a mad gallop to the boundary, "and this blighter looks like staying till Christmas."

"Look here, Tallboy," said Mr. Bredon, as they crossed at the next over. "Keep your eye on the little fat fellow at the other end. He's getting pumped. If this Yorkshire tyke works him like this, something will happen."

It did happen in the next over. The slogger smote a vigorous ball from the factory end, a little too high for a safe boundary, but an almost certain three. He galloped and the fat man galloped. The ball was racing over the grass, and Tallboy racing to intercept it, as they galloped back.

"Come on!" cried the Yorkshireman, already half way down the pitch for the third time. But Fatty was winded; a glance behind showed him Tallboy stooping to the ball. He gasped "No!" and abode, like Dan, in his breeches. The other saw what was happening and turned in his tracks. Tallboy, disregarding the frantic signals of Haagedorn and Garrett, became inspired. He threw from where he stood, not to Garrett, but point-blank at the open wicket. The ball sang through the air and spread-eagled the Yorkshireman's stumps while he was still a yard from the crease, while the batsman, making a frantic attempt to cover himself, flung his bat from his hand and fell prostrate.

"Oh, pretty!" exulted old Mr. Brotherhood. "Oh, well played, sir, well played!"

"He must have taken marvellous aim," said Miss Parton.

"What's the matter with you, Bredon?" asked Ingleby, as the team lolled thankfully on the pitch to await the next man in. "You're looking very white. Touch of the sun?"

"Too much light in my eyes," said Mr. Bredon.

"Well, take it easy," advised Mr. Ingleby. "We shan't have much trouble with them now. Tallboy's a hero. Good luck to him."

Mr. Bredon experienced a slight qualm of nausea.

The remainder of the Brotherhood combination achieved nothing very remarkable, and the side was eventually got out for 114. At 4 o'clock, on a fiery wicket, Mr. Tallboy again sent out his batsmen, faced with the formidable task of making 171 to win.

At 5.30, the thing still looked almost feasible, four wickets having fallen for 79. Then Mr. Tallboy, endeavouring to squeeze a run where there was no run to be got, was run out for 7, and immediately afterwards, the brawny Mr. Pinchley, disregarding his captain's frantic appeals for care, chopped his first ball neatly into the hands of point. The rot had set in. Mr. Miller, having conscientiously blocked through two overs, while Mr. Beeseley added a hard-won 6 to the score, lost his off stump to the gentleman with the leg-break. With the score at 92 by the addition of a couple of byes, and three men to bat, including the well-meaning but inadequate Mr. Haagedorn, defeat appeared to be unavoidable.

"Well," said Mr. Copley, morosely, "it's better than last year. They beat us then by about seven wickets. Am I right, Mr. Tallboy?"

"No," said Mr. Tallboy.

"I beg your pardon, I'm sure," said Mr. Copley, "perhaps it was the year before. You should know, for I believe you were the captain on both occasions."

Mr. Tallboy vouchsafed no statistics, merely saying to Mr. Bredon:

"They draw stumps at 6.30; try and stick it out till then if you can."

Mr. Bredon nodded. The advice suited him excellently. A nice, quiet, defensive game was exactly the game least characteristic of Peter Wimsey. He sauntered tediously to the crease, expended some valuable moments in arranging himself, and faced the bowling with an expression of bland expectation.

All would probably have gone according to calculation, but for the circumstance that the bowler at the garden end of the field was a man with an idiosyncrasy. He started his run from a point in the dim, blue distance, accelerated furiously to within a yard of the wicket, stopped, hopped, and with an action suggestive of a Catherine-wheel, delivered a medium-length, medium-paced, sound straight ball of uninspired but irreproachable accuracy. In executing this manœuvre for the twenty-second time, his foot slipped round about the stop-and-hop period, he staggered, performed a sort of splits and rose, limping and massaging his leg. As a result, he was taken off, and in his place Simmonds, the fast bowler, was put on.

The pitch was by this time not only fast, but bumpy. Mr. Simmonds' third delivery rose wickedly from a patch of bare earth and smote Mr. Bredon violently upon the elbow.

Nothing makes a man see red like a sharp rap over the funny-bone, and it was at this moment that Mr. Death Bredon suddenly and regrettably forgot himself. He forgot his caution and his rôle, and Mr. Miller's braces, and saw only the green turf and the Oval on a sunny day and the squat majesty of the gas-works. The next ball was another of Simmonds' murderous short-pitched bumpers, and Lord Peter Wimsey, opening up wrathful shoulders, strode out of his crease like the spirit of vengeance and whacked it to the wide. The next he clouted to leg for three, nearly braining square-leg and so flummoxing deep-field that he flung it back wildly to the wrong end, giving the Pymmites a fourth for an overthrow. Mr. Simmonds' last ball he treated with the contempt it deserved, snicking it as it whizzed past half a yard wide to leg and running a single.

He was now faced by the merchant with the off-break. The first two balls he treated carefully, then drove the third over the boundary for six. The fourth rose awkwardly and he killed it dead, but the fifth and sixth followed number three. A shout went up, headed by a shrill shriek of admiration from Miss Parton. Lord Peter grinned amiably and settled down to hit the bowling all round the wicket.

As Mr. Haagedorn panted in full career down the pitch, his lips moved in prayer. "Oh, Lord, oh, Lord! don't let me make a fool of myself!" A four was signalled and the field crossed over. He planted his bat grimly, determined to defend his wicket if he died for it. The ball came, pitched, rose, and he hammered it down remorselessly. One. If only he could stick out the other five. He dealt with another the same way. A measure of confidence came to him. He pulled the third ball round to leg and, to his own surprise, found himself running. As the batsmen passed in mid-career, he heard his colleague call: "Good man! Leave 'em to me now."

Mr. Haagedorn asked nothing better. He would run till he burst, or stand still till he hardened into marble, if only he could keep this miracle from coming to an end. He was a poor bat, but a cricketer. Wimsey ended the over with a well-placed three, which left him still in possession of the bowling. He walked down the pitch and Haagedorn came to meet him.

"I'll take everything I can," said Wimsey, "but if anything comes to you, block it. Don't bother about runs. I'll see to them."

"Yes, sir," said Mr. Haagedorn, fervently. "I'll do anything you say. Keep it up, sir, only keep it up."

"All right," said Wimsey. "We'll beat the b——s yet. Don't be afraid of them. You're doing exactly right."

Six balls later, Mr. Simmonds, having been hit to the boundary four times running, was removed, as being too expensive a luxury. He was replaced by a gentleman who was known at Brotherhood's as "Spinner." Wimsey received him with enthusiasm, cutting him consistently and successfully to the off, till Brotherhood's captain moved up his fieldsmen and concentrated them about the off-side of the wicket. Wimsey looked at this grouping with an indulgent smile, and placed the next six balls consistently and successfully to leg. When, in despair, they drew a close net of fielders all round him, he drove everything that was drivable straight down the pitch. The score mounted to 150.

The aged Mr. Brotherhood was bouncing in his seat. He was in an ecstasy. "Oh, pretty, sir! Again! Oh, well played, indeed, sir!" His white whiskers fluttered like flags. "Why on earth, Mr. Tallboy," he asked, severely, "did you send this man in ninth? He's a cricketer. He's the only cricketer among the whole damned lot of you. Oh, well placed!" as the ball skimmed neatly between two agitated fielders who nearly knocked their heads together in the effort to retrieve it. "Look at that! I'm always telling these lads that placing is nine-tenths of the game. This man knows it. Who is he?"

"He's a new member of the staff," said Tallboy, "he's a public-school man and he said he'd done a good deal of country-house cricket, but I hadn't an idea he could play like that. Great Scott!" He paused to applaud a particularly elegant cut, "I never saw anything like it."

"Didn't you?" said the old gentleman with asperity. "Well, now, I've been watching cricket, man and boy, for sixty years, and I've seen something very like it. Let me see, now. Before the War, that would be. Dear, dear—I sometimes think my memory for names isn't what it was, but I fancy that in the 'varsity match of 1910, or it might be 1911—no, not 1910, that was the year in which—"

His tinkling voice was drowned in a yell as the 170 appeared on the score-board.

"One more to win!" gasped Miss Rossiter. "Oh!" For at that moment, Mr. Haagedorn, left for an unfortunate moment to face the bowling, succumbed to a really nasty and almost unplayable ball which curled round his feet like a playful kitten and skittled his leg-stump.

Mr. Haagedorn came back almost in tears, and Mr. Wedderburn, quivering with nervousness, strode forward into the breach. He had nothing to do but to survive four balls and then, except for a miracle, the game was won. The first ball rose temptingly, a little short; he stepped out, missed it, and scuttled back to his crease only just in time. "Oh, be careful! Be careful!" moaned Miss Rossiter, and old Mr. Brotherhood swore. The next ball, Mr. Wedderburn contrived to poke a little way down the pitch. He wiped his forehead. The next was a spinner and, in trying to block it, he tipped it almost perpendicularly into the air. For a moment that seemed like hours the spectators saw the spinning ball—the outstretched hand—then the ball dropped, missed by a hair.

"I'm going to scream," announced Mrs. Johnson to nobody in particular. Mr. Wedderburn, now thoroughly unnerved, wiped his forehead again. Fortunately, the bowler was also unnerved. The ball slipped in his sweating fingers and went down short and rather wide.

"Leave it alone! Leave it alone!" shrieked Mr. Brotherhood, hammering with his stick. "Leave it alone, you numbskull! You imbecile! You—"

Mr. Wedderburn, who had lost his head completely, stepped across to it, raised his bat, made a wild swipe, which missed its object altogether, heard the smack of the leather as the ball went into the wicket-keeper's gloves, and did the only possible thing. He hurled himself bodily back and sat down on the crease, and as he fell he heard the snick of the flying bails.

"How's that?"

"Not out."

"The nincompoop! The fat-headed, thick-witted booby!" yelled Mr. Brotherhood. He danced with fury, "Might have thrown the match away! Thrown it away! That man's a fool. I say he's a fool. He's a fool, I tell you."

"Well, it's all right, Mr. Brotherhood," said Mr. Hankin, soothingly. "At least, it's all wrong for your side, I'm afraid."

"Our side be damned," ejaculated Mr. Brotherhood. "I'm here to see cricket played, not tiddlywinks. I don't care who wins or who loses, sir, provided they play the game. Now, then!"

With five minutes to go, Wimsey watched the first ball of the over come skimming down towards him. It was a beauty. It was jam. He smote it as Saul smote the Philistines. It soared away in a splendid parabola, struck the pavilion roof with a noise like the crack of doom, rattled down the galvanized iron roofing, bounced into the enclosure where the scorers were sitting and broke a bottle of lemonade. The match was won.

Mr. Bredon, lolloping back to the pavilion at 6.30 with 83 runs to his credit, found himself caught and cornered by the ancient Mr. Brotherhood.

"Beautifully played, sir, beautifully played indeed," said the old gentleman. "Pardon me—the name has just come to my recollection. Aren't you Wimsey of Balliol?"

Wimsey saw Tallboy, who was just ahead of them, falter in his stride and look round, with a face like death. He shook his head.

"My name's Bredon," he said.

"Bredon?" Mr. Brotherhood was plainly puzzled. "Bredon? I don't remember ever hearing the name. But didn't I see you play for Oxford in 1911? You have a late cut which is exceedingly characteristic, and I could have taken my oath that the last time I saw you play it was at Lords in 1911, when you made 112. But I thought the name was Wimsey—Peter Wimsey of Balliol—Lord Peter Wimsey —and, now I come to think of it—"

At this very awkward moment an interruption occurred. Two men in police uniform were seen coming across the field, led by another man in mufti. They pushed their way through the crowd of cricketers and guests, and advanced upon the little group by the pavilion fence. One of the uniformed men touched Lord Peter on the arm.

"Are you Mr. Death Bredon?"

"I am," said Wimsey, in some astonishment.

"Then you'll have to come along of us. You're wanted on a charge of murder, and it is my duty to warn you that anything you say may be taken down and used in evidence."

"Murder?" ejaculated Wimsey. The policeman had spoken in unnecessarily loud and penetrating tones, and the whole crowd had frozen into fascinated attention. "Whose murder?"

"The murder of Miss Dian de Momerie."

"Good God!" said Wimsey. He looked round and saw that the man in mufti was Chief-Inspector Parker, who gave a nod of confirmation.

"All right," said Wimsey. "I'll come with you, but I don't know a thing about it. You'd better come with me while I change."

He walked away between the two officers. Mr. Brother-hood detained Parker as he was about to follow them.

"You say that man's called Bredon?"

"Yes, sir," replied Parker, with emphasis. "Bredon is his name. Mister Death Bredon."

"And you want him for murder?"

"For murder of a young woman, sir. Very brutal business."

"Well," said the old gentleman, "you surprise me. Are you sure you've got the right man?"

"Dead sure, sir. Well known to the police."

Mr. Brotherhood shook his head.

"Well," he said again, "his name may be Bredon. But he's innocent. Innocent as day, my good fellow. Did you see him play? He's a damned fine cricketer and he'd no more commit a murder than I would."

"That's as may be, sir," said Inspector Parker, stolidly.

"Just fancy that!" exclaimed Miss Rossiter. "I always *knew* there was *something*. Murder! Only think! We might all have had our throats cut! What do you think, Miss Meteyard? Were you surprised?"

"Yes, I was," said Miss Meteyard. "I was never so surprised in my life. Never!"

CHAPTER XIX

DUPLICATE APPEARANCES
OF A NOTORIOUS PERSONALITY

IT'S a fact, old man," said Parker, as the police-car sped Londonwards. "Dian de Momerie was found this morning with her throat cut in a wood near Maidenhead. Beside the body was a penny whistle and a few yards away there was a black mask caught on a bramble bush, as if some one had flung it away in a hurry. Inquiry among her friends elicited the fact that she had been going about at night with a masked harlequin, one Bredon by name. Strong suspicion was accordingly directed against the said Mr. Bredon, and Scotland Yard, acting with commendable promptitude, tracked the gentleman down to Romford and secured his person. Accused, when charged, replied—"

"I done it," said Wimsey, concluding the sentence for him. "And so, in a sense, I have, Charles. If that girl had never seen me, she'd be alive today."

"Well, she's no great loss," said the Chief-Inspector, callously. "I'm beginning to see their game. They've not yet tumbled to the fact that you're not Death Bredon, and their idea is to put you on ice quietly till they've had time to settle up their affairs. They know you can't get bail on a murder charge."

"I see. Well, they're not quite as smart as I took them to be, or they'd have identified me long since. What happens next?"

"My idea is, that we take immediate steps to establish that Mr. Death Bredon and Lord Peter Wimsey are not one person but two. Is that chap still following us, Lumley?"

"Yes, sir."

"Take care he doesn't lose us in the traffic through Stratford. We're taking you to be questioned at Scotland Yard, and this josser shall see you safely into the building. I've arranged for some pressmen to be there, and we'll prime them with full details of the arrest and a lot about your hideous past. You, as Mr. Bredon, will then telephone to yourself, as Lord Peter Wimsey, to come and see you, with a view to arranging your defence. You will be smuggled out by the back entrance—"

"Disguised as a policeman? Oh, Charles, do let me be a policeman! I should adore it."

"Well, you're a bit under the regulation height, but we might be able to manage it; the helmet is very disguising. Anyway, you go home, or else to your club—"

"Not my club; I couldn't go to the Marlborough dressed up as a cop. Stop a bit, though—the Egotists'—I could go there. I've got a room there, and the Egotists don't care what one does. I like this. Go on."

"All right. You change there, and come down to the Yard in a temper, grumbling loudly about the trouble Mr. Bredon puts you to. You can give an interview about it if you like. Then you go home. The Sunday papers have a long bit about you, with photographs of you both."

"Splendid!"

"And on Monday you go before the magistrate and reserve your defence. It's a pity you can't be in court to hear yourself, but I'm afraid that's rather beyond our powers. Still, you can be seen immediately afterwards doing something conspicuous. You might ride in the Row and fall off—"

"No," said Wimsey. "I absolutely refuse to fall off. There are limits. I don't mind being run away with, and only saving myself by consummate horsemanship."

"Very well; I'll leave that to you. The point is that you must be in the papers."

"I will. I will advertise myself in some way. Advertising is my long suit. By the way, though, that'll mean I can't be at the office on Monday."

"Naturally."

"But that won't do. I've got to get that Whifflets campaign finished. Armstrong wants it particularly; I can't let him down. And besides, I've got interested in the thing."

Parker gazed at him in astonishment.

"Is it possible, Peter, that you are developing a kind of business morality?"

"Dash it all, Charles! You don't understand. It's a really big scheme. It'll be the biggest advertising stunt since the Mustard Club. But if that doesn't stir you, here's another thing. If I'm not at the office, you won't know the Nutrax headline next Tuesday, and won't catch the supplies being delivered."

"We can find that out without you, old man. It won't help us in the least to have you murdered, will it?"

"I suppose not. What I can't understand is, why they haven't murdered Tallboy yet."

"No; I can't understand that, either."

"I'll tell you what I think. They haven't matured their new plans yet. They're leaving him till after next Tuesday, because they've got to deliver one more consignment by the old route. They think that if I'm out of the way they can take the risk."

"Perhaps that's it. We must hope so, any way. Well, here we are. Out you come, and try and look as much like a baffled villain as possible."

"Right-ho!" said Wimsey, distorting his face into a disagreeable sneer. The car turned into the entrance to New Scotland Yard and drew up. The sergeant got out; Wimsey followed, and, glancing round, observed three obvious newspaper men hanging about the courtyard. Just as Parker emerged in his turn from the car, Wimsey tapped the sergeant lightly but efficiently under the chin and sent him staggering, tripped Parker neatly as he jumped from the running-board, and made for the gate like a hare. Two policemen and a reporter dived to intercept him; he dodged the bobbies, tackled the pressman and left him sprawling, swerved through the gateway and led a beautiful ding-dong chase down Whitehall. As he sped, he heard shouts and the blowing of whistles. Foot-passengers joined in the pursuit; motorists accelerated to cut him off; people in buses crowded to the windows and stared. He slipped nimbly into the whirl of traffic, dodged three times round the Cenotaph, doubled back on the opposite side of the street and finally staged a magnificent and sensational capture in the middle of Trafalgar Square. Parker and Lumley came up panting.

" 'Ere 'e is, mister," said the man who had grabbed hold of him—a large and powerful navvy, with a bag of tools. " 'Ere 'e is. Wot's 'e done?"

"He's wanted for murder," announced Parker, briefly and loudly.

A murmur of admiration arose. Wimsey cast an offensively contemptuous glance at Sergeant Lumley.

"You ruddy bobbies are all too fat," he said. "You can't run."

"That's all right," said the sergeant, grimly. "Hold out your hands, my lad. We're taking no more chances."

"As you please, as you please. Are your hands clean? I don't want my cuffs dirtied."

"That's quite enough of it, my lad," said Parker, as the handcuffs snapped home, "we don't want any more trouble from you. Pass along there, please, pass along."

The little procession returned to Scotland Yard.

"Rather prettily done, I flatter myself," said Wimsey.

"Ar!" said Lumley, caressing his jaw. "You didn't need to have hit quite so hard, my lord."

"Verisimilitude," said Wimsey, "verisimilitude. You looked lovely as you went over."

"Ar!" said Sergeant Lumley.

A quarter of an hour later, a policeman whose uniform trousers were a little long for him and whose tunic was slightly too large in the waist, came out from Scotland Yard by a side-entrance, entered a car and was driven along Pall Mall to the discreet entrance of the Egotists' Club. Here he disappeared, and was never seen again, but presently an immaculately dressed gentleman, in evening dress and a silk hat, tripped out and stood on the steps to await a taxi. An elderly gentleman of military appearance stood beside him.

"You will forgive me, Colonel? I shall not be many minutes. This fellow Bredon is an abominable nuisance, but what can one do? I mean to say, one has to do something."

"Quite, quite," said the Colonel.

"I only hope this is the last time. If he's done what they say he has, it *will* be the last."

"Oh, quite," said the Colonel, "my dear Wimsey, quite."

The taxi appeared.

"Scotland Yard," said Wimsey, in very audible tones.

The taxi span away.

Miss Meteyard, skimming the papers in bed on Sunday morning, found her attention held by enormous headlines:

DE MOMERIE MURDER CASE ARREST

FAMOUS DUCAL HOUSE INVOLVED

INTERVIEW WITH LORD PETER WIMSEY

and again:

PENNY WHISTLE MURDER

ARREST OF MASKED MUMMER

CHIEF-INSPECTOR PARKER INTERVIEWED

and once more:

WHISTLING HARLEQUIN CAUGHT

DESPERATE MELEE IN WHITEHALL

PEER'S BROTHER VISITS SCOTLAND YARD

There followed lengthy and picturesque descriptions of the arrest; pictures of the place where the body was found; articles on Lord Peter Wimsey, on the Wimsey family, on their historic seat in Norfolk; on night-life in London and on penny whistles. The Duke of Denver had been interviewed, but refused to say anything; Lord Peter Wimsey, on the other hand, had said a good deal. Finally—and this puzzled Miss Meteyard very much, there was a photograph of Lord Peter and of Death Bredon standing side by side.

"It would be useless," said Lord Peter Wimsey in an interview, "in view of the remarkable resemblance between us, to deny that there is a relationship between this man and myself. In fact, he has on various occasions given trouble by impersonating me. If you were to see us together, you would notice that he is the darker of the two; there are also, of course, slight differences of feature; but, when we are seen separately, it is easy to mistake one of us for the other."

The Death Bredon of the photograph had certainly very much darker hair than the Peter Wimsey; his mouth was set in an unpleasing sneer, and he had that indefinable air of raffish insolence which is the hall-mark of the *chevalier d'industrie*. The newspaper article wandered on to give various unverifiable details.

"Bredon never went to a university, though he sometimes claims Oxford as his Alma Mater. He was educated at a public school in France where English sports are cultivated. He is a very fine natural cricketer, and was actually playing in a cricket match when arrested through the prompt and intelligent action of Chief-Inspector Parker. Under various names he is well known in the night-clubs of London and Paris. He is said to have met the unfortunate girl, with whose murder he is charged, at the house of the late

Major Milligan, who met his death two days ago by being run down by a lorry in Piccadilly. Following representations by the Wimsey family as to his mode of life, he had recently taken a post in a well-known commercial firm, and was supposed to have turned over a new leaf, but . . ."

And so on, and so forth.

Miss Meteyard sat for a long time with the papers strewn about her, smoking cigarettes, while her coffee got cold. Then she went and had a bath. She hoped it might clear her brain.

The excitement at Pym's on the Monday morning was indescribable. The Copy Department sat in the typists' room and did no work at all. Mr. Pym telephoned that he was unwell, and could not come to the office. Mr. Copley was so unnerved that he sat for three hours with a blank sheet of paper before him and then went out for a drink— a thing he had never done in his life. Mr. Willis seemed to be on the verge of nervous collapse. Mr. Ingleby laughed at his colleagues' agitation and said that it was a grand new experience for them all. Miss Parton burst into tears and Miss Rossiter proclaimed that she had always known it. Mr. Tallboy then enlivened the proceedings by fainting in Mr. Armstrong's room, thus giving Mrs. Johnson (who was hysterically inclined) useful occupation for half an hour. And Ginger Joe, of the red head and sunny temper, astonished his companions by having a fit of the sulks and then suddenly cuffing Bill's head for no reason whatever.

At 1 o'clock Miss Meteyard went out to lunch, and read in the *Evening Banner* that Mr. Death Bredon had appeared before the magistrates at 10 a.m. on the murder charge, and had reserved his defence. At 10.30, Lord Peter Wimsey (picturesquely described as "the second protagonist in this drama of dope and death") had, while riding in the Row, narrowly escaped injury, owing to his horse's having been startled by a back-fire from a racing car; the animal had bolted and only Lord Peter's consummate horseman-ship had averted a nasty accident. There was a photograph of Mr. Bredon entering the court at Bow Street in a dark lounge suit and soft hat; there was also a photograph of Lord Peter Wimsey returning from his ride in neat breeches and boots and a bowler; there was, needless to say, no photograph of the metamorphosis of the one gentleman into another, behind the drawn blinds of a Daimler saloon while traversing the quiet squares north of Oxford Street.

On Monday night, Lord Peter Wimsey attended a per-formance of *Say When!* at the Frivolity, companioning a Royal personage.

On Tuesday morning, Mr. Willis arrived at the office late and in a great state of excited importance. He beamed at everybody, presented the typists' room with a four-pound box of chocolates and an iced cake, and informed the sympathetic Miss Parton that he was engaged to be married. At coffee-time, the name of the lady was known to be Miss Pamela Dean. At 11.30, it was divulged that the ceremony would take place at the earliest possible moment, and at 11.45 Miss Rossiter was collecting subscriptions for a wedding-present. By 2 o'clock, the subscribers were already divided into two opinionated and bitterly hostile factions, the one advocating the purchase of a handsome dining-room clock with Westminster chimes, and the other voting with passion for a silver-plated electric chafing-dish. At 4 o'clock, Mr. Jollop had turned down successively, "Sigh no more, Ladies," "Oh, Dry those Tears" and "Weeping Late and Weeping Early," which Mr. Toule had previously passed, and rejected with derision the proposed substitution of "If you have Tears," "O Say, What are You Weeping For?" and "A Poor Soul Sat Sighing." Mr. Ingleby, stimulated by a frantic request for new headlines, had flown into a passion because the *Dictionary of Quotations* had mysteriously disappeared. At 4.30 Miss Rossiter, feverishly typing, had completed "I Weep, I know not Why" and "In Silence and in Tears," while the distracted Mr. Ingleby was seriously contemplating "In that Deep Midnight of the Mind" (for, as he observed, "they'll never know it's Byron unless we tell them"), when Mr. Armstrong sent up word to say that he had persuaded Mr. Jollop to accept the copy of "O Say, What are you Weeping For?" combined with the headline "Flat, Stale, and Unprofitable," and would Mr. Ingleby kindly verify at once whether it was "Flat, Stale" or "Stale, Flat," and get the thing re-typed and hand it to Mr. Tallboy immediately.

"Isn't Mr. Armstrong marvellous?" said Miss Rossiter. "He always finds a way out. Here you are, Mr. Ingleby— I've looked it up—it's "Stale, Flat." The first sentence will want altering, I suppose. You can't have this bit about 'Sometimes you are tempted to ask yourself, in the words of the old game,' can you?"

"I suppose not," grunted Ingleby. "Better make it: 'Sometimes you may be tempted, like Hamlet, to exclaim' —then the whole quote—and go on, 'yet if anybody were to ask you why—' and join it up there. That'll do. Courses of the world, please, not curses."

"T'chk!" said Miss Rossiter.

"Here's Wedderburn, panting for his copy. How's Tallboy, Wedder?"

"Gone home," said Mr. Wedderburn. "He didn't want to go, but he's fagged out. He oughtn't to have come to the office at all today, but he would do it. Is this the thing?"

"Yes. They'll want a new sketch, of course."

"Of course," said Mr. Wedderburn, gloomily. "How they ever expect things to look right when they chop and change like this— Oh, well! What is it? 'Picture of Hamlet.' Have the Studio got a reference for Hamlet?"

"Of course not; they never have anything. Who does

these sketches? Pickering? You'd better take him my illustrated Shakespeare with my compliments, and request him
not to cover it with Indian ink and rubber solution."

"All right."

"And to return it sometime before Christmas."

Wedderburn grinned and departed on his errand.

About ten minutes later, the telephone tinkled in the
typists' room.

"Yes?" said Miss Rossiter, in mellifluous accents. "Who
is it, please?"

"Tallboy speaking," said the telephone.

"Oh!" Miss Rossiter altered her voice from the tone reserved for clients and directors to a tarter one (for she was
not too well pleased with Mr. Tallboy), modified by the
sympathy due to ill-health:

"Oh, yes? Are you feeling better, Mr. Tallboy?"

"Yes, thanks. I've been trying to get Wedderburn, but
he doesn't seem to be in his room."

"I expect he's in the Studio, making poor Mr. Pickering
work overtime on a new Nutrax sketch."

"Oh! that's what I wanted to know. Did Jollop pass that
copy?"

"No—he turned the whole lot down. It's a new one—at
least, new headline with the 'What are you Weeping for?'
copy."

"Oh, a new headline? What is it?"

"Stale, Flat and Unprofitable. Shakespeare, you know."

"Oh! Oh, good! Glad something managed to get through.
It was worrying me."

"It's quite all right, Mr. Tallboy." Miss Rossiter rang off.
"Touching devotion to business," she observed to Miss Parton. "As if the world would stop turning just because *he*
wasn't here!"

"I expect he was afraid old Copley would be butting in
again," said Miss Parton, with a snort.

"Oh, him!" said Miss Rossiter.

"Well, now, young man," said the policeman, "and what do *you* want?"

"I want to see Chief-Inspector Parker."

"Ho!" said the policeman. "Don't want much, do you? Sure you wouldn't rather see the Lord Mayor o' London? Or Mister Ramsay MacDonald?"

"I say, are you always as funny as that? Cor lumme, don't it 'urt yer sometimes? You better buy yourself a new pair o' boots or you'll be gettin' too big for wot yer wearin'. You tell Chief-Inspector Parker as Mr. Joe Potts wants ter see 'im about this 'ere 'Arlequin murder. And look snappy, 'cos I gotter git 'ome ter me supper."

"About the 'Arlequin murder, eh? And wot do you know about that?"

"Never you mind. Jest tell 'im wot I say. Tell 'im it's Joe Potts as works at Pym's Publicity and you'll 'ave 'im steppin' aht ter meet me wiv' a crimson carpet and a bokay."

"Oh! you're from Pym's. Got something to say about this Bredon, is that it?"

"That's it. Now, you 'op it, and don't waste time."

"You'd better come in here, young Cocky—and be'ave yourself."

"Right-oh! it's all the same to me."

Mr. Joseph Potts wiped his boots neatly on the mat, took his seat upon a hard bench, drew out a Yo-Yo from his pocket, and began nonchalantly throwing a handsome series of loops, while the policeman retired defeated.

Presently he returned and, sternly commanding Mr. Joseph Potts to put his top away, conducted him through a series of passages to a door, upon which he knocked. A voice said "Come in," and Mr. Potts found himself in a good-sized room, furnished with two desks, a couple of comfortable arm-chairs and several other seats of penitential appearance. At the farther desk sat a man in mufti, writing, with his back to the door; at the nearer, facing the door, was another man in a grey suit, with a pile of documents before him.

"The boy, sir," announced the policeman, and retired.

"Sit down," said the man in grey, briefly, indicating one of the penitential chairs. "Now then, what's all this you've got to tell us, eh?"

"Excuse me, sir, are you Chief-Inspector Parker?"

"This is a very cautious witness," observed the man in grey to the world in general. "Why do you particularly want to see Chief-Inspector Parker?"

" 'Cos it's important and confidential, see?" said Mr. Joseph Potts, pertly. "Information, that's wot it is. I likes ter do business with the boss, especially if there's anythink ain't bein' 'andled as it should be."

"Oh!"

"I want to tell this Parker that this case ain't bein' 'andled right. See? Mr. Bredon ain't got nothink to do with it."

"Indeed. Well, I'm Chief-Inspector Parker. What do you know about Bredon?"

"This 'ere." Ginger Joe extended an inky forefinger. "You been 'ad. Mr. Bredon ain't no crook, 'e's a great detective, and I'm 'is assistant. We're 'ard on the track of a murderer, see? And this 'ere is just a mashi—macki—I mean it's jest a booby-trap set by the 'ideous gang as 'e's out ter track to its lair. You been boobies ter let yerselves be took in by it, see? 'E's a sport, is Mr. Bredon, and he ain't never murdered no young woman, let alone bein' such a fool as ter leave penny whistles be'ind 'im. If you wants a murderer, Mr. Bredon's got 'is eye on one now, and you're jest playin' into the 'ands of the Black Spider and 'is gang —meaning to say, 'oever done this. Wot I meantersay, the time 'as come fer me ter divulge wot I know, and I ain't agoin'—cor lumme!"

The man at the farther desk had turned round and was grinning at Ginger over the back of his chair.

"That'll do, Ginger," said this person. "We know all about that here. I am obliged to you for your testimonial. I hope you haven't been divulging anything in other direc-tions."

"Me, sir? No, sir. I ain't said a word, Mr. Bredon, sir. But seein' as 'ow—"

"That's all right; I believe you. Now, Charles, I think this is just the lad we want. You can get that headline from him and save ringing up Pym's. Ginger, was the Nutrax headline passed this afternoon?"

"Yes, sir. 'Stale, Flat and Unprofitable,' that's what it was. And lor', wasn't there a to-do about it! Took 'em all afternoon, it did, and Mr. Ingleby wasn't 'arf wild."

"He would be," said Wimsey. "Now, you'd better cut along home, Ginger, and not a word, mind."

"No, sir."

"We're much obliged to you for coming," added Parker, "but you see, we aren't quite such boobies as you think. We know a good deal about Mr. Bredon here. And by the way, let me introduce you to Lord Peter Wimsey."

Ginger Joe's eyes nearly popped out of his head.

"Cool Lord Peter—where's Mr. Bredon, then? This *is* Mr. Bredon. You're pulling my leg."

"I promise," said Wimsey, "to tell you all about it this time next week. Cut along now, there's a good chap. We're busy."

On Wednesday morning, Mr. Parker received a communication from St. Martin's-le-Grand. Inside the official envelope was another, addressed in Tallboy's hand to S. Smith, Esq." at Cummings' address in Old Broad Street.

"That settles it," said Wimsey. He consulted the marked Telephone Directory. "Here you are. The Stag at Bay, Drury Lane. Make no mistake this time."

It was not until Thursday evening that Miss Meteyard made up her mind to speak to Mr. Tallboy.

CHAPTER XX

APPROPRIATE EXIT
OF AN UNSKILLED MURDERER

Is LORD PETER WIMSEY at home?"

The manservant raked his questioner with a swift glance, which took in everything from his hunted eyes to his respectable middle-class boots. Then he said, inclining a respectful head:

"If you will be good enough to take a seat, I will ascertain if his Lordship is at leisure. What name shall I say, sir?"

"Mr. Tallboy."

"Who, Bunter?" said Wimsey. "Mr. Tallboy? This is a little embarrassing. What does he look like?"

"He looks, my lord, if I may so poetically express myself, as though the Hound of Heaven had got him, so to say, cornered, my lord."

"You are probably right. I should not be surprised if a hound of hell or so were knocking about the neighbourhood as well. Take a squint out of the window, Bunter."

"Very good, my lord. . . . I can observe nobody, but I retain a distinct impression that, when I opened the door to Mr. Tallboy, I overheard a footstep on the floor below."

"Very likely. Well, it can't be helped. Show him in."

"Very good, my lord."

The young man came in and Wimsey rose to greet him.

"Good evening, Mr. Tallboy."

"I have come," began Tallboy, and then broke off. "Lord Peter—Bredon—for God's sake, which are you?"

"Both," said Wimsey, gravely. "Won't you sit down?"

"Thanks, I'd rather . . . I don't want . . . I came . . ."

"You're looking rather rotten. I really think you'd better sit down, and have a spot of something."

Tallboy's legs seemed to give way under him, and he sat down without further protest.

"And how," inquired Wimsey, pouring him out a stiff whisky, "is the Whifflets campaign getting on without me?"

"Whifflets?"

"It doesn't matter. I only asked to show you that I really was Bredon. Put that straight down. Is that better?"

"Yes. I'm sorry to have made a fool of myself. I came to you—"

"You came to find out how much I knew?"

"Yes—no. I came because I couldn't stick it out any longer. I came to tell you all about it."

"Wait a minute. There's something I must tell you first. It's all out of my hands now. You understand? As a matter of fact, I don't think there's very much you can tell me. The game's up, old man. I'm sorry—I'm really sorry, because I think you've been having a perfectly bloody time. But there it is."

Tallboy had gone very white. He accepted another drink without protest, and then said:

"Well, I'm rather glad in a way. If it wasn't for my wife and the kid—oh, God!" He hid his face in his hands, and Wimsey walked over to the window and glanced at the lights of Piccadilly, pale in the summer dusk. "I've been a bloody fool," said Tallboy.

"Most of us are," said Wimsey. "I'm damned sorry, old chap."

He came back and stood looking down at him.

"Look here," he said, "you need not tell me a thing, if you don't want to. But if you do, I want you to understand that it won't really make any difference. I mean, if you feel like getting it off your chest, I don't think it will prejudice matters for you at all."

"I'd like to tell you," said Tallboy. "I think you might

understand. I realize that it's all up, anyhow." He paused.
"I say, what put you on to this?"

"That letter of Victor Dean's. You remember it? The
one he threatened to write to Pym. He showed it to you,
I fancy."

"The little swine. Yes, he did. Didn't he destroy it?"

"No, he didn't."

"I see. Well, I'd better begin at the beginning. It all
started about two years ago. I was rather hard up and I
wanted to get married. I'd been losing money on horses,
as well, and things were not too good. I met a man in a
restaurant."

"What restaurant?"

Tallboy gave the name. "He was a middle-aged, ordinary
sort of person. I've never seen him since. But we got talking
about one thing and another, and how tight money was and
so on, and I happened to mention where I was working.
He seemed to be thinking a bit after that, and asked a
good many questions about how advertisements were put
together and sent to the papers, and so on, and whether
I was in a position to know beforehand what the headlines were going to be. So I said, of course, that there were
some accounts I knew all about, such as Nutrax, and others
I didn't. So then he mentioned the *Morning Star* half-
double, and asked when I knew about the headlines of
that, and I said, on Tuesday afternoon. Then he suddenly
asked me if I could do with an extra thousand a year, and
I said, 'Couldn't I? Lead me to it.' So then he came out
with his proposal. It sounded pretty innocent. At least, it
was quite obviously a dirty trick, but it wasn't criminal,
the way he put it. He said, if I would let him know, every
Tuesday, the initial letter of the headline for the following
Friday, I should be well paid for it. Of course, I made a
fuss about breach of confidence and so on and he raised
his terms to twelve hundred. It sounded damned tempting,
and I couldn't see, for the life of me, how it was going to
harm the firm in any way. So I said I'd do it, and we fixed
up a code—"

"I know all about that," said Wimsey. "It was very ingenious and simple. I suppose he told you that the address was simply an accommodation address."

"Yes. Wasn't it? I went to see the place once; it was a tobacconist's."

Wimsey nodded. "I've been there. It's not exactly an accommodation address, in the sense you mean. Didn't this man give you any reason for this rather remarkable request?"

"Yes, he did, and of course I oughtn't to have had anything to do with him after that. He said he was fond of having a bit of a bet with some friends of his about one thing and another, and his idea was to bet on the initial letter of each week's headline—"

"Oh, I see. And he would be betting on a certainty as often as he liked. Plausible; not criminal, but just dirty enough to explain the insistence on secrecy. Was that it?"

"Yes. I fell for it. . . . I was damned hard up. . . . I can't excuse myself. And I suppose I ought to have guessed that there was more to it than that. But I didn't want to guess. Besides, at first I thought it was all a leg-pull, but I wasn't risking anything, so I buzzed off the first two code-letters, and at the end of the fortnight I got my fifty pounds. I was heavily in debt, and I used it. After that—well, I hadn't the courage to chuck it."

"No, it would be rather hard, I should think."

"Hard? You don't know, Bredon—Wimsey—you don't know what it means to be stuck for money. They don't pay any too well at Pym's, and there are heaps of fellows who want to get out and find something better, but they daren't. Pym's is safe—they're kind and decent, and they don't sack you if they can help it—but you live up to your income and you simply daren't cut loose. The competition is so keen, and you marry and start paying for your house and furniture, and you must keep up the instalments, and you can't collect the capital to sit round for a month or two while you look for a new job. You've got to keep going, and it breaks your heart and takes all the stuffing out of you. So

I went on. Of course, I kept hoping that I might be able to save money and get out of it, but my wife fell ill and one thing and another, and I was spending every penny of my salary and Smith's money on top of it. And then, somehow, that little devil Dean got hold of it; God knows how!"

"I can tell you that," said Wimsey, and told him.

"I see. Well, he started to put the screw on. First of all he wanted to go fifty-fifty, and then he demanded more. The devil of it was, that if he split on me, I should lose my job as well as Smith's money, and things were getting pretty awful. My wife was going to have a baby, and I was behind with the income-tax, and I think it was just because everything seemed too utterly hopeless that I got mixed up with the Vavasour girl. Naturally, that only made things worse in the long run. And then, one day, I felt I couldn't stand it any longer and told Dean I was chucking the whole show and he could do as he damn well pleased. And it wasn't till then that he told me what it was all about, and pointed out that I might easily get twelve years' penal servitude for helping to run the dope-traffic."

"Dirty," said Wimsey, "very dirty. It never occurred to you, I suppose, to turn King's Evidence and expose the whole system."

"No; not at first. I was terrified and couldn't think properly. And even if I'd done that, there'd have been awful trouble. Still, I did think of it after a bit, and told Dean that that was what I would do. And then he informed me that he was going to get his shot in first, and showed me that letter he was sending to Pym. That finished me, and I begged him to hold off for a week or two, while I thought things over. What happened about that letter exactly?"

"His sister found it among his things and sent it on to Pym, and he engaged me, through a friend, to enquire into it. He didn't know who I was. I thought there probably wasn't much in it, but I took the job on for the experience."

Tallboy nodded.

"Well, you've had your experience. I hope you haven't

paid as heavily for it as I have. I could see no way out
of it—".

He stopped speaking, and glanced at Wimsey.

"Perhaps I'd better tell you the next bit," said the latter.
"You thought it over, and decided that Victor Dean was a
wart and a scab, and would be no great loss to the world.
One day, Wedderburn came along to your room, chuckling
because Mrs. Johnson had caught Ginger Joe with a catapult and had confiscated it and put it in her desk. You knew
you were a wonderfully good shot with any sort of missile—
the kind of man who could spread-eagle a wicket from the
other end of a cricket-field—and you realized how easily
a man could be plugged through the skylight as he went
down the iron staircase. If the blow didn't kill him, then
the fall might, and it was well worth trying."

"You really do know all about it, then?"

"Nearly. You pinched the catapult, opening the drawer
with Mrs. Johnson's keys during the lunch-hour, and you
did a few practice shots from day to day. You left a pebble
there once, you know."

"I know. Somebody came along, before I could find it."

"Yes. Well, then, the day came for putting Dean away—a
nice bright day, when all the skylights were open. You
dodged about the building a good bit, so that nobody
should know exactly where you were at any particular
minute, and then you went up on the roof. How, by the
way, did you ensure that Dean would go down the iron
staircase at the right moment? Oh, yes, and the scarab?
It was a very good idea to use the scarab, because if anybody found it, they would naturally think it had tumbled
out of his pocket as he fell."

"I'd seen the scarab on Dean's desk after lunch; I knew
he often kept it there. And I had *The Times Atlas* in my
room. I sent Wedderburn down to the Vouchers for something or other, and then I rang up Dean on my telephone.
I said I was speaking for Mr. Hankin from the Big Conference Room, and would Mr. Dean please come down
about the Crunchlets copy and bring *The Times Atlas*

with him from my room. While he went for it, I pinched the scarab and slipped up on to the roof. I knew it would take him a bit of time to find the atlas, because I'd buried it under a whole heap of files, and I was pretty sure he'd go by the iron staircase, because that was the nearest way from my room to the Conference Room. As a matter of fact, it might have gone wrong at that point, because he didn't come that way at all. I think he must have gone back to his own room for something after getting the atlas, but of course, I don't know. Anyway, he came along all right and I shot at him through the skylight when he was about four steps down the staircase."

"How did you know so exactly where to hit him?"

"Curiously enough, I had a young brother who was accidentally killed by being hit in just that place with a golf-ball. But I went and looked it up in a book at the British Museum to make sure. Apparently he broke his neck as well; I hadn't expected that. I stayed up on the roof till the fuss was over, and then came down quietly by the stairs. I didn't meet a soul, of course, they were all holding post-mortems and hanging round the corpse. When I knew I'd succeeded, I didn't care. I was glad. And I tell you this, if I hadn't been found out, I shouldn't care now."

"I can sympathize with that," said Wimsey.

"They asked me for a shilling for the little beast's wreath." Tallboy laughed. "I'd gladly have given twenty shillings, or twenty pounds even. . . . And then you came along. . . . I didn't suspect anything . . . till you started to talk about catapults. . . . And then I got badly frightened, and I . . . and I . . ."

"We'll draw a veil over that," said Wimsey. "You must have got a bit of a shock when you found you'd slugged the wrong man. I suppose that was when you struck a light to look for Pamela Dean's letter."

"Yes. I knew her writing—I'd seen it in Dean's room— and I knew her writing-paper, too. I really came round to find out whether you knew anything or whether you were just drawing a bow at a venture—that's rather appropriate, isn't it? Drawing a catapult at a venture would be better. When I saw that letter I felt sure there must be something in it. And Willis, too—he'd told me that you and Pamela Dean were as thick as thieves. I thought the letter might be telling you all about Dean and me. I don't know quite what I thought, to tell you the truth. Then, when I'd found out my mistake, I got frightened and thought I'd better not try again."

"I was expecting you. When nothing came of it, I began to think it hadn't been you at all, but somebody else."

"Did you know by then that the other thing was me?"

"I didn't know it was you; you were one of several possibles. But after the Nutrax row and the £50 in notes—"

Tallboy looked up with a shy, fleeting smile.

"You know," he said, "I was horribly careless and incompetent all through. Those letters—I ought never to have sent them from the office."

"No; and the catapult. You should have taken the trouble to make your own. A catapult without fingerprints is something very unusual."

"So that was it. I'm afraid I've made an awful mess of everything. Couldn't even do a simple murder. Wimsey—how much of this will have to come out? Everything, I suppose? Even that Vavasour girl . . . ?"

"Ah!" said Wimsey, without replying to the question. "Don't talk about the Vavasour girl. I felt a cad about that. You know, I did tell you not to thank me."

"You did, and it frightened me badly, because you sounded as if you meant it. I knew then that it hadn't been an accident about the catapult. But I hadn't an idea who you were till that infernal cricket match."

"I was careless then. But that damned fellow Simmonds rapping me on the funny-bone got my goat. You didn't fall for my impressive arrest then?"

"Oh, yes, I did. I believed in it implicitly and put up the most heartfelt thanksgivings. I thought I'd got off."

"Then what brought you round here tonight?"

"Miss Meteyard. She got hold of me last night. She said

she'd believed first of all that you and Bredon were the same person, but now she thought you couldn't be. But she said that Bredon would be dead sure to split on me by way of currying favour with the police, and I had better get out in time."

"She said that? Miss Meteyard? Do you mean to say she knew all about it?"

"Not about the Nutrax business. But she knew about Dean."

"Good God!" Wimsey's natural conceit received a shattering blow. "How in Heaven's name did *she* know?"

"Guessed. Said she'd once seen me look at Dean when I didn't know she was there—and apparently he had once let out something to her. Apparently she'd always thought there was something odd about his death. She said she'd made up her mind not to interfere either way, but after your arrest she decided you were the bigger crook of the two. She could stand Lord Peter Wimsey doing a proper investigation, but not Mr. Dirty Bredon squealing to save his skin. She's an odd woman."

"Very. I'd better forget about all this, hadn't I? She seems to have taken the whole thing very coolly."

"She did. You see, she knew Dean. He tried to blackmail her once, about some man or the other. You wouldn't think it to look at her, would you?" said Tallboy, naïvely. "There was nothing much in it, she said, but it was the kind of thing old Pym would have been down on like a sledge-hammer."

"And what did she do?" asked Wimsey, fascinated.

"Told him to publish and be damned. And I wish to God I'd done the same. Wimsey—how much longer is it going to hang on? I've been in torment—I've been trying to give myself up—I—my wife—why haven't I been arrested before this?"

"They've been waiting," said Wimsey, thoughtfully, for his mind was pursuing two trains of thought at the same time. "You see, you aren't really as important as this dope-gang. Once you were arrested, they would stop their little game, and we didn't want them to stop. I'm afraid you're being the tethered kid, left there to trap the tigers."

All this time, his ear was alert to catch the tinkle of the telephone, which would tell him that the raid on the Stag at Bay had succeeded. Once the arrests were made and the gang broken, the sinister watcher in the street would be harmless. He would fly for his life and Tallboy would be able to go home to whatever awaited him there. But if he were to go now—

"When?" Tallboy was saying urgently, "when?"

"Tonight."

"Wimsey—you've been frightfully decent to me—tell me —there's no way out? It isn't myself, exactly, but my wife and the kid. Pointed at all their lives. It's damnable. You couldn't give me twenty-four hours?"

"You would not pass the ports."

"If I were alone I'd give myself up. I would, honestly."

"There is an alternative."

"I know. I've thought about that. I suppose that's—" he stopped and laughed suddenly—"that's the public school way out of it. I—yes—all right. They'll hardly make a headline of it, though, will they? 'Suicide of Old Dumble-tonian' wouldn't have much news-value. Never mind, damn it! We'll show 'em that Dumbleton can achieve the Eton touch. Why not?"

"Good man!" said Wimsey. "Have a drink. Here's luck!"

He emptied his glass and stood up.

"Listen!" he said. "I think there is one other way out. It won't help you, but it may make all the difference to your wife and your child."

"How?" said Tallboy, eagerly.

"They need never know anything about all this. Nothing. Nobody need ever know anything, if you do as I tell you."

"My God, Wimsey! What do you mean? Tell me quickly. I'll do anything."

"It won't save you."

"That doesn't matter. Tell me."

"Go home now," said Wimsey. "Go on foot, and not too fast. And don't look behind you."

Tallboy stared at him; the blood drained away from his face, leaving even his lips as white as paper.

"I think I understand. . . . Very well."

"Quickly, then," said Wimsey. He held out his hand.

"Good-night, and good luck."

"Thank you. Good-night."

From the window, Wimsey watched him come out into Piccadilly, and walk quickly away towards Hyde Park Corner. He saw the shadow slip from a neighbouring door-way and follow him.

"—and from thence to the place of execution . . . and may the Lord have mercy upon your soul."

Half an hour later, the telephone rang.

"Bagged the whole crew," said Parker's cheerful voice. "We let the stuff go up to town. What do you think it went as? Traveller's samples—one of those closed cars with blinds all round."

"That's where they made it into packets, then."

"Yes. We watched our man into the Stag; then we pulled in the motor-boat and the car. Then we kept our eye on the pub. and let the birds hop out into our arms, one after the other. It went off beautifully. No hitch at all. Oh, and by the way—their code-word. We ought to have thought of that. It was just anything to do with Nutrax. Some of them had the *Morning Star*, showing the ad., and some of them just mentioned Nutrax for Nerves. One chap had a bottle of the stuff in his pocket, another had it written on a shopping-list and so on. And one frightfully ingenious chap was bursting with information about some new tracks for greyhound racing. Simple as pie, wasn't it?"

"That explains Hector Puncheon."

"Hector—? Oh, the newspaper fellow. Yes. He must have had his copy of the *Morning Star* with him. We've got old Cummings, too, of course. He turns out to be the actual top-dog of the whole show, and as soon as we collared him he coughed up the whole story, the mangy little blighter. That doctor fellow who shoved Mountjoy under the train is in it—we've got definite information about him, and we've also got our hands on Mountjoy's loot. He's got a safe-deposit somewhere, and I think I know where to find the key. He kept a woman in Maida Vale, bless his heart. The whole thing is most satisfactory. Now we have only got to rake in your murderer chap, what's his name, and everything in the garden will be lovely."

"Lovely," said Wimsey, with a spice of bitterness in his tone, "simply lovely."

"What's the matter? You sound a bit peeved. Hang on a minute till I've cleared up here and we'll go round somewhere and celebrate."

"Not tonight," said Wimsey. "I don't feel quite like celebrating."

CHAPTER XXI

DEATH DEPARTS FROM PYM'S PUBLICITY

So YOU see," said Wimsey to Mr. Pym, "the thing need never come into the papers at all, if we're careful. We've plenty of evidence against Cummings without that, and there's no need to take the public into our confidence about the details of their distributing system."

"Thank Heaven!" said Mr. Pym. "It would have been a terrible thing for Pym's Publicity. How I have lived through this last week, I really don't know. I suppose you will be leaving the advertising?"

"I'm afraid so."

"Pity. You have a natural flair for copy-writing. You will have the satisfaction of seeing your Whifflets scheme go through."

"Splendid! I shall begin to collect coupons at once."

"Just fancy!" said Miss Rossiter. "Charge withdrawn."

"I always *said* Mr. Bredon was a darling," triumphed Miss Parton. "Of course the *real* murderer was one of those horrible dope-trafficking beasts. That was far more likely. I said so at the time."

"I didn't hear you, dear," snapped Miss Rossiter. "I say, Miss Meteyard, you've seen the news? You've seen that our Mr. Bredon is discharged and never did any murder at all?"

"I've done better," replied Miss Meteyard. "I've seen Mr. Bredon."

"No, where?"

"Here."

"*No!*"

"And he isn't Mr. Bredon, he's Lord Peter Wimsey."

"What! ! !"

Lord Peter poked his long nose round the door.

"Did I hear my name?"

"You did. She says you're Lord Peter Wimsey."

"Quite right."

"Then what were you doing here?"

"I came here," said his lordship, unabashed, "for a bet. A friend of mine laid me ten to one I couldn't earn my own living for a month. I did it, though, didn't I? May I have a cup of coffee?"

They would gladly have given him anything.

"By the way," said Miss Rossiter, when the first tumult had subsided, "you heard about poor Mr. Tallboy?"

"Yes, poor chap."

"Knocked down and killed on his way home—wasn't it dreadful? And poor Mrs. Tallboy with a small baby—it does seem awful! Goodness knows what they'll have to live on, because—well, you know! And that reminds me, while you're here, could I have your shilling for a wreath? At least, I suppose you'll be leaving Pym's now, but I expect you'd like to contribute."

"Yes, rather. Here you are."

"Thanks awfully. Oh, and I say! There's Mr. Willis' wedding-present. You know he's getting married?"

"No, I didn't. Everything seems to happen while I'm away. Whom is he marrying?"

"Pamela Dean."

"Oh, good work. Yes, of course. How much for Willis?"

"Well, most people are giving about two bob, if you can spare it."

"I think I can manage two bob. What are we giving him, by the way?"

"Well," said Miss Rossiter, "there's been *rather* a fuss

about that. The Department was awfully keen on a clock, but Mrs. Johnson and Mr. Barrow went off on their own and bought an electric chafing-dish—such a silly thing, because I'm sure they'll never use it. And in any case, Mr. Willis did belong to the Copy Department and we ought to have had a voice in it, don't you think? So there are going to be two presents—the staff as a whole is giving the chafing-dish and the Department is giving its own present. I'm afraid we shan't be able to manage a chiming clock, though, because you can't very well ask people for more than two bob or so, though Hankie and Armstrong have been very decent and stumped up half a quid each."

"I'd better made it half a quid too."

"Oh, no," said Miss Rossiter. "You're a lamb, but it isn't fair."

"It's quite fair," said Wimsey. "There are excellent reasons why I should contribute largely to a wedding present for Mr. Willis."

"Are there? I thought you and he didn't get on very well. I expect I'm being tactless, as usual. If you're quite sure—oh, I forgot, I *am* a fool. Of course, if you're Lord Peter Wimsey, you're simply frightfully rich, aren't you?"

"Fair to middling," confessed Wimsey. "It might run to a cake for tea."

He had a word with Miss Meteyard.

"I'm sorry, you know," he said.

She shrugged her angular shoulders.

"It's not your fault. Things have to happen. You're one of the sort that pushes round and makes them happen. I prefer to leave them alone. You've got to have both kinds."

"Perhaps your way is wiser and more charitable."

"It isn't. I shirk responsibility, that's all. I just let things rip. I don't make it my business to interfere. But I don't blame the people who do interfere. In a way, I rather admire them. They do make something, even if it's only mischief. My sort make nothing. We exploit other people's folly, take the cash and sneer at the folly. It's not admirable. Never mind. You'd better run along now. I've got to get out a new series for Sopo. 'Sopo Day is Cinema Day.' 'Leave the Laundry to ruin itself while you addle your brains at the Talkies.' Muck! Dope! And they pay me £10 a week for that sort of thing. And yet, if we didn't do it, what would happen to the trade of this country? You've got to advertise."

Mr. Hankin tripped along the passage and encountered them.

"So you're leaving us, Mr. Bredon? In fact, I understand that we've been nursing a cuckoo in the nest."

"Not so bad as that, sir. I'm leaving a few of the original nestlings behind me."

Miss Meteyard evaporated quietly, and Mr. Hankin continued:

"A very sad business. Mr. Pym is very grateful for the discretion you have shown. I hope you will lunch with me some day. Yes, Mr. Smayle?"

"Excuse me, sir—about this window-bill for Green Pastures?"

Wimsey made his way out, exchanging mechanical hand-grips and farewells. At the foot of the lift, in the lower vestibule, he found Ginger, with his arms full of parcels.

"Well, Ginger," said Wimsey, "I'm off."

"Oh, sir!"

"By the way, I've still got your catapult."

"I'd like you to keep it, please, sir. You see, sir—" Ginger struggled with a variety of emotions—"if I was ter keep that there catapult, I might get telling some of the boys about it, not meaning to, like. Wot I meantersay, it's 'istorical, like, ain't it, sir?"

"So it is." Wimsey sympathized with the temptation. It is not every fellow whose catapult has been borrowed for the purpose of committing a murder. "Well, I'll keep it, and thank you very much for all your help. Look here, I'll tell you what. I'll give you something in exchange. Which would you rather have—a model aeroplane, or the pair of scissors with which the steward of the *Nancy Belle* stabbed the captain and the purser?"

"Ooh, sir! 'As the scissors got the marks on 'em, sir?"

"Yes, Ginger. Genuine, original bloodstains."

"Then, please, sir, I'd like the scissors."

"You shall have them."

"Thank you *very* much, sir."

"And you'll never say one word to anybody about you know what?"

"Not if you was to roast me alive, sir."

"Right you are; good-bye, Ginger."

"Good-bye, sir."

Wimsey stepped out into Southampton Row. Facing him was a long line of hoardings. Enormous in its midst stretched a kaleidoscopic poster:

NUTRAX FOR NERVES

In the adjoining space, a workman with a broom and a bucket of paste was unfolding a still more vast and emphatic display in blue and yellow:

ARE YOU A WHIFFLER?
IF NOT, WHY NOT?

A 'bus passed, bearing a long ribbon display upon its side:

WHIFFLE YOUR WAY ROUND BRITAIN!

The great campaign had begun. He contemplated his work with a kind of amazement. With a few idle words on a sheet of paper he had touched the lives of millions. Two men, passing, stopped to stare at the hoarding.

"What's this Whiffling business, Alf?"

"I dunno. Some advertising stunt or other. Cigarettes, ain't it?"

"Oh, Whifflets?"

"I suppose so."

"Wonderful how they think of it all. What's it about, anyway?"

"Gawd knows. Here, let's get a packet and see."

"All right. I don't mind."

They passed on.

Tell England. Tell the world. Eat more Oats. Take Care of your Complexion. No More War. Shine your Shoes with Shino. Ask your Grocer. Children Love Laxamalt. Prepare to meet thy God. Bung's Beer is Better. Try Dogsbody's Sausages. Whoosh the Dust Away. Give them Crunchlets. Snagsbury's Soups are Best for the Troops. *Morning Star,* best Paper by Far. Vote for Punkin and Protect your Profits. Stop that Sneeze with Snuffo. Flush your Kidneys with Fizzlets. Flush your Drains with Sanfect. Wear Woolfleece next the Skin. Popp's Pills Pep you Up. Whiffle your Way to Fortune. . . .

Advertise, or go under.

STRONG POISON

STRONG POISON

BY

DOROTHY L. SAYERS

HARPER & ROW, PUBLISHERS
New York, Hagerstown, San Francisco, London

Library of Congress catalog card number: 58-8893

CHAPTER I

THERE were crimson roses on the bench; they looked like splashes of blood.

The judge was an old man; so old, he seemed to have outlived time and change and death. His parrot-face and parrot-voice were dry, like his old, heavily-veined hands. His scarlet robe clashed harshly with the crimson of the roses. He had sat for three days in the stuffy court, but he showed no sign of fatigue.

He did not look at the prisoner as he gathered his notes into a neat sheaf and turned to address the jury, but the prisoner looked at him. Her eyes, like dark smudges under the heavy square brows, seemed equally without fear and without hope. They waited.

"Members of the jury—"

The patient old eyes seemed to sum them up and take stock of their united intelligence. Three respectable tradesmen—a tall, argumentative one, a stout, embarrassed one with a drooping moustache, and an unhappy one with a bad cold; a director of a large company, anxious not to waste valuable time; a publican, incongruously cheerful; two youngish men of the artisan class; a nondescript, elderly man, of educated appearance, who might have been anything; an artist with a red beard disguising a weak chin; three women—an elderly spinster, a stout capable woman who kept a sweet-shop, and a harassed wife and mother whose thoughts seemed to be continually straying to her abandoned hearth.

"Members of the jury—you have listened with great patience and attention to the evidence in this very distressing case, and it is now my duty to sum up the facts and arguments which have been put before you by the learned

Attorney-General and by the learned Counsel for the Defence, and to put them in order as clearly as possible, so as to help you in forming your decision.

"But first of all, perhaps I ought to say a few words with regard to that decision itself. You know, I am sure, that it is a great principle of English law that every accused person is held to be innocent unless and until he is proved otherwise. It is not necessary for him, or her, to prove innocence; it is, in the modern slang phrase, 'up to' the Crown to prove guilt, and unless you are quite satisfied that the Crown has done this beyond all reasonable doubt, it is your duty to return a verdict of 'Not Guilty.' That does not necessarily mean that the prisoner has established her innocence by proof; it simply means that the Crown has failed to produce in your minds an undoubted conviction of her guilt."

Salcombe Hardy, lifting his drowned-violet eyes for a moment from his reporter's note-book, scribbled two words on a slip of paper and pushed them over to Waffles Newton. "Judge hostile." Waffles nodded. They were old hounds on this blood-trail.

The judge creaked on.

"You may perhaps wish to hear from me exactly what is meant by those words 'reasonable doubt.' They mean, just so much doubt as you might have in every-day life about an ordinary matter of business. This is a case of murder, and it might be natural for you to think that, in such a case, the words mean more than this. But that is not so. They do not mean that you must cast about for fantastical solutions of what seems to you plain and simple. They do not mean those nightmare doubts which sometimes torment us at four o'clock in the morning when we have not slept very well. They only mean that the proof must be such as you would accept about a plain matter of buying and selling, or some such commonplace transaction. You must not strain your belief in favour of the prisoner any more, of course, than you must accept proof of her guilt without the most careful scrutiny.

"Having said just these few words, so that you may not feel too much overwhelmed by the heavy responsibility laid upon you by your duty to the State, I will now begin at the beginning and try to place the story that we have heard, as clearly as possible before you.

"The case for the Crown is that the prisoner, Harriet Vane, murdered Philip Boyes by poisoning him with arsenic. I need not detain you by going through the proofs offered by Sir James Lubbock and the other doctors who have given evidence as to the cause of death. The Crown say he died of arsenical poisoning, and the defence do not dispute it. The evidence is, therefore, that the death was due to arsenic, and you must accept that as a fact. The only question that remains for you is whether, in fact, that arsenic was deliberately administered by the prisoner with intent to murder.

"The deceased, Philip Boyes, was, as you have heard, a writer. He was thirty-six years old, and he had published five novels and a large number of essays and articles. All these literary works were of what is sometimes called an 'advanced' type. They preached doctrines which may seem to some of us immoral or seditious, such as atheism, and anarchy, and what is known as free love. His private life appears to have been conducted, for some time at least, in accordance with these doctrines.

"At any rate, at some time in the year 1927, he became acquainted with Harriet Vane. They met in some of those artistic and literary circles where 'advanced' topics are discussed, and after a time they became very friendly. The prisoner is also a novelist by profession, and it is very important to remember that she is a writer of so-called 'mystery' or 'detective' stories, such as deal with various ingenious methods of committing murder and other crimes.

"You have heard the prisoner in the witness-box, and

you have heard the various people who came forward to give evidence as to her character. You have been told that she is a young woman of great ability, brought up on strictly religious principles, who, through no fault of her own was left, at the age of twenty-three, to make her own way in the world. Since that time—and she is now twenty-nine years old—she has worked industriously to keep herself, and it is very much to her credit that she has, by her own exertions, made herself independent in a legitimate way, owing nothing to anybody and accepting help from no one.

"She has told us herself, with great candour, how she became deeply attached to Philip Boyes, and how, for a considerable time, she held out against his persuasions to live with him in an irregular manner. There was, in fact, no reason at all why he should not have married her honourably; but apparently he represented himself as being conscientiously opposed to any formal marriage. You have the evidence of Sylvia Marriott and Eiluned Price that the prisoner was made very unhappy by this attitude which he chose to take up, and you have heard also that he was a very handsome and attractive man, whom any woman might have found it difficult to resist.

"At any rate, in March of 1928, the prisoner, worn out, as she tells us, by his unceasing importunities, gave in, and consented to live on terms of intimacy with him, outside the bonds of marriage.

"Now you may feel, and quite properly, that this was a very wrong thing to do. You may, after making all allowances for this young woman's unprotected position, still feel that she was a person of unstable moral character. You will not be led away by the false glamour which certain writers contrive to throw about 'free love,' into thinking that this was anything but an ordinary, vulgar act of misbehavior. Sir Impey Biggs, very rightly using all his great eloquence on behalf of his client, has painted this action of Harriet Vane's in very rosy colours; he has spoken of unselfish sacrifice and self-immolation, and has reminded you that, in such a situation, the woman always has to pay more heavily than the man. You will not, I am sure, pay too much attention to this. You know quite well the difference between right and wrong in such matters, and you may think that, if Harriet Vane had not become to a certain extent corrupted by the unwholesome influences among which she lived, she would have shown a truer heroism by dismissing Philip Boyes from her society.

"But, on the other hand, you must be careful not to attach the wrong kind of importance to this lapse. It is one thing for a man or woman to live an immoral life, and quite another thing to commit murder. You may perhaps think that one step into the path of wrongdoing makes the next one easier, but you must not give too much weight to that consideration. You are entitled to take it into account, but you must not be too much prejudiced."

The judge paused for a moment, and Freddy Arbuthnot jerked an elbow into the ribs of Lord Peter Wimsey, who appeared to be a prey to gloom.

"I should jolly well hope not. Damn it, if every little game led to murder, they'd be hanging half of us for doin' in the other half."

"And which half would *you* be in?" enquired his lordship, fixing him for a moment with a cold eye and then returning his glance to the dock.

"Victim," said the Hon. Freddy, "victim. Me for the corpse in the library."

"Philip Boyes and the prisoner lived together in this fashion," went on the judge, "for nearly a year. Various friends have testified that they appeared to live on terms of the greatest mutual affection. Miss Price said that, although Harriet Vane obviously felt her unfortunate position very acutely—cutting herself off from her family friends and refusing to thrust herself into company where her social outlawry might cause embarrassment and so on—yet she was extremely loyal to her lover and expressed herself proud and happy to be his companion.

"Nevertheless, in February 1929 there was a quarrel, and the couple separated. It is not denied that the quarrel took place. Mr. and Mrs. Dyer, who occupy the flat immediately above Philip Boyes', say that they heard loud talking in angry voices, the man swearing and the woman crying, and that the next day, Harriet Vane packed up all her things and left the house for good. The curious feature in the case, and one which you must consider very carefully, is the reason assigned for the quarrel. As to this, the only evidence we have is the prisoner's own. According to Miss Marriott, with whom Harriet Vane took refuge after the separation, the prisoner steadily refused to give any information on the subject, saying only that she had been painfully deceived by Boyes and never wished to hear his name spoken again.

"Now it might be supposed from this that Boyes had given the prisoner cause for grievance against him, by unfaithfulness, or unkindness, or simply by a continued refusal to regularise the situation in the eyes of the world. But the prisoner absolutely denies this. According to her statement—and on this point her evidence is confirmed by a letter which Philip Boyes wrote to his father—Boyes did at length offer her legal marriage, and this was the cause of the quarrel. You may think this a very remarkable statement to make, but that is the prisoner's evidence on oath.

"It would be natural for you to think that this proposal of marriage takes away any suggestion that the prisoner had a cause of grievance against Boyes. Anyone would say that, under such circumstances, she could have no motive for wishing to murder this young man, but rather the contrary. Still, there is the fact of the quarrel, and the prisoner herself states that this honourable, though belated, proposal was unwelcome to her. She does not say—as she might very reasonably say, and as her counsel has most forcefully and impressively said for her, that this marriage-offer completely does away with any pretext for enmity on her part towards Philip Boyes. Sir Impey Biggs says so, but that is not what the prisoner says. She says—and you must try to put yourselves in her place and understand her point of view if you can—that she was angry with Boyes because, after persuading her against her will to adopt his principles of conduct, he then renounced those principles and so, as she says, 'made a fool of her.'

"Well, that is for you to consider: whether the offer which was in fact made could reasonably be construed into a motive for murder. I must impress upon you that no other motive has been suggested in evidence."

At this point the elderly spinster on the jury was seen to be making a note—a vigorous note, to judge from the action of her pencil on the paper. Lord Peter Wimsey shook his head slowly two or three times and muttered something under his breath.

"After this," said the judge, "nothing particular seems to have happened to these two people for three months or so, except that Harriet Vane left Miss Marriott's house and took a small flat of her own in Doughty Street, while Philip Boyes, on the contrary, finding his solitary life depressing, accepted the invitation of his cousin, Mr. Norman Urquhart, to stay at the latter's house in Woburn Square. Although living in the same quarter of London, Boyes and the accused do not seem to have met very often after the separation. Once or twice there was an accidental encounter at the house of a friend. The dates of these occasions cannot be ascertained with any certainty—they were informal parties—but there is some evidence that there was a meeting towards the end of March, another in the second week in April, and a third some time in May. These times are worth noting, though, as the exact day is left doubtful, you must not attach too much importance to them.

"However, we now come to a date of the very greatest importance. On April 10th, a young woman, who has been identified as Harriet Vane, entered the chemist's shop kept by Mr. Brown in Southampton Row, and purchased two ounces of commercial arsenic, saying that she needed it to destroy rats. She signed the poison-book in the name of Mary Slater, and the handwriting has been identified as that of the prisoner. Moreover, the prisoner herself admits having made this purchase, for certain reasons of her own. For this reason it is comparatively unimportant—but you may think it worth noting—that the housekeeper of the flats where Harriet Vane lives has come here and told you that there are no rats on the premises, and never have been in the whole time of her residence there.

"On May 5th. we have another purchase of arsenic. The prisoner, as she herself states, this time procured a tin of arsenical weed-killer, of the same brand that was mentioned in the Kidwelly poisoning case. This time she gave the name of Edith Waters. There is no garden attached to the flats where she lives, nor could there be any conceivable use for weed-killer on the premises.

"On various occasions also, during the period from the middle of March to the beginning of May, the prisoner purchased other poisons, including prussic acid (ostensibly for photographic purposes) and strychnine. There was also an attempt to obtain aconitine, which was not successful. A different shop was approached and a different name given in each case. The arsenic is the only poison which directly concerns this case, but these other purchases are of some importance, as throwing light on the prisoner's activities at this time.

"The prisoner has given an explanation of these purchases which you must consider for what it is worth. She says that she was engaged at that time in writing a novel about poisoning, and that she bought the drugs in order to prove by experiment how easy it was for an ordinary person to get hold of deadly poisons. In proof of this, her publisher, Mr. Trufoot, has produced the manuscript of the book. You have had it in your hands, and you will be given it again, if you like, when I have finished my summing-up, to look at in your own room. Passages were read out to you, showing that the subject of the book was murder by arsenic, and there is a description in it of a young woman going to a chemist's shop and buying a considerable quantity of this deadly substance. And I must mention here what I should have mentioned before, namely, that the arsenic purchased from Mr. Brown was the ordinary commercial arsenic, which is coloured with charcoal or indigo, as the law requires, in order that it may not be mistaken for sugar or any other innocent substance."

Salcombe Hardy groaned: "How long, O Lord, how long shall we have to listen to all this tripe about commercial arsenic? Murderers learn it now at their mother's knee."

"I particularly want you to remember those dates—I will give them to you again—the 10th. April and the 5th. May." (The Jury wrote them down. Lord Peter Wimsey murmured: "They all wrote down on their slates, 'She doesn't believe there's an atom of meaning in it.'" The Hon. Freddy said "What? What?" and the judge turned over another page of his notes.)

"About this time, Philip Boyes began to suffer from renewed attacks of a gastric trouble to which he had been subject from time to time during his life. You have read the evidence of Dr. Green, who attended him for something of the sort during his University career. That is some time ago; but there is also Dr. Weare, who, in 1925 prescribed for a similar attack. Not grave illnesses, but painful and exhausting, with sickness and so on, and aching in the limbs. Plenty of people have such troubles from time to time. Still, there is a coincidence of dates here which may be significant. We get these attacks—noted in Dr. Weare's case-book—one on the 31st. of March, one on the 15th. of April and one on the 12th. of May. Three sets of coincidences—as you may perhaps think them to be—Harriet Vane and Philip Boyes meet 'towards the end of March,' and he has an attack of gastritis on March 31st; on 10th. April Harriet Vane purchases two ounces of arsenic—they meet again 'in the second week in April,' and on April 15th, he has another attack; on 5th. May, there is the purchase of weed-killer—'some time in May' there is another meeting, and on the 12th. May he is taken ill for the third time. You may think that is rather curious, but you must not forget that the Crown have failed to prove any purchase of arsenic before the meeting in March. You must bear that in mind when considering this point.

"After the third attack—the one in May—the doctor advises Boyes to go away for a change, and he selects the north-west corner of Wales. He goes to Harlech, and spends a very pleasant time there and is much better. But he has a friend to accompany him, Mr. Ryland Vaughan, whom you have seen, and this friend says that 'Philip was not happy'. In fact. Mr. Vaughan formed the opinion that he was fretting after Harriet Vane. His bodily health improved, but he grew mentally depressed. And so on June 16th, we find him writing a letter to Miss Vane. Now that is an important letter, so I will read it to you once more:

'Dear Harriet,

Life is an utter mess-up. I can't stick it out here any longer. I've decided to cut adrift and take a trip out West. But before I go, I want to see you once again and find out if it isn't possible to put things straight again. You must do as you like, of course, but I still cannot understand the attitude you take up. If I can't make you see the thing in the right perspective this time I'll chuck it for good. I shall be in town on the 20th. Let me have a line to say when I can come round.

Yours,

P.'

"Now that, as you have realised, is a most ambiguous letter. Sir Impey Biggs, with arguments of great weight, has suggested that by the expressions 'cut adrift and take a trip out west,' 'I can't stick it out here,' and 'chuck it for good,' the writer was expressing his intention to make away with himself if he could not effect a reconciliation with the accused. He points out that 'to go west' is a well-known metaphor for dying, and that, of course, may be convincing to you. But Mr. Urquhart, when examined on the subject by the Attorney-General, said that he supposed the letter to refer to a project which he himself had suggested to the deceased, of taking a voyage across the Atlantic to Barbados, by way of change of scene. And the learned Attorney-General makes this other point that when the writer says, 'I can't stick it out *here* any longer,' he means, here in Britain, or perhaps merely 'here at Harlech,' and that if the phrase had reference to suicide it would read simply, 'I can't stick it out any longer.'

"No doubt you have formed your own opinion on this point. It is important to note that the deceased asks for an appointment on the 20th. The reply to this letter is before us; it reads:

'Dear Phil,
     You can come round at 9.30 on the 20th. if you like, but you certainly will not make me change my mind.'

"And it is signed simply 'M.' A very cold letter, you may think—almost hostile in tone. And yet the appointment is made for 9.30.

"I shall not have to keep your attention very much longer, but I do ask for it at this point, specially—though you have been attending most patiently and industriously all the time—because we now come to the actual day of the death itself."

The old man clasped his hands one over the other upon the sheaf of notes and leaned a little forward. He had it all in his head, though he had known nothing of it until the last three days. He had not reached the time to babble of green fields and childhood ways; he still had firm hold of the present; he held it pinned down flat under his wrinkled fingers with their grey, chalky nails.

"Philip Boyes and Mr. Vaughan came back to town together on the evening of the 19th, and there would seem to be no doubt at all that Boyes was then in the best of health. Boyes spent the night with Mr. Vaughan, and they breakfasted together in the usual way upon bacon and eggs, toast, marmalade and coffee. At 11 o'clock Boyes had a Guinness, observing that, according to the advertisements it was 'Good for you.' At 1 o'clock he ate a hearty lunch at his club, and in the afternoon he played several sets at tennis with Mr. Vaughan and some other friends. During the game the remark was made by one of the players that Harlech had done Boyes good, and he replied that he was feeling fitter than he had done for many months.

"At half-past seven he went round to have dinner with his cousin, Mr. Norman Urquhart. Nothing at all unusual in his manner or appearance was noticed, either by Mr. Urquhart or by the maid who waited at table. Dinner was served at 8 o'clock exactly, and I think it would be a good thing if you were to write down that time (if you have not already done so) and also the list of things eaten and drunk.

"The two cousins dined alone together, and first, by way of cocktail, each had a glass of sherry. The wine was a fine Oloroso of 1847, and the maid decanted it from a fresh bottle and poured it into the glasses as they sat in the library. Mr. Urquhart retains the dignified old-fashioned custom of having the maid in attendance throughout the meal, so that we have here the advantage of two witnesses during this part of the evening. You saw the maid, Hannah Westlock, in the box, and I think you will say she gave the impression of being a sensible and observant witness.

"Well, there was the sherry. Then came a cup of cold

bouillon, served by Hannah Westlock from the tureen on the sideboard. It was very strong, good soup, set to a clear jelly. Both men had some, and, after dinner, the bouillon was finished by the cook and Miss Westlock in the kitchen.

"After the soup came a piece of turbot with sauce. The portions were again carved at the sideboard, the sauce-boat was handed to each in turn, and the dish was then sent out to be finished in the kitchen.

"Then came a *poulet en casserole*—that is, chicken cut up and stewed slowly with vegetables in a fireproof cooking utensil. Both men had some of this, and the maids finished the dish.

"The final course was a sweet omelette, which was made at the table in a chafing-dish by Philip Boyes himself. Both Mr. Urquhart and his cousin were very particular about eating an omelette the moment it came from the pan—and a very good rule it is, and I advise you all to treat omelettes in the same way and never to allow them to stand, or they will get tough. Four eggs were brought to the table in their shells, and Mr. Urquhart broke them one by one into a bowl, adding sugar from a sifter. Then he handed the bowl to Mr. Boyes, saying: 'You're the real dab at omelettes, Philip—I'll leave this to you'. Philip Boyes then beat the eggs and sugar together, cooked the omelette in the chafing-dish, filled it with hot jam, which was brought in by Hannah Westlock, and then himself divided it into two portions, giving one to Mr. Urquhart and taking the remainder himself.

"I have been a little careful to remind you of all these things, to show that we have good proof that every dish served at dinner was partaken of by two people at least, and in most cases by four. The omelette—the only dish which did not go out to the kitchen—was prepared by Philip Boyes himself and shared by his cousin. Neither Mr. Urquhart, Miss Westlock nor the cook, Mrs. Pettican, felt any ill-effects from this meal.

"I should mention also that there was one article of diet which was partaken of by Philip Boyes alone, and that was a bottle of Burgundy. It was a fine old Corton, and was brought to the table in its original bottle. Mr. Urquhart drew the cork and then handed the bottle intact to Philip Boyes, saying that he himself would not take any—he had been advised not to drink at mealtimes. Philip Boyes drank two glassfuls and the remainder of the bottle was fortunately preserved. As you have already heard, the wine was later analysed and found to be quite harmless.

"This brings us to 9 o'clock. After dinner, coffee is offered, but Boyes excuses himself on the ground that he does not care for Turkish coffee, and moreover will probably be given coffee by Harriet Vane. At 9.15 Boyes leaves Mr. Urquhart's house in Woburn Square, and is driven in a taxi to the house where Miss Vane has her flat, No. 100 Doughty Street—a distance of about half a mile. We have it from Harriet Vane herself, from Mrs. Bright, a resident in the ground floor flat, and from Police Constable D.1234 who was passing along the street at the time, that he was standing on the doorstep, ringing the prisoner's bell, at 25 minutes past 9. She was on the look-out for him and let him in immediately.

"Now, as the interview was naturally a private one, we have no account of it to go upon but that of the prisoner. She has told us that as soon as he came in, she offered him 'a cup of coffee which was standing ready upon the gas-ring.' Now, when the learned Attorney-General heard the prisoner say that, he immediately asked what the coffee was standing ready in. The prisoner, apparently not quite understanding the purport of the question, replied 'in the fender, to keep hot.' When the question was repeated more clearly, she explained that the coffee was made in a saucepan, and that it was this which was placed upon the gas-ring in the fender. The Attorney-General then drew the prisoner's attention to her previous statement made to the police, in which this expression appeared: 'I had a cup of coffee ready for him on his arrival.' You will see at once the importance of this. If the cups of coffee were prepared and poured out separately before the arrival of the deceased, there was every opportunity to place poison in one of the cups beforehand and offer the prepared cup to Philip Boyes; but if the coffee was poured out from the saucepan in the deceased's presence, the opportunity would be rather less, though of course the thing might easily be done while Boyes' attention was momentarily distracted. The prisoner explained that in her statement she used the phrase 'a cup of coffee' merely as denoting 'a certain quantity of coffee.' You yourselves will be able to judge whether that is a usual and natural form of expression. The deceased is said by her to have taken no milk or sugar in his coffee, and you have the testimony of Mr. Urquhart and Mr. Vaughan that it was his usual habit to drink his after-dinner coffee black and unsweetened.

"According to the prisoner's evidence, the interview was not a satisfactory one. Reproaches were uttered on both sides, and at 10 o'clock or thereabouts, the deceased expressed his intention of leaving her. She says that he appeared uneasy and remarked that he was not feeling well, adding that her behaviour had greatly upset him.

"At ten minutes past ten—and I want you to note these times very carefully, the taxi-driver Burke, who was standing on the rank in Guilford Street, was approached by Philip Boyes and told to take him to Woburn Square. He says that Boyes spoke in a hurried and abrupt tone, like that of a person in distress of mind or body. When the taxi stopped before Mr. Urquhart's house, Boyes did not get out, and Burke opened the door to see what was the matter. He found the deceased huddled in a corner with his hand pressed over his stomach and his face pale and covered with perspiration. He asked him whether he was ill, and the deceased replied: 'Yes, rotten.' Burke helped him

out and rang the bell, supporting him with one arm as
they stood on the doorstep. Hannah Westlock opened the
door. Philip Boyes seemed hardly able to walk; his body
was bent almost double, and he sank groaning into a hall-
chair and asked for brandy. She brought him a stiff brandy-
and-soda from the dining-room, and after drinking this,
Boyes recovered sufficiently to take money from his pocket
and pay for the taxi.

"As he still seemed very ill, Hannah Westlock summoned
Mr. Urquhart from the library. He said to Boyes, 'Hullo,
old man—what's the matter with you?' Boyes replied, 'God
knows! I feel awful. It can't have been the chicken.' Mr.
Urquhart said he hoped not, he hadn't noticed anything
wrong with it, and Boyes answered, No, he supposed it was
one of his usual attacks, but he'd never felt anything like
this before. He was taken upstairs to bed, and Dr. Grainger
was summoned by telephone, as being the nearest physician available.

"Before the doctor's arrival, the patient vomited violently, and thereafter continued to vomit persistently. Dr.
Grainger diagnosed the trouble as acute gastritis. There
was a high temperature and rapid pulse, and the patient's
abdomen was acutely painful to pressure, but the doctor
found nothing indicative of any trouble in the nature of
appendicitis or peritonitis. He therefore went back to his
surgery, and made up a soothing medicine to control the
vomiting—a mixture of bicarbonate of potash, tincture of
oranges, and chloroform—no other drugs.

"Next day the vomiting still persisted, and Dr. Weare
was called in to consult with Dr. Grainger, as he was well
acquainted with the patient's constitution."

Here the judge paused and glanced at the clock.

"Time is getting on, and as the medical evidence has still
to be passed in review, I will adjourn the Court now for
lunch."

"He would," said the Hon. Freddy, "just at the beastliest moment when everybody's appetite is thoroughly taken away. Come on, Wimsey, let's go and fold a chop into the system, shall we?—Hullo!"

Wimsey had pushed past without heeding him, and was making his way down into the body of the court, where Sir Impey Biggs stood conferring with his juniors.

"Seems to be in a bit of a stew," said Mr. Arbuthnot, meditatively. "Gone to put an alternative theory of some kind, I expect. Wonder why I came to this bally show. Tedious, don't you know, and the girl's not even pretty. Don't think I'll come back after grub."

He struggled out, and found himself face to face with the Dowager Duchess of Denver.

"Come and have lunch, Duchess," said Freddy, hopefully. He liked the Dowager.

"I'm waiting for Peter, thanks, Freddy. Such an interesting case and interesting people, too, don't you think, though what the jury make of it I don't know, with faces like hams most of them, except the artist, who wouldn't have any features at all if it wasn't for that dreadful tie and his beard, looking like Christ, only not really Christ but one of those Italian ones in a pink frock and blue top thing. Isn't that Peter's Miss Climpson on the jury, how does she get there, I wonder?"

"He's put her into a house somewhere round about, I fancy," said Freddy, "with a typewriting office to look after and live over the shop and run those comic charity stunts of his. Funny old soul, isn't she? Stepped out of a magazine of the 'nineties. But she seems to suit his work all right and all that."

"Yes—such a good thing too, answering all those shady advertisements and then getting the people shown up and so courageous too, some of them the horridest oily people, and murderers I shouldn't wonder with automatic thingummies and life-preservers in every pocket, and very likely a gas-oven full of bones like Landru, so clever, wasn't he?

And really *such* women—born murderees as somebody says —quite pig-faced but not of course deserving it and possibly the photographs don't do them justice, poor things.

The Duchess was even more rambling than usual, thought Freddy, and as she spoke her eyes wandered to her son with a kind of anxiety unusual in her.

"Top-hole to see old Wimsey back, isn't it?" he said, with simple kindliness. "Wonderful how keen he is on this sort of thing, don't you know. Rampages off the minute he gets home like the jolly old war-horse sniffing the T.N.T. Regularly up to the eyes in it."

"Well, it's one of Chief-Inspector Parker's cases, and they're such great friends, you know, quite like David and Beersheba—or do I mean Daniel?"

Wimsey joined them at this complicated moment, and tucked his mother's arm affectionately in his own.

"Frightfully sorry to keep you waiting, Mater, but I had to say a word to Biggy. He's having a rotten time, and that old Jeffreys of a judge looks as though he was getting measured for a black cap. I'm going home to burn my books. Dangerous to know too much about poisons, don't you think? Be thou as chaste as ice, as pure as snow, thou shalt not escape the old Bailey."

"The young woman doesn't seem to have tried that recipe, does she?" remarked Freddy.

"You ought to be on the jury," retorted Wimsey, with unusual acidity, "I bet that's what they're all saying at this moment. I'm convinced that that foreman is a teetotaller— I saw ginger-beer going into the jury-room, and I only hope it explodes and blows his inside through the top of his skull."

"All right, all right," returned Mr. Arbuthnot, soothingly, "what you want is a drink."

CHAPTER II

THE SCRAMBLE for places subsided; the jury returned; the prisoner reappeared in the dock suddenly, like a jack-in-the-box; the judge resumed his seat. Some petals had spilt from the roses. The old voice took up its tale where it had left off.

"Members of the jury—there is no need, I think, for me to recall the course of Philip Boyes' illness in great detail. The nurse was called in on June 21st, and during that day the doctors visited the patient three times. His condition grew steadily worse. There was persistent vomiting and diarrhoea, and he could not keep any food or medicine down at all. On the day after, the 22nd, he was worse still —in great pain, the pulse growing weaker, and the skin about the mouth getting dry and peeling off. The doctors gave him every attention, but could do nothing for him. His father was summoned, and when he arrived he found his son conscious, but unable to lift himself. He was able to speak, however, and in the presence of his father and Nurse Williams he made the remark, 'I'm going out, Dad, and I'm glad to be through with it. Harriet'll be rid of me now—I didn't know she hated me quite so much.' Now that was a very remarkable speech, and we have heard two very different interpretations put upon it. It is for you to say whether, in your opinion, he meant: 'She has succeeded in getting rid of me; I didn't know she hated me enough to poison me,' or whether he meant, 'When I realised she hated me so much, I decided I did not want to live any longer'—or whether, perhaps, he meant neither of these things. When people are very ill, they sometimes get fantastic ideas, and sometimes they wander in their minds; perhaps you may feel that it is not profitable to take too much for granted. Still, those words are part of the evidence, and you are entitled to take them into account.

"During the night he became gradually weaker and lost consciousness, and at 3 o'clock in the morning he died, without ever regaining it. That was on the 23rd. of June.

"Now, up to this time, no suspicion of any kind had been aroused. Both Dr. Grainger and Dr. Weare formed the opinion that the cause of death was acute gastritis, and we need not blame them for coming to this conclusion, because it was quite consistent both with the symptoms of the illness and with the past history of the patient. A death-certificate was given in the usual way, and the funeral took place on the 28th.

"Well, then something happened which frequently does happen in cases of this kind, and that is that somebody begins to talk. It was Nurse Williams who talked in this particular case, and while you will probably think that this was a very wrong and a very indiscreet thing for a nurse to do, yet, as it turns out, it was a good thing that she did. Of course, she ought to have told Dr. Weare or Dr. Grainger of her suspicions at the time, but she did not do this, and we may at least feel glad to know that, in the doctor's opinions, even if she had done so, and if they had discovered that the illness was caused by arsenic, they would not have been able to do anything more to save the life of this unfortunate man. At any rate, what happened was that Nurse Williams was sent, during the last week of June, to nurse another patient of Dr. Weare's, who happened to belong to the same literary set in Bloomsbury as Philip Boyes and Harriet Vane, and while she was there, she spoke about Philip Boyes, and said that, in her opinion, the illness looked very much like poisoning, and she even mentioned the word arsenic. Well, you know how a thing like that gets about. One person tells another and it is discussed at tea-parties, or what are known, I believe, as cocktail parties, and very soon a story gets spread about, and people mention names and take sides. Miss Marriott and Miss Price were told about it, and it also got to the ears of Mr. Vaughan. Now Mr. Vaughan had been greatly distressed and surprised by Philip Boyes' death, especially as he had been with him in Wales, and knew how much he had improved in health while on his holiday, and he also felt very strongly that Harriet Vane had behaved badly about the love-affair. Mr. Vaughan felt that some action ought to be taken about the matter, and went to Mr. Urquhart and put the story before him. Now Mr. Urquhart is a solicitor, and is therefore inclined to take a cautious view of rumours and suspicions, and he warned Mr. Vaughan that it was not wise to go about making accusations against people, for fear of an action for libel. At the same time, he naturally felt uneasy that such a thing should be said about a relation who had died in his house. He took the course—the very sensible course—of consulting Dr. Weare and suggesting that, if he was quite certain that the illness was due to gastritis and nothing else, he should take steps to rebuke Nurse Williams and put an end to the talk. Dr. Weare was naturally very much surprised and upset to hear what was being said, but, since the suggestion had been made, he could not deny that—taking the symptoms only into account—there was just the bare possibility of something of the sort, because, as you have already heard in the medical evidence, the symptoms of arsenical poisoning and of acute gastritis are really indistinguishable.

"When this was communicated to Mr. Vaughan, he was confirmed in his suspicions, and wrote to the elder Mr. Boyes suggesting an enquiry. Mr. Boyes was naturally very much shocked, and said at once that the matter should be taken up. He had known of the liaison with Harriet Vane, and had noticed that she did not come to enquire after Philip Boyes, nor attend the funeral, and this had struck him as heartless behaviour. In the end, the police were communicated with and an exhumation order obtained.

"You have heard the result of the analysis made by Sir James Lubbock and Mr. Stephen Fordyce. There was a great deal of discussion about methods of analysis and the way that arsenic behaves in the body and so on, but, I think we need not trouble too much about those fine details. The chief points in the evidence seemed to me to be these, which you may note down if you care to do so.

"The analysts took certain organs of the body—the stomach, intestines, kidneys, liver and so on, and analyzed portions of these and found that they all contained arsenic. They were able to weigh the quantity of arsenic found in these various portions, and they calculated from that the quantity of arsenic present in the whole body. Then they had to allow so much for the amount of arsenic eliminated from the body by the vomiting and diarrhoea and also through the kidneys, because the kidneys play a very large part in the elimination of this particular poison. After making allowance for all these things, they formed the opinion that a large and fatal dose of arsenic—four or five grains, perhaps, had been taken about three days before the death.

"I do not know whether you quite followed all the technical arguments about this. I will try to tell you the chief points as I understood them. The nature of arsenic is to pass through the body very quickly, especially if it is taken with food or immediately following a meal, because the arsenic irritates the lining of the internal organs and speeds up the process of elimination. The action would be quicker if the arsenic were taken in liquid than if it were taken in the form of a powder. Where arsenic was taken with, or immediately on top of a meal, nearly the whole of it would be evacuated within twenty-four hours after the onset of the illness. So you see that, although the actual quantities found in the body may seem to you and me very small indeed, the mere fact that they were found there at all, after three days of persistent vomiting and diarrhoea and so on, points to a large dose having been taken at some time.

"Now there was a great deal of discussion about the time at which the symptoms first set in. It is suggested by the defence that Philip Boyes may have taken the arsenic himself at some time between leaving Harriet Vane's flat and hailing the taxi in Guilford Street; and they bring forward books which show that in many cases the onset of symptoms takes place in a very short time after taking the arsenic—a quarter of an hour, I think, was the shortest time mentioned where the arsenic was taken in liquid form. Now the prisoner's statement—and we have no other—is that Philip Boyes left her at 10 o'clock, and at ten minutes past he was in Guilford Street. He was then looking ill. It would not take many minutes to drive to Woburn Square at that hour of night, and by the time he got there, he was already in acute pain and hardly able to stand. Now Guilford Street is a very short way from Doughty Street—perhaps three minutes' walk—and you must ask yourselves, if the prisoner's statement is correct, what he did with those ten minutes. Did he occupy himself in going to some quiet spot and taking a dose of arsenic, which he must in that case have brought with him in anticipation of an unfavourable interview with the prisoner? And I may remind you here, that the defence have brought no evidence to show that Philip Boyes ever bought any arsenic, or had access to any arsenic. That is not to say he could not have obtained it—the purchases made by Harriet Vane show that the law about the sale of poisons is not always as effective as one would like it to be—but the fact remains that the defence have not been able to show that the deceased ever had arsenic in his possession. And while we are on this subject, I will mention that, curiously enough, the analysts could find no traces of the charcoal, or indigo, with which commercial arsenic is supposed to be mixed. Whether it was bought by the prisoner or by the deceased himself, you would expect to find traces of the colouring matter. But you may think it likely that all such traces would be removed from the body by the vomiting and purging which took place.

"As regards the suggestion of suicide, you will have to ask yourselves about those ten minutes—whether Boyes was taking a dose of arsenic, or whether, as is also possible, he felt unwell and sat down somewhere to recover himself, or whether, perhaps, he was merely roaming about in the vague way we sometimes do when we are feeling upset and unhappy. Or you may think that the prisoner was mistaken, or not speaking the truth, about the time he left the flat.

"You have also the prisoner's statement that Boyes mentioned, before he left her, that he was feeling unwell. If you think this had anything to do with the arsenic, it of course disposes of the suggestion that he took poison after leaving the flat.

"Then, when one looks into it, one finds that this question about the onset of symptoms is left very vague. Various doctors came here and told you about their own experiences and the cases quoted by medical authorities in books, and you will have noticed that there is no certainty at all about the time when the symptoms may be expected to appear. Sometimes it is a quarter of an hour or half an hour, sometimes two hours, sometimes as much as five or six, and, I believe, in one case as much as seven hours after taking the poison."

Here the Attorney-General rose respectfully and said: "In that case, me lud, I think I am right in saying that the poison was taken on an empty stomach."

"Thank you, I am much obliged to you for the reminder. That was a case in which the poison was taken on an empty stomach. I only mention these cases to show that we are dealing with a very uncertain phenomenon, and that is why I was particular to remind you of all the occasions on which

Philip Boyes took food during the day—the 20th of June, since there is always the possibility that you may have to take them into consideration."

"A beast, but a just beast," murmured Lord Peter Wimsey.

"I have purposely left out of consideration until now another point which arose out of the analysis, and that is the presence of arsenic in the hair. The deceased had curly hair, which he wore rather long; the front portion, when straightened out, measured about six or seven inches in places. Now, in this hair, arsenic was found, at the end closest to the head. It did not extend to the tips of the longest hair, but it was found near the roots, and Sir James Lubbock says that the quantity was greater than could be accounted for in any natural way. Occasionally, quite normal people are found to have minute traces of arsenic in the hair and skin and so on, but not to the amount found here. That is Sir James' opinion.

"Now you have been told—and the medical witnesses all agree in this—that if a person takes arsenic, a certain proportion of it will be deposited in the skin, nails and hair. It will be deposited in the root of the hair, and as the hair grows, the arsenic will be carried along with the growth of the hair, so that you get a rough idea, from seeing the position of the arsenic in the hair, how long the administration of arsenic has been going on. There was a good deal of discussion about this, but I think there was a fairly general agreement that, if you took a dose of arsenic, you might expect to find traces of it in the hair, close to the scalp, after about ten weeks. Hair grows at the rate of about six inches in a year, and the arsenic will grow out with it till it reaches the far end and is cut off. I am sure that the ladies on the jury will understand this very well, because I believe that the same thing occurs in the case of what is termed a 'permanent wave.' The wave is made in a certain portion of the hair, and after a time it grows out, and the hair near the scalp comes up straight and has to be waved again. You can tell by the position of the wave, how long ago the waving was done. In the same way, if a finger-nail is bruised, the discolouration will gradually grow up the nail until it reaches the point where you can cut it off with the scissors.

"Now it has been said that the presence of arsenic in and about the roots of Philip Boyes' hair indicates that he must have taken arsenic three months at least before his death. You will consider what importance is to be attached to this in view of the prisoner's purchases of arsenic in April and May, and of the deceased's attacks of sickness in March, April and May. The quarrel with the prisoner took place in February; he was ill in March and he died in June. There are five months between the quarrel and the death, and four months between the first illness and the death, and you may think that there is some significance in these dates.

"We now come to the enquiries made by the police. When suspicion was aroused, detectives investigated Harriet Vane's movements and subsequently went to her flat to take a statement from her. When they told her that Boyes was found to have died of arsenic poisoning, she appeared very much surprised, and said, 'Arsenic? What an extraordinary thing!' And then, she laughed, and said, 'Why, I am writing a book all about arsenic poisoning.' They asked her about the purchases of arsenic and other poisons which she had made and she admitted them quite readily and at once gave the same explanation that she gave here in court. They asked what she had done with the poisons, and she replied that she had burnt them because they were dangerous things to have about. The flat was searched, but no poisons of any kind were found, except such things as aspirin and a few ordinary medicines of that kind. She absolutely denied having administered arsenic or any kind of poison to Philip Boyes. She was asked whether the arsenic could possibly have got into the coffee by accident, and replied that that was quite impossible, as she had destroyed all the poisons before the end of May."

Here Sir Impey Biggs interposed and begged with submission to suggest that his lordship should remind the jury of the evidence given by Mr. Challoner.

"Certainly, Sir Impey, I am obliged to you. You remember that Mr. Challoner is Harriet Vane's literary agent. He came here to tell us that he had discussed with her as long ago as last December the subject of her forthcoming book, and she then told him that it was to be about poisons, and very probably about arsenic. So you may think it is a point in the prisoner's favour that this intention of studying the purchase and administration of arsenic was already in her mind some time before the quarrel with Philip Boyes took place. She evidently gave considerable thought to the subject, for there were a number of books on her shelves dealing with forensic medicine and toxicology, and also the reports of several famous poison trials, including the Madeleine Smith case, the Seddon case and the Armstrong case—all of which were cases of arsenical poisoning.

"Well, I think that is the case as it is presented to you. This woman is charged with having murdered her former lover by arsenic. He undoubtedly did take arsenic, and if you are satisfied that she gave it to him with intent to injure or kill him, and that he died of it, then it is your duty to find her guilty of murder.

"Sir Impey Biggs, in his able and eloquent speech, has put it to you that she had very little motive for such a murder, but I am bound to tell you that murders are very often committed for what seem to be most inadequate motives—if, indeed, any motive can be called adequate for such a crime. Especially where the parties are husband and wife, or have lived together as husband and wife, there are likely to be passionate feelings which may tend to crimes of violence in persons with inadequate moral standards and of unbalanced mind.

"The prisoner had the means—the arsenic—she had the expert knowledge, and she had the opportunity to administer it. The defence say that this is not enough. They say the Crown must go further and prove that the poison could not have been taken in any other way—by accident, or with suicidal intent. That is for you to judge. If you feel that there is any reasonable doubt that the prisoner gave this poison to Philip Boyes deliberately, you must bring her in Not Guilty of murder. You are not bound to decide how it was given, if it was not given by her. Consider the circumstances of the case as a whole, and say what conclusion you have come to."

CHAPTER III

"THEY won't be long, I shouldn't think," said Waffles
Newton, "it's pretty damned obvious. Look here, old man,
I'm going to push my stuff in. Will you let me know what
happens?"

"Sure," said Salcombe Hardy, "if you don't mind dropping mine in at our place as you go. You couldn't send me
a drink by 'phone, could you? My mouth's like the bottom
of a parrot's cage." He looked at his watch. "We shall miss
the 6.30 edition, I'm afraid, unless they hurry up. The old
man is careful but he's damned slow."

"They can't in decency not make a pretence of consulting about it," said Newton. "I give them twenty minutes.
They'll want a smoke. So do I. I'll be back at ten to, in
case."

He wriggled his way out. Cuthbert Logan, who reported
for a morning paper, and was a man of more leisure, settled down to write up a word-picture of the trial. He was
a phlegmatic and sober person and could write as comfortably in court as anywhere else. He liked to be on the spot
when things happened, and to note down glances, tones of
voice, colour effects and so forth. His copy was always entertaining, and sometimes even distinguished.

Freddy Arbuthnot, who had not, after all, gone home
after lunch, thought it was time to do so now. He fidgeted,
and Wimsey frowned at him. The Dowager Duchess made
her way along the benches and squeezed in next to Lord
Peter. Sir Impey Biggs, having watched over his client's interests to the last, disappeared, chatting cheerfully to the
Attorney-General, and followed by the smaller legal fry.
The dock was deserted. On the bench the red roses stood
solitary, their petals dropping.

Chief-Inspector Parker, disengaging himself from a group of friends, came slowly up through the crowd and greeted the Dowager. "And what do you think of it, Peter?" he added, turning to Wimsey, "rather neatly got up, eh?"

"Charles," said Wimsey, "you ought not to be allowed out without me. You've made a mistake, old man."

"Made a mistake?"

"She didn't do it."

"Oh, come!"

"She did not do it. It's very convincing and water-tight, but it's all wrong."

"You don't really think that."

"I do."

Parker looked distressed. He had confidence in Wimsey's judgment, and, in spite of his own interior certainty, he felt shaken.

"My dear man, where's the flaw in it?"

"There isn't one. It's damnably knife-proof. There's nothing wrong about it at all, except that the girl's innocent."

"You're turning into a common or garden psychologist," said Parker, with an uneasy laugh, "isn't he, Duchess?"

"I wish I had known that girl," replied the Dowager, in her usual indirect manner, "so interesting and a really remarkable face, though perhaps not strictly good-looking, and all the more interesting for that, because good-looking people are so often cows. I have been reading one of her books, really quite good and so well-written, and I didn't guess the murderer till page 200, rather clever, because I usually do it about page 15. So very curious to write books about crimes and then be accused of a crime one's self, some people might say it was a judgment. I wonder whether, if she didn't do it, she has spotted the murderer herself? I don't suppose detective writers detect much in real life, do they, except Edgar Wallace of course, who always seems to be everywhere and dear Conan Doyle and

the black man what was his name and of course the Slater
person, such a scandal, though now I come to think of it
that was in Scotland where they have such very odd laws
about everything particularly getting married. Well, I suppose we shall soon know now, not the truth, necessarily,
but what the jury have made of it.

"Yes; they are being rather longer than I expected. But,
I say, Wimsey, I wish you'd tell me—"

"Too late, too late, you cannot enter now. I have locked
my heart in a silver box and pinned it wi' a golden pin.
Nobody's opinion matters now, except the jury's. I expect
Miss Climpson is telling 'em all about it. When once she
starts she doesn't stop for an hour or two."

"Well, they've been half-an-hour now," said Parker.

"Still waiting?" said Salcombe Hardy, returning to the
press-table.

"Yes—so this is what you call twenty minutes! Three-
quarters of an hour, I make it."

"They've been out an hour-and-a-half," said a girl to
her fiancé, just behind Wimsey. "What can they be discussing?"

"Perhaps they don't think she did it after all."

"What nonsense! Of course she did it. You could see it
by her face. Hard, that's what I call it, and she never once
cried or anything."

"Oh, I dunno," said the young man.

"You don't mean to say you admired her, Frank?"

"Oh, well, I dunno. But she didn't look to me like a
murderess."

"And how do you know what a murderess looks like?
Have you ever met one?"

"Well, I've seen them at Madame Tussaud's."

"Oh, wax-works. Everybody looks like a murderer in a
wax-works."

"Well, p'raps they do. Have a choc."

"Two hours and a quarter," said Waffles Newton, impatiently. "They must have gone to sleep. Have to be a special edition. What happens if they are all night about it?"

"We sit here all night, that's all."

"Well, it's my turn for a drink. Let me know, will you?"

"Right-ho!"

"I've been talking to one of the ushers," said the Man Who Knows the Ropes, importantly, to a friend. "The judge has just sent round to the jury to ask if he can help them in any way."

"Has he? And what did they say?"

"I don't know."

"They've been out three hours and a half now," whispered the girl behind Wimsey. "I'm getting fearfully hungry."

"Are you, darling? Shall we go?"

"No—I want to hear the verdict. We've waited so long now, we may as well stop on."

"Well, I'll go out and get some sandwiches."

"Oh, that would be nice. But don't be long, because I'm sure I shall get hysterics when I hear the sentence."

"I'll be as quick as ever I can. Be glad you're not the jury—they're not allowed anything at all."

"What, nothing to eat or drink?"

"Not a thing. I don't think they're supposed to have light or fire either."

"Poor things! But it's central-heated, isn't it?"

"It's hot enough here, anyway. I'll be glad of a breath of fresh air."

Five hours.

"There's a terrific crowd in the street," said the Man Who Knows the Ropes, returning from a reconnaissance. "Some people started booing the prisoner and a bunch of men attacked them, and one fellow has been carried off in an ambulance."

"Really, how amusing! Look! There's Mr. Urquhart; he's

come back. I'm so sorry for him, aren't you? It must be horrid having somebody die in your house."

"He's talking to the Attorney-General. They've all had a proper dinner, of course."

"The Attorney-General isn't as handsome as Sir Impey Biggs. Is it true he keeps canaries?"

"The Attorney-General?"

"No, Sir Impey."

"Yes, quite true. He takes prizes with them."

"What a funny idea!"

"Bear up, Freddy," said Lord Peter Wimsey. "I perceive movements. They are coming, my own, my sweet, were it never so airy a tread."

The court rose to its feet. The judge took his seat. The prisoner, very white in the electricity, re-appeared in the dock. The door leading to the jury-room opened.

"Look at their faces," said the fiancée, "they say if it's going to be Guilty they never look at the prisoner. Oh, Archie, hold my hand!"

The Clerk of Assizes addressed the jury in tones in which formality struggled with reproach.

"Members of the jury, have you all agreed upon your verdict?"

The foreman rose with an injured and irritable countenance.

"I am sorry to say that we find it impossible to come to an agreement."

A prolonged gasp and murmur went round the court. The judge leaned forward, very courteous and not in the least fatigued.

"Do you think that with a little more time you may be able to reach an agreement?"

"I'm afraid not, my lord." The foreman glanced savagely at one corner of the jury-box, where the elderly spinster sat with her head bowed and her hands tightly clasped. "I see no prospect at all of our ever agreeing."

"Can I assist you in any way?"

"No, thank you, my lord. We quite understand the evidence, but we cannot agree about it."

"That is unfortunate. I think perhaps you had better try again, and then, if you are still unable to come to a decision, you must come back and tell me. In the meantime, if my knowledge of the law can be of any assistance to you, it is, of course, quite at your disposal."

The jury stumbled sullenly away. The judge trailed his scarlet robes out at the back of the bench. The murmur of conversation rose and swelled into a loud rumble.

"By jove," said Freddy Arbuthnot, "I believe it's your Miss Climpson that's holdin' the jolly old show up, Wimsey. Did you see how the foreman glared at her?"

"Good egg," said Wimsey, "oh, excellent, excellent egg! She has a fearfully tough conscience—she may stick it out yet."

"I believe you've been corrupting the jury, Wimsey. Did you signal to her or something?"

"I didn't," said Wimsey. "Believe me or believe me not, I refrained from so much as a lifted eyebrow."

"And he himself has said it," muttered Freddy, "and it's greatly to his credit. But it's damned hard on people who want their dinners."

Six hours. Six hours and a half.

"At last!"

As the jury filed back for the second time, they showed signs of wear and tear. The harassed woman had been crying and was still choking into her handkerchief. The man with the bad cold looked nearly dead. The artist's hair was rumpled into an untidy bush. The company director and the foreman looked as though they would have liked to strangle somebody, and the elderly spinster had her eyes shut and her lips moving as though she were praying.

"Members of the jury, are you agreed upon your verdict?"

"No; we are quite sure that it is impossible for us ever to agree."

"You are quite sure?" said the judge. "I do not wish to hurry you in any way. I am quite prepared to wait here as long as ever you like."

The snarl of the company director was audible even in the gallery. The foreman controlled himself, and replied in a voice ragged with temper and exhaustion.

"We shall never agree, my lord—not if we were to stay here till Doomsday."

"That is very unfortunate," said the judge, "but in that case, of course, there is nothing for it but to discharge you and order a fresh trial. I feel sure that you have all done your best and that you have brought all the resources of your intelligence and conscience to bear on this matter to which you have listened with so much patient and zealous attention. You are discharged, and you are entitled to be excused from all further jury service for the next twelve years."

Almost before the further formalities were completed, and while the judge's robes still flared in the dark little doorway, Wimsey had scrambled down into the well of the court. He caught the defending counsel by the gown.

"Biggy—well done! You've got another chance. Let me in on this and we'll pull it off."

"You think so, Wimsey? I don't mind confessing that we've done better than I ever expected."

"We'll do better still next time. I say, Biggy, swear me in as a clerk or something. I want to interview her."

"Who, my client?"

"Yes, I've got a hunch about this case. We've got to get her off, and I know it can be done."

"Well, come and see me tomorrow. I must go and speak to her now. I'll be in my chambers at ten. Good-night."

Wimsey darted off and rushed round to the side-door, from which the jury were emerging. Last of them all, her hat askew and her mackintosh dragged awkwardly round her shoulders, came the elderly spinster. Wimsey dashed up to her and seized her hand.

"Miss Climpson!"

"Oh, Lord Peter. Oh, dear! What a dreadful day it has been. Do you know, it was me that caused the trouble, mostly, though two of them most bravely backed me up, and oh, Lord Peter, I hope I haven't done wrong, but I couldn't, no I *couldn't* in conscience say she had done it when I was sure she hadn't, could I? Oh, dear, oh, dear!"

"You're absolutely right. She didn't do it, and thank God you stood up to them and gave her another chance. I'm going to prove she didn't do it. And I'm going to take you out to dinner, and—I say, Miss Climpson!"

"Yes?"

"I hope you won't mind, because I haven't shaved since this morning, but I'm going to take you round the next quiet corner and kiss you."

CHAPTER IV

THE FOLLOWING day was a Sunday, but Sir Impey Biggs cancelled an engagement to play golf (with the less regret as it was pouring cats and dogs), and held an extraordinary council of war.

"Well, now, Wimsey," said the advocate, "what is your idea about this? May I introduce Mr. Crofts of Crofts & Cooper, solicitors for the defence."

"My idea is that Miss Vane didn't do it," said Wimsey. "I dare say that's an idea which has already occurred to you, but with the weight of my great mind behind it, no doubt it strikes the imagination more forcibly."

Mr. Crofts, not being quite clear whether this was funny or fatuous, smiled deferentially.

"Quite so," said Sir Impey, "but I should be interested to know how many of the jury saw it in that light."

"Well, I can tell you that, at least, because I know one of them. One woman and half a woman and about three-quarters of a man."

"Meaning precisely?"

"Well, the woman I know stuck out for it that Miss Vane wasn't that sort of person. They bullied her a good deal, of course, because she couldn't lay a finger on any real weakness in the chain of evidence, but she said the prisoner's demeanour was part of the evidence and that she was entitled to take that into consideration. Fortunately, she is a tough, thin, elderly woman with a sound digestion and a militant High-Church conscience of remarkable staying-power, and her wind is excellent. She let 'em all gallop themselves dead, and then said she still didn't believe it and wasn't going to say she did."

"Very useful," said Sir Impey. "A person who can believe

all the articles of the Christian faith is not going to boggle
over a trifle of adverse evidence. But we can never hope for
a whole jury-box full of ecclesiastical diehards. How about
the other woman and the man?"

"Well, the woman was rather unexpected. She was the
stout, prosperous party who keeps a sweet-shop. She said
she didn't think the case was proved, and that it was perfectly possible that Boyes had taken the stuff himself, or
that his cousin had given it to him. She was influenced,
rather oddly, by the fact that she had attended one or two
arsenic trials, and had not been satisfied by the verdict in
some other cases—notably the Seddon trial. She has no
opinion of men in general (she has buried her third) and
she disbelieves all expert evidence on principle. She said
that, personally, she thought Miss Vane might have done
it, but she wouldn't really hang a dog on medical evidence.
At first she was ready to vote with the majority, but she
took a dislike to the foreman, who tried to bear her down
by his male authority, and eventually she said she was going
to back up my friend Miss Climpson."

Sir Impey laughed.

"Very interesting. I wish we always got this inside information about juries. We sweat like hell to prepare evidence,
and then one person makes up her mind on what isn't
really evidence at all, and another supports her on the
ground that evidence can't be relied on. How about the
man?"

"The man was the artist, and the only person who really
understood the kind of life these people were leading. He
believed your client's version of the quarrel, and said that,
if the girl really felt like that about the man, the last thing
she would want to do would be to kill him. She'd rather
stand back and watch him ache, like the man with the
hollow tooth in the comic song. He was also able to believe
the whole story about purchasing the poisons, which to the
others, of course, seemed extremely feeble. He also said

that Boyes, from what he had heard, was a conceited prig, and that anybody who disposed of him was doing a public service. He had had the misfortune to read some of his books, and considered the man an excrescence and a public nuisance. Actually he thought it more than likely that he had committed suicide, and if anybody was prepared to take that point of view he was ready to second it. He also alarmed the jury by saying that he was accustomed to late hours and a stale atmosphere, and had not the slightest objection to sitting up all night. Miss Climpson also said that, in a righteous cause, a little personal discomfort was a trifle, and added that her religion had trained her to fasting. At that point, the third woman had hysterics and another man, who had an important deal to put through next day, lost his temper, so, to prevent bodily violence, the foreman said he thought they had better agree to disagree. So that's how it was."

"Well, they've given us another chance," said Mr. Crofts, "so it's all to the good. It can't come on now till the next sessions, which gives us about a month, and we'll probably get Bancroft next time, who's not such a severe judge as Crossley. The thing is, can we do anything to improve the look of our case?"

"I'm going to have a strenuous go at it," said Wimsey. "There must *be* evidence somewhere, you know. I know you've all worked like beavers, but I'm going to work like a king beaver. And I've got one big advantage over the rest of you."

"More brains?" suggested Sir Impey, grinning.

"No—I should hate to suggest that, Biggy. But I do believe in Miss Vane's innocence."

"Damn it, Wimsey, didn't my eloquent speeches convince you that I was a whole-hearted believer?"

"Of course they did. I nearly shed tears. Here's old Biggy, I said to myself, going to retire from the Bar and cut his throat if this verdict goes against him, because he won't believe in British justice any more. No—it's your triumph at having secured a disagreement that gives you away, old horse. More than you expected. You said so. By the way, if it's not a rude question, who's paying you, Biggy?"

"Crofts and Cooper," said Sir Impey, slyly.

"They're in the thing for their health, I take it?"

"No, Lord Peter. As a matter of fact, the costs in this case are being borne by Miss Vane's publishers and by a—well, a certain newspaper, which is running her new book as a serial. They expect a scoop as the result of all this. But frankly, I don't quite know what they'll say to the expense of a fresh trial. I'm expecting to hear from them this morning."

"The vultures," said Wimsey. "Well, they'd better carry on, but tell 'em I'll see they're guaranteed. Don't bring my name in, though."

"This is very generous—"

"Not at all. I wouldn't lose the fun of all this for the world. Sort of case I fairly wallow in. But in return you must do something for me. I want to see Miss Vane. You must get me passed in as part of your outfit, so that I can hear her version of the story in reasonable privacy. Get me?"

"I expect that can be done," said Sir Impey. "In the meantime you have nothing to suggest?"

"Haven't had time yet. But I'll fish out something, don't you worry. I've already started to undermine the confidence of the police. Chief-Inspector Parker has gone home to twine willow-wreaths for his own tomb-stone."

"You'll be careful," said Sir Impey. "Anything we can discover will come in much more effectively if the prosecution don't know of it beforehand."

"I'll walk as on egg-shells. But if I find the real murderer (if any), you won't object to my having him or her arrested, I take it?"

"No; I won't object to that. The police may. Well, gentlemen, if there's nothing further at the moment, we'd better adjourn the meeting. You'll get Lord Peter the facilities he wants, Mr. Crofts?"

Mr. Crofts exerted himself with energy, and on the following morning, Lord Peter presented himself at the gates of Holloway Gaol, with his credentials.

"Oh, yes, my lord. You are to be treated on the same footing as the prisoner's solicitor. Yes, we have had a separate communication from the police and that will be quite all right, my lord. The warder will take you down, and explain the regulations to you."

Wimsey was conducted through a number of bare corridors to a small room with a glass door. There was a long deal table in it and a couple of repellent chairs, one at either end of the table.

"Here you are, my lord. You sit at one end and the prisoner at the other, and you must be careful not to move from your seats, nor to pass any object over the table. I shall be outside and see you through the glass, my lord, but I shan't be able to overhear nothing. If you will take a seat, they'll bring the prisoner in, my lord."

Wimsey sat down and waited, a prey to curious sensations. Presently there was a noise of footsteps, and the prisoner was brought in, attended by a female wardress. She took the chair opposite to Wimsey, the wardress withdrew and the door was shut. Wimsey, who had risen, cleared his throat.

"Good afternoon, Miss Vane," he said, unimpressively.

The prisoner looked at him.

"Please sit down," she said, in the curious, deep voice which had attracted him in Court. "You are Lord Peter Wimsey, I believe, and have come from Mr. Crofts."

"Yes," said Wimsey. Her steady gaze was unnerving him. "Yes. I—er—I heard the case and all that, and—er—I thought there might be something I could do, don't you know."

"That was very good of you," said the prisoner.

"Not at all, not at all, dash it! I mean to say, I rather enjoy investigating things, if you know what I mean."

"I know. Being a writer of detective stories, I have naturally studied your career with interest."

She smiled suddenly at him and his heart turned to water.

"Well, that's rather a good thing in a way, because you'll understand that I'm not really such an ass as I'm looking at present."

That made her laugh.

"You're not looking an ass—at least, not more so than any gentleman should under the circumstances. The background doesn't altogether suit your style, but you are a very refreshing sight. And I'm really very grateful to you, though I'm afraid I'm rather a hopeless case."

"Don't say that. It can't be hopeless, unless you actually did it, and I know you didn't."

"Well, I didn't, as a matter of fact. But I feel it's like one book I wrote, in which I invented such a perfectly water-tight crime that I couldn't devise any way for my detective to prove it, and had to fall back on the murderer's confession."

"If necessary, we'll do the same. You don't happen to know who the murderer is, I suppose?"

"I don't think there is one. I really believe Philip took the stuff himself. He was rather a defeatist sort of person, you know."

"I suppose he took your separation pretty hard?"

"Well, I daresay it was partly that. But I think it was more that he didn't feel he was sufficiently appreciated. He was apt to think that people were in league to spoil his chances."

"And were they?"

"No, I don't think so. But I do think he offended a great many people. He was rather apt to demand things as a right—and that annoys people, you know."

"Yes, I see. Did he get on all right with his cousin?"

"Oh, yes; though of course he always said it was no more than Mr. Urquhart's duty to look after him. Mr. Urquhart is fairly well off, as he has quite a big professional connection, but Philip really had no claim on him, as it wasn't family money or anything. His idea was that great artists deserved to be boarded and lodged at the expense of the ordinary man."

Wimsey was fairly well acquainted with this variety of the artistic temperament. He was struck, however, by the tone of the reply, which was tinged, he thought, with bitterness and even some contempt. He put his next question with some hesitation.

"Forgive my asking, but—you were very fond of Philip Boyes?"

"I must have been, mustn't I—under the circumstances?"

"Not necessarily," said Wimsey, boldly, "you might have been sorry for him—or bewitched by him—or even badgered to death by him."

"All those things."

Wimsey considered for a moment.

"Were you friends?"

"No." The word broke out with a kind of repressed savagery that startled him. "Philip wasn't the sort of man to make a friend of a woman. He wanted devotion. I gave him that. I did, you know. But I couldn't stand being made a fool of. I couldn't stand being put on probation, like an office-boy, to see if I was good enough to be condescended to. I quite thought he was honest when he said he didn't believe in marriage—and then it turned out that it was a test, to see whether my devotion was abject enough. Well, it wasn't. I didn't like having matrimony offered as a bad-conduct prize."

"I don't blame you," said Wimsey.

"Don't you?"

"No. It sounds to me as if the fellow was a prig—not to say a bit of a cad. Like that horrid man who pretended to be a landscape-painter and then embarrassed the unfortunate young woman with the burden of an honour unto which she was not born. I've no doubt he made himself perfectly intolerable about it, with his ancient oaks and family plate, and the curtseying tenantry and all the rest of it."

Harriet Vane laughed once more.

"Yes—it's ridiculous—but humiliating too. Well, there it is. I thought Philip had made both himself and me ridiculous, and the minute I saw that—well, the whole thing simply shut down—flop!"

She sketched a gesture of finality.

"I quite see that," said Wimsey. "Such a Victorian attitude, too, for a man with advanced ideas. He for God only, she for God in him, and so on. Well, I'm glad you feel like that about it."

"Are you? It's not going to be exactly helpful in the present crisis."

"No; I was looking beyond that. What I mean to say is, when all this is over, I want to marry you, if you can put up with me and all that."

Harriet Vane, who had been smiling at him, frowned, and an indefinable expression of distaste came into her eyes.

"Oh, are you another of them? That makes forty-seven."

"Forty-seven what?" asked Wimsey, much taken aback.

"Proposals. They come in by every post. I suppose there are a lot of imbeciles who want to marry anybody who's at all notorious."

"Oh," said Wimsey. "Dear me, that makes it very awkward. As a matter of fact, you know, I don't need any notoriety. I can get into the papers off my own bat. It's no treat to me. Perhaps I'd better not mention it again."

His voice sounded hurt, and the girl eyed him rather remorsefully.

"I'm sorry—but one gets rather a bruised sort of feeling in my position. There have been so many beastlinesses."

"I know," said Lord Peter. "It was stupid of me—"

"No, I think it was stupid of me. But why—?"

"Why? Oh, well—I thought you'd be rather an attractive person to marry. That's all. I mean, I sort of took a fancy to you. I can't tell you why. There's no rule about it, you know."

"I see. Well, it's very nice of you."

"I wish you wouldn't sound as if you thought it was rather funny. I know I've got a silly face, but I can't help that. As a matter of fact, I'd like somebody I could talk sensibly to, who would make life interesting. And I could give you a lot of plots for your books, if that's any inducement."

"But you wouldn't want a wife who wrote books, would you?"

"But I should; it would be great fun. So much more interesting than the ordinary kind that is only keen on clothes and people. Though of course, clothes and people are all right too, in moderation. I don't mean to say I object to clothes."

"And how about the old oaks and the family plate?"

"Oh, you wouldn't be bothered with them. My brother does all that. I collect first editions and incunabulae, which is a little tedious of me, but you wouldn't need to bother with them either unless you liked."

"I don't mean that. What would your family think about it?"

"Oh, my mother's the only one that counts, and she likes you very much from what she's seen of you."

"So you had me inspected?"

"No—dash it all, I seem to be saying all the wrong things today. I was absolutely stunned that first day in court, and I rushed off to my mater, who's an absolute dear, and the kind of person who really understands things, and I said, 'Look here! here's the absolutely one and only woman, and she's being put through a simply ghastly awful business and for God's sake come and hold my hand!' You simply don't know how foul it was."

"That does sound rather rotten. I'm sorry I was brutal. But, by the way, you're bearing in mind, aren't you, that I've had a lover?"

"Oh, yes. So have I, if it comes to that. In fact, several. It's the sort of thing that might happen to anybody. I can produce quite good testimonials. I'm told I make love rather nicely—only I'm at a disadvantage at the moment. One can't be very convincing at the other end of a table with a bloke looking in at the door."

"I will take your word for it. But, however entrancing it is to wander unchecked through a garden of bright images, are we not enticing your mind from another subject of almost equal importance? It seems probable—"

"And if you can quote *Kai Lung*, we should certainly get on together."

"It seems very probable that I shall not survive to make the experiment."

"Don't be so damned discouraging," said Wimsey. "I have already carefully explained to you that this time *I* am investigating this business. Anybody would think you had no confidence in me."

"People have been wrongly condemned before now."

"Exactly; simply because I wasn't there."

"I never thought of that."

"Think of it now. You will find it very beautiful and in-spiring. It might even help to distinguish me from the other forty-six, if you should happen to mislay my features, or anything. Oh, by the way—I don't positively repel you or anything like that, do I? Because, if I do, I'll take my name off the waiting-list at once."

"No," said Harriet Vane, kindly and a little sadly. "No, you don't repel me."

"I don't remind you of white slugs or make you go goose-flesh all over?"

"Certainly not."

"I'm glad of that. Any minor alterations, like parting the old mane, or growing a tooth-brush, or cashiering the eyeglass, you know, I should be happy to undertake, if it suited your ideas."

"Don't," said Miss Vane, "please don't alter yourself in any particular."

"You really mean that?" Wimsey flushed a little. "I hope it doesn't mean that nothing I could do would make me even passable. I'll come in a different set of garments each time, so as to give you a good all-round idea of the subject. Bunter—my man, you know—will see to that. He has excellent taste in ties, and socks, and things like that. Well, I suppose I ought to be going. You—er—you'll think it over, won't you, if you have a minute to spare. There's no hurry. Only don't hesitate to say if you think you couldn't stick it at any price. I'm not trying to blackmail you into matrimony, you know. I mean, I should investigate this for the fun of the thing, whatever happened, don't you see."

"It's very good of you—"

"No, no, not at all. It's my hobby. Not proposing to people, I don't mean, but investigating things. Well, cheer-frightfully-ho and all that. And I'll call again, if I may."

"I will give the footman orders to admit you," said the prisoner, gravely; "you will always find me at home."

Wimsey walked down the dingy street with a feeling of being almost light-headed.

"I do believe I'll pull it off—she's sore, of course—no wonder, after that rotten brute—but she doesn't feel repelled—one couldn't cope with being repulsive—her skin is like honey—she ought to wear deep red—and old garnets—and lots of rings, rather old-fashioned ones—I could take a house, of course—poor kid, I would damn well work to make it up to her—she's got a sense of humour too—brains —one wouldn't be dull—one would wake up, and there'd be a whole day for jolly things to happen in—and then one would come home and go to bed—that would be jolly, too—and while she was writing, I could go out and mess round, so we shouldn't either of us be dull—I wonder if Bunter was right about this suit—it's a little dark, I always think, but the line is good—"

He paused before a shop window to get a surreptitious view of his own reflection. A large coloured window-bill caught his eye:—

GREAT SPECIAL OFFER
ONE MONTH ONLY

"Oh, God!" he said softly, sobered at once. "One month—four weeks—thirty-one days. There isn't much time. And I don't know where to begin."

CHAPTER V

W<small>ELL</small> now," said Wimsey, "why do people kill people?"

He was sitting in Miss Katharine Climpson's private office. The establishment was ostensibly a typing bureau, and indeed there were three efficient female typists who did very excellent work for authors and men of science from time to time. Apparently the business was a large and flourishing one, for work frequently had to be refused on the ground that the staff was working at full pressure. But on other floors of the building there were other activities. All the employees were women—mostly elderly, but a few still young and attractive—and if the private register in the steel safe had been consulted, it would have been seen that all these women were of the class unkindly known as "superfluous." There were spinsters with small fixed incomes, or no incomes at all; widows without family; women deserted by peripatetic husbands and living on a restricted alimony, who, previous to their engagement by Miss Climpson, had had no resources but bridge and boardinghouse gossip. There were retired and disappointed school-teachers; out-of-work actresses; courageous people who had failed with hat-shops and tea-parlours; and even a few Bright Young Things, for whom the cocktail-party and the night-club had grown boring. These women seemed to spend most of their time in answering advertisements. Unmarried gentlemen who desired to meet ladies possessed of competences, with a view to matrimony; sprightly sexagenarians, who wanted housekeepers for remote country districts; ingenious gentlemen with financial schemes on the look-out for capital; literary gentlemen, anxious for female collaborators; plausible gentlemen about to engage talent for productions in the provinces; benevolent gentlemen, who could tell people

49

how to make money in their spare time—gentlemen such as these were very liable to receive applications from members of Miss Climpson's staff. It may have been coincidence that these gentlemen so very often had the misfortune to appear shortly afterwards before the magistrate on charges of fraud, blackmail or attempted procuration, but it is a fact that Miss Climpson's office boasted a private telephone-line to Scotland Yard, and that few of her ladies were quite so unprotected as they appeared. It is also a fact that the money which paid for the rent and upkeep of the premises might, by zealous enquirers, have been traced to Lord Peter Wimsey's banking account. His lordship was somewhat reticent about this venture of his, but occasionally, when closeted with Chief-Inspector Parker or other intimate friends, referred to it as "My Cattery."

Miss Climpson poured out a cup of tea before replying. She wore a quantity of little bangles on her spare, lace-covered wrists, and they chinked aggressively with every movement.

"I really don't know," she said, apparently taking the problem as a psychological one, "it is so *dangerous*, as well as so terribly *wicked*, one wonders that anybody has the *effrontery* to undertake it. And very often they gain so *little* by it."

"That's what I mean," said Wimsey, "what do they set out to gain? Of course, some people seem to do it for the fun of the thing, like that German female, what's her name, who enjoyed seeing people die."

"Such a *strange* taste," said Miss Climpson. "No sugar, I think?—You know, dear Lord Peter, it has been my melancholy duty to attend *many* death-beds, and, though a number of them—such as my dear father's—were *most* Christian and beautiful, I could not call them *fun*. People have very different ideas of fun, of course, and personally I have never greatly cared for George Robey, though Charlie Chaplin always makes me laugh—still, you know, there are *disagreeable details* attending *any* death-bed which one would think could hardly be to anybody's taste, however depraved."

"I quite agree with you," said Wimsey. "But it must be fun, in one sense, to feel that you can control the issues of life and death, don't you know."

"That is an *infringement* upon the prerogative of the Creator," said Miss Climpson.

"But rather jolly to know yourself divine, so to speak. Up above the world so high, like a tea-tray in the sky. I admit the fascination. But for practical purposes that theory is the devil—I beg your pardon, Miss Climpson, respect for sacred personages—I mean, it's unsatisfactory, because it would suit one person just as well as another. If I've got to find a homicidal maniac, I may as well cut my throat at once."

"Don't say *that*," pleaded Miss Climpson, "even in jest. Your work here—so good, so valuable—would be worth living for in spite of the *saddest* personal disappointments. And I have known jokes of that kind turn out very badly, in the most surprising ways. There was a young man we used to know, who was given to talking in a sadly *random* way—a long time ago, dear Lord Peter, while you were still in the nursery, but young men were wild, even then, whatever they say now about the 'eighties—and he said one day to my poor, dear Mother, 'Mrs. Climpson, if I don't make a good bag today, I shall shoot myself' (for he was very fond of sport), and he went out with his gun and as he was getting over a stile, he caught the trigger in the hedge and the gun went off and blew his head to pieces. I was quite a girl, and it upset me *dreadfully*, because he was a very handsome young man, with whiskers which we all admired very much, though today they would be smiled at, and they were burnt *right off* him with the explosion, and a shocking hole in the side of his head, so they said, for of course I was not allowed to see him."

"Poor chap," said his lordship. "Well, let's dismiss homicidal mania from our minds for the moment. What else do people kill people for?"

"There is—passion," said Miss Climpson, with a slight initial hesitation at the word, "for I should not like to call it *love*, when it is so unregulated."

"That is the explanation put forward by the prosecution," said Wimsey. "I don't accept it."

"Certainly not. But—it might be possible, might it not, that there was some other unfortunate young woman who was attached to this Mr. Boyes, and felt vindictively towards him?"

"Yes, or a man who was jealous. But the time is the difficulty. You've got to have some plausible pretext for giving a bloke arsenic. You can't just catch him standing on a doorstep, and say, 'Here, have a drink of this,' can you?"

"But there were ten minutes unaccounted for," said Miss Climpson, shrewdly. "Might he not have entered some public-house for refreshment, and there met an enemy?"

"By jove, that's a possibility." Wimsey made a note, and shook his head dubiously. "But it's rather a coincidence. Unless there was a previous appointment to meet there. Still, it's worth looking into. At any rate, it's obvious that Mr. Urquhart's house and Miss Vane's flat were not the only conceivable places where Boyes might have eaten or drunk between seven and 10.10 that evening. Very well: under the head 'Passion' we find 1) Miss Vane (ruled out ex hypothesi), 2) jealous lover, 3) ditto rival. Place, Public-house (query). Now we go on to the next motive, and that's Money. A very good motive for murdering anybody who has any, but a poor one in Boyes' case. Still, let us say, Money. I can think of three sub-headings for that: 1) Robbery from the person (very improbable); 2) insurance; 3) inheritance."

"What a clear mind you have," said Miss Climpson.

"When I die you will find 'Efficiency' written on my heart."

I don't know what money Boyes had on him, but I shouldn't think it was much. Urquhart and Vaughan might know; still, it's not very important, because arsenic isn't a sensible drug to use on anyone you want to rob. It takes a long time, comparatively, to begin business, and it doesn't make the victim helpless enough. Unless we suppose the taxi-driver drugged and robbed him, there was no one who could possibly profit by such a silly crime."

Miss Climpson agreed, and buttered a second tea-cake.

"Then, insurance. Now we come to the region of the possible. Was Boyes insured? It doesn't seem to have occurred to anybody to find out. Probably he wasn't. Literary blokes have very little forethought, and are careless about trifles like premiums. But one ought to know. Who might have an insurable interest? His father, his cousin (possibly), other relations (if any), his children (if any) and—I suppose —Miss Vane, if he took out the policy while he was living with her. Also, anybody who may have lent him money on the strength of such insurance. Plenty of possibilities there. I'm feeling better already, Miss Climpson, fitter and brighter in every way. Either I'm getting a line on the thing, or else it's your tea. That's a good, stout-looking pot. Has it got any more in it?"

"Yes, indeed," said Miss Climpson, eagerly. "My dear father used to say I was a great hand at getting the *utmost* out of a tea-pot. The secret is to *fill* up as you *go* and never empty the pot completely."

"Inheritance," pursued Lord Peter. "Had he anything to leave? Not much, I shouldn't think. I'd better hop round and see his publisher. Or had he lately come into anything? His father or cousin would know. The father is a parson— 'slashing trade, that,' as the naughty bully says to the new boy in one of Dean Farrar's books. He has a thread-bare look. I shouldn't think there was much money in the family. Still, you never know. Somebody might have left Boyes a fortune for his *beaux yeux* or out of admiration for his books. If so, to whom did Boyes leave it? Query: did he make a will? But surely the defence must have thought of these things. I am getting depressed again."

"Have a sandwich," said Miss Climpson.

"Thank you," said Wimsey, "or some hay. There is nothing like it when you are feeling faint, as the White King truly remarked. Well, that more or less disposes of the money motive. There remains Blackmail."

Miss Climpson, whose professional connection with the Cattery had taught her something about blackmail, assented with a sigh.

"Who was this fellow Boyes?" enquired Wimsey rhetorically. "I know nothing about him. He may have been a blackguard of the deepest dye. He may have known unmentionable things about all his friends. Why not? Or he may have been writing a book to show somebody up, so that he had to be suppressed at all costs. Dash it all, his cousin's a solicitor. Suppose he has been embezzling Trust deeds or something, and Boyes was threatening to split on him? He'd been living in Urquhart's house, and had every opportunity for finding out. Urquhart drops some arsenic into his soup, and—Ah! there's the snag. He puts arsenic into the soup and eats it himself. That's awkward. I'm afraid Hannah Westlock's evidence rather knocks that on the head. We shall have to fall back on the mysterious stranger in the pub."

He considered a little, and then said:

"And there's suicide, of course, which is what I'm really rather inclined to believe in. Arsenic is tomfool stuff to commit suicide with, but it has been done. There was the duc de Praslin, for instance—if his *was* suicide. Only, where's the bottle?"

"The bottle?"

"Well, he must have carried it in something. It might be in a paper, if he took the powdered form, though that would be awkward. Did anybody look for a bottle or paper?"

"Where would they look for it?" asked Miss Climpson.

"That's the rub. If it wasn't on him, it would be anywhere round about Doughty Street, and it's going to be a job looking for a bottle or paper that was chucked away six months ago. I do loathe suicides—they're so difficult to prove. Oh, well, faint heart never won so much as a scrap of paper. Now look here, Miss Climpson. We've got about a month to work this out in. The Michaelmas Term ends on the 21st; this is the 15th. They can't very well bring it up before then, and the Hilary term starts on January 12th. They'll probably take it early, unless we can show reason for delay. Four weeks to get fresh evidence. Will you reserve the best efforts of yourself and the staff? I don't know yet what I shall want, but I shall probably want something done."

"Of course I will, Lord Peter. You know that it is only *too* great a pleasure to do *anything* for you—even if the whole office were not your own property, which it *is*. Only let me know, at *any* minute of the night or day, and I will do my *very* best to help you."

Wimsey thanked her, made a few enquiries about the work of the bureau and departed. He hailed a taxi and was immediately driven to Scotland Yard.

.   .   .   .

Chief Detective-Inspector Parker was, as usual, delighted to see Lord Peter, but there was a worried expression on his plain though pleasant face as he greeted his visitor.

"What is it, Peter? The Vane case again?"

"Yes. You've come a mucker over this, old man, you really have."

"Well, I don't know. It looked pretty straightforward to us."

"Charles, acushla, distrust the straight-forward case, the man who looks you straight in the eyes, and the tip straight from the horse's mouth. Only the most guileful deceiver can afford to be so aggressively straight. Even the path of the light is curved—or so they tell us. For God's sake, old man, do what you can to put the thing right before next assizes. If you don't, I'll never forgive you. Damn it, you don't *want* to hang the wrong person, do you?—especially a woman and all that."

"Have a fag," said Parker. "You're looking quite wild about the eyes. What have you been doing with yourself? I'm sorry if we've got the wrong pig by the ear, but it's the defence's business to point out where we're wrong, and I can't say they put up a very convincing show."

"No, confound them. Biggy did his best, but that fool and beast Crofts gave him no materials at all. Blast his ugly eyes! I know the brute thinks she did it. I hope he will fry in hell and be served up with cayenne pepper on a red-hot dish!"

"What eloquence!" said Parker, unimpressed. "Anybody would think you'd gone goopy over the girl."

"That's a damned friendly way to talk," said Wimsey, bitterly. "When you went off the deep end about my sister, I may have been unsympathetic—I daresay I was—but I swear I didn't dance on your tenderest feelings and call your manly devotion 'going goopy over a girl.' I don't know where you pick up such expressions, as the clergyman's wife said to the parrot. 'Goopy,' indeed! I never heard anything so vulgar!"

"Good lord," exclaimed Parker, "you don't seriously say—"

"Oh, no!" retorted Wimsey, bitterly. "I'm not expected to be serious. A buffoon, that's what I am. I now know exactly what Jack Point feels like. I used to think the 'Yeomen' sentimental tosh, but it is all too true. Would you like to see me dance in motley?"

"I'm sorry," said Parker, taking his cue rather from the

tone than the words. "If it's like that, I'm damned sorry, old man. But what can I do?"

"Now you're talking. Look here—the most likely thing is that this unsavoury blighter Boyes committed suicide. The unspeakable defence haven't been able to trace any arsenic to his possession—but then they probably couldn't trace a herd of black cattle over a snow-bound field in broad noonday with a microscope. I want your people to take it up."

"Boyes—query arsenic," said Parker, making a note on a pad. "Anything else?"

"Yes. Find out if Boyes visited any pub. in the neighbourhood of Doughty Street between, say, 9.50 and 10.10 on the night of Jan. 20th—if he met anybody, and what he took to drink."

"It shall be done. Boyes—query pub." Parker made another note. "Yes?"

"Thirdly, if any bottle or paper that might have contained arsenic was picked up in that district."

"Oh, indeed? And would you like me to trace the 'bus ticket dropped by Mrs. Brown outside Selfridge's in the last Christmas rush? No use making it too easy."

"A bottle is more likely than a paper," went on Wimsey, ignoring him, "because I think the arsenic must have been taken in liquid form to work so quickly."

Parker made no further protest, but noted down "Boyes —Doughty Street—query bottle," and paused expectantly. "Yes?"

"That's all for the moment. By the way, I should try the garden in Mecklenburgh Square. A thing might lie quite a long time under those bushes."

"Very well. I'll do my best. And if you find out anything which really proves that we've been on the wrong tack, you'll let us know, won't you? We don't want to make large and ignominious public mistakes."

"Well—I've just earnestly promised the defence that I'll

do no such thing. But if I spot the criminal, I'll let you arrest him."

"Thanks for small mercies. Well, good luck! Funny for you and me to be on opposite sides, isn't it?"

"Very," said Wimsey. "I'm sorry about it, but it's your own fault."

"You shouldn't have been out of England. By the way——"

"Yes?"

"You realise that probably all our young friend did during those missing ten minutes was to stand about in Theobalds Road or somewhere, looking for a stray taxi."

"Oh, shut up!" said Wimsey, crossly, and went out.

CHAPTER VI

The next day dawned bright and fair, and Wimsey felt a certain exhilaration as he purred down to Tweedling Parva. "Mrs. Merdle" the car, so called because, like that celebrated lady, she was averse to "row," was sparking merrily on all twelve cylinders, and there was a touch of frost in the air. These things conduce to high spirits.

Wimsey reached his destination about 10 o'clock, and was directed to the vicarage, one of those large, rambling and unnecessary structures which swallow the incumbent's income during his life and land his survivors with a heavy bill for dilapidations as soon as he is dead.

The Rev. Arthur Boyes was at home, and would be happy to see Lord Peter Wimsey.

The clergyman was a tall, faded man, with lines of worry deeply engraved upon his face, and mild blue eyes a little bewildered by the disappointing difficulty of things in general. His black coat was old, and hung in depressed folds from his stooping, narrow shoulders. He gave Wimsey a thin hand and begged him to be seated.

Lord Peter found it a little difficult to explain his errand. His name evidently aroused no associations in the mind of this gentle and unworldly parson. He decided not to mention his hobby of criminal investigation, but to represent himself, with equal truth, as a friend of the prisoner's. That might be painful, but it would be at least intelligible. Accordingly, he began, with some hesitation:

"I'm fearfully sorry to trouble you, especially as it's all so very distressin' and all that, but it's about the death of your son, and the trial and so on. Please don't think I'm wanting to make an interfering nuisance of myself, but I'm deeply interested—personally interested. You see, I know

59

Miss Vane—I—in fact I like her very much, don't you know, and I can't help thinking there's a mistake somewhere and —and I should like to get it put right if possible."

"Oh—oh, yes!" said Mr. Boyes. He carefully polished a pair of pince-nez and balanced them on his nose, where they sat crookedly. He peered at Wimsey and seemed not to dislike what he saw, for he went on:

"Poor misguided girl! I assure you, I have no vindictive feelings—that is to say, nobody would be more happy than myself to know that she was innocent of this dreadful thing. Indeed, Lord Peter, even if she were guilty, it would give me great pain to see her suffer the penalty. Whatever we do, we cannot bring back the dead to life, and one would infinitely prefer to leave all vengeance in the hand of Him to whom it belongs. Certainly, nothing could be more terrible than to take the life of an innocent person. It would haunt me to the end of my days if I thought there were the least likelihood of it. And I confess that, when I saw Miss Vane in court, I had grievous doubts whether the police had done rightly in accusing her."

"Thank you," said Wimsey, "it is very kind of you to say that. It makes the job much easier. Excuse me, you say, 'when you saw her in court.' You hadn't met her previously?"

"No. I knew, of course, that my unhappy son had formed an illicit connection with a young woman, but—I could not bring myself to see her—and indeed, I believe that she, with very proper feeling, refused to allow Philip to bring her into contact with any of his relations. Lord Peter, you are a younger man than I am, you belong to my son's generation, and you will perhaps understand that—though he was not bad, not depraved, I will never think that—yet somehow there was not that full confidence between us which there should be between father and son. No doubt I was much to blame. If only his mother had lived—"

"My dear sir," mumbled Wimsey, "I perfectly understand. It often happens. In fact, it's continually happening. The post-war generation and so on. Lots of people go off the rails a bit—no real harm in 'em at all. Just can't see eye to eye with the older people. It generally wears off in time. Nobody really to blame. Wild oats and, er, all that sort of thing."

"I could not approve," said Mr. Boyes, sadly, "of ideas so opposed to religion and morality—perhaps I spoke my mind too openly. If I had sympathised more—"

"It can't be done," said Wimsey. "People have to work it out for themselves. And, when they write books and so on, and get into that set of people, they tend to express themselves rather noisily, if you see what I mean."

"Maybe, maybe. But I reproach myself. Still, this does not help you at all. Forgive me. If there is any mistake and the jury were evidently not satisfied, we must use all our endeavours to put it right. How can I assist?"

"Well, first of all," said Wimsey, "and I'm afraid this is rather a hateful question, did your son ever say anything, or write anything to you which might lead you to think that he—was tired of his life or anything of that kind? I'm sorry."

"No, no—not at all. I was, of course, asked the same question by the police and by the counsel for the defence. I can truly say that such an idea never occurred to me. There was nothing at all to suggest it."

"Not even when he parted company with Miss Vane?"

"Not even then. In fact, I gathered that he was rather more angry than despondent. I must say that it was a surprise to me to hear that, after all that had passed between them, she was unwilling to marry him. I still fail to comprehend it. Her refusal must have come as a great shock to him. He wrote so cheerfully to me about it beforehand. Perhaps you remember the letter?" He fumbled in an untidy drawer. "I have it here, if you would like to look at it."

"If you would just read the passage, sir," suggested Wimsey.

"Yes, oh, certainly. Let me see. Yes. 'Your morality will be pleased to hear, Dad, that I have determined to regularise the situation, as the good people say.' He had a careless way of speaking and writing sometimes, poor boy, which doesn't do justice to his good heart. Dear me. Yes. 'My young woman is a good little soul, and I have made up my mind to do the thing properly. She really deserves it, and I hope that when everything is made respectable, you will extend your paternal recognition to her. I won't ask you to officiate—as you know, the registrar's office is more in my line, and though she was brought up in the odour of sanctity, like myself, I don't think she will insist on the Voice that Breathed o'er Eden. I will let you know when it's to be, so that you can come and give us your blessing (quâ father if not quâ parson) if you should feel so disposed.' You see, Lord Peter, he quite meant to do the right thing, and I was touched that he should wish for my presence."

"Quite so," said Lord Peter, and thought, "If only that young man were alive, how dearly I should love to kick his bottom for him."

"Well, then there is another letter, saying that the marriage had fallen through. Here it is. 'Dear Dad—sorry, but I'm afraid your congratulations must be returned with thanks. The wedding is off, and the bride has run away. There's no need to go into the story. Harriet has succeeded in making a fool of herself and me, so there's no more to be said.' Then later I heard that he had not been feeling well—but all that you know already."

"Did he suggest any reason for these illnesses of his?"

"Oh, no—we took it for granted that it was a recurrence of the old gastric trouble. He was never a very robust lad. He wrote in very hopeful mood from Harlech, saying that he was much better, and mentioning his plan of a voyage to Barbados."

"He did?"

"Yes. I thought it would do him a great deal of good, and take his mind off other things. He spoke of it only as a vague project, not as though anything were settled."

"Did he say anything more about Miss Vane?"

"He never mentioned her name to me again until he lay dying."

"Yes—and what did you think of what he said then?"

"I didn't know what to think. We had no idea of any poisoning then, naturally, and I fancied it must refer to the quarrel between them that had caused the separation."

"I see. Well now, Mr. Boyes. Supposing it was not self-destruction—"

"I really do not think it could have been."

"Now is there anybody else at all who could have an interest in his death?"

"Who could there be?"

"No—no other woman, for instance?"

"I never heard of any. And I think I should have done. He was not secretive about these things, Lord Peter. He was remarkably open and straightforward."

"Yes," commented Wimsey internally, "liked to swagger about it, I suppose. Anything to give pain. Damn the fellow." Aloud he merely said: "There are other possibilities. Did he, for instance, make a will?"

"He did. Not that he had much to leave, poor boy. His books were very cleverly written—he had a fine intellect, Lord Peter—but they did not bring him in any great sums of money. I helped him with a little allowance, and he managed on that and on what he made from his articles in the periodicals."

"He left his copyrights to somebody, though, I take it?"

"Yes. He wished to leave them to me, but I was obliged to tell him that I could not accept the bequest. You see,

I did not approve of his opinions, and I should not have
thought it right to profit by them. No; he left them to his
friend Mr. Vaughan."

"Oh!—may I ask when this will was made?"

"It is dated at the period of his visit to Wales. I believe
that before that he had made one leaving everything to
Miss Vane."

"Indeed!" said Wimsey. "I suppose she knew about it."
His mind reviewed a number of contradictory possibilities,
and he added: "But it would not amount to an important
sum, in any case?"

"Oh, no. If my son made £50 a year by his books, that
was the utmost. Though they tell me," added the old gentleman, with a sad smile, "that, after this, his new book will
do better."

"Very likely," said Wimsey. "Provided you get into the
papers, the delightful reading public don't mind what it's
for. Still— Well, that's that. I gather he would have no
private money to leave?"

"Nothing whatever. There has never been any money in
our family, Lord Peter, nor yet in my wife's. We're quite
the proverbial Church mice." He smiled faintly at this little
clerical jest. "Except, I suppose, for Cremorna Garden."

"For—I beg your pardon?"

"My wife's aunt, the notorious Cremorna Garden of the
'sixties."

"Good lord, yes—the actress?"

"Yes. But she, of course, was never, never mentioned.
One did not enquire into the way she got her money. No
worse than others, I dare say—but in those days we were
very easily shocked. We have seen and heard nothing of her
for well over fifty years. I believe she is quite childish now."

"By jove! I'd no idea she was still alive!"

"Yes, I believe she is, though she must be well over
ninety. Certainly Philip never had any money from her."

"Well, that rules money out. Was your son's life insured, by any chance?"

"Not that I ever heard of. We found no policy among his papers, and so far as I know, nobody has made any claim."

"He left no debts?"

"Only trifling ones—tradesmen's accounts and so on. Perhaps fifty pounds' worth altogether."

"Thank you so much," said Wimsey, rising, "that has cleared the ground a good deal."

"I am afraid it has not got you much farther."

"It tells me where not to look, at any rate," said Wimsey, "and that all saves time, you know. It's frightfully decent of you to be bothered with me."

"Not at all. Ask me anything you want to know. Nobody would be more glad than myself to see that unfortunate young woman cleared."

Wimsey again thanked him and took his leave. He was a mile up the road before a regretful thought overtook him. He turned Mrs. Merdle's bonnet round, skimmed back to the church, stuffed a handful of treasury notes with some difficulty into the mouth of a box labelled "Church expenses," and resumed his way to town.

. . . . . .

As he manoeuvred the car through the City, a thought struck him, and instead of heading for Piccadilly, where he lived, he turned off into a street south of the Strand, in which was situated the establishment of Messrs. Grimsby & Cole, who published the works of Mr. Philip Boyes. After a little delay, he was shown into Mr. Cole's office.

Mr. Cole was a stout and cheerful person, and was much interested to hear that the notorious Lord Peter Wimsey was concerning himself with the affairs of the equally notorious Mr. Boyes. Wimsey represented that, as a collector of First Editions, he would be glad to secure copies of all Philip Boyes' works. Mr. Cole regretted extremely that he could not help him, and, under the influence of an expensive cigar, became quite confidential.

"Without wishing to seem callous, my dear Lord Peter," he said, throwing himself back in his chair, and creasing his three chins into six or seven as he did so, "between you and me, Mr. Boyes could not have done better for himself than to go and get murdered like this. Every copy was sold out a week after the result of the exhumation became known, two large editions of his last book were diposed of before the trial came on—at the original price of 7/6, and the libraries clamoured so for the early volumes that we had to reprint the lot. Unfortunately we had not kept the type standing, and the printers had to work night and day, but we did it. We are rushing the three-and-sixpennies through the binders' now, and the shilling edition is arranged for. Positively, I don't think you could get a First Edition in London for love or money. We have nothing here but our own file copies, but we are putting out a special memorial edition, with portraits, on hand-made paper, limited and numbered, at a guinea. Not the same thing of course, but—"

Wimsey begged to put his name down for a set at a guinea a-piece, adding:

"Sad and all that, don't you know, that the author can't benefit by it, what?"

"Deeply distressing," agreed Mr. Cole, compressing his fat cheeks by two longitudinal folds from the nostril to the mouth. "And sadder still that there can be no more work to come from him. A very talented young man, Lord Peter. We shall always feel a melancholy pride, Mr. Grimsby and myself, in knowing that we recognised his quality, before there was any likelihood of financial remuneration. A *succès d'estime*, that was all, until this very grievous occurrence. But when the work is good, it is not our habit to boggle about monetary returns."

"Ah, well!" said Wimsey, "it sometimes pays to cast your bread upon the waters. Quite religious, isn't it—you know, the bit about 'plenteously bringing out good works may of thee be plenteously rewarded.' Twenty-fifth after Trinity."

"Quite," said Mr. Cole, with a certain lack of enthusiasm, possibly because he was imperfectly acquainted with the book of Common Prayer, or possibly because he detected a hint of mockery in the other's tone. "Well, I have very much enjoyed this chat. I am sorry I can do nothing for you about First Editions."

Wimsey begged him not to mention it, and with a cordial farewell ran hastily down the stairs.

His next visit was to the office of Mr. Challoner, Harriet Vane's agent. Challoner was an abrupt, dark, militant-looking little man, with untidy hair and thick spectacles.

"Boom?" said he, when Wimsey had introduced himself and mentioned his interest in Miss Vane. "Yes, of course there is a boom. Rather disgusting, really, but one can't help that. We have to do our best for our client, whatever the circumstances. Miss Vane's books have always sold reasonably well—round about the three or four thousand mark in this country—but of course this business has stimulated things enormously. The last book has gone to three new editions, and the new one has sold seven thousand before publication."

"Financially, all to the good, eh?"

"Oh, yes—but frankly I don't know whether these artificial sales do very much good to an author's reputation in the long run. Up like a rocket, down like the stick, you know. When Miss Vane is released—"

"I am glad you say 'when.'"

"I am not allowing myself to contemplate any other possibility. But *when* that happens, public interest will be liable to die down very quickly. I am, of course, securing the most advantageous contracts I possibly can at the moment, to cover the next three or four books, but I can only really control the advances. The actual receipts will depend on the sales, and that is where I foresee a slump.

I am, however, doing well with serial rights, which are important from the point of view of immediate returns."

"On the whole, as a business man, you are not altogether glad that this has happened?"

"Taking the long view, I am not. Personally, I need not say that I am extremely grieved, and feel quite positive that there is some mistake."

"That's my idea," said Wimsey.

"From what I know of your lordship, I may say that your interest and assistance are the best stroke of luck Miss Vane could have had."

"Oh, thanks—thanks very much. I say—this arsenic book—you couldn't let me have a squint at it, I suppose?"

"Certainly, if it would help you." He touched a bell. "Miss Warburton, bring me a set of galleys of '*Death in the Pot.*' Trufoot's are pushing publication on as fast as possible. The book was still unfinished when the arrest took place. With rare energy and courage, Miss Vane has put the finishing touches and corrected the proofs herself. Of course, everything had to go through the hands of the prison authorities. However, we were anxious to conceal nothing. She certainly knows all about arsenic, poor girl. These are complete, are they, Miss Warburton? Here you are. Is there anything else?"

"Only one thing. What do you think of Messrs. Grimsby & Cole?"

"I never contemplate them," said Mr. Challoner. "Not thinking of doing anything with them, are you, Lord Peter?"

"Well, I don't know that I am—seriously."

"If you do, read your contract carefully. I won't say, bring it to us—"

"If ever I do publish with Grimsby & Cole," said Lord Peter, "I'll promise to do it through you."

CHAPTER VII

LORD PETER WIMSEY almost bounced into Holloway Prison next morning. Harriet Vane greeted him with a kind of rueful smile.

"So you've reappeared?"

"Good lord, yes! Surely you expected me to. I fancied I'd left that impression. I say—I've thought of a good plot for a detective story."

"Really?"

"Top-hole. You know, the sort people bring out and say, 'I've often thought of doing it myself, if I could only find time to sit down and write it.' I gather that sitting down is all that is necessary for producing masterpieces. Just a moment, though. I must get through my business first. Let me see—" He made believe to consult a notebook. "Ah, yes? Do you happen to know whether Philip Boyes made a will?"

"I believe he did, when we were living together."

"In whose favour?"

"Oh, in mine. Not that he had much to leave, poor man. It was chiefly that he wanted a literary executor."

"Are you, in point of fact, his executrix now?"

"Good heavens! I never thought of that. I took it for granted he would have altered it when we parted. I think he must have, or I should have heard about it when he died, shouldn't I?"

She looked candidly at him, and Wimsey felt a little uncomfortable.

"You didn't *know* he had altered it, then? Before he died, I mean?"

"I never thought a word more about it, as a matter of

fact. If I had thought—of course I should have assumed it. Why?"

"Nothing," said Wimsey. "Only I'm rather glad the will wasn't brought up at the thingummy bob."

"Meaning the trial? You needn't be so delicate about mentioning it. You mean, if I had thought I was still his heir, I might have murdered him for his money. But it didn't amount to a hill of beans, you know. I was making four times as much as he was."

"Oh, yes. It was only this silly plot I'd got in my mind. But it *is* rather silly, now I come to think of it."

"Tell me."

"Well, you see—" Wimsey choked a little, and then rattled his idea out with an exaggerated lightness.

"Well—it's about a girl (or a man would do, but we'll call it a girl) who writes novels—crime stories, in fact. And she has a—a friend who also writes. Neither of them best-sellers, you see, but just ordinary novelists."

"Yes? That's a kind of thing that might happen."

"And the friend makes a will, leaving his money—receipts from books and so on—to the girl."

"I see."

"And the girl—who has got rather fed up with him, you know, thinks of a grand scoop, that will make both of them best-sellers."

"Oh, yes?"

"Yes. She polishes him off by the same method she has used in her latest crime-thriller."

"A daring stroke," said Miss Vane, with grave approval.

"Yes. And of course, his books immediately become best-sellers. And she grabs the pool."

"That's really ingenious. An entirely new motive for murder—the thing I've been looking for for years. But don't you think it would be a little dangerous? She might even be suspected of the murder."

"Then *her* books would become best-sellers, too."

"How true that is! But possibly she wouldn't live to enjoy the profits."

"That, of course," said Wimsey, "is the snag."

"Because, unless she were suspected and arrested and tried, the scoop would only half come off."

"There you are," said Wimsey. "But, as an experienced mystery-monger, couldn't you think of a way round that?"

"I daresay. She might prove an ingenious alibi, for instance. Or, if she were very wicked, manage to push the blame on somebody else. Or lead people to suppose that her friend had made away with himself."

"Too vague," said Wimsey. "How would she do that?"

"I can't say, off-hand. I'll give it careful thought and let you know. Or—here's an idea!"

"Yes?"

"She is a person with a monomania—no, no—not a homicidal one. That's dull, and not really fair to the reader. But there is somebody she wishes to benefit—somebody, say a father, mother, sister, lover or cause, that badly needs money. She makes a will in his, her or its favour, and lets herself be hanged for the crime, knowing that the beloved object will then come in for the money. How's that?"

"Great!" cried Wimsey, carried away. "Only—wait a minute. They wouldn't give her the friend's money, would they? You're not allowed to profit by a crime."

"Oh, hang! That's true. It would only be her own money, then. She could make that over by a deed of gift. Yes—look! If she did that immediately after the murder—a deed of gift of everything she possessed—that would include everything she came into under the friend's will. It would then all go direct to the beloved object, and I don't believe the law could stop it!"

She faced him with dancing eyes.

"See here," said Wimsey. "You're not safe. You're too clever by half. But, I say, it's a good plot, isn't it?"

"It's a winner! Shall we write it?"

"By jove, let's!"

"Only, you know, I'm afraid we shan't get the chance."

"You're not to say that. Of course we're going to write it. Damn it, what am I here for? Even if I could be reconciled to losing you, I couldn't lose the chance of writing my best-seller!"

"But what you've done so far is to provide me with a very convincing motive for murder. I don't know that that's going to help us a great lot."

"What I've done," said Wimsey, "is to prove that that was not the motive, anyway."

"Why?"

"You wouldn't have told me if it had been. You would have gently led me away from the subject. And besides——"

"Well?"

"Well, I've seen Mr. Cole of Grimsby & Cole, and I know who is going to get the major part of Philip Boyes' profits. And I don't somehow fancy that he is the beloved object."

"No?" said Miss Vane, "and why not? Don't you know that I passionately dote on every chin on his face?"

"If it's chins you admire," said Wimsey, "I will try to grow some, though it will be rather hard work. Anyway, keep smiling—it suits you."

.   .   .   .

"It's all very well, though," he thought to himself, when the gates had closed behind him. "Bright back-chat cheers the patient, but gets us no forrarder. How about this fellow Urquhart? He looked all right in court, but you never can tell. I think I'd better pop round and see him."

He presented himself accordingly in Woburn Square, but was disappointed. Mr. Urquhart had been called away to a sick relative. It was not Hannah Westlock who answered the door, but a stout elderly woman, whom Wimsey supposed to be the cook. He would have liked to question her, but felt that Mr. Urquhart would hardly receive him well if he discovered that his servants had been pumped behind his back. He therefore contented himself with enquiring how long Mr. Urquhart was likely to be away.

"I couldn't rightly say, sir. I understand it depends how the sick lady gets on. If she gets over it, he'll be back at once, for I know he is very busy just now. If she should pass away, he would be engaged some time, with settling up the estate."

"I see," said Wimsey. "It's a bit awkward, because I wanted to speak to him rather urgently. You couldn't give me his address, by any chance?"

"Well, sir, I don't rightly know if Mr. Urquhart would wish it. If it's a matter of business, sir, they could give you information at his office in Bedford Row."

"Thanks very much," said Wimsey, noting down the number. "I'll call there. Possibly they'd be able to do what I want without bothering him."

"Yes, sir. Who should I say called?"

Wimsey handed over his card, writing at the top, "In re R. v. Vane," and added:

"But there is a chance he may be back quite soon?"

"Oh, yes, sir. Last time he wasn't away more than a couple of days, and a merciful providence I am sure that was, with poor Mr. Boyes dying in that dreadful manner."

"Yes, indeed," said Wimsey, delighted to find the subject introducing itself of its own accord. "That must have been a shocking upset for you all."

"Well, there," said the cook, "I don't hardly like to think of it, even now. A gentleman dying in the house like that, and poisoned too, when one's had the cooking of his dinner —it do seem to bring it home to one, like."

"It wasn't the dinner that was at fault, anyway," said Wimsey, genially.

"Oh, dear, no, sir—we proved that most careful. Not that any accident could happen in my kitchen—I should like to see it! But people do say such things if they get half a chance. Still, there wasn't a thing ate but master and Hannah and I had some of it, and very thankful I was for that, I needn't tell you."

"You must be; I am sure." Wimsey was framing a further enquiry, when the violent ringing of the area bell interrupted them.

"There's that butcher," said the cook, "you'll excuse me, sir. The parlour-maid's in bed with the influenza, and I'm single-handed this morning. I'll tell Mr. Urquhart you called."

She shut the door, and Wimsey departed for Bedford Row, where he was received by an elderly clerk, who made no difficulty about supplying Mr. Urquhart's address.

"Here it is, my lord. Care of Mrs. Wrayburn, Applefold, Windle, Westmorland. But I shouldn't think he would be very long away. In the meantime, could we do anything for you?"

"No, thanks. I rather wanted to see him personally, don't you know. As a matter of fact, it's about that very sad death of his cousin, Mr. Philip Boyes."

"Indeed, my lord? Shocking affair, that. Mr. Urquhart was greatly upset, with it happening in his own house. A very fine young man, was Mr. Boyes. He and Mr. Urquhart were great friends, and he took it greatly to heart. Were you present at the trial, my lord?"

"Yes. What did you think of the verdict?"

The clerk pursed up his lips.

"I don't mind saying I was surprised. It seemed to me a very clear case. But juries are very unreliable, especially nowadays, with women on them. We see a good deal of the fair sex in this profession," said the clerk, with a sly smile, "and very few of them are remarkable for possessing the legal mind."

"How true that is," said Wimsey. "If it wasn't for them, though, there'd be much less litigation, so it's all good for business."

"Ha, ha! Very good, my lord. Well, we have to take

things as they come, but in my opinion—I'm an old-fashioned man—the ladies were most adorable when they
adorned and inspired and did not take an active part in
affairs. Here's our young lady clerk—I don't say she wasn't
a good worker—but a whim comes over her and away she
goes to get married, leaving me in the lurch, just when Mr.
Urquhart is away. Now, with a young man, marriage
steadies him, and makes him stick closer to his job, but
with a young woman, it's the other way about. It's right she
should get married, but it's inconvenient, and in a solicitor's
office one can't get temporary assistance, very well. Some
of the work is confidential, of course, and in any case, an
atmosphere of permanence is desirable."

Wimsey sympathised with the head-clerk's grievance, and
bade him an affable good-morning. There is a telephone
box in Bedford Row, and he darted into it and immediately rang up Miss Climpson.

"Lord Peter Wimsey speaking—oh, hullo, Miss Climpson!
How is everything? All bright and beautiful? Good!—Yes,
now listen. There's a vacancy for a confidential female clerk
at Mr Norman Urquhart's, the solicitor's, in Bedford Row—
Have you got anybody?—Oh, good!—'Yes, send them all
along—I particularly want to get someone in there—Oh,
no! no special enquiry—just to pick up any gossip about
the Vane business—Yes, pick out the steadiest-looking, not
too much face-powder, and see that their skirts are the regulation four inches below the knee—the head-clerk's in
charge, and the last girl left to be married, so he's feeling
anti-sex-appeal. Right ho! Get her in and I'll give her her
instructions. Bless you, may your shadow never grow
bulkier!"

CHAPTER VIII

"Bunter!"

"My lord?"

Wimsey tapped with his fingers a letter he had just received.

"Do you feel at your brightest and most truly fascinating? Does a livelier iris, winter weather notwithstanding, shine upon the burnished Bunter? Have you got that sort of conquering feeling? The Don Juan touch, so to speak?"

Bunter, balancing the breakfast tray on his fingers, coughed deprecatingly.

"You have a good, upstanding, impressive figure, if I may say so," pursued Wimsey, "a bold and roving eye when off duty, a ready tongue, Bunter—and, I am persuaded, you have a way with you. What more should any cook or house-parlourmaid want?"

"I am always happy," replied Bunter, "to exert myself to the best of my capacity in your lordship's service."

"I am aware of it," admitted his lordship. "Again and again I say to myself, Wimsey, this cannot last. One of these days this worthy man will cast off the yoke of servitude and settle down in a pub. or something, but nothing happens. Still, morning by morning, my coffee is brought, my bath is prepared, my razor laid out, my ties and socks sorted and my bacon and eggs brought to me in a lordly dish. No matter. This time I demand a more perilous devotion—perilous for us both, my Bunter, for if you were to be carried away, a helpless martyr to matrimony, who then would bring my coffee, prepare my bath, lay out my razor and perform all those other sacrificial rites? And yet—"

"Who is the party, my lord?"

"There are two of them, Bunter, two ladies lived in a

bower, Binnorie, O Binnorie! The parlourmaid you have
seen. Her name is Hannah Westlock. A woman in her thirties, I fancy, and not ill-favored. The other, the cook—I
cannot lisp the tender syllables of her name, for I do not
know it, but doubtless it is Gertrude, Cecily, Magdalen,
Margaret, Rosalys or some other sweet symphonious sound
—a fine woman, Bunter, on the mature side, perhaps, but
none the worse for that."

"Certainly not, my lord. If I may say so, the woman of
ripe years and queenly figure is frequently more susceptible
to delicate attentions than the giddy and thoughtless young
beauty."

"True. Let us suppose, Bunter, that you were to be the
bearer of a courteous missive to one Mr. Norman Urquhart
of Woburn Square. Could you, in the short space of time at
your disposal, insinuate yourself, snakelike, as it were, into
the bosom of the household?"

"If you desire it, my lord, I will endeavour to insinuate
myself to your lordship's satisfaction."

"Noble fellow. In case of an action for breach, or any
consequence of that description, the charges will, of course,
be borne by the management."

"I am obliged to your lordship. When would your lordship wish me to commence?"

"As soon as I have written a note to Mr. Urquhart. I will
ring."

"Very good, my lord."

Wimsey moved over to the writing-desk. After a few moments he looked up, a little peevishly.

"Bunter, I have a sensation of being hovered over. I do
not like it. It is unusual and it unnerves me. I implore you
not to hover. Is the proposition distasteful, or do you want
me to get a new hat? What is troubling your conscience?"

"I beg your lordship's pardon. It had occurred to my
mind to ask your lordship, with every respect—"

"Oh, God, Bunter—don't break it gently. I can't bear it. Stab and end the creature—to the heft! What is it?"

"I wished to ask you, my lord, whether your lordship thought of making any changes in your establishment?"

Wimsey laid down his pen and stared at the man.

"Changes, Bunter? When I have just so eloquently expressed to you my undying attachment to the loved routine of coffee, bath, razor, socks, eggs and bacon and the old, familiar faces? You're not giving me warning, are you?"

"No, indeed, my lord. I should be very sorry to leave your lordship's service. But I had thought it possible that, if your lordship was about to contract new ties—"

"I *knew* it was something in the haberdashery line! By all means, Bunter, if you think it necessary. Had you any particular pattern in mind?"

"Your lordship misunderstands me. I referred to domestic ties, my lord. Sometimes, when a gentleman reorganizes his household on a matrimonial basis, the lady may prefer to have a voice in the selection of the gentleman's personal attendant, in which case—"

"Bunter!" said Wimsey, considerably startled, "may I ask where you have contracted these ideas?"

"I ventured to draw an inference, my lord."

"This comes of training people to be detectives. Have I been nourishing a sleuth-hound on my own hearth-stone? May I ask if you have gone so far as to give a name to the lady?"

"Yes, my lord."

There was a pause.

"Well?" said Wimsey, in a rather subdued tone, "what about it, Bunter?"

"A very agreeable lady, if I may say so, my lord."

"It strikes you that way, does it? The circumstances are unusual, of course."

"Yes, my lord. I might perhaps make so bold as to call them romantic."

"You may make so bold as to call them damnable, Bunter."

"Yes, my lord," said Bunter, in a tone of sympathy.

"You won't desert the ship, Bunter?"

"Not on any account, my lord."

"Then don't come frightening me again. My nerves are not what they were. Here is the note. Take it round and do your best."

"Very good, my lord."

"Oh, and, Bunter."

"My lord?"

"It seems that I am being obvious. I have no wish to be anything of the kind. If you see me being obvious, will you drop me a hint?"

"Certainly, my lord."

Bunter faded gently out, and Wimsey stepped anxiously to the mirror.

"I can't see anything," he said to himself. "No lily on my cheek with anguish moist and fever-dew. I suppose, though, it's hopeless to try and deceive Bunter. Never mind. Business must come first. I've stopped one, two, three, four earths. What next? How about this fellow Vaughan?"

.   .   .   .   .

When Wimsey had any researches to do in Bohemia, it was his custom to enlist the help of Miss Marjorie Phelps. She made figurines in porcelain for a living, and was therefore usually to be found either in her studio or in some one else's studio. A telephone-call at 10 a.m. would probably catch her scrambling eggs over her own gas-stove. It was true that there had been passages, about the time of the Bellona Club affair,* between her and Lord Peter which made it a little embarrassing and unkind to bring her in on the subject of Harriet Vane, but with so little time in which to pick and choose his tools, Wimsey was

* See "The Unpleasantness at the Bellona Club," published 1928.

past worrying about gentlemanly scruples. He put the call through and was relieved to hear an answering "Hullo!"

"Hullo, Marjorie! This is Peter Wimsey. How goes it?"

"Oh, fine, thanks. Glad to hear your melodious voice again. What can I do for the Lord High Investigator?"

"Do you know one Vaughan, who is mixed up in the Philip Boyes murder mystery?"

"Oh, Peter! Are you on to that? How gorgeous! Which side are you taking?"

"For the defence."

"Hurray!"

"Why this pomp of jubilee?"

"Well, it's much more exciting and difficult, isn't it?"

"I'm afraid it is. Do you know Miss Vane, by the way?"

"Yes and no. I've seen her with the Boyes-Vaughan crowd."

"Like her?"

"So-so."

"Like him? Boyes, I mean?"

"Never stirred a heart-beat."

"I said, did you like him?"

"One didn't. One either fell for him or not. He wasn't the merry bright-eyed pal of the period, you know."

"Oh! What's Vaughan?"

"Hanger-on."

"Oh?"

"House-dog. Nothing must interfere with the expansion of my friend the genius. That sort."

"Oh!"

"Don't keep saying 'Oh!' Do you want to meet the man Vaughan?"

"If it's not too much trouble."

"Well, turn up to-night with a taxi and we'll go the rounds. We're certain to drop across him somewhere. Also the rival gang, if you want them—Harriet Vane's supporters."

"Those girls who gave evidence?"

"Yes. You'll like Eiluned Price, I think. She scorns everything in trousers, but she's a good friend at a pinch."

"I'll come, Marjorie. Will you dine with me?"

"Peter, I'd adore to, but I don't think I will. I've got an awful lot to do."

"Right-ho! I'll roll round about nine, then."

Accordingly, at 9 o'clock, Wimsey found himself in a taxi with Marjorie Phelps, headed for a round of the studios.

"I've been doing some intensive telephoning," said Marjorie, "and I think we shall find him at the Kropotkys'. They are pro-Boyes, Bolshevik and musical, and their drinks are bad, but their Russian tea is safe. Does the taxi wait?"

"Yes; it sounds as if we might want to beat a retreat."

"Well, it's nice to be rich. It's down the court here, on the right, over the Petrovitchs' stable. Better let me grope first."

They stumbled up a narrow and encumbered stair, at the top of which a fine confused noise of a piano, strings and the clashing of kitchen utensils announced that some sort of entertainment was in progress.

Marjorie hammered loudly on a door, and, without waiting for an answer, flung it open. Wimsey, entering on her heels, was struck in the face, as by an open hand, by a thick muffling wave of heat, sound, smoke and the smell of frying.

It was a very small room, dimly lit by a single electric bulb, smothered in a lantern of painted glass, and it was packed to suffocation with people, whose silk legs, bare arms and pallid faces loomed at him like glow-worms out of the obscurity. Coiling wreaths of tobacco-smoke swam slowly to and fro in the midst. In one corner an anthracite stove, glowing red and mephitical, vied with a roaring gas-oven in another corner to raise the atmosphere to roasting-pitch. On the stove stood a vast and steaming kettle; on a side-table stood a vast and steaming samovar; over the gas, a dim figure stood turning sausages in a pan with a fork, while an assistant attended to something in the oven, which Wimsey, whose nose was selective, identified among the other fragrant elements in this compound atmosphere, and identified rightly, as kippers. At the piano, which stood just inside the door, a young man with bushy red hair was playing something of a Czecho-Slovakian flavour, to a violin obligato by an extremely loose-jointed person of indeterminate sex in a Fair-Isle jumper. Nobody looked round at their entrance. Marjorie picked her way over the scattered limbs on the floor and, selecting a lean young woman in red, bawled into her ear. The young woman nodded and beckoned to Wimsey. He negotiated a passage and was introduced to the lean. woman by the simple formula: "Here's Peter—this is Nina Kropotky."

"So pleased," shouted Madame Kropotky through the clamour. "Sit by me. Vanya will get you something to drink. It is beautiful, yes? That is Stanislas—such a genius —his new work on the Piccadilly Tube Station—great, n'estce-pas? Five days he was continually travelling upon the escalator to absorb the tone-values."

"Colossal!" yelled Wimsey.

"So—you think? Ah! you can appreciate! You understand it is really for the big orchestra. On the piano it is nothing. It needs the brass, the effects, the timpani-b'rrrrrrr! So! But one seizes the form, the outline! Ah! it finishes! Superb! Magnificent!"

The enormous clatter ceased. The pianist mopped his face and glared haggardly round. The violinist put down its instrument and stood up, revealing itself, by its legs, to be female. The room exploded into conversation. Madame Kropotky leapt over her seated guests and embraced the perspiring Stanislas on both cheeks. The frying-pan was lifted from the stove in a fusillade of spitting fat, a shriek went up for 'Vanya!' and presently a cadaverous face was pushed down to Wimsey's, and a deep guttural voice barked at him: "What will you drink?" while simultaneously a plate of kippers came hovering perilously over his shoulder.

"Thanks," said Wimsey, "I have just dined—just *dined*," he roared despairingly, "full up, complet!"

Marjorie came to the rescue with a shriller voice and more determined refusal.

"Take those dreadful things away, Vanya. They make me sick. Give us some tea, tea, tea!"

"Tea!" echoed the cadaverous man, "they want tea! What do you think of Stanislas' tone-poem? Strong, modern, eh? The soul of rebellion in the crowd—the clash, the revolt at the heart of the machinery. It gives the bourgeois something to think of, oh, yes!"

"Bah!" said a voice in Wimsey's ear, as the cadaverous man turned away, "it is nothing. Bourgeois music. Programme music. Pretty!—You should hear Vrilovitch's 'Ecstasy on the letter Z.' That is pure vibration with no antiquated pattern in it. Stanislas—he thinks much of himself, but it is old as the hills—you can sense the resolution at the back of all his discords. Mere harmony in camouflage. Nothing in it. But he takes them all in because he has red hair and reveals his bony structure."

The speaker certainly did not err along these lines, for he was as bald and round as a billiard-ball. Wimsey replied soothingly:

"Well, what can you do with the wretched and antiquated instruments of our orchestra? A diatonic scale, bah! Thirteen miserable, bourgeois semi-tones, pooh! To express the infinite complexity of modern emotion, you need a scale of thirty-two notes to the octave."

"But why cling to the octave?" said the fat man. "Till you can cast away the octave and its sentimental associations, you walk in fetters of convention."

"That's the spirit!" said Wimsey. "I would dispense with all definite notes. After all, the cat does not need them for his midnight melodies, powerful and expressive as they are. The love-hunger of the stallion takes no account of octave or interval in giving forth the cry of passion. It is only man, trammelled by a stultifying convention—Oh, hullo, Marjorie, sorry—what is it?"

"Come and talk to Ryland Vaughan," said Marjorie. "I have told him you are a tremendous admirer of Philip Boyes' books. Have you read them?"

"Some of them. But I think I'm getting light-headed."

"You'll feel worse in an hour or so. So you'd better come now." She steered him to a remote spot near the gas-oven, where an extremely elongated man was sitting curled up on a floor cushion, eating caviare out of a jar with a pickle-fork. He greeted Wimsey with a sort of lugubrious enthusiasm.

"Hell of a place," he said, "hell of a business altogether. This stove's too hot. Have a drink. What the devil else can one do? I come here, because Philip used to come here. Habit, you know. I hate it, but there's nowhere else to go."

"You knew him very well, of course," said Wimsey, seating himself in a waste-paper basket, and wishing he was wearing a bathing-suit.

"I was his only real friend," said Ryland Vaughan, mournfully. "All the rest only cared to pick his brains. Apes! parrots! all the bloody lot of them."

"I've read his books and thought them very fine," said Wimsey, with some sincerity. "But he seemed to me an unhappy soul."

"Nobody understood him," said Vaughan. "They called him difficult—who wouldn't be difficult with so much to fight against? They sucked the blood out of him, and his damned thieves of publishers took every blasted coin they could lay their hands on. And then that bitch of a woman poisoned him. My God, what a life!"

"Yes, but what made her do it—if she did do it?"

"Oh, she did it all right. Sheer, beastly spite and jealousy,

that's all there was to it. Just because she couldn't write anything but tripe herself. Harriet Vane's got the bug all these
damned women have got—fancy they can do things. They
hate a man and they hate his work. You'd think it would
have been enough for her to help and look after a genius
like Phil, wouldn't you? Why, damn it, he used to ask her
advice about his work, her advice, good lord!"

"Did he take it?"

"Take it? She wouldn't give it. Told him she never gave
opinions on other authors' work. *Other* authors! The impudence of it! Of course she was out of things among us all,
but why couldn't she realise the difference between her
mind and his? Of course it was hopeless from the start for
Philip to get entangled with that kind of woman. Genius
must be served, not argued with. I warned him at the time,
but he was infatuated. And then, to want to marry her—"

"Why did he?" asked Wimsey.

"Remains of parsonical upbringing, I suppose. It was
really pitiful. Besides, I think that fellow Urquhart did a
lot of mischief. Sleek family lawyer—d'you know him?"

"No."

"He got hold of him—put up to it by the family, I
imagine. I saw the influence creeping over Phil long before
the real trouble began. Perhaps it's a good thing he's dead.
It would have been ghastly to watch him turn conventional
and settle down."

"When did this cousin start getting hold of him, then?"

"Oh—about two years ago—a little more, perhaps. Asked
him to dinner and that sort of thing. The minute I saw him
I knew he was out to ruin Philip, body and soul. What he
wanted—what Phil wanted, I mean—was freedom and room
to turn about in, but what with the woman and the cousin
and the father in the background—oh, well! It's no use crying about it now. His work is left, and that's the best part
of him. He's left me that to look after, at least. Harriet
Vane didn't get her finger in that pie, after all."

"I'm sure it's absolutely safe in your hands," said Wimsey.

"But when one thinks what there might have been," said Vaughan, turning his blood-shot eyes miserably on Lord Peter, "it's enough to make one cut one's throat, isn't it?"

Wimsey expressed agreement.

"By the way," he said, "you were with him all that last day, till he went to his cousin's. You don't think he had anything on him in the way of—poison or anything? I don't want to seem unkind—but he was unhappy—it would be rotten to think that he—"

"No," said Vaughan, "no. That I'll swear he never did. He would have told me—he trusted me in those last days. I shared all his thoughts. He was miserably hurt by that damned woman, but he wouldn't have gone without telling me or saying good-bye. And besides—he wouldn't have chosen that way. Why should he? I could have given him—"

He checked himself, and glanced at Wimsey, but, seeing nothing in his face beyond sympathetic attention, went on:

"I remember talking to him about drugs. Hyoscine—veronal—all that sort of thing. He said, 'If ever I want to go out, Ryland, you'll show me the way.' And I would have—if he'd really wanted it. But arsenic! Philip, who loved beauty so much—do you think he would have chosen arsenic?—the suburban poisoner's outfit? That's absolutely impossible."

"It's not an agreeable sort of thing to take, certainly," said Wimsey.

"Look here," said Vaughan, hoarsely and impressively—he had been putting a constant succession of brandies on top of the caviare, and was beginning to lose his reserve—"Look here! See this!" He pulled a small bottle from his breast-pocket. "That's waiting, till I've finished editing Phil's books. It's a comfort to have it there to look at, you know. Peaceful. Go out through the ivory gate—that's classical—they brought me up on the classics. These people would laugh at a fellow, but you needn't tell them I said it

—funny, the way it sticks—'tendebantque manus ripae ulterioris amore, ulterioris amore'—what's that bit about the souls thronging thick as leaves in Vallombrosa—no, that's Milton—'amorioris ultore—ultoriore—damn it—poor Phil!"

Here Mr. Vaughan burst into tears and patted the little bottle.

Wimsey, whose head and ears were thumping as though he were sitting in an engine-room, got up softly and withdrew. Somebody had begun a Hungarian song and the stove was white-hot. He made signals of distress to Marjorie, who was sitting in a corner with a group of men. One of them appeared to be reading his own poems with his mouth nearly in her ear, and another was sketching something on the back of an envelope, to the accompaniment of yelps of merriment from the rest. The noise they made disconcerted the singer, who stopped in the middle of a bar, and cried angrily:

"Ach! this noise! these interruptions! they are intolerable! I lose myself! Stop! I begin all over again, from the beginning."

Marjorie sprang up, apologising.

"I'm a brute—I'm not keeping your menagerie in order, Nina—we're being perfect nuisances. Forgive me, Marya, I'm in a bad temper. I'd better pick up Peter and toddle away. Come and sing to me another day, darling, when I'm feeling better and there is more room for my feelings to expand. Good-night, Nina—we've enjoyed it frightfully —and, Boris, that poem's the best thing you've done, only I couldn't hear it properly. Peter, tell them what a rotten mood I'm in to-night and take me home."

"That's right," said Wimsey, "nervy, you know—bad effect on the manners and so on."

"Manners," said a bearded gentleman suddenly and loudly, "are for the bourgeois."

"Quite right," said Wimsey. "Beastly bad form, and gives

you repressions in the what-not. Come on, Marjorie, or we shall all be getting polite."

"I begin again," said the singer, "from the beginning."

"Whew!" said Wimsey, on the staircase.

"Yes, I know. I think I'm a perfect martyr to put up with it. Anyway, you've seen Vaughan. Nice dopey specimen, isn't he?"

"Yes, but I don't think he murdered Philip Boyes, do you? I had to see him to make sure. Where do we go next?"

"We'll try Joey Trimbles.' That's the stronghold of the opposition show."

Joey Trimbles occupied a studio over a mews. Here there was the same crowd, the same smoke, more kippers, still more drinks and still more heat and conversation. In addition there was a blaze of electric light, a gramophone, five dogs and a strong smell of oil-paints. Sylvia Marriott was expected. Wimsey found himself involved in a discussion of free love, D. H. Lawrence, the prurience of prudery and the immoral significance of long skirts. In time, however, he was rescued by the arrival of a masculine-looking middle-aged woman with a sinister smile and a pack of cards, who proceeded to tell everybody's fortune. The company gathered around her, and at the same time a girl came in and announced that Sylvia had sprained her ankle and couldn't come. Everybody said warmly, "Oh, how sickening, poor dear!" and forgot the subject immediately.

"We'll scoot off," said Marjorie. "Never mind about saying good-bye. Nobody marks you. It's good luck about Sylvia, because she'll be at home and can't escape us. I sometimes wish they'd all sprain their ankles. And yet, you know, nearly all those people are doing very good work. Even the Kropotky crowd. I used to enjoy this kind of thing myself, once."

"We're getting old, you and I," said Wimsey. "Sorry, that's rude. But do you know, I'm getting on for forty, Marjorie."

"You wear well. But you are looking a bit fagged tonight, Peter dear. What's the matter?"

"Nothing at all but middle-age."

"You'll be settling down if you're not careful."

"Oh, I've been settled for years."

"With Bunter and the books. I envy you sometimes, Peter."

Wimsey said nothing. Marjorie looked at him almost in alarm, and tucked her arm in his.

"Peter—do please be happy. I mean, you've always been the comfortable sort of person that nothing could touch. Don't alter, will you?"

That was the second time Wimsey had been asked not to alter himself; the first time, the request had exalted him; this time, it terrified him. As the taxi lurched along the rainy Embankment, he felt for the first time the dull and angry helplessness which is the first warning stroke of the triumph of mutability. Like the poisoned Athulf in the *Fool's Tragedy*, he could have cried, "Oh, I am changing, changing, fearfully changing." Whether his present enterprise failed or succeeded, things would never be the same again. It was not that his heart would be broken by a disastrous love—he had outlived the luxurious agonies of youthful blood, and in this very freedom from illusion he recognised the loss of something. From now on, every hour of light-heartedness would be, not a prerogative but an achievement—one more axe or case-bottle or fowling-piece, rescued, Crusoe-fashion, from a sinking ship.

For the first time, too, he doubted his own power to carry through what he had undertaken. His personal feelings had been involved before this in his investigations, but they had never before clouded his mind. He was fumbling—grasping uncertainly here and there at fugitive and mocking possibilities. He asked questions at random, doubtful of his object, and the shortness of the time, which would once have stimulated, now frightened and confused him.

"I'm sorry, Marjorie," he said, rousing himself, "I'm afraid I'm being damned dull. Oxygen-starvation, probably. D'you mind if we have the window down a bit? That's better. Give me good food and a little air to breathe and I will caper, goat-like, to a dishonourable old age. People will point me out, as I creep, bald and yellow and supported by discreet corsetry, into the night-clubs of my great-grandchildren, and they'll say, 'Look, darling! that's the wicked Lord Peter, celebrated for never having spoken a reasonable word for the last ninety-six years. He was the only aristocrat who escaped the guillotine in the revolution of 1960. We keep him as a pet for the children.' And I shall wag my head and display my up-to-date dentures and say, 'Ah, ha! They don't have the fun we used to have in my young days, the poor, well-regulated creatures!'"

"There won't be any night-clubs then for you to creep into, if they're as disciplined as all that."

"Oh, yes—nature will have her revenge. They will slink away from the Government Communal Games to play solitaire in catacombs over a bowl of unsterilised skim-milk. Is this the place?"

"Yes; I hope there's someone to let us in at the bottom, if Sylvia's bust her leg. Yes—I hear footsteps. Oh, it's you, Eiluned; how's Sylvia?"

"Pretty all right, only swelled up—the ankle, that is. Coming up?"

"Is she visible?"

"Yes, perfectly respectable."

"Good, because I'm bringing Lord Peter Wimsey up, too."

"Oh," said the girl. "How do you do? You detect things, don't you? Have you come for the body or anything?"

"Lord Peter's looking into Harriet Vane's business for her."

"Is he? That's good. Glad somebody's doing something about it." She was a short, stout girl with a pugnacious nose and a twinkle. "What do you say it was? I say he did it himself. He was the self-pitying sort, you know. Hullo, Syl—here's Marjorie, with a bloke who's going to get Harriet out of jug."

"Produce him instantly!" was the reply from within. The door opened upon a small bed-sitting room, furnished with the severest simplicity, and inhabited by a pale, spectacled young woman in a Morris chair, her bandaged foot stretched out upon a packing-case.

"I can't get up, because, as Jenny Wren said, my back's bad and my leg's queer. Who's the champion, Marjorie?"

Wimsey was introduced, and Eiluned Price immediately inquired, rather truculently:

"Can he drink coffee, Marjorie? Or does he require masculine refreshment?"

"He's perfectly godly, righteous and sober, and drinks anything but cocoa and fizzy lemonade."

"Oh! I only asked because some of your male belongings need stimulating, and we haven't got the wherewithal, and the pub's just closing."

She stumped over to a cupboard, and Sylvia said:

"Don't mind Eiluned; she likes to treat 'em rough. Tell me, Lord Peter, have you found any clues or anything?"

"I don't know," said Wimsey. "I've put a few ferrets down a few holes. I hope something may come up the other end."

"Have you seen the cousin yet—the Urquhart creature?"

"Got an appointment with him for tomorrow. Why?"

"Sylvia's theory is that he did it," said Eiluned.

"That's interesting. Why?"

"Female intuition," said Eiluned, bluntly. "She doesn't like the way he does his hair."

"I only said he was too sleek to be true," protested Sylvia. "And who else could it have been? I'm sure it wasn't Ryland Vaughan; he's an obnoxious ass, but he is genuinely heart-broken about it all."

Eiluned sniffed scornfully, and departed to fill a kettle at a tap on the landing.

"And whatever Eiluned thinks, I can't believe Phil Boyes did it himself."

"Why not?" asked Wimsey.

"He talked such a lot," said Sylvia. "And he really had too high an opinion of himself. I don't think he would have wilfully deprived the world of the privilege of reading his books."

"He would," said Eiluned. "He'd do it out of spite, to make the grown-ups sorry. No, thanks," as Wimsey advanced to carry the kettle, "I'm quite capable of carrying six pints of water."

"Crushed again!" said Wimsey.

"Eiluned disapproves of conventional courtesies between the sexes," said Marjorie.

"Very well," replied Wimsey, amiably. "I will adopt an attitude of passive decoration. Have you any idea, Miss Marriott, why this over-sleek solicitor should wish to make away with his cousin?"

"Not the faintest. I merely proceed on the old Sherlock Holmes basis, that when you have eliminated the impossible, then whatever remains, however improbable, must be true."

"Dupin said that before Sherlock. I grant the conclusion, but in this case I question the premises. No sugar, thank you."

"I thought all men liked to make their coffee into syrup."

"Yes, but then I am very unusual. Haven't you noticed it?"

"I haven't had much time to observe you, but I'll count the coffee as a point in your favour."

"Thanks frightfully. I say—can you people tell me just what was Miss Vane's reaction to the murder?"

"Well—" Sylvia considered a moment. "When he died —she was upset, of course—"

"She was startled," said Miss Price, "but it's my opinion she was thankful to be rid of him. And no wonder. Selfish beast! He'd made use of her and nagged her to death for a year and insulted her at the end. And he was one of your greedy sort that wouldn't let go. She *was* glad, Sylvia—what's the good of denying it?"

"Yes, perhaps. It was a relief to know he was finished with. But she didn't know then that he'd been murdered."

"No. The murder spoilt it a bit—if it was a murder, which I don't believe. Philip Boyes was always determined to be a victim, and it was very irritating of him to succeed in the end. I believe that's what he did it for."

"People do do that kind of thing," said Wimsey, thoughtfully. "But it's difficult to prove. I mean, a jury is much more inclined to believe in some tangible sort of reason, like money. But I can't find any money in this case."

Eiluned laughed.

"No, there never was much money, except what Harriet made. The ridiculous public didn't appreciate Phil Boyes. He couldn't forgive her that, you know."

"Didn't it come in useful?"

"Of course, but he resented it all the same. She ought to have been ministering to his work, not making money for them both with her own independent trash. But that's men all over."

"You haven't much opinion of us, what?"

"I've known too many borrowers," said Eiluned Price, "and too many that wanted their hands held. All the same, the women are just as bad, or they wouldn't put up with it. Thank Heaven, I've never borrowed and never lent—except to women, and they pay back."

"People who work hard usually do pay back, I fancy," said Wimsey, "—except geniuses."

"Women geniuses don't get coddled," said Miss Price, grimly, "so they learn not to expect it."

"We're getting rather off the subject, aren't we?" said Marjorie.

"No," replied Wimsey, "I'm getting a certain amount of light on the central figures in the problem—what journalists like to call the protagonists." His mouth gave a wry little twist. "One gets a lot of illumination in that fierce light that beats upon a scaffold."

"Don't say that," pleaded Sylvia.

A telephone rang somewhere outside, and Eiluned Price went out to answer it.

"Eiluned's anti-man," said Sylvia, "but she's a very reliable person."

Wimsey nodded.

"But she's wrong about Phil—she couldn't stick him, naturally, and she's apt to think—"

"It's for you, Lord Peter," said Eiluned, returning. "Fly at once—all is known. You're wanted by Scotland Yard."

Wimsey hastened out.

"That you, Peter? I've been scouring London for you. We've found the pub."

"Never!"

"Fact. And we're on the track of a packet of white powder."

"Good God!"

"Can you run down first thing tomorrow? We may have it for you."

"I will skip like a ram and hop like a high hill. We'll beat you yet, Mr. Bleeding Chief-Inspector Parker."

"I hope you will," said Parker, amiably, and rang off.

Wimsey pranced back into the room.

"Miss Price's price has gone to odds on," he announced. "It's suicide, fifty to one and no takers. I am going to grin like a dog and run about the city."

"I'm sorry I can't join you," said Sylvia Marriott, "but I'm glad if I'm wrong."

"I'm glad I'm right," said Eiluned Price, stolidly.

"And you are right and I am right and everything is quite all right," said Wimsey.

Marjorie Phelps looked at him and said nothing. She suddenly felt as though something inside her had been put through a wringer.

CHAPTER IX

By what ingratiating means Mr. Bunter had contrived to turn the delivery of a note into the acceptance of an invitation to tea was best known to himself. At half-past four on the day which ended so cheerfully for Lord Peter, he was seated in the kitchen of Mr. Urquhart's house, toasting crumpets. He had been trained to a great pitch of dexterity in the preparation of crumpets, and if he was somewhat lavish in the matter of butter, that hurt nobody except Mr. Urquhart. It was natural that the conversation should turn to the subject of murder. Nothing goes so well with a hot fire and buttered crumpets as a wet day without and a good dose of comfortable horrors within. The heavier the lashing of the rain and the ghastlier the details, the better the flavour seems to be. On the present occasion, all the ingredients of an enjoyable party were present in full force.

" 'Orrible white, he looked, when he came in," said Mrs. Pettican the cook. "I see him when they sent for me to bring up the 'ot bottles. Three of them, they 'ad, one to his feet and one to his back and the big rubber one to 'is stummick. White and shiverin', he was, and that dreadful sick, you never would believe. And he groaned pitiful."

"Green, he looked to me, Cook," said Hannah Westlock, "or you might perhaps call it a greenish-yellow. I thought it was jaundice a-coming on—more like them attacks he had in the Spring."

"He was a bad colour then," agreed Mrs. Pettican, "but nothink like to what he was that last time. And the pains and cramps in his legs was agonising. That struck Nurse Williams very forcible—a nice young woman she was, and not stuck-up like some as I could name. 'Mrs. Pettican,' she said to me, which I call it better manners than callin'

95

you Cook as they mostly do, as though they paid your wages for the right of callin' you out of your name—'Mrs. Petti-can,' said she, 'never did I see anythink to equal them cramps except in one other case that was the dead spit of this one,' she said, 'and you mark my words, Mrs. Pettican, them cramps ain't there for nothin'. Ah! little did I under-stand her meanin' at the time."

"That's a regular feature of these arsenical cases, or so his lordship tells me," replied Bunter. "A very distressing symp-tom. Had he ever had anything of the sort before?"

"Not what you could call cramps," said Hannah, "though I remember when he was ill in the Spring he complained of getting the fidgets in the hands and feet. Something like pins-and-needles, by what I understood him to say. It was a worrit to him, because he was finishing one of his articles in a hurry, and what with that and his eyes being so bad, the writing was a trial to him, poor thing."

"From what the gentleman for the prosecution said, talk-ing it out with Sir James Lubbock," said Mr. Bunter, "I gathered that those pins-and-needles, and bad eyes and so on, were a sign he'd been given arsenic regularly, if I may so phrase it."

"A dreadful wicked woman she must 'a' been," said Mrs. Pettican, "—'ev another crumpet, do, Mr. Bunter—a-tor-turin' of the poor soul that long-winded way. Bashin' on the 'ed or the 'asty use of a carvin' knife when roused I can understand, but the 'orrors of slow poisonin' is the work of a fiend in 'uman form, in my opinion."

"Fiend is the only word, Mrs. Pettican," agreed the vis-itor.

"And the wickedness of it," said Hannah, "quite apart from the causing of a painful death to a fellow-being. Why, it's only the mercy of Providence we weren't all brought under suspicion."

"Yes, indeed," said Mrs. Pettican. "Why, when master told us about them diggin' poor Mr. Boyes up and findin'

him full of that there nasty arsenic, it give me sech a turn, I felt as if the room was a-goin' round like the gallopin' 'orses at the roundabouts. 'Oh, sir!' I ses, 'what, in our 'ouse!' That's what I ses, and he ses, 'Mrs. Pettican,' he ses, 'I sincerely hope not.'"

Mrs. Pettican, having imparted this Macbeth-like flavour to the story, was pleased with it, and added:

"Yes, that's what I said to 'im. 'In our 'ouse.' I said, and I'm sure I never slep' a wink for three nights afterwards, what with the police and the fright and one thing and another."

"But of course you had no difficulty in proving that it hadn't happened in this house?" suggested Bunter. "Miss Westlock gave her evidence so beautifully at the trial, I'm sure she made it clear as clear could be to judge and jury. The judge congratulated you, Miss Westlock, and I'm sure he didn't say nearly enough—so plainly and well as you spoke up before the whole court."

"Well, I never was one to be shy," confessed Hannah, "and then, what with going through it all so careful with the master and then with the police, I knew what the questions would be and was prepared, as you might say."

"I wonder you could speak so exactly to every little detail, all that time ago," said Bunter, with admiration.

"Well, you see, Mr. Bunter, the very morning after Mr. Boyes was took ill, master comes down to us and he says, sitting in that chair ever so friendly, just as you might be yourself, 'I'm afraid Mr. Boyes is very ill,' he says. 'He thinks he must have ate something as disagreed with him,' he says, 'and perhaps as it might be the chicken. So I want you and Cook,' he says, 'to run through with me everything we had for dinner last night to see if we can think what it could have been.' 'Well, sir,' I said, 'I don't see that Mr. Boyes could have ate anything unwholesome here, for Cook and me had just the same, put aside yourself, sir, and it was all as sweet and good as it could be,' I said."

"And I said the same," said the Cook. "Sech a plain, simple dinner as it was, too—no oysters nor mussels nor anything of that sort, as it's well known shell-fish is poison to some people's stummicks, but a good stren'thenin' drop o' soup, and a bit of nice fish and a casseroled chicken with turnips and carrots done in the gravy, and a omelette, wot could be lighter and better? Not but there's people as can't relish eggs in any form, my own mother was just the same, give her so much as a cake what had bin made with a egg in it and she'd be that sick and come out all over spots like nettle-rash, you'd be surprised. But Mr. Boyes was a great gentleman for eggs, and omelettes was his particular favourite."

"Yes, he made the omelette himself that very night, didn't he?"

"He did," said Hannah, "and well I remember it, for Mr. Urquhart asked particular after the eggs, was they new-laid, and I reminded him they was some he had brought in himself that afternoon from that shop on the corner of Lamb's Conduit Street where they always have them fresh from the farm, and I reminded him that one of them was a little cracked and he'd said, 'We'll use that in the omelette tonight, Hannah,' and I brought out a clean bowl from the kitchen and put them straight in—the cracked one and three more besides, and never touched them again till I brought them to table. 'And what's more, sir,' I said, 'there's the other eight still here out of the dozen, and you can see for yourself they're as good and fresh as they can be.' Didn't I, Cook?"

"Yes, Hannah. And as for the chicken, that was a little beauty. It was that young and tender, I says to Hannah at the time as it seemed a shame to casserole it, for it would 'ave roasted beautiful. But Mr. Urquhart is very partial to a casseroled chicken; he says as there's more flavour to 'em that way, and I dunno but what he's right."

"If done with a good beef stock," pronounced Mr. Bunter, judicially, "the vegetables well packed in layers, on a

foundation of bacon, not too fat, and the whole well sea-
soned with salt, pepper and paprika, there are few dishes
to beat a casseroled chicken. For my own part I would recommend a soupçon of garlic, but I am aware that such is
not agreeable to all tastes."

"I can't a-bear the smell or sight of the stuff," said Mrs.
Pettican, frankly, "but as for the rest I'm with you, always
allowing that the giblets is added to the stock, and I would
personally favour mushrooms when in season, but not them
tinned or bottled sorts as looks pretty but has no more
taste to 'em than boot-buttons if so much. But the secret is
in the cooking, as you know well, Mr. Bunter, the lid being
kep' well sealed down to 'old the flavour and the cookin'
bein' slow to make the juices perambulate through *and*
through each other as you might say. I'm not denyin' as
sech is very 'ighly enjoyable, and so Hannah and me found
it, though fond of a good roast fowl also, when well-basted
with a good rich stuffing to rejuice the dryness. But as to
roasting it, Mr. Urquhart wouldn't hear of it, and bein' as
it's him that pays the bills, he has the right to give his
orders."

"Well," said Bunter, "it's certain if there had been anything unwholesome about the casserole, you and Miss Westlock could scarcely have escaped it."

"No, indeed," said Hannah, "for I won't conceal that,
being blessed with hearty appetites, we finished it every
bit, except a little piece I gave to the cat. Mr. Urquhart
asked to see the remains of it next day, and seemed quite
put out to find it was all gone and the dish washed up—as
though any washing-up was ever left over-night in *this*
kitchen."

"I couldn't abear myself if I had to begin the day with
dirty dishes," said Mrs. Pettican. "There was a drop of the
soup left—not much, jest a wee drain, and Mr. Urquhart
took that up to show to the doctor, and he tasted it and
said it was very good, so Nurse Williams told us, though
she didn't have none of it herself."

"And as for the burgundy," said Hannah Westlock, "which was the only thing Mr. Boyes had to himself, like, Mr. Urquhart told me to cork it up tight and keep it. And just as well we did, because, of course, the police asked to see it when the time came."

"It was very far-seeing of Mr. Urquhart to take such precautions," said Bunter, "when there wasn't any thought at the time but that the poor man died naturally."

"That's what Nurse Williams said," replied Hannah, "but we put it down to him being a solicitor and knowing what ought to be done in a case of sudden death. Very particular he was, too—got me to put a bit of sticking-plaster over the mouth of the bottle and write my initials on it, so that it shouldn't be opened accidental. Nurse Williams always said he expected an inquest, but Dr. Weare being there to speak to Mr. Boyes having had these kind of bilious attacks all his life, of course there was no question raised about giving the certificate."

"Of course not," said Bunter, "but it's very fortunate as it turns out that Mr. Urquhart should have understood his duty so well. Many's the case his lordship has seen in which an innocent man has been brought near to the gallows for lack of a simple little precaution like that."

"And when I think how near Mr. Urquhart was to being away from 'ome at the time," said Mrs. Pettican, "the thought fair gives me palpitations. Called away, he was, to that tiresome old woman what's always a-dying and never dies. Why, he's there now—Mrs. Wrayburn, up in Windle. Rich as Sneezes, she is, by all accounts, and no good to nobody, for she's gone quite childish, so they say. A wicked old woman she was, too, in 'er day, and 'er other relations wouldn't 'ave nothink to do with 'er, only Mr. Urquhart, and I don't suppose 'e wouldn't, neither, only 'e's her solicitor and it's his duty so to do."

"Duty does not always lie in pleasant places," commented Mr. Bunter, "as you and I well know, Mrs. Pettican."

"Them that are rich," said Hannah Westlock, "find no

difficulty about getting their duties performed for them. Which I will make bold to say, Mrs. Wrayburn would not have done if she had been poor, great-aunt or no great-aunt, knowing Mr. Urquhart."

"Ah!" said Bunter.

"I pass no comments," said Miss Westlock, "but you and me, Mr. Bunter, know how the world goes."

"I suppose Mr. Urquhart stands to gain something when the old woman does peg out," suggested Bunter.

"That's as may be; he's not a talker," said Hannah, "but it stands to reason he wouldn't be always giving up his time and tearing off to Westmorland for nothing. Though I wouldn't care myself to put my hand to money that's wickedly come by. It would not bring a blessing with it, Mr. Bunter."

"It's easy talking, my girl, when you ain't likely to be put in the way of temptation," said Mrs. Pettican. "There's many great families in the Kingdom what never would a bin 'eard of if somebody 'adn't bin a little easier in their ways than what we've bin brought up to. There's skelintons in a many cupboards if the truth was known."

"Ah!" said Bunter, "I believe you. I've seen diamond necklaces and fur coats that should have been labelled Wages of Sin if deeds done in the dark were to be proclaimed upon the house-tops, Mrs. Pettican. And there are families that hold their heads high that wouldn't ever have existed but for some king or other taking his amusements on the wrong side of the blanket as the old saying goes."

"They say as some that was high up wasn't too high to take notice of old Mrs. Wrayburn in her young days," said Hannah, darkly. "Queen Victoria wouldn't never allow her to act before the Royal Family—she knew too much about her goings-on."

"An actress, was she?"

"And a very beautiful one, they say, though I can't rightly recollect what her stage name was," mused Mrs. Pettican. "It was a queer one, I know—'Yde Park, or some-

think of that. This Wrayburn as she married, 'e was nobody—jest to kiver up the scandal that's what she married
'im for. Two children she 'ad—but 'ose I would not take it
upon me to say—and they both died in the cholera, which
no doubt it was a judgment."

"That's not what Mr. Boyes called it," said Hannah,
with a self-righteous sniff. "The devil took care of his own,
that was his way of putting it."

"Ah! he talked careless," said Mrs. Pettican, "and no
wonder, seeing the folks he lived with. But he'd a sobered
down in time if he'd bin spared. A very pleasant way he
'ad with 'im when 'e liked. Come in here, he would, and
chat upon one thing and another, very amusing-like."

"You're too soft with the gentlemen, Mrs. Pettican," said
Hannah. "Anyone as has taking ways and poor health is
ewe-lambs to you."

"So Mr. Boyes knew all about Mrs. Wrayburn?"

"Oh, yes—it was all in the family, you see, and no doubt
Mr. Urquhart would a told him more than he'd say to us.
Which train did Mr. Urquhart say he was a-comin' by,
Hannah?"

"He said dinner for half-past seven. That'll be the six-
thirty, I should think."

Mrs. Pettican glanced at the clock and Bunter, taking
this as a hint, rose and made his farewells.

"And I 'opes as you'll come again, Mr. Bunter," said the
Cook, graciously. "The master makes no objections to respectable gentlemen visitors at tea-time. Wednesday is my
'arf-day."

"Mine is Friday," added Hannah, "and every other Sunday. If you should be Evangelical, Mr. Bunter, the Rev.
Crawford in Judd Street is a beautiful preacher. But maybe
you'll be going out of town for Christmas."

Mr. Bunter replied that that season would undoubtedly
be spent at Duke's Denver, and departed in a shining halo
of vicarious splendour.

CHAPTER X

HERE you are, Peter," said Chief-Inspector Parker, "and here is the lady you are anxious to meet. Mrs. Bulfinch, allow me to introduce Lord Peter Wimsey."

"Pleased, I am sure," said Mrs. Bulfinch. She giggled, and dabbed her large, blonde face with powder.

"Mrs. Bulfinch, before her union with Mr. Bulfinch, was the life and soul of the saloon bar at the Nine Rings in Grays Inn Road," said Mr. Parker, "and well-known to all for her charm and wit."

"Go on," said Mrs. Bulfinch, "you're a one, aren't you? Don't you pay no attention to him, your lordship. You know what these police fellows are."

"Sad dogs," said Wimsey, shaking his head. "But I don't need his testimonials, I can trust my own eyes and ears, Mrs. Bulfinch, and I can only say that, if I had had the happiness to make your acquaintance before it was too late, it would have been my life-time's ambition to wipe Mr. Bulfinch's eye."

"You're every bit as bad as he is," said Mrs. Bulfinch, highly gratified, "and what Bulfinch would say to you I *don't* know. Quite upset, he was, when the officer came round to ask me to pop along to the Yard. 'I don't like it, Gracie,' he says, 'we've always bin respectable in this house and no trouble with disorderlies nor drinks after hours, and once you get among them fellows you don't know the things you may be asked.' 'Don't be so soft,' I tells him, 'the boys all know me and they haven't got nothing against me, and if it's just to tell them about the gentleman that left the packet behind him at the Rings, I haven't no objection to tell them, having nothing to reproach myself with. What'd they think,' I said, 'if I refused to go? Ten to one they'd think there was something funny about it.' 'Well,' he says, 'I'm coming with you.' 'Oh, are you?' I says, 'and how about the new barman you was going to engage this morning? For,' I said, 'serve in the jug and bottle I will not, never having been accustomed to it, so you can do as you like.' So I came away and left him to it. Mind you, I like him for it. I ain't saying nothing against Bulfinch, but police or no police, I reckon I know how to take care of myself."

"Quite so," said Parker, patiently. "Mr. Bulfinch need feel no alarm. All we want you to do is to tell us, to the best of your recollection, about that young man you spoke of and help us to find the white-paper packet. You may be able to save an innocent person from being convicted, and I am sure your husband could not object to that."

"Poor thing!" said Mrs. Bulfinch, "I'm sure when I read the account of the trial I said to Bulfinch——"

"Just a moment. If you wouldn't mind beginning at the beginning, Mrs. Bulfinch, Lord Peter would understand better what you have to tell us."

"Why, of course. Well, my lord, before I was married I was barmaid at the Nine Rings, as the Chief-Inspector says. Miss Montague I was then—it's a better name than Bulfinch, and I was almost sorry to say good-bye to it, but there! a girl has to make a lot of sacrifices when she marries and one more or less is nothing to signify. I never worked there but in the saloon bar, for I wouldn't undertake the four-ale business, it not being a refined neighbourhood, though there's a lot of very nice legal gentlemen drops in of an evening on the saloon side. Well, as I was saying, I was working there up to my marriage, which was last August Bank Holiday, and I remember one evening a gentleman coming in——"

"Could you remember the date, do you think?"

"Not within a day or so I couldn't, for I wouldn't wish to swear to a fib, but it wasn't far off the longest day, for

I remember making that same remark to the gentleman for something to say, you know."

"That's near enough," said Parker. "Round about June 20th, or 21st, or something like that?"

"That's right, as near as I can speak to it. And as to the time of night, that I *can* tell you—knowing how keen you 'tecs always are on the hands of the clock." Mrs. Bulfinch giggled again and looked archly round for applause. "There was a gentleman sitting there—I didn't know him, he was a stranger to the district—and he asked what was our closing hour and I told him 11 o'clock, and he said, 'Thank God! I thought I was going to be turned out at 10.30,' and I looked at the clock and said, 'Oh, you're all right, anyhow, sir; we always keep that clock a quarter of an hour fast.' The clock said twenty past, so I know it must have been five past ten really. So we got talking a bit about these prohibitionists and the way they had been trying it on again to get our licensing-hour altered to half-past ten, only we had a good friend on the Bench in Mr. Judkins, and while we was discussing it, I remember so well, the door was pushed open hurried-like and a young gentleman comes in, almost falls in, I might say, and he calls, 'Give me a double brandy, quick.' Well, I didn't like to serve him all at once, he looked so white and queer, I thought he'd had one or two over the eight already, and the boss was most particular about that sort of thing. Still, he spoke all right—quite clear and not repeating himself nor nothing, and his eyes, though they did look a bit funny, weren't fixed-like, if you understand me. We get to size folks up pretty well in our business, you know. He sort of held on to the bar, all scrunched up together and bent double, and he says, "Make it a stiff one, there's a good girl, I'm feeling awful bad.' The gentleman I'd been talking to, he says to him, 'Hold up,' he says, 'what's the matter?' and the gentleman says, 'I'm going to be ill.' And he puts his hands across his waistcoat like so!"

Mrs. Bulfinch clasped her waist and rolled her big blue eyes dramatically.

"Well, then I see he wasn't drunk, so I mixed him a double Martell with just a splash of soda and he gulps it down, and says, 'That's better.' And the other gentleman puts his arm round him and helps him to a seat. There was a good many other people in the bar, but they didn't notice much, being full of the racing news. Presently the gentleman asks me for a glass of water, and I fetched it to him, and he says: 'Sorry if I frightened you, but I've just had a bad shock, and it must have gone to my inside. I'm subject to gastric trouble,' he says, 'and any worry or shock always affects my stomach. However,' he says, 'perhaps this will stop it.' And he takes out a white paper packet with some powder in it, and drops it into the glass of water and stirs it up with a fountain-pen and drinks it off."

"Did it fizz or anything?" asked Wimsey.

"No; it was just a plain powder, and it took a bit of a time to mix. He drank it off and said, 'That settles it,' or 'That'll settle it,' or something of that sort. And then he says, 'Thanks very much. I'm better now and I'd better get home in case it takes me again.' And he raised his hat—he was quite the gentleman—and off he goes."

"How much powder do you think he put in?"

"Oh, a good dollop. He didn't measure it or anything, just shot it in out of the packet. Near a dessert spoonful it might have been."

"And what happened to the packet?" prompted Parker.

"Ah, there you are." Mrs. Bulfinch took a glance at Wimsey's face and seemed pleased with the effect she was producing.

"We'd just got the last customer out—about five past eleven, that would be, and George was locking the door, when I see something white on the seat. Somebody's handkerchief I thought it was, but when I picked it up, I see it was the paper packet. So I said to George, 'Hullo! the gentleman's left his medicine behind him.' So George asked what gentleman, and I told him, and he said, 'What is it?' and I looked, but the label had been torn off. It was just one of them chemist's packets, you know, with the ends turned up and a label stuck across, but there wasn't a bit of the label left."

"You couldn't even see whether it had been printed in black or in red?"

"Well, now." Mrs. Bulfinch considered. "Well, no, I couldn't say that. Now you mention it, I do seem to recollect that there was something red about the packet, somewhere, but I can't clearly call it to mind. I wouldn't swear. I know there wasn't any name or printing of any kind, because I looked to see what it was."

"You didn't try tasting it, I suppose?"

"Not me. It might have been poison or something. I tell you, he was a funny-looking customer." (Parker and Wimsey exchanged glances.)

"Was that what you thought at the time?" enquired Wimsey, "or did it only occur to you later on—after you'd read about the case, you know?"

"I thought it at the time, of course," retorted Mrs. Bulfinch, snappishly. "Aren't I telling you that's why I didn't taste it? I said so to George at the time, what's more. Besides, if it wasn't poison, it might be 'snow' or something. 'Best not touch it,' that's what I said to George, and he said 'Chuck it in the fire.' But I wouldn't have that. The gentleman might have come back for it. So I stuck it up on the shelf behind the bar, where they keep the spirits, and never thought of it again from that day to yesterday, when your policeman came round about it."

"It's been looked for there," said Parker, "but they can't seem to find it anywhere."

"Well, I don't know about that. I put it there and I left the Rings in August, so what's gone with it I can't say. Daresay they threw it away when they were cleaning. Wait a bit, though—I'm wrong when I say I never thought about it again. I did just wonder about it when I read the report of the trial in the *News of the World*, and I said to George, 'I wouldn't be surprised if that was the gentleman who came into the Rings one night and seemed so poorly—just fancy!' I said—just like that. And George said, 'Now don't you get fancies, Gracie my girl; you don't want to get mixed up in a police case.' George has always held his head high, you see."

"It's a pity you didn't come forward with this story," said Parker, severely.

"Well, how was I to know it was important? The taxi-driver had seen him a few minutes afterwards and he was ill then, so the powder couldn't have had anything to do with it, if it was him, which I couldn't swear to. And anyhow, I didn't see about it till the trial was all over and finished with."

"There will be a new trial, though," said Parker, "and you may have to give evidence at that."

"You know where to find me," said Mrs. Bulfinch, with spirit. "I shan't run away."

"We're very much obliged to you for coming now," added Wimsey, pleasantly.

"Don't mention it," said the lady. "Is that all you want, Mr. Chief-Inspector?"

"That's all at present. If we find the packet, we may ask you to identify it. And, by the way, it's advisable not to discuss these matters with your friends, Mrs. Bulfinch. Sometimes ladies get talking, and one thing leads to another, and in the end they remember incidents that never took place at all. You understand."

"I never was one for talking," said Mrs. Bulfinch, offended. "And it's my opinion, when it comes to putting two-and-two together to make five of 'em, the ladies aren't in it with the gentlemen."

"I may pass this on to the solicitors for the defence, I

suppose?" said Wimsey, when the witness had departed.

"Of course," said Parker, "that's why I asked you to come and hear it—for what it's worth. Meanwhile, we shall of course have a good hunt for the packet."

"Yes," said Wimsey, thoughtfully, "yes—you will have to do that—naturally."

. . . .

Mr. Crofts did not look best pleased when this story was handed on to him.

"I warned you, Lord Peter," he said, "what might come of showing our hand to the police. Now they've got hold of this incident, they will have every opportunity to turn it to their own advantage. Why didn't you leave it to us to make the investigation?"

"Damn it," said Wimsey angrily, "it was left to you for about three months and you did absolutely nothing. The police dug it up in three days. Time's important in this case, you know."

"Very likely, but don't you see that the police won't rest now till they've found this precious packet?"

"Well?"

"Well, and suppose it isn't arsenic at all? If you'd left it in our hands, we could have sprung the thing on them at the last moment, when it was too late to make enquiries, and then we should have knocked the bottom out of the prosecution. Give the jury Mrs. Bulfinch's story as it stands and they'd have to admit there was some evidence that the deceased poisoned himself. But now, of course, the police will find or fake something and show that the powder was perfectly harmless."

"And supposing they find it and it *is* arsenic?"

"In *that* case, of course," said Mr. Crofts, "we shall get an acquittal. But do you believe in that possibility, my lord?"

"It's perfectly evident that *you* don't," said Wimsey, hotly. "In fact, you think your client's guilty. Well, I don't."

Mr. Crofts shrugged his shoulders.

"In our client's interests," he said, "we are bound to look at the unfavourable side of all evidence, so as to anticipate the points that are likely to be made by the prosecution. I repeat, my lord, that you have acted indiscreetly."

"Look here," said Wimsey, "I'm not out for a verdict of 'Not Proven.' As far as Miss Vane's honour and happiness are concerned, she might as well be found guilty as acquitted on a mere element of doubt. I want to see her absolutely cleared and the blame fixed in the right quarter. I don't want any shadow of doubt about it."

"Highly desirable, my lord," agreed the solicitor, "but you will allow me to remind you that it is not merely a question of honour or happiness, but of saving Miss Vane's neck from the gallows."

"And I say," said Wimsey, "that it would be better for her to be hanged outright than to live and have everybody think her a murderess who got off by a fluke."

"Indeed?" said Mr. Crofts, "I fear that is not an attitude that the defence can very well adopt. May I ask if it is adopted by Miss Vane herself?"

"I shouldn't be surprised if it was," said Wimsey. "But she's innocent, and I'll make you damn well believe it before I've done."

"Excellent, excellent," said Mr. Crofts, suavely, "nobody will be more delighted than myself. But I repeat that, in my humble opinion, your lordship will be wiser not to betray too many confidences to Chief-Inspector Parker."

.   .   .   .

Wimsey was still simmering inwardly from this encounter when he entered Mr. Urquhart's office in Bedford Row. The head-clerk remembered him and greeted him with the deference due to an exalted and expected visitor. He begged his lordship to take a seat for a moment, and vanished into an inner office.

A woman typist, with a strong, ugly, rather masculine

face, looked up from her machine as the door closed, and nodded abruptly to Lord Peter. Wimsey recognized her as one of the "Cattery," and put a commendatory mental note against Miss Climpson's name for quick and efficient organisation. No words passed, however, and in a few moments the head-clerk returned and begged Lord Peter to step inside.

Norman Urquhart rose from his desk and held out a friendly hand of greeting. Wimsey had seen him at the trial, and noted his neat dress, thick, smooth dark hair and general appearance of brisk and business-like respectability. Seeing him now more closely, he noticed that he was rather older than he had appeared at a distance. He put him down as being somewhere about the middle forties. His skin was pale and curiously clear, except for a number of little freckles, like sun-spots, rather unexpected at that time of the year, and in a man whose appearance conveyed no other suggestion of an out-door life. The eyes, dark and shrewd, looked a little tired, and were blistered about the orbits, as though anxiety were not unknown to them.

The solicitor welcomed his guest in a high, pleasant voice and asked what he could do for him.

Wimsey explained that he was interested in the Vane poisoning trial, and that he had the authority of Messrs. Crofts & Cooper to come and bother Mr. Urquhart with questions, adding, as usual, that he was afraid he was being a nuisance.

"Not at all, Lord Peter, not at all. I'm only too delighted to help you in any way, though really I'm afraid you have heard all I know. Naturally, I was very much taken aback by the result of the autopsy, and rather relieved, I must admit, to find that no suspicion was likely to be thrown on me, under the rather peculiar circumstances."

"Frightfully tryin' for you," agreed Wimsey. "But you seem to have taken the most admirable precautions at the time."

"Well, you know, I suppose we lawyers get into a habit of taking precautions. Not that I had any idea of poison at the time—or, needless to say, I should have insisted on an enquiry then and there. What was in my mind was more in the nature of some kind of food-poisoning; not botulism, the symptoms were all wrong for that, but some contamination from cooking utensils or from some bacillus in the food itself. I am glad it turned out not to be that, though the reality was infinitely worse in one way. I suppose, really, in all cases of sudden and unaccountable illness, an analysis of the secretions ought to be made as a routine part of the business, but Dr. Weare appeared perfectly satisfied, and I trusted entirely to his judgment."

"Obviously," said Wimsey. "One doesn't naturally jump to the idea that people are bein' murdered—though I dare say it happens more often than one is apt to suppose."

"It probably does, and if I'd ever had the handling of a criminal case, the suspicion might have occurred to me, but my work is almost entirely conveyancing and that sort of business—and probate and divorce and so on."

"Talkin' of probate," said Wimsey, carelessly, "had Mr. Boyes any sort of financial expectations?"

"None at all that I know of. His father is by no means well off—the usual country parson with a small stipend and a huge Vicarage and tumble-down Church. In fact, the whole family belongs to the unfortunate professional middle-class—over-taxed and with very little financial stamina. I shouldn't think there were more than a few hundred pounds to come to Philip Boyes, even if he had outlived the lot of them."

"I had an idea there was a rich aunt somewhere."

"Oh, no—unless you're thinking of old Cremorna Garden. She's a great-aunt, on the mother's side. But she hasn't had anything to do with them for very many years."

At this moment Lord Peter had one of those bursts of illumination which come suddenly when two unrelated

facts make contact in the mind. In the excitement of hearing Parker's news about the white paper packet, he had
paid insufficient attention to Bunter's account of the tea-
party with Hannah Westlock and Mrs. Pettican, but now
he remembered something about an actress, with a name
like ''Yde Park or something of that.' The readjustment
made itself so smoothly and mechanically in his mind that
his next question followed almost without a pause.

"Isn't that Mrs. Wrayburn of Windle in Westmorland?"

"Yes," said Mr. Urquhart. "I've just been up to see her,
as a matter of fact. Of course, yes, you wrote to me there.
She's been quite childish, poor old lady, for the last five
years or so. A wretched life—dragging on like that, a misery
to herself and everybody else. It always seems to me a cruel
thing that one may not put these poor old people out of
the way, as one would a favourite animal—but the law will
not let us be so merciful."

"Yes, we'd be hauled over the coals by the N.S.P.C.A. if
we let a cat linger on in misery," said Wimsey. "Silly, isn't
it? But it's all of a piece with the people who write to the
papers about keepin' dogs in draughty kennels and don't
give a hoot—or a penny—to stop landlords allowin' a family
of thirteen to sleep in an undrained cellar with no glass in
the windows and no windows to put it in. It really makes
me quite cross, sometimes, though I'm a peaceful sort of
idiot as a rule. Poor old Cremorna Garden—she must be
gettin' on now, though. Surely she can't last much longer."

"As a matter of fact, we all thought she'd gone the other
day. Her heart is giving out—she's over ninety, poor soul,
and she gets these attacks from time to time. But there's
amazing vitality in some of these ancient ladies."

"I suppose you're about her only living relation now."

"I suppose I am, except for an uncle of mine in Australia." Mr. Urquhart accepted the fact of the relationship
without enquiring how Wimsey came to know about it.
"Not that my being there can do her any good. But I'm her

man of business, too, so it's just as well I should be on the spot when anything happens."

"Oh, quite, quite. And being her man of business, of course you know how she has left her money."

"Well, yes, of course. Though I don't quite see, if you'll forgive my saying so, what that has to do with the present problem."

"Why, don't you see," said Wimsey, "it just occurred to me that Philip Boyes might have got himself into some kind of financial mess-up—it happens to the best of men—and have, well, taken the short way out of it. But, if he had any expectations from Mrs. Wrayburn, and the old girl, I mean, the poor old lady, was so near shuffling off this mortal thingummy, why, then, don't you know, he would have waited, or raised the wind on the strength of a post-orbit or something or the other. You get my meaning, what?"

"Oh, I see—you are trying to make out a case for suicide. Well, I agree with you that it's the most hopeful defense for Miss Vane's friends to put up, and as far as that goes, I can support you. Inasmuch, that is, as Mrs. Wrayburn did not leave Philip anything. Nor, so far as I know, had he the smallest reason to suppose she would do so."

"You're positive of that?"

"Quite. As a matter of fact," Mr. Urquhart hesitated, "well, I may as well tell you that he asked me about it one day, and I was obliged to tell him that he hadn't the least chance of getting anything from her."

"Oh—he did actually ask?"

"Well, yes, he did."

"That's rather a point, isn't it? How long ago would that be?"

"Oh—about eighteen months ago, I fancy. I couldn't be sure."

"And as Mrs. Wrayburn is now childish, I suppose he couldn't entertain any hope that she would ever alter the will?"

"Not the slightest."

"No, I see. Well, I think we might make something of that. Great disappointment, of course—one would make out that he had counted a good deal upon it. Is it much, by the way?"

"Pretty fair—about seventy or eighty thousand."

"Very sickening, to think of all that good stuff going west and not getting a look-in one's self. By the way, how about you? Don't you get anything? I beg your pardon, fearfully inquisitive and all that, but I mean to say, considering you've been looking after her for years and are her only available relation so to speak, it would be a trifle thick, what?"

The solicitor frowned, and Wimsey apologised.

"I know, I know—I've been fearfully impudent. It's a failing of mine. And anyhow, it'll all be in the papers when the old lady does pop off, so I don't know why I should be so anxious to pump you. Wash it out—I'm sorry."

"There's no real reason why you shouldn't know," said Mr. Urquhart, slowly, "though one's professional instinct is to avoid disclosing one's clients' affairs. As a matter of fact, I am the legatee myself."

"Oh?" said Wimsey, in a disappointed voice. "But in that case—that rather weakens the story, doesn't it? I mean to say, your cousin might very well have felt, in that case, that he could look to you for—that is—of course I don't know what your ideas might have been—"

Mr. Urquhart shook his head.

"I see what you are driving at, and it is a very natural thought. But actually, such a disposal of the money would have been directly contrary to the expressed wish of the testatrix. Even if I could legally have made it over, I should have been morally bound not to do so, and I had to make that clear to Philip. I might, of course, have assisted him with casual gifts of money from time to time, but, to tell the truth, I should hardly have cared to do so. In my opinion, the only hope of salvation for Philip would have been to make his way by his own work. He was a little inclined—though I don't like speaking ill of the dead—to—to rely too much on other people."

"Ah, quite. No doubt that was Mrs. Wrayburn's idea also?"

"Not exactly. No. It went rather deeper than that. She considered that she had been badly treated by her family. In short, well, as we have gone so far, I don't mind giving you her *ipsissima verba.*"

He rang a bell on his desk.

"I haven't got the will itself here, but I have the draft. Oh, Miss Murchison, would you kindly bring me in the deed-box labelled 'Wrayburn'? Mr. Pond will show it to you. It isn't heavy."

The lady from the "Cattery" departed silently in quest of the box.

"This is all rather irregular, Lord Peter," went on Mr. Urquhart, "but there are times when too much discretion is as bad as too little, and I should like you to see exactly why I was forced to take up this rather uncompromising attitude towards my cousin. Ah, thank you, Miss Murchison."

He opened the deed-box with a key attached to a bunch which he took from his trousers' pocket, and turned over a quantity of papers. Wimsey watched him with the expression of a rather foolish terrier who expects a tit-bit.

"Dear, dear," ejaculated the solicitor, "it doesn't seem to be—oh! of course, how forgetful of me. I'm so sorry, it's in my safe at home. I got it out for reference last June, when the previous alarm occurred about Mrs. Wrayburn's illness, and in the confusion which followed on my cousin's death I quite forgot to bring it back. However, the gist of it was—"

"Never mind," said Wimsey, "there's no hurry. If I called at your house tomorrow, perhaps I could see it then."

"By all means, if you think it important. I do apologise for my carelessness. In the meantime, is there anything else I can tell you about the matter?"

Wimsey asked a few questions, covering the ground already traversed by Bunter in his investigations, and took his departure. Miss Murchison was again at work in the outer office. She did not look up as he passed.

"Curious," mused Wimsey, as he pattered along Bedford Row, "everybody is so remarkably helpful about this case. They cheerfully answer questions which one has no right to ask and burst into explanations in the most unnecessary manner. None of them seem to have anything to conceal. It's quite astonishing. Perhaps the fellow really did commit suicide. I hope he did. I wish I could question *him*. I'd put him through it, blast him. I've got about fifteen different analyses of his character already—all different . . . It's very ungentlemanly to commit suicide without leaving a note to say you've done it—gets people into trouble. When I blow my brains out—"

He stopped.

"I hope I shan't want to," he said. "I hope I shan't need to want to. Mother wouldn't like it, and it's messy. But I'm beginning to dislike this job of getting people hanged. It's damnable for their friends. . . . I won't think about hanging. It's unnerving."

CHAPTER XI

Wimsey presented himself at Mr. Urquhart's house at 9 o'clock the next morning, and found that gentleman at breakfast.

"I thought I might catch you before you went down to the office," said his lordship, apologetically. "Thanks awfully, I've had my morning nosebag. No, really, thanks—I never drink before eleven. Bad for the inside."

"Well, I've found the draft for you," said Mr. Urquhart pleasantly. "You can cast your eye over it while I drink my coffee, if you'll excuse my going on. It exposes the family skeleton a little, but it's all ancient history now."

He fetched a sheet of typescript from a side-table and handed it to Wimsey, who noticed, mechanically, that it had been typed on a Woodstock machine, with a chipped lower case p, and an A slightly out of alignment.

"I'd better make quite clear the family connection of the Boyes's and the Urquharts's," he went on, returning to the breakfast-table, "so that you will understand the will. The common ancestor is old John Hubbard, a highly respectable banker at the beginning of the last century. He lived in Nottingham, and the bank, as usual in those days, was a private, family concern. He had three daughters, Jane, Mary and Rosanna. He educated them well, and they ought to have been heiresses in a mild way, but the old boy made the usual mistakes, speculated unwisely, allowed his clients too much rope—the old story. The bank broke, and the daughters were left penniless. The eldest, Jane, married a man called Henry Brown. He was a schoolmaster and very poor and quite repellantly moral. They had one daughter, Julia, who eventually married a curate, the Rev. Arthur Boyes, and was the mother of Philip Boyes. The second daughter, Mary, did rather better financially, though socially she married beneath her. She accepted the hand of one Josiah Urquhart, who was engaged in the lace-trade. This was a blow to the old people, but Josiah came originally of a fairly decent family, and was a most worthy person, so they made the best of it. Mary had a son, Charles Urquhart, who contrived to break away from the degrading associations of trade. He entered a solicitor's office, did well, and finally became a partner in the firm. He was my father, and I am his successor in the legal business.

"The third daughter, Rosanna, was made of different stuff. She was very beautiful, a remarkably fine singer, a graceful dancer and altogether a particularly attractive and spoilt young person. To the horror of her parents she ran away and went on the stage. They erased her name from the family Bible. She determined to justify their worst suspicions. She became the spoilt darling of fashionable London. Under her stage name of Cremorna Garden, she went from one disreputable triumph to another. And, mind you, she had brains—nothing of the Nell Gwyn business about her. She was the take-it-and-keep-it sort. She took everything—money, jewels, apartments meublés, horses, carriages, all the rest of it, and turned it into good consolidated funds. She was never prodigal of anything except her person, which she considered to be a sufficient return for all favours, and I daresay it was. I never saw her till she was an old woman, but before she had the stroke which destroyed her brain and body, she still kept the remains of remarkable beauty. She was a shrewd old woman in her way, and grasping. She had those tight little hands, plump and narrow, that give nothing away—except for cash down. You know the sort.

"Well, the long and the short of it was that the eldest sister, Jane—the one who married the schoolmaster—would have nothing to do with the family black sheep. She and her husband wrapped themselves up in their virtue and

shuddered when they saw the disgraceful name of Cremorna
Garden billed outside the Olympic or the Adelphi. They
returned her letters unopened and forbade her the house,
and the climax was reached when Henry Brown tried to
have her turned out of the Church on the occasion of his
wife's funeral.

"My grand-parents were less strait-laced. They didn't call
on her and didn't invite her, but they occasionally took a
box for her performances and they sent her a card for their
son's wedding, and were polite in a distant kind of way.
In consequence, she kept up a civil acquaintance with my
father, and eventually put her business into his hands. He
took the view that property was property, however acquired, and said that if a lawyer refused to handle dirty
money he would have to show half his clients the door.

"The old lady never forgot or forgave anything. The very
mention of the Brown-Boyes connection made her foam at
the mouth. Hence, when she came to make her will, she put
in that paragraph you have before you now. I pointed out
to her that Philip Boyes had had nothing to do with the
persecution, as, indeed, neither had Arthur Boyes, but the
old sore rankled still, and she wouldn't hear a word in his
favour. So I drew up the will as she wanted it; if I hadn't,
somebody else would have done so, you know."

Wimsey nodded, and gave his attention to the will, which
was dated eight years previously. It appointed Norman
Urquhart as sole executor, and, after a few legacies to
servants and to theatrical charities, it ran as follows:—

"All the rest of my property whatsoever and wheresoever
situated I give to my great-nephew Norman Urquhart of
Bedford Row Solicitor for his lifetime and at his death
to be equally divided among his legitimate issue but if the
said Norman Urquhart should decease without legitimate
issue the said property to pass to (here followed the names
of the charities previously specified). And I make this disposition of my property in token of gratitude for the con-

sideration shown to me by my said great-nephew Norman
Urquhart and his father the late Charles Urquhart throughout their lives and to ensure that no part of my property
shall come into the hands of my great-nephew Philip Boyes
or his descendants. And to this end and to mark my sense
of the inhuman treatment meted out to me by the family
of the said Philip Boyes I enjoin upon the said Norman
Urquhart as my dying wish that he neither give, lend or
convey to the said Philip Boyes any part of the income derived from the said property enjoyed by him the said Norman Urquhart during his lifetime nor employ the same to
assist the said Philip Boyes in any manner whatsoever."

"H'm!" said Wimsey, "that's pretty clear, and pretty
vindictive."

"Yes, it is—but what are you to do with old ladies who
won't listen to reason? She looked pretty sharply to see that
I had got the wording fierce enough before she would put
her name to it."

"It must have depressed Philip Boyes all right," said
Wimsey. "Thank you—I'm glad I've seen that; it makes the
suicide theory a good deal more probable."

In theory it might do so, but the theory did not square
as well as Wimsey could have wished with what he had
heard about the character of Philip Boyes. Personally, he
was inclined to put more faith in the idea that the final
interview with Harriet had been the deciding factor in the
suicide. But this, too, was not quite satisfactory. He could
not believe that Philip had felt that particular kind of
affection for Harriet Vane. Perhaps, though, it was merely
that he did not want to think well of the man. His emotions, he feared, clouding his judgment a little.

He went back home and read the proofs of Harriet's
novel. Undoubtedly she could write well, but undoubtedly
she knew only too much about the administration of arsenic. Moreover, the book was about two artists who lived
in Bloomsbury and led an ideal existence, full of love and

laughter and poverty, till somebody unkindly poisoned the young man and left the young woman inconsolable and passionately resolved to avenge him. Wimsey ground his teeth and went down to Halloway Gaol, where he very nearly made a jealous exhibition of himself. Fortunately, his sense of humour came to the rescue when he had cross-examined his client to the verge of exhaustion and tears.

"I'm sorry," he said; "the fact is, I'm most damnably jealous of this fellow Boyes. I oughtn't to be, but I am."

"That's just it," said Harriet, "and you always would be."

"And if I was, I shouldn't be fit to live with. Is that it?"

"You would be very unhappy. Quite apart from all the other drawbacks."

"But, look here," said Wimsey, "if you married me I shouldn't be jealous, because then I should know that you really liked me and all that."

"You think you woundn't be. But you would."

"Should I? Oh, surely not. Why should I? It's just the same as if I married a widow. Are all second husbands jealous?"

"I don't know. But it's not quite the same. You'd never really trust me, and we should be wretched."

"But damn it all," said Wimsey, "if you would once say you cared a bit about me it would be all right. I should be-lieve that. It's because you won't say it that I imagine all sorts of things."

"You would go on imagining things in spite of yourself. You couldn't give me a square deal. No man ever does."

"Never?"

"Well, hardly ever."

"That would be rotten," said Wimsey, seriously. "Of course, if I turned out to be that sort of idiot, things would be pretty hopeless. I know what you mean. I knew a bloke once who got that jealous bug. If his wife wasn't always hanging round his neck, he said it showed he meant noth-ing to her, and if she did express her affection he called

her a hypocrite. It got quite impossible, and she ran away
with somebody she didn't care twopence for, and he went
about saying that he had been right about her all along.
But everybody else said it was his own silly fault. It's all
very complicated. The advantage seems to be with the person who gets jealous first. Perhaps you could manage to be
jealous of me. I wish you would, because it would prove
that you took a bit of interest in me. Shall I give you some
details of my hideous past?"

"Please don't."

"Why not?"

"I don't want to know about all the other people."

"Don't you, by jove? I think that's rather hopeful. I
mean, if you just felt like a mother to me, you would be
anxious to be helpful and understanding. I loathe being
helped and understood. And, after all, there was nothing
in any of them—except Barbara, of course."

"Who was Barbara?" asked Harriet, quickly.

"Oh, a girl. I owe her quite a lot, really," replied Wimsey, musingly. "When she married the other fellow, I took
up sleuthing as a cure for wounded feelings, and it's really
been great fun, take it all in all. Dear me, yes—I was very
much bowled over that time. I even took a special course
in logic for her sake."

"Good gracious!"

"For the pleasure of repeating 'Barbara celarent darii
ferio baralipton.' There was a kind of mysterious romantic
lilt about the thing which was somehow expressive of passion. Many a moonlight night have I murmured it to the
nightingales which haunt the gardens of St. Johns—though,
of course, I was a Balliol man myself, but the buildings are
adjacent."

"If anybody ever marries you, it will be for the pleasure
of hearing you talk piffle," said Harriet, severely.

"A humiliating reason, but better than no reason at all."

"I used to piffle rather well myself," said Harriet, with

tears in her eyes, "but it's got knocked out of me. You know—I was really meant to be a cheerful person—all this gloom and suspicion isn't the real me. But I've lost my nerve, somehow."

"No wonder, poor kid. But you'll get over it. Just keep on smiling, and leave it to Uncle Peter."

When Wimsey got home, he found a note awaiting him.

Dear Lord Peter,
   As you saw, I got the job. Miss Climpson sent six of us, all with different stories and testimonials, of course, and Mr. Pond (the head-clerk) engaged me, subject to Mr. Urquhart's approval.

   I've only been here a couple of days, so there isn't very much I can tell you about my employer, personally, except that he has a sweet tooth and keeps secret stores of chocolate cream and Turkish delight in his desk, which he surreptitiously munches while he is dictating. He seems pleasant enough.

   But there's just one thing. I fancy it would be interesting to investigate his financial activities. I've done a good bit one way and another with stockbroking, you know, and yesterday in his absence I took a call for him which I wasn't meant to hear. It wouldn't have told the ordinary person anything, but it did me, because I knew something about the man at the other end. Find out if Mr. U. had been doing anything with the Megatherium Trust before their big crash.

   Further reports when anything turns up.
                                   Yours sincerely,
                                       Joan Murchison.

"Megatherium Trust?" said Wimsey. "That's a nice thing for a respectable solicitor to get mixed up with. I'll ask Freddy Arbuthnot. He's an ass about everything except stocks and shares, but he does understand them, for some ungodly reason."

He read the letter again, mechanically noting that it was

typed on a Woodstock machine, with a chipped lower case p, and a capital A that was out of alignment.

Suddenly he woke up and read it a third time, noticing by no means mechanically, the chipped p and the irregular capital A.

Then he sat down, wrote a line on a sheet of paper, folded it, addressed it to Miss Murchison and sent Bunter out to post it.

For the first time, in this annoying case, he felt the vague stirring of the waters as a living idea emerged slowly and darkly from the innermost deeps of his mind.

CHAPTER XII

Wimsey was accustomed to say, when he was an old man and more talkative even than usual, that the recollection of that Christmas at Duke's Denver had haunted him in nightmares, every night regularly, for the following twenty years. But it is possible that he remembered it with advantages. There is no doubt that it tried his temper severely. It began inauspiciously at the tea-table, when Mrs. "Freak" Dimsworthy fluted out in her high, overriding voice: "And is it true, Lord Peter dear, that you are defending that frightful poisoning woman?" The question acted like the drawing of a champagne cork. The whole party's bottled-up curiosity about the Vane case creamed over in one windy gust of stinging froth.

"I've no doubt she did it, and I don't blame her," said Captain Tommy Bates, "perfectly foul blighter. Has his photograph on the dust-cover of his books, you know, that's the sort of squit he was. Wonderful, the rotters these highbrow females will fall for. The whole lot of 'em ought to be poisoned like rats. Look at the harm they do to the country."

"But he was a very fine writer," protested Mrs. Featherstone, a lady in her thirties, whose violently compressed figure suggested that she was engaged in a perpetual struggle to compute her weight in terms of the first syllables of her name rather than the last. "His books are positively Gallic in their audacity and restraint. Audacity is not rare—but that perfect concision of style is a gift which—"

"Oh, if you like dirt," interrupted the Captain, rather rudely.

"I wouldn't call it that," said Mrs. Featherstone. "He is frank, of course, and that is what people in this country will not forgive. It is part of our national hypocrisy. But the beauty of the writing puts it all on a higher plane."

"Well, I wouldn't have the muck in the house," said the Captain, firmly. "I caught Hilda with it, and I said, 'Now you send that book straight back to the library.' I don't often interfere, but one must draw the line somewhere."

"How did you know what it was like?" asked Wimsey, innocently.

"Why, James Douglas' article in the *Express* was good enough for me," said Captain Bates. "The paragraphs he quoted were filthy, positively filthy."

"Well, it's a good thing we've all read them," said Wimsey. "Forewarned is forearmed."

"We owe a great debt of gratitude to the press," said the Dowager Duchess, "so kind of them to pick out all the plums for us and save the trouble of reading the books, don't you think, and such a joy for the poor dear people who can't afford seven-and-sixpence, or even a library subscription, I suppose, though I'm sure that works out cheaply enough if one is a quick reader. Not that the cheap ones will take those books for I asked my maid, such a superior girl and so keen on improving her mind, which is more than I can say for most of my friends, but no doubt it is all due to free education for the people and I suspect her in my heart of voting labour though I never ask because I don't think it's fair, and besides, if I did, I couldn't very well take any notice of it, could I?"

"Still, I don't suppose the young woman murdered him on that account," said her daughter-in-law. "From all accounts she was just as bad as he was."

"Oh, come," said Wimsey, "you can't think that, Helen. Damn it, she writes detective stories and in detective stories virtue is always triumphant. They're the purest literature we have."

"The devil is always ready to quote scripture when it pays him to do so," said the younger Duchess, "and they say the wretched woman's sales are going up by leaps and bounds."

"It's my belief," said Mr. Harringay, "that the whole thing is a publicity stunt gone wrong." He was a large, jovial man, extremely rich and connected with the City. "You never know what these advertising fellows are up to."

"Well, it looks like a case of hanging the goose that lays the golden eggs this time," said Captain Bates, with a loud laugh. "Unless Wimsey means to pull off one of his conjuring tricks."

"I hope he does," said Miss Titterton. "I adore detective stories. I'd commute the sentence to penal servitude on condition that she turned out a new story every six months. It would be much more useful than picking oakum or sewing mail-bags for the post-office to mislay."

"Aren't you being a bit previous?" suggested Wimsey, mildly. "She's not convicted yet."

"But she will be next time. You can't fight facts, Peter."

"Of course not," said Captain Bates. "The police know what they're about. They don't put people into the dock if there isn't something pretty shady about 'em."

Now this was a fearful brick, for it was not so many years since the Duke of Denver had himself stood his trial on a mistaken charge of murder. There was a ghastly silence, broken by the Duchess, who said icily: "Really, Captain Bates!"

"What? eh? Oh, of course, I mean to say, I know mistakes do happen sometimes, but that's a very different thing. I mean to say, this woman, with no morals at all, that is, I mean—"

"Have a drink, Tommy," said Lord Peter, kindly. "You aren't quite up to your usual standard of tact today."

"No, but do tell us, Lord Peter," cried Mrs. Dimsworthy, "what the creature is *like*. Have you talked to her? I thought she had rather a nice voice, though she's as plain as a pancake."

"Nice voice, Freakie? Oh, no," said Mrs. Featherstone. "I should have called it rather sinister. It absolutely thrilled me, I got shudders all the way down my spine. A genuine *frisson*. And I think she would be quite attractive, with those queer, smudgy eyes, if she were properly dressed. A sort of *femme fatale*, you know. Does she try to hypnotise you, Peter?"

"I saw in the papers," said Miss Titterton, "that she had had hundreds of offers of marriage."

"Out of one noose into the other," said Harringay, with his noisy laugh.

"I don't think I should care to marry a murderess," said Miss Titterton, "especially one that's been trained on detective stories. One would be always wondering whether there was anything funny about the taste of the coffee."

"Oh, these people are all mad," said Mrs. Dimsworthy. "They have a morbid longing for notoriety. It's like the lunatics who make spurious confessions and give themselves up for crimes they haven't committed."

"A murderess might make quite a good wife," said Harringay. "There was Madeleine Smith, you know—she used arsenic too, by the way—she married somebody and lived happily to a respectable old age."

"But did her husband live to a respectable old age?" demanded Miss Titterton. "That's more to the point, isn't it?"

"Once a poisoner, always a poisoner, *I* believe," said Mrs. Featherstone. "It's a passion that grows upon you—like drink or drugs."

"It's the intoxicating sensation of power," said Mrs. Dimsworthy. "But, Lord Peter, *do* tell us—"

"Peter!" said his mother, "I do wish you'd go and see what's happened to Gerald. Tell him his tea is getting cold. I think he's in the stables talking to Freddy about thrush or cracked heels or something, so tiresome the way horses are always getting something the matter with them. You haven't trained Gerald properly, Helen, he used to be quite punctual as a boy. Peter was always the tiresome one, but he's becoming almost human in his old age. It's that wonderful man of his who keeps him in order, really a remarkable character and so intelligent, quite one of the old sort, you know, a perfect autocrat, and such manners too. He would be worth thousands to an American millionaire, most impressive, I wonder Peter isn't afraid he'll give warning one of these days, but I really believe he is positively attached to him, Bunter attached to Peter, I mean, though the other way on would be true too, I'm sure Peter pays more attention to his opinion than he does to mine."

Wimsey had escaped, and was by now on his way to the stables. He met Gerald, Duke of Denver, returning, with Freddy Arbuthnot in tow. The former received the Dowager's message with a grin.

"Got to turn up, I suppose," he said. "I wish nobody had ever invented tea. Ruins your nerves and spoils your appetite for dinner."

"Beastly sloppy stuff," agreed the Hon. Freddy. "I say, Peter, I've been wanting to get hold of you."

"Same here," said Wimsey, promptly. "I'm feelin' rather exhausted with conversation. Let's wander through the billiard-room and build our constitutions up before we face the barrage."

"Today's great thought," said Freddy, enthusiastically. He pattered happily after Wimsey into the billiard-room, and flung himself down in a large chair. "Great bore, Christmas, isn't it? All the people one hates most gathered together in the name of goodwill and all that."

"Bring a couple of whiskies," said Wimsey to the footman. "And, James, if anybody asks for Mr. Arbuthnot or me, you rather think we have gone out. Well, Freddy, here's luck! Has anything transpired, as the journalists say?"

"I've been sleuthing like stink on the tracks of your man," said Mr. Arbuthnot. "Really, don't you know, I shall

soon be qualified to set up in your line of business. Our
financial column, edited by Uncle Buthie—that sort of
thing. Friend Urquhart has been very careful, though.
Bound to be—respectable family lawyer and all that. But I
saw a man yesterday who knows a fellow who had it from a
chappie that said Urquhart had been dipping himself a bit
recklessly off the deep end."

"Are you sure, Freddy?"

"Well, not to say sure. But this man, you see, owes me
one, so to speak, for having warned him off the Megatherium before the band began to play, and he thinks, if he
can get hold of the chappie that knows, not the fellow that
told him, you understand, but the other one, that he might
be able to get something out of him, don't you see, especially if I was able to put this other chappie in the way of
something or the other, what?"

."And no doubt you have secrets to sell."

"Oh, well, I daresay I could make it worth this other
chappie's while, because I've got an idea, through this other
fellow that my bloke knows, that the chappie is rather up
against it, as you might say, through being caught short on
some Airways stock, and if I was to put him in touch with
Goldberg, don't you see, it might get him out of a hole and
so on. And Goldberg will be all right, because, don't you
see, he's a cousin of old Levy's, who was murdered, you
know, and all these Jews stick together like leeches and as
a matter of fact, I think it's very fine of them."

"But what has old Levy got to do with it?" asked
Wimsey, his mind running over the incidents in that half-
forgotten murder-episode.

"Well, as a matter of fact," said the Hon. Freddy, a little
nervously, "I've—er—done the trick as you might say. Rachel
Levy is—er, in fact—going to become Mrs. Freddy and all
that sort of thing."

"The devil she is," said Wimsey, ringing the bell. "Tremendous congratters and all that. It's been a long time working up, hasn't it?"

"Why, yes," said Freddy. "Yes, it has. You see, the trouble was that I was a Christian—at least, I was christened and all that, though I pointed out I wasn't at all a good one, except, of course, that one keeps up the family pew and turns out on Christmas Day and so on. Only it seems they didn't mind that so much as my bein' a Gentile. Well that, of course, is past prayin' for. And then there was the difficulty about the kids—if any. But I explained that I didn't mind what they counted them as—and I don't, you know, because, as I was saying, it would be all to the little beggars' advantage to be in with the Levy and Goldberg crowd, especially if the boys were to turn out anything in the financial way. And then I rather got round Lady Levy by sayin' I had served nearly seven years for Rachel—that was rather smart, don't you think?"

"Two more whiskies, James," said Lord Peter. "It was brilliant, Freddy. How did you come to think of it?"

"In church," said Freddy, "at Diana Rigby's wedding. The bride was fifty minutes late and I had to do something, and somebody had left a Bible in the pew. I saw that—I say, old Laban was a bit of a tough, wasn't he?—and I said to myself, 'I'll work that off next time I call,' and so I did, and the old lady was uncommonly touched by it."

"And the long and the short of it is, you're fixed up," said Wimsey. "Well, cheerio, here's to it. Am I best man, Freddy, or do you bring it off at the Synagogue?"

"Well, yes—it is to be at the Synagogue—I had to agree to that," said Freddy, "but I believe some sort of bridegroom's friend comes into it. You'll stand by me, old bean, won't you? You keep your hat on, don't forget."

"I'll bear it in mind," said Wimsey, "and Bunter will explain the procedure to me. He's bound to know. He knows everything. But look here, Freddy, you won't forget about this little enquiry, will you?"

"I won't, old chap—upon my word I won't. I'll let you know the very second I hear anything. But I really think you may count on there being something in it."

Wimsey found some consolation in this. At any rate, he so far pulled himself together as to be the life and soul of the rather restrained revels at Duke's Denver. The Duchess Helen, indeed, observed rather acidly to the Duke that Peter was surely getting too old to play the buffoon, and that it would be better if he took things seriously and settled down.

"Oh, I dunno," said the Duke, "Peter's a weird fish— you never know what he's thinkin' about. He pulled me out of the soup once and I'm not going to interfere with him. You leave him alone, Helen."

Lady Mary Wimsey, who had arrived late on Christmas Eve, took another view of the matter. She marched into her younger brother's bedroom at 2 o'clock on the morning of Boxing Day. There had been dinner and dancing and charades of the most exhausting kind. Wimsey was sitting thoughtfully over the fire in his dressing-gown.

"I say, old Peter," said Lady Mary, "you're being a bit fevered, aren't you? Anything up?"

"Too much plum-pudding," said Wimsey, "and too much county. I'm a martyr, that's what I am—burning in brandy to make a family holiday."

"Yes, it's ghastly, isn't it? But how's life? I haven't seen you for an age. You've been away such a long time."

"Yes—and you seem very much taken up with this house-decorating job you're running."

"One must do something. I get rather sick of being aimless, you know."

"Yes. I say, Mary, do you ever see anything of old Parker these days?"

Lady Mary stared into the fire.

"I've had dinner with him once or twice, when I was in town."

"Have you? He's a very decent sort. Reliable, homespun—that sort of thing. Not amusing, exactly."

"A little solid."

"As you say—a little solid." Wimsey lit a cigarette. "I should hate anything upsettin' to happen to Parker. He'd take it hard. I mean to say, it wouldn't be fair to muck about with his feelin's and so on."

Mary laughed.

"Worried, Peter?"

"N-no. But I'd rather like him to have fair play."

"Well, Peter—I can't very well say yes or no till he asks me, can I?"

"Can't you?"

"Well, not to him. It would upset his ideas of decorum, don't you think?"

"I suppose it would. But it would probably upset them just as much if he did ask you. He would feel that the mere idea of hearing a butler announce 'Chief-Detective-Inspector and Lady Mary Parker' would have something shocking about it."

"It's stalemate, then, isn't it?"

"You could stop dining with him."

"I could do that, of course."

"And the mere fact that you don't—I see. Would it be any good if I demanded to know his intentions in the true Victorian manner?"

"Why this sudden thirst for getting your family off your hands, old man? Peter—nobody's being horrible to you, are they?"

"No, no. I'm just feeling rather like a benevolent uncle, that's all. Old age creeping on. That passion for being useful which attacks the best of us when we're getting past our prime."

"Like me with the house-decorating. I designed these pajamas, by the way. Don't you think they're rather entertaining? But I expect Chief-Inspector Parker prefers the old-fashioned night-gown, like Dr. Spooner or whoever it was."

"That would be a wrench," said Wimsey.

"Never mind. I'll be brave and devoted. Here and now I cast off my pajamas for ever!"

"No, no," said Wimsey, "not here and now. Respect a brother's feelings. Very well. I am to tell my friend Charles Parker, that if he will abandon his natural modesty and propose, you will abandon your pajamas and say yes."

"It will be a great shock for Helen, Peter."

"Blast Helen. I daresay it won't be the worst shock she'll get."

"Peter, you're plotting something devilish. All right. If you want me to administer the first shock and let her down by degrees—I'll do it."

"Right-ho!" said Wimsey, casually.

Lady Mary twisted one arm about his neck and bestowed on him one of her rare sisterly caresses.

"You're a decent old idiot," she said, "and you look played-out. Go to bed."

"Go to blazes," said Lord Peter, amiably.

CHAPTER XIII

Miss Murchison felt a touch of excitement in her well-regulated heart, as she rang the bell of Lord Peter's flat. It was not caused by the consideration of his title or his wealth or his bachelorhood, for Miss Murchison had been a business woman all her life, and was accustomed to visiting bachelors of all descriptions without giving a second thought to the matter. But his note had been rather exciting.

Miss Murchison was thirty-eight, and plain. She had worked in the same financier's office for twelve years. They had been good years on the whole, and it was not until the last two that she had even begun to realise that the brilliant financier who juggled with so many spectacular undertakings was juggling for his life under circumstances of increasing difficulty. As the pace grew faster, he added egg after egg to those which were already spinning in the air. There is a limit to the number of eggs which can be spun by human hands. One day an egg slipped and smashed—then another—then a whole omelette of eggs. The juggler fled from the stage and escaped abroad, his chief assistant blew out his brains, the audience booed, the curtain came down, and Miss Murchison, at 37, was out of a job.

She had put an advertisement in the papers and had answered many others. Most people appeared to want their secretaries young and cheap. It was discouraging.

Then her own advertisement had brought an answer, from a Miss Climpson, who kept a typing bureau.

It was not what she wanted, but she went. And she found that it was not quite a typing bureau after all, but something more interesting.

Lord Peter Wimsey, mysteriously at the back of it all,

had been abroad when Miss Murchison entered the "Cattery," and she had never seen him till a few weeks ago. This would be the first time she had actually spoken to him. An odd-looking person, she thought, but people said he had brains. Anyhow—

The door was opened by Bunter, who seemed to expect her and showed her at once into a sitting-room lined with bookshelves. There were some fine prints on the walls, an Aubusson carpet, a grand piano, a vast Chesterfield and a number of deep and cosy chairs, upholstered in brown leather. The curtains were drawn, a wood-fire blazed on the hearth, and before it stood a table, with a silver tea-service whose lovely lines were delightful to the eye.

As she entered, her employer uncoiled himself from the depths of an armchair, put down a black-letter folio which he had been studying and greeted her in the cool, husky and rather languid tones which she had already heard in Mr. Urquhart's office.

"Frightfully good of you to come round, Miss Murchison. Beastly day, isn't it? I'm sure you want your tea. Can you eat crumpets? Or would you prefer something more up-to-date?"

"Thanks," said Miss Murchison, as Bunter hovered obsequiously at her elbow, "I like crumpets very much."

"Oh, good! Well, Bunter, we'll struggle with the teapot ourselves. Give Miss Murchison another cushion and then you can toddle off. Back at work, I suppose? How's our Mr. Urquhart?"

"He's all right." Miss Murchison had never been a chatty girl. "There's one thing I wanted to tell you—"

"Plenty of time," said Wimsey. "Don't spoil your tea." He waited on her with a kind of anxious courtesy which pleased her. She expressed admiration of the big bronze chrysanthemums heaped here and there about the room.

"Oh! I'm glad you like them. My friends say they give a feminine touch to the place, but Bunter sees to it, as a matter of fact. They make a splash of colour and all that, don't you think?"

"The books look masculine enough."

"Oh, yes—they're my hobby, you know. Books—and crime, of course. But crime's not very decorative, is it? I don't care about collecting hangmen's ropes and murderers' overcoats. What are you to do with 'em? Is the tea all right? I ought to have asked you to pour out, but it always seems to me rather unfair to invite a person and then make her do all the work. What do you do when you're not working, by the way? Do you keep a secret passion for anything?"

"I go to concerts," said Miss Murchison. "And when there isn't a concert I put something on the gramophone."

"Musician?"

"No—never could afford to learn properly. I ought to have been, I daresay. But there was more money in being a secretary."

"I suppose so."

"Unless one is absolutely first-class, and I should never have been that. And third-class musicians are a nuisance."

"They have a rotten time, too," said Wimsey. "I hate to see them in cinemas, poor beasts, playing the most ghastly tripe, sandwiched in with snacks of Mendelssohn and torn-off gobbets of the 'Unfinished.' Have a sandwich. Do you like Bach? or only the Moderns?"

He wriggled on to the piano stool.

"I'll leave it to you," said Miss Murchison, rather surprised.

"I feel rather like the Italian Concerto this evening. It's better on the harpsichord, but I haven't got one here. I find Bach good for the brain. Steadying influence and all that."

He played the Concerto through, and then, after a few seconds' pause went on to one of the "Forty-eight." He played well, and gave a curious impression of controlled power, which, in a man so slight and so fantastical in manner, was unexpected and even a little disquieting. When he had finished, he said, still sitting at the piano:

"Did you make the enquiry about the typewriter?"

"Yes; it was bought new three years ago."

"Good. I gather, by the way, that you are probably right about Urquhart's connection with the Megatherium Trust. That was a very helpful observation of yours. Consider yourself highly commended."

"Thank you."

"Anything fresh?"

"No—except that the evening after you called at Mr. Urquhart's office, he stayed on a long time after we had gone, typing something."

Wimsey sketched an arpeggio with his right hand and demanded:

"How do you know how long he stayed and what he was doing if you had all gone?"

"You said you wanted to know of anything, however small, that was in the least unusual. I thought it might be unusual for him to stay on by himself, so I walked up and down Princeton Street and round Red Lion Square till half past seven. Then I saw him put the light out and go home. Next morning I noticed that some papers I had left just inside my typewriter cover had been disturbed. So I concluded that he had been typing."

"Perhaps the charwoman disturbed them?"

"Not she. She never disturbs the dust, let alone the cover."

Wimsey nodded.

"You have the makings of a first-class sleuth, Miss Murchison. Very well. In that case, our little job will have to be undertaken. Now, look here—you quite understand that I'm going to ask you to do something illegal?"

"Yes, I understand."

"And you don't mind?"

"No. I imagine that if I'm taken up you will pay any necessary costs."

"Certainly."

"And if I go to prison?"

"I don't think it will come to that. There's a slight risk, I admit—that is, if I'm wrong about what I think is happening—that you might be brought up for attempted theft or for being in possession of safebreaking tools, but that is the most that could happen."

"Oh! well, it's all in the game, I suppose."

"You mean that?"

"Yes."

"Splendid. Well—you know that deed-box you brought in to Mr. Urquhart's room the day I was there?"

"Yes, the one marked Wrayburn."

"Where is it kept? In the outer office, where you could get hold of it?"

"Oh, yes—on a shelf with a lot of others."

"Good. Would it be possible for you to get left alone in the office any day for, say, half an hour?"

"Well—at lunch-time I'm supposed to go out at half-past twelve and come back at half-past one. Mr. Pond goes out then, but Mr. Urquhart sometimes comes back. I couldn't be certain that he wouldn't pop out on me. And it would look funny if I wanted to stay on after four-thirty, I expect. Unless I pretended I had made a mistake and wanted to stay and put it right. I could do that. I might come extra early in the morning when the charwoman is there—or would it matter her seeing me?"

"It wouldn't matter very much," said Wimsey, thoughtfully. "She'd probably think you had legitimate business with the box. I'll leave it to you to choose the time."

"But what am I to do? Steal the box?"

"Not quite. Do you know how to pick a lock?"

"Not in the least, I'm afraid."

"I often wonder what we go to school for," said Wimsey. "We never seem to learn anything really useful. I can pick quite a pretty lock myself, but, as we haven't much time and as you'll need some rather intensive training, I think I'd better take you to an expert. Should you mind putting your coat on and coming round with me to see a friend?"

"Not at all. I should be delighted."

"He lives in the Whitechapel Road, but he's a very pleasant fellow, if you can overlook his religious opinions. Personally, I find them rather refreshing. Bunter! Get us a taxi, will you?"

On the way to the East End, Wimsey insisted upon talking music—rather to Miss Murchison's disquietude; she began to think there was something a little sinister in this pointed refusal to discuss the object of their journey.

"By the way," she ventured, interrupting something Wimsey was saying about fugal form, "this person we are going to see—has he a name?"

"Now you mention it, I believe he has, but he's never called by it. It's Rumm."

"Not very, perhaps, if he—er—gives lessons in lock-picking."

"I mean, his name's Rumm."

"Oh; what is it then?"

"Dash it! I mean, Rumm is his name."

"Oh! I beg your pardon."

"But he doesn't care to use it, now that he is a total abstainer."

"Then what does one call him?"

"I call him Bill," said Wimsey, as the taxi drew up at the entrance to a narrow court, "but when he was at the head of his profession, they called him 'Blindfold Bill.' He was a very great man in his time."

Paying off the taxi-man (who had obviously taken them for welfare-workers till he saw the size of his tip, and now did not know what to make of them), Wimsey steered his companion down the dirty alleyway. At the far end was a small house, from whose lighted windows poured forth the loud strains of a chorus of voices, supported by a harmonium and other instruments.

"Oh, dear!" said Wimsey, "we've struck a meeting. It can't be helped. Here goes."

Pausing until the strains of "Glory, glory, glory" had

been succeeded by a sound as of fervent prayer, he hammered lustily at the door. Presently a small girl put her head out and, seeing Lord Peter, uttered a shrill cry of delight.

"Hullo, Esmeralda Hyacinth," said Wimsey. "Is Dad in?"

"Yes, sir, please, sir, they'll be so pleased, will you step in and oh, please?"

"Well?"

"Please, sir, will you sing 'Nazareth'?"

"No, I will not sing 'Nazareth' on any account, Esmeralda; I'm surprised at you."

"Daddy says 'Nazareth' isn't worldly, and you do sing it so beautiful," said Esmeralda, her mouth drooping.

Wimsey hid his face in his hands.

"This comes of having done a foolish thing once," he said. "One never lives it down. I won't promise, Esmeralda, but we'll see. But I want to talk business with Dad when the meeting's over."

The child nodded; at the same moment, the praying voice within the room ceased, amid ejaculations of "Alleluia!" and Esmeralda, profiting by this momentary pause, pushed open the door and said loudly:

"Here's Mr. Peter and a lady."

The room was small, very hot and very full of people. In one corner was the harmonium, with the musicians grouped about it. In the middle, standing by a round table covered with a red cloth, was a stout, square man, with a face like a bull-dog. He had a book in his hand, and appeared to be about to announce a hymn, but, seeing Wimsey and Miss Murchison, he came forward, stretching out a large and hearty hand.

"Welcome one and welcome all!" he said. "Brethren, 'ere is a dear brother and sister in the Lord as is come out of the 'aunts of the rich and the riotous living of the Westend to join with us in singing the Songs of Zion. Let us sing and give praise. Alleluia! We know that many shall come from the East *and* from the West and sit down at the Lord's feast, while many that thinks theirselves chosen shall be cast into outer darkness. Therefore let us not say, because this man wears a shiny eye-glass, that he is not a chosen vessel, or because this woman wears a di'mond necklace and rides in 'er Rolls-Royce, she will not therefore wear a white robe and a gold crown in the New Jerusalem, nor because these people travels in the Blue Train to the Rivereera, therefore they shall not be seen a-castin' down their golden crowns by the River of the Water of Life. We 'ears that there talk sometimes in 'Yde Park o' Sundays, but it's bad and foolish and leads to strife and envyings and not to charity. All we like sheep 'ave gone astray and well I may say so, 'avin' been a black and wicked sinner myself till this 'ere gentleman, for such 'e truly·is, laid 'is 'and upon me as I was a-bustin' of 'is safe and was the instrument under God of turnin' me from the broad way that leadeth to destruction. Oh, brethren, what a 'appy day that was for me, alleluia! What a shower of blessings come to me by the grace of the Lord! Let us unite now in thanksgiving for 'Eaven's mercies in Number One 'Undred and Two. (Esmeralda, give our dear friends a 'ymn-book)."

"I'm sorry," said Wimsey to Miss Murchison. "Can you bear it? I fancy this is the final outbreak."

The harmonium, harp, sackbut, psaltery, dulcimer and all kinds of music burst out with a blare which nearly burst the ear-drum, the assembly lifted its combined voices, and Miss Murchison, to her amazement, found herself joining— at first self-consciously and then with a fine fervour in that stirring chant—

> "Sweeping through the gates,
> Sweeping through the gates of the New Jerusalem,
> Washed in the Blood of the Lamb."

Wimsey, who appeared to find it all very good fun, carolled away happily, without the slightest embarrassment;

whether because he was accustomed to the exercise, or merely because he was one of those imperturbably self-satisfied people who cannot conceive of themselves as being out of place in any surroundings, Miss Murchison was unable to determine.

To her relief, the religious exercise came to an end with the hymn, and the company took their leave, with many hand-shakings all round. The musicians emptied the condensed moisture from their wind-instruments politely into the fireplace and the lady who played the harmonium drew the cover over the keys and came forward to welcome the guests. She was introduced simply as Bella and Miss Murchison concluded, rightly, that she was the wife of Mr. Bill Rumm and the mother of Esmeralda.

"Well, now," said Bill, "it's dry work preachin' and singin'—you'll take a cup of tea or coffee, now, won't you?"

Wimsey explained that they had just had tea, but begged that the family might proceed with their own meal.

"It ain't 'ardly supper-time yet," said Mrs. Rumm. "P'raps if you was to do your business with the lady and gentleman, Bill, they might feel inclined to take a bite with us later. It's trotters," she added, hopefully.

"It's very kind of you," said Miss Murchison, hesitatingly.

"Trotters want a lot of beating," said Wimsey, "and since our business may take a little time we'll accept with pleasure—if you're sure we're not putting you out."

"Not at all," said Mrs. Rumm, heartily. "Eight beautiful trotters they is, and with a bit of cheese they'll go round easy. Come along, 'Meraldy—your Dad's got business."

"Mr. Peter's going to sing," said the child, fixing reproachful eyes on Wimsey.

"Now don't you worrit his lordship," rebuked Mrs. Rumm, "I declare I'm ashamed of you."

"I'll sing after supper, Esmeralda," said Wimsey. "Hop along now like a good girl or I'll make faces at you. Bill, I've brought you a new pupil."

"Always 'appy to serve you, sir, knowing as it's the Lord's work. Glory be."

"Thank you," said Wimsey, modestly. "It's a simple matter, Bill, but as the young lady is inexperienced with locks and so on, I've brought her along to be coached. You see, Miss Murchison, before Bill here saw the light—"

"Praise God!" put in Bill.

"He was the most accomplished burglar and safe-breaker in the three kingdoms. He doesn't mind my telling you this, because he's taken his medicine and finished with it all and is now a very honest and excellent locksmith of the ordinary kind."

"Thanks be to Him that giveth the victory!"

"But from time to time, when I need a little help in a righteous cause, Bill gives me the benefit of his great experience."

"And oh! what 'appiness it is, miss, to turn them talents which I so wickedly abused to the service of the Lord. His 'oly Name be blessed that bringeth good out of evil."

"That's right," said Wimsey, with a nod. "Now, Bill, I've got my eye on a solicitor's deed-box, which may or may not contain something which will help me to get an innocent person out of trouble. This young lady can get access to the box, Bill, if you can show her the way inside it."

"If?" grunted Bill, with sovereign contempt. " 'Course I can! Deed-box, that's nuffin'. That ain't no field for a man's skill. Robbin' the kids' money-box, that's what it is with they trumpery little locks. There ain't a deed-box in this 'ere city wot I couldn't open blindfold in boxing-gloves with a stick of boiled macaroni."

"I know, Bill; but it isn't you that's got to do it. Can you teach the lady how to work it?"

"Sure I can. What kinder lock is it, lidy?"

"I don't know," said Miss Murchison. "An ordinary lock, I think. I mean, it has the usual sort of key—not a Bramah, or anything of that kind. Mr.—that is, the solicitor has one set of keys and Mr. Pond has another—just plain keys with barrels and wards."

"Ho!" said Bill, "then 'arf an hour will teach you all you want, miss." He went to a cupboard and brought out half a dozen lock-plates and a bunch of curious, thin wire hooks, strung on a ring like keys.

"Are those pick-locks?" asked Miss Murchison, curiously.

"That's what they are, miss. Ingines of Satan!" He shook his head as he lovingly fingered the bright steel. "Many's the time sech keys as these 'ave let pore sinners in by the back gate into 'ell."

"This time," said Wimsey, "they'll let a poor innocent out of prison into the sunshine—if any, in this beastly climate."

"Praise Him for His manifold mercies! Well, miss, the fust thing is to understand the construction of a lock. Now jest you look 'ere."

He picked up one of the locks and showed how, by holding up the spring, the catch could be thrust back.

"There ain't no need of all them fancy wards, you see, miss. The barrel and the spring—that's all there is to it. Jest you try."

Miss Murchison accordingly tried, and forced several locks with an ease that astonished her.

"Well now, miss, the difficulty is, you see, that when the lock's in place, you can't use your eyes, but you 'as your 'earin' and you 'as the feelin' in your fingers, giv' you by Providence (praise His Name!) for that purpose. Now what you 'as to do, miss, is to shet your eyes and see with your fingers, like, w'en you've got your spring 'ooked back sufficient ter let the catch go past."

"I'm afraid I'm very clumsy," said Miss Murchison, at the fifth or sixth attempt.

"Now don't you fret, miss. Jest take it easy and you'll find the right way of it come to you all of a sudden, like. Jest feel when it seems to go sweet and use your 'ands independent. Would you like to 'ave a little go at a Combination while you're 'ere, sir? I've got a beauty 'ere. Giv' to me it was by Sam, you know 'oo I mean. Many's the time I've tried to show 'im the error of 'is ways. 'No, Bill,' 'e ses, 'I ain't got no use for religion,' 'e ses, pore lost sheep, 'but I ain't got no quarrel with you, Bill,' ses 'e, 'and I'd like for ter give you this 'ere little sooveneer.' "

"Bill, Bill," said Wimsey, shaking a reproachful finger, "I'm afraid this wasn't honestly come by."

"Well, sir, if I knowed the owner I'd 'and it over to 'im with the greatest of pleasure. It's quite good, you see. Sam put the soup in at the 'inges and it blowed the 'ole front clean off, lock and all. It's small, but it's a real beauty—new pattern to me, that is. But I mastered it," said Bill, with unregenerate pride, "in an hour or two."

"It'd have to be a good bit of work to beat you, Bill"; Wimsey set the lock up before him, and began to manipulate the knob, his fingers moving with micrometer delicacy and his ear bent to catch the fall of the tumblers.

"Lord!" said Bill—this time with no religious intention—"wot a cracksman you'd a-made, if you'd a-given your mind to it—which the Lord in His mercy forbid you should!"

"Too much work in that life for me, Bill," said Wimsey. "Dash it! I lost it that time."

He turned the knob back and started over again.

By the time the trotters arrived, Miss Murchison had acquired considerable facility with the more usual types of lock and a greatly enhanced respect for burglary as a profession.

"And don't you let yourself be 'urried, miss," was Bill's final injunction, "else you'll leave scratches on the lock and do yourself no credit. Lovely bit of work, that, ain't it, Lord Peter, sir?"

"Beyond me, I'm afraid," said Wimsey, with a laugh.

"Practice," said Bill, "that's all it is. If you'd a-started early enough you'd a-been a beautiful workman." He

sighed. "There ain't many of 'em now-a-days—glory be!—
that can do a real artistic job. It fair goes to my 'eart to see
a elegant bit o' stuff like that blowed all to bits with gelignite. Wot's gelignite? Any fool can 'andle it as doesn't mind
makin' a blinkin' great row. Brutal, I calls it."

"Now, don't you get 'ankerin' back after them things,
Bill," said Mrs. Rumm, reprovingly. "Come along, do, now
and eat yer supper. Ef anybody's goin' ter do sech a wicked
thing as breakin' safes, wot do it matter whether it's done
artistic or inartistic?"

"Ain't that jest like a woman?—beggin' your pardon,
miss."

"Well, you know it's true," said Mrs. Rumm.

"I know those trotters look very artistic," said Wimsey,
"and that's quite enough for me."

The trotters having been eaten, and "Nazareth" duly
sung, to the great admiration of the Rumm family, the
evening closed pleasantly with the performance of a hymn,
and Miss Murchison found herself walking up the Whitechapel Road, with a bunch of picklocks in her pocket and
some surprising items of knowledge in her mind.

"You make some very amusing acquaintances, Lord
Peter."

"Yes—rather a jape, isn't it? But Blindfold Bill is one of
the best. I found him on my premises one night and struck
up a sort of an alliance with him. Took lessons from him
and all that. He was a bit shy at first, but he got converted
by another friend of mine—it's a long story—and the long
and short of it was, he got hold of this locksmith business,
and is doing very well at it. Do you feel quite competent
about locks now?"

"I think so. What am I to look for when I get the box
open?"

"Well," said Wimsey, "the point is this. Mr. Urquhart
showed me what purported to be the draft of a will made
five years ago by Mrs. Wrayburn. I've written down the gist
of it on a bit of paper for you. Here it is. Now the snag

about it is that that draft was typed on a machine which, as you tell me, was bought new from the makers only three years ago."

"Do you mean that's what he was typing that evening he stayed late at the office?"

"It looks like it. Now, why? If he had the original draft, why not show me that? Actually, there was no need for him to show it to me at all, unless it was to mislead me about something. Then, though he said he had the thing at home, and must have known he had it there, he pretended to search for it in Mrs. Wrayburn's box. Again, why? To make me think that it was already in existence when I called. The conclusion I drew is that, if there is a will, it's not along the lines of the one he showed me."

"It looks rather like that, certainly."

"What I want you to look for is the real will—either the original or the copy ought to be there. Don't take it away, but try to memorise the chief points in it, especially the names of the chief legatee or legatees and of the residuary legatee. Remember that the residuary legatee gets everything which isn't specifically left to somebody else, or anything which falls in by a legatee's dying before the testatrix. I specially want to know whether anything was left to Philip Boyes or if any mention of the Boyes family is made in the will. Failing a will, there might be some other interesting document, such as a secret trust, instructing the executor to dispose of the money in some special way. In short, I want particulars of any document which may seem to be of interest. Don't waste too much time making notes. Carry the provisions in your head if you can and note them down privately when you get away from the office. And be sure you don't leave those skeleton keys about for people to find."

Miss Murchison promised to observe these instructions, and, a taxi coming up at that moment, Wimsey put her into it and sped her to her destination.

CHAPTER XIV

Mr. Norman Urquhart glanced at the clock, which stood at 4.15, and called through the open door:

"Are those affidavits nearly ready, Miss Murchison?"

"I am just on the last page, Mr. Urquhart."

"Bring them in as soon as you've finished. They ought to go round to Hanson's tonight."

"Yes, Mr. Urquhart."

Miss Murchison galloped noisily over the keys, slamming the shift-lever over with unnecessary violence, and causing Mr. Pond once more to regret the intrusion of female clerks. She completed her page, ornamented the foot of it with a rattling row of fancy lines and dots, threw over the release, spun the roller, twitching the foolscap sheets from under it in vicious haste, flung the carbons into the basket, shuffled the copies into order, slapped them vigorously on all four edges to bring them into symmetry, and bounced with them into the inner office.

"I haven't had time to read them through," she announced.

"Very well," said Mr. Urquhart.

Miss Murchison retired, shutting the door after her. She gathered her belongings together, took out a hand-mirror and unashamedly powdered her rather large nose, stuffed a handful of odds-and-ends into a bulging hand-bag, pushed some papers under her typewriter cover ready for the next day, jerked her hat from the peg and crammed it on her head, tucking wisps of hair underneath it with vigorous and impatient fingers.

Mr. Urquhart's bell rang—twice.

"Oh, bother!" said Miss Murchison, with heightened colour.

She snatched the hat off again, and answered the summons.

"Miss Murchison," said Mr. Urquhart, with an expression of considerable annoyance, "do you know that you have left out a whole paragraph on the first page of this?"

Miss Murchison flushed still more deeply.

"Oh, have I? I'm very sorry."

Mr. Urquhart held up a document resembling in bulk that famous one of which it was said that there was not truth enough in the world to fill so long an affidavit.

"It is very annoying," he said. "It is the longest and most important of the three, and is urgently required first thing tomorrow morning."

"I can't think how I could have made such a silly mistake," muttered Miss Murchison. "I will stay on this evening and re-type it."

"I'm afraid you will have to. It is unfortunate, as I shall not be able to look it through myself, but there is nothing else to be done. Please check it carefully this time, and see that Hanson's have it before ten o'clock tomorrow."

"Yes, Mr. Urquhart. I will be extremely careful. I am very sorry indeed. I will make sure that it is quite correct and take it round myself."

"Very well, that will do," said Mr. Urquhart. "Don't let it happen again."

Miss Murchison picked up the papers and came out, looking flustered. She dragged the cover off the typewriter with much sound and fury, jerked out the desk-drawers till they slammed against the drawer-stops, shook the top-sheet, carbons and flimsies together as a terrier shakes a rat, and attacked the machine tempestuously.

Mr. Pond, who had just locked his desk, and was winding a silk scarf about his throat, looked at her in mild astonishment.

"Have you some more typing to do tonight, Miss Murchison?"

"Got to do the whole bally thing again," said Miss Murchison. "Left out a paragraph on page one—it would be page one, of course—and he wants the tripe round at Hanson's by 10 o'clock."

Mr. Pond groaned slightly and shook his head.

"Those machines make you careless," he reproved her. "In the old days, clerks thought twice about making foolish mistakes, when it meant copying the whole document out again by hand."

"Glad I didn't live then," said Miss Murchison, shortly. "One might as well have been a galley-slave."

"And we didn't knock off at half-past four, either," said Mr. Pond. "We *worked* in those days."

"You may have worked longer," said Miss Murchison, "but you didn't get through as much in the time."

"We worked accurately and neatly," said Mr. Pond, with emphasis, as Miss Murchison irritably disentangled two keys which had jammed together under her hasty touch.

Mr. Urquhart's door opened and the retort on the typist's lips was silenced. He said good-night and went out. Mr. Pond followed him.

"I suppose you will have finished before the cleaner goes, Miss Murchison," he said. "If not, please remember to extinguish the light and to hand the key to Mrs. Hodges in the basement."

"Yes, Mr. Pond. Good-night."

"Good-night."

His steps pattered through the entrance, sounded again loudly as he passed the window, and died away in the direction of Brownlow Street. Miss Murchison continued typing till she calculated that he was safely on the tube at Chanoery Lane. Then she rose, with a quick glance round her and approached a higher tier of shelves, stacked with black deed-boxes, each of which bore the name of a client in bold white letters.

WRAYBURN was there, all right, but had mysteriously

shifted its place. This in itself was unaccountable. She clearly remembered having replaced it, just before Christmas, on top of the pile MORTIMER—SCROGGINS—LORD COOTE—DOLBY BROS. AND WINGFIELD; and here it was, on the day after Boxing Day, at the bottom of a pile, heaped over and kept down by BODGERS—SIR J. PENKRIDGE—FLATSBY & COATEN—TRUBODY LTD. and UNIVERSAL BONE TRUST. Somebody had been spring-cleaning, apparently, over the holidays, and Miss Murchison thought it improbable that it was Mrs. Hodges.

It was tiresome, because all the shelves were full, and it would be necessary to lift down all the boxes and stand them somewhere before she could get out WRAYBURN. And Mrs. Hodges would be in soon, and though Mrs. Hodges didn't really matter, it might look odd . . .

Miss Murchison pulled the chair from her desk (for the shelf was rather high) and, standing on it, lifted down UNIVERSAL BONE TRUST. It was heavyish, and the chair (which was of the revolving kind, and not the modern type with one spindly leg and a stiffly sprung back, which butts you in the lower spine and keeps you up to your job) wobbled unsteadily, as she carefully lowered the box and balanced it on the narrow top of the cupboard. She reached up again and took down TRUBODY LTD., and placed it on BONE TRUST. She reached up for the third time and seized FLATSBY & COATEN. As she stooped with it a step sounded in the doorway and an astonished voice said behind her:

"Are you looking for something, Miss Murchison?"

Miss Murchison started so violently that the treacherous chair swung through a quarter-turn, nearly shooting her into Mr. Pond's arms. She came down awkwardly, still clasping the black deed-box.

"How you startled me, Mr. Pond! I thought you had gone."

"So I had," said Mr. Pond, "but when I got to the Underground I found I had left a little parcel behind me. So tiresome—I had to come back for it. Have you seen it any where? A little round jar, done up in brown paper."

Miss Murchison set FLATSBY & COATEN on the seat of the chair and gazed about her.

"It doesn't seem to be in my desk," said Mr. Pond. "Dear, dear, I shall be so late. And I can't go without it, because it's wanted for dinner—in fact, it's a little jar of caviare. We have guests tonight. Now, where can I have put it?"

"Perhaps you put it down when you washed your hands," suggested Miss Murchison, helpfully.

"Well now, perhaps I did." Mr. Pond fussed out and she heard the door of the little lavabo in the passage open with a loud creak. It suddenly occurred to her that she had left her handbag open on her desk. Suppose the skeleton keys were visible. She darted towards the bag, just as Mr. Pond returned in triumph.

"Much obliged to you for your suggestion, Miss Murchison. It was there all the time. Mrs. Pond would have been so much upset. Well, good-night again." He turned towards the door. "Oh, by the way, were you looking for something?"

"I was looking for a mouse," replied Miss Murchison with a nervous giggle. "I was just sitting working when I saw it run along the top of the cupboard and—er—up the wall behind those boxes."

"Dirty little beasts," said Mr. Pond, "the place is over-run with them. I have often said we ought to have a cat here. No hope of catching it now, though. You're not afraid of mice apparently?"

"No," said Miss Murchison, holding her eyes, by a strenuous physical effort, on Mr. Pond's face. If the skeleton keys were—as it seemed to her they must be—indecently exposing their spidery anatomy on her desk, it would be madness to look in that direction. "No—in your days I suppose all women were afraid of mice."

"Yes, they were," admitted Mr. Pond, "but then, of course, their garments were longer."

"Rotten for them," said Miss Murchison.

"They were very graceful in appearance," said Mr. Pond. "Allow me to assist you in replacing those boxes."

"You will miss your train," said Miss Murchison.

"I have missed it already," replied Mr. Pond, glancing at his watch. "I shall have to take the 5.30." He politely picked up FLATSBY & COATEN and climbed perilously with it in his hands to the unsteady seat of the rotatory chair.

"It's extremely kind of you," said Miss Murchison, watching him as he restored it to its place.

"Not at all. If you would kindly hand me up the others—"

Miss Murchison handed him TRUBODY LTD., and UNIVERSAL BONE TRUST.

"There!" said Mr. Pond, completing the pile and dusting his hands. "Now let us hope the mouse has gone for good. I will speak to Mrs. Hodges about procuring a suitable kitten."

"That would be a very good idea," said Miss Murchison. "Good-night, Mr. Pond."

"Good-night, Miss Murchison."

His footsteps pattered down the passage, sounded again more loudly beneath the window and for the second time died away in the direction of Brownlow Street.

"Whew!" said Miss Murchison. She darted to her desk. Her fears had deceived her. The bag was shut and the keys invisible.

She pulled her chair back to its place and sat down as a clash of brooms and pails outside announced the arrival of Mrs. Hodges.

"Ho!" said Mrs. Hodges, arrested on the threshold at sight of the lady clerk industriously typing away, "beg your pardon, miss, but I didn't know as how anybody was here."

"Sorry, Mrs. Hodges, I've got a little bit of work to finish. But you carry on. Don't mind me."

"That's all right, miss," said Mrs. Hodges, "I can do Mr. Partridge's office fust."

"Well, if it's all the same to you," said Miss Murchison. "I've just got to type a few pages and—er—make a précis—notes you know, of some documents for Mr. Urquhart."

Mrs. Hodges nodded and vanished again. Presently a loud bumping noise overhead proclaimed her presence in Mr. Partridge's office.

Miss Murchison waited no longer. She dragged her chair to the shelves again, took down swiftly, one after the other, BONE TRUST, TRUBODY LTD., FLATSBY & COATEN, SIR J. PENK-RIDGE and BODGERS. Her heart beat heavily as at last she seized WRAYBURN and carried it across to her desk.

She opened her bag and shook out its contents. The bunch of picklocks clattered upon the desk, mixed up with a handkerchief, a powder compact and a pocket-comb. The thin and shining steel barrels seemed to burn her fingers.

As she picked the bunch over, looking for the most suitable implement, there came a loud rap at the window.

She wheeled round, terrified. There was nothing there. Thrusting the picklocks into the pocket of her sports-coat, she tiptoed across and looked out. In the lamplight she observed three small boys engaged in climbing the iron railings which guard the sacred areas of Bedford Row. The foremost child saw her and gesticulated, pointing downwards. Miss Murchison waved her hand and cried, "Be off with you!"

The child shouted something unintelligible and pointed again. Putting two and two together, Miss Murchison deduced from the rap at the window, the gesture and the cry, that a valuable ball had fallen into the area. She shook her head with severity and returned to her task.

But the incident had reminded her that the window had no blinds and that, under the glare of the electric light, her movements was as visible to anybody in the street as though she stood on a lighted stage. There was no reason to suppose that Mr. Urquhart or Mr. Pond was about, but her uneasy conscience vexed her. Moreover, if a policeman should pass by, would he not be able to recognise picklocks a hundred yards away? She peered out again. Was it her agitated fancy, or was that a sturdy form in dark blue emerging from Hand Court?

Miss Murchison fled in alarm and, snatching up the deed-box, carried it bodily into Mr. Urquhart's private office.

Here, at least, she could not be overlooked. If anybody came in—even Mrs. Hodges—her presence might cause surprise but she would hear them coming and be warned in advance.

Her hands were cold and shaking, and she was not in the best condition to profit by Blindfold Bill's instructions. She drew a few deep breaths. She had been told not to hurry herself. Very well, then, she would not.

She chose a key with care and slipped it into the lock. For years, as it seemed to her, she scratched about aimlessly, till at length she felt the spring press against the hooked end. Pushing and lifting steadily with one hand, she introduced her second key. She felt the lever move—in another moment there was a sharp click and the lock was open.

There were not a great many papers in the box. The first document was a long list of securities, endorsed "Securities deposited with Lloyd's Bank." Then came the copies of some title-deeds, of which the originals were similarly deposited. Then came a folder filled with correspondence. Some of this consisted of letters from Mrs. Wrayburn herself, the latest letter being dated five years previously. In addition there were letters from tenants, bankers and stockbrokers, with copies of the replies written from the office and signed by Norman Urquhart.

Miss Murchison hastened impatiently through all this.

There was no sign of a will or copy of a will—not even of the dubious draft that the solicitor had shown to Wimsey. Two papers only now remained at the bottom of the box. Miss Murchison picked up the first. It was a Power of Attorney, dated January 1925, giving Norman Urquhart full powers to act for Mrs. Wrayburn. The second was thicker and tied neatly with red tape. Miss Murchison slipped this off and unfolded the document.

It was a Deed of Trust, making over the whole of Mrs. Wrayburn's property to Norman Urquhart, in trust for herself, and providing that he should pay into her current account, from the estate, a certain fixed annual sum for personal expenses. The deed was dated July 1920 and attached to it was a letter, which Miss Murchison hastily read through:

Appleford, Windle.
15th May, 1920.

My dear Norman,

Thank you very much, my dear boy, for your birthday letter and the pretty scarf. It is good of you to remember your old aunt so faithfully.

It has occurred to me that, now that I am over eighty years old, it is time that I put my business into your hands entirely. You and your father have managed very well for me all these years, and you have, of course, always very properly consulted me before taking any step with regard to investments. But I am getting such a *very old woman now* that I am quite out of touch with the modern world, and I cannot pretend that my opinions are of any real value. I am a *tired* old woman, too, and though you always explain everything *most clearly*, I find the *writing of letters a gêne* and a burden to me at my advanced age.

So I have determined to put my property in Trust with you for my lifetime, so that you may have full power to handle everything according to your own discretion, without having to consult me every time. And also, though I am strong and healthy yet, I am glad to say, and have my wits quite about me, still, that happy state of things might

alter at any time. I might become paralysed or feeble in
my head, or want to make some foolish use of my money,
as silly old women have done before now.

So will you draw up a deed of this kind and bring it to
me and I will sign it. And at the same time I will give you
instructions about my will.

Thanking you again for your good wishes,

> Your affec. Great-Aunt,
> Rosanna Wrayburn.

"Hurray!" said Miss Murchison. "There *was* a will, then!
And this Trust—that's probably important, too."

She read the letter again, skimmed through the clauses
of the Trust, taking particular notice that Norman Urquhart was named as sole Trustee, and finally made a mental
note of some of the larger and more important items in the
list of securities. Then she replaced the documents in their
original order, re-locked the box—which yielded to treatment like an angel—carried it out, replaced it, piled the
other boxes above it, and was back at her machine, just as
Mrs. Hodges re-entered the office.

"Just finished, Mrs. Hodges," she called out cheerfully.

"I wondered if yer would be," said Mrs. Hodges, "I
didn't hear the typewriter a-going."

"I was making notes by hand," said Miss Murchison. She
crumpled together the spoiled front page of the affidavit
and threw it into the waste-paper basket together with the
re-type which she had begun. From her desk-drawer she
produced a correctly typed first page, provided beforehand for the purpose, added it to the bundle of script, put
the top copy and the required sets of flimsies into an envelope, sealed it, addressed it to Messrs. Hanson & Hanson,
put on her hat and coat and went out, bidding a pleasant
farewell to Mrs. Hodges at the door.

A short walk brought her to Messrs. Hanson's office,
where she delivered the affidavit through the letter-box.
Then, with a brisk step and humming to herself, she made

for the 'bus-stop at the junction of Theobald's Road and Gray's Inn Road.

"I think I deserve a little supper in Soho," said Miss Murchison.

She was humming again as she walked from Cambridge Circus into Frith Street. "What *is* this beastly tune?" she asked herself abruptly. A little consideration reminded her that it was "Sweeping through the gates, Sweeping through the gates . . ."

"Bless me!" said Miss Murchison. "Going dotty, that's what I am."

CHAPTER XV

LORD PETER congratulated Miss Murchison and gave her a rather special lunch at Rules, where there is a particularly fine old Cognac for those that appreciate such things. Indeed, Miss Murchison was a little late in returning to Mr. Urquhart's office, and in her haste omitted to hand back the skeleton keys. But when the wine is good and the company agreeable one cannot always think of everything.

Wimsey himself, by a great act of self-control, had returned to his own flat to think, instead of bolting away to Halloway Gaol. Although it was a work of charity and necessity to keep up the spirits of the prisoner (it was in this way that he excused his almost daily visits) he could not disguise from himself that it would be even more useful and charitable to get her innocence proved. So far, he had not made much real progress.

The suicide theory had been looking very hopeful when Norman Urquhart had produced the draft of the will; but his belief in·that draft had now been thoroughly undermined. There was still a faint hope of retrieving the packet of white powder from the "Nine Rings," but as the days passed remorselessly on, that hope diminished almost to vanishing-point. It irked him to be taking no action in the matter—he wanted to rush to the Gray's Inn Road, to cross-question, bully, bribe, ransack every person and place in and about the "Rings" but he knew that the police could do this better than he could.

Why had Norman Urquhart tried to mislead him about the will? He could so easily have refused all information. There must be some mystery about it. But if Urquhart were not, in fact, the legatee, he was playing rather a dangerous game. If the old lady died, and the will was proved, the facts would probably be published—and she might die any day.

How easy it would be, he thought, regretfully, to hasten Mrs. Wrayburn's death a trifle. She was ninety-three and very frail. An over-dose of something—a shake—a slight shock, even—it did not do to think after that fashion. He wondered idly who lived with the old woman and looked after her. . . .

It was the 30th. of December, and he still had no plan. The stately volumes on his shelves, rank after rank of Saint, historian, poet, philosopher, mocked his impotence. All that wisdom and all that beauty, and they could not show him how to save the woman he imperiously wanted from a sordid death by hanging. And he had thought himself rather clever at that kind of thing. The enormous and complicated imbecility of things was all round him like a trap. He ground his teeth and raged helplessly, striding about the suave, wealthy, futile room. The great Venetian mirror over the fireplace showed him his own head and shoulders. He saw a fair, foolish face, with straw-coloured hair sleeked back; a monocle clinging incongruously under a ludicrously twitching brow; a chin shaved to perfection, hairless, epicene; a rather high collar, faultlessly starched, a tie elegantly knotted and matching in colour the handkerchief which peeped coyly from the breast-pocket of an expensive Savile-Row-tailored suit. He snatched up a heavy bronze from the mantelpiece—a beautiful thing, even as he snatched it, his fingers caressed the patina—and the impulse seized him to smash the mirror and smash the face—to break out into great animal howls and gestures.

Silly! One could not do that. The inherited inhibitions of twenty civilised centuries tied one hand and foot in bonds of ridicule. What if he did smash the mirror? Nothing would happen. Bunter would come in, unmoved and unsurprised, would sweep up the débris in a dust-pan, would prescribe a hot bath and massage. And next day a new mirror would be ordered, because people would come in and ask questions, and civilly regret the accidental damage to the old one. And Harriet Vane would still be hanged, just the same.

Wimsey pulled himself together, called for his hat and coat, and went away in a taxi to call on Miss Climpson.

"I have a job," he said to her, more abruptly than was his wont, "which I should like you to undertake yourself. I can't trust anybody else."

"How *kind* of you to put it like that," said Miss Climpson.

"The trouble is, I can't in the least tell you how to set about it. It all depends on what you find when you get there. I want you to go to Windle in Westmorland and get hold of an imbecile and paralysed old lady called Mrs. Wrayburn, who lives at a house called Appleford. I don't know who looks after her, or how you are to get into the house. But you've got to do it, and you've got to find out where her will is kept, and, if possible, see it."

"Dear me!" said Miss Climpson.

"And what's worse," said Wimsey, "you've only got about a week to do it in."

"That's a very short time," said Miss Climpson.

"You see," said Wimsey, "unless we can give some very good reason for delay, they're bound to take the Vane case almost first thing next sessions. If I could persuade the lawyers for the defence that there is the least chance of securing fresh evidence, they could apply for a postponement. But at present I have nothing that could be called evidence—only the vaguest possible hunch."

"I see," said Miss Climpson. "Well, none of us can do more than our best, and it is very necessary to have Faith. That moves mountains, we are told."

"Then for Heaven's sake lay in a good stock of it," said Wimsey, gloomily, "because as far as I can see, this job is like shifting the Himalayas and the Alps, with a spot of frosty Caucasus and a touch of the Rockies thrown in."

"You may count on me to do my poor best," replied Miss Climpson, "and I will ask the dear vicar to say a Mass of special intention for one engaged in a difficult undertaking. When would you like me to start?"

"At once," said Wimsey. "I think you had better go just as your ordinary self, and put up at the local hotel—no— a boarding-house, there will be more opportunities for gossip. I don't know much about Windle, except that there is a boot-factory there and rather a good view, but it's not a large place, and I should think everybody would know about Mrs. Wrayburn. She is very rich, and was notorious in her time. The person you'll have to cotton on to is the female—there must be one of some sort—who nurses and waits on Mrs. Wrayburn and is, generally speaking, about her path and about her bed and all that. When you find out her special weakness, drive a wedge into it like one o'clock. Oh! by the way—it's quite possible the will isn't there at all, but in the hands of a solicitor-fellow called Norman Urquhart who hangs out in Bedford Row. If so, all you can do is to get the pump to work and find out anything—anything at all—to his disadvantage. He's Mrs. Wrayburn's great-nephew, and he goes to see her sometimes."

Miss Climpson made a note of these instructions.

"And now I'll tootle off and leave you to it," said Wimsey. "Draw on the firm for any money you want. And if you need any special outfit, send me a wire."

On leaving Miss Climpson, Lord Peter Wimsey again found himself a prey to Weltschmerz and self-pity. But it now took the form of a gentle, pervading melancholy. Convinced of his own futility, he determined to do what little good lay in his power before retiring to a monastery or to the frozen wastes of the Antarctic. He taxied purposefully round to Scotland Yard, and asked for Chief-Inspector Parker.

Parker was in his office, reading a report which had just come in. He greeted Wimsey with an expression which seemed more embarrassed than delighted.

"Have you come about that packet of powder?"

"Not this time," said Wimsey, "I don't suppose you'll ever hear anything more of that. No. It's—rather a more—er—delicate matter. It's about my sister."

Parker started and pushed the report to one side.

"About Lady Mary?"

"Er—yes. I understand she's been going about with you —er—dining—and all that sort of thing, what?"

"Lady Mary has honoured me—on one or two occasions —with her company," said Parker. "I did not think—I did not know—that is, I understood—"

"Ah! but *did* you understand, that's the point?" said Wimsey, solemnly. "You see, Mary's a very nice-minded sort of girl, though I say it, and—"

"I assure you," said Parker, "that there is no need to tell me that. Do you suppose that I should misinterpret her kindness. It is the custom now-a-days for women of the highest character to dine unchaperoned with their friends, and Lady Mary has—"

"I'm not suggesting a chaperon," said Wimsey, "Mary wouldn't stick it for one thing, and I think it's all bosh, anyhow. Still, bein' her brother, and all that—it's Gerald's job really, of course, but Mary and he don't altogether hit it off, you know, and she wouldn't be likely to burble any secrets into his ear, especially as it would all be handed on to Helen—what was I going to say? Oh, yes—as Mary's brother, you know, I suppose it's my so to speak duty to push round and drop the helpful word here and there."

Parker jabbed the blotting-paper thoughtfully.

"Don't do that," said Wimsey, "it's bad for your pen. Take a pencil."

"I suppose," said Parker, "I ought not to have presumed—"

"What did you presume, old thing?" said Wimsey, his head cocked, sparrow-fashion.

"Nothing to which anybody could object," said Parker, hotly. "What are you thinking of, Wimsey? I quite see that it is unsuitable, from your point of view, that Lady Mary Wimsey should dine in public restaurants with a policeman, but if you imagine I have ever said a word to her that could not be said with the greatest propriety—"

"—in the presence of her mother, you wrong the purest and sweetest woman that ever lived, and insult your friend," interrupted Peter, snatching the words from his mouth and rattling them to a glib conclusion. "What a perfect Victorian you are, Charles. I should like to keep you in a glass case. Of course you haven't said a word. What I want to know is, why?"

Parker stared at him.

"For the last five years or so," said Wimsey, "you have been looking like a demented sheep at my sister, and starting like a rabbit whenever her name is mentioned. What do you mean by it? It is not ornamental. It is not exhilarating. You unnerve the poor girl. You give me a poor idea of your guts, if you will pardon the expression. A man doesn't like to see a man go all wobbly about his sister —at least, not with such a prolonged wobble. It's unsightly. It's irritating. Why not slap the manly thorax and say, 'Peter, my dear old mangel-wurzel, I have decided to dig myself into the old family trench and be a brother to you'? What's stopping you? Is it Gerald? He's an ass, I know, but he's not a bad old stick, really. Is it Helen? She's a bit of a wart, but you needn't see much of her. Is it me? Because, if so, I'm thinking of becoming a hermit—there was a Peter the Hermit, wasn't there?—So I shouldn't be in your way. Cough up the difficulty, old thing, and we will have it removed in a plain van. Now, then!"

"Do you—are you asking me—?"

"I'm asking you your intentions, damn it!" said Wimsey, "and if that's not Victorian enough, I don't know what is. I quite understand your having given Mary time to recover from that unfortunate affair with Cathcart and the Goyles fellow, but, dash it all, my dear man, one can overdo the delicacy business. You can't expect a girl to stand on and off for ever, can you? Are you waiting for Leap Year, or what?"

"Look here, Peter, don't be a damned fool. How can I ask your sister to marry me?"

"*How* you do it is your affair. You might say: 'What about a spot of matrimony, old dear?' That's up-to-date, and plain and unmistakable. Or you could go down on one knee and say, 'Will you honour me with your hand and heart?' which is pretty and old-fashioned and has the merit of originality in these times. Or you could write, or wire, or telephone. But I leave that to your own individual fancy."

"You're not serious."

"Oh, God! Shall I ever live down this disastrous reputation for tom-foolery? You're making Mary damned unhappy, Charles, and I wish you'd marry her and have done with it."

"Making her unhappy?" said Parker, almost in a shout, "me—her—unhappy?"

Wimsey tapped his forehead significantly.

"Wood—solid wood! But the last blow seems to have penetrated. Yes, you—her—unhappy—do you get it now?"

"Peter—if I really thought that—"

"Now don't go off the deep end," said Wimsey, "it's wasted on me. Keep it for Mary. I've done my brotherly duty and there's an end of it. Calm yourself. Return to your reports—"

"Oh, lord, yes," said Parker. "Before we go any farther, I've got a report for you."

"You have? Why didn't you say so at first."

"You wouldn't let me."

"Well, what is it?"

"We've found the packet."

"What?"

"We've found the packet."

"Actually found it?"

"Yes. One of the barmen—"

"Never mind the barmen. You're sure it's the right packet?"

"Oh, yes; we've identified it."

"Get on. Have you analysed it?"

"Yes, we've analysed it."

"Well, what is it?"

Parker looked at him with the eyes of one who breaks bad news, and said, reluctantly:

"Bicarbonate of soda."

CHAPTER XVI

Mr. Crofts, excusably enough, said, "I told you so"; Sir Impey Biggs observed curtly, "Very unfortunate."

To chronicle Lord Peter Wimsey's daily life during the ensuing week would be neither kind nor edifying. An enforced inactivity will produce irritable symptoms in the best of men. Nor did the imbecile happiness of Chief-Inspector Parker and Lady Mary Wimsey tend to soothe him, accompanied as it was by tedious demonstrations of affection for himself. Like the man in Max Beerbohm's story, Wimsey "hated to be touching." He was only moderately cheered by hearing from the industrious Freddy Arbuthnot that Mr. Norman Urquhart was found to be more or less deeply involved in the disasters of the Megatherium Trust.

Miss Kitty Climpson, on the other hand, was living in what she herself liked to call a "whirl of activity." A letter, written the second day after her arrival in Windle, furnishes us with a wealth of particulars.

> Hillside View,
> Windle, Westmorland.
> 1st Jan. 1930.

My dear Lord Peter,

I feel sure you will be anxious to hear, at the *earliest possible* moment *how* things are *going,* and though I have only been here *one* day, I really think I have *not* done so *badly,* all things considered!

My train got in quite late on Monday night, after a *most dreary* journey, with a *lugubrious* wait at *Preston,* though thanks to your kindness in insisting that I should travel *First-class,* I was not really at all tired! Nobody can realise what a *great* difference these extra comforts make, especially when one is *getting on* in years, and after the *uncomfortable* travelling which I had to endure in my days

of poverty, I feel that I am living in almost *sinful* luxury!
The carriage was *well* heated—indeed, *too much* so and I
should have liked the window down, but that there was a
very fat business man, *muffled* up to the eyes in *coats* and
woolly waistcoats who *strongly* objected to fresh air!' Men
are such HOT-HOUSE PLANTS nowadays, are they not, quite
unlike my dear father, who would never permit a *fire* in the
house *before* November the 1st, or *after* March 31st even
though the thermometer was at *freezing-point!*

I had *no* difficulty in getting a comfortable room at the
Station Hotel, *late* as it was. In the *old* days, an *unmarried*
woman arriving *alone* at *midnight* with a *suitcase* would
hardly have been considered *respectable*—what a wonderful difference one finds today! I am *grateful* to have lived
to see such changes, because whatever old-fashioned people
may say about the greater *decorum* and *modesty* of women
in Queen Victoria's time, those who can remember the old
conditions know how *difficult* and *humiliating* they were!

Yesterday morning, of course, my *first* object was to find
a *suitable boarding-house,* in accordance with your instructions, and I was *fortunate* enough to hit upon this house at
the *second* attempt. It is very well run and *refined,* and
there are three *elderly ladies* who are *permanent* boarders
here, and are *well up* in all the GOSSIP of the town, so that
nothing could be more *advantageous* for our purpose!!

As soon as I had engaged my room, I went out for a
little *voyage of discovery.* I found a very helpful *policeman*
in the High Street, and asked him where to find Mrs. Wrayburn's house. He knew it quite well, and told me to take
the *omnibus* and it would be a penny ride to the "Fisherman's Arms" and then about 5 minutes' walk. So I followed
his directions, and the 'bus took me right into the country to a *cross-roads* with the "Fisherman's Arms" at the
corner. The conductor was most polite and helpful and
showed me the way, so I had *no difficulty* in finding the
house.

It is a *beautiful old place,* standing in its own grounds—
quite a *big* house built in the *eighteenth century,* with an
Italian porch and a lovely green lawn with a cedar-tree and
formal flower-beds, and in summer must be really a *garden*

of Eden. I looked at it from the road for a little time—I did not think this would be at all *peculiar* behaviour, if anybody saw me, because *anybody* might be interested in such a fine old place. Most of the *blinds* were down, as though the greater part of the house were *uninhabited,* and I could not see any *gardener* or anybody about—I suppose there is not very much to be done in the garden this time of the year. One of the *chimneys* was smoking, however, so there were *some* signs of life about the place.

I took a little *walk* down the road and then turned back and passed the house again, and this time I saw a servant just passing round the corner of the house, but of course she was *too far off* for me to speak to. So I took the omnibus back again and had lunch at Hillside View, so as to make acquaintance with my fellow-boarders.

Naturally I did not want to seem *too eager* all at once, so I said nothing about Mrs. Wrayburn's house *at first,* but just talked *generally* about Windle. I had some difficulty in parrying the *questions* of the good ladies, who *wondered* very much *why* a stranger had come to Windle at this time of year, but without telling many actual *untruths* I think I left them with the *impression* that I had come into a little fortune (!) and was visiting the Lake District to find a suitable spot in which to settle next *summer!* I talked about *sketching*—as girls we were *all* brought up to dabble a little in water-colours, so that I was able to display quite sufficient *technical knowledge to satisfy them!*

That gave me quite a *good* opportunity to ask about the *house!!* Such a *beautiful* old place, I said, and did anybody live there? (Of *course* I did not blurt this out *all at once*—I waited till they had told me of the many *quaint spots* in the district that would interest an artist!) Mrs. Pegler, a very *stout,* PUSSY old lady, with a LONG TONGUE (!) was able to tell me *all* about it. My dear Lord Peter, what I do *not* know now about the *abandoned wickedness* of Mrs. Wrayburn's early life is really NOT WORTH KNOWING!! But what was *more to the point* is that she told me the *name of* Mrs. Wrayburn's *nurse-companion.* She is a MISS BOOTH, a retired nurse, about *sixty* years old, and she lives *all alone* in the house with Mrs. Wrayburn, except for the *servants,* and a *housekeeper*. When I heard that Mrs. Wrayburn was so *old*, and *paralysed* and *frail*, I said was it not very *dangerous* that Miss Booth should be the only attendant, but Mrs. Pegler said the housekeeper was a *most trustworthy* woman who had been with Mrs. Wrayburn for many years, and was *quite* capable of looking after her any time when Miss Booth was out. So it appears that Miss Booth does go out sometimes! Nobody in this house seems to *know* her *personally*, but they say she is often to be seen in the town in *nurse's uniform*. I managed to extract quite a good description of her, so if I should happen to meet her, I daresay I shall be *smart* enough to *recognise* her!

That is really *all* I have been able to discover in *one* day. I hope you will not be *too* disappointed, but I was obliged to listen to a terrible amount of *local history* of one kind and another, and of course I could not FORCE the conversation round to Mrs. Wrayburn in any suspicious way.

I will let you know as *soon* as I get the *least bit* more information.

                                    Most sincerely yours,
                              Katharine Alexandra Climpson.

Miss Climpson finished her letter in the privacy of her bedroom, and secured it carefully in her capacious hand-bag before going downstairs. A long experience of board-ing-house life warned her that to display openly an enve-lope addressed even to a minor member of the nobility would be to court a quite unnecessary curiosity. True, it would establish her status, but at that moment Miss Climp-son hardly wished to move in the limelight. She crept quietly out at the hall door, and turned her steps towards the centre of the town.

On the previous day, she had marked down one principal tea-shop, two rising and competitive tea-shops, one slightly passé and declining tea-shop, a Lyons and four obscure and, on the whole, negligible tea-shops which combined the service of refreshments with a trade in sweets. It was now half-past ten. In the next hour and a half she could, with a

little exertion, pass in review all that part of the Windle
population which indulged in morning coffee.

She posted her letter and then debated with herself where
to begin. On the whole, she nclined to leave the Lyons for
another day. It was an ordinary plain Lyons, without orchestra or soda-fountain. She thought that its clientèle
would be chiefly housewives and clerks. Of the other four,
the most likely was, perhaps, the "Central." It was fairly
large, well-lighted and cheerful and strains of music issued
from its doors. Nurses usually like the large, well-lighted
and melodious. But the "Central" had one drawback. Anyone coming from the direction of Mrs. Wrayburn's house
would have to pass all the others to get to it. This fact
unfitted it for an observation post. From this point of view,
the advantage lay with "Ye Cosye Corner," which com-
manded the 'bus-stop. Accordingly, Miss Climpson decided
to start her campaign from that spot. She selected a table
in the window, ordered a cup of coffee and a plate of
digestive biscuits and entered upon her vigil.

After half an hour, during which no woman in nurse's
costume had been sighted, she ordered another cup of coffee and some pastries. A number of people—mostly women
—dropped in, but none of them could by any possibility be
identified with Miss Booth. At half-past eleven, Miss Climpson felt to stay any longer would be conspicuous and might
annoy the management. She paid her bill and departed.

The "Central" had rather more people in it than "Ye
Cosye Corner," and was in some ways an improvement,
having comfortable wicker chairs instead of fumed oak
settles, and brisk waitresses instead of languid semi-gentle-
women in art-linen. Miss Climpson ordered another cup of
coffee and a roll and butter. There was no window-table
vacant, but she found one close to the orchestra from which
she could survey the whole room. A fluttering dark-blue
veil at the door made her heart beat, but it proved to belong to a lusty young person with two youngsters and a

perambulator, and hope withdrew once more. By twelve o'clock, Miss Climpson decided that she had drawn blank at the "Central."

Her last visit was to the "Oriental"—an establishment singularly ill-adapted for espionage. It consisted of three very small rooms of irregular shape, dimly lit by forty-watt bulbs in Japanese shades, and further shrouded by bead curtains and draperies. Miss Climpson, in her inquisitive way, wandered into all its nooks and corners, disturbing several courting couples, before returning to a table near the door and sitting down to consume her fourth cup of coffee. Half-past twelve came, but no Miss Booth. "She can't come now," thought Miss Climpson, "she will have to get back and give her patient lunch."

She returned to Hillside View with but little appetite for the joint of roast mutton.

At half-past three she sallied out again, to indulge in an orgy of teas. This time she included the Lyons and the fourth tea-shop, beginning at the far end of the town and working her way back to the 'bus-stop. It was while she was struggling with her fifth meal, in the window of "Ye Cosye Corner," that a hurrying figure on the pavement caught her eye. The winter evening had closed in, and the street-lights were not very brilliant, but she distinctly saw a stoutish middle-aged nurse in a black veil and grey cloak pass along on the nearer pavement. By craning her neck, she could see her make a brisk spurt, scramble on the 'bus at the corner and disappear in the direction of the "Fisherman's Arms."

"How vexatious!" said Miss Climpson, as the vehicle disappeared. "I must have just missed her somewhere. Or perhaps she was having tea in a private house. Well, I'm afraid this is a blank day. And I do feel so *full* of tea!"

It was fortunate that Miss Climpson had been blest by Heaven with a sound digestion, for the next morning saw a repetition of the performance. It was possible, of course, that Miss Booth only went out two or three times a week, or that she only went out in the afternoon, but Miss Climpson was taking no chances. She had at least achieved the certainty that the 'bus-stop was the place to watch. This time she took up her post at "Ye Cosye Corner" at 11 o'clock and waited till twelve. Nothing happened and she went home.

In the afternoon she was there again at three. By this time the waitress had got to know her, and betrayed a certain amused and tolerant interest in her comings and goings. Miss Climpson explained that she liked so much to watch the people pass, and spoke a few words in praise of the Café and its service. She admired a quaint old inn on the opposite side of the street, and said she thought of making a sketch of it.

"Oh, yes," said the girl, "there's a many artists comes here for that."

This gave Miss Climpson a bright idea, and the next morning she brought a pencil and sketch-book with her.

By the extraordinary perversity of things in general, she had no sooner ordered her coffee, opened the sketch-book and started to outline the gables of the inn, than a 'bus drew up, and out of it stepped the stout nurse in the black and grey uniform. She did not enter "Ye Cosye Corner," but marched on at a brisk pace down the opposite side of the street, her veil flapping like a flag.

Miss Climpson uttered a sharp exclamation of annoyance, which drew the waitress's attention.

"How provoking!" said Miss Climpson. "I have left my rubber behind. I must just run out and buy one."

She dropped the sketch-book on the table and made for the door.

"I'll cover your coffee up for you, miss," said the girl, helpfully. "Mr. Bulteel's, down near the 'Bear,' is the best stationer's."

"Thank you, thank you," said Miss Climpson, and darted out.

The black veil was still flapping in the distance. Miss Climpson pursued breathlessly, keeping to the near side of the road. The veil dived into a chemist's shop. Miss Climpson crossed the road a little behind it and stared into a window full of baby-linen. The veil came out, fluttered undecidedly on the pavement, turned, passed Miss Climpson and went into a boot-shop.

"If it's shoe-laces, it'll be quick," thought Miss Climpson, "but if it's trying-on it may be all morning." She walked slowly past the door. By good luck a customer was just coming out, and, peering past him, Miss Climpson just caught a glimpse of the black veil vanishing into the back premises. She pushed the door boldly open. There was a counter for sundries in the front of the shop, and the doorway through which the nurse had vanished was labelled "Ladies' Department."

While buying a pair of brown silk laces, Miss Climpson debated with herself. Should she follow and seize this opportunity? Trying on shoes is usually a lengthy business. The subject is marooned for long periods in a chair, while the assistant climbs ladders and collects piles of cardboard boxes. It is also comparatively easy to enter into conversation with a person who is trying on shoes. But there is a snag in it. To give colour to your presence in the Fitting department, you must yourself try on shoes. What happens? The assistant first disables you by snatching off your right-hand shoe, and then disappears. And supposing, meanwhile, your quarry completes her purchase and walks out? Are you to follow, hopping madly on one foot? Are you to arouse suspicion by hurriedly replacing your own footgear and rushing out with laces flying and an unconvincing murmur about a forgotten engagement? Still worse, suppose you are in an amphibious condition, wearing one shoe of your own and one of the establishment's? What impression will you make by suddenly bolting with goods to which

you are not entitled? Will not the pursuer very quickly
become the pursued?

Having weighed this problem in her mind, Miss Climpson paid for her shoelaces and retired. She had already
bilked a tea-shop, and one misdemeanour in a morning
was about as much as she could hope to get away with.

The male detective, particularly when dressed as a workman, an errand-boy or a telegraph-messenger, is favourably
placed for "shadowing." He can loaf without attracting attention. The female detective must not loaf. On the other
hand, she can stare into shop-windows for ever. Miss Climpson selected a hat-shop. She examined all the hats in both
windows attentively, coming back to gaze in a purposeful
manner at an extremely elegant model with an eye-veil and
a pair of excrescences like rabbits'-ears. Just at the moment
when any observer might have thought that she had at last
made up her mind to go in and ask the price, the nurse
came out of the boot-shop. Miss Climpson shook her head
regretfully at the rabbits'-ears, darted back to the other
window, looked, hovered, hesitated—and tore herself away.

The nurse was now about thirty yards ahead, moving
well, with the air of a horse that sights his stable. She
crossed the street again, looked into a window piled with
coloured wools, thought better of it, passed on, and turned
in at the door of the Oriental Café.

Miss Climpson was in the position of one who, after prolonged pursuit, has clapped a tumbler over a moth. For
the moment the creature is safe and the pursuer takes
breath. The problem now is to extract the moth without
damage.

It is easy, of course, to follow a person into a café and
sit down at her table, if there is room there. But she may
not welcome you. She may feel it perverse in you to thrust
yourself upon her when other tables are standing empty. It
is better to offer some excuse, such as restoring a dropped
handkerchief or drawing attention to an open handbag.

If the person will not provide you with an excuse, the next best thing is to manufacture one.

The stationer's shop was only a few doors off. Miss Climpson went in and purchased an indiarubber, three picture post-cards, a BB pencil and a calendar, and waited while they were made up into a parcel. Then she slowly made her way across the street and turned into the "Oriental."

In the first room she found two women and a small boy occuping one recess, an aged gentleman drinking milk in another, and a couple of girls consuming coffee and cakes in a third.

"Excuse me," said Miss Climpson to the two women, "but does this parcel belong to you? I picked it up just outside the door."

The elder woman, who had evidently been shopping, hastily passed in review a quantity of miscellaneous packages, pinching each one by way of refreshing her memory as to the contents.

"I don't think it's mine, but really I can't say for certain. Let me see. That's eggs and that's bacon and—what's this, Gertie? Is that the mouse-trap? No, wait a minute, that's cough-mixture, that is—and that's Aunt Edith's cork soles, and that's Nugget—no, bloater paste, this here's the Nugget—why, bless my soul, I believe I *have* been and gone and dropped the mouse-trap—but that don't look like it to me."

"No, Mother," said the younger woman, "don't you remember, they were sending round the mouse-trap with the bath."

"Of course, so they were. Well, that accounts for that. The mouse-trap and the two frying-pans, they was all to go with the bath, and that's all except the soap, which you've got, Gertie. No, thank you very much, all the same, but it isn't ours; somebody else must have dropped it."

The old gentleman repudiated it firmly, but politely,

and the two girls merely giggled at it. Miss Climpson passed on. Two young women with their attendant young men duly thanked her in the second room, but said the parcel was not theirs.

Miss Climpson passed into the third room. In one corner was a rather talkative party of people with an Airedale, and at the back, in the most obscure and retired of all the Oriental nooks and corners, sat the nurse, reading a book.

The talkative party had nothing to say to the parcel, and Miss Climpson, with her heart beating fast, bore down upon the nurse.

"Excuse me," she said, smiling graciously, "but I think this little parcel must be yours. I picked it up just in the doorway and I've asked all the other people in the café."

The nurse looked up. She was a grey-haired, elderly woman, with those curious large blue eyes which disconcert the beholder by their intense gaze, and are usually an index of some emotional instability. She smiled at Miss Climpson and said pleasantly:

"No, no, it isn't mine. So kind of you. But I have all my parcels here."

She vaguely indicated the cushioned seat which ran round three sides of the alcove, and Miss Climpson, accepting the gesture as an invitation, promptly sat down.

"How very odd," said Miss Climpson, "I made sure someone must have dropped it coming in here. I wonder what I had better do with it." She pinched it gently. "I shouldn't think it was valuable, but one never knows. I suppose I ought to take it to the police-station."

"You could hand it to the cashier," suggested the nurse, "in case the owner came back here to claim it."

"Well now, so I could," cried Miss Climpson. "How clever of you to think of it. Of course, yes, that would be the best way. You must think me very foolish, but the idea never occurred to me. I'm not a very practical person, I'm afraid, but I do so admire the people who are. I should never do to take up *your* profession, should I? Any little emergency leaves me *quite* bewildered."

The nurse smiled again.

"It is largely a question of training," she said. "And of *self*-training, too, of course. All these little weaknesses can be cured by placing the mind under a Higher Control— don't you believe that?"

Her eyes rested hypnotically upon Miss Climpson's.

"I suppose that is true."

"It is such a mistake," pursued the nurse, closing her book and laying it down on the table, "to imagine that anything in the mental sphere is large or small. Our least thoughts and actions are equally directed by the higher centres of spiritual power, if we can bring ourselves to believe it."

A waitress arrived to take Miss Climpson's order.

"Oh, dear! I seem to have intruded myself upon your table . . ."

"Oh, don't get up," said the nurse.

"Are you sure? Really? because I don't want to interrupt you—"

"Not at all. I live a very solitary life, and I am always glad to find a friend to talk to."

"How nice of you. I'll have scones and butter, please, and a pot of tea. This is such a nice little café, don't you think? —so quiet and peaceful. If only those people wouldn't make such a noise with that dog of theirs. I don't like those great big animals, and I think they're quite dangerous, don't you?"

The reply was lost on Miss Climpson, for she had suddenly seen the title of the book on the table, and the Devil, or a Ministering Angel (she was not quite sure which) was, so to speak, handing her a fullblown temptation on a silver salver. The book was published by the Spiritualist Press and was called "*Can the Dead Speak?*"

In a single moment of illumination, Miss Climpson saw her plan complete and perfect in every detail. It involved a course of deception from which her conscience shrank appalled, but it was certain. She wrestled with the demon. Even in a righteous cause, could anything so wicked be justified?

She breathed what she thought was a prayer for guidance, but the only answer was a small whisper in her ear, "Oh, jolly good work, Miss Climpson!" and the voice was the voice of Peter Wimsey.

"Pardon me," said Miss Climpson, "but I see you are a student of spiritualism. How interesting that is!"

If there was one subject in the world about which Miss Climpson might claim to know something, it was Spiritualism. It is a flower which flourishes bravely in a boarding-house atmosphere. Time and again, Miss Climpson had listened while the apparatus of planes and controls, correspondences and veridical communications, astral bodies, auras and ectoplastic materialisations was displayed before her protesting intelligence. That to the Church it was a forbidden subject she knew well enough, but she had been paid companion to so many old ladies and had been forced so many times to bow down in the House of Rimmon.

And then there had been the quaint little man from the Psychical Research Society. He had stayed a fortnight in the same private hotel with her at Bournemouth. He was skilled in the investigation of haunted houses and the detection of poltergeists. He had rather liked Miss Climpson, and she had passed several interesting evenings hearing about the tricks of mediums. Under his guidance she had learnt to turn tables and produce explosive cracking noises; she knew how to examine a pair of sealed slates for the marks of the wedges which let the chalk go in on a long black wire to write spirit-passages. She had seen the ingenious rubber gloves which leave the impression of spirit hands in a bucket of paraffin-wax, and which, when deflated, can be drawn delicately from the hardened wax through a hole narrower than a child's wrist. She even knew theoretically, though she had never tried it, how to hold her hands to be tied behind her back so as to force that first deceptive knot which makes all subsequent knots useless, and how to flit about the room banging tambourines in the twilight in spite of having been tied up in a black cabinet with both fists filled with flour. Miss Climpson had wondered greatly at the folly and wickedness of mankind.

The nurse went on talking, and Miss Climpson answered mechanically.

"She's only a beginner," said Miss Climpson to herself. "She's reading a text-book. . . . And she is quite uncritical. . . . Surely she knows that that woman was exposed long ago. . . . People like her shouldn't be allowed out alone— they're living incitements to fraud. . . . I don't know this Mrs. Craig she is talking about, but I should say she was as twisty as a corkscrew. . . . I must avoid Mrs. Craig, she probably knows too much . . . if the poor deluded creature will swallow that, she'll swallow anything."

"It does seem *most* wonderful, doesn't it?" said Miss Climpson, aloud. "But isn't it a wee bit *dangerous?* I've been told I'm sensitive myself, but I have never dared to *try.* Is it *wise* to open one's mind to these supernatural influences?"

"It's not dangerous if you know the right way," said the nurse. "One must learn to build up a shell of pure thoughts about the soul, so that no evil influences can enter it. I have had the most marvellous talks with the dear ones who have passed over. . . ."

Miss Climpson refilled the tea-pot and sent the waitress for a plate of sugary cakes.

". . . unfortunately I am not mediumistic myself—not yet, that is. I can't get anything when I'm alone. Mrs. Craig says that it will come by practice and concentration. Last night I was trying with the Ouija board, but it would only write spirals."

"Your conscious mind is too active, I expect," said Miss Climpson.

"Yes, I daresay that is it. Mrs. Craig says that I am wonderfully sympathetic. We get the most wonderful results when we sit together. Unfortunately she is abroad just now."

Miss Climpson's heart gave a great leap, so that she nearly spilled her tea.

"You yourself are a medium, then?" went on the nurse.

"I have been told so," said Miss Climpson, guardedly.

"I wonder," said the nurse, "whether if we sat together—" She looked hungrily at Miss Climpson.

"I don't really like—"

"Oh, do! You are such a sympathetic person. I'm sure we should get good results. And the spirits are so pathetically anxious to communicate. Of course, I wouldn't like to try unless I was sure of the person. There are so many fraudulent mediums about"— ("So you do know that much!" thought Miss Climpson)—"but with somebody like yourself one is absolutely safe. You would find it made such a difference in your life. I used to be so unhappy over all the pain and misery in the world—we see so much of it, you know—till I realised the certainty of survival and how all our trials are merely sent to fit us for life on a higher plane."

"Well," said Miss Climpson, slowly, "I'm willing just to try. But I can't say I really *believe* in it, you know."

"You would—you would."

"Of course, I've see one or two strange things happen— things that couldn't be tricks, because I knew the people— and which I couldn't explain—"

"Come up and see me this evening, now do!" said the nurse, persuasively. "We'll just have one quiet sitting and then we shall see whether you really are a medium. I've no doubt you are."

"Very well," said Miss Climpson. "What is your name, by the way?"

"Caroline Booth—Miss Caroline Booth. I'm nurse to an old, paralysed lady in the big house along the Kendal Road."

"Thank goodness for that, anyway," thought Miss Climpson. Aloud she said:

"And my name is Climpson; I think I've got a card somewhere. No—I've left it behind. But I'm staying at Hillside View. How do I get to you?"

Miss Booth mentioned the address and the time of the 'bus, and added an invitation to supper, which was accepted. Miss Climpson went home and wrote a hurried note:

My dear Lord Peter—

I am sure you have been *wondering* what has *happened* to me. But *at last* I have NEWS! I have STORMED THE CITA-DEL!!! I am going to the *house tonight* and you may expect GREAT THINGS!!!

In *haste*,

Yours very sincerely,

Katharine A. Climpson.

Miss Climpson went out into the town again after lunch. First, being an honest woman, she retrieved her sketch-book from "Ye Cosye Corner" and paid her bill, explaining that she had run across a friend that morning and been detained. She then visited a number of shops. Eventually she selected a small metal soap-box which suited her requirements. Its sides were slightly convex, and when closed and pinched slightly, it sprang back with a hearty cracking noise. This, with a little contrivance and some powerful sticking-plaster, she fixed to a strong elastic garter. When clasped about Miss Climpson's bony knee and squeezed sharply against the other knee, the box emitted a series of cracks so satisfying as to convince the most sceptical. Miss Climpson, seated before the looking-glass, indulged in an hour's practice before tea, till the crack could be produced with the minimum of physical jerk.

Another purchase was a length of stiff black-bound wire, such as is used for making hat-brims. Used double, neatly bent to a double angle and strapped to the wrist, this contrivance was sufficient to rock a light table. The weight of a heavy table would be too much for it, she feared, but she had had no time to order blacksmith's work. She could try, anyway. She hunted out a black velvet rest-gown with long, wide sleeves, and satisfied herself that the wires could be sufficiently hidden.

At six o'clock, she put on this garment, fastened the soap-box to her leg—turning the box outward, lest untimely cracks should startle her fellow-travellers, muffled herself in a heavy rain-cloak of Inverness cut, took hat and umbrella and started on her way to steal Mrs. Wrayburn's will.

CHAPTER XVII

Supper was over. It had been served in a beautiful old panelled room with an Adam ceiling and fireplace, and the food had been good. Miss Climpson felt braced and ready.

"We'll sit in my own room, shall we?" said Miss Booth. "It's the only really comfortable place. Most of this house is shut up, of course. If you'll excuse me, dear, I will just run up and give Mrs. Wrayburn her supper and make her comfortable, poor thing, and then we can begin. I shan't be more than half an hour or so."

"She's quite helpless, I suppose?"

"Yes, quite."

"Can she speak?"

"Not to say speak. She mumbles sometimes, but one can't make anything of it. It's sad, isn't it, and her so rich. It will be a happy day for her when she passes over."

"Poor soul!" said Miss Climpson.

Her hostess led her into a small, gaily-furnished sitting-room and left her there among the cretonne covers and the ornaments. Miss Climpson ran her eyes rapidly over the books, which were mostly novels, with the exception of some standard works on Spiritualism, and then turned her attention to the mantelpiece. It was crowded with photographs, as the mantelpieces of nurses usually are. Conspicuous among hospital groups and portraits inscribed "From your grateful patient," was a cabinet photograph of a gentleman in the dress and moustache of the 'nineties, standing beside a bicycle, apparently upon a stone balcony in mid-air with a distant view over a rocky gorge. The frame was silver, heavy and ornate.

"Too young for a father," said Miss Climpson, as she turned it over and pulled back the catch of the frame, "either sweetheart or favourite brother. H'm! 'My dearest Lucy from her ever-loving Harry.' Not a brother, I fancy. Photographer's address, Coventry. Cycle trade, possibly. Now what happened to Harry? Not matrimony, obviously. Death, or infidelity. First-class frame and central position; bunch of hot-house narcissus in a vase—I think Harry has passed over. What next? Family group? Yes. Names conveniently beneath. Dearest Lucy in a fringe, Papa and Mamma, Tom and Gertrude. Tom and Gertrude are older, but they may be still alive. Papa is a parson. Largeish house—country rectory, perhaps. Photographer's address, Maidstone. Wait a minute. Here's Papa in another group, with a dozen small boys. Schoolmaster, or takes private pupils. Two boys have straw hats with zig-zag ribbons—school, probably, then. What's that silver cup? Thos. Booth and three other names—Pembroke College Fours 1883. Not an expensive college. Wonder whether Papa objected to Harry on account of the cycle-manufacturing connection? That book over there looks like a school prize. It is. Maidstone Ladies' College—for distinction in English Literature. Just so. Is she coming back?—No, false alarm. Young man in khaki, 'Your loving nephew, G. Booth'—ah! Tom's son, I take it. Did he survive, I wonder? Yes—she is coming, this time."

When the door opened, Miss Climpson was sitting by the fire, deeply engaged in *Raymond*.

"So sorry to keep you waiting," said Miss Booth, "but the poor old dear is rather restless this evening. She'll do now for a couple of hours, but I shall have to go up again later. Shall we begin at once? I'm *so* eager to try."

Miss Climpson readily agreed.

"We usually use this table," said Miss Booth, bringing forward a small, round table of bamboo, with a shelf between its legs. Miss Climpson thought she had never seen a piece of furniture more excellently adapted for the faking of phenomena, and heartily approved of Mrs. Craig's choice.

"Do we sit in the light?" she enquired.

"Not in full light," said Miss Booth. "Mrs. Craig explained to me that the blue rays of daylight or electricity are too hard for the spirits. They shatter the vibrations, you see. So we usually put out the light and sit in the firelight, which is quite bright enough for taking notes. Will you write down, or shall I?"

"Oh, I think you had better do it as you're more accustomed to it," said Miss Climpson.

"Very well." Miss Booth fetched a pencil and a pad of paper and switched off the light.

"Now we just sit down and place our thumbs and finger-tips lightly on the table, near the edge. It's better to make a circle, of course, but one can't do that with two people. And just at first, I think it's better not to talk—till a rapport is established, you know. Which side will you sit?"

"Oh, this will do for me," said Miss Climpson.

"You don't mind the fire on your back?"

Miss Climpson most certainly did not.

"Well, that's a good arrangement, because it helps to screen the rays from the table."

"That's what I thought," said Miss Climpson, truthfully.

They placed thumbs and finger-tips on the table and waited.

Ten minutes passed.

"Did you feel any movement?" whispered Miss Booth.

"No."

"It sometimes takes a little time."

Silence.

·"Ah! I thought I felt something then."

"I've got a feeling like pins and needles in my fingers."

"So have I. We shall get something soon."

A pause.

"Would you like to rest a little?"

"My wrists ache rather."

"They do till you get used to it. It's the power coming through them."

Miss Climpson lifted her fingers and rubbed each wrist gently. The thin black hooks came quietly down to the edge of her black velvet sleeve.

"I feel sure there is power all about us. I can feel a cold thrill on my spine."

"Let's go on," said Miss Climpson. "I'm quite rested now."

Silence.

"I feel," whispered Miss Climpson, "as though something was gripping the back of my neck."

"Don't move."

"And my arms have gone dead from the elbow."

"Hush! so have mine."

Miss Climpson might have added that she had a pain in her deltoids, if she had known the name for them. This is not an uncommon result of sitting with the thumbs and fingers on a table without support for the wrist.

"I'm tingling from head to foot," said Miss Booth.

At this moment the table gave a violent lurch. Miss Climpson had over-estimated the force necessary to move bamboo furniture.

"Ah!"

After a slight pause for recuperation, the table began to move again, but more gently, till it was rocking with a regular see-saw motion. Miss Climpson found that by gently elevating one rather large foot, she could take practically all the weight off her wrist-hooks. This was fortunate, as she was doubtful whether their constitution would stand the strain.

"Shall we speak to it?" asked Miss Climpson.

"Wait a moment," said Miss Booth. "It wants to go side-ways."

Miss Climpson was surprised by this statement, which

seemed to argue a high degree of imagination, but she obligingly imparted a slight gyratory movement to the table.

"Shall we stand up?" suggested Miss Booth.

This was disconcerting, for it is not easy to work a vibrating table while stooping and standing on one leg. Miss Climpson decided to fall into a trance. She dropped her head on her chest and uttered a slight moan. At the same time she pulled back her hands, releasing the hooks, and the table continued to revolve jerkily, spinning beneath their fingers.

A coal fell from the fire with a crash, sending up a bright jet of flame. Miss Climpson started, and the table ceased spinning and came down with a little thud.

"Oh, dear!" exclaimed Miss Booth. "The light has dispersed the vibrations. Are you all right, dear?"

"Yes, yes," said Miss Climpson, vaguely. "Did anything happen?"

"The power was tremendous," said Miss Booth. "I've never felt it so strong."

"I think I must have fallen asleep," said Miss Climpson.

"You were entranced," said Miss Booth. "The control was taking possession. Are you very tired, or can you go on?"

"I feel quite all right," said Miss Climpson, "only a little drowsy."

"You're a wonderfully strong medium," said Miss Booth.

Miss Climpson, surreptitiously flexing her ankle, was inclined to agree.

"We'll put a screen before the fire this time," said Miss Booth. "That's better. Now!"

The hands were replaced on the table, which began to rock again almost immediately.

"We won't lose any more time," said Miss Booth. She cleared her throat slightly, and addressed the table.

"Is there a spirit here?"

Crack!

The table ceased moving.

"Will you give me one knock for 'Yes' and two for 'No'?"

Crack!

The advantage of this method of interrogation is that it obliges the enquirer to put leading questions.

"Are you the spirit of one who has passed over?"

"Yes."

"Are you Fedora?"

"No."

"Are you one of the spirits who have visited me before?"

"No."

"Are you friendly to us?"

"Yes."

"Are you pleased to see us?"

"Yes. Yes. Yes."

"Are you happy?"

"Yes."

"Are you here to ask anything for yourself?"

"No."

"Are you anxious to help us personally?"

"No."

"Are you speaking on behalf of another spirit?"

"Yes."

"Does he want to speak to my friend?"

"No."

"To me, then?"

"Yes. Yes. Yes. Yes." (The table rocked violently.)

"Is it the spirit of a woman?"

"No."

"A man?"

"Yes."

A little gasp.

"Is it the spirit I have been trying to communicate with?"

"Yes."

A pause and a tilting of the table.

"Will you speak to us by means of the alphabet? One knock for A, two for B, and so on?"

("Belated caution," thought Miss Climpson.)

"Crack!"

"What is your name?"

Eight taps, and a long indrawn breath.

One tap—

"H—A—"

A long succession of taps.

"Was that an R? You go too fast."

"Crack!"

"H—A—R—is that right?"

"Yes."

"Is it Harry?"

"Yes, yes, yes."

"Oh, Harry! At last! How are you? Are you happy?"

"Yes—no—lonely."

"It wasn't my fault, Harry."

"Yes. Weak."

"Ah, but I had my duty to think of. Remember who came between us."

"Yes. F-A-T-H-E-"

"No, no, Harry! It was mo—"

"—A-D!" concluded the table, triumphantly.

"How can you speak so unkindly?"

"Love comes first."

"I know that now. But I was only a girl. Won't you forgive me now?"

"All forgiven. Mother forgiven too."

"I'm so glad. What do you do where you are, Harry?"

"Wait. Help Atone."

"Have you any special message for me?"

"Go to Coventry!" (Here the table became agitated.)

This message seemed to overwhelm the seeker.

"Oh, it really is you, Harry! You haven't forgotten the dear old joke. Tell me—"

The table showed great signs of excitement at this point
and poured out a volley of unintelligible letters.

"What do you want?"

"G—G—G—"

"It must be somebody else interrupting," said Miss Booth.
"Who is that, please?"

"G-E-O-R-G-E" (very rapidly).

"George? I don't know any George, except Tom's boy.
Has anything happened to him, I wonder."

"Ha! ha! ha! not George Booth, George Washington."

"George Washington?"

"Ha! ha!" (The table became convulsively agitated, so
much so that the medium seemed hardly able to hold it.
Miss Booth, who had been noting down the conversation,
now put her hands back on the table, which stopped caper-
ing and began to rock.)

"Who is here now?"

"Pongo."

"Who is Pongo?"

"Your control."

"Who was that talking just now?"

"Bad spirit. Gone now."

"Is Harry still there?"

"Gone."

"Does anybody else want to speak?"

"Helen."

"Helen who?"

"Don't you remember? Maidstone."

"Maidstone? Oh, do you mean Ellen Pate?"

"Yes, Pate."

"Fancy that! Good-evening, Ellen. How nice to hear from
you."

"Remember row."

"Do you mean the big row in the dormitory?"

"Kate bad girl."

"No, I don't remember Kate, except Kate Hurley. You don't mean her, do you?"

"Naughty Kate. Lights out."

"Oh, I *know* what she's trying to say. The cakes after lights were out."

"That's right."

"You still spell badly, Ellen."

"Miss—Miss—"

"Mississippi? Haven't you learnt it yet?"

"Funny."

"Are there many of our class where you are?"

"Alice and Mabel. Send love."

"How sweet of them. Give them my love too."

"Yes. All love. Flowers. Sunshine."

"What do you—"

"P," said the table, impatiently.

"Is that Pongo again?"

"Yes. Tired."

"Do you want us to stop?"

"Yes. Another time."

"Very well, good-night."

"Good-night."

The medium leaned back in her chair with an air of exhaustion which was perfectly justified. It is very tiring to rap out letters of the alphabet, and she was afraid the soap-box was slipping.

Miss Booth turned on the light.

"That was wonderful!" said Miss Booth.

"Did you get the answers you wanted?"

"Yes, indeed. Didn't you hear them?"

"I didn't follow it all," said Miss Climpson.

"It is a little difficult, counting, till you're used to it. You must be dreadfully tired. We'll stop now and make some tea. Next time perhaps we could use the Ouija. It doesn't take nearly so long to get the answers with that."

Miss Climpson considered this. Certainly it would be less

wearisome, but she was not sure of being able to manipulate it.

Miss Booth put the kettle on the fire and glanced at the
clock.

"Dear me! it's nearly eleven. How the time has flown!
I must run up and see to my old dear. Would you like
to read through the questions and answers? I don't suppose
I shall be many minutes."

Satisfactory, so far, thought Miss Climpson. Confidence
was well established. In a few days' time, she would be able
to work her plan. But she had nearly tripped up over
George. And it was stupid to have said 'Helen.' Nellie
would have done for either—there was a Nellie in every
school forty-five years ago. But after all, it didn't much
matter what you said—the other person was sure to help
you out of it. How desperately her legs and arms were aching. Wearily she wondered if she had missed the last bus.

"I'm afraid you have," said Miss Booth, when the question was put to her on her return. "But we'll ring up a taxi.
At my expense, of course, dear. I insist, as you were so good
in coming all this way, entirely to please me. Don't you
think the communications are too marvellous? Harry would
never come before—poor Harry! I'm afraid I was very unkind to him. He married, but you see he has never forgotten me. He lived at Coventry and we used to have a
joke about it—that's what he meant by saying that. I wonder which Alice and Mabel that was. There was an Alice
Gibbons and an Alice Roach—both such nice girls; I think
Mabel must be Mabel Herridge. She married and went out
to India years and years ago. I can't remember her married name and I've never heard from her since, but she
must have passed to the other side. Pongo is a new control.
We must ask him who he is. Mrs. Craig's control is Fedora
—she was a slave-girl at the court of Poppaea."

"Really!" said Miss Climpson.

"She told us her story one night. So romantic. She was

thrown to the lions because she was a Christian and refused to have anything to do with Nero."

"How very interesting."

"Yes, isn't it? But she doesn't speak very good English, and it's sometimes rather hard to understand her. And she sometimes lets the tiresome ones in. Pongo was very quick at getting rid of George Washington. You will come again, won't you? Tomorrow night?"

"Certainly, if you like."

"Yes, please do. And next time you must ask for a message for yourself."

"I will indeed," said Miss Climpson. "It has all been *such* a revelation—quite *wonderful*. I never *dreamed* that I had such a gift."

And that was true, also.

CHAPTER XVIII

It was, of course, useless for Miss Climpson to try to conceal from the boarding-house ladies where she had been and what she had been doing. Her return at midnight in a taxi had already aroused the liveliest curiosity, and she told the truth to avoid being accused of worse dissipations.

"My dear Miss Climpson," said Mrs. Pegler, "you will not, I trust, think me interfering, but I must caution you against having anything to do with Mrs. Craig or her friends. I have no doubt Miss Booth is an excellent woman, but I do not like the company she keeps. Nor do I approve of spiritualism. It is a prying into matters which we are not intended to know about, and may lead to very undesirable results. If you were a married woman, I could explain myself more clearly, but you may take it from me that these indulgences may have serious effects upon the character in more ways than one."

"Oh, Mrs. Pegler," said Miss Etheredge, "I don't think you should say that. One of the most beautiful characters I know—a woman whom it is a privilege to call one's friend—is a spiritualist, and she is a real saint in her life and influence."

"Very likely, Miss Etheredge," replied Mrs. Pegler, drawing her stout figure to its most impressive uprightness, "but that is not the point. I do not say that a spiritualist *may* not live a good life, but I *do* say that the majority of them are most unsatisfactory people, and far from truthful."

"I have happened to meet with a number of so-called mediums in the course of my life," agreed Miss Lweall, acidly, "and all of them, without *any* exception, were people I would not have trusted any further than I could see them—if as far."

"That is very true of a great many of them," said Miss Climpson, "and I am sure *nobody* could have better opportunities of judging than *myself*. But I think and hope that some of them are at least *sincere* if *mistaken* in their claims. What do *you* think, Mrs. Liffey?" she added, turning to the proprietress of the establishment.

"We-ll," said Mrs. Liffey—obliged, in her official capacity, to agree as far as possible with all parties. "I must say, from what I have read, and that is not a great deal, for I have little time for reading—still, I think there is a certain amount of evidence to show that, in certain cases and under strictly safeguarded conditions, there is possibly some foundation of truth beneath the spiritualists' claims. Not that I should care to have anything to do with it personally; as Mrs. Pegler says, I do not as a rule care very much for the sort of people who go in for it, though doubtless there are many exceptions. I think perhaps that the subject should be left to properly qualified investigators."

"There I agree with you," said Mrs. Pegler. "No words can express the disgust I feel at the intrusion of women like this Mrs. Craig into realms that should be sacred to us all. Imagine, Miss Climpson, that that woman—whom I do not know and have no intention of knowing—actually had the impertinence once to write to me and say that she had received a message at one of her séances, as she calls them, purporting to come from my dear husband. I cannot tell you what I felt. To have the General's name actually brought up, in public, in connection with such wicked nonsense! And of course it was the purest invention, for the General was the *last* man to have anything to do with goings-on. 'Pernicious poppy-cock,' he used to call it in his bluff military way. And when it came to telling me, his widow, that he had come to Mrs. Craig's house and played the accordion and asked for special prayers to deliver him from a place of punishment, I could only look on it as a calculated insult. The General was a regular Church-goer and

entirely opposed to prayers for the dead or anything
popish; and as to being in any undesirable place, he was
the best of men, even if he was a little abrupt at times. As
for accordions, I hope, wherever he is, he has something
better to do with his time."

"A most shameful business," said Miss Tweall.

"Who is this Mrs. Craig?" asked Miss Climpson.

"Nobody knows," said Mrs. Pegler, ominously.

"She is said to be a doctor's widow," said Mrs. Liffey.

"It's my opinion," said Miss Tweall, "that she is no
better than she should be."

"A woman of her age," said Mrs. Pegler, "with henna'd
hair and earrings a foot long——"

"And going about in those extraordinary clothes," said
Miss Tweall.

"And having such very odd people to stay with her," said
Mrs. Pegler. "You remember that black man, Mrs. Liffey,
who wore a green turban and used to say his prayers in the
front garden, till the police interfered."

"What I should like to know," said Miss Tweall, "is,
where she gets her money from."

"If you ask me, my dear, the woman's on the make.
Heaven knows what she persuades people to do in these
spiritualistic meetings."

"But what brought her to Windle?" asked Miss Climpson. "I should have thought London, or some big town,
would have been a better place for her if she is the kind of
person you describe."

"I shouldn't be surprised if she was in hiding," said Miss
Tweall, darkly. "There is such a thing as making a place
too hot to hold you."

"Without altogether subscribing to your wholesale con-
demnation," said Miss Climpson, "I must agree that psychical research can be *very dangerous indeed* in the *wrong
hands*, and from what Miss Booth tells me, I do doubt *very
much* whether Mrs. Craig is a suitable guide for the inex-

perienced. Indeed, I quite felt it my *duty* to put Miss Booth on her guard, and that is what I am endeavouring to do. But, as you know, one has to do that kind of thing *very* tactfully—otherwise one may merely, so to speak, put the person's back up. The first step is to gain her *confidence*, and then, little by little, one may be able to induce a more wholesome frame of mind."

"That's *so* true," said Miss Etheredge, eagerly, her pale blue eyes lighting with something that was almost animation. "I very nearly fell under the influence of a dreadful, fraudulent person myself, till my dear friend showed me a better way."

"Maybe," said Mrs. Pegler, "but in my opinion the whole thing is best left alone."

Undeterred by this excellent advice, Miss Climpson kept her appointment. After a spirited exhibition of table-rocking, Pongo consented to communicate by means of the Ouija board, though at first he was rather awkward with it. He attributed this, however, to the fact that he had never learned to write while on earth. Asked who he was, he explained that he was an Italian acrobat of the Renaissance period, and that his full name was Pongocelli. He had lived a sadly irregular life, but had redeemed himself by heroically refusing to abandon a sick child during the time of the Great Plague in Florence. He had caught the plague and died of it, and was now working out the period of probation for his sins by serving as guide and interpreter to other spirits. It was a touching story, and Miss Climpson was rather proud of it.

George Washington was rather intrusive, and the séance also suffered from a number of mysterious interruptions from what Pongo described as a "jealous influence." Nevertheless, "Harry" reappeared and delivered some consolatory messages, and there were further communications from Mabel Herridge, who gave a vivid description of her life in

India. On the whole, and taking the difficulties into account, a successful evening.

On Sunday there was no séance, owing to the revolt of the medium's conscience. Miss Climpson felt that she could not, really could not, bring herself to do it. She went to church instead, and listened to the Christmas message with a distracted mind.

On Monday, however, the two enquirers again took their seats about the bamboo table, and the following is the report of the séance, as noted down by Miss Booth.

7.30 p.m.

On this occasion proceedings were begun at once with the Ouija board; after a few minutes, a loud succession of raps announced the presence of a control.

Question: Good-evening. Who is that?

Answer: Pongo here. Good-evening! Heaven bless you.

Q. We are very glad to have you with us, Pongo.

A. Good—very good. Here we are again!

Q. Is that you, Harry?

A. Yes, only to give my love. Such a crowd.

Q. The more the better. We are glad to meet all our friends. What can we do for you?

A. Attend. Obey the spirits.

Q. We will do all we can, if you will tell us what to do.

A. Boil your heads!

Q. Go away, George, we don't want you.

A. Get off the line, silly.

Q. Pongo, can't you send him away?

(Here the pencil drew the sketch of an ugly face.)

Q. Is that your portrait?

A. That's me. G. W. Ha, ha!

(The pencil zig-zagged violently and drove the board right over the edge of the table. When it was replaced it started to write in the hand we associate with Pongo.)

A. I have sent him away. Very noisy tonight. F. jealous

and sends him to disturb us. Never mind. Pongo more powerful.

Q. Who do you say is jealous?

A. Never mind. Bad person. Maladetta.

Q. Is Harry still there?

A. No. Other business. There is a spirit here who wishes your help.

Q. Who is it?

A. Very hard. Wait.

(The pencil made a series of wide loops.)

Q. What letter is that?

A. Silly! don't be impatient. There is difficulty. I will try again.

(The pencil scribbled for a few minutes and then wrote a large C.)

Q. We have got the letter C. Is that right?

A. C-C-C

Q. We have got C.

A. C-R-E

(Here there was another violent interruption.)

A. (in Pongo's writing) She is trying, but there is much opposition. Think helpful thoughts.

Q. Would you like us to sing a hymn?

A. (Pongo again, very angry) Stupid! Be quiet! (Here the writing changed again) M-O-

Q. Is that part of the same word?

A. R-N-A.

Q. Do you mean Cremorna?

A. (in the new writing) Cremorna, Cremorna. Through! Glad, glad, glad!

At this point, Miss Booth turned to Miss Climpson and said in a puzzled voice:

"This is very strange. Cremorna was Mrs. Wrayburn's stage name. I do hope—surely she can't have passed away suddenly. She was perfectly comfortable when I left her. Had I better go and see?"

"Perhaps it's another Cremorna?" suggested Miss Climpson.

"But it's such an unusual name."

"Why not ask who it is?"

Q. Cremorna—what is your second name?

A. (The pencil writing very fast) Rosegarden—easier now.

Q. I don't understand you.

A. Rose—Rose—Rose—Silly!

Q. Oh!—(My dear, she's mixing up the two names)—Do you mean Cremorna Garden?

A. Yes.

Q. Rosanna Wrayburn?

A. Yes.

Q. Have you passed over?

A. Not yet. In exile.

Q. Are you still in the body?

A. Neither in the body nor out of the body. Waiting. (Pongo interposing) When what you call the mind is departed, the spirit waits in exile for the Great Change. Why can't you understand? Make haste. Great difficulties.

Q. We are so sorry. Are you in trouble about something?

A. Great trouble.

Q. I hope it isn't anything in Dr. Brown's treatment, or mine—

A. (Pongo) Do not be so foolish. (Cremorna) My will.

Q. Do you want to alter your will?

A. No.

Miss Climpson. That is fortunate, because I don't think it would be legal. What do you want us to do about it, dear Mrs. Wrayburn?

A. Send it to Norman.

Q. To Mr. Norman Urquhart?

A. Yes. He knows.

Q. He knows what is to be done with it?

A. He wants it.

Q. Very well. Can you tell us where to find it?

A. I have forgotten. Search.

Q. Is it in the house?

A. I tell you I have forgotten. Deep waters. No safety. Failing, failing . . .

(Here the writing became very faint and irregular.)

Q. Try to remember.

A. In the B—B—B—(a confusion and the pencil staggering wildly)—No good. (Suddenly, in a different hand and very vigorously) Get off the line, get off the line, get off the line.

Q. Who is that?

A. (Pongo) She has gone. The bad influence back. Ha, ha! Get off! Finished now. (The pencil ran right out of the medium's control, and on being replaced on the table, refused to answer any further questions.)

"How dreadfully vexatious!" exclaimed Miss Booth.

"I suppose you have no idea where the will is?"

"Not the least. 'In the B—' she said. Now, what could that be?"

"In the Bank, perhaps," suggested Miss Climpson.

"It might be. If so, of course, Mr. Urquhart would be the only person who could get it out."

"Then why hasn't he? She said he wanted it."

"Of course. Then it must be somewhere in the house. What could B stand for?"

"Box, Bag, Bureau—?"

"Bed? It might be almost anything."

"What a pity she couldn't finish the message. Shall we try again? Or shall we look in all the likely places?"

"Let's look first, and then, if we can't find it, we can try again."

"That's a good idea. There are some keys in one of the bureau drawers that belong to her boxes and things."

"Why not try them?" said Miss Climpson, boldly.

"We will. You'll come and help, won't you?"

"If you think it advisable. I'm a stranger, you know."

"The message came to you as much as to me. I'd rather you came with me. You might be able to suggest places."

Miss Climpson made no further ado, and then went upstairs. It was a queer business—practically robbing a helpless woman in the interests of someone she had never seen. Queer. But the motive must be a good one, if it was Lord Peter's.

At the top of the beautiful staircase with its ample curve was a long, wide corridor, the walls hung thickly from floor to ceiling with portraits, sketches, framed autograph letters, programmes, and all the reminiscent bric-à-brac of the green-room.

"All her life is here and in these two rooms," said the nurse. "If this collection was to be sold, it would fetch a lot of money. I suppose it will be, some day."

"Whom does the money go to, do you know?"

"Well, I've always thought it would be to Mr. Norman Urquhart—he's a relation of hers, about the only one, I believe. But I've never been told anything about it."

She pushed open a tall door, graceful with curved panels and classical architrave, and turned on the light.

It was a stately great room, with three tall windows and a ceiling gracefully moulded with garlands of flowers and flambeaux. The purity of its lines was, however, defaced and insulted by a hideous rose-trellised wall-paper, and heavy plush curtains of a hot crimson with thick gold fringes and ropes, like the drop-curtain of a Victorian playhouse. Every foot of space was crammed thick with furniture—buhl cabinets incongruously jostling mahogany chiffoniers; whatnot tables strewn with ornaments cuddling the bases of heavy German marbles and bronzes; lacquer screens, Sheraton bureaux, Chinese vases, alabaster lamps, chairs, ottomans of every shape, colour and period, clustered thick as plants wrestling for existence in a tropical jungle. It was the room of a woman without taste or moderation, who refused nothing and surrendered nothing, to

whom the fact of possession had become the one steadfast
reality in a world of loss and change.

"It may be in here or in the bedroom." said Miss Booth.
"I'll get her keys."

She opened a door on the right. Miss Climpson, endlessly
inquisitive, tip-toed in after her.

The bedroom was even more of a nightmare than the
sitting-room. A small electric reading-lamp burned dimly
by the bed, huge and gilded, with hangings of rose brocade
cascading in long folds from a tester supported by fat
golden cupids. Outside the narrow circle of light loomed
monstrous wardrobes, more cabinets, tall chests of drawers.
The dressing-table, frilled and flounced, held a wide, three-
fold mirror, and a monstrous cheval-glass in the centre of
the room darkly reflected the towering and shadowy outlines of the furniture.

Miss Booth opened the middle door of the largest wardrobe. It swung back with a creak, letting out a great gush
of frangipani. Nothing, evidently, had been altered in this
room since silence and paralysis had struck the owner down.

Miss Climpson stepped softly up to the bed. Instinct
made her move cautiously as a cat, though it was evident
that nothing would ever startle or surprise its occupant.

An old, old face, so tiny in the vast expanse of sheet and
pillow that it might have been a doll, stared up at her with
unblinking, unseeing eyes. It was covered with fine surface-
wrinkles, like a hand sodden with soapy water, but all the
great lines carved by experience had been smoothed out
with the relaxing of the helpless muscles. It was both puffed
and crumpled. It reminded Miss Climpson of a child's pink
balloon, from which nearly all the air has leaked away.
The escaping breath puffed through the lax lips in little
blowing, snorting sounds and added to the resemblance.
From under the frilled night-cap straggled a few lank wisps
of whitened hair.

"Funny, isn't it," said Miss Booth, "to think that with her lying like that, her spirit can communicate with us."

Miss Climpson was overcome by a sense of sacrilege. It was only by a great effort that she prevented herself from confessing the truth. She had pulled the garter with the soap-box above her knee for safety, and the elastic was cutting painfully into the muscles of her leg—a kind of reminder of her iniquities.

But Miss Booth had already turned away, and was pulling open the drawers of one of the bureaux.

Two hours passed, and they were still searching. The letter B. opened up a particularly wide field of search. Miss Climpson had chosen it on that account, and her foresight was rewarded. By a little ingenuity, that useful letter could be twisted to fit practically any hiding-place in the house. The things that were neither bureaux, beds, bags, boxes, baskets nor bibelot-tables could usually be described as big, black, brown or buhl or, at a pinch, as being bedroom or boudoir furniture, and since every shelf, drawer and pigeon-hole in every object was crammed full of newspaper-cuttings, letters and assorted souvenirs, the searchers soon found their heads, legs and backs aching with effort.

"I'd no idea," said Miss Booth, "that there could be so many possible places."

Miss Climpson, sitting on the floor, with her back hair uncoiling itself and her decent black petticoats tucked up nearly to the soap-box, agreed wearily.

"It's dreadfully exhausting, isn't it?" said Miss Booth. "Wouldn't you like to stop? I can go on searching tomorrow by myself. It's a shame to tire you out in this way."

Miss Climpson turned this over in her mind. If the will were found in her absence and sent to Norman Urquhart, would Miss Murchison be able to get hold of it before it was again hidden away or destroyed? She wondered.

Hidden away, not destroyed. The mere fact that the will had been sent to him by Miss Booth would prevent the solicitor from making away with it, for there would be a witness to its existence. But he might successfully conceal it for a considerable time—and time was of the essence of the adventure.

"Oh, I'm not a scrap tired," she said brightly, sitting up on her heels and restoring her coiffure to something more like its usual neatness. She had a black note-book in her hand, taken from a drawer in one of the Japanese cabinets, and was turning its pages mechanically. A line of figures caught her eye: 12, 18, 4, 0, 9, 3, 15, and she wondered vaguely what they referred to.

"We've looked through everything here," said Miss Booth. "I don't believe we've missed anything—unless, of course, there is a secret drawer somewhere."

"Could it be in a book, do you think?"

"A book! Why, of course it might. How silly of us not to think of that! In detective stories, wills are always hidden in books."

"More often than in real life," thought Miss Climpson, but she got up and dusted herself and said cheerfully:

"So they are. Are there many books in the house?"

"Thousands," said Miss Booth. "Downstairs in the library."

"I shouldn't have expected Mrs. Wrayburn to be a great reader, somehow."

"Oh, I don't think she was. The books were bought with the house, so Mr. Urquhart told me. They're nearly all old ones, you know—big things bound in leather. Dreadfully dull. I've never found a thing to read there. But they're just the sort of books to hide wills in."

They emerged into the corridor.

"By the way," said Miss Climpson, "won't the servants think it funny of us to be wandering about the place so late?"

"They all sleep in the other wing. Besides, they know that I sometimes have visitors. Mrs. Craig has often been here as late as this when we have had interesting sittings. There's a spare bedroom where I can put people up when I want to."

Miss Climpson made no more objections, and they went downstairs and along the hall into the library. It was big, and books filled the walls and bays in serried ranks—a heart-breaking sight.

"Of course," said Miss Booth, "if the communication hadn't insisted on something beginning with B—"

"Well?"

"Well—I should have expected any papers to be in the safe down here."

Miss Climpson groaned in spirit. The obvious place, naturally! If only her misplaced ingenuity—well! one must make the best of it.

"Why not look?" she suggested. "The letter B. may have been referring to something quite different. Or it may have been an interruption from George Washington. It would be quite like him to use words beginning with a B, don't you think?"

"But if it was in the safe, Mr. Urquhart would know about it."

Miss Climpson began to feel that she had let her invention play about too freely.

"It wouldn't do any harm to make sure," she suggested.

"But I don't know the combination," said Miss Booth. "Mr. Urquhart does, of course. We could write and ask him."

An inspiration came to Miss Climpson.

"I believe I know it," she exclaimed. "There was a row of seven figures in that black note-book I was looking at just now, and it passed through my mind that they must be a memorandum of something."

"Black Book!" cried Miss Booth. "Why, there you are! How could we have been so silly! Of course, Mrs. Wrayburn was trying to tell us where to find the combination!"

Miss Climpson again blessed the all-round utility of the letter B.

"I'll run up and fetch it," she cried.

When she came down again, Miss Booth was standing before a section of the bookshelves, which had swung out from the wall, disclosing the green door of a built-in safe. With trembling hands, Miss Climpson touched the milled knob and turned it.

The first attempt was unsuccessful, owing to the fact that the note did not make it clear which way the knob should be turned first, but at the second attempt the pointer swung over on the seventh figure with a satisfying click.

Miss Booth seized the handle, and the heavy door moved and stood open.

A bundle of papers lay inside. On the top, staring them in the face, was a long, sealed envelope. Miss Climpson pounced upon it.

"Will of Rosanna Wrayburn
5 June 1920."

"Well, isn't that marvellous?" cried Miss Booth. On the whole, Miss Climpson agreed with her.

CHAPTER XIX

Miss Climpson stayed the night in the spare bedroom.

"The best thing," she said, "will be for you to write a little letter to Mr. Urquhart, explaining about the séance, and saying that you thought it best and safest to send the will on to him."

"He will be very much surprised," said Miss Booth. "I wonder what he will say. Lawyers don't believe in spirit communications as a rule. And he'll think it rather funny that we should have managed to open the safe."

"Well, but the spirit led us directly to the combination, didn't it? He could hardly expect you to ignore a message like that, could he? The proof of your good faith is that you are sending the will straight to him. And it would be as well, don't you think, if you asked him to come up and check the other contents of the safe and have the combination altered."

"Wouldn't it be better if I kept the will and asked him to come for it?"

"But perhaps he requires it urgently?"

"Then why hasn't he been to fetch it?"

Miss Climpson noted with some irritation that, where spiritualistic messages were not concerned, Miss Booth showed signs of developing an independent judgment.

"Perhaps he doesn't know yet that he wants it. Perhaps the spirits foresaw an urgent need that will only arise to-morrow."

"Oh, yes, that's quite likely. If only people would avail themselves more fully of the marvellous guidance given to them, so much might be foreseen and provided for! Well, I think you are right. We will find a big envelope to fit it, and I will write a letter and we will send it by the first post tomorrow."

"It had better be registered," said Miss Climpson. "If you will entrust it to me, I will take it down to the post office first thing."

"Will you? That will be a great relief to my mind. Well now, I'm sure you're as tired as I am, so I'll put on a kettle for the hot-water bottles and we'll turn in. Will you make yourself comfy in my sitting-room? I've only got to put the sheets on your bed. What? No, indeed, I can do it in a moment; *please* don't bother. I'm so used to making beds."

"Then I'll see to the kettles," said Miss Climpson. "I simply *must* make myself useful."

"Very well. It won't take long. The water is quite hot in the kitchen boiler."

Left alone in the kitchen, with a kettle bumping and singing on its way to boiling-point, Miss Climpson wasted no time. She tip-toed quickly out again and stood with ear cocked at the foot of the stairs, listening to the nurse's footsteps as they pattered into the distance. Then she slipped into the little sitting-room, took up the will in its sealed envelope, and a long thin paper-knife which she had already marked down as a useful weapon, and hastened back to the kitchen.

It is astonishing how long a kettle which seems to be on the verge of boiling will take before the looked-for jet of steady steam emerges from its spout. Delusive little puffs and deceptive pauses in the song tantalise the watcher interminably. It seemed to Miss Climpson that there would have been time to make twenty beds before the kettle boiled that evening. But even a watched pot cannot absorb heat for ever. After what appeared to be an hour, but was actually about seven minutes, Miss Climpson, guilty and furtive, was holding the flap of the envelope before the scalding steam.

"I mustn't hurry," said Miss Climpson, "oh, blessed saints, I mustn't hurry, or I shall tear it."

She slipped the paper-knife under the flap; it lifted; it opened cleanly, just as Miss Booth's step resounded in the passage.

Miss Climpson adroitly dropped the paper-knife behind the stove and thrust the envelope, with the flap doubled back to prevent it from re-sticking itself, behind a dish-cover on the wall.

"The water's ready!" she cried blithely. "Where are the bottles?"

It is a tribute to her nerve that she filled them with a steady hand. Miss Booth thanked her, and departed upstairs, a bottle in each hand.

Miss Climpson pulled the will from its hiding-place, drew it from its envelope and glanced swiftly through it.

It was not a long document, and in spite of the legal phraseology, its purport was easily gathered. Within three minutes she had replaced it, moistened the gum and stuck the flap down again. She put it in her petticoat-pocket— for her garments were of a useful and old-fashioned kind— and went to hunt in the pantry. When Miss Booth returned, she was making tea peacefully.

"I thought it would refresh us after our labours," she remarked.

"A very good idea," said Miss Booth; "in fact, I was just going to suggest it."

Miss Climpson carried the tea-pot to the sitting-room, leaving Miss Booth to follow with the cups, milk and sugar on a tray. With the tea-pot on the hob and the will once more lying innocently on the table, she smiled and breathed deeply. Her mission was accomplished.

.   .   .   .

Letter from Miss Climpson to Lord Peter Wimsey.

Tuesday, Jan. 7, 1930.

My dear Lord Peter,

As my *telegram* this morning will have informed you, I have SUCCEEDED!! Though what excuse I can find in my *conscience* for the *methods* I have used, I *don't* KNOW! but I believe the Church takes into account the necessity of *deception* in certain *professions*, such as that of a *police-detective* or a SPY in time of WARFARE, and I *trust* that my *subterfuges* may be allowed to come under that *category*. However, you will not want to hear about my *religious scruples!* So I will hasten to let you know *what* I have DIS-COVERED!!

In my last letter I explained the *plan* I had in mind, so you will know what to do about the *Will itself*, which was duly *despatched* by *Registered Post* this morning under cover to *Mr. Norman Urquhart*. How surprised he will be to get it!!! Miss Booth wrote an excellent *covering letter*, which I *saw* before it went, which explains the circumstances and *mentions* NO NAMES!! I have wired to Miss Murchison to *expect* the package, and I hope that when it comes she will contrive to be *present* at the opening, so as to constitute *yet another* WITNESS to its existence. In any case, I should not think he would *venture* to *tamper* with it. Perhaps Miss Murchison may be able to INVESTIGATE it in detail, which I had not *time* to do (it was all *most* adventurous! and I am looking forward to *telling* you ALL ABOUT IT when I come back), but in case she is *not* able to do so, I will give you the *rough outline*.

The property consists of *real estate* (the house and grounds) and a *personalty* (am I not *good* at legal terms??) which I am not able to calculate *exactly*. But the gist of it all is this:—

The *real estate* is left to *Philip Boyes*, absolutely.

Fifty thousand pounds is left to *Philip Boyes* also, in *cash*.

The remainder (is not this called the residue?) is left to NORMAN URQUHART, who is appointed sole executor.

There are a few *small legacies* to Stage Charities, of which I did not manage to memorise any *particulars*.

There is a special paragraph, explaining that the greater

part of the property is left to *Philip Boyes* in token that the
testatrix FORGIVES the ill-treatment meted out to her by *his
family*, for which he was *not responsible*.

The date of the Will is 5 June 1920, and the *witnesses* are
Eva Gubbins, housekeeper, and *John Briggs*, gardener.

I hope, dear Lord Peter, that this information will be
enough for your purpose. I had hoped that even *after* Miss
Booth had enclosed the Will in a *covering envelope* I might
be able to take it out and *peruse* it at leisure, but unfortunately she *sealed* it for greater security with Mrs. Wrayburn's *private seal*, which I had not sufficient *dexterity* to
remove and replace, though I understand it is possible to
do so with a *hot knife*.

You will *understand* that I cannot leave Windle *just yet*
—it would look so odd to do so immediately after this occurrence. Besides, I am hoping, in a further series of "sittings," to *warn* Miss Booth against Mrs. Craig and her
"control" Fedora, as I am *quite sure* that this person is
quite as great a *charlatan* as I AM!!!—and without my
altruistic motives!! So you will not be surprised if I am
away from Town for, say, *another week!* I am a little worried about the *extra expense* of this, but if you do not think
it *justified* for the sake of safety, *let me know*—and I will
alter my arrangements accordingly.

Wishing you *all success*, dear Lord Peter,
Most sincerely yours,
Katharine A. Climpson.

P.S. I managed to do the "job" *very nearly* within the
stipulated week, you see. I am *so sorry* it was not *quite*
finished yesterday, but I was so *terrified* of *spoiling* the
WHOLE THING by *rushing* it!!

.   .   .   .

"Bunter," said Lord Peter, looking up from this letter,
"I *knew* there was something fishy about that will."

"Yes, my lord."

"There is something about wills which brings out the
worst side of human nature. People who under ordinary
circumstances are perfectly upright and amiable, go as

curly as corkscrews and foam at the mouth, whenever they hear the words 'I devise and bequeath.' That reminds me, a spot of champagne in a silver tankard is no bad thing to celebrate on. Get up a bottle of the Pommery and tell Chief-Inspector Parker I should be glad of a word with him. And bring me those notes of Mr. Arbuthnot's. And oh, Bunter!"

"My lord?"

"Get Mr. Crofts on the 'phone and give him my compliments, and say I have found the criminal and the motive and hope presently to produce proof of the way the crime was done, if he will see that the case is put off for a week or so."

"Very good, my lord."

"All the same, Bunter, I really don't know how it *was* done."

"That will undoubtedly suggest itself before long, my lord."

"Oh, yes," said Wimsey, airily. "Of course. Of course. I'm not worrying about a trifle like that."

CHAPTER XX

T'ch! t'ch!" said Mr. Pond, clicking his tongue against his denture.

Miss Murchison looked up from her typewriter.

"Is anything the matter, Mr. Pond?"

"No, nothing," said the head-clerk, testily. "A foolish letter from a foolish member of your sex, Miss Murchison."

"That's nothing new."

Mr. Pond frowned, conceiving the tone of his subordinate's voice to be impertinent. He picked up the letter and its enclosure and took them into the inner office.

Miss Murchison nipped swiftly across to his desk and glanced at the registered envelope which lay upon it, open. The post-mark was 'Windle.'

"That's luck," said Miss Murchison, to herself. "Mr. Pond is a better witness than I should be. I'm glad he opened it."

She regained her place. In a few minutes Mr. Pond emerged, smiling slightly.

Five minutes later, Miss Murchison, who had been frowning over her shorthand note-book, rose up and came over to him.

"Can you read short-hand, Mr. Pond?"

"No," said the head-clerk. "In my day it was not considered necessary."

"I can't make out this outline," said Miss Murchison. "It looks like 'give consent to,' but it may be only 'give consideration to'—there's a difference, isn't there?"

"There certainly is," said Mr. Pond, drily.

"P'raps I'd better not risk it," said Miss Murchison. "It's got to go off this morning. I'd better ask him."

Mr. Pond snorted—not for the first time—over the care-lessness of the female typist.

Miss Murchison walked briskly across the room and opened the inner door without knocking—an informality which left Mr. Pond groaning again.

Mr. Urquhart was standing up with his back to the door, doing something or other at the mantelpiece. He turned round sharply, with an exclamation of annoyance.

"I have told you before, Miss Murchison, that I like you to knock before entering."

"I am very sorry; I forgot."

"Don't let it happen again. What is it?"

He did not return to his desk, but stood leaning against the mantelshelf. His sleek head, outlined against the drab-painted panelling, was a little thrown back, as though—Miss Murchison thought—he were protecting or defying somebody.

"I could not quite make out my shorthand note of your letter to Tewke & Peabody," said Miss Murchison, "and I thought it better to come and ask you."

"I wish," said Mr. Urquhart, fixing a stern eye upon her, "that you would take your notes clearly at the time. If I am going too fast for you, you should tell me so. It would save trouble in the end—wouldn't it?"

Miss Murchison was reminded of a little set of rules which Lord Peter Wimsey—half in jest and half in earnest—had once prepared for the guidance of "The Cattery." Of Rule Seven, in particular, which ran: "Always distrust the man who looks you straight in the eyes. He wants to prevent you from seeing something. Look for it."

She shifted her eyes under her employer's gaze.

"I'm very sorry, Mr. Urquhart. I won't let it occur again," she muttered. There was a curious dark line at the edge of the panelling just behind the solicitor's head, as though the panel did not quite fit its frame. She had never noticed it before.

"Well, now, what is the trouble?"

Miss Murchison asked her question, got her answer and retired. As she went, she cast a glance over the desk. The will was not there.

She went back and finished her letters. When she took them in to be signed, she seized the opportunity to look at the panelling again. There was no dark line to be seen.

Miss Murchison left the office promptly at half-past four. She had a feeling that it would be unwise to linger about the premises. She walked briskly away through Hand Court, turned to the right along Holborn, dived to the right again through Featherstone Buildings, made a detour through Red Lion Street and debouched into Red Lion Square. Within five minutes she was at her old walk round the square, and up Princeton Street. Presently, from a safe distance, she saw Mr. Pond come out, thin, stiff and stooping, and walk down Bedford Row towards Chancery Lane Station. Before very long, Mr. Urquhart followed. He stood a moment on the threshold, glancing to left and right, then came straight across the street towards her. For a moment she thought he had seen her, and she dived hurriedly behind a van that was standing at the kerb. Under its shelter, she withdrew to the corner of the street, where there is a butcher's shop, and scanned a windowful of New Zealand lamb and chilled beef. Mr. Urquhart came nearer. His steps grew louder—then paused. Miss Murchison glued her eyes on a round of meat marked 4½lb. ¾d. A voice said: "Good evening, Miss Murchison. Choosing your supper-chop?"

"Oh! Good evening, Mr. Urquhart. Yes—I was just wishing that Providence had seen fit to provide more joints suitable for single people."

"Yes—one gets tired of beef and mutton."

"And pork is apt to be indigestible."

"Just so. Well, you should cease to be single, Miss Murchison."

Miss Murchison giggled.

"But this is so sudden, Mr. Urquhart."

Mr. Urquhart flushed under his curious freckled skin.

"Good-night," he said abruptly, and with extreme coldness.

Miss Murchison laughed to herself as he strode off.

"Thought that would settle him. It's a great mistake to be familiar with your subordinates. They take advantage of you."

She watched him out of sight on the far side of the Square, then returned along Princeton Street, crossed Bedford Row and re-entered the office building. The charwoman was just coming downstairs.

"Well, Mrs. Hodges, it's me again! Do you mind letting me in? I've lost a pattern of silk. I think I must have left it in my desk, or dropped it on the floor. Have you come across it?"

"No, miss, I ain't done your office yet."

"Then I'll have a hunt round for it. I want to get up to Bourne's before half-past six. It's such a nuisance."

"Yes, miss, and such a crowd always with the buses and things. Here you are, miss."

She opened the door, and Miss Murchison darted in.

"Shall I 'elp you to look for it, miss?"

"No, thank you, Mrs. Hodges, please don't bother. I don't expect it's far off."

Mrs. Hodges took up a pail and went to fill it at a tap in the back yard. As soon as her heavy steps had ascended again to the first floor, Miss Murchison made for the inner office.

"I must and will see what's behind that panelling."

The houses in Bedford Row are Hogarthian in type, tall, symmetrical, with the glamour of better days upon them. The panels in Mr. Urquhart's room, though defaced by many coats of paint, were handsomely designed, and over the mantelpiece ran a festoon of flowers and fruit, rather florid for the period, with a ribbon and basket in the center. If the panel was controlled by a concealed spring, the boss that moved it was probably to be found among this decorative work. Pulling a chair to the fireplace, Miss Murchison ran her fingers quickly over the festoon, pushing and pressing with both hands, while keeping her ear cocked for intruders.

This kind of investigation is easy for experts, but Miss Murchison's knowledge of secret hiding places was only culled from sensational literature; she could not find the trick of the thing. After nearly a quarter of an hour, she began to despair.

Thump—thump—thump—Mrs. Hodges was coming downstairs.

Miss Murchison sprang away from the panelling so hastily that the chair slipped, and she had to thrust hard at the wall to save herself. She jumped down, restored the chair to its place, glanced up—and saw the panel standing wide open.

At first she thought it was a miracle, but soon realised that in slipping she had thrust sideways at the frame of the panel. A small square of woodwork had slipped away sideways, and exposed an inner panel with a keyhole in the middle.

She heard Mrs. Hodges in the outer room, but she was too excited to bother about what Mrs. Hodges might be thinking. She pushed a heavy chair across the door, so that nobody could enter without noise and difficulty. In a moment Blindfold Bill's keys were in her hand—how fortunate that she had not returned them! How fortunate, too, that Mr. Urquhart had relied on the secrecy of the panel, and had not thought it worth while to fit his cache with a patent lock!

A few moments' quick work with the keys, and the lock turned. She pulled the little door open.

Inside was a bundle of papers. Miss Murchison ran them

over—at first quickly—then again, with a puzzled face. Receipts for securities—Share certificates—Megatherium Trust —surely the names of those investments were familiar— where had she . . . ?

Suddenly Miss Murchison sat down, feeling quite faint, the bundle of papers in her hand.

She realised now what had happened to Mrs. Wrayburn's money, which Norman Urquhart had been handling under that confiding Deed of Trust, and why the matter of the will was so important. Her head whirled. She picked up a sheet of paper from the desk and began jotting down in hurried shorthand the particulars of the various transactions of which these documents were the evidence.

Somebody bumped at the door.

"Are you in here, miss?"

"Just a moment, Mrs. Hodges. I think I must have dropped it on the floor in here."

She gave the big chair a sharp push, effectually closing the door.

She must hurry. Anyway she had got down enough to convince Lord Peter that Mr. Urquhart's affairs needed looking into. She put the papers back into the cupboard, in the exact place from which she had taken them. The will was there, too, she noticed, laid on one side by itself. She peered in. There was something else, tucked away at the back. She thrust her hand in and pulled the mysterious object out. It was a white paper packet, labelled with the name of a foreign chemist. The end had been opened and tucked in again. She pulled the paper apart, and saw that the packet contained about two ounces of a fine white powder.

Next to hidden treasure and mysterious documents, nothing is more full of sensational suggestion than a packet of anonymous white powder. Miss Murchison caught up another sheet of clean paper, tipped a thimbleful of the powder into it, replaced the packet at the back of the cupboard and re-locked the door with the skeleton key. With trembling fingers she pushed the panel back into place, taking care to shut it completely, so as to show no betraying dark line.

She rolled the chair away from the door and cried out gaily:

"I've got it, Mrs. Hodges!"

"There, now!" said Mrs. Hodges, appearing in the doorway.

"Just fancy!" said Miss Murchison. "I was looking through my patterns when Mr. Urquhart rang, and this one must have stuck to my frock and dropped on the floor in here."

She held up a small piece of silk triumphantly. She had torn it from the lining of her bag in the course of the afternoon—a proof, if any were needed, of her devotion to her work, for the bag was a good one.

"Dearie me," said Mrs. Hodges. "What a good thing you found it, wasn't it, miss?"

"I nearly didn't," said Miss Murchison, "it was right in this dark corner. Well, I must fly to get there before the shop shuts. Good-night, Mrs. Hodges."

But long before the accommodating Messrs. Bourne & Hollingsworth had closed their doors, Miss Murchison was ringing the second floor bell at 11Ca, Piccadilly.

.   .   .   .

She found a council in progress. There was the Hon. Freddy Arbuthnot, looking amiable, Chief-Inspector Parker, looking worried, Lord Peter, looking somnolent, and Bunter, who, having introduced her, retired to a position on the fringe of the assembly and hovered there looking correct.

"Have you brought us news, Miss Murchison? If so, you have come at the exact right moment to find the eagles gathered together. Mr. Arbuthnot, Chief-Inspector Parker, Miss Murchison. Now let's all sit down and be happy together. Have you had tea? or will you absorb a spot of something?"

Miss Murchison declined refreshment.

"H'm!" said Wimsey. "The patient refuses food. Her eyes glitter wildly. The expression is anxious. The lips are parted. The fingers fumble with the clasp of the bag. The symptoms point to an acute attack of communicativeness. Tell us the worst, Miss Murchison."

Miss Murchison needed no urging. She told her adventures, and had the pleasure of holding her audience enthralled from the first word to the last. When she finally produced the screw of paper containing the white powder, the sentiments of the company expressed themselves in a round of applause, in which Bunter joined discreetly.

"Are you convinced, Charles?" asked Wimsey.

"I admit that I am heavily shaken," said Parker. "Of course, the powder must be analysed—"

"It shall, embodied caution," said Wimsey. "Bunter, make ready the rack and thumbscrew. Bunter has been taking lessons in Marsh's test, and performs it to admiration. You know all about it too, Charles, don't you?"

"Enough for a rough test."

"Carry on then, my children. In the meanwhile, let us sum up our feelings."

Bunter went out and Parker, who had been making entries in a note-book, cleared his throat.

"Well," he said, "the matter stands, I take it, like this. You say that Miss Vane is innocent, and you undertake to prove this by bringing a convincing accusation against Norman Urquhart. So far, your evidence against him is almost entirely concerned with motive, bolstered up by proofs of intent to mislead enquiry. You say that your investigations have brought the case against Urquhart to a point at which the police can, and ought to, take it up, and I am inclined to agree with you. I warn you, however, that you still have to establish evidence as to means and opportunity."

"I know that. Tell us a new one."

"All right, as long as you know it. Very well. Now Philip Boyes and Norman Urquhart are the only surviving relations of Mrs. Wrayburn, or Cremorna Garden, who is rich, and has money to leave. A number of years ago, Mrs. Wrayburn put all her affairs into the hands of Urquhart's father, the only member of the family with whom she remained on friendly terms. On his father's death, Norman Urquhart took over those affairs himself, and in 1920, Mrs. Wrayburn executed a Deed of Trust, giving him sole authority to handle her property. She also made a will, dividing her property unequally between her two great-nephews. Philip Boyes got all the real estate and £50,000, while Norman Urquhart took whatever was left and was also sole executor. Norman Urquhart when questioned about this Will, deliberately told you an untruth, saying that the bulk of the money was left to him, and even went so far as to produce a document purporting to be a draft of such a will. The pretended date of this draft is subsequent to that of the Will discovered by Miss Climpson, but there is no doubt that the draft itself was drawn out by Urquhart, certainly within the last three years and probably within the last few days. Moreover, the fact that the actual Will, though lying in a place accessible to Urquhart, was not destroyed by him, suggests that it was not, in fact, superseded by any subsequent testamentary disposition. By the way, Wimsey, why didn't he simply take the will and destroy it? As the sole surviving heir, he would then inherit without dispute."

"Perhaps it didn't occur to him. Or there might even be other relatives surviving. How about that uncle in Australia?"

"True. At any rate he didn't destroy it. In 1925 Mrs. Wrayburn became completely paralysed and imbecile, so that there was no possibility of her ever enquiring into the disposition of her estate or making another will.

"About this time, as we know from Mr. Arbuthnot, Urquhart took the dangerous step of plunging into speculation. He made mistakes, lost money, plunged more deeply to recover himself, and was involved to a large extent in the great crash of Megatherium Trust, Ltd. He certainly lost far more than he could possibly afford, and we now find, from Miss Murchison's discoveries—of which I must say that I should hate to have to take official notice—that he had been consistently abusing his position as Trustee and employing Mrs. Wrayburn's money for his private speculations. He deposited her holdings as security for large loans, and embarked the money thus raised in the Megatherium and other wild-cat schemes.

"As long as Mrs. Wrayburn lived, he was fairly safe, for he only had to pay to her the sums necessary to keep up her house and establishment. In fact, all the household bills and so on were settled by him as her man of affairs under Power of Attorney, all salaries were paid by him, and so long as he did this, it was nobody's business to ask what he had done with the capital. But as soon as Mrs. Wrayburn died, he would have to account to the other heir, Philip Boyes, for the capital which he had misappropriated.

"Now in 1929, just about the time that Philip Boyes quarrelled with Miss Vane, Mrs. Wrayburn had a serious attack of illness and very nearly died. The danger passed, but might recur at any moment. Almost immediately afterwards we find him becoming friendly with Philip Boyes and inviting him to stay at his house. While living with Urquhart, Boyes has three attacks of illness, attributed by his doctor to gastritis, but equally consistent with arsenical poisoning. In June 1929, Philip Boyes goes away to Wales and his health improves.

"While Philip Boyes is absent, Mrs. Wrayburn has another alarming attack, and Urquhart hastens up to Windle, possibly with the idea of destroying the will in case the worst happens. It does not happen, and he comes back to London, just in time to receive Boyes on his return from

Wales. That night, Boyes is taken ill with symptoms similar to those of the previous spring, but much more violent. After three days he dies.

"Urquhart is now perfectly safe. As residuary legatee, he will receive, at Mrs. Wrayburn's death, all the money bequeathed to Philip Boyes. That is, he will not get it, because he has already taken it and lost it, but he will no longer be called upon to produce it and his fraudulent dealings will not be exposed.

"So far, the evidence as to motive is extremely cogent, and far more convincing than the evidence against Miss Vane.

"But here is your snag, Wimsey. When and how was the poison administered? We know that Miss Vane possessed arsenic and that she could easily have given it to him without witnesses. But Urquhart's only opportunity was at the dinner he shared with Boyes, and if anything in this case is certain, it is that the poison was not administered at that dinner. Everything which Boyes ate or drank was equally eaten and drunk by Urquhart and the servants, with the single exception of the burgundy, which was preserved and analysed and found to be harmless."

"I know," said Wimsey, "but that is what is so suspicious. Did you ever hear of a meal hedged round with such precautions? It's not natural, Charles. There's the sherry, poured out by the maid from the original bottle, the soup, fish and casseroled chicken—so impossible to poison in one portion without poisoning the whole—the omelette, so ostentatiously prepared at the table by the hands of the victim—the wine, sealed up and marked—the remnants consumed in the kitchen—you would think the man had gone out of his way to construct a suspicion-proof meal. The wine is the final touch which makes the thing incredible. Do you tell me that at that earliest moment when everybody supposes the illness to be a natural one, and when the affectionate cousin ought to be overwhelmed with anxiety

for the sick man, it is natural or believable that an innocent person's mind should fly to accusations of poisoning?
If he was innocent himself, then he suspected something.
If he did suspect, why didn't he tell the doctor and have the
patient's secretions and so on analysed? Why should he
ever have thought of protecting himself against accusation
when no accusation had been made, unless he knew that an
accusation would be well-founded? And then there's the
business about the nurse."

"Exactly. The nurse did have her suspicions."

"If he knew about them, he ought to have taken steps to
refute them in the proper way. But I don't think he did
know about them. I was referring to what you told us today. The police have got in touch with the nurse again,
Miss Williams, and she tells them that Norman Urquhart
took special pains never to be left alone with the patient,
and never to give him any food or medicine, even when
she herself was present. Doesn't that argue a bad conscience?"

"You won't find any lawyer or jury to believe it, Peter."

"Yes, but look here, doesn't it strike you as funny? Listen
to this, Miss Murchison. One day the nurse was doing something or the other in the room, and she had got the medicine there on the mantelpiece. Something was said about it,
and Boyes remarked, 'Oh, don't bother, Nurse. Norman can
give me my dope.' Does Norman say, 'Right-ho, old man!'
as you or I would? No! He says: 'No, I'll leave it to Nurse
—I might make a mess of it.' Pretty feeble, what?"

"Lots of people are nervous about looking after invalids,"
said Miss Murchison.

"Yes, but most people can pour stuff out of a bottle into
a glass. Boyes wasn't *in extremis*—he was speaking quite
rationally and all that. I say the man was deliberately protecting himself."

"Possibly," said Parker, "but after all, old man, when
did he administer the poison?"

"Probably not at the dinner at all," said Miss Murchison. "As you say, the precautions seem rather obvious. They may have been intended to make people concentrate on the dinner and forget other possibilities. Did he have a whisky when he arrived or before he went out or anything?"

"Alas, he did not. Bunter has been cultivating Hannah Westlock almost to breach of promise point, and she says that she opened the door to Boyes on his arrival, that he went straight upstairs to his room, that Urquhart was out at the time and only came in a quarter of an hour before dinner-time, and that the two men met for the first time over the famous glass of sherry in the library. The folding-doors between the library and dining-room were open and Hannah was buzzing round the whole time laying the table, and she is sure that Boyes had the sherry and nothing but the sherry."

"Not so much as a digestive tablet?"

"Nothing."

"How about after dinner?"

"When they had finished the omelette, Urquhart said something about coffee. Boyes looked at his watch and said, 'No time, old chap, I've got to be getting along to Doughty Street.' Urquhart said he would ring up a taxi, and went out to do so. Boyes folded up his napkin, got up and went into the hall. Hannah followed and helped him on with his coat. The taxi arrived. Boyes got in and off he went without seeing Urquhart again."

"It seems to me," said Miss Murchison, "that Hannah is an exceedingly important witness for Mr. Urquhart's defence. You don't think—I hardly like to suggest it—but you don't think that Bunter is allowing his feelings to overcome his judgment?"

"He says," replied Lord Peter, "that he believes Hannah to be a sincerely religious woman. He has sat beside her in chapel and shared her hymn-book."

"But that may be the merest hypocrisy," said Miss Murchison, rather warmly, for she was militantly rationalist. "I don't trust these unctuous people."

"I didn't offer that as a proof of Hannah's virtue," said Wimsey, "but of Bunter's unsusceptibility."

"But he looks like a deacon himself."

"You've never seen Bunter off duty," said Lord Peter, darkly. "I have, and I can assure you that a hymn-book would be about as softening to his heart as neat whisky to an Anglo-Indian liver. No; if Bunter says Hannah is honest, then she *is* honest."

"Then that definitely cuts out the drinks and the dinner," said Miss Murchison, unconvinced, but willing to be open-minded. "How about the water-bottle in the bedroom?"

"The devil!" cried Wimsey. "That's one up to you, Miss Murchison. We didn't think of that. The water-bottle—yes —a perfectly fruity idea. You recollect, Charles, that in the Bravo case, it was suggested that a disgruntled servant had put tartar emetic in the water-bottle. Oh, Bunter—here you are! Next time you hold Hannah's hand, will you ask her whether Mr. Boyes drank any water from his bedroom water-bottle before dinner?"

"Pardon me, my lord, the possibility had already presented itself to my mind."

"It had?"

"Yes, my lord."

"Do you never overlook anything, Bunter?"

"I endeavour to give satisfaction, my lord."

"Well then, don't talk like Jeeves. It irritates me. What about the water-bottle?"

"I was about to observe, my lord, when this lady arrived, that I had elicited a somewhat peculiar circumstance relating to the water-bottle."

"Now we're getting somewhere," said Parker, flattening out a new page of his note-book.

"I would not go so far as to say that, sir. Hannah in-

formed me that she showed Mr. Boyes into his bedroom
on his arrival and withdrew, as it was her place to do.
She had scarcely reached the head of the staircase, when
Mr. Boyes put his head out of the door and recalled her.
He then asked her to fill his water-bottle. She was considerably astonished at this request, since she had a perfect
recollection of having previously filled it when she put the
room in order."

"Could he have emptied it himself?" asked Parker,
eagerly.

"Not into his interior, sir—there had not been time. Nor
had the drinking-glass been utilised. Moreover, the bottle
was not merely empty, but dry inside. Hannah apologised
for the neglect, and immediately rinsed out the bottle and
filled it from the tap."

"Curious," said Parker. "But it's quite likely she never
filled it at all."

"Pardon me, sir. Hannah was so much surprised by the
episode that she mentioned it to Mrs. Pettican, the cook,
who said that she distinctly recollected seeing her fill the
bottle that morning."

"Well, then," said Parker, "Urquhart or somebody must
have emptied it and dried it out. Now, why? What would
one naturally do if one found one's water-bottle empty?"

"Ring the bell," said Wimsey, promptly.

"Or shout for help," added Parker.

"Or," said Miss Murchison, "if one wasn't accustomed to
be waited on, one might use the water from the bedroom
jug."

"Ah! . . . of course Boyes was used to a more or less
Bohemian life."

"But surely," said Wimsey, "that's idiotically roundabout.
It would be much simpler just to poison the water in the
bottle. Why direct attention to the thing by making it
more difficult? Besides, you couldn't count on the victim's
using the jug-water—and, as a matter of fact, he didn't."

"And he *was* poisoned," said Miss Murchison, "so the poison wasn't either in the jug or the bottle."

"No—I'm afraid there's nothing to be got out of the jug and bottle department. Hollow, hollow, hollow all delight, Tennyson."

"All the same," said Parker, "that incident convinces me. It's too complete, somehow. Wimsey's right; it's not natural for a defence to be so perfect."

"My God," said Wimsey, "we have convinced Charles Parker. Nothing more is needed. He is more adamantine than any jury."

"Yes," said Parker, modestly, "but I'm more logical, I think. And I'm not being flustered by the Attorney-General. I should feel happier with a little evidence of a more objective kind."

"You would. You want some real arsenic. Well, Bunter, what about it?"

"The apparatus is quite ready, my lord."

"Very good. Let us go and see if we can give Mr. Parker what he wants. Lead and we follow."

In a small apartment usually devoted to Bunter's photographic work, and furnished with a sink, a bench and a bunsen burner, stood the apparatus necessary for making a Marsh's test of arsenic. The distilled water was already bubbling gently in the flask, and Bunter lifted the little glass tube which lay across the flame of the burner.

"You will perceive, my lord," he observed, "that the apparatus is free from contamination."

"I see nothing at all," said Freddy.

"That, as Sherlock Holmes would say, is what you may expect to see when there is nothing there," said Wimsey, kindly. "Charles, you will pass the water and the flask and the tube, old Uncle Tom Cobley and all as being arsenic-free."

"I will."

"Wilt thou love, cherish and keep her, in sickness or in

health—sorry! turned over two pages at once. Where's that
powder? Miss Murchison, you identify this sealed envelope
as being the one you brought from the office, complete with
mysterious white powder from Mr. Urquhart's secret
hoard?"

"I do."

"Kiss the Book. Thank you. Now then—"

"Wait a sec," said Parker, "you haven't tested the envelope separately."

"That's true. There's always a snag somewhere. I suppose, Miss Murchison, you haven't such a thing as another
office envelope about you?"

Miss Murchison blushed, and fumbled in her handbag.

"Well—there's a little note I scribbled this afternoon to
a friend—"

"*In* your employer's time, *on* your employer's paper,"
said Wimsey. "Oh, how right Diogenes was when he took
his lantern to look for an honest typist! Never mind. Let's
have it. Who wills the end, wills the means."

Miss Murchison extracted the envelope and freed it from
the enclosure. Bunter, receiving it respectfully on a developing dish, cut it into small pieces which he dropped
into the flask. The water bubbled brightly, but the little
tube still remained stainless from end to end.

"Does something begin to happen soon?" enquired Mr.
Arbuthnot. "Because I feel this show's a bit lackin' in pep,
what?"

"If you don't sit still I shall take you out," retorted
Wimsey. "Carry on, Bunter. We'll pass the envelope."

Bunter accordingly opened the second envelope, and delicately dropped the white powder into the wide mouth of
the flask. All five heads bent eagerly over the apparatus.
And presently, definitely, magically, a thin silver stain
began to form in the tube where the flame impinged upon
it. Second by second it spread and darkened to a deep
brownish-black ring with a shining metallic centre.

"Oh, lovely, lovely," said Parker, with professional delight.

"Your lamp's smoking or something," said Freddy.

"Is that arsenic?" breathed Miss Murchison, gently.

"I hope so," said Wimsey, gently detaching the tube and holding it up to the light. "It's either arsenic or antimony."

"Allow me, my lord. The addition of a small quantity of solute chlorinated lime should decide the question beyond reach of cavil."

He performed this further test amid an anxious silence. The stain dissolved out and vanished under the bleaching solution.

"Then it is arsenic," said Parker.

"Oh, yes," said Wimsey, nonchalantly, "of course it is arsenic. Didn't I tell you?" His voice wavered a little with suppressed triumph.

"Is that all?" inquired Freddy, disappointed.

"Isn't it enough?" said Miss Murchison.

"Not quite," said Parker, "but it's a long way towards it. It proves that Urquhart has arsenic in his possession, and by making an official enquiry in France, we can probably find out whether this packet was already in his possession last June. I notice, by the way, that it is ordinary white arsenious acid, without any mixture of charcoal or indigo, which agrees with what was found at the post-mortem. That's satisfactory, but it would be even more satisfactory if we could provide an opportunity for Urquhart to have administered it. So far, all we have done is to demonstrate clearly that he couldn't have given it to Boyes either before, during or after dinner, during the period required for the symptoms to develop. I agree that an impossibility so bolstered up by testimony is suspicious in itself, but, to convince a jury, I should prefer something better than a *credo quia impossibile*."

"Riddle-me-right, and riddle-me-ree," said Wimsey, imperturbably. "We've overlooked something, that's all.

Probably something quite obvious. Give me the statutory dressing-gown and ounce of shag, and I will undertake to dispose of this little difficulty for you in a brace of shakes. In the meantime, you will no doubt take steps to secure, in an official and laborious manner, the evidence which our kind friends here have already so ably gathered in by unconventional methods, and will stand by to arrest the right man when the time comes?"

"I will," said Parker, "gladly. Apart from all personal considerations, I'd far rather see that oily-haired fellow in the dock than any woman, and if the Force has made a mistake, the sooner it's put right the better for all concerned."

   .   .   .   .

Wimsey sat late that night in the black-and-primrose library, with the tall folios looking down at him. They represented the world's accumulated hoard of mellow wisdom and poetical beauty, to say nothing of thousands of pounds in cash. But all these counsellors sat mute upon their shelves. Strewn on tables and chairs lay the bright scarlet volumes of the Notable British Trials—Palmer, Pritchard, Maybrick, Seddon, Armstrong, Madeleine Smith—the great practitioners in arsenic—huddled together with the chief authorities on Forensic Medicine and Toxicology.

The theatre-going crowds surged home in saloon and taxi, the lights shone over the empty width of Piccadilly, the heavy night-lorries rumbled slow and seldom over the black tarmac, the long night waned and the reluctant winter dawn struggled wanly over the piled roofs of London. Bunter, silent and anxious, sat in his kitchen, brewing coffee on the stove and reading the same page of the "British Journal of Photography" over and over again.

At half-past eight the library bell rang.

"My lord?"

"My bath, Bunter."

"Very good, my lord."

"And some coffee."

"Immediately, my lord."

"And put back all the books except these."

"Yes, my lord."

"I know now how it was done."

"Indeed, my lord? Permit me to offer my respectful congratulations."

"I've still got to prove it."

"A secondary consideration, my lord."

Wimsey yawned. When Bunter returned a minute or two later with the coffee, he was asleep.

Bunter put the books quietly away, and looked with some curiosity at the chosen few left open on the table. They were: "The Trial of Florence Maybrick"; Dixon Mann's "Forensic Medicine and Toxicology"; a book with a German title which Bunter could not read; and A. E. Housman's "A Shropshire Lad."

Bunter studied these for a few moments, and then slapped his thigh softly.

"Why, of course!" he said under his breath, "why, what a mutton-headed set of chumps we've all been!" He touched his master lightly on the shoulder,

"Your coffee, my lord."

CHAPTER XXI

"THEN you won't marry me?" said Lord Peter.

The prisoner shook her head.

"No. It wouldn't be fair to you. And besides—"

"Well?"

"I'm frightened of it. One couldn't get away. I'll live with you, if you like, but I won't marry you."

Her tone was so unutterably dreary that Wimsey could feel no enthusiasm for this handsome offer.

"But that sort of thing doesn't always work," he expostulated. "Dash it all, you ought to know—forgive my alluding to it and all that—but it's frightfully inconvenient, and one has just as many rows as if one was married."

"I know that. But you could cut loose any time you wanted to."

"But I shouldn't want to."

"Oh, yes, you would. You've got a family and traditions, you know. Caesar's wife and that sort of thing."

"Blast Caesar's wife! And as for the family traditions—they're on my side, for what they're worth. Anything a Wimsey does is right and heaven help the person who gets in the way. We've even got a damned old family motto about it—'I hold by my Whimsy'—quite right too. I can't say that when I look in the glass I exactly suggest to myself the original Gerald de Wimsey, who bucked about on a cart horse at the Siege of Acre, but I do jolly well intend to do what I like about marrying. Who's to stop me? They can't eat me. They can't even cut me, if it comes to that. Joke, unintentional, officers, for the use of."

Harriet laughed.

"No, I suppose they can't cut you. You wouldn't have to slink abroad with your impossible wife and live at obscure

237

continental watering-places like people in Victorian novels."

"Certainly not."

"People would forget I'd had a lover?"

"My dear child, they're forgetting that kind of thing every day. They're experts at it."

"And was supposed to have murdered him?"

"And were triumphantly acquitted of having murdered him, however greatly provoked."

"Well, I won't marry you. If people can forget all that, they can forget we're not married."

"Oh, yes, *they* could. I couldn't, that's all. We don't seem to be progressing very fast with this conversation. I take it the general idea of living with me does not hopelessly repel you?"

"But this is all so preposterous," protested the girl. "How can I say what I should or shouldn't do if I were free and certain of—surviving?"

"Why not? I can imagine what I should do even in the most unlikely circumstances, whereas this really is a dead cert, straight from the stables."

"I can't," said Harriet, beginning to wilt. "Do please stop asking me. I don't know. I can't think. I can't see beyond the—beyond the—beyond the next few weeks. I only want to get out of this and be left alone."

"All right," said Wimsey, "I won't worry you. Not fair. Abusing my privilege and so on. You can't say 'Pig' and sweep out, under the circs., so I won't offend again. As a matter of fact I'll sweep out myself, having an appointment—with a manicurist. Nice little girl, but a trifle refained in her vowels. Cheerio!"

.   .   .   .

The manicurist, who had been discovered by the help of Chief-Inspector Parker and his sleuths, was a kitten-faced child with an inviting manner and a shrewd eye. She made no bones about accepting her client's invitation to dine, and showed no surprise when he confidentially murmured that he had a little proposition to put before her. She put her plump elbows on the table, cocked her head at a coy angle, and prepared to sell her honour dear.

As the proposition unfolded itself, her manner underwent an alteration that was almost comical. Her eyes lost their round innocence, her very hair seemed to grow less fluffy, and her eyebrows puckered in genuine astonishment.

"Why, of course I could," she said finally, "but whatever do you want them for? Seems funny to me."

"Call it just a joke," said Wimsey.

"No." Her mouth hardened. "I wouldn't like it. It doesn't make sense, if you see what I mean. What I mean, it sounds a queer sort of joke and that kind of thing might get a girl into trouble. I say, it's not one of those, what do they call 'em?—there was a bit about it in Madame Crystal's column last week, in *Susie's Snippets*—spells, you know, witchcraft—the occult, that sort of thing? I wouldn't like it if it was to do any harm to anybody."

"I'm not going to make a waxen image, if that's what you mean. Look here, are you the sort of girl who can keep a secret?"

"Oh, I don't talk. I never was one to let my tongue wag around. I'm not like ordinary girls."

"No, I thought you weren't. That's why I asked you to come out with me. Well, listen, and I'll tell you."

He leaned forward and talked. The little painted face upturned to his grew so absorbed and so excited that a bosom friend, dining at a table some way off, grew quite peevish with envy, making sure that darling Mabel was being offered a flat in Paris, a Daimler car and a thousand-pound necklace, and quarrelled fatally with her own escort in consequence.

"So you see," said Wimsey, "it means a lot to me."

Darling Mabel gave an ecstatic sigh.

"Is that all true? You're not making it up? It's better than any of the talkies."

"Yes, but you mustn't say one word. You're the only person I've told. You won't give me away to him?"

"Him? He's a stingy pig. Catch me giving him anything. I'm on. I'll do it for you. It'll be a bit difficult, 'cause I'll have to use the scissors, which we don't do as a rule. But I'll manage. You trust me. They won't be big ones, you know. He comes in pretty often, but I'll give you all I get. And I'll fix Fred. He always has Fred. Fred'll do it if I ask him. What'll I do with them when I get them?"

Wimsey drew an envelope from his pocket.

"Sealed up inside this," he said, impressively, "there are two little pill-boxes. You mustn't take them out till you get the specimens, because they've been carefully prepared so as to be absolutely chemically clean, if you see what I mean. When you're ready, open the envelope, take out the pill-boxes, put the parings into one and the hair into the other, shut them up at once, put them into a clean envelope and post them to this address. Get that?"

"Yes." She stretched out an eager hand.

"Good girl. And not a word."

"Not—one—word!" She made a gesture of exaggerated caution.

"When's your birthday?"

"Oh, I don't have one. I never grow up."

"Right; then I can send you an unbirthday present any day in the year. You'd look nice in mink, I think."

"Mink, I think," she mocked him. "Quite a poet, aren't you?"

"You inspire me," said Wimsey, politely.

CHAPTER XXII

I HAVE come round," said Mr. Urquhart, "in answer to your letter. I am greatly interested to hear that you have some fresh information about my unfortunate cousin's death. Of course I shall be delighted to give you any assistance I can."

"Thank you," said Wimsey. "Do sit down. You have dined, of course? But you will have a cup of coffee. You prefer the Turkish variety, I fancy. My man brews it rather well."

Mr. Urquhart accepted the offer, and complimented Bunter on having achieved the right method of concocting that curiously syrupy brew, so offensive to the average Occidental.

Bunter thanked him gravely for his good opinion, and proffered a box of that equally nauseating mess called Turkish Delight, which not only gluts the palate and glues the teeth, but also smothers the consumer in a floury cloud of white sugar. Mr. Urquhart immediately plugged his mouth with a large lump of it, murmuring indistinctly that it was the genuine Eastern variety. Wimsey, with an austere smile, took a few sips of strong black coffee without sugar or milk, and poured himself out a glass of old brandy. Bunter retired, and Lord Peter, laying a note-book open upon his knee, glanced at the clock and began his narrative.

He recapitulated the circumstances of Philip Boyes' life and death at some length. Mr. Urquhart, yawning surreptitiously, ate, drank and listened.

Wimsey, still with his eye on the clock, then embarked upon the story of Mrs. Wrayburn's will.

Mr. Urquhart, considerably astonished, set his coffee-cup aside, wiped his sticky fingers upon his handkerchief, and stared.

Presently he said:

"May I ask how you have obtained this very remarkable information?"

Wimsey waved his hand.

"The police," he said, "wonderful thing, police organisation. Surprisin' what they find out when they put their minds to it. You're not denying any of it, I presume?"

"I am listening," said Mr. Urquhart, grimly. "When you have finished this extraordinary statement, I may perhaps discover exactly what it is I have to deny."

"Oh, yes," said Wimsey, "I'll try to make that clear. I'm not a lawyer, of course, but I'm tryin' to be as lucid as I can."

He droned remorselessly on, and the hands of the clock went round.

"So far as I make it out," he said, when he had reviewed the whole question of motive, "it was very much to your interest to get rid of Mr. Philip Boyes. And indeed the fellow was, in my opinion, a pimple and a wart, and in your place I should have felt much the same about him."

"And is this the whole of your fantastic accusation?" enquired the solicitor.

"By no means. I am now coming to the point. Slow but sure is the motto of yours faithfully. I notice that I have taken up seventy minutes of your valuable time, but believe me, the hour has not been unprofitably spent."

"Allowing that all this preposterous story were true, which I most emphatically deny," observed Mr. Urquhart, "I should be greatly interested to know how you imagine that I administered the arsenic. Have you worked out something ingenious for that? Or am I supposed to have suborned my cook and parlourmaid to be my accomplices? A little rash of me, don't you think, and affording remarkable opportunities for blackmail?"

"So rash," said Wimsey, "that it is quite out of the question for a man so full of forethought as yourself. The sealing-up of that bottle of burgundy, for example, argues a mind alive to possibilities—unusually so. In fact, the episode attracted my attention from the start."

"Indeed?"

"You ask me how and when you administered the poison. It was not before dinner, I think. The thoughtfulness shown in emptying the bedroom water-bottle—oh, no! that point was not missed—the care displayed in meeting your cousin before a witness and never being left alone with him—I think that rules out the period before dinner."

"I should think it might."

"The sherry," pursued Wimsey, thoughtfully. "It was a new bottle, freshly decanted. The disappearance of the remains might be commented on. I fancy we can absolve the sherry."

Mr. Urquhart bowed ironically.

"The soup—it was shared by the cook and parlourmaid and they survived. I am inclined to pass the soup, and the same thing applies to the fish. It would be easy to poison a portion of fish, but it would involve the co-operation of Hannah Westlock, and that conflicts with my theory. A theory is a sacred thing to me, Mr. Urquhart—almost a what d'you call it—a dogma."

"An unsafe attitude of mind," remarked the lawyer, "but in the circumstances I will not quarrel with it."

"Besides," said Wimsey, "if the poison had been given in the soup or the fish, it might have started to work before Philip—I may call him so, I hope?—had left the house. We come to the casserole. Mrs. Pettican and Hannah Westlock can give the casserole a clean bill of health, I fancy. And by the way, from the description it must have been most delicious. I speak as a man with some considerable experience in gastronomic matters, Mr. Urquhart."

"I am well aware of it," said Mr. Urquhart, politely.

"And now there remains only the omelette. A most admirable thing when well made and eaten—that is so important—eaten immediately. A charming idea to have the eggs and sugar brought to the table and prepared and cooked on the spot. By the way, I take it there was no omelette left over for the kitchen? No, no! One does not let a good thing like that go out half-eaten. Much better that the good cook should make a fine, fresh omelette for herself and her colleague. Nobody but yourself and Philip partook of the omelette, I am sure."

"Quite so," said Mr. Urquhart, "I need not trouble to deny it. But you will bear in mind that I did partake of it, without ill-effects. And moreover, that my cousin made it himself."

"So he did. Four eggs, if I remember rightly, with sugar and jam from what I may call the common stock. No—there would be nothing wrong with the sugar or the jam. Er—I believe I am right in saying that one of the eggs was cracked when it came to the table?"

"Possibly. I do not really remember."

"No? Well, you are not on oath. But Hannah Westlock remembers that when you brought the eggs in—you purchased them yourself, you know, Mr. Urquhart—you mentioned that one was cracked and particularly desired that it should be used for the omelette. In fact, you yourself laid it in the bowl for that purpose."

"What about it?" asked Mr. Urquhart, perhaps a trifle less easily than before.

"It is not very difficult to introduce powdered arsenic into a cracked egg," said Wimsey. "I have made the experiment myself with a small glass tube. Perhaps a small funnel would be even easier. Arsenic is a fairly heavy substance—7 or 8 grains will go into a tea-spoon. It collects at one end of the egg, and any traces on the exterior of the shell can be readily wiped off. Liquid arsenic could be poured in still more easily, of course, but for a particular reason I made my experiment with the ordinary white powder. It is fairly soluble."

Mr. Urquhart had taken a cigar from his case, and was making rather a business of lighting it.

"Do you suggest," he enquired, "that in the whisking together of four eggs, one particular poisoned egg was somehow kept miraculously separated from the rest and deposited with its load of arsenic at one end of the omelette only? Or that my cousin deliberately helped himself to the poisoned end and left the rest to me?"

"Not at all, not at all," said Wimsey. "I suggest merely that the arsenic was in the omelette and came there by way of the egg."

Mr. Urquhart threw his match into the fireplace.

"There seem to be some flaws in your theory, as well as in the egg."

"I haven't finished the theory yet. My next bit of it is built up from very trifling indications. Let me enumerate them. Your disinclination to drink at dinner, your complexion, a few nail-parings, a snipping or so from your very well-kept hair—I put these together, add a packet of white arsenic from the secret cupboard in your office, rub the hands a little—so—and produce—hemp, Mr. Urquhart, hemp."

He sketched the shape of a noose lightly in the air.

"I don't understand you," said the solicitor, hoarsely.

"Oh *you* know," said Wimsey. "Hemp—what they make ropes of. Great stuff, hemp. Yes, well, about this arsenic. As you know, it's not good for people in a general way, but there are some people—those tiresome peasants in Styria one hears so much about—who are supposed to eat it for fun. It improves their wind, so they say, and clears their complexions and makes their hair sleek, and they give it to their horses for the same reason; bar the complexion, that is, because a horse hasn't much complexion, but you know what I mean. Then there was that horrid man Maybrick—he used to take it, or so they say. Anyhow, it's well known that some people do take it and manage to put away large dollops after a bit of practice—enough to kill any ordinary person. But you know all this."

"This is the first time I've heard of such a thing."

"Where *do* you expect to go to? Never mind. We'll pretend this is all new to you. Well, some fellow—I've forgotten his name,* but it's all in Dixon Mann—wondered how the dodge was worked, and he got going on some dogs and things and he dosed 'em and killed a lot of 'em I daresay, and in the end he found that whereas liquid arsenic was dealt with by the kidneys and was uncommonly bad for the system, solid arsenic could be given day by day, a little bigger dose each time, so that in time the doings—what an old lady I knew in Norfolk called 'the tubes'—got used to it and could push it along without taking any notice of it, so to speak. I read a book somewhere which said it was all done by leucocytes—those jolly little white corpuscles, don't you know—which sort of got round the stuff and bustled it along so that it couldn't do any harm. At all events, the point is that if you go on taking solid arsenic for a good long time—say a year or so—you establish a what-not, an immunity, and can take six or seven grains at a time without so much as a touch of indijaggers."

"Very interesting," said Mr. Urquhart.

"Apparently these beastly Styrian peasants do it that way, and they're very careful not to drink for two hours or thereabouts after taking it, for fear it should all get washed into the kidneys and turn poisonous on 'em. I'm not bein' very technical, I'm afraid, but that's the gist of it. Well, it occurred to me, don't you see, old horse, that if you'd had the bright idea to immunise yourself first, you could easily have shared a jolly old arsenical omelette with a friend. It would kill him and it wouldn't hurt you."

"I see."

The solicitor licked his lips.

* Valetta.

"Well, as I say, you have a nice clear complexion—except that I notice the arsenic has pigmented the skin here and there (it does sometimes), and you've got the sleek hair and so on, and I noticed you were careful not to drink at dinner, and I said to myself, 'Peter, my bright lad, what about it?' And when they found a packet of white arsenic in your cupboard—never mind how for the moment!—I said, 'Hullo, hullo, how long has this been going on?' Your handy foreign chemist has told the police two years—is that right? About the time of the Megatherium crash that would be, wouldn't it? All right, don't tell me if you don't want to. Then we got hold of some bits of your hair and nails, and lo and behold, they were bung-full of arsenic. And we said 'What-ho!' So that's why I asked you to come along and have a chat with me. I thought you might like to offer some sort of suggestion, don't you know."

"I can only suggest," said Urquhart, with a ghastly face but a strictly professional manner, "that you should be careful before you communicate this ludicrous theory to anybody. What you and the police—whom, frankly, I believe to be capable of anything—have been planting on my premises I do not know, but to give out that I am addicted to drug-taking habits is slander and criminal. It is quite true that I have for some time been taking a medicine which contains slight traces of arsenic—Dr. Grainger can furnish the prescription—and that may very likely have left a deposit in my skin and hair, but further than that, there is no foundation for this monstrous accusation."

"None?"

"None."

"Then how is it," asked Wimsey, coolly, but with something menacing in his rigidly controlled voice, "how is it that you have this evening consumed, without apparent effect, a dose of arsenic sufficient to kill two or three ordinary people? That disgusting sweetmeat on which you have been gorging yourself in, I may say, a manner wholly unsuited to your age and position, is smothered in white arsenic. You ate it, God forgive you, an hour and a half ago. If arsenic can harm you, you should have been rolling about in agonies for the last hour."

"You devil!"

"Couldn't you try to get up a few symptoms?" said Wimsey, sarcastically. "Shall I bring you a basin? Or fetch the doctor? Does your throat burn? Is your inside convulsed with agony? It is rather late in the day, but with a little goodwill you could surely produce *some* display of feeling, even now."

"You are lying. You wouldn't dare to do such a thing! It would be murder."

"Not in this case, I fancy. But I am willing to wait and see."

Urquhart stared at him. Wimsey got out of his chair in a single swift movement and stood over him.

"I wouldn't use violence if I were you. Let the poisoner stick to his bottle. Besides, I am armed. Pardon the melodrama. Are you going to be sick or not?"

"You're mad."

"Don't say that. Come, man—pull yourself together. Have a shot at it. Shall I show you the bathroom?"

"I'm ill."

"Of course; but your tone is not convincing. Through the door, along the passage, and third on the left."

The lawyer stumbled out. Wimsey returned to the library and rang the bell.

"I think, Bunter, Mr. Parker may require some assistance in the bathroom."

"Very good, my lord."

Bunter departed and Wimsey waited. Presently there were sounds of a scuffle in the distance. A group appeared at the door. Urquhart, very white, his hair and clothes disordered, flanked by Parker and Bunter, who held him firmly by the arms.

"Was he sick?" asked Wimsey, with interest.

"No, he wasn't," said Parker, grimly, snapping the handcuffs on his prey. "He cursed you fluently for five minutes, then tried to get out of the window, saw it was a three-story drop, charged in through the dressing-room door and ran straight into me. Now don't struggle, my lad, you'll only hurt yourself."

"And he still doesn't know whether he's poisoned or not?"

"He doesn't seem to think he is. At any rate, he made no effort about it. His one idea was to hop it."

"That's feeble," said Wimsey, "if I wanted people to think I'd been poisoned I'd put up a better show than that."

"Stop talking, for God's sake," said the prisoner. "You've got me, by a vile, damnable trick. Isn't that enough? You can shut up about it."

"Oh," said Parker, "we've got you, have we? Well, I warned you not to talk, and if you *will* do it, it's not my fault. By the way, Peter, I don't suppose you did actually poison him, did you? It doesn't seem to have hurt him, but it'll affect the doctor's report."

"No, I didn't, as a matter of fact," said Wimsey. "I only wanted to see how he'd react to the suggestion. Well, cheerio! I can leave it to you now."

"We'll look after him," said Parker. "But you might let Bunter ring up a taxi."

When the prisoner and his escort had departed, Wimsey turned thoughtfully to Bunter, glass in hand.

"*Mithridates he died old*, says the poet. But I doubt it, Bunter. In this case I very much doubt it."

CHAPTER XXIII

There were golden chrysanthemums on the judge's bench; they looked like burning banners.

The prisoner, too, had a look in her eyes that was a challenge to the crowded court, as the clerk read the indictment. The judge, a plump, elderly man with an eighteenth-century face, looked expectantly at the Attorney-General.

"My lord—I am instructed that the Crown offers no evidence against this prisoner."

The gasp that went round the room sounded like the rustle of trees in a rising wind.

"Do I understand that the charge against the prisoner is withdrawn?"

"Those are my instructions, my lord."

"In that case," said the judge, impassively, turning to the jury, "there is nothing left for you but to return a verdict of 'Not Guilty.' Usher, keep those people quiet in the gallery."

"One moment, my lord." Sir Impey Biggs rose up, large and majestic.

"On my client's behalf—on Miss Vane's behalf, my lord, I beg your lordship's indulgence for a few words. A charge has been brought against her, my lord, the very awful charge of murder, and I should like it to be made clear, my lord, that my client leaves this court without a stain upon her character. As I am informed, my lord, this is not a case of the charge being withdrawn in default of evidence. I understand, my lord, that further information has come to the police which definitely proves the entire innocence of my client. I also understand, my lord, that a further arrest has been made and that an inquiry will follow, my lord, in due course. My lord, this lady must go forth into the world acquitted, not only at this bar, but at the bar of public opinion. Any ambiguity would be intolerable, and I am sure, my lord, that I have the support of the learned Attorney-General for what I say."

"By all means," said the Attorney. "I am instructed to say, my lord, that in withdrawing the charge against the prisoner, the Crown proceeds from complete conviction of her absolute innocence."

"I am very glad to hear it," said the judge. "Prisoner at the bar, the Crown, by unreservedly withdrawing this dreadful charge against you, has demonstrated your innocence in the clearest possible way. After this, nobody will be able to suppose that the slightest imputation rests upon you, and I most heartily congratulate you on this very satisfactory ending to your long ordeal. Now, please—I sympathise very much with the people who are cheering, but this is not a theatre or a football match, and if they are not quiet, they will have to be put out. Members of the jury, do you find the Prisoner Guilty or Not Guilty?"

"Not Guilty, my lord."

"Very good. The prisoner is discharged without a stain upon her character. Next case."

So ended, sensational to the last, one of the most sensational murder trials of the century.

. . . . .

Harriet Vane, a free woman, found Eiluned Price and Sylvia Marriott waiting for her as she descended the stairs.

"Darling!" said Sylvia.

"Three loud cheers!" said Eiluned.

Harriet greeted them a little vaguely.

"Where is Lord Peter Wimsey?" she enquired. "I must thank him."

"You won't," said Eiluned, bluntly. "I saw him drive off the moment the verdict was given."

"Oh!" said Miss Vane.

"He'll come and see you," said Sylvia.

"No, he won't," said Eiluned.

"Why not?" said Sylvia.

"Too decent," said Eiluned.

"I'm afraid you're right," said Harriet.

"I like that young man," said Eiluned. "You needn't grin. I do like him. He's not going to do the King Cophetua stunt, and I take off my hat to him. If you want him, you'll have to send for him."

"I won't do that," said Harriet.

"Oh, yes, you will," said Sylvia. "I was right about who did the murder, and I'm going to be right about this."

.   .   .   .

Lord Peter Wimsey went down to Duke's Denver that same evening. He found the family in a state of perturbation, all except the Dowager, who sat placidly making a rug in the midst of the uproar.

"Look here, Peter," said the Duke, "you're the only person with any influence over Mary. You've got to do something. She wants to marry your policeman friend."

"I know," said Wimsey. "Why shouldn't she?"

"It's ridiculous," said the Duke.

"Not at all," said Lord Peter. "Charles is one of the best."

"Very likely," said the Duke, "but Mary can't marry a policeman."

"Now, look here," said Wimsey, tucking his sister's arm in his, "you leave Polly alone. Charles made a bit of a mistake at the beginning of this murder case, but he doesn't make many, and one of these days he'll be a big man, with a title, I shouldn't wonder, and everything handsome about him. If you want to have a row with somebody, have it with me."

"My God!" said the Duke, "you're not going to marry a policewoman?"

"Not quite," said Wimsey. "I intend to marry the prisoner."

"What?" said the Duke. "Good lord, what, what?"

"If she'll have me," said Lord Peter Wimsey.